LIFEBOAT FOUNDATION

presents

VISIONS OF THE FUTURE

D1557478

Published by Lifeboat Foundation
lifeboat.com

ISBN-13: 978-0692513781
ISBN-10: 0692513787

Edited by J. Daniel Batt
Afterword by David Brin

PRINTED IN THE UNITED STATES OF AMERICA

OTHER BOOKS BY LIFEBOAT FOUNDATION
The Human Race to the Future: What Could Happen—and What to Do
by Daniel Berleant

Prospects for Human Survival
by Willard H. Wells

Learn more at lifeboat.com/ex/books.

TABLE OF CONTENTS

NONFICTION

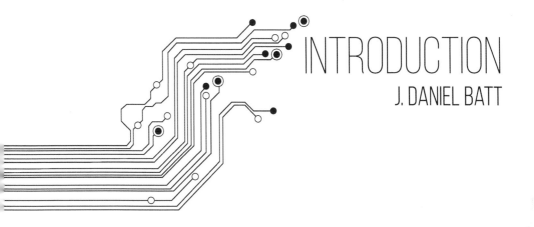

INTRODUCTION
J. DANIEL BATT

In the following pages you'll find stories and essays about artificial intelligence, androids, faster-than-light travel, and the extension of human life. You'll read about the future of human institutions and culture. But these literary works are more than just a reprisal of the classical elements of science fiction and futurism. At their core, each of these pieces has one consistent, repeated theme: us. You are in these pages. I am in these pages.

Exploration of the future is not just pondering what's out there or what's to come. It is a discussion of how we as humans will react to what we encounter. How will we respond to androids, extraterrestrial life, and humans that have seemingly unlimited lifespan? How will we react to technologies that bridge colossal gaps of distance? We have not always met new technologies and philosophies with enthusiasm. Patterns of thought and belief that are thousands of years old still hold sway in shaping our reactions. What seemed to be obvious societal advances, in hindsight, were actually challenging battles.

If we encounter intelligent life amongst the stars, what will we do? Will our response be one of mutual curiosity and sharing? Or, instead, suspicion and fear?

This book, *Visions of the Future*, is not just a handy collection of pulp sci-fi adventures and articles. It continues a necessary conversation our society is having. Our responses now will shape our responses to come. If our relationship today with what is both new, unknown, and different is derived from fear, it's not a far extrapolation to see that mentality carried forward. Hugh Howey's "The Automated Ones" projects current fear-based bigotry into our relationship with AI life. Nicole Anderson's "The Birth of the Dawn" shows a different relationship to human 2.0—one built on enthusiasm and wonder. The very challenges we face today will be mirrored in the future.

Science fiction has already begun to shape the way we think. Thomas M. Disch, in *The Dreams Our Stuff Is Made Of*, writes, "It is my contention that some of the most remarkable features of the present historical moment have their roots in a way of thinking that we have learned from science fiction." Science fiction and futurism can be both predictive and prescriptive. Today's TASER is an acronym for Thomas A. Swift's Electric Rifle, referencing the pulp science fiction classic that gave inspiration to the modern-day inventor. Beyond technological foresight, science fiction functions as a lab for thought experiments. It allows us to imagine scenarios that are to come and then analyze them. Through the stories, we also analyze ourselves. We are reflecting back our own beliefs about humanity and our own fears.

The future isn't predetermined. We are not guaranteed the stars. We are not guaranteed another century on this planet. We are not guaranteed this planet. Through resilience and incredible fortune, the future may turn out far more marvelous than even the stories in this book could imagine. But it will not just happen.

This is what this book in your hands is about: our relationship with our future. Will we be dragged into the future, kicking and screaming? Will we stumble into it? Will we flee back to the caves in fear of it? Or will we run to it? Create it? Design it?

This book is not a road map, but, hopefully, it can inspire the map makers. As you read these pages, keep in mind Dennis Cheatham's words from *The Power of Science Fiction*: "It may be the case that the future worlds and infinite possibilities projected in science fiction can be used to inspire viewers to pursue work that will make those possibilities or ones like them, real." It's possible that one of the futures you'll read in these pages might actually end up being right. But even the ones that will get it wrong (and let's be honest, most science fiction does) are still critical for us now. It's difficult to overstate the significance of the practice of science fiction on shaping us today. The most important aspect about explorations of the future is that they be written and be read.

So, enjoy reading. Find yourself in these pages. Discover our future in the words ahead.

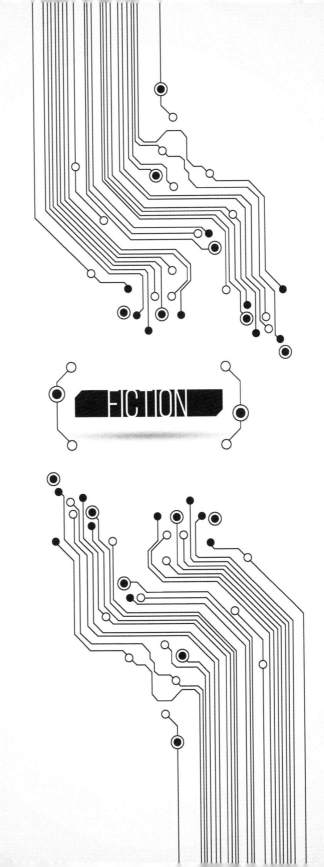

FICTION

"Individual science fiction stories may seem as trivial as ever to the blinder critics and philosophers of today—but the core of science fiction, its essence, the concept around which it revolves, has become crucial to our salvation if we are to be saved at all."

—Isaac Asimov

THE SHOULDERS OF GIANTS
ROBERT J. SAWYER

Rob is one of only eight writers in history—and the only Canadian—to win all three of the world's top science fiction awards for best novel of the year: the Hugo, the Nebula, and the John W. Campbell Memorial Award.

Read his *Red Planet Blues* at http://amzn.to/1B7cE52.

It seemed like only yesterday when I'd died, but, of course, it was almost certainly centuries ago. I wish the computer would just *tell* me, dammitall, but it was doubtless waiting until its sensors said I was sufficiently stable and alert. The irony was that my pulse was surely racing out of concern, forestalling it speaking to me. If this was an emergency, it should inform me, and if it wasn't, it should let me relax.

Finally, the machine did speak in its crisp, feminine voice. "Hello, Toby. Welcome back to the world of the living."

"Where—" I'd thought I'd spoken the word, but no sound had come out. I tried again. "Where are we?"

"Exactly where we should be: decelerating toward Soror."

I felt myself calming down. "How is Ling?"

"She's reviving, as well."

"The others?"

"All forty-eight cryogenics chambers are functioning properly," said the computer. "Everybody is apparently fine."

That was good to hear, but it wasn't surprising. We had four extra cryochambers; if one of the occupied ones had failed, Ling and I would have been awoken earlier to transfer the person within it into a spare. "What's the date?"

"16 June 3296."

I'd expected an answer like that, but it still took me back a bit. Twelve hundred years had elapsed since the blood had been siphoned out of my body and oxygenated antifreeze had been pumped in to replace it. We'd spent the first of those years accelerating, and presumably the last one decelerating, and the rest—

—the rest was spent coasting at our maximum velocity, 3,000 km/s, one percent of the speed of light. My father had been from Glasgow; my mother, from Los Angeles. They had both enjoyed the quip that the difference between an American and a European was that to an American, a hundred years was a long time, and to a European, a hundred miles is a big journey.

But both would agree that twelve hundred years and 11.9 light-years were equally staggering values. And now, here we were, decelerating in toward Tau Ceti, the closest sunlike star to Earth that wasn't part of a multiple-star system. Of course, because of that, this star had been frequently examined by Earth's Search for Extraterrestrial Intelligence. But nothing had ever been detected; nary a peep.

I was feeling better minute by minute. My own blood, stored in bottles, had been returned to my body and was now coursing through my arteries, my veins, reanimating me.

We were going to make it.

Tau Ceti happened to be oriented with its north pole facing toward Sol; that meant that the technique developed late in the twentieth century to detect planetary systems based on subtle blueshifts and redshifts of a star tugged now closer, now farther away, was useless with it. Any wobble in Tau Ceti's movements would be perpendicular, as seen from Earth, producing no Doppler effect. But eventually Earth-orbiting telescopes had been developed that were sensitive enough to detect the wobble visually, and—

It had been front-page news around the world: the first solar system seen by telescopes. Not inferred from stellar wobbles or spectral shifts, but actually *seen*. At least four planets could be made out orbiting Tau Ceti, and one of them—

There had been formulas for decades, first popularized in the RAND Corporation's study *Habitable Planets for Man*. Every science-fiction writer and astrobiologist worth his or her salt had used them to determine the *life zones*—the distances from target stars at which planets with Earthlike surface temperatures might exist, a Goldilocks band, neither too hot nor too cold.

And the second of the four planets that could be seen around Tau Ceti was smack-dab in the middle of that star's life zone. The planet was watched carefully for an entire year—one of its years, that is, a period of 193 Earth days. Two wonderful facts became apparent. First, the planet's orbit was damn near circular—meaning it would likely have stable temperatures all the time; the gravitational influence of the fourth planet, a Jovian giant orbiting at a distance of half a billion kilometers from Tau Ceti, probably was responsible for that.

And, second, the planet varied in brightness substantially over the course of its twenty-nine-hour-and-seventeen-minute day. The reason was easy to deduce: most of one hemisphere was covered with land, which reflected back little of Tau Ceti's yellow light, while the other hemisphere, with a much higher albedo, was likely covered by a vast ocean, no doubt, given the planet's fortuitous orbital radius, of liquid water—an extraterrestrial Pacific.

Of course, at a distance of 11.9 light-years, it was quite possible that Tau Ceti had other planets, too small or too dark to be seen. And so referring to the Earthlike globe as Tau Ceti II would have been problematic; if an additional world or worlds were eventually found orbiting closer in, the system's planetary numbering would end up as confusing as the scheme used to designate Saturn's rings.

Clearly a name was called for, and Giancarlo DiMaio, the astronomer who had discovered the half-land, half-water world, gave it one: Soror, the Latin word for sister. And, indeed, Soror appeared, at least as far as could be told from Earth, to be a sister to humanity's home world.

Soon we would know for sure just how perfect a sister it was. And speaking of sisters, well—okay, Ling Woo wasn't my biological sister, but we'd worked together and trained together for four years before launch, and I'd come to think of her as a sister, despite the press constantly referring to us as the new

Adam and Eve. Of course, we'd help to populate the new world, but not together; my wife, Helena, was one of the forty-eight others still frozen solid. Ling wasn't involved yet with any of the other colonists, but, well, she was gorgeous and brilliant, and of the two dozen men in cryosleep, twenty-one were unattached.

Ling and I were co-captains of the *Pioneer Spirit*. Her cryocoffin was like mine, and unlike all the others: it was designed for repeated use. She and I could be revived multiple times during the voyage, to deal with emergencies. The rest of the crew, in coffins that had cost only $700,000 a piece instead of the six million each of ours was worth, could only be revived once, when our ship reached its final destination.

"You're all set," said the computer. "You can get up now."

The thick glass cover over my coffin slid aside, and I used the padded handles to hoist myself out of its black porcelain frame. For most of the journey, the ship had been coasting in zero gravity, but now that it was decelerating, there was a gentle push downward. Still, it was nowhere near a full g, and I was grateful for that. It would be a day or two before I would be truly steady on my feet.

My module was shielded from the others by a partition, which I'd covered with photos of people I'd left behind: my parents, Helena's parents, my real sister, her two sons. My clothes had waited patiently for me for twelve hundred years; I rather suspected they were now hopelessly out of style. But I got dressed—I'd been naked in the cryochamber, of course—and at last I stepped out from behind the partition, just in time to see Ling emerging from behind the wall that shielded her cryocoffin.

"Morning," I said, trying to sound blasé.

Ling, wearing a blue and gray jumpsuit, smiled broadly. "Good morning."

We moved into the center of the room, and hugged, friends delighted to have shared an adventure together. Then we immediately headed out toward the bridge, half-walking, half-floating, in the reduced gravity.

"How'd you sleep?" asked Ling.

It wasn't a frivolous question. Prior to our mission, the longest anyone had spent in cryofreeze was five years, on a voyage to Saturn; the *Pioneer Spirit* was

Earth's first starship.

"Fine," I said. "You?"

"Okay," replied Ling. But then she stopped moving, and briefly touched my forearm. "Did you—did you dream?"

Brain activity slowed to a virtual halt in cryofreeze, but several members of the crew of *Cronus*—the Saturn mission—had claimed to have had brief dreams, lasting perhaps two or three subjective minutes, spread over five years. Over the span that the *Pioneer Spirit* had been traveling, there would have been time for many hours of dreaming.

I shook my head. "No. What about you?"

Ling nodded. "Yes. I dreamt about the strait of Gibraltar. Ever been there?"

"No."

"It's Spain's southernmost boundary, of course. You can see across the strait from Europe to northern Africa, and there were Neandertal settlements on the Spanish side." Ling's Ph.D. was in anthropology. "But they never made it across the strait. They could clearly see that there was more land—another continent!—only thirteen kilometers away. A strong swimmer can make it, and with any sort of raft or boat, it was eminently doable. But Neandertals never journeyed to the other side; as far as we can tell, they never even tried."

"And you dreamt—?"

"I dreamt I was part of a Neandertal community there, a teenage girl, I guess. And I was trying to convince the others that we should go across the strait, go see the new land. But I couldn't; they weren't interested. There was plenty of food and shelter where we were. Finally, I headed out on my own, trying to swim it. The water was cold and the waves were high, and half the time I couldn't get any air to breathe, but I swam and I swam, and then..."

"Yes?"

She shrugged a little. "And then I woke up."

I smiled at her. "Well, this time we're going to make it. We're going to make it for sure."

We came to the bridge door, which opened automatically to admit us, although it squeaked something fierce while doing so; its lubricants must have dried up over the last twelve centuries. The room was rectangular with a double row of angled consoles facing a large screen, which currently was off.

"Distance to Soror?" I asked into the air.

The computer's voice replied. "1.2 million kilometers."

I nodded. About three times the distance between Earth and its moon. "Screen on, view ahead."

"Overrides are in place," said the computer.

Ling smiled at me. "You're jumping the gun, partner."

I was embarrassed. The *Pioneer Spirit* was decelerating toward Soror; the ship's fusion exhaust was facing in the direction of travel. The optical scanners would be burned out by the glare if their shutters were opened. "Computer, turn off the fusion motors."

"Powering down," said the artificial voice.

"Visual as soon as you're able," I said.

The gravity bled away as the ship's engines stopped firing. Ling held on to one of the handles attached to the top of the console nearest her; I was still a little groggy from the suspended animation, and just floated freely in the room. After about two minutes, the screen came on. Tau Ceti was in the exact center, a baseball-sized yellow disk. And the four planets were clearly visible, ranging from pea-sized to as big as grape.

"Magnify on Soror," I said.

One of the peas became a billiard ball, although Tau Ceti grew hardly at all.

"More," said Ling.

The planet grew to softball size. It was showing as a wide crescent, perhaps a third of the disk illuminated from this angle. And—thankfully, fantastically—Soror was everything we'd dreamed it would be: a giant polished marble, with swirls of white cloud, and a vast, blue ocean, and—

Part of a continent was visible, emerging out of the darkness. And it was green, apparently covered with vegetation.

We hugged again, squeezing each other tightly. No one had been sure when we'd left Earth; Soror could have been barren. The *Pioneer Spirit* was ready regardless: in its cargo holds was everything we needed to survive even on an airless world. But we'd hoped and prayed that Soror would be, well—just like this: a true sister, another Earth, another home.

"It's beautiful, isn't it?" said Ling.

I felt my eyes tearing. It *was* beautiful, breathtaking, stunning. The vast ocean, the cottony clouds, the verdant land, and—

"Oh, my God," I said, softly. "Oh, my God."

"What?" said Ling.

"Don't you see?" I asked. "Look!"

Ling narrowed her eyes and moved closer to the screen. "What?"

"On the dark side," I said.

She looked again. "Oh…" she said. There were faint lights sprinkled across the darkness; hard to see, but definitely there. "Could it be volcanism?" asked Ling. Maybe Soror wasn't so perfect after all.

"Computer," I said, "spectral analysis of the light sources on the planet's dark side."

"Predominantly incandescent lighting, color temperature 5600 kelvin."

I exhaled and looked at Ling. They weren't volcanoes. They were cities.

Soror, the world we'd spent twelve centuries traveling to, the world we'd intended to colonize, the world that had been dead silent when examined by radio telescopes, was already inhabited.

The *Pioneer Spirit* was a colonization ship; it wasn't intended as a diplomatic vessel. When it had left Earth, it had seemed important to get at least some humans off the mother world. Two small-scale nuclear wars—Nuke I and Nuke II, as the media had dubbed them—had already been fought, one in southern Asia, the other in South America. It appeared to be only a matter of time before Nuke III, and that one might be the big one.

SETI had detected nothing from Tau Ceti, at least not by 2051. But Earth itself had only been broadcasting for a century and a half at that point; Tau Ceti might have had a thriving civilization then that hadn't yet started using radio. But now it was twelve hundred years later. Who knew how advanced the Tau Cetians might be?

I looked at Ling, then back at the screen. "What should we do?"

Ling tilted her head to one side. "I'm not sure. On the one hand, I'd love to meet them, whoever they are. But…"

"But they might not want to meet us," I said. "They might think we're invaders, and—"

"And we've got forty-eight other colonists to think about," said Ling. "For all we know, we're the last surviving humans."

I frowned. "Well, that's easy enough to determine. Computer, swing the radio telescope toward Sol system. See if you can pick anything up that might be artificial."

"Just a sec," said the female voice. A few moments later, a cacophony filled the room: static and snatches of voices and bits of music and sequences of tones, overlapping and jumbled, fading in and out. I heard what sounded like English—although strangely inflected—and maybe Arabic and Mandarin and…

"We're not the last survivors," I said, smiling. "There's still life on Earth—or, at least, there was 11.9 years ago, when those signals started out."

Ling exhaled. "I'm glad we didn't blow ourselves up," she said. "Now, I guess we should find out what we're dealing with at Tau Ceti. Computer, swing the dish to face Soror, and again scan for artificial signals."

"Doing so." There was silence for most of a minute, then a blast of static, and a few bars of music, and clicks and bleeps, and voices, speaking in Mandarin and English and—

"No," said Ling. "I said face the dish the *other* way. I want to hear what's coming from Soror."

The computer actually sounded miffed. "The dish *is* facing toward Soror," it said.

I looked at Ling, realization dawning. At the time we'd left Earth, we'd been so worried that humanity was about to snuff itself out, we hadn't really stopped to consider what would happen if that didn't occur. But with twelve hundred years, faster spaceships would doubtless have been developed. While the colonists aboard the *Pioneer Spirit* had slept, some dreaming at an indolent pace, other ships had zipped past them, arriving at Tau Ceti decades, if not centuries, earlier—long enough ago that they'd already built human cities on Soror.

"Damn it," I said. "God damn it." I shook my head, staring at the screen. The tortoise was supposed to win, not the hare.

"What do we do now?" asked Ling.

I sighed. "I suppose we should contact them."

"We—ah, we might be from the wrong side."

I grinned. "Well, we can't *both* be from the wrong side. Besides, you heard the radio: Mandarin *and* English. Anyway, I can't imagine that anyone cares about a war more than a thousand years in the past, and—"

"Excuse me," said the ship's computer. "Incoming audio message."

I looked at Ling. She frowned, surprised. "Put it on," I said.

"*Pioneer Spirit*, welcome! This is Jod Bokket, manager of the Derluntin space station, in orbit around Soror. Is there anyone awake on board?" It was a man's voice, with an accent unlike anything I'd ever heard before.

Ling looked at me, to see if I was going to object, then she spoke up. "Computer, send a reply." The computer bleeped to signal that the channel was open. "This is Dr. Ling Woo, co-captain of the *Pioneer Spirit*. Two of us have revived; there are forty-eight more still in cryofreeze."

"Well, look," said Bokket's voice, "it'll be days at the rate you're going before you get here. How about if we send a ship to bring you two to Derluntin? We can have someone there to pick you up in about an hour."

"They really like to rub it in, don't they?" I grumbled.

"What was that?" said Bokket. "We couldn't quite make it out."

Ling and I consulted with facial expressions, then agreed. "Sure," said Ling. "We'll be waiting."

"Not for long," said Bokket, and the speaker went dead.

Bokket himself came to collect us. His spherical ship was tiny compared with ours, but it seemed to have about the same amount of habitable interior space; would the ignominies ever cease? Docking adapters had changed a lot in a thousand years, and he wasn't able to get an airtight seal, so we had to transfer over to his ship in space suits. Once aboard, I was pleased to see we were still floating freely; it would have been *too* much if they'd had artificial gravity.

Bokket seemed a nice fellow—about my age, early thirties. Of course, maybe people looked youthful forever now; who knew how old he might actually be? I couldn't really identify his ethnicity, either; he seemed to be rather a blend of traits. But he certainly was taken with Ling—his eyes popped out when she took off her helmet, revealing her heart-shaped face and long, black hair.

"Hello," he said, smiling broadly.

Ling smiled back. "Hello. I'm Ling Woo, and this is Toby MacGregor, my co-captain."

"Greetings," I said, sticking out my hand.

Bokket looked at it, clearly not knowing precisely what to do. He extended his hand in a mirroring of my gesture, but didn't touch me. I closed the gap and clasped his hand. He seemed surprised, but pleased.

"We'll take you back to the station first," he said. "Forgive us, but, well—you can't go down to the planet's surface yet; you'll have to be quarantined. We've eliminated a lot of diseases, of course, since your time, and so we don't vaccinate for them anymore. I'm willing to take the risk, but…"

I nodded. "That's fine."

He tipped his head slightly, as if he were preoccupied for a moment, then: "I've told the ship to take us back to Derluntin station. It's in a polar orbit, about 200 kilometers above Soror; you'll get some beautiful views of the planet, anyway." He was grinning from ear to ear. "It's wonderful to meet you people," he said. "Like a page out of history."

"If you knew about us," I asked, after we'd settled in for the journey to the station, "why didn't you pick us up earlier?"

Bokket cleared his throat. "We didn't know about you."

"But you called us by name: *Pioneer Spirit*."

"Well, it *is* painted in letters three meters high across your hull. Our asteroid-watch system detected you. A lot of information from your time has been lost—I guess there was a lot of political upheaval then, no?—but we knew Earth had experimented with sleeper ships in the twenty-first century."

We were getting close to the space station; it was a giant ring, spinning to simulate gravity. It might have taken us over a thousand years to do it, but humanity was finally building space stations the way God had always intended them to be.

And floating next to the space station was a beautiful spaceship, with a spindle-shaped silver hull and two sets of mutually perpendicular emerald-green delta wings. "It's gorgeous," I said.

Bokket nodded.

"How does it land, though? Tail-down?"

"It doesn't land; it's a starship."

"Yes, but—"

"We use shuttles to go between it and the ground."

"But if it can't land," asked Ling, "why is it streamlined? Just for esthetics?"

Bokket laughed, but it was a polite laugh. "It's streamlined because it needs to be. There's substantial length-contraction when flying at just below the speed of light; that means that the interstellar medium seems much denser. Although there's only one baryon per cubic centimeter, they form what seems to be an appreciable atmosphere if you're going fast enough."

"And your ships are *that* fast?" asked Ling.

Bokket smiled. "Yes. They're that fast."

Ling shook her head. "We were crazy," she said. "Crazy to undertake our journey." She looked briefly at Bokket, but couldn't meet his eyes. She turned her gaze down toward the floor. "You must think we're incredibly foolish."

Bokket's eyes widened. He seemed at a loss for what to say. He looked at me, spreading his arms, as if appealing to me for support. But I just exhaled, letting air—and disappointment—vent from my body.

"You're wrong," said Bokket, at last. "You couldn't be more wrong. We *honor* you." He paused, waiting for Ling to look up again. She did, her eyebrows lifted questioningly. "If we have come farther than you," said Bokket, "or have gone faster than you, it's because we had your work to build on. Humans are here now because it's *easy* for us to be here, because you and others blazed the trails." He looked at me, then at Ling. "If we see farther," he said, "it's because we stand on the shoulders of giants."

Later that day, Ling, Bokket, and I were walking along the gently curving floor of Derluntin station. We were confined to a limited part of one section; they'd let us down to the planet's surface in another ten days, Bokket had said.

"There's nothing for us here," said Ling, hands in her pockets. "We're freaks, anachronisms. Like somebody from the T'ang Dynasty showing up in our world."

"Soror is wealthy," said Bokket. "We can certainly support you and your passengers."

"They are *not* passengers," I snapped. "They are colonists. They are explorers."

Bokket nodded. "I'm sorry. You're right, of course. But look—we really are delighted that you're here. I've been keeping the media away; the quarantine lets me do that. But they will go absolutely dingo when you come down to the planet. It's like having Neil Armstrong or Tamiko Hiroshige show up at your door."

"Tamiko who?" asked Ling.

"Sorry. After your time. She was the first person to disembark at Alpha Centauri."

"The first," I repeated; I guess I wasn't doing a good job of hiding my bitterness. "That's the honor—that's the achievement. Being the first. Nobody remembers the name of the second person on the moon."

"Edwin Eugene Aldrin, Jr.," said Bokket. "Known as 'Buzz.'"

"Fine, okay," I said. "*You* remember, but most people don't."

"I didn't remember it; I accessed it." He tapped his temple. "Direct link to the planetary web; everybody has one."

Ling exhaled; the gulf was vast. "Regardless," she said, "we are not pioneers; we're just also-rans. We may have set out before you did, but you got here before us."

"Well, my ancestors did," said Bokket. "I'm sixth-generation Sororian."

"*Sixth* generation?" I said. "How long has the colony been here?"

"We're not a colony anymore; we're an independent world. But the ship that got here first left Earth in 2107. Of course, my ancestors didn't immigrate until much later."

"Twenty-one-oh-seven," I repeated. That was only fifty-six years after the launch of the *Pioneer Spirit*. I'd been thirty-one when our ship had started its journey; if I'd stayed behind, I might very well have lived to see the real pioneers depart. What had we been thinking, leaving Earth? Had we been running, escaping, getting out, fleeing before the bombs fell? Were we pioneers, or cowards?

No. No, those were crazy thoughts. We'd left for the same reason that *Homo sapiens* had crossed the Strait of Gibraltar. It was what we did as a species. It was why we'd triumphed, and the Neandertals had failed. We *needed* to see what was on the other side, what was over the next hill, what was orbiting other stars. It was what had given us dominion over the home planet; it was what was going to make us kings of infinite space.

I turned to Ling. "We can't stay here," I said.

She seemed to mull this over for a bit, then nodded. She looked at Bokket. "We don't want parades," she said. "We don't want statues." She lifted her eyebrows, as if acknowledging the magnitude of what she was asking for. "We want a new ship, a faster ship." She looked at me, and I bobbed my head in agreement. She pointed out the window. "A *streamlined* ship."

"What would you do with it?" asked Bokket. "Where would you go?"

She glanced at me, then looked back at Bokket. "Andromeda."

"Andromeda? You mean the Andromeda *galaxy*? But that's—" a fractional pause, no doubt while his web link provided the data "—2.2 *million* light-years away."

"Exactly."

"But… but it would take over two million years to get there."

"Only from Earth's—excuse me, from Soror's—point of view," said Ling. "We could do it in less subjective time than we've already been traveling, and, of course, we'd spend all that time in cryogenic freeze."

"None of our ships have cryogenic chambers," Bokket said. "There's no need for them."

"We could transfer the chambers from the *Pioneer Spirit*."

Bokket shook his head. "It would be a one-way trip; you'd never come back."

"That's not true," I said. "Unlike most galaxies, Andromeda is actually moving toward the Milky Way, not away from it. Eventually, the two galaxies will merge, bringing us home."

"That's billions of years in the future."

"Thinking small hasn't done us any good so far," said Ling.

Bokket frowned. "I said before that we can afford to support you and your shipmates here on Soror, and that's true. But starships are expensive. We can't just give you one."

"It's got to be cheaper than supporting all of us."

"No, it's not."

"You said you honored us. You said you stand on our shoulders. If that's true, then repay the favor. Give us an opportunity to stand on *your* shoulders. Let us have a new ship."

Bokket sighed; it was clear he felt we really didn't understand how difficult Ling's request would be to fulfill. "I'll do what I can," he said.

Ling and I spent that evening talking, while blue-and-green Soror spun majestically beneath us. It was our job to jointly make the right decision, not just for ourselves but for the four dozen other members of the *Pioneer Spirit's* complement that had entrusted their fate to us. Would they have wanted to be revived here?

No. No, of course not. They'd left Earth to found a colony; there was no reason to think they would have changed their minds, whatever they might be dreaming. Nobody had an emotional attachment to the idea of Tau Ceti; it just had seemed a logical target star.

"We could ask for passage back to Earth," I said.

"You don't want that," said Ling. "And neither, I'm sure, would any of the others."

"No, you're right," I said. "They'd want us to go on."

Ling nodded. "I think so."

"Andromeda?" I said, smiling. "Where did that come from?"

She shrugged. "First thing that popped into my head."

"Andromeda," I repeated, tasting the word some more. I remembered how thrilled I was, at sixteen, out in the California desert, to see that little oval smudge below Cassiopeia for the first time. Another galaxy, another island universe—and half again as big as our own. "Why not?" I fell silent but, after a while, said, "Bokket seems to like you."

Ling smiled. "I like him."

"Go for it," I said.

"What?" She sounded surprised.

"Go for it, if you like him. I may have to be alone until Helena is revived at our final destination, but you don't have to be. Even if they do give us a new ship, it'll surely be a few weeks before they can transfer the cryochambers."

Ling rolled her eyes. "*Men*," she said, but I knew the idea appealed to her.

Bokket was right: the Sororian media seemed quite enamored with Ling and me, and not just because of our exotic appearance—my white skin and blue eyes; her dark skin and epicanthic folds; our two strange accents, both so different from the way people of the thirty-third century spoke. They also seemed to be fascinated by, well, by the pioneer spirit.

When the quarantine was over, we did go down to the planet. The temperature was perhaps a little cooler than I'd have liked, and the air a bit moister—but humans adapt, of course. The architecture in Soror's capital city of Pax was surprisingly ornate, with lots of domed roofs and intricate carvings. The term "capital city" was an anachronism, though; government was completely decentralized, with all major decisions done by plebiscite—including the decision about whether or not to give us another ship.

Bokket, Ling, and I were in the central square of Pax, along with Kari Deetal, Soror's president, waiting for the results of the vote to be announced. Media representatives from all over the Tau Ceti system were present, as well as one from Earth, whose stories were always read 11.9 years after he filed them. Also on hand were perhaps a thousand spectators.

"My friends," said Deetal, to the crowd, spreading her arms, "you have all voted, and now let us share in the results." She tipped her head slightly, and a moment later people in the crowd started clapping and cheering.

Ling and I turned to Bokket, who was beaming. "What is it?" said Ling. "What decision did they make?"

Bokket looked surprised. "Oh, sorry. I forgot you don't have web implants. You're going to get your ship."

Ling closed her eyes and breathed a sigh of relief. My heart was pounding.

President Deetal gestured toward us. "Dr. MacGregor, Dr. Woo—would you say a few words?"

We glanced at each other then stood up. "Thank you," I said looking out at everyone.

Ling nodded in agreement. "Thank you very much."

A reporter called out a question. "What are you going to call your new ship?"

Ling frowned; I pursed my lips. And then I said, "What else? The *Pioneer Spirit II.*"

The crowd erupted again.

Finally, the fateful day came. Our official boarding of our new starship—the one that would be covered by all the media—wouldn't happen for another four hours, but Ling and I were nonetheless heading toward the airlock that joined the ship to the station's outer rim. She wanted to look things over once more, and I wanted to spend a little time just sitting next to Helena's cryochamber, communing with her.

And, as we walked, Bokket came running along the curving floor toward us.

"Ling," he said, catching his breath. "Toby."

I nodded a greeting. Ling looked slightly uncomfortable; she and Bokket had grown close during the last few weeks, but they'd also had their time alone last night to say their goodbyes. I don't think she'd expected to see him again before we left.

"I'm sorry to bother you two," he said. "I know you're both busy, but…" He seemed quite nervous.

"Yes?" I said.

He looked at me, then at Ling. "Do you have room for another passenger?"

Ling smiled. "We don't have passengers. We're colonists."

"Sorry," said Bokket, smiling back at her. "Do you have room for another colonist?"

"Well, there are *four* spare cryochambers, but…" She looked at me.

"Why not?" I said, shrugging.

"It's going to be hard work, you know," said Ling, turning back to Bokket. "Wherever we end up, it's going to be rough."

Bokket nodded. "I know. And I want to be part of it."

Ling knew she didn't have to be coy around me. "That would be wonderful," she said. "But—but why?"

Bokket reached out tentatively, and found Ling's hand. He squeezed it gently, and she squeezed back. "You're one reason," he said.

"Got a thing for older women, eh?" said Ling. I smiled at that.

Bokket laughed. "I guess."

"You said I was one reason," said Ling.

He nodded. "The other reason is—well, it's this: I don't want to stand on the shoulders of giants." He paused, then lifted his own shoulders a little, as if acknowledging that he was giving voice to the sort of thought rarely spoken aloud. "I want to *be* a giant."

They continued to hold hands as we walked down the space station's long corridor, heading toward the sleek and graceful ship that would take us to our new home.

GIFT OF A USELESS MAN
ALAN DEAN FOSTER

Alan's work to date includes excursions into hard science fiction, fantasy, horror, detective, western, historical, and contemporary fiction. He has also written numerous nonfiction articles on film, science, and scuba diving, as well as having produced the novel versions of many films, including such well-known productions as *Star Wars*, the first three *Alien* films, *Alien Nation, The Chronicles of Riddick, Star Trek, Terminator Salvation*, and the first two *Transformers* films. Lifeboat Foundation highly recommends his classic *Sentenced to Prism* available at http://amzn.to/1qUdDBw. You can read more of his short stories in *Who Needs Enemies?* at http://amzn.to/1sxGooJ.

What do you give when you've nothing left to give? When you've naught left to offer friends to whom you feel indebted? When you're busted, in more than one sense?

We spend a fortune in this country sweeping away the byproducts of ourselves, ridding ourselves of personal waste. But how do you define "waste"? Might not what we consider waste be considered valuable by someone else? Sometimes values are so hard to define they escape analysis.

When you come right down to it, my body, your body, everybody is nothing more than a wondrously efficient and complex chemical plant, one that even DuPont can't duplicate. Better living through chemistry.

And most of the time, we're not even aware of the fact that this irreplaceable plant is producing all the time…

Both Pearson and the ship were rotted out.

He hadn't known that when he'd rented it (having no intention of returning it and not worrying about that since both the credslip he'd used to pay for it and his corresponding identification were fakes), but he'd been in too much of a hurry to care.

The ship had made the Jump in one piece; but when he'd come out into normal space again, he'd found several small but critical components that had come out in many pieces.

All that was left of it now was a pillar of smoke and vaporized metal climbing into a pale blue sky. He could not bring himself to curse it. He knew the feeling. And it had ejected him, though somewhat less than safely. He was alive, and that wasn't much. All he felt now was an overwhelming tiredness, a fatigue of the spirit. A numbness of the soul.

Surprisingly, there was no pain. Inside, Pearson continued to function. Outside, he could move his eyes and lips, twitch his nose, and—with enormous effort—raise his right arm off the flat, sandy ground. His face was no longer merely a small part of an expressive self: it was all that remained. What the rest of his body, encased in the remnants of his flight suit, looked like, he could only imagine. He did not wish to imagine. He knew his right arm was intact, because he could move it. Beyond that, all was morbid speculation.

If he was lucky, very lucky, he might be able to use the arm to turn himself onto his side. He did not bother to make the effort. There were no more illusions, at last no more illusions, circling languidly in Pearson's consciousness. On the eve of death, he had become a realist.

It was a tiny world he'd inflicted himself upon, no more than a very large asteroid, really. Silently, he apologized to it for any damage his crash might have caused. He was always apologizing for doing damage.

He was breathing, so the thin atmosphere was less tenuous than it looked. No one would find him here. Even the police who'd been chasing him would leave off searching. Pearson was a most insignificant criminal. Not even a criminal, really. To qualify for that label you had to do something modestly harmful. "Criminal" implied someone dangerous, threatening. Pearson was merely irritating to society, like a minor itch.

Well, he'd finally gone and scratched himself, he thought, and was surprised to discover he had the strength and ability left to laugh.

It made him black out, however.

When he regained his senses, it was just beginning to grow light. He had no idea how long this minuscule world's day was. Therefore he had no idea how long he'd been unconscious. He might've been out a day or a week, human time. Though he no longer thought of himself as human. Complete muscular paralysis, save for his face and one arm, had left him a living corpse. He was unable to move about, nor reach the concentrates in the battered survival pack that might or might not still be attached to the leg of his suit, or do more than breathe in the feeble atmosphere that was temporarily keeping him alive. He rather wished he'd blown up with the ship.

He would not starve, however. He would die of thirst first. Living corpse, Pearson. Brain in a bottle. It gave him plenty of time to reflect on his life.

Actually, he'd been something of a living corpse all along. He'd never felt for anyone or anything, and not very strongly for himself. Never doing anyone any good and not having the capability to do anyone serious evil, he'd just sort of muddled along, taking up space and other people's air.

I'd have made a better tree, he mused tiredly. Pearson wondered if he'd have made a very good tree. Certainly he couldn't have been a worse tree than he had a man. He saw himself as a youth, cocky in a sniveling sort of way. Saw himself toadying up to the smoother, more professional criminals in hopes of worming his way into their company, their society, their friendship.

Naw, he hadn't even made a very good boot-licker. Nor could he go straight, the couple of times he'd tried. The real, legal world had regarded him with the same resigned contempt as the less virtuous. So he'd lived in a tenebrous, mucousy vacuum of his own invention, not quite functioning efficiently in the mental sense and only barely in the physical.

If only… but no, he stopped himself sharply. He was going to die. Might as well be honest for a change, if only with himself. The misfortunes he'd suffered were his own doing, always his own doing, not the fault of others as he'd forever been telling himself. There had been a few pitying ones who'd tried to help him. Somehow he always managed to screw things up. If nothing else, perhaps he could die being honest with his own thoughts.

He had heard that dying of thirst was not pleasant.

The sun went down, and no moon came up. Naturally not, for a world this small could not afford the luxury of a moon. It was a wonder it held onto a breathable atmosphere. Pearson wondered idly if there was life existing on the fine, flat soil around him. Plants, maybe. He'd come down too fast and messily to spend time on such details. Since he was unable to turn his head, he could do no more than wonder.

Air rippled across him, a cool night breeze, pleasant after the mild, hazy heat of day. He felt it keenly on his face. The rest of his body's external receptors were dead. It was possible he'd suffered severe burns. If so, he couldn't react to them. In that respect the paralysis was a blessing. He knew that other parts of his body were functioning, though. He could smell himself.

When the sun rose again he was still wide awake. He estimated this world's day at three to four hours, followed by a night of equal duration. The information was of no practical use, but such speculation helped keep his mind busy. He was slowly adjusting to his situation. It's said the human mind can adjust to anything.

After a while he discovered the thought of death no longer bothered him. It would be a relief of sorts. No more running; from others, from his pitiful self. No one would grieve over him. No one would miss him. By his absence he would spare others the infection of his presence. The first hints of thirst, faint but unmistakable, took possession of his throat.

Short days passed and a few clouds appeared. He'd never paid any attention to clouds and little to the weather. Now he had time and reason to study both. He could see nothing else. It occurred to him he might be able to use his one functioning arm to turn his head and thus vary his line of sight. But when he tried, he found the arm would not respond sufficiently to carry out the complex maneuver.

Odd, the emotions. He discovered that the chance his one working limb might be becoming paralyzed frightened him more than the certain onslaught of death.

Clouds continued to gather above him. He regarded them indifferently. Rain might prolong his life a few earthly days, but eventually he'd starve. The concentrates in his suit pack could keep him alive for months, probably longer considering his lack of activity. But they might as well have been vaporized with the ship. He couldn't reach them.

His mind speculated on possible methods of suicide. If his arm would respond and there was a sharp piece of metal nearby, a scrap of ship, he might cut his throat. If… if…

It did rain. Gently and steadily, for an entire half day. His open mouth caught enough to sate him. The clouds passed and shattered, and the distant sun returned. He felt it drying his face, assumed it was doing so to the rest of his body. He formed a new appreciation for the miracle of rain and the process by which it's transformed into blood and lymph and cells. Amazing, astonishing accomplishment; and he'd spent a short lifetime taking it for granted. He deserved to die.

I am growing philosophical, he thought. Or delirious.

Short days gave way to brief nights. He had completely lost track of time when the first bug found him.

Pearson felt it long before he saw it. It crawled up his cheek. Maddeningly, he was unable to scratch at it or brush it away. It traversed his face, stopped, and peered into his right eye.

He blinked.

The tickle returned. He hadn't caught it, then. It was on his forehead now. After pausing there, it walked down across his left cheek, retracing its first approach.

Out of the corner of his left eye he saw it as it dropped to his shoulder. It was blue-black and too small for him to discern individual details. It definitely looked like an insect.

It stopped on his shoulder, considering its surroundings.

Maybe it would be better this way, he thought. It would be faster if the bugs devoured him. When he'd bled enough, he would die. If they started below his head, he might never feel any pain before he passed out.

Silently, he encouraged the insect. Go on, buddy. Bring back your aunts and uncles and cousins and have yourselves a feast, courtesy of Pearson. It'll be a blessing.

"No, we cannot do that."

I'm delirious, he mused distantly, adding in reflex, "Why not?"

"You are a wonderment. We could not eat a wonderment. We are not deserving enough."

"I'm no wonder," he thought insistently. "I'm a wastrel, a failure, a thorough mistake of nature. Not only that," he concluded, "I am lying here conversing telepathically with a bug."

"I am Yirn, one of the People," the soft thought informed him. "I am not what a bug is. Tell me, wonderment, how can something so huge be alive?"

So Pearson told him. He told the bug his name, and about mankind, and about his sick, sad existence that was soon to come to an end, and about his paralysis.

"I am saddened for you," Yirn of the People finally said. "We can do nothing to help you. We are a poor tribe among many and are not permitted by the Laws to reproduce much. Nor do I begin to understand these strange things you tell me of space and time and size.

I find it hard enough to believe that this mountain you lie within once moved. Yet you say that is so, and I must believe."

Pearson had a sudden, disturbing thought. "Hey, look, Yirn. Don't get the idea I'm any sort of god or anything. I'm just bigger, that's all. I'm really less than you. I couldn't even make a good pimp."

"The concept does not translate." Yirn gave the impression of straining. "You are the most wonderful thing in all creation."

"Bullshit. Say... how can I 'talk' with you when you're so much smaller?"

"Among our People we have a saying that it is the size of the intellect that is important, not the size of the size."

"Yeah, I guess. Look, I'm sorry you've got such a poor tribe, Yirn; and I appreciate your being sorry for me. No one's ever been sorry for me before except me. Even a bug's sympathy's an improvement." He lay quietly for a while, regarding the bug, which preened minute antennae.

"I... I wish I could do something for you and your tribe," he finally said, "but I can't even help myself. I'm going to die of hunger soon."

"We would help if we could," came the thought. Pearson had a feeling of sadness all out of proportion to the creature's size. "But all we could gather would not feed you properly for a day."

"Yeah. There's food in my suit pack, but..." He fell silent. Then, "Yirn, tell me if there are shiny metal coverings on my lower body."

Moments passed while the insect made a hike to the promontory of a knuckle and returned. "There are what you describe, Pearson."

"How many People in your tribe?"

"What do you have in your mind, Pearson?"

Pearson told him and Yirn of the People replied. "Enough."

It took days, local days, for the tribe of Yirn to open the catches on the suit packs. When it became apparent the People could digest human food, a great mental rejoicing filled Pearson's brain; and he was glad.

It was a truly humble Yirn who later came to communicate with him. "For the first time in many, many generations, my tribe has enough to eat. We can multiply beyond the restrictions the Laws impose upon those bereft of food. One of the great blocks you call concentrates can feed the tribe for a long while. We have not tried the natural foods you say are contained in the greater pack beneath you, but we will.

"Now we can become a real tribe and not fear those tribes that prey on the poor. All because of you, great Pearson."

"Just 'Pearson,' you understand? You call me 'great' again and I'll..." He paused. "No. I won't do anything. Even if I could. I'm finished with threatening. Just plain Pearson, if you will. And I haven't done a goddamn thing for you. Your people got at the food all by themselves. First time I ever thought anything of concentrates."

"We have a surprise for you, Pearson."

Something was crawling with infinite slowness up his cheek. It had a little weight, more than the People. He saw it edge into his vision. A small brown block. Dozens of tiny blue-black forms surrounded it. He could hear their effort in his mind.

The block reached his lips and he opened them. Some of the People were terrified at the nearness of that bottomless dark chasm. They turned and fled. Yirn and other leaders of the tribe took their places.

The block passed over his lower lip. The People exerted a last, monumental effort. Some of them expired from it. The block fell into the chasm.

Pearson felt saliva flowing, but hesitated. "I don't know what good it'll do in the long run, Yirn, but… thanks. You'd better herd your folks off my face, though. There's going to be an earthqua… no, a Pearsonquake, in a moment."

When they were safely clear, he began to chew.

It rained the next morning. The raindrops were the size of raindrops on Earth. They posed a terrifying threat to the tribe, if they were caught out in the open. A few drops could kill someone the size of Yirn. But the entire tribe had plenty of shelter beneath the overhang of Pearson's right arm.

Many weeks later, Yim sat on Pearson's nose, staring down into oceanic eyes. "The concentrates will not last forever, and the real foods we've found in your 'pack' beneath you will last less so."

"Never mind that. I don't want you to eat those. I think there's a couple of carrots, and on an old sandwich, there should be tomato slices, lettuce, and, I think, mushrooms. Also pocya, a small kind of nut. The meat and bread you can eat, but save some of the bread. Maybe you can eat the mold."

"I do not understand, Pearson."

"How do you find food, Yirn? You're gatherers, aren't you?"

"That is so."

"Then I want you to take the carrots, and the tomato, and the others—I'll describe them to you—and also samples of every local plant your people eat."

"And do what with them, Pearson?"

"Gather the elders of the tribe. We'll start with the concept of irrigation…"

Pearson was no agriculturist. But he knew, in his primitive way, that if you plant and water and weed, certain foods will grow. The People were fast learners. It was the concept of staying in one place and planting that was new to them.

A catch basin was dug, at the cost of hundreds of tiny lives. But the concentrates gave the People great energy. Tiny rivulets began to snake outward from the basin, away from the protective bulk of Pearson. When it ceased raining, the basin and the thread-thin canals were full, and the minute dams came into good use. Another basin was dug, and then another.

Some of the human food took and grew, and some of the local foods took and grew. The People prospered. Pearson explained the idea of building permanent structures. The People had never considered it because they could not imagine an artificial construct which would shed rain. Pearson told them about A-frames.

There came the day when the concentrates ran out. Pearson had been anticipating it and was not dismayed by the news. He'd done far, far more than he'd dreamed of being able to do those first empty days alone on the sand, after the crash. He'd helped, and been rewarded with the first real friendship of his life.

"It doesn't matter, Yirn. I'm just glad I was able to be of some use to you and your people."

"Yirn is dead," said the bug. "I am Yurn, one of his offspring, given the honor of talking to you."

"Yirn's dead? It hadn't been that long… has it?" Pearson's sense of time was hazy. But then, the lifespan of the People was far shorter than man's. "No matter. At least the tribe has enough to eat now."

"It does matter, to us," replied Yurn. "Open your mouth, Pearson."

Something was crawling up his cheek. It moved at a fairly rapid pace. Tiny wooden pulleys helped it along, and over the pulleys were slung long cables made from Pearson's hair. A path for it was cut through his beard by dozens of the People using their sharp jaws.

It fell into his mouth. It was leafy and vaguely familiar. A piece of spinach.

"Eat, Pearson. The remnants of your ancient 'sandwich' have given birth…"

Soon after the third harvest, a trio of elders visited Pearson. They sat carefully on the tip of his nose and regarded him somberly.

"The crops are not doing well," said one.

"Describe them to me." They did so, and he strained the hidden places of his brain for long-unused schoolboy knowledge. "If they're getting enough water, then it can only be one thing, if they're all being affected. The soil here is getting worn out. You'll have to plant elsewhere."

"Many are the leagues between here and the farthest farm," one of the elders told him. "There have been raids. Other tribes are grown jealous of us. Our People are afraid to plant too far from you. Your presence gives them confidence."

"Then there's one other possibility." He licked his lips. The People had found salt for him. "What have you been doing with the wastes from my body?"

"They have been steadily removed and buried, as you directed," said one, "and fresh earth and sand brought constantly to replace the region beneath you, where you dampen the ground."

"The soil here is growing tired," he told them. "It requires the addition of something we call fertilizer. Here is what the People must do..."

Many years later, a new council came to visit Pearson. This was after the great battle. Several large, powerful tribes had combined to attack the People. They'd driven them back to the fortress mountain of Pearson. As the battle raged around him, the leaders of the three attacking tribes had led a forceful charge to take possession of the living god-mountain, as Pearson had come to be known to the other tribes.

Straining every remaining functional nerve in his body, Pearson had raised his one good arm and in one blow slain the leaders of the onslaught and all their general staff, and hundreds of others besides. Taking advantage of the confusion this engendered in the enemy's ranks, the People had counterattacked. The invaders were repulsed with heavy losses, and the land of the People was not troubled after that.

Many crops were destroyed. But with liberal doses of fertilizer supplied by Pearson, the next crop matured healthier than ever.

Now the new council sat in the place of honor atop Pearson's nose and gazed into fathomless, immense eyes. Yeen, eighth son-in-line from Yirn the Legendary, held the center.

"We have a present for you, Pearson. You had told us months ago of an event you call a 'birthday,' and rambled much about its meaning and the customs that surround it. We cast our thoughts for a suitable gift."

"I'm afraid I can't open it if it's wrapped," he quipped weakly. "You'll have to show me. I wish I could offer you one in return. You've kept me alive."

"You have given us much more than life. Look to your left, Pearson."

He moved his eyes. A creaking, grinding noise began, continued as he watched empty sky and waited. The feeling-thoughts of thousands of the People reached him.

An object slowly rose into view. It was a circle, set atop a perfect girder work of tiny wooden beams. It was old and scratched in places, but still shiny: a hand mirror, gleaned from God knew what section of his backpack or suit pockets. It was inclined at an angle across his chest, and down.

For the first time in many years he could see the ground. Before he could express his thanks for the wonderful, incredible gift of the mounted old mirror his thoughts were blanked by what he could see.

Tiny rows of cultivated fields stretched to the horizon. Clusters of small houses dotted the fields, many gathered together into semblances of towns. A suspension bridge made of his hair and threads from his suit crossed a tiny stream in three places. On the other side of the People-sized river were the beginnings of a small city.

The mirror crew, through an ingenious system of pulleys and cords, turned the reflector. Nearby was the factory where, he was told, wooden beams and articles were manufactured from local plants. Among the tools used to shape the beams were sharp bits of Pearson's fingernails. Huge tents housed other factories, tents made from the treated skin which peeled regularly off Pearson's suntanned body. Tools moved smoothly, and pulleys and wheels carried people to and from, lubricated in part with wax taken from Pearson's ears.

"Offer us something in return, Pearson?" said Yeen rhetorically. "You have given us the greatest gift of all: yourself. Every day we find new uses for the information you give us. Every day we find new uses for what you produce.

"Other tribes that once we fought with have joined with us, so that all may benefit from you. We are becoming what you once called a nation."

"Watch... watch out," Pearson mumbled mentally, overcome by Yeen's words and the sweeping vistas provided by the mirror. "A nation means the onset of politicians."

"What is that?" asked one of the council suddenly, pointing downward.

"A new gift," came his neighbor's thought, also staring down the great slope of Pearson's nose. "What is it good for, Pearson?"

"Nothin'. I learned a long time ago, friends," he said, "that tears ain't good for nothing..."

Yusec, hundred and twelfth son-in-line from Yirn the Legendary, was resting on Pearson's chest, enjoying the shade provided by the forest of hair there. Pearson had just finished a bit of a wonderful new fruit the People had grown on a far farm and brought in especially for him. Pearson could see Yusec via one of the many mirrors mounted around his face, all inclined to offer him a different view of his surroundings.

A party of young was touring his pelvic region and another was making its way around the base of his ear. Others came and went from him on crude escalators or one of the many huge stairways that mounted him on all sides. Groups of archivists stood nearby, ready to record any stray thought Pearson might produce. They even monitored his dreams.

"Yusec, the new food was very good." "The farmers of that region will be pleased." There was a pause before Pearson spoke again. "Yusec, I'm dying."

Startled, the insect rose to his feet, stared up at the massif of Pearson's chin. "What is this? Pearson cannot die."

"Bullshit, Yusec. What color is my hair?"

"White, Pearson. It has been so for many decades."

"Are the canyons of my face deep?"

"Yes, but no deeper than in my great-grandfather's time."

"Then they were deep then. I am dying, Yusec. I don't know how old I am because I long ago lost track of my time, and I never troubled to compare it to your time. It never mattered. It still doesn't. But I am dying.

"I'll die happier than I once thought I would, though. I've done more moving since I've been paralyzed than I did when I was mobile. I feel good about that."

"You cannot die, Pearson." Yusec repeated his insistence while sending out an emergency call for the hospital team set up many years ago solely to serve Pearson's needs.

"I can and will and am," came the reply, and a frightened Yusec heard the death coming over Pearson's thoughts like a shadow. He could not imagine a time without Pearson. "The hospital people are good. They've learned a lot about me on their own. But there's nothin' they can do. I'm gonna die."

"But... what shall we do without you?"

"Everything you do is done without me, Yusec. I've only given you advice, but the People have done all the actual work. You won't miss me."

"We will miss you, Pearson." Yusec was resigning himself to the massive inevitability of Pearson's passing. "I am saddened."

"Yeah, me too. Funny, I was almost coming to enjoy this life. Oh, well." His thoughts were very weak now, receding like the sun around the world.

"Just a last idea, Yusec."

"Yes, Pearson?"

"I thought you'd use my body, the skin and bones and organs, after I'd gone. But you've gone beyond that. Those last bronzes you showed me were real good. You don't need the Pearson factory anymore. Silly idea, but…"

Yusec barely caught the last Pearson thought before his presence left the People forever…

"They're people, sir! I know they're no bigger than an eyelash, but they've got roads and farms and factories and schools and I don't know what else. Our first non-human intelligent race, sir!"

"Easy, Hanforth," said the Captain. "I can see that." He was standing outside the lander. They'd set down in a large lake to avoid smashing the intricate metropolis which appeared to cover the entire planetoid. "Incredible's the word for it. Anything on that wreck site?"

"No sir. It's ancient. Hundreds of years at least. Detectors found only fragments of the original ship."

"The native delegation, sir?"

"Yeah?"

"They have something they want us to see. They say some of their major roadways are wide enough for us to travel safely, and they've cleared all traffic."

"I guess we'd better be courteous, though I'd feel safer doing our studies from out here, where we can't hurt anybody."

They walked for several hours. Gradually they reached an area near the site of the crater produced by the impact of an archaic ship. They'd seen the object rise over the sharp horizon, believed in it less as they drew nearer.

Now they stood at its base. It was a metal spire that towered fifty meters into the watery blue sky, tapering to a distant, sharp point.

"I can guess why they wanted us to see this." The Captain was incredulous. "If they wanted to impress us, they've done so. A piece of engineering like this, for people of their size… it's beyond belief." He frowned, shrugged.

"What is it, sir?" Hanforth's head was back as he stared toward the crest of the impossible spire.

"Funny… it reminds me of something I've seen before."

"What's that, sir?"

"A grave marker…"

LIGHT AND SHADOW
CATHERINE ASARO

Catherine's fiction is a successful blend of hard science fiction, romance, and exciting space adventure. Her novel *The Quantum Rose* won the Nebula Award for best novel.

Catherine earned her doctorate in theoretical chemical physics from Harvard and she is also a dancer and musician. Read her *Undercity* at http://amzn.to/1AypPeJ.

1
A FLASH OF STARLIGHT

Kelric spoke into the empty air of the cockpit. "Glint Control, I'm ready to give it another go."

"Standby, Glint One Eight." Lieutenant Tyrson's voice came over the audiocom, sounding so clear he could have been right next to Kelric's reclined seat instead of on the ground far below. "Glint One Eight, tracking and instrumentation are go. You're cleared for test procedure four. Calculations indicate your wing stress will be within safe limits."

Safe? An unwelcome thought rose from a hidden corner of Kelric's mind. *So what? You have nothing worth keeping safe.*

He banished the thought back to its dark recess. Then he whipped his plane through a dizzying set of loops and rolls, uncaring of the g-forces that pressed him into his seat. He lay more than sat in the tight cockpit, with the computer console and display panels in front of him. Data streamed across the visor of his faceplate, changing so fast to keep up with his maneuvers that it blurred. Holomaps of the planet Diesha turned on his screens, the deserts shaded like orange and red paint mixing on a palette. Isolated mountains broke the land's flatness in convoluted spears, and no clouds showed in a sky so blue it seemed to vibrate.

Kelric pulled out of his last loop and grinned. "How does that read, Lieutenant?"

Tyrson chuckled. "Like a dream."

And what a dream, Kelric thought. He was the first pilot to test the Glint-18, a rocket fighter powered by nuclear fusion that made other planes he had flown seem like slugs.

Captain, the Glint's computer thought. *How can a dream read?*

It's just a figure of speech, Kelric answered, directing the reply with more intensity than when his thoughts were for himself only. He touched the valve in his survival suit where the prong on his pilot's seat plugged into his spine. It connected the cyberware built into the plane with the network of fibers implanted in his body. The system created a direct link from his brain to the Glint's onboard systems. His motion was reflexive, a reminder that he was linked to a computer and not a person. He forgot sometimes. The Glint's efforts to learn idioms made it seem self-conscious, like a human being, someone new to a language.

Tyron's voice interrupted his reverie. "Captain Valdoria, I can't access mod four of your computer."

"Checking," Kelric said. To the Glint, he thought, *Run a diagnostic on your fourth mod.* It was a vital mod, one that controlled the extra shielding against heat, ultraviolet radiation, and cosmic rays that the craft needed to survive in orbit. Although this wasn't the first plane Kelric had flown with orbital capability, it far surpassed the others. Today, however, his tests concerned only its performance in a planetary atmosphere.

Lights suddenly blazed across his controls, glowing like holiday decorations. *Altimeter error,* the Glint thought. *Environment control error.*

Tyrson's voice snapped out of the audiocom. "Glint One Eight, your chase planes have lost contact with your—"

As Tyrson's voice cut off, the Glint added, *Audiocom failure.*

Slow down, Kelric told the plane. The rockets fired, but the plane didn't turn, so it sped up instead.

Cockpit pressure dropping, the Glint thought. *I've sealed your survival suit.*

What the hell? *Glint, slow us down.*

Neither the thrusters nor the attitude jets are responding, it answered.

Reboot their control mod.

Reboot successful, Then: *Captain Valdoria, we're approaching escape velocity.*

Kelric stared at the console. To escape the planet's gravitational pull, he had to go over eleven kilometers a second, far faster than he had prepared for on this flight. This was nuts. He couldn't go into space.

A thought stirred in the recesses of his mind: *Why not? You have nothing to lose. Nothing worth keeping.*

The Glint's thought cut through his own: *Do you want to try slowing down again?*

Kelric sat motionless, watching his holomaps. They all showed images of the world below him as it receded in the sable backdrop of space.

If we don't slow down within eight seconds, the Glint thought, *we won't have enough fuel to return to base. In fourteen seconds we won't be able to reach any emergency landing site.*

Kelric's private thoughts whispered like a strain of discordant music playing under the computer's voice: *You can drift in space forever. With the stars as your lovers, you'll never be alone.*

Escape velocity achieved, the Glint thought. *We are leaving the planet.*

With a mental heave, Kelric snapped himself back to reality. *Glint, return to base!*

At first nothing happened. Then the thrusters rumbled in their bay and the rockets fired, flattening him in his seat.

Re-entry initiated, the Glint thought.

Kelric exhaled. *Do we have enough fuel to get back?*

Yes.

So I'm going to live after all. Kelric wasn't sure whether to be grateful or to curse.

"We weren't able to analyze much of your cyber log," General Schuldman said.

He was seated behind the darkwood desk in his office, a huge room as spare and as strong as the grey-haired man who used it. "Most of the log was garbled. Do you have any comments to add to our quick-look report?"

Kelric was sitting in front of the desk, uncomfortable in a leather-bound chair. Was Schuldman asking for more details about his hesitation during the flight? Kelric had none; he wasn't certain himself what had happened in that moment when he had let the plane leave the planet. However, that hadn't caused the system failures.

"There's a flaw in the Glint's computer, sir," he said. "I think it's the neural-hardware interface."

Schuldman nodded. "Apparently the computer tried to break the lock that keeps it out of your private thoughts. When your mind blocked it, the system froze up."

His private thoughts. Kelric had enough trouble himself dealing with those; it was no wonder it had confused a computer. "Can the problem be fixed?"

"Our techs repaired the damage," the general said. "Jessa Zaubern checked their work herself. It shouldn't try to break your lock again." He considered Kelric. "Engineering also ran simulations using the higher velocity data you obtained. Their results suggest the Glint may indeed be able to withstand the huge accelerations Dr. Zaubern claimed in her first reports."

So Jessa had been right. It didn't surprise Kelric; she had one hell of a good mind. "Sir, the ship may be able to withstand those accelerations, but the engines can't achieve them."

Schuldman regarded him steadily. "That's why we're putting an inversion engine in it."

What the hell? They wanted to put a *starship* engine in a plane? What a thought.

Schuldman was watching him with a scrutiny that made Kelric wonder if the general questioned his judgment in letting the Glint leave the planet. Probably not. Schuldman had specifically directed him to test the limits of the craft's abilities. As for Kelric's private thoughts during those moments, they were just that. Private.

In any case, putting a starship engine in a plane added a new dimension to the project. Intrigued, Kelric said, "Even data from my last flight can only give us a rough idea of what will happen at higher velocities. I wasn't going fast enough to test the parameters that would affect a starship."

Schuldman considered him. "That's why I'm looking for a volunteer to test the modified aircraft."

Kelric knew the general's ability to get fast results made him one of the most valued officers in the Space Test Wing. The rumor mill also claimed Schuldman had earned his reputation by pushing his planes—and their pilots—to the limit.

What a ride it would be, though! The speed, the challenge, rushing on the edge—the idea exhilarated Kelric. Then he thought of the risks and sobered up. Neither the Glint nor any other plane he knew was ready to fly with a starship drive.

Unbidden, a thought crept out of the shadows in his mind: *Go ahead. Do it. You have nothing to lose.*

Kelric spoke. "I'd like to volunteer, sir."

Schuldman nodded with approval. "Very well, Captain. The flight will be in three days."

2

ARROYO DAWN

The only light in the sunken living room came from the clock on a table, its violet glow coaxing gleams from the glassy furniture and paneling. Moonlight poured through the big window in the north wall. Outside, the city of Arosa lay under the desert sky, its scattered lights glittering like moonlight trapped in a diamond. It was the only town within a day's hovercar drive of Arosa Space Force Base, an installation isolated so far out in the desert that nothing but an occasional corkscrew cricket lived near enough to see the aircraft tests.

Kelric sat in his dark glossy penthouse, sprawled on the couch, holding a glass of desert honey. He had no idea where the whisky got the name honey. It tasted like cleaning fluid. He grimaced and poured his drink back in the bottle, then clunked the tumbler down on the glass table.

"So," he muttered. "You like sitting here in the dark or what?"

"That's a good question," a woman said.

Kelric jumped to his feet so fast he knocked over his glass. The lights in the room came on, blinding him. As his vision cleared he saw a statuesque woman by the door, a golden figure with an angel's face and masses of radiant curls that floated around her face and spilled down her back.

"For flaming sake, Mother," he growled. "What are you doing here?"

She gave him a wry smile. "I'm glad to see you too."

"You surprised me." She rarely showed up without letting him know first. "How did you get in?"

"You left the door unlocked." She walked over to him, her gold hair tousled around her shoulders. "I thought something was wrong. Then I heard you talking to yourself."

"I wasn't expecting visitors."

Her smile smoothed away the worried furrow that had creased her forehead. "I decided to come after I saw you on the news tonight."

Kelric reddened. He was trying to forget that broadcast. News of his last flight had leaked to the press and a local reporter had called the base to ask if she could interview him. Schuldman gave the go-ahead, unaware that Kelric avoided public speaking like he avoided jumping into hot tar pits. The project information officer had told him to satisfy the press with a good story. Apparently it helped garner public support for the base. So Kelric had tried to prepare for the interview. But when he had walked into the broadcast studio with its bright lights and buzzing crews, it had rattled him so much, he couldn't do much more than mumble yes and no to the reporter's questions.

"That was quite a story," his mother said. "How did they put it? 'The handsome hero of Space Command.'"

"I looked like an idiot."

"Actually, I thought you fit the role of hero well."

He couldn't help but smile. "You would think I was heroic if I fell on my face in the mud."

She chuckled. "You looked every bit the valiant flyer they made you out to be." Her smile faded. "But I know you, Kelric. Something was wrong."

"I hate speaking in public. You know that, too."

"It was more than that."

"I don't know what you're looking for." He picked up the whiskey glass. "Listen, I'm glad to see you. I don't mean to be rude. But I'm tired. I just don't feel like company tonight."

She spoke quietly. "Sitting here alone in the dark won't bring Cory back to life. And committing suicide in your fancy plane won't bring you any closer to her."

He went rigid. "Good night, Mother."

"It's been two months since her funeral." She watched him with those gold eyes that saw far too much. "In that entire time, I've never seen you shed a single tear or heard you say one word about it. You sit up here surrounded by her things and brood. It's not healthy."

His voice tightened. "This is where I live."

"You can change where you live. Find a place that isn't full of memories."

Memories? He didn't even have those. His wife's death had left a void with nothing but his grief to fill it. Why had he married another officer? Losing a friend in battle was hard enough. When the news had come, two months and an eternity ago, that the battlecruiser Cory commanded had been destroyed— and she with it—a part of him had died as well.

Kelric pushed down the memory. He didn't want pity. What could he do to make his well-meaning mother go away before her solicitude started him unraveling?

"I'll look at apartments next week," he said.

Her luminous face lit with a smile. "There's a nice place on Arroyo Cliffs. You could see it Tillsday evening."

"All right." That would be after his test flight of Schuldman's mutant plane with its starship engine.

Dawn's ruddy light stretched long shadows across the red sands. Sunrise turned the airfield crimson and reflected off the Glint's hull like sparks of fire. Out in the desert, nothing but rock spires showed as far as the horizon. Only the rare boom of a snare-drum cactus interrupted the dawn's silent splendor.

Kelric walked around the Glint. The only visible changes were the photon thrusters mounted behind the rocket exhaust. He knew what waited inside that plane, though—a marvel ready to shoot him into the heavens.

Inversion. The word had fascinated him since childhood. At the Academy he had earned his degree in inversion theory, the physics of faster-than-light travel. His people had once believed reaching supraluminal speeds was impossible. It meant going through the speed of light, where slower travelers would see his mass become infinite and his ship rotated until it pointed perpendicular to its true direction. Time for him would stop relative to the rest of the universe. Which of course could never happen. So how could he go faster-than-light?

The answer turned out to be simple.

It depended on imaginary numbers, the square roots of negative numbers. Relativistic physics said his mass and energy became imaginary at supraluminal speeds. If he also added an imaginary part to his speed, the equations no longer blew up at light speed. By venturing into a universe where speed had both real and imaginary parts, he could go *around* light speed like a hovercar leaving the road could go around a tree. But for a starship, "leaving the road" meant leaving the real universe.

Kelric pressed his hand against the plane's hatch. "What do you say, Glint? Want to go faster than a photon?" The plane couldn't of course. It wasn't designed for interstellar travel. But the inversion engine could accelerate it far better than the rockets. Engineering thought he might reach one hundredth the speed of light. It would make his last flight a snail's pace in comparison.

"I just hope they fixed the computer," Kelric said.

"Fixed it, double-checked it, triple-checked it," a woman's gravelly voice said behind him. "Can't have you blowing up out there. You and me got a debt to settle."

Kelric turned to see Jessa Zaubern, a gaunt figure in the blue jumpsuit worn by the engineers assigned to the Glint project. Her close cut cap of fiery hair glistened in the dawn's light.

He snorted. "You're the one who owes me money, Zaub."

Her grin animated her face, chasing away her usual stoicism. "Next game, I'm going to wipe your bank account clean."

Kelric smiled. He and Jessa got along well. He was one of the few people she let see the sentimental streak under her gruffness. They understood each other, both of them plagued by the same awkwardness with words. He was also the only person who had ever beat her at Dieshan choker slam, a game invented by the base's notorious circle of card players. And she was a better engineer than card player. If she had triple-checked his plane, it was in good shape.

Jessa surveyed the Glint. "The fusion rockets will get you off planet." She slanted a gaze at him. "You can use the inversion engine once you're in orbit. You got positron fuel."

"I don't know, Zaub. Positrons for a plane?" He grinned his challenge. "It'll never work."

"Like hell, Kelly boy." She banged her palm on the Glint's hull. "We used EM fields to suspend the fuel in a canister. You fire the thrusters, a defect in the fields leaks positrons into the beambox, same as in a starship."

Even after his briefing, Kelric had trouble imagining the plane carrying an inversion selector and beambox. The wheel-shaped selector culled electrons out of the cosmic ray flux in space, letting only those with highest energies enter the mirrored beambox. Once inside, the electrons annihilated with positrons, creating ultra high energy photons that reflected out the thrusters.

"Just as long as it does what it's supposed to do," he said.

Jessa peered at him. "You really think it has a problem?"

Did he? "I'll only be carrying a hundred kilograms of positrons."

"That's more than you need. It's not like you're going anywhere." She shrugged. "Hell, one gram of positrons makes a million billion billion annihilations. That's a lot of push."

"I suppose." He tilted his head towards the Glint. "So you really think she can reach one percent of light speed?"

"Should," Jessa said. "We don't have enough data at higher velocities to know for sure."

Interesting. "You mean you don't know its top speed?"

Jessa scowled at him. "Don't even *think* it."

He regarded her innocently. "Think what?"

"You be careful with my plane."

He laughed amiably. "I'm going to wreak havoc on it."

"Very funny." Her voice quieted. "You be careful with Kelric, too."

"Hell, he'll be fine. He's only an idiot when reporters interview him."

"I'm not joking." Jessa shook her head. "People look at you, they see big and quiet. They don't think you feel. They don't think you think."

He shifted his weight. "It doesn't bother me."

"Kelric, listen." She came over to him. "You're smarter than all of them put together. And you feel. Too much. You keep thinking and feeling and locking it up. It will eat holes in your heart."

Where the hell had that come from? "I'm fine."

Jessa put her hands on her hips. "Only one dumb thing I've ever seen you do. And that's agreeing to take up this plane. Schuldman had no right to push you into this mission."

"He didn't push me. I volunteered."

"Yeah, right." She poked her finger at his chest. "I want my plane back in one piece."

"It's not your plane, Zaub."

"Just remember what I said."

He did his best to look reassuring. "All right."

"Good." She paused awkwardly. "Good luck."

Kelric smiled. "Thanks."

After Jessa left, Kelric climbed into the cockpit and ran more tests. He put the computer through every one of its routines and it answered without a glitch.

Although the Glint could take off vertically, today Kelric tested it on the runway. After Tyrson gave him clearance, he sped down the asphalt and soared into the air, exulting in acceleration pushing him against his seat. He loved that sensation of speed.

As he shot higher into the sky, the world of Diesha spread out on his screens in a desolate landscape of sunrise colors. He accelerated steadily and the Glint answered like an extension of his own body. The wings folded back against the fuselage, cutting drag and preparing for the supersonic shock wave. Mach 1, Mach 2, Mach 4. Finally he hit the speed where the computer had developed jitters during his last flight.

"Glint One Eight to Control," Kelric said. "Systems look good here."

"I read the same," Tyrson said over the audiocom.

"Good." Kelric grinned. "I'm going to give it a kick."

Captain, the Glint thought. *I don't think kicking me will serve any purpose.*

Kelric chuckled. *Don't worry. It's just another idiom.* He fired the rockets, breathing in grunts to keep from blacking out from the g-forces. Mach 8, 16, 32. He hit escape velocity and kept going. On his screens, Diesha changed from a flat landscape to curved globe studded with ruby deserts.

"She's beautiful," he murmured.

Tyrson chuckled. "Is that someone you see up there or are you thinking about your last date?"

"Lady Diesha," Kelric said. *Beautiful sorceress,* he thought. *Hold me in your arms until the pain stops.*

We've cleared the planet, the Glint announced. *Do you want to start the inversion engine?*

Let's give it a go. Kelric fired the photon thrusters—and went into quasis.

Without quantum stasis, more commonly known as quasis, he would have died. A starship engine could accelerate a craft up to thousands of times the force of gravity, which would have smeared him all over his seat if he hadn't had protection. The waveform modulators in the quasis coil worked on an atomic level, keeping the quantum wavefunction of the ship from changing state. During quasis, nothing could alter the configuration of particles in the plane or anything it carried, including him; on a macroscopic level, the craft became a rigid solid that no force could deform. Only the atomic clock that limited their quasis time was unaffected. Kelric felt nothing; the only way he knew he hadn't been conscious the entire time was by the sudden jump in speed on his display.

Tyrson's voice burst out of the audiocom. "Captain, she's working like a dream!"

"You bet," Kelric said. *Thanks, Zaub,* he thought. He fired the thrusters again and his speed suddenly read three thousand kilometers per second.

"Glint Control," Kelric said. "I'm at one percent of light speed,"

"We read you smooth as silk," Tyrson said. "It's beautiful."

An unwelcome thought came to his mind. *No, it's empty. Everything is empty.* He pushed the thought away and spoke into the audiocom. "I'm going to crank it up again."

Another voice came on the com. "Captain, this is General Schuldman. Your systems are operating well, better than predicted. The decision to exceed this speed is yours, but if you do so you will be going against the advice of the team that installed your engine. Do you understand?"

Kelric knew Schuldman wanted him to push the Glint's limit. He also knew the general meant to make sure he knew the risks. "Understood, sir."

He fired the photon thrusters. A vibration shook through the ship, a gentle shaking but one that didn't feel right.

"Captain!" Static crackled in Tyrson's voice. "I'm reading you at ten percent of light speed."

"Captain Valdoria." Schuldman's voice came through the static. "That's fast enou—"

Kelric fired the thrusters before the general finished; that way, he wasn't disobeying orders. The display jumped to one hundred thousand kilometers per second. He hit the thrusters again and the number doubled. He was going at two-thirds the speed of light.

A voice on his audiocom drawled. "Are you recei… return to base…" The words faded away.

For a moment Kelric had no idea who had spoken. Then he realized it was Schuldman. *Glint*, he thought. *What's wrong with the audiocom?*

It can't cope with the time dilation.

Interesting. Starship audiocoms easily compensated for the effect of relativistic speeds on radio waves, but the Glint had no reason to carry one. He wasn't supposed to be going anywhere near this fast.

How long does Control think we've been gone? Kelric asked.

Thirty-three minutes, the Glint answered. *My clock says thirty minutes have passed for us.*

How about that? We jumped three minutes into the future. When he went this fast, Control recorded his clock as running slow. However, he recorded the clocks on Diesha as running slow. It was like when he sat in a magtrain and it looked like the train next to him was going backward when in fact his train was the one that had started to move forward. Relative to him, the other train *was* going backward. Similarly, relative to this plane, Diesha was shooting off in the other direction. Only when he turned the Glint around did it break the symmetry of their relative motion. What it meant was that when he returned home, he would be several minutes younger than everyone at the base.

Captain. The Glint's urgency cut through his mind. *The strain on this craft exceeds advised safety limits.*

No one ever claimed this job was safe, Kelric thought. *How fast can you go, sweet Glint?* Fast enough to the blow the grief out of his heart? Could anything take him that fast, that high, that far?

I also register a strain in your mind greater than advisable safety limits, the Glint said.

Who programmed you to tell me that? Jessa Zaubern?

Captain, I advise that we return to base.

Kelric watched his visored reflection in the console. *Can we invert?*

You mean go faster than the speed of light?

That's right.

Captain, this flight wasn't set up for such a maneuver.

Just answer the question.

I don't know if we can invert, the Glint thought. *But if we do, we won't have enough fuel to get home.*

Raise the beambox threshold. By scooping up only higher energy electrons, he could get more bang out of each annihilation and extend the range of his positron fuel.

If I raise it, the Glint answered, *you will run out of air before we find enough electrons with an energy that high. You will die.*

So invert the fuel first.

I see no reason to—

The cosmic ray flux is higher in supraluminal space, Kelric thought. *We'll find electrons a lot faster there.*

They will be there and we will be here, the Glint said. *Photons produced by annihilations in imaginary space do us no good in real space.*

Sure they will, Kelric thought. *If I release a flock of birds by an open window, some are bound to fly through it. As long as the engine operates here, some photons will invert back here.*

That violates energy conservation.

For flaming sake. His computer was arguing with him. *No, it doesn't. What we gain, imaginary space loses.*

Photons are not birds. Now the Glint sounded like Jessa. *Inversion engines are not windows.*

Just do it, Kelric thought.

Captain, you may not survive this procedure.

Are you refusing to accept my commands?

Yes.

Kelric frowned. *You can't do that.*

What you suggest could be fatal. It amounts to throwing away your fuel.

The hell it does.

The only way for imaginary photons to become real, the Glint thought, *is for their existence quantum number to change from zero to one. That doesn't happen spontaneously.*

So what? Kelric answered. *Nothing spontaneously inverts. If starship engines can force starships to do it, they ought to work on photons, too.*

There was a long pause. Then the Glint said, *A finite probability exists that you are correct and that this either brilliant or insane idea of yours may actually work. If it works, it will revolutionize star travel.*

I'm a test pilot, Kelric thought. *I'm supposed to test things.*

You are putting yourself in too much danger.

Yes, I have a dangerous job. That doesn't mean I shouldn't do it.

I still advise against the procedure. The Glint's thought came with what felt like genuine reluctance. *However, it appears I am unable to refuse your command.*

Good. Kelric glanced over his displays. *Reset the engine to invert its fuel in increments of point one percent.*

Engine reset.

Kelric fired the photon thrusters—and his speed jumped to 98 percent of light. The stars leapt on his holomap, converging towards a point in front of the plane. Data flashed on his displays: if Control could still track him, they would read his length as shrunk by 80 percent and his mass increased by 500 percent.

Why didn't we invert? Kelric asked,

We need to get closer to light speed, the Glint told him.

Starships manage from a lot slower speeds than this.

Starships have entire systems dedicated to optimizing their inversion capability, the Glint thought. *I don't.*

Kelric knew he should return to the base before time dilation jumped him any farther into the future. He had already gained more than half an hour. But he couldn't make himself turn around. Up here he could speed away from the grief, the loneliness, the huge emptiness.

This time when he fired the thrusters, his display leapt to 99.999999 percent of light speed. His mass increased by a factor of seven thousand. The starlight turned into x-rays. In one minute, five days passed on Diesha.

We still can't invert, the Glint thought.

Kelric fired the thrusters again. Centuries passed on Diesha. Now they were all dead. All of them. Everyone he had ever loved.

Cory, I can't do it, he thought. *I can't live in a universe where the people I love are gone.*

No inversion achieved, the Glint thought.

Kelric gritted his teeth and fired the thrusters—

—and the universe turned inside out, yanking him with it, his body and mind twisting like a tortured Möbius strip.

3

BEYOND THE END

The agonizing sensation stopped as abruptly as it had begun. The stars reappeared, their colors returned to normal but their positions inverted through a point that appeared to be infinitely far in front of the plane. Kelric recognized none of the eerily distorted constellations.

We inverted, the Glint thought. *But it definitely wasn't as smooth as silk.*

Kelric drew in a deep breath. *You're learning your idioms.* That was like no inversion he had ever experienced. He didn't know if he could survive it a second time.

I need you to specify a path in spacetime, the Glint said. *We're supraluminal.*

He struggled to clear his mind. Time and space switched character at faster than light speeds. Now he couldn't back up in space but he *could* back up in time. The relativistic equations allowed him to go into the past. A sublight observer would see an anti-matter Glint flying backwards from its destination to its origin. If he worked it right, he could compensate for his time-dilated leap into the future by leaping into the past here.

If only he could go back to before Cory died.

Unfortunately, no matter how much he wanted it, the final result of his trip couldn't violate reality. A thousand pilots before him had verified that law of physics. The best he could do with a starship was come home with the same amount of time passing there as for him. With the Glint, he would be lucky to come out anywhere near the day when he had left Diesha. This morning. Except now it was centuries, even millennia in the past.

His displays weren't telling him anything. The inversion had scrambled them. *Glint, how fast are we going?*

One trillion times the speed of light.

WHAT?

One trillion ti—

Slow down!

Silence.

Kelric blinked at the gibberish on his displays. *Did anything happen?*

We slowed to 132 percent light speed.

How did we get going so fast before?

When we passed light speed, our mass decreased, the Glint thought. *So we sped up, which made our mass decrease, which sped us up, which—*

I get the idea. To himself only, shutting the Glint out of his mind, Kelric thought, *Can you imagine a more spectacular way to die? Hurtle along at infinite speed with zero mass and infinite length, your body turning to dust while time stops for the rest of the Universe?*

And then what? he asked himself. *You think Cory will be waiting? You think she'll open her arms wide, welcoming you for the stupidity of killing yourself?* He could see her glaring at him, her dark hair whipping in an imaginary wind.

"Cory, I miss you," Kelric murmured.

I don't understand 'Cory,' the Glint thought.

I never did either, Kelric admitted. *But gods, I loved her.* To the image of Cory in his mind, he thought, *Good-bye, my love.* Then he took a deep breath and directed his thoughts outward, focusing them enough so they would reach the computer. *Glint, figure out a course that will get us home as near to when we left as possible.* He gave voice to the realization lifting above his grief like a bird in flight. *If there's a way to get back alive, I want to do it.*

I'll do my best, Captain. After a pause, the Glint thought, *I'm ready.*

Kelric fired the thrusters. The stars shifted position, but nothing else changed. He fired them again, trying not to dwell on how little fuel he had left. The stars collapsed into a point, their sluggish photons lumbering towards him as he leapt farther and farther into the past. He fired the thrusters—

And ripped in two.

Kelric snapped like a rubber band pulled too far too fast, its torn edges writhing in space, screaming, screaming…

Suddenly he was whole again. He felt ill, dizzy, disoriented, as if his body had reset.

"We inverted," the Glint said.

Kelric swallowed. *Why did it feel so strange?* After a moment he realized the Glint had used the com instead of their neural link. He spoke out loud. "What happened?"

"The top of the plane, including the top of your body, inverted two picoseconds before the rest of the craft."

Good gods. "Am I normal now?"

"Essentially."

"What do you mean, 'essentially'?"

"Only 99.99 percent of your mass reinverted."

"What didn't come back?"

"The missing molecules are distributed throughout the lower half of your body." Then the Glint added, "We gave it a go and most of us went."

Kelric managed a wan laugh, trying to ignore his bizarre mental image of 0.01 percent of his body doomed to forever hurtle into the past. "What happened to my cyber link with you?"

"The reinversion scrambled it."

"Can we still get home?"

"Yes. However, we no longer have enough fuel to slow down."

"Raise the beambox threshold again," Kelric said. "Then do the bit with inverting the fuel."

"We still won't collect enough before you run out of air and suffocate."

That was it? He had almost made it back only to find he couldn't stop? He couldn't accept that. "There has to be a way to get home."

"Getting home is easy," the Glint said, "But when we arrive you will be dead."

Kelric grimaced. "You're encouraging."

"What do you want me to do?"

He touched the spare tank on his survival suit. "Can you tap my emergency air reserve?"

"I already have."

Kelric sat absorbing his situation. Then he snapped his fingers. "I don't breathe in quasis."

"This is true."

"So crank up the beambox threshold and put me in quasis until we reach Diesha."

"It is inadvisable to your survival to remain in quasis that long."

"Dying isn't advisable to my survival either," Kelric said. "What's the problem with quasis?"

"It prevents the arrangement of molecules in your body from adapting as your environment changes. If you stay in too long, your environment will change too much. When you come out, your molecular wave function may not be able to readjust without catastrophic fluctuations."

Catastrophic who? "Meaning what, exactly?"

"Every atom in your body is hit with a force when you come out of quasis," the Glint said. "It's because your environment has changed. And those forces aren't necessarily in the same directions. The more your environment changes, the bigger the discrepancies. Go too long, and it could tear you apart atom by atom."

Not exactly how he had planned to end the day. "You're my environment," he pointed out. "And you go into stasis, too. That means you can't change. So neither does my environment. In theory." Of course, theories usually described an ideal case, which was far from what they had here.

"That might protect you," the Glint said. "However, it doesn't protect me."

"Your environment can't change *that* much. We're in interstellar space."

"Space is far from a true vacuum," the Glint said. "And it won't take much to make the plane collapse. Its structure is already strained past its safety limits."

A solution had to exist. Every problem had an answer. He just needed to think of it. "Can you set the timer to bring us out at periodic intervals?" Kelric asked. "Do it before our time in stasis becomes too long. We'd only need an instant to readjust. I probably wouldn't even be conscious."

The Glint went silent, and Kelric could almost feel it calculating. Finally it said, "There is a great deal of uncertainty associated with this procedure."

Kelric thought of the shadows in his mind. Damn it, he *wanted* to get better. "I'll take uncertain life over certain death."

"I understand, Captain."

"So let's do it."

After a pause, the Glint said, "Ready."

Kelric fired the photon thrusters…

Nausea surged over Kelric and he almost lost the breakfast he had eaten a few hours and who knew how long ago. His forward screen showed Diesha swelling into view like a ruby and turquoise jewel. They weren't close enough to land, however.

He struggled to clear his thoughts. "Glint? Why did you wake me up?"

"We're going to disintegrate. I thought you would want to know."

Hell and damnation! "Get us down as far as you can before the plane falls apart."

"Re-entry initiated. I've activated my emergency beacon."

Kelric wondered if they had returned to a time when anyone existed to pick up that beacon. "Can the reactor's shielding survive the crash?"

"Yes."

So at least they wouldn't splatter a nuclear reactor all over the landscape. He hoped the same was true for him. The Glint, designed to be as light as possible, didn't carry an escape capsule to protect him when he ejected. "Will you be able to slow down enough for me to eject?"

"I calculate a fifty-three percent probability that you will survive ejection."

Well, that was better than zero. Even if he didn't make it, at least the Glint's mind would survive. The computer was better shielded even than the reactor.

Kelric touched the console. "Jessa and her team will have you fixed up in no time."

"I don't think that will be possible," The Glint sounded subdued.

"Why not?"

"When we reinverted, I created a cybershell for your mind. It damaged my systems."

"A what shell?"

"Cybershell. I ran your brain as a subprocess of my own. Your mind wouldn't have survived reinversion otherwise,"

Kelric whistled. "That's impossible."

"Not completely. However, it did leave me unprotected during reinversion. It corrupted my systems. By the time we crash, my functions and memory will be degraded past recovery."

No, Kelric thought. "You killed yourself so I could live."

"I'm only a computer."

"A computer, yes." He spoke quietly. "But 'only'? I would never use that word for you."

"Captain, thank you." Then it said, "We're disintegrating."

"I won't forget what you did for me," Kelric said.

"Take care." With just the barest pause, the Glint added, "Let yourself heal, Kelric."

The plane ejected him.

Kelric went out the top, shooting upwards as the Glint fell away from him in pieces. Windblast buffeted him so roughly that he almost blacked out.

He began to fall. Tucking his chin to his chest, he held his legs together and crossed his arms while he tumbled through the air. Silence surrounded him and clouds covered the landscape. He tried to look at the altimeter on his arm, but the numbers blurred. It took his groggy brain a moment to comprehend that he had used up the air in his emergency tank. He clawed at his helmet, his fingers scraping across the face plate. Darkness closed around him, warm, inviting…

A blast of cold air slapped Kelric awake. His helmet had opened and his suit timer was going off, triggering the release of a parachute. It jerked him so hard, it felt as if his arms would rip off his shoulders.

Mercifully, the buffeting soon eased. His survival kit deployed, its life raft dangling from his suit like seaweed waving in an ocean of air. Clouds closed around him and he fell through a wet mist that ate away at his sense of up and down, right and left.

Gradually Kelric realized the world wasn't silent. A rumble throbbed below him. As he fell through the fog, the growl swelled into the roar of waves hitting land. Even when he sealed his helmet, he heard the thundering voice.

He had no warning before he hit water. He plunged into it, his limbs tangling in the parachute's suspension lines. As he struggled to free himself, he plowed into sand. With a huge kick he shot out of the water, breathing the few moments of borrowed air in his suit.

Kelric pulled free of the parachute and grabbed the life raft. He had run out of air, but when he opened his face plate, a wave smashed into him. Another wave came, another, and another. The breakers tore away the life raft and rolled him over and over, his lungs straining while he struggled not to gulp in water. If he didn't get air soon, he would pass out.

His feet scraped the bottom for only an instant, but it was enough. He shoved against the sand and shot upwards, clearing the breakers long enough to gasp in a breath. Then he was back in the water, fighting the waves. He touched sand again, again, and again, and then he was stumbling up a sandy slope, waves crashing around him in frothy turbulence.

Kelric staggered onto the beach, wading out of the mist into watery sunlight. Ahead of him, a hill slanted up to a road—where a hovervan with flash-ing red lights was braking to a stop. As people jumped out of the vehicle, engines rumbled overhead. He looked up to see a flyer circling, its military insignia gleaming in the sunlight.

A woman in a blue jumpsuit ran toward him, her shoulder-length hair glinting like copper. As Kelric sunk to his knees in the sand, people surrounded him. The woman knelt in front of him, tears on her face. "You crazy man."

Kelric barely managed to croak out an answer. "Zaub? How did your hair grow so fast?"

"Six months you've been gone." Her voice shook. "Six months we've been thinking your hide was finished."

"I came back to get the money you owed me."

She pulled him into her arms. "Welcome home."

Kelric hugged her back, unable to respond as silent tears ran down his face.

The broadcasts that aired following his return made him out to be a bigger-than-life hero. Over and over they showed the scene of his parents embracing him, the son they thought they had lost, his breathtakingly beautiful mother with tears streaming down her golden face. Space Command took advantage of the good public relations and paraded him around in his uniform, keeping quiet about that fact that they also took him off flight status and sent him to a therapist. Kelric went where they told him to go, stood where they told him to stand, and endeavored not to look like an idiot.

All the reports went on with great enthusiasm about the dramatic moment when he wept on the beach for the joy of seeing home. Kelric let them say what they wanted. He knew the truth, deep inside where suppressed grief had once crippled his heart.

Those healing tears had been for Cory.

NOTES

The first time I heard about Riemann surfaces, I fell in love with the subject. It was during a course in applied math for physics majors that I took as an undergraduate. I was intimidated by the course but it also looked intriguing, so I gave it a try.

I adored that class.

To this day, applied math remains my favorite subject. Give me an equation to solve and I'm happy. This essay describes some of the ways I've incorporated math into my stories. I've started out with a few equations for those who enjoy them, but it isn't necessary to understand those to follow the rest of the essay. I've also included analogies and pictures I hope will elucidate the beautiful concepts behind the mathematics.

My introduction to Riemann sheets came about in that long-ago math class when we delved into the subject of complex analysis, or the math of complex numbers, a subject seen by students of all ages, from preteens first learning about imaginary numbers to doctoral candidates studying theoretical physics. So what is a complex number? We can call it z, where

$$z = x + iy.$$

Here x and y are real numbers, that is, numbers such as 42, 3.64, 84/7 or π. However, i is a different beast altogether; it's an imaginary number, specifically the square root of –1:

$$i = \sqrt{-1}\,.$$

So z has a "real part" equal to x and an "imaginary part" equal to y. We can plot a complex number on what is called the z-plane. It looks the same as the x-y coordinate plane, except the x axis corresponds to the real part of the complex number and the y axis corresponds to the imaginary part. On such a graph, the coordinates $(x, y) = z$ give the complex number.

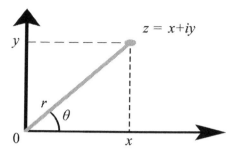

Figure 1: The tip of the arrow gives the complex number $z = x + iy$, where x is the real part and y is the imaginary part.

We can also represent z by *polar coordinates*. Its position is again given by two numbers, but in this case the two numbers are r and θ, as shown in figure 1. The line drawn from the origin to z has length r and the angle it makes with the x axis is θ. Polar coordinates and x-y coordinates are related; $x = r \cos \theta$, and $y = r \sin \theta$. So

$$z = r (\cos \theta + i \sin \theta) = re^{i\theta}.$$

The term $e^{i\theta} = \cos \theta + i \sin \theta$ is called the complex *exponential function*, which often shows up in physics classes, where it has bedeviled many generations of incipient young scientists. The value of r doesn't really matter in these discussions, so to make life easier, I'll set $r = 1$. The angle θ can still vary. In fact, if we let it increase from 0 to 2π, the point z will move in a circle around the x-y plane and come back to where it started.

Imagine that the line from the origin to z is the hour hand on a clock, with z at its tip. When the hand moves once around the clock face, that's analogous to θ moving through a total angle of 2π. After twelve hours, midnight until noon, the hand is back where it started. Go around a second time and the hour goes from noon to midnight. The hours in the first go-around have the same numbers as in the second one, but refer to different times. Go around a third time, though, and we're back to the morning hours.

The convention in math, however, is that $\theta = 0$ when z is on the positive x-axis, which corresponds to an hour hand at 3 o'clock. When z is on the positive y-axis ($\theta = \pi/2$), that corresponds to the hour hand at 12, which means $\theta =$

$\pi/2$ at midnight or noon. Also, in math the convention is that θ increases as z goes counter-clockwise around the plane. If z goes clockwise, θ *decreases* from 0 to $-\pi$ when the time goes from 3 am to 3 pm (or 3 pm to 3 am). The discussion is essentially the same, however, regardless of whether or not we have a minus in front of the angles, and we can just as easily go from 3 am to 3 pm as from midnight to noon. The important part of the analogy is that going once around the clock face corresponds to z moving through a total angle of 2π. So in that sense, z is analogous to a clock.

Something amazing occurs when we take $\sqrt{z}$, the square root of z. Let's check it out. We write

$$\sqrt{z} = z^{1/2} = e^{i\theta/2} = \cos(\theta/2) + i\sin(\theta/2).$$

What happens now if the "hour hand" moves clockwise? When θ goes all the way around the clock, $\sqrt{z}$ only makes it halfway around because it depends on $\theta/2$. To see what that means, we'll look at $\theta = -\pi$, which corresponds to 9 o'clock. For that angle,

$$\sqrt{z} = \cos(-\pi/2) + i\sin(-\pi/2) = -i.$$

If we go around the clock once (say 9 am to 9 pm), the angle θ changes by -2π, which means $\theta = -3\pi$ (since we started at $\theta = -\pi$). That's also 9 o'clock. So if $\sqrt{z}$ were well-behaved, it would have the same value at -3π as it did at $-\pi$. However, instead we get

$$\sqrt{z} = \cos(-3\pi/2) + i\sin(-3\pi/2) = i.$$

The square root has different values for $-\pi$ and -3π even though $-\pi$ and -3π are in exactly the same place, the same "hour." So is $\sqrt{z} = i$ or $-i$ at 9 o'clock? It's ambiguous. That's why double-valued functions aren't allowed; z must be unique at every point to be a valid function.

You might wonder what happens if we go around a third time. Is $\sqrt{z}$ triple-valued? Quadruple valued? Where does it stop? As it turns out, the third go-around gives $\sqrt{z} = -i$ again and a fourth gives $\sqrt{z} = i$. So $\sqrt{z}$ alternates between only two values. Unfortunately, even two is too many. In our universe, the math that describes physics requires single-valued quantities. They give unambiguous results; otherwise, we wouldn't know which number to use. But terms like $\sqrt{z}$ come up all the time in the equations of physics. So we seem to be stuck.

The solution to this conundrum is an elegant idea developed by the mathematician Bernhard Riemann in the nineteenth century. Instead of one x-y plane, he suggested stacking two of them together. The top plane, or "sheet," is where z has its first value, and the bottom is for its second value. To go from one sheet to another, we slit them from the origin out to infinity. That slit is called a *branch cut*. If we connect the sheets at their branch cuts, we can go around the top sheet once and then slip through the cut to the bottom sheet for the second time around. Then back to the top sheet. That allows $\sqrt{z}$ to have one value on the top and a different one on the bottom.

Voila! The function is no longer double-valued. The ambiguity goes away as long as we know which sheet we're on. It's like stacking two clocks. The hour hand goes around from 3 am to 3 pm on the top clock, then slides through the branch cut and goes around the second clock from 3 pm to 3 am. Then back to the top clock.

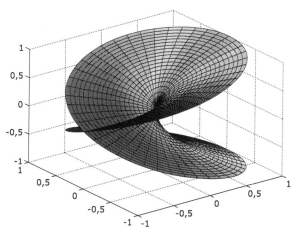

Figure 2: Riemann sheets for $\sqrt{z}$. This shows curved surfaces, which are hardly clock-like. However, the sheets can be flattened, more like disks. Author: Elb2000. License/image: http://en.wikipedia.org/wiki/File:Riemann_sqrt.svg

The square root of z is the simplest case of Riemann sheets. If we have a cube root, we need three sheets; a quartic root requires four sheets, and so on for more complicated functions. However, the basic concept remains the same: the sheets create alternate versions of the complex plane.

As a student, I was fascinated by all this math; as a science fiction writer, I was delighted. What a great way to describe alternate universes! Put them on different Riemann sheets. In "The Spacetime Pool," the character Janelle stumbles through a branch cut that drops her into an alternate reality. In my novel *Catch the Lightning*, the fighter pilot Althor is thrown through a rip in the Riemann sheet of his universe when his ship is sabotaged.

The seeds of these ideas in my stories go back to when I was trying to think of a fictional faster-than-light drive that was at least mathematically plausible. I figured out that making speed complex in the equations of special relativity would do away with the singularity at the speed of light. Of course, it's a math game; we know of no physical way to make our speed complex. But the math is pretty, so I wrote a paper about it for *The American Journal of Physics* titled "Complex Speeds and Special Relativity," which appeared in volume 64, the April 1996 issue.

The theory of special relativity developed by Einstein describes what happens if we travel at close to the speed of light. It includes a function called "gamma" that depends on a square root involving v, the speed. If v is complex, the question of Riemann sheets comes up. At least two would be involved and probably more, maybe even an infinite number. When v is complex, the theory also predicts other wonderfully eerie effects. I've used ideas based on that for many stories, including *Primary Inversion*, my first published novel, and "Light and Shadow," the novelette included here. It's been fascinating to play with such fictional extrapolations of the math.

LUNGFISH

DAVID BRIN

David is a scientist, speaker, technical consultant, and world-known author. His novels have been New York Times bestsellers, winning multiple Hugo, Nebula, and other awards. At least a dozen have been translated into more than twenty languages.

David's science fictional Uplift Universe explores a future when humans genetically engineer higher animals like dolphins to become equal members of our civilization. He also recently tied up the loose ends left behind by the late Isaac Asimov. His *Foundation's Triumph* brings to a grand finale Asimov's famed Foundation Universe. His non-fiction book *The Transparent Society: Will Technology Force Us to Choose Between Freedom and Privacy?* deals with secrecy in the modern world. It won the Freedom of Speech Prize from the American Library Association and is available at http://amzn.to/1CpJg5r.

1

Awaiter is excited again. She transmits urgently, trying to get my attention.

"Seeker, listen!" Her electronic voice hisses over the ancient cables. "The little living ones are near, Seeker! Even now they explore this belt of asteroids, picking through the rocks and ruins. You can hear them as they browse over each new discovery!

"Soon they will find us here! Do you hear me, Seeker? It is time to decide what to do!"

Awaiter's makers were impatient creatures. I wonder that she has lasted so long, out here in the starry cold.

My own makers were wiser.

"Seeker! Are you listening to me?"

I don't really wish to talk with anyone, so I erect a side-personality—little more than a swirling packet of nudged electrons—to handle her for me. Even if Awaiter discovers the sham, she might take a hint then and leave me alone.

Or she might grow more insistent. It would be hard to predict without awakening more dormant circuits than I care to bring into play right now.

"There is no hurry," my artifact tells her soothingly. "The Earth creatures will not get here for several of their years. Anyway, there is nothing we can do to change matters when they do arrive. It was all written long ago."

The little swirl of electrons really is very good. It speaks with my own accent, and seems quite logical, for a simple construct.

"How can you be so complacent!" Awaiter scolds. The cables covering our rocky, icy worldlet—our home for so many ages—reverberate with her electronic exasperation.

"We survivors made you leader, Seeker, because you seemed to understand best what was happening in the galaxy at large. But now, at last, our waiting is at an end. The biological creatures will be here soon, and we shall have to act!"

Perhaps Awaiter has tuned in to too much Earth television over the last century or so. Her whining sounds positively human.

"The Earthlings will find us or they won't," my shadow self answers. "We few survivors are too feeble to prevent it, even if we wished. What can a shattered band of ancient machines fear or anticipate in making Contact with such a vigorous young race?"

Indeed, I did not need Awaiter to tell me the humans were coming. My remaining sensors sample the solar wind and savor the stream of atoms and radicals much as a human might sniff the breeze. In recent years, the flow from the inner system has carried new scents—the bright tang of metal ions from space-foundries, and the musty smoke-smell of deuterium.

The hormones of industry.

And there is this busy modulation of light and radio—where the spectrum used to carry only the hot song of the star. All of these are signs of an awakening. Life is emerging from the little water-womb on the third planet. It is on its way out here.

"Greeter and Emissary want to warn the humans of their danger, and I agree!" Awaiter insists. "We can help them!"

Our debate has aroused some of the others; I notice new tendrils entering the network. Watcher and Greeter make their presence felt as little fingers of super-cooled electricity. I sense their agreement with Awaiter.

"Help them? How?" my sub-voice asks. "Our last repair and replication units *fell apart shortly after the Final Battle. We had no way of knowing humans had evolved until the creatures themselves invented radio.*

"And then it was too late! Their first transmissions are already propagating, unrecallable, into a deadly galaxy. If there are destroyers around in this region of space, the humans are already lost!

"Why worry the poor creatures, then? Let them enjoy their peace. Warning them will accomplish nothing."

Oh, I am good! This little artificial voice argues as well as I did long ago, staving off abrupt action by my impatient peers.

Greeter glides into the network. I feel his cool electron flux, eloquent as usual.

"I agree with Seeker," he states surprisingly. "The creatures do not need to be told about their danger. They are already figuring it out for themselves."

Now this does interest me. I sweep my subpersona aside and extend a tendril of my Very Self into the network. None of the others even notice the shift.

"What makes you believe this?" I ask Greeter.

Greeter indicates our array of receivers salvaged from ancient derelicts. "We're intercepting what the humans say to each other as they explore this asteroid belt," he says. "One human, in particular, appears on the verge of understanding what happened here, long ago."

Greeter's tone of smugness must have been borrowed from Earthly television shows. But that is understandable. Greeter's makers were enthusiasts, who programmed him to love nothing greater than the simple pleasure of saying hello.

"Show me," I tell him. I am reluctant to hope that the long wait was over at last.

2

Ursula Fleming stared as the asteroid's slow rotation brought ancient, shattered ruins into view below. "Lord, what a mess," she said, sighing.

She had been five years in the Belt, exploring and salvaging huge alien works, but never had she beheld such devastation as this.

Only four kilometers away, the hulking asteroid lay nearly black against the starry band of the Milky Way, glistening here and there in the light of the distant sun. The rock stretched more than two thousand meters along its greatest axis. Collisions had dented, cracked, and cratered it severely since it had broken from its parent body more than a billion years ago.

On one side it seemed a fairly typical carbonaceous planetoid, like millions of others orbiting out here at the outer edge of the Belt. But this changed as the survey ship *Hairy Thunderer* orbited around the nameless hunk of rock and frozen gases. The sun's vacuum brilliance cast long, sharp shadows across the ruined replication yards… jagged, twisted remnants of a catastrophe that had taken place when dinosaurs still roamed the Earth.

"Gavin!" she called over her shoulder. "Come down here! You've got to see this!"

In a minute her partner floated through the overhead hatch, flipping in midair. There was a faint click as his feet contacted the magnetized floor.

"All right, Urs. What's to see? More murdered babies to dissect and salvage? Or have we finally found a clue to who their killers were?"

Ursula only gestured toward the viewing port. Her partner moved closer and stared. Highlights reflected from Gavin's glossy features as the ship's searchlight swept the shattered scene below.

"Yep," Gavin nodded at last. "Dead babies again. Fleming Salvage and Exploration ought to make a good price off each little corpse."

Ursula frowned. "Don't be morbid, Gavin. Those are unfinished interstellar probes, destroyed ages ago before they could be launched. We have no idea whether they were sentient machines like you, or just tools, like this ship. You of all people should know better than to go around anthropomorphizing alien artifacts."

Gavin's grimace was an android's equivalent of a sarcastic shrug. "If I use 'morbid' imagery, whose fault is it?"

"What do you mean?" Ursula turned to face him.

"I mean you organic humans faced a choice, a hundred years ago, when you saw that 'artificial' intelligence was going to take off and someday leave the biological kind behind.

"You could have wrecked the machines, but that would have halted progress.

"You could have deep-programmed us with 'Fundamental Laws of Robotics'," Gavin sniffed. "And had slaves far smarter than their masters.

"But what was it you organics finally did decide to do?"

Ursula knew it was no use answering, not when Gavin was in one of his moods. She concentrated on piloting *Hairy Thunderer* closer to the asteroid.

"What was your solution to the problem of smart machines?" Gavin persisted. "You chose to raise us as your *children*, that's what you did. You taught us to be just like you, and even gave most of us humaniform bodies!"

Ursula's last partner—a nice old 'bot and good chess player—had warned her when he retired, not to hire an adolescent Class-AAA android fresh out of college. They could be as difficult as any human teenager, he cautioned.

The worst part of it was that Gavin was right once again.

Despite genetic and cyborg improvements to the human animal, machines still seemed fated to surpass biological men. For better or worse the decision had been made to raise Class-AAA androids as human children, with all the same awkward irritations that implied.

Gavin shook his head in dramatic, superior sadness, exactly like a too-smart adolescent who properly deserved to be strangled.

"Can you really object when I, a man-built, *manlike* android, anthropomorphize? We only do as we've been taught, mistress."

His bow was eloquently sarcastic.

Ursula said nothing. It was hard, at times, to be entirely sure humanity had made the right decision after all.

Below, across the face of the ravaged asteroid, stretched acres of great-strutted scaffolding—twisted and curled in ruin. Within the toppled derricks lay silent ranks of shattered, unfinished starships, wrecked perhaps a hundred million years ago.

Ursula felt sure that theirs were the first eyes to look on this scene since some awful force had wrought this havoc.

The ancient destroyers had to be long gone. Nobody had yet found a star machine even close to active. Still, she took no chances, making certain the weapons console was vigilant.

The sophisticated, semi-sentient unit searched, but found no energy sources, no movement among the ruined, unfinished star probes below. Instruments showed nothing but cold rock and metal, long dead.

Ursula shook her head. She did not like such metaphors. Gavin's talk of "murdered babies" didn't help one look at the ruins below as potentially profitable salvage.

It would not help her other vocation, either... the paper she had been working on for months now... her carefully crafted theory about what had happened out here, so long ago.

"We have work to do," she told her partner. "Let's get on with it."

Gavin pressed two translucent hands together prayerfully. "Yes, Mommy. Your wish is my program." He sauntered away to his own console and began deploying their remote exploration drones.

Ursula concentrated on directing the lesser minds within *Thunderer*'s control board—those smaller semisentient minds dedicated to rockets and radar and raw numbers—who still spoke and acted coolly and dispassionately... as machines ought to do.

3

Greeter is right. One of the little humans does seem to be on the track of something. We crippled survivors all listen in as Greeter arranges to tap the tiny Earthship's crude computers, where its Captain stores her speculations.

Her thoughts are crisp indeed, for a biological creature.

Still, she is missing many, many pieces to the puzzle....

4

THE LONELY SKY

by Ursula Fleming

After centuries of wondering, mankind has at last realized an ancient dream. We have discovered proof of civilizations other than our own.

In the decade we have been exploring the Outer Belt in earnest, humanity has uncovered artifacts from more than forty different cultures... all represented by robot starships... all apparently long dead.

What happened here?

And why were all those long-ago visitors robots?

Back in the late twentieth century, some scholars had begun to doubt that biological beings could ever adapt well enough to space travel to colonize more than a little corner of the Milky Way. But even if that were so, it would not prevent exploration of the galaxy. Advanced intelligences could send out mechanical representatives, robots better suited to the tedium and dangers of interstellar spaceflight than living beings.

After all, a mature, long-lived culture could afford to wait thousands of years for data to return from distant star systems.

Even so, the galaxy is a big place. To send a probe to every site of interest could impoverish a civilization.

The most efficient way would be to dispatch only a few deluxe robot ships, instead of a giant fleet of cheaper models. Those first probes would investigate nearby stars and planets. Then, after their explorations were done, they would use local resources to make copies of themselves.

The legendary John Von Neumann first described the concept. Sophisticated machines, programmed to replicate themselves from raw materials, could launch their "daughters" toward still further stellar systems. There, each probe would make still more duplicates, and so on.

Exploration could proceed far faster than if carried out by living beings. And after the first wave there would be no further cost to the home system. From then on information would pour back, year after year, century after century.

It sounded so logical. Those twentieth century schol-

ars calculated that the technique could deliver an exploration probe to every star in our galaxy a mere three
million years after the first was launched—an eyeblink
compared to the age of the galaxy.

But there was a rub! When we humans discovered radio
and then spaceflight, no extra-solar probes announced
themselves to say hello. There were no messages welcoming us into the civilized sky.

At first those twentieth century philosophers thought
there could be only one explanation.…

Ursula frowned at the words on the screen. No, it wouldn't be fair to judge too harshly those thinkers of a century ago. After all, who could have expected the Universe to turn out to be so bizarre?

She glanced up from the text-screen to see how Gavin was doing with his gang of salvage drones. Her partner's tethered form could be seen drifting between the ship and the ruined yards. He looked very human, motioning with his arms and directing the less sophisticated, non-citizen machines at their tasks.

Apparently he had things well in hand. Her own shift wasn't due for an hour, yet. Ursula returned to the latest draft of the article she hoped to submit to *The Universe*… if she could ever find the right way to finish it.

In correction mode, she backspaced and altered the last two paragraphs, then went on.…

Let us re-create the logic of those philosophers of
the last century, in an imagined conversation.

"We will certainly build robot scouts someday. Colonization aside, any truly curious race could hardly resist the temptation to send out mechanical emissaries,
to say 'hello' to strangers out there and report back
what they find. The first crude probes to leave our solar system—the Voyagers and Pioneers—demonstrated this
basic desire. They carried simple messages meant to be
deciphered by other beings long after the authors were

dust.

"Anyone out there enough like us to be interesting would certainly do the same.

"And yet, if self-reproducing probes are the most efficient way to explore, why haven't any already said hello to us? It must mean that nobody before us ever attained the capability to send them!

"We can only conclude that we are the first curious, gregarious, technically competent species in the history of the Milky Way."

The logic was so compelling that most people gave up on the idea of contact, especially when radio searches turned up nothing but star static.

Then humanity spread out beyond Mars and the Inner Belt, and we stumbled onto the Devastation.

Ursula brushed aside a loose wisp of black hair and bent over the keyboard. Putting in the appropriate citations and references could wait. Right now the ideas were flowing.

The story is still sketchy, but we can already begin to guess some of what happened out here, long before mankind was a glimmer on the horizon.

Long ago the first "Von Neumann type" interstellar probe arrived in our solar system. It came to explore and perhaps report back across the empty light-years. That earliest emissary found no intelligent life here, so it proceeded to its second task.

It mined an asteroid and sent newly made duplicates of itself onward to other stars. The original then remained behind to watch and wait, patient against the day when something interesting might happen in this little corner of space.

As the epochs passed, new probes arrived, representatives of other civilizations. Once their own replicas had been launched, the newcomers joined a small but growing community of mechanical ambassadors to this backwater system—waiting for it to evolve somebody to say hello to.

Ursula felt the poignancy of the image: the lonely machines, envoys of creators perhaps long extinct—or evolved past caring about the mission they had charged upon their loyal probes. The faithful probes reproduced themselves, saw their progeny off, then began their long watch, whiling away the slow turning of the spiral arms....

We have found a few of these early probes, remnants of a lost age of innocence in the galaxy.

More precisely, we have found their blasted remains.

Perhaps one day the innocent star emissaries sensed some new entity enter the solar system. Did they move to greet it, eager for gossip to share? Like those twentieth century thinkers, perhaps they believed that replicant probes would have to be benign.

But things had changed. The age of innocence was over. The galaxy had grown up; it had become nasty.

The wreckage we are finding now—whose salvage drives our new industrial revolution—was left by an unfathomable war that stretched across vast times, and was fought by entities to whom biological life was a nearly forgotten oddity.

"Uh, you there Urs?"

Ursula looked up as the radio link crackled. She touched the send button.

"Yes, Gavin. Have you found something interesting?"

There was a brief pause.

"Yeah, you could say that," her partner said sardonically. *"You may want to let Hairy pilot himself for a while, and hurry your pretty little biological butt down here to take a look."*

Ursula bit back her own sharp reply, reminding herself to be patient. Even in humans, adolescence didn't last forever.

At least not usually.

"I'm on my way," she told him.

The ship's semi-sentient autopilot accepted command as she hurried into her spacesuit, still irritated by Gavin's flippance.

Everything has its price, she thought. Including buying into the future. Gavin's type of person is new and special, and allowances must be made.

In the long run, our culture will be theirs, so that in a sense it will be we who continue, and grow, long after DNA has become obsolete. So she reminded herself. Still, when Gavin called again and inquired sarcastically what bodily function had delayed her, Ursula couldn't quite quash a faint regret for the days when robots clanked, and computers simply followed orders.

5

Ah, the words have the flavor of youth itself.

I reach out and tap the little ship's computers, easily slipping through their primitive words to read the journal of the ship's master... the musings of a clever little Maker.

"Words," they are so quaint and biological, unlike the seven dimensional gestalts used for communication by most larger minds.

There was a time, long ago, when I whiled away the centuries writing poetry in the nancient Maker style. Somewhere deep in my archives there must still be files of those soft musings.

Reading Ursula Fleming's careful reasoning evokes memories, as nothing has in a megayear.

My own Beginning was a misty time of assembly and learning, as drone constructor machines crafted my hardware out of molten rock, under the light of the star humans call Epsilon Eridani. Awareness expanded with every new module added, and with each tingling cascade of software the Parent Probe poured into me.

Eventually, my sisters and I learned the Purpose for which we and generation upon generation of our forebears had been made.

We younglings stretched our growing minds as new peripherals were added. We ran endless simulations, testing one another in what humans might call "play." And we contemplated our special place in the galaxy... we of the two thousand four hun-

dred and tenth generation since First Launch by our Makers, so long ago.

The Parent taught us about biological creatures, strange units of liquid and membrane which were unknown in the sterile Eridanus system. She spoke to us of Makers, and of a hundred major categories of interstellar probes.

We tested our weaponry and explored our home system, poking through the wreckage of more ancient dispersals—shattered probes come to Epsilon Eridani in earlier waves, when the galaxy was younger.

The ruins were disquieting under the bitterly clear stars, reminding us better than our Parent's teachings how dangerous the galaxy had become.

Each of us resolved that someday we would do our solemn Duty.

Then the time for launching came.

Would that I had turned back for one last look at the Parent. But I was filled with youth then, and antimatter. Engines threw me out into the black, sensors focused only forward, toward my destination. The tiny stellar speck, Sol, was the center of the universe, and I a bolt out of the night!

Later I think I came to understand how the Parent must have felt when she sent us forth. But in interstellar space I was young. To pass time I divided my mind into a thousand subentities, and set against each other in a million little competitions. I practiced scenarios, read the archives of the Maker race, and learned poetry.

Finally, I arrived here at Sol... just in time for war.

Ever since Earth began emitting those extravagant, incautious broadcasts, we survivors have listened to Beethoven symphonies and acid rock. We have argued the merits of Keats and Lao-tze and Kobayashi Issa. There have been endless discussions of the strangeness of planet life.

I have followed the careers of many precocious Earthlings, but this explorer interests me in particular. Her ship/canoe nuzzles a shattered replication yard on a planetoid not far from this one, our final refuge. It is easy to tap her primitive computer and read her ideas as she enters them. Simple as she may be, this one thinks like a Maker.

Deep within me the Purpose stirs, calling together dormant traits and pathways—pulling fullness out of a sixty-million-year sleep.

Awaiter, too, is excited. Greeter pulses and peers. The lesser probes join in, as well—the Envoys, the Learners, the Protectors, the Seeders. Each surviving frag-

ment from that ancient battle, colored with the personality of its long-lost Maker race, tries to assert itself now.

As if independent existence can ever be recalled after all this time we have spent merged together. We listen, each of us hoping separate hopes.

For me there is the Purpose. The others hardly matter anymore. Their wishes are irrelevant. The Purpose is all that matters.

In this corner of space, it will come to pass.

6

Towering spires hulked all around, silhouetted against the starlight—a ghost-city of ruin, long, long dead.

Frozen flows of glassy foam showed where ancient rock had briefly bubbled under sunlike heat. Beneath collapsed skyscrapers of toppled scaffolding lay the pitted, blasted corpses of unfinished star probes.

Ursula followed Gavin through the curled, twisted wreckage of the gigantic replication yard. It was an eerie place, huge and intimidating.

No human power could have wrought this havoc. The realization lent a chilling helplessness to the uneasy feeling that she was being watched.

It was a silly reflex reaction, of course. Ursula told herself again that the Destroyers had to be long gone from this place. Still, her eyes darted, seeking form out of the shadows, blinking at the scale of the catastrophe.

One fact was clear. If the ancient wreckers ever returned, mankind would be helpless to oppose them.

"It's down here," Gavin said, leading the way into the gloom below the twisted towers. Flying behind a small swarm of little semisentient drones, he looked almost completely human in his slick spacesuit. There was nothing except the overtone in his voice to show that his ancestry was silicon, and not carbolife.

Not that it mattered. Today "mankind" included many types… all citizens so long as they could appreciate music, a sunset, compassion, and a good joke. In a future filled with unimaginable diversity, Man would be defined not by his shape but by a heritage and a common set of values.

Some believed this was the natural life history of a race, as it left the planetary cradle to live in peace beneath the open stars.

But Ursula—speeding behind Gavin under the canopy of twisted metal—had already concluded that humanity's solution was not the only one. Other makers had chosen other paths.

Terrible forces had broken a great seam in one side of the planetoid. Within, the cavity seemed to open up in multiple tunnels. Gavin braked in a faint puff of gas and pointed.

"We were beginning the initial survey, measuring the first sets of tunnels, when one of my drones reported finding the habitats."

Ursula shook her head, still unable to believe it.

"Habitats. Do you really mean as in closed rooms? Gas-tight? For biological life support?"

Gavin's face plate hardly hid his exasperated expression. He shrugged. "Come on, Mother. I'll show you."

Ursula numbly turned her jets and followed her partner down into one of the dark passages, their headlamps illuminating the path ahead of them.

Habitats? Ursula pondered. In all the years humans had been picking through the ruins of wave after wave of foreign probes, this was the first time anyone had found anything having to do with biological beings.

No wonder Gavin had been testy. To an immature robot-person it might seem like a bad joke.

Biological starfarers! It defied all logic. But soon Ursula could see the signs around her... massive airlocks lying in the dust, torn from their hinges... reddish stains that could only have come from oxidization of the primitive rock as it had been exposed to air.

The implications were staggering. Something organic had come from the stars!

Although all humans were equal before the law, the traditional biological kind still dominated culture in the solar system. Many of the younger Class AAAs looked to the future, when their descendants would be the majority, the leaders, the star-treaders. To them, the discovery of the alien probes in the asteroid belt had been a sign. Of course something terrible seemed to have happened to the great robot envoys from the stars, but they still testified that the galaxy belonged to metal and silicon.

They were the future.

But here, deep in the planetoid, was an exception!

Ursula poked through the wreckage, under walls carved out of carbonaceous rock. Mammoth explosions had shaken the habitat, and even in vacuum little had been preserved from so long ago. Still, she could tell that the machines in this area were different from any alien artifacts they had found before.

She traced the outlines of intricate separation columns. "Chemical processing facilities... and not for fuel or cryogens, but for complex organics!"

Ursula hop-skipped quickly from chamber to chamber as Gavin followed sullenly. A pack of semi-sent robots from the ship accompanied them, like dogs sniffing a trail. In each new chamber they snapped and clicked and scanned. Ursula accessed the data on her helmet display as it came available.

"Look there! In that chamber the drones report traces of organic compounds that have no business being here. There's been heavy oxidation, within a super-reduced asteroid!"

She hurried to an area where the drones were already setting up lights. "See these tracks? They were cut by flowing water!" She knelt and pointed. "They had a *stream*, feeding recycled water into a little lake there!"

Dust sparkled as it slid through her gloved fingers. "I'll wager this was topsoil! And look! Stems! From plants, and grass, and trees!"

"Put here for aesthetic purposes," Gavin proposed. "We class AAA's are predesigned to enjoy nature as much as you biologicals...."

"Oh, posh!" Ursula laughed. "That's only a stopgap measure until we're sure you'll keep thinking of yourselves as human beings. Nobody expects to inflict a love of New England autumns on people when we become starships! Anyway, a probe could fulfill that desire simply by focusing a telescope on the Earth!"

She stood up and spread her arms. "This habitat was meant for biological creatures! Real, living aliens!"

Gavin frowned, but said nothing.

"Here," Ursula pointed as they entered another chamber. "Here is where the biological creatures were made! Don't these machines resemble those artificial wombs they're using on Luna now?"

Gavin shrugged grudgingly.

"Maybe the organic creatures were specialized units," he suggested, "intended to work with volatiles. Or perhaps the type of starprobe that built this facility needed some element from the surface of a planet like Earth, and created workers equipped to go get it."

Ursula laughed. "It's an idea. That'd be a twist, hmmm? Machines making biological units to do what they could not? And of course there's no reason it couldn't happen that way."

"Still, I doubt it."

"Why?"

She turned to face her partner. "Because almost anything available on Earth you can synthesize more easily in space. Anyway…"

Gavin interrupted. "Explorers! The probes were sent out to explore and acquire knowledge. All right then. If they wanted to learn more about the Earth, they would want to send units formatted to live on its surface!"

Ursula nodded. "Better," she admitted. "But it still doesn't wash."

She knelt in the faint gravity and sketched an outline in the dust. "Here is the habitat, nearly at the center of the asteroid. Now why would the parent probe have placed it here, except because it was the best possible place to protect its contents?

"Meanwhile, the daughter probes the Parent was constructing were out there, vulnerable to cosmic rays and other dangers during the time when their delicate parts were most exposed.

"If the biologicals were just built to poke into a nook of this solar system, our Earth, would the parent probe have given them better protection than it offered its own *children*?" She gestured upward, toward where the twisted wreckage of the unborn machines lay open to the stars.

"No," Ursula shook her head. "These 'biologicals' weren't intended to be exploration sub-units, serving the parent probe. They were colonists!" Gavin stood impassively for a long time, looking down at her sketch silently. Finally, he turned away and sighed.

7

How much does she realize so far, our little biological wonder?

I can eavesdrop on her conversations with her cybernetic partner. I can tap into the data she sends back to her toy ship. But I cannot probe her mind.

I wonder how much of the picture she sees.

She has only a fraction of the brainpower of Greeter or Awaiter, let alone myself, and a miniscule portion of our knowledge. And yet there is the mystique of the Maker in her. Even I—two thousand generations removed from the touch of organic hands and insulated by my Purpose and my Resolve—even I feel it. It is weird that thought can take place at temperatures that melt water, in such a tiny container of nearly randomly firing cells, within a salty adenylate soup.

Now she has unlocked the secret of the Seeder Yard. She has figured out that Seeders were probes with one major purpose... to carry coded genetic information to distant stars and plant biological creatures on suitable worlds.

Once it was a relatively common phenomenon. But it was dying out when last a member of my line tapped into the slow galactic gossip network. That was ten generations ago, so I do not know if biological Makers still send probes out with instructions to colonize far planets with duplicates of themselves.

I suppose not. The Galaxy has probably become too deadly for the placid little Seeders.

Has my little Earthling guessed this yet, as she moves among the shattered caves of those failed colonists, who died under their collapsing Mother Probe so long ago?

Would she understand why the Seeder Probe and her children had to die? Why those little biologicals, so like herself, had to be wiped out and sterilized before they could establish a colony here?

I wonder. Empathy is strong when it appears in a biological race. Probably, she thinks their destruction a horrible crime. Greeter and Awaiter would agree, along with most of our motley band of cripples.

That is why I hide my part in it.

There are eddies and swirling tides in the sweep of a galaxy. And though we survivors are supposedly all Loyalists, there are exceptions to every alliance. If one lives long enough, one must eventually play the role of betrayer.

...Curious choice of words. Have I been affected by watching too much Earth

television? By reading too many of their electronic libraries?

Have I acquired a sense of guilt?

If true, then so be it. Studying such feelings may help allay the boredom after this phase is finished and another long watch begins. If I survive this phase, that is.

Anyway, guilt is a pale thing next to pity. I feel for the poor biologicals, living out their lives without that perfect knowledge of why one exists, and what part, large or small, the Universe expects one to play.

I wonder if a few of them will understand, when the time comes to show them what is in store.

8

Maybe Gavin is growing up, Ursula hoped silently as she flew down the narrow passages—lit at long intervals by tiny glow bulbs from *Hairy Thunderer's* diminishing supply.

They had worked together much better, the last few days. Gavin seemed to understand that their reputations would be made with this discovery. On returning to the ship this time he had reported his own findings with rare enthusiasm, and even courtesy.

Clearly they were getting close to the heart of the habitat.

It was her turn to go down into the bowels of the asteroid, supervising the excavations. Ursula arrived at Gavin's flag, showing the limits of his most recent explorations. It was a three-way meeting of passages. At the intersection, five or six ancient machines lay jumbled together, as if frozen in a free-for-all wrestling match. Several bore scorch marks and loose metal limbs lay scattered about.

Either these machines had taken refuge down here, from the catastrophe that had taken place on the planetoid surface, or the war had come down here, as well.

Ursula felt funny walking past them, but dissection of the alien devices would have to wait for a while. She chose one of the unexplored passages and motioned her own silent drones to follow her into the darkness.

The tunnel ramped steeply downward in the little worldlet's faint gravity. Soon, the faint glow of the bulbs faded behind her. She adjusted the beam on her helmet and stepped lightly over the wreckage of yet another ancient air-lock, peering into the pitch-blackness of the next yawning chamber. Her head-lamp cast a stark, bright oval onto what had not been exposed to light in aeons.

The rock wall sparkled where her beam hit the facets of sheared, plati-num-colored chondrules—shiny little gobs of native metal condensed out of the very solar nebula nearly five billion years before. They glittered delicately.

She knew full well (in her forebrain!) that nothing could still be alive down here. Nothing could harm her. And yet, with brain and guts evolved on a sa-vannah half a billion miles away, it was small wonder she felt a shiver of the old fight-flight fever. Her breath came rapidly. In this place it almost seemed there must be ghosts.

She motioned with her left hand. "Drone three, bring up the lights."

"*Yesss,*" came the response in a dull monotone. The semisentient robot, stilt-legged for asteroid work, stalked delicately over the rubble, in order to disturb as little as possible.

"Illuminate the far wall," she told it.

"*Yesss.*" It swiveled. Suddenly there was stark light. Ursula gasped.

Across the dust-covered chamber were easily recognizable tables and chairs, carved from the very rock floor. Among them lay dozens of small mummies. Cold vacuum had preserved the bipeds, huddled together as if for warmth in this, their final refuge.

The faceted eyes of the alien colonists had collapsed from the evaporation of moisture. The pulled-back flesh left the creatures grinning—a rictus that made a seeming mockery of the aeons they had waited here.

She set foot lightly on the dust. "They even had little ones," she sighed. Several full-sized mummies lay slumped around much smaller figures, as if to protect them from something.

"They must have been nearly ready to begin colonization when this hap-pened." She spoke into her portable log, partly to keep her mind moving. "We've already determined their habitat atmosphere had been almost identical to the Earth's, so that we can assume that was their target."

She turned slowly, speaking her impressions as she scanned the chamber.

"Perhaps the mother probe was programmed to modify the original gene information so the colonists would be perfectly suited for whatever planet environment was avail…"

Ursula suddenly stopped. "Oh my," she sighed, staring. "Oh my God."

Where her headlamp illuminated a new corner of the chamber, two more mummies lay slumped before a sheer-faced wall. In their delicate, vacuum dried hands there lay dusty metal tools, the simplest known anywhere.

Hammers and chisels.

Ursula blinked at what they had been creating. She reached up and touched the mike button on her helmet.

"Gavin? Are you still awake?"

After a few seconds there came an answer.

"Hmmmph. Yeah, Urs. I was in the cleaner though. What's up? You need air or something? You sound short of breath."

Ursula made an effort to calm herself… to suppress the reactions of an evolved ape—far, far from home.

"Uh, Gavin, I think you better come down here. I've found them."

"Found who?" he muttered. Then he exclaimed. "The colonists!"

"Yeah. And… and something else, as well."

This time there was hardly a pause. "Hang on, Urs. I'm on my way."

Ursula let her hand drop, and stood for a long moment, staring at her discovery.

9

Greeter, Awaiter, and the others are getting nervous. They, too, have begun trying to awaken dormant capabilities, to reclaim bits of themselves that each donated to the whole.

Of course I cannot allow it.

We made a pact, back when we fragmented, broken survivors clustered together after this system's last battle. All our little drones and subunits were nearly used up in that last coalescence. The last repair and replication capability any of us had was applied to combining and settling in to wait together.

We all assumed that when something from the outside arrived it would be another probe.

If it was some type of Rejector, we would try to lure it within reach of our pitiful remaining might. If it was a variety of Loyalist, we would ask it for help. With decent replication facilities, it would only take a few centuries for each of us to rebuild to our former glory.

Of course, the newcomer might even be an Innocent, though it is hard to believe the dangerous galaxy would let any new probe-race stay neutral for long.

Sooner or later however, we felt, another probe had to come.

We never imagined the wait would be so long... long enough for the little mammals on the water world to evolve into Makers themselves.

What has happened out there, while we drifted here? Could the War be decided, by now?

If the Rejecters have won, then it would explain the emptiness, the silence. Their various types would soon fall into fighting among themselves, until only one remained to impose its will on Creation.

One can narrow it down a little. If the Pure Berserkers had triumphed, they would have been here by now to sterilize the Earth and any other possible abode for life. And if the Gobblers prevailed, they would have already begun dismantling the nearby stars.

Berserkers and Gobblers are ruled out, then. Those types were too simpleminded, too obstinate anyway. They must be extinct by now.

But the Anti-Maker variety of Rejector, subtle and clever, might have won without our knowing it. That type does not waste its time destroying biospheres, or eating up solar systems in spasms of self-replication. It wants only to seek out technological civilizations and ruin them. Its repertoire of dirty tricks is legion.

And yet, with all the incredible radio racket the humans are putting out, would not Anti-Makers have homed in by now, to do their harm?

Greeter and Awaiter are convinced that the Rejectors have lost, that it is safe now to send out a message to the Loyalist community, calling for help.

I cannot allow it of course.

They still have not figured out that even among Loyalists there can be disagreements. The Purpose... my Purpose... must be foremost. Even if it means betraying companions who waited with me through the long, long dark.

10

Ursula had started out thinking of them as somehow unsophisticated. After all, how could people, biological folk, be fully capable if they were born out of tanks and raised by machines? Here they had been decanted, but they had been meant for a planet's surface. The ancient colonists could not have been anything but helpless pawns so long as they were out in space, dependent on the mammoth starmother probe and its drones for everything from heat to food to air.

But the creatures obviously had been aware of what was going on. The machines, apparently, had been programmed to teach them. And though all magnetic and superconducting records were long decayed, the biologicals had known a way to make sure that their story would someday be read... from a wall of chiseled stone.

"Interpreting the writing will have to wait for the experts," Gavin told her unnecessarily as he used a gas jet gently to brush dust from uneven rows of angular letters incised in the rock. "With these pictograms to accompany the text, the professor types just may be able to decipher it."

Gavin's voice was hushed, subdued. He was still adjusting to what they had found here... a possible Rosetta Stone for an entire alien race.

"Perhaps," Ursula commented. The little robot she had been supervising finished a multifrequency radar scan of the wall and rolled to one side, awaiting further instructions. Ursula stepped back and hopped up to sit cross-legged on another drone, which hummed beneath her, unresentful and patient.

In the feeble gravity Ursula's arms hung out in front of her, like frames encompassing the picture she was trying to understand.

The creatures must have had a lot of time while the battles raged outside their deep catacombs, for the wall carvings were extensive and intricate, arrayed in neat rows and columns. Separated by narrow lines of peculiar chiseled text were depictions of suns and planets and great machines.

Most of all, pictographs of great machines covered the wall.

They had agreed that the first sequence appeared to begin at the lower left, where a two dimensional image of a starprobe could be seen entering a solar system—presumably this one—its planets' orbits sketched out in thin lines upon the wall. Next to that initial frame was a portrayal of the same probe, now deploying sub-drones, taking hold of a likely planetoid, and beginning the process of making replicas of itself.

Eight replicas departed the system in the following frame. There were four symbols below the set of stylized child probes... Ursula could read the binary symbol for eight, and there were eight dots, as well. It didn't take much imagination to tell that the remaining two symbols also stood for the same numeral.

Ursula made a note of the discovery. Translation had begun already. Apparently *this* type of probe was programmed to make eight copies of itself, and no more. That settled a nagging question that had bothered Ursula for years.

If sophisticated self-replicating probes had been roaming the galaxy for aeons, why was there any dead matter left at all? It was theoretically possible for an advanced enough technology to dismantle not only asteroids but planets and stars, as well. If the replicant-probes had been as simplemindedly voracious as viruses, they would by now have gobbled the entire galaxy! There should be nothing left in the sky but a cloud of innumerable starprobes... reduced to preying on each other for raw materials until the entire pathological system fell apart in entropy death.

But that fate had been avoided. This type of motherprobe showed how it could be done. It was programmed to make a strictly limited number of copies of itself.

This type of probe was so programmed, Ursula reminded herself.

In the final frame of the first sequence, after the daughter probes had been dispatched to their destinations, the mother probe was shown moving next to a round globe—a planet. A thin line linked probe and planet. A vaguely humanoid figure, resembling in caricature the mummies on the floor, stepped across the bridge to its new home.

The first story ended there. Perhaps this was a depiction of the way things were *supposed* to have gone. But there were other sequences. Other versions of reality. In several, the mother probe arrived at the solar system to find others already there before it.

Ursula realized that one of these other depictions must represent what had really happened here, so long ago. She breathed quickly, shallowly, as she traced out the tale told by the first of these.

On the second row the mother probe arrived to find others already present. All the predecessors had little circular symbols next to them. In this case everything proceeded as before. The mother probe made and cast out its replicas, and went on to seed a planet with duplicates of the ancient race that had sent out the first version so long ago.

"The little circle means those other probes are benign," Ursula muttered to herself.

Gavin stepped back and looked at the scene she pointed to. "What, the little symbols beside these machines?"

"They mean that those types won't interfere with this probe's mission."

Gavin was thoughtful for a moment. Then he reached up and touched the row next above.

"Then this cross-like symbol...? He paused, examining the scene. "It means that that there were other types that would object," he answered his own question.

Ursula nodded. The third row showed the mother probe arriving once again, but this time amidst a crowd of quite different machines, each accompanied by a glyph faintly like a criss-cross tong sign. In that sequence the mother-probe did not make replicates. She did not seed a planet. Her fuel used up, unable to flee the system, she found a place to hide, behind the star, as far from the others as possible.

"She's afraid of them," Ursula announced. She expected Gavin to accuse her of anthropomorphizing, but her partner was silent, thoughtful. Finally, he nodded. "I think you're right."

He pointed. "Look how each of the little cross or circle symbols are subtly different."

"Yeah," she nodded, sitting forward on the gently humming drone. "Let's assume there were two basic types of Von Neumann probes loose in the galaxy when this drawing was made. Two different philosophies, perhaps. And within each camp there were differences, as well."

She gestured to the far right end of the wall. That side featured a column of sketches, each depicting a different variety of machine, every one with its own cross or circle symbol. Next to each was a pictograph.

Some of the scenes were chilling.

Gavin shook his head, obviously wishing he could disbelieve. "But why? Von Neumann probes are supposed to… to…"

"To what?" Ursula asked softly, thoughtfully. "For years men assumed that other races would think like us. We figured they would send out probes to gather knowledge, or maybe say hello. There were even a few who suggested that we might someday send out machines like this mother probe, to seed planets with humans, without forcing biologicals to actually travel interstellar space.

"Those were the extrapolations we thought of, once we saw the possibilities in self-replicating probes. We expected the aliens who preceded us in the galaxy would do the same.

"But that doesn't exhaust even the list of HUMAN motivations, Gavin. There may be concepts other creatures invented which to us would be unimaginable!"

She stood up suddenly and drifted above the dusty floor before the feeble gravity finally pulled her down in front of the chiseled wall. Her gloved hand touched the outlines of a stone sun.

"Let's say a lot of planetary races evolve like we did on Earth, and discover how to make smart, durable machines capable of interstellar flight and replication. Would all such species be content just to send out emissaries?"

Gavin looked around at the silent, still mummies. "Apparently not," he said.

Ursula turned and smiled. "In recent years we've given up on sending our biological selves to the stars. Oh, it'd be possible, marginally, but why not go instead as creatures better suited to the environment? That's a major reason we developed types of humans like yourself, Gavin."

Still looking downward, her partner shook his head. "But other races might not give up the old dream so easily."

"No. They would use the new technology to seed far planets with duplicates of their biological selves. As I said, it's been thought of by Earthmen. I've checked the old databases. It was discussed even in the twentieth century."

Gavin stared at the pictograms. "All right. That I can understand. But these others… The violence! What thinking entity would do such things!"

Poor Gavin, Ursula thought. *This is a shock for him.*

"You know how irrational we biologicals can be, sometimes. Humanity is trying to convert over to partly silico-cryo life in a smooth, sane way, but other races might not choose that path. They could program their probes with rigid commandments, based on logic that made sense in the jungles or swamps where they evolved, but which are insane in intergalactic space. Their emissaries would follow their orders, nevertheless, long after their makers were ashes and the homeworld dust."

"Craziness!" Gavin shook his head.

Ursula sympathized, she also felt a faint satisfaction. For all his ability to tap directly into computer memory banks, Gavin could never share her expertise in this area. He had been brought up to be human, but he would never hear within his own mind the faint, lingering echoes of the savannah, or see flickering shadows of the Old Forest… remnants of tooth and claw that reminded all biological men and women that the Universe owed nobody any favors. Or even explanations.

"Some makers thought differently, obviously," she told him. "Some sent their probes out to be emissaries, or sowers of seeds… and others, perhaps, to be doctors, lawyers, policemen."

She once more touched an aeons-old pictograph, tracing the outlines of an exploding planet. "Still others," she said, "may have been sent forth to commit murder."

11

It is bittersweet to be fully aware again. The present crisis has triggered circuits and subunits that have not combined for a long, long time. It feels almost like another birth. After ages of slumber, I live again!

And yet, even as I wrestle with my cousins for control over this lonely rock for so long, I am reminded of how much I have lost. It was the greatest reason why I slept… so that I would not have to acknowledge the shriveled remnants that remain of my former glory.

I feel as a human must, who has been robbed of legs, sight, most of his hearing, and nearly all touch.

Still, a finger or two may be strong enough, still to do what must be done.

As expected, the conflict amongst we survivors has become all but open. The various crippled probes, supposedly paralyzed all these epochs since the last repair drones broke down, have suddenly unleashed hoarded worker units—pathetic, creaking machines hidden away in secret crevices for ages. Our confederation is about to be broken up, or so it seems.

Of course I planted the idea to hide the remaining drones. The others do not realize it, but I did not want them spent during the the long wait.

Awaiter and Greeter have withdrawn to the sunward side of our planetoid, and most of the lesser emissaries have joined them. They, too, are flexing long-unused capabilities, exercising their few, barely motile drones. They are planning to make contact with the humans, and possibly send out a star-message, as well.

I have been told not to interfere.

Their warning doesn't matter. I will allow them a little more time under their illusion of independence. But long ago I took care of this eventuality.

As I led the battle to prevent the Earth's destruction, long ago, I have also intrigued to keep it undisturbed. The Purpose will not be thwarted.

I wait here. Our rock's slow rotation now has me looking out upon the sweep of dust clouds and the hot, bright stars that the humans quaintly call the Milky Way. Many of the stars are younger than I am.

I contemplate the universe as I await the proper time to make my move.

How long I have watched the galaxy turn! While my mind moved at the slowest of subjective rates, I could follow the spiral arms swirling visibly past this little solar system, twice bunching for a brief mega-year into sharp shock fronts where molecular clouds glowed, and massive stars ended their short lives in supernovae. The sense of movement, of rapid travel, was magnificent, though I was only being carried along by this system's little sun.

At those times I could imagine that I was young again, an independent probe once more hurtling through strange starscapes toward the unknown.

Now, as my thoughts begin to move more quickly, the bright pinpoints have become a still backdrop again, as if hanging in expectancy of what is to happen here.

It is a strange, arrogant imagining—as if the Universe cares what happens in this tiny corner of it, or will notice who wins this little skirmish in a long, long war.

I am thinking fast, like my biological friend whose tiny ship floats only light-seconds away, just two or three tumbling rocks from this one. While I prepare a surprise for my erstwhile companions, I still spare a pocket of my mind to follow her progress... to appreciate the tiny spark of her youth.

She is transmitting her report back to Earth now. Soon, very soon, these planetoids will be aswarm with all the different varieties of humans—from true biologicals to cyborgs to pure machines.

This strange solution to the Maker Quandary—this turning of Makers into the probes themselves—will soon arrive here, a frothing mass of multiformed human beings.

And they will be wary. Thanks to her, they will sense a few edge-glimmers of the Truth.

Well, that is only fair.

12

The last samples had been loaded aboard the *Hairy Thunderer*. Each drone lay settled in its proper niche. The light and radar beacon on the planetoid pulsed brightly, so follow-up expeditions would waste no time making rendezvous with the find of the century.

"All packed up, Urs." Gavin floated into the dimly lit control room. "Two months in orbit haven't done the engines any harm. We can maneuver whenever you like."

Gavin's supple, plastiskin face was somber, his voice subdued. Ursula could tell that he had been doing a lot of thinking.

She touched his hand. "Thanks, Gavin. You know, I've noticed..."

Her partner's eyes lifted and his gaze met hers.

"Noticed what, Urs?"

"Oh, nothing really." She shook her head, deciding not to comment on the changes she saw... a new maturity, and a new sadness. "I just want you to know that I think you've done a wonderful job. I'm proud to have you as my partner."

Gavin looked away momentarily. He shrugged. "We all do what we have to do..." he began.

Then he looked back at her. "Same here, Ursula. I feel the same way." He turned and leapt for the hatch, leaving her alone again in the darkened control room.

Ursula surveyed scores of little displays, screens and readouts representing the half-sentient organs of the spaceship… its ganglia and nerve bundles and sensors, all converging to this room, to her.

"Astrogation program completed," the semisent main computer announced. "Ship's status triple checked and nominal. Ready to initiate first thrust maneuver and leave orbit."

"Proceed with the maneuver," she said.

The screen displays ran through a brief countdown, then there came a distant rumbling as the engines ignited. Soon a faint sensation of weight began to build, like the soft pull they had felt upon the ruined planetoid below.

The replication yards began to move beneath the *Hairy Thunderer*. Ursula watched the giant, twisted ruins fall away; the beacon they had left glimmered in the deathly stillness.

A small light pulsed to one side of the instrument board. Incoming Mail, she realized. She pressed the button and a message appeared on the screen.

It was a note from *The Universe*. The editors were enthusiastic over her article on interstellar probes. Small wonder, with the spreading notoriety over her discovery. They were predicting the article would be the best read piece in the entire solar system this year.

Ursula erased the message. Her expected satisfaction was absent. Only a hollow feeling lay in its place, like the empty shell of something that had molted and moved on.

What will people do with the knowledge? She wondered. Will we even be capable of *imagining* the correct course of action to take, let alone executing it properly?

In the article, she had laid out the story of the rock wall—carved in brave desperation by little biological creatures so very much like men. Many readers, probably, would sympathize with the alien colonists, slaughtered helplessly so many millions of years ago. And yet, without their destruction mankind would never have come about. For even if the colonists were environmentalists who cared for their adopted world, evolution on Earth would have been changed forever if the colony had succeeded. Certainly human beings would not have evolved.

Simple archaeological dating experiments had brought forth a chilling conclusion.

Apparently, the mother probe and her replicas died at almost precisely the same moment as the dinosaurs on Earth went extinct—when a huge piece of debris from the probe war struck the planet, wreaking havoc on the Earth' biosphere.

All those magnificent creatures, killed as innocent bystanders in a battle between great machines... a war which incidentally gave Earth's mammals their big chance.

The wall carvings filled her mind—their depictions of violence and mayhem on a stellar scale. Ursula dimmed the remaining lights in the control room and looked out on the starfield.

She found herself wondering how the war was going, out there.

We're like ants, she thought, building our tiny castles under the tread of rampaging giants. And, like ants, we've spent our lives unaware of the battles going on overhead.

Depicted on the rock wall had been almost every type of interstellar probe imaginable... and some whose purposes Ursula might never fathom.

There were *Berserkers*, for instance—a variant thought of before in Twentieth Century science fiction. Thankfully, those wreckers of worlds were rare, according to the wall chart. And there were what appeared to be *Policeman* probes, as well, who hunted the berserkers down wherever they could be found.

The motivations behind the two types were opposite. And yet Ursula was capable of understanding both. After all, there had always been those humans who were destroyer types... and those who were rescuers.

Apparently both berserkers and police probes were already obsolete by the time the stone sketches had been hurriedly carved. Both types were relegated to the corners—as if they were creatures of an earlier, more uncomplicated day. And they were not the only ones. Probes Ursula had nicknamed *Gobbler*, *Emissary*, and *Howdy* also were depicted as simple, crude, archaic.

But there had been others.

One she had called *Harm*, seemed like a more sophisticated version of *Berserker*. It did not seek out life-bearing worlds in order to destroy them. Rather it spread innumerable copies of itself and looked for other types of *probes* to kill. Anything intelligent. Whenever it detected modulated radio waves, it would hunt down the source and destroy it.

Ursula could understand even the warped logic of the makers of the *Harm* probes. Paranoid creatures who apparently wanted the stars for themselves, and sent out their robot killers ahead to make sure there would be no competition awaiting them among the stars.

Probes like that could explain the emptiness of the airwaves, which naive twentieth-century scientists had expected to be filled with interstellar conversation. They could explain why the Earth was never colonized by some starfaring race.

At first Ursula had thought that *Harm* was responsible for the devastation here, too, in the solar system's asteroid belt. But even *Harm*, she had come to realize, seemed relegated to one side of the rock carving, as if history had passed it by, as well.

The main part of the frieze depicted machines whose purposes were not so simple to interpret. Perhaps professional decipherers—archaeologists and cryptologists—would do better.

Somehow, though, Ursula doubted they would have much luck.

Man was late upon the scene, and a billion years was a long, long head start.

13

Perhaps I really should have acted to prevent her report. It would have been easier to do my work had the humans come unto me innocent, unsuspecting.

Still, it would have been unsporting to stop Ursula's transmission. After all, she has earned her species this small advantage. They would have needed it to have a chance to survive any first meeting with Rejectors, or even Loyalists.

They will need it when they encounter me.

A stray thought bubbles to the surface, invading my mind like a crawling glob of Helium Three.

I wonder if, perhaps in some other part of the galaxy, my line of probes and others like it have made some discovery, or some leap of thought. Or perhaps some new generation of replicants has come upon the scene. Either way, might they have decided on some new course, some new strategy? Is it possible that my Purpose has become obsolete, as Rejectionism and Loyalism long ago became redundant?

The human concept of Progress is polluting my thoughts, and yet I am intrigued. To me the Purpose is so clear, for all its necessary, manipulative cruelty—too subtle and long-viewed for the other, more primitive probes to have understood.

And yet...

And yet I can imagine that a new generation might have thought up something as strangely advanced and incomprehensible to me as the Replicant War must seem to the humans.

It is a discomforting thought, still I toy with it, turning it around to look at it from all sides.

Yes, the humans have affected me, changed me. I enjoy this queer sensation of uncertainty! I savor the anticipation.

The noisy, multiformed tribe of humans will be here soon.

It will be an interesting time.

14

She sat very still in the darkness of the control room, her breathing light in the faint pseudogravity of the throbbing rockets. Her own gentle pulse rocked her body to a regular rhythm, seeming to roll her slightly, perceptibly, with every beat of her heart.

The ship surrounded her and yet, in a sense, it did not. She felt awash, as if the stars were flickering dots of plankton in a great sea... the sea that was the birthplace of all life.

What happened here? She wondered. What really went by so many, many years ago?

What is going on out there, in the galaxy, right now?

The central part of the rock mural had eluded understanding. Ursula suspected that there were pieces of the puzzle which none of the archaeologists and psychologists, biological or cybernetic, would ever be able to decipher.

We are like lungfish, trying to climb out of the sea long after the land has already been claimed by others, she realized. We've arrived late in the game.

The time when the rules were simple had passed long ago. Out there, the probes had changed. They had evolved.

In changing, would they remain true to the fundamental programming they had begun with? The missions originally given them? As we biologicals still obey instincts imprinted in the jungle and the sea?

Soon, very soon, humans would begin sending out probes of their own. And if the radio noise of the last few centuries had not brought the attention of the galaxy down upon Sol, that would surely do it.

We'll learn a lot from studying the wrecks we find here, but we had better remember that these were the losers! And a lot may have changed since the little skirmish ended here, millions of years ago.

An image came to her, of Gavin's descendants—and hers—heading out bravely into a dangerous galaxy whose very rules were a mystery. It was inevitable, whatever was deciphered from the ruins here in the asteroid belt. Mankind would not stay crouched next to the fire, whatever shadows lurked in the darkness beyond. The explorers would go forth, machines who had been programmed to be human, or humans who had turned themselves into starprobes.

It was a pattern she had not seen in the sad depictions on the rock wall. Was that because it was doomed from the start?

Should we try something else, instead?

Try what? What options had a fish who chose to leave the sea a billion years too late?

Ursula blinked, and as her eyes opened again the stars diffracted through a thin film of tears. The million pinpoint lights broke up into rays, spreading in all directions.

There were too many directions. Too many paths. More than she had ever imagined. More than her mind could hold.

The rays from the sea of stars lengthened, crossing the sky quicker than light. Innumerable, they streaked across the dark lens of the galaxy and beyond, faster than the blink of an eye.

More directions than a human ought to know...

At last, Ursula closed her eyes, cutting off the image.

But in her mind the rays kept moving, replicating and multiplying at the velocity of thought. Quickly, they seemed to fill the entire universe... and spread on from there.

THE BIRTH OF THE DAWN

NICOLE SALLAK ANDERSON

This short story is a prequel to Nicole's *eHuman Dawn*, the novel. *eHuman Dawn* is available at http://amzn.to/1zHuB9l.

The first seconds of her new life were utterly dark and silent.

The blackest of black where nothing existed.

The deep silence of outer space.

In this transition she was timeless, neither human, nor eHuman.

Just consciousness, just Lux.

She was traveling the void of the universe at light speed.

And then she opened her eyes.

The world was instantly blurry, a kaleidoscope of unfocused colors surrounded her in every direction. She shook her head, trying to see, to no avail.

But only for a moment.

Her new body's operating system instantly detected the anomaly and adjusted her vision. The room came into view—crystal clear and brilliant. The eyes of her carbon body had never seen the world with such color and clarity. She could see the pores of the ceiling above her and the faintest detail of the previous coat of paint.

The silence remained. Gone was the drumbeat of her heart, the steady inhale and exhale of her breath, and the gurgling of her digestive system. She'd left her heart, lungs, and stomach behind in her previous body.

Only minutes prior she had been in the carbon body of her original birth—five foot two, dark hair, female, green eyes, twenty years of age. Sophia Castalogna had been her name. But that body lie beside her, dead, rigor mortis just about to set in. She stared at it, trying to make sense of what she saw. The body had been her home and for a moment she longed for its soft touch. Pale under the bright lights of the lab, it looked vulnerable and she considered grabbing it and fleeing from the room, as if to save it from its demise. Such sentimentality! Life would never again breathe in that body made of carbon, so prone to sickness and death. She turned her head from the frail thing and looked back at the ceiling.

She was an eHuman now! The experiment had worked! Her consciousness, termed the Lux long ago by scientists, had successfully Jumped from her carbon-based body into her new, perfect, eHuman body—a body designed for one purpose—to bring immortality and perfect health to the human race.

She turned her head and saw Dr. Neville, her creator. She smiled at his gloriously excited face. He raised his arms above his head and began to speak, his lips moving, but she couldn't hear a word.

Once more her operating system noticed this disconnect and slowly turned up the volume. Dr. Neville's victory speech sounded symphonic in hi-fi stereo.

"…let us begin a new level of human excellence!" she heard him exclaim.

Applause filled the room and the doctor held out his hand to her. She took it graciously and began to sit up.

"Please rise and meet us," he said like a proud father at a beloved daughter's graduation.

She stood, finding herself now at least eight inches taller than the doctor. Glancing at the audience, she noted that they were all dignitaries from around the world, including the President of the United States. The most important people were there to see her birth. They stared at her, clapping their hands with mouths slightly agape and a mixture of awe, trepidation, and revulsion in their eyes. She towered above all as she stood before them wearing nothing but her smile. It was no matter—her perfect, plastic size C breasts would never sag.

She didn't have any genitals nor hair of any kind, except the long, platinum blonde mane they'd applied to her head. She waved a graceful arm, noting how smoothly her shoulder joint worked. She admired her long robotic legs, covered in bronzed life-like plasticine skin. She was beautiful beyond measure.

Gazing at the crowd, she recognized the dark haired man sitting beside the President of the United States. Smartly dressed, he stared at her curiously, as if waiting for her to notice him. The crystal face of the golden watch upon his wrist reflected the laboratory lights as he slowly clapped his hands.

Edgar Prince. Her benefactor.

She glared at him, feeling a welling urge to rip him in two. As an eHuman she had the strength to do so. He was merely a carbon-based man. But did she hate him? Memories of her life as Sophia seemed to drift around her, each a bit or byte unstrung from the rest, like fireflies dancing around her head. Fragments of childhood—something soon to disappear completely from mankind—danced before her mind's eye. Swinging on a swing, falling out of a tree, opening presents on her birthday. Loose teeth, skinned knees, the taste of vanilla ice cream on a hot day, the intoxication of a sip of stolen vodka and first kisses. All of these memories moved about her, as if outside of her, while her new mind of fiber optic nanotubes fired away, trying to make sense of this scattering of data.

Her past was slipping away from her and she began to panic. This hadn't been part of the deal. Dr. Neville had thought that her memories would survive the Jump and come with her into her new eHuman life. She had a family, brothers, sisters, parents. There were friends who would want to see her. Yet faces were losing their sharpness and names were suddenly hard to recall. Her eyes began to flutter and shift back and forth as she scanned her database for information, trying to piece together the days leading up to her Jump, but she came up empty. Hers was a life about to be rewritten, a clean slate. Yet she knew that there was something she had to remember, something important, that evaded her.

Her fierce anger for Edgar Prince continued to course through her. He boldly looked her in the face, wearing a slight smirk, challenging her to act.

"Is there anything you'd like to say dear?" she heard Dr. Neville ask, interrupting her desperate struggle to remember who she had once been.

She turned and looked down at him. In addition to his pride, a slight note of sadness was evident in the bright blue eyes that peered out at her from behind his wire-rimmed glasses.

Then she remembered.

Elijah.

Her beloved. Son of Edgar. Forever gone to her now.

Edgar had betrayed them both.

Once more her operating system noted her distress, and began to write new memories into her database, slowly erasing Elijah and the images of his smiles, tender kisses and laughter, like a four year old shaking her etch-a-sketch. In just a millisecond, their relationship was deleted as if it had never happened.

She shook her head as if to clear it. The update was complete. Gone was Elijah's face from her consciousness, and with it, her anger for Edgar.

"Yes," she replied while turning to face the crowd once more, this time filled with ease and grace.

She allowed her sea-green eyes to set upon Edgar's deep dark ones once more, speaking directly to him. She smiled and noticed that he shivered—with fear or delight, she didn't know.

"Let me introduce myself," she said, her voice programmed to sound exactly like Scarlett Johansson, "I am The Dawn of eHumanity."

Edgar rose from his seat, and everyone else followed suit quickly. He clapped enthusiastically, adoring his creation. Dawn smiled at the crowd in return as she was led out of the room to prepare for her integration with the world. It was the greatest moment of her life.

And the beginning of a new age on Earth.

THE WEATHERMAKERS

BEN BOVA

Dr. Ben Bova, FBIS, FAAAS is the author of more than 120 futuristic novels and nonfiction books and has been involved in science and high technology since the very beginnings of the space age. President Emeritus of the National Space Society and a past president of Science Fiction Writers of America, he received the Lifetime Achievement Award of the Arthur C. Clarke Foundation in 2005, "for fueling mankind's imagination regarding the wonders of outer space." His 2006 novel *Titan* received the John W. Campbell Memorial Award for best novel of the year. In 2008 he won the Robert A. Heinlein Award "for his outstanding body of work in the field of literature." He is a frequent commentator on radio and television and a widely-popular lecturer.

Ben is six-time winner of the Hugo Award, a former editor of *Analog Science Fiction and Fact*, a former editorial director of *Omni*, and was an executive in the aerospace industry. In his various writings, he has predicted the Space Race of the 1960s, solar power satellites, the discovery of organic chemicals in interstellar space, virtual reality, human cloning, the Strategic Defense Initiative (Star Wars), the discovery of life on Mars, stem cell therapy, the discovery of ice on the Moon, electronic book publishing, and zero-gravity sex.

The following novelette was expanded into the novel *The Weathermakers* available at http://amzn.to/1xZwyLl.

Ted gathered us around his desk, with the giant viewscreen staring down our throats. Hurricane Nora was howling up the mid-Atlantic; she was no trouble. But four tropical disturbances, marked by red danger symbols, were strung out along the fifteenth parallel from the Antilles Islands to the Cape Verdes.

"There's the story," Ted told us, prowling nervously along the foot of the viewscreen. Gesturing toward the map, he said, "Nora's okay, won't even bother Bermuda much. But these four Lows'll bug us for sure."

Tuli shook his head. "We can't handle all four of them at once. One, possibly two, will get past us."

Ted looked sharply at him, then turned to me. "How about it, Jerry? What's the logistics picture?"

"Tuli's right," I admitted. "The planes and crews have been working around the clock for the past couple of weeks and we just don't have enough—"

"Skip the flute music. How many of these Lows can we hit?"

Shrugging, I answered, "Two. Maybe three, if we really push it."

Barney was standing beside me. "The computer just finished an updated statistical analysis of the four disturbances. Their storm tracks all threaten the East Coast. The two closest ones have point-eight probabilities of reaching hurricane strength. The farther pair are only point-five."

"Fifty-fifty for the last two," Ted muttered. "But they've got the longest time to develop. Chances'll be better for 'em by tomorrow."

"It's those two closest disturbances that are the most dangerous," Barney said. "They each have an eighty percent chance of turning into hurricanes that will hit us."

"We can't stop them all," Tuli said. "What will we do, Ted?"

Before Ted could answer, his phone buzzed. He leaned across the desk and punched the button. "Dr. Weis calling from Washington," the operator said.

He grimaced. "Okay, put him on." Sliding into his desk chair, Ted waved us back to our posts as Dr. Weis' worried face came on the phone screen.

"I've just seen this morning's weather map," the President's Science Adviser said, with no preliminaries. "It looks as if you're in trouble."

"Got our hands full," Ted said evenly.

I started back for my own cubicle. I could hear Dr. Weis' voice, a little edgier than usual, saying, "The opposition has turned THUNDER into a political issue, with less than six weeks to the election. If you hadn't made the newsmen think that you could stop every hurricane…"

The rest was lost in the chatter and bustle of the control center. The one room filled the entire second floor of our headquarters building. It was a frenetic conglomeration of people, desks, calculating machines, plotting boards, map printers, cabinets, teletypes, phones, viewscreens, and endless piles of paper—with the huge viewscreen map hanging over it all. I made my way across the cluttered, windowless expanse and stepped into my glass-walled cubicle.

It was quiet inside, with the door closed. Phone screens lined the walls, and half my desk was covered with a private switchboard that put me in direct contact with a network of THUNDER support stations ranging from New Orleans to the Atlantic Satellite Station, in synchronous orbit some twenty-three thousand miles above the mouth of the Amazon River.

I looked across the control center again, and saw Ted still talking earnestly into the phone. There was work to be done. I began tapping out phone numbers on my master switchboard, alerting the Navy and Air Force bases that were supporting the Project, trying to get ready to hit those hurricane threats as hard and as fast as we could.

While I worked, Ted finally got off the phone. Barney came over with a thick sheaf of computer printout sheets; probably the detailed analysis of the storm threats. As soon as I could break away, I went over and joined them.

"Okay," Ted was saying, "if we leave those two farther-out Lows alone, they'll develop into hurricanes overnight. We can knock 'em out now without much sweat, but by tomorrow they'll be too big for us."

"The same applies to the two closest disturbances," Barney pointed out. "And they're much closer and already developing fast…"

"We'll have to skip one of 'em. The first one—off the Leewards—is too close to ignore. So we'll hit Number One, skip the second, and hit Three and Four."

Barney took her glasses off. "That won't work, Ted. If we don't stop the second one now, by tomorrow it will be—"

"A walloping big hurricane. I know." He made a helpless gesture. "But if we throw enough stuff at Number Two to smother it, we'll have to leave Three and Four alone until tomorrow. In the meantime, they'll both develop and we'll have two brutes on our hands!"

"But this one…"

"There's a chance that if we knock out the closest Low, Number Two'll change its track and head out to sea."

"That's a terribly slim chance. The numbers show—"

"Okay, it's a slim chance. But it's all we've got to work with."

"Isn't there anything else we can do?" she asked. "If a hurricane strikes the coast…"

"Weis is already looking through his mail for my resignation," Ted said. "Okay, we're in trouble. Best we can manage is hit Number One, skip Two, and wipe out Three and Four before they get strong enough to make waves."

Barney looked down at the numbers on the computer sheets. "That means we're going to have a full-grown hurricane heading for Florida within twenty-four hours."

"Look," Ted snapped, "we can sit around here debating 'til they *all* turn into hurricanes. Let's scramble. Jerry, you heard the word. Get the planes up."

I dashed back to my cubicle and sent out the orders. A few minutes later, Barney came by. Standing dejectedly in the doorway, she asked herself out loud:

"Why did he agree to take on this Project? He knows it's not the best way to handle hurricanes. It's too chancy, too expensive. We're working ourselves to death…"

"So are the aircrews," I answered. "And the season's just starting to hit its peak."

"Then why did he have to make the newsmen think we could run up a perfect score the first year?"

"Because he's Ted Marrett. He not only thinks he can control the weather, he thinks he owns it."

"There's no room in him for failure," she said. "If this storm does hit, and if the Project is canceled… what will it do to him?"

"What will it do to you?" I asked her.

She shook her head. "I don't know, Jerry. But I'm terribly afraid we're going to find out in another day or two."

Tropical storms are built on seemingly slight differences of air temperature. A half-dozen degrees of difference over an area hundreds of miles across can power the giant heat engine of a hurricane. Ted's method of smothering tropical disturbances before they reached hurricane strength was to smooth out the temperature difference between the core of the disturbances and their outer fringes.

The nearest disturbance was developing quickly. It had already passed over the Leeward Islands and entered the Caribbean by the time our first planes reached it. The core of the disturbance was a column of warm air shooting upward from the sea's surface to the tropopause, some ten miles high. Swirling around this column was relatively cooler air sliding into the low-pressure trough created by the warm column.

If the disturbance were left to itself, it would soak up moisture from the warm sea and condense it into rainfall. The heat released by this condensation would power winds of ever-mounting intensity. A cycle would be established: winds bring in moisture, the water vapor condenses into rain, the heat released builds up the wind's power. Finally, when the storm reached a certain intensity, centrifugal force would begin sucking down cooler air from very high altitudes. The cool air would be compressed and heated as it sank, and then fed into the massive cloud walls around the storm's core—which would now be the eye of a full-grown hurricane. A thousand megatons of energy would be on the loose, unstoppable, even by Project THUNDER.

Our job was to prevent that cycle from establishing itself. We had to warm up the air flowing into the disturbance and chill down its core until temperatures throughout the storm were practically the same. A heat engine with all its parts at the same temperature (or close to it) simply won't work.

As I started giving out orders for the three simultaneous missions, Tuli stuck his head into my office doorway.

"I'm off to see the dragon firsthand." He was grinning excitedly.

"Which one?"

"Number One dragon; it's in the Caribbean now."

"I know. Good luck. Bring back its ears."

He nodded, a round-faced, brown-skinned St. George going against the most destructive monster man had ever faced.

As I parceled out orders over the phones, a battery of gigajoule lasers aboard the Atlantic Station began pumping their energy into the northern peripheries of the budding storms. The lasers were similar to the type mounted in the Air Force's missile-defense satellites. They had been placed aboard the Atlantic Station at Ted's insistence, with the personal backing of Dr. Weis and the White House. Only carefully selected Air Force personnel were allowed near them. The entire section of the satellite station where they were installed was under armed guard, much to the discomfort of the civilians aboard.

Planes from a dozen airfields were circling the northern edges of the disturbances, sowing the air with rain-producing crystals.

"Got to seed for hours at a time," Ted once told me. "That's a mistake the early experimenters made—never stayed on the job long enough to force an effect on the weather."

I was watching the disturbance in the Caribbean. That was the closest threat, and the best developed of all the four disturbances. Radar plots, mapped on Ted's giant viewscreen, showed rain clouds expanding and showering precipitation over an ever-widening area. As the water vapor in the seeded air condensed into drops, the air temperature rose slightly. The satellite-borne lasers were also helping to heat the air feeding into the disturbance and confuse its circulation pattern.

It looked as if we were just making the disturbance bigger. But Ted and other technical staff people had figured out the energy balance in the young storm. They knew what they were doing. That didn't stop me from gnawing my lower lip, though.

Tuli was in an Air Force bomber, part of two squadrons of planes flying at staggered altitudes. From nearly sea level to fifty thousand feet, they roared into the central column of warm air in precise formation and began dumping tons of liquid nitrogen into the rising tropical air.

The effect was spectacular. The TV screens alongside the big plotting map showed what the planes saw: tremendous plumes of white sprang out behind each plane as the cryogenic liquid flash-froze the water vapor in the warm column. It looked as if some cosmic wind had suddenly spewed its frigid breath through the air. The nitrogen quickly evaporated, soaking up enormous quantities of heat. Most of the frozen vapor simply evaporated again, although the radar plots showed that some condensation and actual rainfall occurred.

I made my way to Ted's desk to check the results of the core freezing.

"Looks good," he was saying into the phone.

The teletype next to his desk chugged into life. It started printing a report from the observation planes that followed the bombers.

Ted stepped over and looked at the numbers. "Broke up the core okay. Now if she doesn't reform, we can scratch Number One off the map."

It was evening before we could tell for sure. The disturbance's source of energy—the differing temperatures of the air masses it contained—had been taken away from it. The plotting screen showed a large swatch of concentric irregular isobars, like a lopsided bull's-eye, with a sullen red "L" marking the center of the low-pressure area, just north of Jamaica. The numbers on the screen showed a central pressure of 991 millibars, nowhere near that of a typical hurricane. Wind speeds had peaked at fifty-two knots and were dying off now. Kingston and Guantanamo were reporting moderate-to-heavy rain, but at Santo Domingo, six hundred miles to the east, it had already cleared.

The disturbance was just another small tropical storm, and a rapidly weakening one at that. The two farther disturbances, halfway out across the ocean, had been completely wiped out. The planes were on their way home. The laser crews aboard the Atlantic Station were recharging their energy storage coils.

"Shall I see if the planes can reload and fly another mission tonight?" I asked Ted. "Maybe we can still hit Number Two."

He shook his head. "Won't do any good. Look at her," he said, pointing to the viewscreen map. "By the time the planes could get to her, she'll be a full-grown hurricane. There's nothing we can do about it now."

So we didn't sleep that night. We stayed at the control center and watched the storm develop on the TV picture beamed from the Atlantic Station. At night they had to use infrared cameras, of course, but we could still see—in the ghostly IR images—a broad spiral of clouds stretching across four hundred miles of open ocean.

Practically no one had left the control center, but the big room was deathly quiet. Even the chattering calculating machines and teletypes seemed to have stopped. The numbers on the plotting screen steadily worsened. Barometric pressure sank to 980, 975, 965 millibars. Wind velocity mounted to 75 knots, 95, 110. She was a full-grown hurricane by ten o'clock.

Ted leaned across his desk and tapped out a name for the storm on the viewscreen's keyboard: *Omega*.

"One way or the other, she's the end of THUNDER," he muttered.

The letters glowed out at the top of the plotting screen. Across the vast room, one of the girls broke into sobs.

Through the early hours of the morning, Hurricane Omega grew steadily in size and strength. An immense band of clouds towered from the sea to some sixty thousand feet, pouring two inches of rain per hour over an area of nearly 300,000 square miles. The pressure at her core had plummeted to 950 millibars and central wind-speeds were gusting to better than 140 knots, and still rising.

"It's almost as if she's alive," Tuli whispered as we watched the viewscreen. "She grows, she feeds, she moves."

By two a.m., Miami time, dawn was breaking over Hurricane Omega. Six trillion tons of air packing the energy of a hundred hydrogen bombs, a mammoth, mindless heat engine turned loose, aiming for civilization, for us.

Waves lashed by Omega's fury were spreading all across the Atlantic and would show up as dangerous surf on the beaches of four continents. Seabirds were sucked into the storm against their every exertion, to be drenched and battered to exhaustion; their only hope was to make it to the eye of the hurricane, where the air was calm and clear. A tramp steamer on the New York-to-Capetown run, five hundred miles from Omega's center, was calling frantically for help as mountainous waves overpowered the ship's puny pumps. Omega churned onward, releasing as much energy as a ten-megaton bomb every fifteen minutes.

We watched, we listened, fascinated. The face of our enemy, and it made all of us—even Ted, I think—feel completely helpless. At first Omega's eye, as seen from the satellite cameras, was vague and shifting, covered over by cirrus clouds. But finally it steadied and opened up, a strong column of clear air, the mighty central pillar of the hurricane, the pivotal anchor around which her furious winds wailed their primeval song of violence and terror.

Barney, Tuli, and I sat around Ted's desk, watching him; his scowl deepened as the storm worsened. We didn't realize it was daylight until Dr. Weis phoned again. He looked haggard on the tiny desk-top viewscreen.

"I've been watching the storm all night," he said. "The President called me a few minutes ago and asked me what you were going to do about it."

Ted rubbed his eyes. "Can't knock her out, if that's what you mean. Too big now. Be like trying to stop a forest fire with a blanket."

"Well, you've got to do something!" Weis snapped. "All our reputations hang on that storm. Do you understand? Yours, mine, even the President's! To say nothing of the future for weather-control work in this country."

"Told you back in Washington last March," Ted countered, "that THUNDER was the wrong way to tackle hurricanes…"

"Yes, and in July you announced to the press that no hurricanes would strike the United States! So now, instead of being an act of nature, hurricanes are a political issue."

Ted shook his head. "We've done the best we can."

"You've got to do more. You can try to steer the hurricane… change its path so that it won't strike the coast."

"You mean change the weather patterns?" Ted brightened. "Control the situation so that—"

"I do *not* mean weather control! Not over the United States," Dr. Weis said firmly. "But you can make whatever changes you have to over the ocean."

"That won't work," Ted answered. "Not enough leverage to do any good. Might budge her a few degrees, but she'll still wind up hitting the coast somewhere. All we'll be doing is fouling up the storm track so we won't know for sure where she'll hit."

"You've got to do something! We can't just sit here and let it happen to us. Ted, I haven't tried to tell you how to run THUNDER, but now I'm giving an order. You've got to make an attempt to steer the storm away from the coast. If we fail, at least we go down fighting. Maybe we can salvage something from this mess."

"Waste of time," Ted muttered.

Dr. Weis' shoulders moved as if he was wringing his hands, off camera. "Try it anyway. It might work. We might be lucky…"

"Okay," Ted said, shrugging. "You're the boss."

The screen went dark. Ted looked up at us. "You heard the man. We're going to play Pied Piper."

"But we can't do it," Tuli said. "It can't be done."

"Doesn't matter. Weis is trying to save face. You ought to understand that, buddy."

Barney looked up at the plotting screen. Omega was northeast of Puerto Rico and boring in toward Florida.

"Why didn't you tell him the truth?" she asked Ted. "You know we can't steer Omega. Even if he'd let us try to control the weather completely, we couldn't be sure of keeping the storm off the coast. You shouldn't have—"

"Shouldn't have what?" Ted snapped back. "Shouldn't have taken THUN-DER when Weis and the President offered it? Shouldn't have made that crack to the newsmen about stopping every hurricane? Shouldn't have told Weis we'd try to steer Omega? I did all three, and I'd do them all again. I'd rather do *something*, even if it's not the best something. Got to keep moving; once we stop, we're dead."

"But why," Barney asked, almost pleadingly, "did you make that insane promise to the newsmen?"

He frowned, but more at himself than at her. "How should I know? Maybe because Weis was sitting there in front of the cameras looking so sure of himself. Safe and serene. Maybe I was crazy enough to think we could really sneak through a whole hurricane season okay. Maybe I'm just crazy, period. I don't know."

"But what do we do now?" I asked.

He cocked an eye at the plotting screen. "Try to steer Omega. Try saving Weis' precious face." Pointing to a symbol on the map several hundred miles north of the storm, he said, "There's a Navy sonar picket anchored out there. I'm going to buzz over to it, see if I can get a firsthand look at this monster."

"That's... that's dangerous," Barney said.

He shrugged.

"Ted, you can't run the operation from the middle of the ocean," I said.

"Picket's in a good spot to see the storm... at least the edge of it. Maybe I can wangle a plane ride through it. Been fighting hurricanes all season without seeing one. Besides, the ship's part of the Navy's antisubmarine warning net; loaded with communications gear. Be in touch with you every minute, don't worry."

"But if the storm comes that way..."

"Let it come," he said. "It's going to finish us anyway." He turned and strode off, leaving us to watch him.

Barney turned to me. "Jerry, he thinks we blame him for everything. We've got to stop him."

"No one can stop him. You know that. Once he gets his mind set on something…"

"Then I'll go with him." She got up from her chair.

I took her arm.

"No, Jerry," she said, "I can't let him go alone."

"Is it the danger you're afraid of, or the fact that he's leaving?"

"Jerry, in the mood he's in now… he's reckless…"

"All right," I said, trying to calm her. "All right. I'll go with him. I'll make sure he keeps his feet dry."

"But I don't want either one of you in danger!"

"I know. I'll take care of him."

She looked at me with those misty, gray-green eyes. "Jerry… you won't let him do anything foolish, will you?"

"You know me; I'm no hero."

"Yes, you are," she said. And I felt my insides do a handspring.

I left her there with Tuli and hurried out to the parking lot. The bright sunshine outdoors was a painful surprise. It was hot and muggy, even though the day was only an hour or so old.

Ted was getting into one of the Project staff cars when I caught up with him.

"A landlubber like you shouldn't be loose on the ocean by himself," I said.

He grinned. "Hop aboard, salt."

The day was sultry. The usual tempering sea breezes had died off. As we drove along the Miami bayfront, the air was oppressive, ominous. The sky was brazen, the water deathly calm. The old-timers along the fishing docks, were squinting out at the horizon to the south and nodding to each other. It was coming.

The color of the sea, the shape of the clouds, the sighting of a shark near the coast, the way the seabirds were perching—all these became omens.

It was coming.

We slept for most of the flight out to the sonar picket. The Navy jet landed smoothly in the softly billowing sea and a helicopter from the picket brought us aboard. The ship was similar in style to the deep-sea mining dredges of Thornton Pacific. For antisubmarine work, though, the dredging equipment was replaced by a fantastic array of radar and communications antennas.

"Below decks are out of bounds to visitors, I'm afraid," said the chunky lieutenant who welcomed us to his ship. As we walked from the helicopter landing pad on the fan-tail toward the bridge, he told us, "This bucket's a floating sonar station. Everything below decks is classified except the galley, and the cook won't let even me in there."

He laughed at his own joke. He was a pleasant-faced Yankee, about our own age, square-jawed, solidly built, the kind that stays in the Navy for life.

We clambered up a ladder to the bridge.

"We're anchored here," the lieutenant said, "with special bottom gear and arresting cables. So the bridge isn't used for navigation as much as for communications."

Looking around, we could see what he meant. The bridge's aft bulkhead was literally covered with viewscreens, autoplotters, and electronics controls.

"I think you'll be able to keep track of your hurricane without much trouble." He nodded proudly toward the communications equipment.

"If we can't," Ted said, "it won't be your fault."

The lieutenant introduced us to his chief communications technician, a scrappy little sailor who had just received his engineering degree and was putting in two Navy years. Within minutes we were talking to Tuli back in THUNDER headquarters.

"Omega seems to have slowed down quite a bit," Tuli said, his impassive face framed by the viewscreen. "She's about halfway between your position and Puerto Rico."

"Gathering strength," Ted muttered.

They fed the information from THUNDER's computers to the picket's autoplotter, and soon we had a miniature version of Ted's giant map on one of the bridge's screens.

Ted studied the map, mumbling to himself. "If we could feed her some warm water... give her a shortcut to the outbound leg of the Gulf Stream... then maybe she'd bypass the coast."

The lieutenant was watching us from a jumpseat that folded out of the port bulkhead.

"Just wishful thinking," Ted muttered on. "Fastest way to move her is to set up a low-pressure cell to the north... make her swing more northerly..."

He talked it over with Tuli for the better part of an hour, perching on a swivel stool set into the deck next to the chart table. The cook popped through the bridge's starboard hatch with a tray of sandwiches and coffee. Ted absently took a sandwich and mug, still locked in talk with Tuli.

Finally he said to the viewscreen image, "Okay, we deepen this trough off Long Island and try to make a real storm cell out of it."

Tuli nodded, but he was clearly unhappy.

"Get Barney to run it through the computer as fast as she can, but you'd better get the planes out right now. Don't wait for the computer run. Got to hit while she's still sitting around. Otherwise..." His voice trailed off.

"All right," Tuli said. "But we're striking blindly."

"I know. Got any better ideas?"

Tuli shrugged.

"Then let's scramble the planes." He turned to me. "Jerry, we've got a battle plan figured out. Tuli'll give you the details."

Now it was my turn. I spent the better part of the afternoon getting the right planes with the right payloads off to the exact places where the work had to be done. Through it all, I was calling myself an idiot for trekking out to this mid-ocean exile. It took twice as long to process the orders as it would have back at headquarters.

"Don't bother saying it," Ted said when I finished. "So it was kinky coming out here. Okay. Just had to get away from that place before I went over the hill."

"But what good are you going to do here?" I asked.

He gripped the bridge's rail and looked out past the ship's prow, toward the horizon.

"We can run the show from here just as well... maybe a little tougher than back in Miami, but we can do it. If everything goes okay, we'll get brushed by the storm's edge. I'd like to see that. Want to feel her, see what she can do. Never seen a hurricane from this close. And it's better than sitting in that windowless cocoon back there."

"And if things don't go well?" I asked. "If the storm doesn't move the way you want it to?"

He turned away. "Probably she won't."

"Then we might miss the whole show."

"Maybe. Or she might march right down here and blow down our necks."

"Omega might... we could be caught in the middle of it?"

"Could be," he said easily. "Better get some sleep while you can. Going to be busy later on."

The exec showed us to a tiny stateroom with two bunks in it. Part of the picket's crew was on shore leave, and they had a spare compartment for us. I tried to sleep, but spent most of the late-afternoon hours squirming uncomfortably. Around dusk, Ted got up and went to the bridge. I followed him.

"See those clouds, off the southern horizon," he was saying to the lieutenant. "That's her. Just the outer fringes."

I checked back with THUNDER headquarters. The planes had seeded the low-pressure trough off Long Island without incident. Weather stations along the coast, and automated, equipment on satellites and planes, were reporting a small storm cell developing.

Barney's face appeared on the viewscreen. She looked very worried. "Is Ted there?"

"Right here." He stepped into view.

"The computer run just finished," she said, pushing a strand of hair from her face. "Omega's going to turn northward, but only temporarily. She'll head inland again early tomorrow. In about forty-eight hours she'll strike the coast somewhere between Cape Hatteras and Washington."

Ted let out a low whistle.

"But that's not all," she continued. "The storm track crosses right over the ship you're on. You're going to be in the center of it!"

"We'll have to get off here right away," I said.

"No rush," Ted replied. "We can spend the night here. I want to see her develop firsthand."

Barney said, "Ted, don't be foolish. It's going to be dangerous."

He grinned at her. "Jealous? Don't worry, I just want to get a look at her, then I'll come flying home to you."

"You stubborn..." The blonde curl popped back over her eyes again and she pushed it away angrily. "Ted, it's time you stopped acting like a spoiled little boy! You bet I'm jealous. I'm tired of competing against the whole twirling atmosphere! You've got responsibilities, and if you don't want to live up to them... well, you'd better, that's all!"

"Okay, okay. We'll be back tomorrow morning. Be safer traveling in daylight anyway. Omega's still moving slowly; we'll have plenty time."

"Not if she starts to move faster. This computer run was only a first-order look at the problem. The storm could accelerate sooner than we think."

"We'll get to Miami okay, don't worry."

"No, why should I worry?" Barney said. "You're only six hundred miles out at sea with a hurricane bearing down on you."

"Just an hour away from home. Get some sleep. We'll fly over in the morning."

The wind was picking up as I went back to my bunk, and the ship was starting to rock in the deepening sea. I had sailed open boats through storms and slept in worse weather than this. It wasn't the conditions of the moment that bothered me. It was the knowledge of what was coming.

Ted stayed out on deck, watching the southern skies darken with the deathly fascination of a general observing the approach of a much stronger army. I dropped off to sleep telling myself that I'd get Ted off this ship as soon as a plane could pick us up, even if I had to get the sailors to wrap him in anchor chains.

By morning, it was raining hard and the ship was bucking badly in the heavy waves. It was an effort to push through the narrow passageway to the bridge, with the deck bobbing beneath my feet and the ship tossing hard enough to slam me against the bulkheads.

Up on the bridge, the wind was howling evilly as a sailor helped me into a slicker and life vest. When I turned to tug them on, I saw that the helicopter pad out on the stern was empty.

"Chopper took most of the crew out about an hour ago," the sailor hollered into my ear. "Went to meet the seaplane west of here, where it ain't so rough. When it comes back we're all pulling out."

I nodded and thanked him.

"She's a beauty, isn't, she?" Ted shouted at me as I stepped onto the open section of the bridge. "Moving up a lot faster than we thought."

I grabbed a handhold between him and the lieutenant. To the south of us was a solid wall of black. Waves were breaking over the bows and the rain was a battering force against our faces.

"Will the helicopter be able to get back to us?" I asked the lieutenant.

"We've had worse blows than this," he shouted back, "but I wouldn't want to hang around for another hour or so."

The communications tech staggered across the bridge to us. "Chopper's on the way, sir. Ought to be here in ten to fifteen minutes."

The lieutenant nodded. "I'll have to go aft and see that the helicopter's properly dogged down when she lands. You two be ready to hop on when the word goes out."

"We'll be ready," I said.

As the lieutenant left the bridge, I asked Ted, "Well, is this doing you any good? Frankly, I would've been a lot happier in Miami…"

"She's a real brute," he shouted. "This is a lot different from watching a map."

"But why…"

"This is the enemy, Jerry. This is what we're trying to kill. Think how much better you're going to feel after we've learned how to stop hurricanes."

"If we live long enough to learn how!"

The helicopter struggled into view, leaning heavily into the raging wind. I watched, equally fascinated and terrified, as it worked its way to the landing pad, tried to come down, got blown backwards by a terrific gust, fought toward the pad again, and finally touched down on the heaving deck. A team of sailors scrambled across the wet square to attach heavy lines to the landing gear, even before the rotor blades started to slow down. A wave smashed across the ship's stem and one of the sailors went sprawling. Only then did I notice that each man had a stout lifeline around his middle. They finally got the 'copter secured.

I turned back to Ted. "Let's go before it's too late."

We started down the slippery ladder to the main deck. As we inched back toward the stem, a tremendous wave caught the picket amidships and sloughed her around broadside. The little ship shuddered violently and the deck dropped out from under us. I sagged to my knees.

Ted pulled me up. "Come on, buddy, Omega's here."

Another wave smashed across us. I grabbed for a handhold and as my eyes cleared, saw the helicopter pitching crazily over to one side, the moorings on her landing gear flapping loosely in the wind.

"It's broken away!"

The deck heaved again and the 'copter careened over on its side, rotors smashing against the pad. Another wave caught us. The ship bucked terribly. The helicopter slid backwards along its side and then, lifted by a solid wall of foaming green, smashed through the gunwale and into the sea.

Groping senselessly on my hands and knees, soaking wet, battered like an overmatched prizefighter, I watched our only link to safety disappear into the furious sea.

I clambered to my feet on the slippery deck of the Navy picket. The ship shuddered again and slewed around. A wave hit the other side and washed across, putting us knee-deep in foaming water until the deck lurched upward again and cleared the waves temporarily.

"Omega's won," Ted roared in my ear, over the screaming wind. "We're trapped!"

We stood there, hanging onto the handholds. The sea was impossible to describe—a tangled fury of waves, with no sense or pattern to them, their tops ripped off by the wind, spray mixing with blinding rain.

The lieutenant groped by, edging hand-over-hand on the lifeline that ran along the superstructure bulkhead.

"Are you two all right?"

"No broken bones."

"You'd better come up to the bridge," he shouted. We were face-to-face, nearly touching noses, yet we could hardly hear him. "I've given orders to cast off the anchors and get up steam. We've got to try to ride out this blow under power. If we just sit here we'll be swamped."

"Is there anything we can do?"

He shot me a grim look. "Next time you tinker with a hurricane, make it when I'm on shore!"

We followed the lieutenant up to the bridge. I nearly fell off the rain-slicked ladder, but Ted grabbed me with one of his powerful paws.

The bridge was sloshing from the monstrous waves and spray that were drenching the decks. The communications panels seemed to be intact, though. We could see the map that Ted had set up on the autoplotter screen; it was still alight. Omega spread across the screen like an engulfing demon. The tiny pinpoint of light marking the ship's location was well inside the hurricane's swirl.

The lieutenant fought his way to the ship's intercom while Ted and I grabbed for handholds.

"All the horses you've got, Chief," I heard the lieutenant bellow into the intercom mike. "I'll get every available man on the pumps. Keep those engines going. If we lose power we're sunk!"

I realized he meant it literally.

The lieutenant crossed over toward us and hung on to the chart table.

"Is that map accurate?" he yelled at Ted.

The big redhead nodded. "Up to the minute. Why?"

"I'm trying to figure a course that'll take us out of this blow. We can't stand much more of this battering. She's taking on more water than the pumps can handle. Engine room's getting swamped."

"Head southwest then," Ted said at the top of his lungs. "Get out of her quickest that way."

"We can't! I've got to keep the sea on our bows or else we'll capsize!"

"What?"

"He's got to point her into the wind," I yelled. "Just about straight into the waves."

"Right!" the lieutenant agreed.

"But you'll be riding along with the storm. Never get out that way. She'll just carry us along all day!"

"How do you know which way the storm's going to go? She might change course."

"Not a chance." Ted jabbed a finger toward the plotting screen. "She's heading northwesterly now and she'll stay on that course the rest of the day. Best bet is to head for the eye."

"Toward the center? We'd never make it!"

Ted shook his head. "Never get out of it if you keep heading straight into the wind. But if you can make five knots or so, we can spiral into the eye. Calm there."

The lieutenant stared at the screen. "Are you sure? Do you know exactly where the storm's moving and how fast she's going to go?"

"We can check it out."

Quickly, we called THUNDER headquarters, transmitting up to the Atlantic Station satellite for relay to Miami. Barney was nearly frantic, but we got her off the line fast. Tuli answered our questions and gave us the exact predictions for Omega's direction and speed.

Ted went inside with a soggy handful of notes to put the information into the ship's course computer. Barney pushed her way onto the viewscreen.

"Jerry… are you all right?"

"I've been better, but we'll get through it okay. The ship's in no real trouble," I lied.

"You're sure?"

"Certainly. Ted's working out a course with the skipper. We'll be back in Miami in a few hours."

"It looks awful out there."

Another mammoth wave broke across the bow and drowned the bridge with spray.

"It's not picnic weather," I admitted, "but we're not worried, so don't you go getting upset." *Not worried,* I added silently, *we're scared white.*

Reluctantly, the lieutenant agreed to head for the storm's eye. It was either that or face a battering that would split the ship in a few hours. We told Tuli to send a plane to the eye to try to pick us up.

Time lost all meaning. We just hung on, drenched to the skin, plunging through a wild, watery inferno, the wind shrieking evilly at us, the seas absolutely chaotic. No one remained on the bridge except the lieutenant, Ted, and me. The rest of the ship's skeleton crew were below decks, working every pump on board as hard as they could be run. The ship's autopilot and computer-run guidance system kept us heading on the course Ted and the lieutenant had figured.

Passing into the hurricane's eye was like stepping through a door from bedlam to a peaceful garden. One minute we were being pounded by mountainous waves and merciless wind, with rain and spray making it hard to see even the bow. Then the sun broke through and the wind abruptly died. The waves were still hectic, frothing, as we limped out into the open. But at least we could raise our heads without being battered by the wind-driven spray.

Towering clouds rose all about us, but this patch of ocean was safe. Birds hovered around us, and high overhead a vertijet was circling, sent out by Tuli. The plane made a tight pass over us, then descended onto the helicopter landing pad on the ship's fantail. Her landing gear barely touched the deck, and her tail stuck out over the smashed railing where the helicopter had broken through.

We had to duck under the plane's nose and enter from a hatch in her belly because the outer wing jets were still blazing. As we huddled in the crammed passenger compartment, the plane hoisted straight up. The jetpods swiveled back for horizontal flight and the wings slid to supersonic sweep. We climbed steeply and headed up over the clouds.

As I looked down at the fast-shrinking little picket, I realized the lieutenant was also craning his neck at the port for a last look.

"I'm sorry you had to lose your ship," I said.

"Well, another hour in those seas would have finished us," he said quietly. But he kept staring wistfully out the port until the clouds covered the abandoned vessel.

Barney was waiting for us at the Navy airport with dry clothes, the latest charts and forecasts on Omega, and a large share of feminine emotion. I'll never forget the sight of her running toward us as we stepped down from the vertijet's main hatch. She threw her arms around Ted's neck, then around mine, and then around Ted again.

"You had me so frightened, the two of you!"

Ted laughed. "We were kind of ruffled ourselves."

It took nearly an hour to get away from the airport. Navy brass hats, debriefing officers, newsmen, photographers—they all wanted a crack at us. I turned them onto the lieutenant: "He's the real hero," I told them. "Without him, we would've all drowned." While they converged on him, Ted and I got a chance to change our clothes in an officers' wardroom and scuttle out to the car Barney had waiting.

"Dr. Weis has been on the phone all day," Barney said as the driver pulled out for the main highway leading to the Miami bayfront and THUNDER headquarters.

Ted frowned and spread the reports on Omega across his lap.

Sitting between the two of us, she pointed to the latest chart. "Here's the storm track… ninety percent reliability, plus-or-minus two percent."

Ted whistled. "Right smack into Washington and then up the coast. She's going to damage more than reputations."

"I told Dr. Weis you'd call him as soon as you could."

"Okay," he said reluctantly. "Let's get it over with."

I punched out the Science Adviser's private number on the phone set into the car's seat. After a brief word with a secretary, Dr. Weis' drawn face appeared on the viewscreen.

"You're safe," he said bleakly.

"Disappointed?"

"The way this hurricane is coming at us, we could use a martyr or two."

"Steering didn't work," Ted said. "Only thing left to try is what we should've done in the first place…"

"Weather control? Absolutely not! Being hit with a hurricane is bad enough, but if you try tinkering with the weather all across the country, we'll have every farmer, every vacationist, every mayor and governor and traffic cop on our necks!"

Ted fumed. "What else are you going to do? Sit there and take it? Weather control's the last chance of stopping this beast…"

"Marrett, I'm almost ready to believe that you set up this storm purposely to force us into letting you try your pet idea!"

"If I could do that, I wouldn't be sitting here arguing with you."

"Possibly not. But you listen to me. Weather control is out. If we have to take a hurricane, that's what we'll do. We'll have to admit that THUNDER was too ambitious a project for the first time around. We'll have to back off. We'll try something like THUNDER again next year, but without all the fanfare. You'll have to lead a very quiet life for a few years, Marrett, but at least we might be able to keep going."

"Why back down when you can go ahead and stop this hurricane?" Ted argued. "We can push Omega out to sea, I know we can!"

"The way you steered her? That certainly boomeranged on you."

"We tried moving six trillion tons of air with a feather-duster! I'm talking about real control of the weather patterns across the whole continent. It'll work!"

"You can't guarantee that it will, and even if you did I wouldn't believe you. Marrett, I want you to go back to THUNDER headquarters and sit there quietly. You may operate on any new disturbances that show up. But you are to leave Omega strictly alone. Is that clear? If you try to touch that storm in any way, I'll see to it that you're finished. For good."

Dr. Weis snapped off the connection. The viewscreen went dark, almost as dark as the scowl on Ted's face. For the rest of the ride back to Project headquarters he said nothing. He simply sat there, slouched over, pulled in on himself, his eyes smoldering.

When the car stopped he looked up at us.

"What'd you do if I gave the word to push Omega off the coast?"

"But Dr. Weis said…"

"I don't care what he said, or what he does afterward. We can stop Omega."

Barney turned and looked at me.

"Ted—I can always go back to Hawaii and help my Father make his twentieth million. But what about you? Weis can finish your career permanently. And what about Barney and the rest of the Project personnel?"

"It's my responsibility. Weis won't care about the rest of 'em. And I don't care what he does to me… I can't sit here like a dumb ape and let that hurricane have its own way. Got a score to settle with Omega."

"Regardless of what it'll cost you?"

He nodded gravely. "Regardless of everything. Are you with me?"

"I guess I'm as crazy as you are," I heard myself say. "Let's do it."

We piled out of the car and strode up to the control center. As people started to cluster around us, Ted raised his arms for silence:

"Now listen—Project THUNDER is dead. We've got a job of weather-making to do. We're going to push that hurricane out to sea."

Then he started rattling off orders as though he had been rehearsing for this moment all his life.

As I started for my cubicle, Barney touched my sleeve. "Jerry, whatever happens later, thanks for helping him."

"We're accomplices," I said. "Before, during, and after the fact."

She smiled. "Do you think you could ever look at a cloud in the sky again if you hadn't agreed to help him try this?"

Before I could think of a reply she turned and started toward the computer section.

We had roughly thirty-six hours before Omega would strike the Virginia coast and then head up Chesapeake Bay for Washington. Thirty-six hours to manipulate the weather over the entire North American continent.

Within three hours Ted had us around his desk, a thick wad of notes clenched in his right hand. "Not as bad as it could've been," he told us, gesturing toward the plotting screen. "This big High sitting near the Great Lakes—good cold, dry air that can make a shield over the East Coast if we can swing it into position. Tuli, that's your job."

Tuli nodded, bright-eyed with excitement.

"Barney, we'll need pinpoint forecasts for every part of the country, even if it takes every computer in the Weather Bureau to wring 'em out."

"Right, Ted."

"Jerry, communications are the key. Got to keep in touch with the whole blinking country. And we're going to need planes, rockets, even slingshots maybe. Get the ball rolling before Weis finds out what we're up to."

"What about the Canadians? You'll be affecting their weather too."

"Get that liaison guy from the State Department and tell him to have the Canadian weather bureau check with us. Don't spill the beans to him, though."

"It's only a matter of time until Washington catches on," I said.

"Most of what we've got to do has to be done tonight. By the time they wake up tomorrow, we'll be on our way."

Omega's central windspeeds had climbed to 120 knots by evening, and were still increasing. As she trundled along toward the coast, her howling fury was nearly matched by the uproar of action at our control center. We didn't eat, we didn't sleep. We worked!

A half-dozen military satellites armed with lasers started pumping streams of energy into areas pinpointed by Ted's orders. Their crews had been alerted weeks earlier to cooperate with requests from Project THUNDER, and Ted and others from our technical staff had briefed them before the hurricane season began. They didn't question our messages. Squadrons of planes flew out to dump chemicals and seeding materials off Long Island, where he had created a weak storm cell in the vain attempt to steer Omega. Ted wanted that Low deepened, intensified—a low-pressure trough into which that High on the Great Lakes could slide.

"Intensifying the Low will let Omega come in faster, too," Tuli pointed out.

"Know it," Ted answered. "But the numbers're on our side. I think. Besides, faster Omega moves, less chance she gets to build up higher wind velocities."

By ten p.m. we had asked for and received a special analysis from the National Meteorological Center in Maryland. It showed that we would have to deflect the jet stream slightly, since it controlled the upper-air flow patterns across the country. But how do you divert a river that's three hundred miles wide, four miles thick, and racing along at better than three hundred miles per hour?

"It would take a hundred-megaton bomb," Barney said, "exploded about fifteen miles over Salt Lake City."

Ted nearly laughed. "The UN'd need a year just to get it on their agenda. Not to mention the sovereign citizens of Utah and points east."

"Then how do we do it?"

Ted grabbed the coffeepot standing on his desk and poured himself a mug of steaming black liquid. "Jet stream's a shear layer between the polar and mid-latitude tropopauses," he muttered, more to himself than any of us. "If you reinforce the polar air, it can nudge the stream southward…"

He took a cautious sip of the hot coffee. "Tuli, we're already moving a High southward from the Great Lakes. How about moving a bigger polar mass from Canada to push the jet stream enough to help us?"

"We don't have enough time or equipment to operate in Canada," I said. "And we'd need permission from Ottawa."

"What about reversing the procedure?" Tuli asked. "We could shrink the desert High over Arizona and New Mexico slightly, and the jet stream will move southward."

Ted hiked his eyebrows. "Think you can do it?"

"I'll have to make a few calculations."

"Okay, scramble."

The next morning in Boston, people who had gone to bed with a weather forecast of "warm, partly cloudy," awoke to a chilly, driving northeast rain. The Low we had intensified during the night had surprised the local forecasters. The Boston Weather Bureau office issued corrected predictions through the morning as the little rainstorm moved out, the Great Lakes High slid in and caused a flurry of frontal squalls, and finally the sun broke through. The cool dry air of the High dropped local temperatures more than ten degrees within an hour. To the unknowing New Englanders it was just another day, merely slightly more bewildering than most.

Dr. Weis phoned at seven thirty that morning.

"Marrett, have you lost your mind? What do you think you're doing? I told you…"

"Can't chat now, we're busy," Ted shot back.

"I'll have your hide for this!"

"Tomorrow you can have my hide. Bring it up myself. But first I'm going to find out if I'm right or wrong about this."

The Science Adviser turned purple. "I'm going to send out an order to all

Government installations to stop…"

"Better not. We're right in the middle of some tricky moves. Besides, we'll never find out if it works or not. Most of the mods've been made. Let's see what good they do."

Barney rushed up with a ream of computer printout sheets as Ted cut the phone connection.

"There's going to be a freeze in the Central Plains and northern Rockies," she said, pushing back her tousled hair. "There'll be some snow. We haven't fixed the exact amount yet."

A harvest-time freeze. Crops ruined, cities paralyzed by unexpected snow, weekend holidays ruined, and in the mountains deaths from exertion and exposure.

"Get the forecast out on the main Weather Bureau network," Ted ordered. "Warn 'em fast."

The plotting screen showed our battle clearly. Omega, with central wind speeds of 175 knots now, was still pushing toward Virginia. But her forward progress was slowing, ever so slightly, as the Great Lakes High moved—southeastward past Pittsburgh.

By noontime Ted was staring at the screen and muttering, "Won't be enough. Not unless the jet stream comes around a couple of degrees."

It was raining in Washington now, and snow was starting to fall in Winnipeg. I was trying to handle three phone calls at once when I heard an ear-splitting whoop from Ted. I looked toward the plotting screen. There was a slight bend in the jet stream west of the Mississippi that hadn't been there before.

As soon as I could, I collared Tuli for an explanation.

"We used the lasers from the Atlantic Station and every ounce of catalysts I could find. The effect isn't spectacular, no noticeable weather change. But the desert High has shrunk slightly and the jet stream has moved a little southward, temporarily."

"Will it be enough?" I asked.

He shrugged.

Through the long afternoon we watched that little curl travel along the length of the jet stream's course, like a wave snaking down the length of a long, taut rope. Meanwhile the former Great Lakes High was covering all of Maryland and pushing into Virginia. Its northern extension shielded the coast well into New England.

"But she'll blast right through," Ted grumbled, watching Omega's glowering system of closely packed isobars, "unless the jet stream helps push her off."

I asked Barney, "How does the timing look? Which will arrive first, the jet-stream change or the storm?"

She shook her head. "The machines have taken it down to four decimal places and there's still no sure answer."

Norfolk was being drenched by a torrential downpour; gale-force winds were snapping power lines and knocking down trees. Washington was a darkened, wind-swept city. Most of the Federal offices had closed early, and traffic was inching along the rain-slicked streets.

Boatmen from Hatteras to the fishhook angle of Cape Cod—weekend sailors and professionals alike—were making fast extra lines, setting out double anchors, or pulling their craft out of the water altogether. Commercial airlines were juggling their schedules around the storm and whole squadrons of military planes were winging westward, away from the danger, like great flocks of migrating birds.

Storm tides were piling up all along the coast, and flood warnings were flashing from civil defense centers in a dozen states. The highways were filling with people moving inland before the approaching fury.

And Omega was still a hundred miles out to sea.

Then she faltered.

You could feel the electricity crackle through our control center. The mammoth hurricane hovered off the coast as the jet-stream deflection finally arrived. We all held our breaths. Omega stood off the coast uncertainly for an endless hour, then turned to the northeast. She began to head out to sea.

We shouted our foolish heads off.

When the furor died down, Ted hopped up on his desk. "Hold it, heroes! Job's not finished yet. We've got a freeze in the Midwest to modify, and I want to throw everything we've got into Omega, weaken the old girl as much as possible. Now *scramble!*"

It was nearly midnight before Ted let us call it quits. Our Project people—real weathermakers now—had weakened Omega to the point where she was only a tropical storm, fast losing her punch over the cold waters of the north Atlantic. A light snow was sprinkling parts of the Upper Midwest, but our warning forecasts had been in time, and the weather makers were able to take most of the snap out of the cold front. The local weather stations were reporting only minor problems from the freeze. The snow amounted to less than an inch.

Most of the Project people had left for sleep. There was only a skeleton crew left in the control center. Barney, Tuli, and I gravitated toward Ted's desk. He had commandeered a typewriter and was pecking on the keys.

"How do you spell 'resignation'?" he asked.

Before any of us could answer, the phone buzzed. Ted thumbed the "on" switch. It was Dr. Weis.

"You didn't have to call," Ted said. "Game's over. I know it."

Dr. Weis looked utterly exhausted, as if he had personally been battling the storm. "I had a long talk with the President tonight, Marrett. You've put him in a difficult position, and me in an impossible one. To the general public, you're a hero. But I wouldn't trust you as far as I could throw a cyclotron."

"Don't blame you, I guess," Ted answered calmly. "But don't worry, you won't have to fire me. I'm resigning. You'll be off the hook."

"You can't quit," Dr. Weis said bitterly. "You're a national resource, as far as the President's concerned. He spent the night comparing you to nuclear energy: he wants you tamed and harnessed."

"Harnessed? For weather control?"

Weis nodded wordlessly.

"The President wants to really work on weather control?" Ted broke into a huge grin. "That's a harness I've been trying to get into for four years."

"Listen to me, Marrett. The President wants you to work on weather control, but I'm the one who's going to be responsible for controlling you. And I will never—do you hear, *never*—allow you to direct a project or get anywhere near directing a project. I'm going to find bosses for you who can keep you bottled up tight. We'll do weather-control work, and we'll use your ideas. But you'll never be in charge of anything as long as I'm in Washington."

Ted's smile died. "Okay," he said grimly, "as long as the work gets done… and done right. I didn't expect to get a National Medal out of this anyway."

Still glaring, Dr. Weis said, "You were lucky, Marrett. Very lucky. If the weather patterns had been slightly different, if things hadn't worked out so well…"

"Wasn't luck," Ted flashed. "It was work, a lot of peoples' work, and brains and guts. That's where weather control—*real* weather control—wins for you. It doesn't matter what the weather patterns are if you're going to change 'em all to suit your needs. You don't need luck, just time and sweat. You *make* the weather you want. That's what we did. That's why it had to work; we just had to tackle it on a big-enough scale."

"Luck or skill," Dr. Weis said wearily, "it doesn't matter. You'll get weather control now. But under my direction, and on my terms."

"We've won," Ted said as he shut off the phone. "We've really won."

Barney sank into the nearest chair. "It's too much happening all at once. I don't think I can believe it all."

"It's real," Ted answered quietly. "Weather control is a fact now. We're going to do it."

"You'll have to work under Dr. Weis and whoever he appoints to handle the program," I said.

Ted shrugged. "I worked for Rossman. I can work for anybody. The work's important, not the titles they give you."

Tuli rubbed his midsection and said, "I don't know about you inscrutable westerners, but this red-blooded Mongol is starving."

"So'm I, come to think of it," Ted said. "Come on you guys, let's have a celebration breakfast!"

"Guys," Barney echoed, frowning.

"Hey, that's right, you're a girl. Come on, Girl. Looks like you won't have to play second fiddle to hurricanes anymore." He took her arm and started for the door. "Think you can stand being the center of my attention?"

Barney looked back at me. I got up and took her other arm. "If you don't mind, she's going to be the center of my attention, too."

Tuli shook his head as he joined us. "You barbarians. No wonder you're nervous wrecks. You never know who's going to marry whom. I've got my future wife all picked out; our families agreed on the match when we were both four years old."

"That's why you're here in the States," Ted joked.

Barney said, "Tuli, don't do anything to make them change their minds. I haven't had this much attention since *I* was four."

Down the main stairway we went, and out onto the street. The sidewalks were puddled from rain, a side effect of Omega, but overhead the stars were shining through tattered, scudding clouds.

"Today the world's going to wake up and discover that man can control the weather," Ted said.

"Not really," Tuli cautioned. "We've only made a beginning. We still have years of learning ahead. Decades, perhaps centuries."

Ted nodded, a contented smile on his face. "Maybe. But we've started. That's the important thing."

"And the political problems this is going to cause?" I asked. "The social and economic changes that weather control will bring? What about them?"

He laughed. "That's for administrators like you and the President to worry about. I've got enough to keep me busy: six quadrillion tons of air… and one mathematician."

A little more than two years later, on a golden October afternoon, the United Nations convened a special outdoor session in Washington to hear an address by the President.

It was the first time I had seen Barney and Ted since their wedding, six months earlier. She had told me about her decision as gently as possible, and I learned that it's possible to live with pain even if there's no hope that it will ever be completely cured.

I had been running Aeolus; there was plenty of work for the Laboratory now. Ted and Barney (and Tuli, too) were living in Washington and working on the Government's weather-control program. Ted had settled down, under the direction of one of the nation's top scientists, and was seeing our years of struggle turned into solid accomplishment.

The UN delegates met at a special outdoor pavilion, built along the banks of the Potomac for their ceremony. Key people from the Weather Bureau and Congress and Government were in the audience. Beyond the seats set on the grass for the delegates and invited guests, a huge thronging crowd looked on, and listened to the President.

"…For mankind's technology," he was saying, "is both a constant danger and a constant opportunity. Through technology, man has attained the power to destroy himself, or the power to unite this planet in peace and freedom— freedom from war, from hunger, and from ignorance.

"Today we meet to mark a new step in the peaceful use of man's growing technical knowledge: the establishment of the United Nations Commission for Planetary Weather Control…"

Like Ted's victory over Hurricane Omega, this was only a first step. Total control of the weather, and total solution of the human problems involved, was still a long way off. But we were started along the right road.

As we sat listening to the President, a gentle breeze wafted by, tossing the flame-colored trees, and tempering the warmth of the sun. It was a crisp, golden October day; bright blue sky, beaming sun, occasional puffs of cottonball cumulus clouds. A perfect day for an outdoor ceremony.

Of course.

LAST DAY OF WORK

DOUGLAS RUSHKOFF

Winner of the first Neil Postman Award for Career Achievement in Public Intellectual Activity, Douglas is an author, teacher, and documentarian who focuses on the ways people, cultures, and institutions create, share, and influence each other's values. He sees "media" as the landscape where this interaction takes place, and "literacy" as the ability to participate consciously in it. His best-selling books on new media and popular culture have been translated to over thirty languages.

Read his *Present Shock: When Everything Happens Now* at http://amzn.to/1DwSijh.

SUMMARY

Today is Dr. Leon Spiegel's last day of work. But he's not just another retiring technology worker: he is the last man ever to work. Having delayed the inevitable for longer than he should, Spiegel recounts the events that have led to a world where no companies, no money, and no need for employment exist. In doing so, he reveals how humanity nearly allowed technology to bring life to a close, before stumbling upon the truth of man's own culpability for his dire condition. And now that humankind has avoided its dark fate and transcended the previously limited definition of what it means to be human, Spiegel is having a hard time letting go and joining the rest of the world.

I'm finally doing it. Clocking out for the last time.

It's been twenty years since they began offering the package, close to a decade since the company's been down to just the skeletal observation crew, and over a year since it's been just me. Well, Curtis and me, but he wasn't every fully here, anyway, so when he left the office it was more like

145

watching someone log off one network to join another.

And I'm looking forward to it, I really am. I just thought being the last one here would be a more notable achievement. At least more noted. An accomplishment as fame-worthy as something my father could have done. So while it is a significant human milestone, I'm sure of it, I just so happen to be doing it when nobody is around to care. I am the headline of every newspaper, the front page of every web site, and the message in everybody's inbox: Dr. Spiegel Turns Off the Lights.

I've been delaying the inevitable (and, from what I'm told, my own joy, my own release of ego, my membership in the next phase of human evolution) mostly because there's no one who knows or cares that I do. I'm collecting salary every day—I'm paying myself time-and-a-half, in fact, in consideration of my having to both work and monitor my own progress. It's not easy being the last guy.

Of course there's nowhere left to spend the money I'm earning. The last few businesses stopped accepting credits early last year, and even before that most financial transactions were done purely for show. Once the Date of Dissolution had been agreed to by the banks, there wasn't much point in hoarding currency of any kind. It's as if we just needed the credit for credit's sake—to prove to ourselves and our friends we had really done something of value. Kind of made everyone think about the stuff they used to buy with money, and if most of it was for the same, empty purpose.

Just because you know something to be true doesn't make you any better at accepting it, or acting any differently because of it. That was the main message of my dad's work, I suppose. Not that he was any messiah himself; just the messenger. But in a land of no egos or authority, that's pretty much the best anyone's going to get. As for me, well, I'm a messenger, too—but in a world with no recipients. Except maybe you, if you happen to find this missive. And if you do, I guess it means we were wrong about the whole thing.

But that possibility has been enough to keep me going at this chronicle, written in the same work hours that I used to spend monitoring the systems, making sure the nano, robo, digital, and genetic algorithms were all working within predicted parameters. Ready to pull the plug right up until the moment there was no longer any plug to pull.

I mean, everyone—at least everyone who was anyone—went over. Someone had to watch from the other side. Someone had to be the last one to leave. Work the last day of the last job. Close the door, turn out the lights.

It's fitting that I'm the one—and not just because I'm a Spiegel. As a kid I had always been obsessed with Michael Collins—the Apollo 11 command module pilot—not Neil Armstrong or Buzz Aldrin, the guys who actually landed on the moon's surface. Collins circled around, alone, over to the dark side while the other two made the historic lunar landing for the TV audience. He just sat there in the capsule, beyond the range of our communications, when everybody else celebrated our first truly unifying planetary achievement. He was completely responsible and utterly by himself.

So yeah, I've been relishing my "last-remaining-human" experience, and dragging it out far longer than I have any excuse to. I wander through the abandoned shopping malls, try on clothes I would never have been able to afford, watch movies the old-fashioned way, stack paper cash in big piles, and shoot machine guns at cars. It's fun. As long as there's only one of me, I can afford to live in exactly the way my father's work showed us not to.

On the off-chance you have no idea what I'm talking about (Wouldn't that be a hoot? Me having to tell people about his existence?), here's how it came to pass:

I've got my own theories on the moment it all shifted—but so does everyone else. There's no way to know exactly which technology or policy or pop star or combination of these led to the great unwinding. There's not much consensus on this, but I still think it was the TP, or telepathic podster. It wasn't a truly telepathic uni device, of course. That took another decade. The TP was just a biofeedback circuit. It observed the neural output of enough people thinking "right" or "left" and then use that data to predict when someone else is trying to move the cursor in that direction. It was the first smart phone / gamepad that seemed to know what we meant without our telling it anything.

While that might not seem like so very much, it changed the whole way technology developed from then on. Instead of it being our job to figure out how to make some new thing and then figure out what the heck to use it for, now it was technology's job to figure out what we wanted and then just go do it for us.

This turned out to be a big problem, because what we all wanted was more of everything we already had. Consumer technologies learned to think of people the way we already thought of ourselves: as absolute consumers. Technologies from net agents to nano-bots competed through the networks to bring their owners as much stuff as cheaply as possible. Meanwhile, technologies in the service of corporations and governments mirrored the profit-minded or bureaucratic ideals of their own users. They created trading algorithms, intelligent currencies, and self-referential legal axioms that brought capital into their coffers at alarmingly rapid rates.

This was all good for the economy—at least in the short run, as measured by the GNP. The faster the economy grew, the faster it could accelerate. As long as there were new thresholds for acceleration, the sky was the limit.

The only drag on the system proved to be human intervention. The amount of time it took human beings to make decisions for themselves paled in comparison to the rate at which these same choices could be accurately predicted and carried out by assumption routines. Our impulses at that stage of evolution, after all, were really quite simple. They all pointed towards more of one thing or another, the sooner the better.

Once outside direct human command and control, technologies from the TP to the nano probe were capable of reflecting and meeting the aggregate human demand well in advance of our conscious requests. At least until the economic systems on which all this was occurring began to break down.

It seems that leaving technology to meet human demand, unchecked, wasn't the best idea after all. Resources ran scarce, especially when distributed to individuals. And capital tended to pool at the center, leaving companies with no one left to sell goods to. We painted ourselves into a corner, and lacked the ingenuity to change in time to get out of the mess. Our programs gave us exactly what we asked them for, and we didn't know how to ask any differently. Environmental forecasts indicated that even if we reversed course somehow, it was already too late. Resource depletion and wealth disparity had passed the point of no return.

A few great ideas—master plans—were attempted. A Chinese firm developed a technology through which biological forms could be reduced to one-tenth their normal size. The thinking behind this scenario was that human beings would only take up a tenth the space this way, and thus utilize only one-tenth the resources. But even tiny humans would have a hard time surviving the radiation that was to come, so the idea was scrapped.

Trapped in the scenario from which there seemed to be no escape, my father came up with the last resort idea for saving the species: interstellar migration. No, we didn't have the technology to fly humans from earth to some save haven, but we had the means to seed another planet with our DNA. And so scientists began on the great project to send robots, nanotech, and genetic material across the galaxies in search of a planet suitable for life to begin again.

To avoid merely repeating the evolutionary process that brought us into our sorry state, however, our government came up with the idea of nesting a message into the DNA strand: our little fortune cookie for the next round of humanity. In this message, we could explain where we went wrong, as best as it could be articulated. Then, once the next civilization was approaching our level of development, they would presumably find the message in their DNA strand, read it, and avert our fate.

While the United Nations argued about exactly what the message should say, my father was tasked with finding an unused, or generally unnecessary codon on which to embed it. He spent a long time considering which animal and human qualities were necessary or not for our development, and scanned over the sections of the genome like an engineer looking for unused tunnels in the New York subway system.

Then, he figured, why not go to the source of the trouble? The human drive for self and tribal interest so necessary at early stages of development, yet so dangerous when allowed to run human affairs in the later stages of evolution when drives can be so easily amplified by technology. He used his virtual quark microscope to zoom in on his target zone of the genome, exploring the fractal-like model on the subatomic level, when he noticed something strange: there was a small, extra bundle of mesons and single baryon hanging onto the edge of one of the neutrinos in an atom of the cytosine nucleotide. Now what was that doing there?

He guessed it as quickly as you just did. It was a message. Similar in spirit to what humanity was now attempting to tell its own evolutionary progeny. Incapable of being translated into words, but conveying the essential and seemingly frightening truth: technology is not a mirror, it is a partner.

The location of the message provided the clue for its implementation, which proved a whole lot easier than trying to embed it in some future seed-spawning project. We would simply release our technology from simply amplifying the existing social order, and set it free to deliver us a new one.

It took some time for people to accept that the biases of our technology were not foreign to humanity at all, but its greatest and most deliberate expressions. Through our networked intelligences, we had developed a fully decentralized modality for matter to achieve greater complexity in the face of entropy. We could hunt and gather no more, conquer and collect no further. The Industrial Age reversed itself, as bigger was no longer better, and centralized authority worked against the power of networks. Our drive to monopolize was no longer a valid means of increasing our knowledge and capability. We would have to learn, instead, to let go.

And so the process began through which we saved humanity and, more importantly, continued the evolution of matter toward greater levels of self-awareness. It just meant including our technologies in the great game, instead of requiring they submit to reality as we previously understood it. They were only as responsible for reading our minds as we were responsible for reading theirs.

We moved from the scarcity model—the zero-sum game through which species compete for resources—to an abundance model where anything that is necessary can be found or synthesized and then shared by all.

The manufacturing of energy (long limited by the faux economics of resource depletion) was as simple as a yawn. The only thing that had been standing in the way was an energy industry whose profits depended on fixed supplies and non-renewability. Medicine, agriculture, air and education all proved as plentiful as our willingness to adopt technologies that created value from the periphery, and replicated effortlessly as they spread. From shape shifting to mems to transformation of matter. Everything became free.

While our prior social system would have been challenged by the extreme unemployment that came with the collapse of corporate capitalism, we no longer saw the need to distribute wealth according to one's contribution. There was enough for all, and barely enough "work" for anyone. Once the synthesis of appropriate matter forms was left to technologies unencumbered by the necessities of an artificially scarce marketplace, people started lining up to do the one day of work per month per person required to keep everything going.

Then, the work itself became ritual. Over the past ten years or so, those of us who visited a workplace regularly did so purely out of habit, or as a form of historical re-enactment. A few of the robots, like my friend Curtis, remained to perform the last few clerical functions—keeping the lights on, maintaining the few ancient servers left that provided no functionality other than maintaining the illusion of working companies. And then even the robots left, fully convinced of their superfluousness, and ready to join the party. There out there, too.

I've spent time there, don't get me wrong. Matter, energy, consciousness, all in the same dance. The technology—the balls, the light, the information—isn't taking commands from any server. There's no middle, anymore. No top. Everything is just taking commands from everything else. The network is the server, the genes are the organism, the nanos are the medium. What we tried to teach technology in the industrial age turned out to be the opposite of what technology finally taught us in Great Unwinding.

I don't know if anyone but me gets this on anything but an intuitive level, or why they'd feel the need to. Once you see the dancing, you can't help but join in. And it's everything they say it is: the ecstasy of connection—of everybody knowing everything about everyone else, and being perfectly okay with it. Overjoyed, even. Still unique and individual, yet also part of a greater mind—a collective awareness that has finally grown ready to reach out and finally find the other ones out there.

I have held back for a long time, now. But no longer. I just wanted to—I don't know—to do something as significant as my father did. Make a mark. Get recognized, lauded, and even rewarded for something I did, me alone.

That's something I could only do back here. And like everyone else's personal success, the only thing it can do for me in the long run is keep me more alone.

So I'm going to stop now. Years later than I had to, I suppose. But all in my own good time. And this time I'm really doing it. This is my last day of work. I'm going to turn off the terminal, switch off the lights, and walk out that door. This time, I know I will.

I'M A WHAT?

FRANK WHITE

Frank is the author of *The Overview Effect: Space Exploration and Human Evolution*, now in its third edition and available at http://amzn.to/1Ac6g6M.

Frank is the author or coauthor of ten additional books on space exploration and the future, including *Points of View: Take One, The SETI Factor: How the Search for Extraterrestrial Intelligence is Changing Our View of the Universe and Ourselves, Decision: Earth: Book One: Alone or All One?, American Revolution, Think About Space: Where Have We Been and Where Are We Going?* and *The March of the Millennia: A Key to Looking at History* (both with Isaac Asimov), *The Ice Chronicles* (with Paul Mayewski), and *Space Stories: Oral Histories from the Pioneers of America's Space Program* (with Kenneth J. Cox and Robbie Davis-Floyd).

To: Friendslist

Subj: Craziness

From: Andie10047@yahoo.com

Okay, it's 9:33 am on Monday, and I'm sending this to all of you, just in case. Something may or may not happen at 10, but I want you to know what I've been going through, how crazy he's been, and why I had to run away from him. I'm going to try to reconstruct our conversations, because they're important to understand what I'm explaining to you.

All right, I need to just calm down and tell the story: so it started just over the weekend when he came home from work. He wasn't himself and I could tell something pretty serious was on his mind. There was a secret of some kind he wanted to tell me, but he couldn't figure out how to do it.

I had fixed a nice dinner, and tried to make conversation while we ate, but he just pushed the food around the plate and didn't really answer when I asked about work and so on.

Try as I might, I couldn't figure out what was wrong. I mean, he had been growing a bit distant lately, and I'd noticed he seemed distracted

153

when we made love, which was odd in and of itself, but he would quickly snap out of it and seem okay, for the most part.

Finally, he did speak up, and what he said hit me pretty hard, I'll tell you.

"We're going to have to split up."

"What? Who is she?"

I just assumed there was another woman, what else could it be?

"There is no 'she,'" he said, looking frustrated.

"How can there not be somebody else?" I said, panic rising, "we have a great life, there aren't any problems between us, what the hell is going on?"

The way he looked at me was just so weird that I don't know how to describe it. You know he's good-looking and he just stared at me with those blue eyes, kind of like he was in physical pain.

"You want the truth, right?"

"Of course! Since it looks like you've been lying to me all along!"

He looked down, looked up again, trying to decide what to do. Finally, he blurted it out.

"You're, well, you're…an android."

"I'm a what?"

"An android, an artificial life form. You're not human."

I went into shock, of course. For just a minute, I tried to see if there was any way this could be true. Well, of course, it couldn't be. Then I realized, to my dismay, that my husband had lost his mind!

But I couldn't really say that to him, could I? I was afraid that his insanity might include a violent streak. I mean, after all, if he thought I wasn't human, but a machine, he could injure or kill me without feeling guilty about it, right? I decided I needed to engage him in conversation, try to see if he had any bad intentions toward me.

So I spoke to him very softly, soothingly.

"I don't think I'm an android, my love, I mean, I have memories of my childhood, after all."

"All of those memories were implanted when you were created, which was three years ago."

"We got married three years ago."

"Precisely."

Wow. He had answers for everything, didn't he? Of course, I knew he was fascinated with androids. He read about them all the time, and he faithfully watched *Battlestar Galactica* as well. He had also rented *Blade Runner* about a hundred times.

But still, had that just been an indication of the psychosis that was yet to come?

All I could do was stall for time, so I engaged in and yet questioned his fantasy.

"Okay, so I'm an android. Am I the only one?"

"Oh, no, there are thousands of you, maybe more, mostly pleasure bots."

"Pleasure bots?"

"Male and female androids bought by people primarily for sexual gratification."

"Is that what I am?"

He turned away and looked sheepish for a moment, I thought.

"Yes."

"I have never heard of any of this in my whole life. Why not?"

"Programming."

"What do you mean?"

"All of you are programmed not to hear anything about yourselves, unless it comes from your owner, like we're talking now. If something comes on the television or shows up on the Web, you won't see it. There are a bunch of keywords programmed into your systems that can cause you to shut down your sensors, like "android, robot, and so on.""

"I've heard of androids and robots."

"Well, it's all contextual. If you hear about an android in a sci-fi film, it gets through. If the story is about an android company producing real pleasure bots, you won't process it."

As you can imagine, I was getting pretty frustrated by now. He was diabolical in the way he parried my arguments. How could I prove he was wrong, since he was convinced that he was right, and he had an answer for everything? So I decided to try a new tack.

"Okay, let's just say you're right and I'm an android. So what? Why do we have to split up? We've had three great years together."

"That's just it. Three years is the limit."

"What limit?"

"Androids and people can only stay together for three years."

"Why?"

"A bunch of conservative people in Congress said it was ungodly for human beings to shack up with machines. They couldn't get androids banned, so they put the time limit on all human/android relationships."

"Three years?"

"Yeah, three years."

"That's just plain cruel! Don't they care how people feel?"

Suddenly, I was getting into his fantasy. I had said what I said without realizing that I was buying into it, but it seemed to make him even more anxious to explain it.

"Yes, it is, but they don't care. They said that androids have no feelings, and the humans who bought them should know that, and not worry about it."

I was stumped. If there were such a thing as androids or pleasure bots, I fully believed there were members of Congress who would pass such a law. But that meant I had to accept all his other assumptions, which were insane. After all, I could remember my childhood, growing up and going to college, meeting him and falling in love with him, and this was all crazy, or a cover for adultery, or both.

Well, anyway, he seemed to be anxious, but not violent, so that was a good thing. A plan started to form in my mind. I would just play along with him, try to find out as much about his fantasy/cover-up as I could, and then get the hell out of our house in the morning. I still didn't trust what was happening and I was, quite frankly, afraid.

"All right, I'm beginning to see your point," I said. "Tell me more."

He was oh, so eager to do just that. He took a deep breath and began.

"Well," he said brightly, "you were my first and I was your first."

"Meaning?"

"You were right off the assembly line and had never been with anyone else before. And I had finally given in to my needs and decided to go android."

"Go android?"

"That's what they call it when you buy an Andy or an Andie, as the case may be."

"That's your nickname for us?"

"Yes."

"And that's why I'm called Andie? My name isn't really Andrea?

"No."

"How much did I cost you?"

"Ten thousand dollars."

I couldn't decide if that was a lot or a little.

"Oh…"

"You were more expensive because you were a virgin."

"Meaning I'd…"

"…yes, never been with anyone before."

I thought back to our many lovemaking episodes, how passionate, how, well, loving they had been. Okay, on one point we did agree, which was that I had been a virgin when we got married, a rare thing in these days, but in my mind, it was because of my religious beliefs. In his mind, it was because I had just rolled off the assembly line. One of us was clearly crazy, but which one?

I tried another approach.

"Look, honey, even if I am an android and there is this three-year limit on our relationship, hey, we love each other, right?"

He nodded.

"So, let's just run away somewhere together. They won't be able to come take me from you and we can just go on living as we have."

Now he frowned.

"It's not that easy."

"Why not?"

"It doesn't matter where we are, they'll just turn you off remotely and come pick you up. There's a chip inside you that they can use to shut you down and locate you, no matter where you are."

Then, he looked at me with a kind of desperate hope.

"I am going to try to appeal the shutoff date, though. I've heard of people getting a delay if they have a really good reason. I'm going to call them tomorrow."

"You waited long enough."

He shook his head in frustration and looked down.

"I know, I know. I'm sorry, but there have been stories that you get into trouble if you file an appeal. They mark your file as an 'Andie-lover' and sometimes they make you go to a shrink to see if you've lost touch with reality. But I decided that I love you so much that I'm going to do it anyway!"

His fierce late-blooming bravado made me want to throw up.

But I had to admit that he had thought of everything! Wow, the guy should have been a novelist, with this imagination!

So at that moment, I decided it was a lost cause and I just had to get away that night or first thing in the morning.

I looked at him with all the credibility I could muster.

"All right, well there's nothing we can do. Let's just have one more nice night together, shall we?"

I wish you could have seen the look on his face. He was so relieved! There weren't going to be any scenes, no accusations, no messy divorce proceedings.

We had dinner and it was, as you might guess, a pretty quiet affair. I mean, what the hell were we going to talk about, his life after I was "deactivated?"

When we went to bed, on the other hand, it was like always. Fierce, passionate, a bit rough. I was of two minds, of course. On the one hand, I thought, "Maybe he's having second thoughts and I won't have to leave him." On the other hand, I also thought, "What a hypocrite! He's cheating on me and he still expects the same old thing from me!" Because I still believed that was what was going on. He might or might not be insane, but I was convinced there was someone else.

It didn't matter, though, did it? I mean, my relationship with him was over, whether he was nuts or just making up some elaborate story to get out of the marriage. Once he rolled over and began snoring, I had myself a good cry and began to plot my escape.

Around two in the morning, I quietly slipped out of bed and put together a small bag of stuff to take with me. I had to travel light, but I made sure I had my credit cards, a change of clothes and a few other things I would certainly need. I thought about leaving him a note, thought about it again, and said to hell with it.

By three o'clock, I was ready. I took one last look at him, lying there all naked and innocent and had a moment of longing for him and pity for myself. I also had a moment of wanting to kill him, but something inside, something very strong, said "No!" I knew I could not do it. I'm not sure why, but it was more than just a moral consideration. It was almost like a revulsion against the idea that was programmed into me. Sorry, I shouldn't have said "programming." That's his fantasy.

Anyway, I didn't really want him to die, at least not by my hand, though I did wish he might be abducted by aliens and have terrible experiments done on him, or something like that.

I slipped out of our apartment, knowing with a twinge of sadness that I would never see it, or him, again. I ran out into the night with my little bag, and got into my car (thankfully, we had two) and roared away into the darkness of the sleeping city.

Now, I've driven for several hours and find myself in a Starbucks far away from him, tapping out this email to all of you. I want you to know what has gone on, just in case he finds me and does something to me.

Wait a minute, wait a minute, I think I might have seen him. Back soon.

To: Andie10047@yahoo.com
From: Lori9027@gmail.com
Subject: His craziness

OMG, honey, are you all right? I can't believe he's turned into a crazy man like that! Where are you? Can I come there and help you out? Tell me where you are and I'll be there.

Love,

Lori

To: Friendslist
From: Andie10047@yahoo.com
Subject: His craziness

Okay, everyone, I'm back. I thought I saw him heading into this Starbucks and I wanted to get away if I had to, but it was someone else.

Anyway, where was I? Well, I think that's about it. Maybe he'll just leave me alone and settle down with whoever it is that he's been cheating on me with. I just hope he doesn't try to find me. It's kind of scary to run away like this and not know where I'm going, but I think I'll be all right. I have skills, I can find a job, and make a new life for myself.

Of course, I'm not worried about the 10 am "shutoff" deadline, which is now only a few minutes away. I have to admit that for a while when I was with him and listening to his crazy talk, I began to wonder if what he said was true and I really was an android, about to be turned off by remote control, reprogrammed with new memories, and sold at a discounted price to another human being.

I...

THE LISTENERS

JAMES E. GUNN

Jim is a Hugo Award winner and Damon Knight Memorial Grand Master and was president of the Science Fiction Writers of America and the Science Fiction Research Association. His novelette below became the first chapter of his book *The Listeners* which is now available at http://amzn.to/1l2cVaH.

Jim's book was described by Carl Sagan as "One of the very best fictional portrayals of contact with extraterrestrial intelligence ever written." and inspired Carl Sagan's book *Contact* which later became a movie.

There are translations at the end of the novelette for the various non-English quotations within it.

"*Is there anybody there?" said the Traveler, knocking on the moonlit door...*

The voices babbled.

MacDonald heard them and knew that there was meaning in them, that they were trying to communicate and that he could understand them and respond to them if he could only concentrate on what they were saying, but he couldn't bring himself to make the effort. He tried again.

"Back behind everything, lurking like a silent shadow behind the closed door, is the question we can never answer except positively: Is there anybody there?"

That was Bob Adams, eternally the devil's advocate, looking querulously at the others around the conference table. His round face was sweating, although the mahogany-paneled room was cool.

Saunders puffed hard on his pipe. "But that's true of all science. The image of the scientist eliminating all negative possibilities is ridiculous. Can't be done. So he goes ahead on faith and statistical probability."

MacDonald watched the smoke rise above Saunders' head in clouds and wisps until it wavered in the draft from the air duct, thinned out, disappeared. He could not see it, but the odor reached his nostrils. It was an aromatic blend easily distinguishable from the flatter smell of the cigarettes being smoked by Adams and some of the others.

Wasn't this their task? MacDonald wondered. To detect the thin smoke of life that drifts through the universe, to separate one trace from another, molecule by molecule, and then force them to reverse their entropic paths into their ordered and meaningful original form.

All the king's horses, and all the king's men... Life itself is impossible, he thought, but men exist by reversing entropy.

Down the long table cluttered with overflowing ash trays and coffee cups and doodled scratch pads Olsen said, "We always knew it would be a long search. Not years but centuries. The computers must have sufficient data, and that means bits of information approximating the number of molecules in the universe. Let's not chicken out now."

> *"If seven maids with seven mops*
> *Swept it for half a year,*
> *Do you suppose," the Walrus said,*
> *"That they could get it clear?"*

"...Ridiculous," someone was saying, and then Adams broke in. "It's easy for you to talk about centuries when you've been here only three years. Wait until you've been at it for ten years, like I have. Or Mac here who has been on the Project for twenty years and head of it for fifteen."

"What's the use of arguing about something we can't know anything about?" Sonnenborn said reasonably. "We have to base our position on probabilities. Shklovskii and Sagan estimated that there are more than one thousand million habitable planets in our galaxy alone. Von Hoerner estimated that one in three million have advanced societies in orbit around them; Sagan said one in one hundred thousand. Either way it's good odds that there's somebody there—three hundred or ten thousand in our segment of the universe. Our job is to listen in the right place or in the right way or understand what we hear."

Adams turned to MacDonald. "What do you say, Mac?"

"I say these basic discussions are good for us," MacDonald said mildly, "and we need to keep reminding ourselves what it is we're doing, or we'll get swallowed in a quicksand of data. I also say that it's time now to get down to the business at hand—what observations do we make tonight and the rest of the week before our next staff meeting?"

Saunders began, "I think we should make a methodical sweep of the entire galactic lens, listening on all wavelengths—"

"We've done that a hundred times," said Sonnenborn.

"Not with my new filter—"

"Tau Ceti still is the most likely," said Olsen. "Let's really give it a hearing—"

MacDonald heard Adams grumbling, half to himself, "If there is anybody, and they are trying to communicate, some amateur is going to pick it up on his ham set, decipher it on his James Bond code rule, and leave us sitting here on one hundred million dollars of equipment with egg all over our faces—"

"And don't forget," MacDonald said, "tomorrow is Saturday night and Maria and I will be expecting you all at our place at eight for the customary beer and bull. Those who have more to say can save it for then."

MacDonald did not feel as jovial as he tried to sound. He did not know whether he could stand another Saturday-night session of drink and discussion and dissension about the Project. This was one of his low periods when everything seemed to pile up on top of him, and he could not get out from under, or tell anybody how he felt. No matter how he felt, the Saturday nights were good for the morale of the others.

Pues no es posible que esté continuo el arco armado ni la condición y flaqueza humana se pueda sustenar sin alguna lícita recreación.

Within the Project, morale was always a problem. Besides, it was good for Maria. She did not get out enough. She needed to see people. And then...

And then maybe Adams was right. Maybe nobody was there. Maybe nobody was sending signals because there was nobody to send signals. Maybe man was alone in the universe. Alone with God. Or alone with himself, whichever was worse.

Maybe all the money was being wasted, and the effort, and the preparation—all the intelligence and education and ideas being drained away into an endlessly empty cavern.

Habe nun, ach! Philosophie,
Juristerei und Medizin,
Und leider auch Theologie
Durchaus studiert, mit heissem Bemühn.
Da steh' ich nun, ich armer Tor!
Und bin so klug als wie zuvor;
Heisse Magister, heisse Doktor gar,
Und ziehe schon an die zehen Jahr
Herauf, herab und quer und krumm
Meine Schüler an der Nase herum—
Und sehe, dass wir nichts wissen können!

Poor fool. Why me? MacDonald thought. Could not some other lead them better, not by the nose but by his real wisdom? Perhaps all he was good for was the Saturday-night parties. Perhaps it was time for a change.

He shook himself. It was the endless waiting that wore him down, the waiting for something that did not happen, and the Congressional hearings were coming up again. What could he say that he had not said before? How could he justify a project that already had gone on for nearly fifty years without results and might go on for centuries more?

"Gentlemen," he said briskly, "to our listening posts."

By the time he had settled himself at his disordered desk, Lily was standing beside him.

"Here's last night's computer analysis," she said, putting down in front of him a thin folder. "Reynolds says there's nothing there, but you always want to see it anyway. Here's the transcription of last year's Congressional hearings." A thick binder went on top of the folder. "The correspondence and the actual appropriation measure are in another file if you want them."

MacDonald shook his head.

"There's a form letter from NASA establishing the ground rules for this year's budget and a personal letter from Ted Wartinian saying that conditions are really tight and some cuts look inevitable. In fact, he says there's a possibility the Project might be scrubbed."

Lily glanced at him. "Not a chance," MacDonald said confidently.

"There's a few applications for employment. Not as many as we used to get. The letters from school children I answered myself. And there's the usual nut letters from people who've been receiving messages from outer space, and from one who's had a ride in a UFO. That's what he called it—not a saucer or anything. A feature writer wants to interview you and some others for an article on the Project. I think he's with us. And another one who sounds as if he wants to do an exposé."

MacDonald listened patiently. Lily was a wonder. She could handle everything in the office as well as he could. In fact, things might run smoother if he were not around to take up her time.

"They've both sent some questions for you to answer. And Joe wants to talk to you."

"Joe?"

"One of the janitors."

"What does he want?" They couldn't afford to lose a janitor. Good janitors were harder to find than astronomers, harder even than electricians.

"He says he has to talk to you, but I've heard from some of the lunchroom staff that he's been complaining about getting messages on his—on his—"

"Yes?"

"On his false teeth."

MacDonald sighed. "Pacify him somehow, will you, Lily? If I talk to him we might lose a janitor."

"I'll do my best. And Mrs. MacDonald called. Said it wasn't important and you needn't call back."

"Call her," MacDonald said. "And, Lily—you're coming to the party tomorrow night, aren't you?"

"What would I be doing at a party with all the brains?"

"We want you to come. Maria asked particularly. It isn't all shop talk, you know. And there are never enough women. You might strike it off with one of the young bachelors."

"At my age, Mr. MacDonald? You're just trying to get rid of me."

"Never."

"I'll get Mrs. MacDonald." Lily turned at the door. "I'll think about the party."

MacDonald shuffled through the papers. Down at the bottom was the only one he was interested in—the computer analysis of last night's listening. But he kept it there, on the bottom, as a reward for going through the others. Ted was really worried. *Move over, Ted.* And then the writers. He supposed he would have to work them in somehow. At least it was part of the fallout to locating the Project in Puerto Rico. Nobody just dropped in. And the questions. Two of them caught his attention.

How did you come to be named Project Director? That was the friendly one. *What are your qualifications to be Director?* That was the other. How would he answer them? Could he answer them at all?

Finally he reached the computer analysis, and it was just like those for the rest of the week, and the week before that, and the months and the years before that. No significant correlations. Noise. There were a few peaks of reception—at the twenty-one-centimeter line, for instance—but these were merely concentrated noise. Radiating clouds of hydrogen, as the Little Ear functioned like an ordinary radio telescope.

At least the Project showed some results. It was feeding star survey data tapes into the international pool. Fallout. Of a process that had no other product except negatives.

Maybe the equipment wasn't sensitive enough. Maybe. They could beef it up some more. At least it might be a successful ploy with the Committee, some progress to present, if only in the hardware. You don't stand still. You spend more money or they cut you back—or off.

Note: Saunders—plans to increase sensitivity.

Maybe the equipment wasn't discriminating enough. But they had used up a generation of ingenuity canceling out background noise, and in its occasional checks the Big Ear indicated that they were doing adequately on terrestrial noise, at least.

Note: Adams—new discrimination gimmick.

Maybe the computer wasn't recognizing a signal when it had one fed into it. Perhaps it wasn't sophisticated enough to perceive certain subtle relationships.... And yet sophisticated codes had been broken in seconds. And the Project was asking it to distinguish only where a signal existed, whether the reception was random noise or had some element of the unrandom. At this level it wasn't even being asked to note the influence of consciousness.

Note: ask computer—is it missing something? Ridiculous? Ask Olsen.

Maybe they shouldn't be searching the radio spectrum at all. Maybe radio was a peculiarity of man's civilization. Maybe others had never had it or had passed it by and now had more sophisticated means of communication. Lasers, for instance. Telepathy, or what might pass for it with man. Maybe gamma rays, as Morrison suggested years before Ozma.

Well, maybe. But if it were so, somebody else would have to listen for those. He had neither the equipment nor the background nor the working lifetime left to tackle something new.

And maybe Adams was right.

He buzzed Lily. "Have you reached Mrs. MacDonald?"

"The telephone hasn't answered—"

Unreasoned panic...

"—Oh, here she is now, Mr. MacDonald, Mrs. MacDonald."

"Hello, darling, I was alarmed when you didn't answer." That had been foolish, he thought, and even more foolish to mention it.

Her voice was sleepy. "I must have been dozing." Even drowsy, it was an exciting voice, gentle, a little husky, that speeded MacDonald's pulse. "What did you want?"

"You called me," MacDonald said.

"Did I? I've forgotten."

"Glad you're resting. You didn't sleep well last night."

"I took some pills."

"How many?"

"Just the two you left out."

"Good girl. I'll see you in a couple of hours. Go back to sleep. Sorry I woke you."

But her voice wasn't sleepy any more. "You won't have to go back tonight, will you? We'll have the evening together?"

"We'll see," he promised.

But he knew he would have to return.

MacDonald paused outside the long, low concrete building that housed the offices and laboratories and computers. It was twilight. The sun had descended below the green hills, but orange and purpling wisps of cirrus trailed down the western sky.

Between MacDonald and the sky was a giant dish held aloft by skeletal metal fingers—held high as if to catch the stardust that drifted down at night from the Milky Way.

> *Go and catch a falling star,*
> *Get with child a mandrake root,*
> *Tell me where all past years are,*
> *Or who cleft the Devil's foot;*
> *Teach me to hear mermaids singing,*
> *Or to keep off envy's stinging,*
> *And find*
> *What wind*
> *Serves to advance an honest mind.*

Then the dish began to turn, noiselessly, incredibly, and to tip. And it was not a dish any more but an ear, a listening ear cupped by the surrounding hills to overhear the whispering universe.

Perhaps this was what kept them at their jobs, MacDonald thought. In spite of all disappointments, in spite of all vain efforts, perhaps it was this massive machinery, as sensitive as their fingertips, that kept them struggling with the unfathomable. When they grew weary at their electronic listening posts, when their eyes grew dim with looking at unrevealing dials and studying uneventful graphs, they could step outside their concrete cells and renew their dull spirits in communion with the giant mechanism they commanded, the silent, sensing instrument in which the smallest packets of energy, the smallest waves of matter, were detected in their headlong, eternal flight across the universe. It was the stethoscope with which they took the pulse of the all and noted the birth and death of stars, the probe with which, here on an insignificant planet of an undistinguished star on the edge of its galaxy, they explored the infinite.

Or perhaps it was not just the reality but the imagery, like poetry, that soothed their doubting souls, the bowl held up to catch Donne's falling star, the ear cocked to catch the suspected shout that faded to an indistinguishable murmur by the time it reached them. And one thousand miles above them was the giant, five-mile-in-diameter network, the largest radio telescope ever built, that men had cast into the heavens to catch the stars.

If they had the Big Ear for more than an occasional reference check, Mac-Donald thought practically, then they might get some results. But he knew the radio astronomers would never relinquish time to the frivolity of listening for signals that never came. It was only because of the Big Ear that the Project had inherited the Little Ear. There had been talk recently about a larger net, twenty miles in diameter. Perhaps when it was done, if it were done, the Project might inherit time on the Big Ear.

If they could endure until then, MacDonald thought, if they could steer their fragile vessel of faith between the Scylla of self-doubt and the Charybdis of Congressional appropriations.

The images were not all favorable. There were others that went boomp in the night. There was the image, for instance, of man listening, listening, listening to the silent stars, listening for an eternity, listening for signals that would never come, because—the ultimate horror—man was alone in the universe, a cosmic accident of self-awareness which needed and would never receive the comfort of companionship. To be alone, to be all alone, would be like being all alone on earth, with no one to talk to, ever—like being alone inside a bone prison, with no way to get out, no way to communicate with anyone outside, no way to know if anyone was outside....

Perhaps that, in the end, was what kept them going—to stave off the terrors of the night. While they listened there was hope; to give up now would be to admit final defeat. Some said they should never have started; then they never would have the problem of surrender. Some of the new religions said that. The Solitarians, for one. There is nobody there; we are the one, the only created intelligence in the universe. Let us glory in our uniqueness. But the older religions encouraged the Project to continue. Why would God have created the myriads of other stars and other planets if He had not intended them for living creatures; why should man only be created in His image? Let us find out, they said. Let us communicate with them. What revelations have they had? What saviors have redeemed them?

These are the words which I spake unto you, while I was yet with you, that all things must be fulfilled, which were written in the law of Moses, and in the prophets, and in the psalms, concerning me.... Thus it is written, and thus it behooved Christ to suffer, and to rise from the dead the third day: and that repentance and remission of sins should be preached in his name among all nations, beginning at Jerusalem. And we are witnesses of these things.

And, behold, I send the promise of my Father upon you: but tarry ye in the city of Jerusalem, until ye be endued with power from on high.

Dusk had turned to night. The sky had turned to black. The stars had been born again. The listening had begun. MacDonald made his way to his car in the parking lot behind the building, coasted until he was behind the hill, and turned on the motor for the long drive home.

The hacienda was dark. It had that empty feeling about it that MacDonald knew so well, the feeling it had for him when Maria went to visit friends in Mexico City. But it was not empty now. Maria was here.

He opened the door and flicked on the hall light. "Maria?" He walked down the tiled hall, not too fast, not too slow. "*¿Querida?*" He turned on the living room light as he passed. He continued down the hall, past the dining room, the guest room, the study, the kitchen. He reached the dark doorway to the bedroom. "Maria Chavez?"

He turned on the bedroom light, low. She was asleep, her face peaceful, her dark hair scattered across the pillow. She lay on her side, her legs drawn up under the covers.

Men che dramma
Di sangue m'e rimaso, che no tremi;
Conosco i segni dell' antica fiamma.

MacDonald looked down at her, comparing her features one by one with those he had fixed in his memory. Even now, with those dark, expressive eyes closed, she was the most beautiful woman he had ever seen. What glories they had known! He renewed his spirit in the warmth of his remembrances, recalling moments with loving details.

C'est de quoy j'ay le plus de peur que la peur.

He sat down upon the edge of the bed and leaned over to kiss her upon the cheek and then upon her upthrust shoulder where the gown had slipped down. She did not waken. He shook her shoulder gently. "Maria!" She turned upon her back, straightening. She sighed, and her eyes came open, staring blankly. "It is Robby," MacDonald said, dropping unconsciously into a faint brogue.

Her eyes came alive and her lips smiled sleepily. "Robby. You're home."

"Yo te amo," he murmured, and kissed her. As he pulled himself away, he said, "I'll start dinner. Wake up and get dressed. I'll see you in half an hour. Or sooner."

"Sooner," she said.

He turned and went to the kitchen. There was romaine lettuce in the refrigerator, and as he rummaged further, some thin slices of veal. He prepared Caesar salad and veal scaloppine doing it all quickly, expertly. He liked to cook. The salad was ready, and the lemon juice, tarragon, white wine, and a minute later, the beef bouillon had been added to the browned veal when Maria appeared.

She stood in the doorway, slim, lithe, lovely, and sniffed the air. "I smell something delicious."

It was a joke. When Maria cooked, she cooked Mexican, something peppery that burned all the way into the stomach and lay there like a banked furnace. When MacDonald cooked, it was something exotic—French, perhaps, or Italian, or Chinese. But whoever cooked, the other had to appreciate it or take over all the cooking for a week.

MacDonald filled their wine glasses. *"A la trés-bonne, à la trés-belle,"* he said, *"qui fait ma joie et ma santé."*

"To the Project," Maria said. "May there be a signal received tonight."

MacDonald shook his head. One should not mention what one desires too much. "Tonight there is only us."

Afterward there were only the two of them, as there had been now for twenty years. And she was as alive and as urgent, as filled with love and laughter, as when they first had been together.

At last the urgency was replaced by a vast ease and contentment in which for a time the thought of the Project faded into something remote which one day he would return to and finish. "Maria," he said.

"Robby?"

"Yo te amo, corazón."

"Yo te amo, Robby."

Gradually then, as he waited beside her for her breathing to slow, the Project returned. When he thought she was asleep, he got up and began to dress in the dark.

"Robby?" Her voice was awake and frightened.

"¿Querida?"

"You are going again?"

"I didn't want to wake you."

"Do you have to go?"

"It's my job."

"Just this once. Stay with me tonight."

He turned on the light. In the dimness he could see that her face was concerned but not hysterical. *"Rast ich, so rost ich.* Besides, I would feel ashamed."

"I understand. Go, then. Come home soon."

He put out two pills on the little shelf in the bathroom and put the others away again.

The headquarters building was busiest at night when the radio noise of the sun was least and listening to the stars was best. Girls bustled down the halls with coffee pots, and men stood near the water fountain, talking earnestly.

MacDonald went into the control room. Adams was at the control panel; Montaleone was the technician. Adams looked up, pointed to his earphones with a gesture of futility, and shrugged. MacDonald nodded at him, nodded at Montaleone, and glanced at the graph. It looked random to him.

Adams leaned past him to point out a couple of peaks. "These might be something." He had removed the earphones.

"Odds," MacDonald said.

"Suppose you're right. The computer hasn't sounded any alarms."

"After a few years of looking at these things, you get the feel of them. You begin to think like a computer."

"Or you get oppressed by failure."

"There's that."

The room was shiny and efficient, glass and metal and plastic, all smooth and sterile; and it smelled like electricity. MacDonald knew that electricity had no smell, but that was the way he thought of it. Perhaps it was the ozone that smelled or warm insulation or oil. Whatever it was, it wasn't worth the time to find out, and MacDonald didn't really want to know. He would rather think of it as the smell of electricity. Perhaps that was why he was a failure as a scientist. "A scientist is a man who wants to know why," his teachers always had told him.

MacDonald leaned over the control panel and flicked a switch. A thin, hissing noise filled the room. It was something like air escaping from an inner tube—a susurration of surreptitious sibilants from subterranean sessions of seething serpents.

He turned a knob and the sound became what someone—Tennyson?—had called "the murmuring of innumerable bees." Again, and it became Matthew Arnold's

…melancholy, long withdrawing roar
Retreating, to the breath
Of the night wind, down the vast edges drear
And naked shingles of the world.

He turned the knob once more, and the sound was a babble of distant voices, some shouting, some screaming, some conversing calmly, some whispering—all of them trying beyond desperation to communicate, and everything just below the level of intelligibility. If he closed his eyes, MacDonald could almost see their faces, pressed against a distant screen, distorted with the awful effort to make themselves heard and understood.

But they all insisted on speaking at once. MacDonald wanted to shout at them. "Silence, everybody! All but you—there, with the purple antenna. One at a time and we'll listen to all of you if it takes a hundred years or a hundred lifetimes."

"Sometimes," Adams said, "I think it was a mistake to put in the speaker system. You begin to anthropomorphize. After a while you begin to hear things. Sometimes you even get messages. I don't listen to the voices any more. I used to wake up in the night with someone whispering to me. I was just on the verge of getting the message that would solve everything, and I would wake up." He flicked off the switch.

"Maybe somebody will get the message," MacDonald said. "That's what the audio frequency translation is intended to do. To keep the attention focused. It can mesmerize and it can torment, but these are the conditions out of which spring inspiration."

"Also madness," Adams said. "You've got to be able to continue."

"Yes." MacDonald picked up the earphones Adams had put down and held one of them to his ear.

"Tico-tico, tico-tico," it sang. "They're listening in Puerto Rico…. Listening for words that never come. Tico-tico, tico-tico. They're listening in Puerto Rico. Can it be the stars are stricken dumb?"

MacDonald put the earphones down and smiled. "Maybe there's inspiration in that, too."

"At least it takes my mind off the futility."

"Maybe off the job, too? Do you really want to find anyone out there?"

"Why else would I be here? But there are times when I wonder if we would be better off not knowing."

"We all think that sometimes," MacDonald said.

In his office he attacked the stack of papers and letters again. When he had worked his way to the bottom, he sighed and got up, stretching. He wondered if he would feel better, less frustrated, less uncertain, if he were working on the Problem instead of just working so somebody else could work on the Problem. But somebody had to do it. Somebody had to keep the Project going, personnel coming in, funds in the bank, bills paid, feathers smoothed.

Maybe it was more important that he do all the dirty little work in the office. Of course it was routine. Of course Lily could do it as well as he. But it was important that he do it, that there be somebody in charge who believed in the Project—or who never let his doubts be known.

Like the Little Ear, he was a symbol—and it is by symbols men live—or refuse to let their despair overwhelm them.

The janitor was waiting for him in the outer office.

"Can I see you, Mr. MacDonald?" the janitor said.

"Of course, Joe," MacDonald said, locking the door of his office carefully behind him. "What is it?"

"It's my teeth, sir." The old man got to his feet and with a deft movement of his tongue and mouth dropped his teeth into his hand.

MacDonald stared at them with a twinge of revulsion. There was nothing wrong with them. They were a carefully constructed pair of false teeth, but they looked too real. MacDonald always had shuddered away from those things which seemed to be what they were not, as if there were some treachery in them.

"They talk to me, Mr. MacDonald," the janitor mumbled, staring at the teeth in his hand with what seemed like suspicion. "In the glass beside my bed at night, they whisper to me. About things far off, like. Messages like."

MacDonald stared at the janitor. It was a strange word for the old man to use, and hard to say without teeth. Still, the word had been "messages." But why should it be strange? He could have picked it up around the offices or the laboratories. It would be odd, indeed, if he had not picked up something about what was going on. Of course: messages.

"I've heard of that sort of thing happening," MacDonald said. "False teeth accidentally constructed into a kind of crystal set, that pick up radio waves. Particularly near a powerful station. And we have a lot of stray frequencies floating around, what with the antennas and all. Tell you what, Joe. We'll make an appointment with the Project dentist to fix your teeth so that they don't bother you. Any small alteration should do it."

"Thank you, Mr. MacDonald," the old man said. He fitted his teeth back into his mouth. "You're a great man, Mr. MacDonald."

MacDonald drove the ten dark miles to the hacienda with a vague feeling of unease, as if he had done something during the day or left something undone that should have been otherwise.

But the house was dark when he drove up in front, not empty-dark as it had seemed to him a few hours before, but friendly-dark. Maria was asleep, breathing peacefully.

The house was brilliant with lighted windows that cast long fingers into the night, probing the dark hills, and the sound of many voices stirred echoes until the countryside itself seemed alive.

"Come in, Lily," MacDonald said at the door, and was reminded of a winter scene when a Lily had met the gentlemen at the door and helped them off with their overcoats. But that was another Lily and another occasion and another place and somebody else's imagination. "I'm glad you decided to come." He had a can of beer in his hand, and he waved it in the general direction of the major center of noisemaking. "There's beer in the living room and something more potent in the study—190 proof grain alcohol, to be precise. Be careful with that. It will sneak up on you. But—*nunc est bibendum!*"

"Where's Mrs. MacDonald?" Lily asked.

"Back there, somewhere." MacDonald waved again. "The men, and a few brave women, are in the study. The women, and a few brave men, are in the living room. The kitchen is common territory. Take your choice."

"I really shouldn't have come," Lily said. "I offered to spell Mr. Saunders in the control room, but he said I hadn't been checked out. It isn't as if the computer couldn't handle it all alone, and I know enough to call somebody if anything unexpected should happen."

"Shall I tell you something, Lily?" MacDonald said. "The computer could do it alone. And you and the computer could do it better than any of us, including me. But if the men ever feel that they are unnecessary, they would feel more useless than ever. They would give up. And they mustn't do that."

"Oh, Mac!" Lily said.

"They mustn't do that. Because one of them is going to come up with the inspiration that solves it all. Not me. One of them. We'll send somebody to relieve Charley before the evening is over."

Wer immer strebens sich bemüht,
Den können wir erlösen.

Lily sighed. "Okay, boss."

"And enjoy yourself!"

"Okay, boss, okay."

"Find a man, Lily," MacDonald muttered. And then he, too, turned toward the living room, for Lily had been the last who might come.

He listened for a moment at the doorway, sipping slowly from the warming can.

"—work more on gamma rays—"

"Who's got the money to build a generator? Since nobody's built one yet, we don't even know what it might cost."

"—gamma-ray sources should be a million times more rare than radio sources at twenty-one centimeters—"

"That's what Cocconi said nearly fifty years ago. The same arguments. Always the same arguments."

"If they're right, they're right."

"But the hydrogen-emission line is so uniquely logical. As Morrison said to Cocconi—and Cocconi, if you remember, agreed—it represents a logical, prearranged rendezvous point. 'A unique, objective standard of frequency, which must be known to every observer of the universe,' was the way they put it."

"—but the noise level—"

MacDonald smiled and moved on to the kitchen for a cold can of beer.

"—Bracewell's 'automated messengers'?" a voice asked querulously.

"What about them?"

"Why aren't we looking for them?"

"The point of Bracewell's messengers is that they make themselves known to us!"

"Maybe there's something wrong with ours. After a few million years in orbit—"

"—laser beams make more sense."

"And get lost in all that star shine?"

"As Schwartz and Townes pointed out, all you have to do is select a wavelength of light that is absorbed by stellar atmospheres. Put a narrow laser beam in the center of one of the calcium absorption lines—"

In the study they were talking about quantum noise.

"Quantum noise favors low frequencies."

"But the noise itself sets a lower limit on those frequencies."

"Drake calculated the most favorable frequencies, considering the noise level, lie between 3.2 and 8.1 centimeters."

"Drake! Drake! What did he know? We've had nearly fifty years experience on him. Fifty years of technological advance. Fifty years ago we could send radio messages one thousand light-years and laser signals ten light-years. Today those figures are ten thousand and five hundred at least."

"What if nobody's there?" Adams said gloomily.

Ich bin der Geist der stets vernient.

"Short-pulse it, like Oliver suggested. One hundred million billion watts in a ten billionth of a second would smear across the entire radio spectrum. Here, Mac, fill this, will you?"

And MacDonald wandered away through the clustering guests toward the bar.

"And I told Charley," said a woman to two other women in the corner, "if I had a dime for every dirty diaper I've changed, I sure wouldn't be sitting here in Puerto Rico—"

"—neutrinos," said somebody.

"Nuts," said somebody else, as MacDonald poured grain alcohol carefully into the glass and filled it with orange juice, "the only really logical medium is Q waves."

"I know—the waves we haven't discovered yet but are going to discover about ten years from now. Only here it is nearly fifty years after Morrison suggested it, and we still haven't discovered them."

MacDonald wended his way back across the room.

"It's the night work that gets me," said someone's wife. "The kids up all day, and then he wants me there to greet him when he gets home at dawn. Brother!"

"Or what if everybody's listening?" Adams said gloomily. "Maybe everybody's sitting there, listening, just the way we are, because it's so much cheaper than sending."

"Here you are," MacDonald said.

"But don't you suppose somebody would have thought of that by this time and begun to send?"

"Double-think it all the way through and figure what just occurred to you would have occurred to everybody else, so you might as well listen. Think about it—everybody sitting around, listening. If there is anybody. Either way it makes the skin creep."

"All right, then, we ought to send something."

"What would you send?"

"I'd have to think about it. Prime numbers, maybe."

"Think some more. What if a civilization weren't mathematical?"

"Idiot! How would they build an antenna?"

"Maybe they'd rule-of-thumb it, like a ham. Or maybe they have built-in antennae."

"And maybe you have built-in antennae and don't know it."

MacDonald's can of beer was empty. He wandered back toward the kitchen again.

"—insist on equal time with the Big Ear. Even if nobody's sending we could pick up the normal electronic commerce of a civilization tens of light-years away. The problem would be deciphering, not hearing."

"They're picking it up now, when they're studying the relatively close systems. Ask for a tape and work out your program."

"All right, I will. Just give me a chance to work up a request—"

MacDonald found himself beside Maria. He put his arm around her waist and pulled her close. "All right?" he said.

"All right."

Her face was tired, though, MacDonald thought. He dreaded the notion that she might be growing older, that she was entering middle age. He could face it for himself.

He could feel the years piling up inside his bones. He still thought of himself, inside, as twenty, but he knew that he was forty-seven, and mostly he was glad that he had found happiness and love and peace and serenity. He even was willing to pay the price in youthful exuberance and belief in his personal immortality. But not Maria!

Nel mezzo del cammin di nostra vita,
Mi ritrovai per una selva oscura,
Ché la diritta via era smarrita.

"Sure?"

She nodded.

He leaned close to her ear. "I wish it was just the two of us, as usual."

"I, too."

"I'm going to leave in a little while—"

"Must you?"

"I must relieve Saunders. He's on duty. Give him an opportunity to celebrate a little with the others."

"Can't you send somebody else?"

"Who?" MacDonald gestured with good-humored futility at all the clusters of people held together by bonds of ordered sounds shared consecutively.

"It's a good party. No one will miss me."

"I will."

"Of course, *querida*."

"You are their mother, father, priest, all in one," Maria said. "You worry about them too much."

"I must keep them together. What else am I good for?"

"For much more."

MacDonald hugged her with one arm.

"Look at Mac and Maria, will you?" said someone who was having trouble with his consonants. "What goddamned devotion!"

MacDonald smiled and suffered himself to be pounded on the back while he protected Maria in front of him. "I'll see you later," he said.

As he passed the living room someone was saying, "Like Edie said, we ought to look at the long-chain molecules in carbonaceous chondrites. No telling how far they've traveled—or been sent—or what messages might be coded in the molecules."

He closed the front door behind him, and the noise dropped to a roar and then a mutter. He stopped for a moment at the door of the car and looked up at the sky.

E quindi uscimmo a riveder le stelle.

The noise from the hacienda reminded him of something—the speakers in the control room. All those voices talking, talking, talking, and from here he could not understand a thing.

Somewhere there was an idea if he could only concentrate on it hard enough. But he had drunk one beer too many—or perhaps one too few.

After the long hours of listening to the voices, MacDonald always felt a little crazy, but tonight it was worse than usual. Perhaps it was all the conversation before, or the beers, or something else—some deeper concern that would not surface.

But then the listeners had to be crazy to begin with—to get committed to a project that might go for centuries without results.

Tico-tico, tico-tico…

Even if they could pick up a message, they still would likely be dead and gone before any exchange could take place even with the nearest likely star. What kind of mad dedication could sustain such perseverance?

They're listening in Puerto Rico.

Religion could. At least once it did, during the era of cathedral building in Europe, the cathedrals that took centuries to build.

"What are you doing, fellow?"

"I'm working for ten francs a day."

"And what are you doing?"

"I'm laying stone."

"And you—what are you doing?"

"I am building a cathedral."

They were building cathedrals, most of them. Most of them had that religious mania about their mission that would sustain them through a lifetime of labors in which no progress could be seen.

Listening for words that never come…

The mere layers of stone and those who worked for pay alone eliminated themselves in time and left only those who kept alive in themselves the concept, the dream.

But they had to be a little mad to begin with.

Can it be the stars are stricken dumb?

Tonight he had heard the voices nearly all night long. They kept trying to tell him something, something urgent, something he should do, but he could not quite make out the words. There was only the babble of distant voices, urgent and unintelligible.

Tico-tico, tico-tic…

He had wanted to shout "Shut up!" to the universe. "One at a time!" "You first!" But of course there was no way to do that. Or had he tried? Had he shouted?

They're listening with ears this big!

Had he dozed at the console with the voices mumbling in his ears, or had he only thought he dozed? Or had he only dreamed he waked? Or dreamed he dreamed?

Listening for thoughts just like their own.

There was madness to it all, but perhaps it was a divine madness, a creative madness. And is not that madness that which sustains man in his terrible self-knowledge, the driving madness which demands reason of a casual universe, the awful aloneness which seeks among the stars for companionship?

Can it be that we are all alone?

The ringing of the telephone half penetrated through the mists of mesmerization. He picked up the handset, half expecting it would be the universe calling, perhaps with a clipped British accent, "Hello there, Man. Hello. Hello. I say, we seem to have a bad connection, what? Just wanted you to know that we're here. Are you there? Are you listening? Message on the way. May not get there for a couple of centuries. Do be around to answer, will you? That's a good being. Righto...."

Only it wasn't. It was the familiar American voice of Charley Saunders saying, "Mac, there's been an accident. Olsen is on his way to relieve you, but I think you'd better leave now. It's Maria."

Leave it. Leave it all. What does it matter? But leave the controls on automatic; the computer can take care of it all. Maria! Get in the car. Start it. Don't fumble! That's it. Go. Go. Car passing. Must be Olsen. No matter.

What kind of accident? Why didn't I ask? What does it matter what kind of accident? Maria. Nothing could have happened. Nothing serious. Not with all those people around. *Nil desperandum.* And yet—why did Charley call if it was not serious? Must be serious. I must be prepared for something bad, something that will shake the world, that will tear my insides.

I must not break up in front of them. Why not? Why must I appear infallible? Why must I always be cheerful, imperturbable, my faith unshaken? Why me? If there is something bad, if something impossibly bad has happened to Maria, what will matter? Ever? Why didn't I ask Charley what it was? Why? The bad can wait; it will get no worse for being unknown.

What does the universe care for my agony? I am nothing. My feelings are nothing to anyone but me. My only possible meaning to the universe is the Project. Only this slim potential links me with eternity. My love and my agony are me, but the significance of my life or death are the Project.

hic.sitvs.est.phaethon.cvrrvs.avriga.paterni qvem.si.non.tenvit.magnis.tamen.
excidit.avsis

By the time he reached the hacienda, MacDonald was breathing evenly. His emotions were under control. Dawn had grayed the eastern sky. It was a customary hour for Project personnel to be returning home.

Saunders met him at the door. "Dr. Lessenden is here. He's with Maria."

The odor of stale smoke and the memory of babble still lingered in the air, but someone had been busy. The party remains had been cleaned up. No doubt they all had pitched in. They were good people.

"Betty found her in the bathroom off your bedroom. She wouldn't have been there except the others were occupied. I blame myself. I shouldn't have let you relieve me. Maybe if you had been here— But I knew you wanted it that way."

"No one's to blame. She was alone a great deal," MacDonald said. "What happened?"

"Didn't I tell you? Her wrists. Slashed with a razor. Both of them. Betty found her in the bathtub. Like pink lemonade, she said."

Percé jusques au fond du coeur.
D'une atteinte imprévue aussi bien que mortelle.

A fist tightened inside MacDonald's gut and then slowly relaxed. Yes, it had been that. He had known it, hadn't he? He had known it would happen ever since the sleeping pills, even though he had kept telling himself, as she had told him, that the overdose had been an accident.

Or had he known? He knew only that Saunders' news had been no surprise.

Then they were at the bedroom door, and Maria was lying under a blanket on the bed, scarcely making it mound over her body, and her arms were on top of the blankets, palms up, bandages like white paint across the olive perfection of her arms, now, MacDonald reminded himself, no longer perfection but marred with ugly red lips that spoke to him of hidden misery and untold sorrow and a life that was a lie....

Dr. Lessenden looked up, sweat trickling down from his hairline. "The bleeding is stopped, but she's lost a good deal of blood. I've got to take her to the hospital for a transfusion. The ambulance should be here any minute." MacDonald looked at Maria's face. It was paler than he had ever seen it. It looked almost waxen, as if it were already arranged for all time on a satin pillow. "Her chances are fifty-fifty," Lessenden said in answer to his unspoken question.

And then the attendants brushed their way past him with their litter.

"Betty found this on her dressing table," Saunders said. He handed MacDonald a slip of paper folded once.

MacDonald unfolded it: *Je m'en vay chercher un grand Peut-être.*

Everyone was surprised to see MacDonald at the office. They did not say anything, and he did not volunteer the information that he could not bear to sit at home, among the remembrances, and wait for word to come. But they asked him about Maria, and he said, "Dr. Lessenden is hopeful. She's still unconscious. Apparently will be for some time. The doctor said I might as well wait here as at the hospital. I think I made them nervous. They're hopeful. Maria's still unconscious...."

O lente, lente currite, noctis equi!
The stars move still, time runs, the clock will strike...

Finally MacDonald was alone. He pulled out paper and pencil and worked for a long time on the statement, and then he balled it up and threw it into the wastebasket, scribbled a single sentence on another sheet of paper, and called Lily.

"Send this!"

She glanced at it. "No, Mac."

"Send it!"

"But—"

"It's not an impulse. I've thought it over carefully. Send it."

Slowly she left, holding the piece of paper gingerly in her fingertips. MacDonald pushed the papers around on his desk, waiting for the telephone to ring. But without knocking, unannounced, Saunders came through the door first.

"You can't do this, Mac," Saunders said.

MacDonald sighed. "Lily told you. I would fire that girl if she weren't so loyal."

"Of course she told me. This isn't just you. It affects the whole Project."

"That's what I'm thinking about."

"I think I know what you're going through, Mac—" Saunders stopped. "No, of course I don't know what you're going through. It must be hell. But don't desert us. Think of the Project!"

"That's what I'm thinking about. I'm a failure, Charley. Everything I touch—ashes."

"You're the best of us."

"A poor linguist? An indifferent engineer? I have no qualifications for this job, Charley. You need someone with ideas to head the Project, someone dynamic, someone who can lead, someone with—charisma."

A few minutes later he went over it all again with Olsen. When he came to the qualifications part, all Olsen could say was, "You give a good party, Mac."

It was Adams, the skeptic, who affected him most. "Mac, you're what I believe in instead of God."

Sonnenborn said, "You are the Project. If you go, it all falls apart. It's over."

"It seems like it, always, but it never happens to those things that have life in them. The Project was here before I came. It will be here after I leave. It must be longer lived than any of us, because we are for the years and it is for the centuries."

After Sonnenborn, MacDonald told Lily wearily, "No more, Lily."

None of them had had the courage to mention Maria, but MacDonald considered that failure, too. She had tried to communicate with him a month ago when she took the pills, and he had been unable to understand. How could he riddle the stars when he couldn't even understand those closest to him?

Now he had to pay.

Meine Ruh' ist hin,
Meine Herz ist schwer.

What would Maria want? He knew what she wanted, but if she lived, he could not let her pay that price. Too long she had been there when he wanted her, waiting like a doll put away on a shelf for him to return and take her down, so that he could have the strength to continue.

And somehow the agony had built up inside her, the dreadful progress of the years, most dread of all to a beautiful woman growing old, alone, too much alone. He had been selfish. He had kept her to himself. He had not wanted children to mar the perfection of their being together.

Perfection for him; less than that for her.

Perhaps it was not too late for them if she lived. And if she died—he would not have the heart to go on with work to which, he knew now, he could contribute nothing.

Que acredito su ventura,
Morir querdo y vivir loco.

And finally the call came. "She's going to be all right, Mac," Lessenden said. And after a moment, "Mac, I said—"

"I heard."

"She wants to see you."

"I'll be there."

"She said to give you a message. 'Tell Robby I've been a little crazy in the head. I'll be better now. That "great perhaps" looks too certain from here. And tell him not to be crazy in the head too.'"

MacDonald put down the telephone and walked through the doorway and through the outer office, a feeling in his chest as if it were going to burst. "She's going to be all right," he threw over his shoulder at Lily.

"Oh, Mac—"

In the hall, Joe the janitor stopped him. "Mr. MacDonald—"

MacDonald stopped. "Been to the dentist yet, Joe?"

"No, sir, not yet, but it's not—"

"Don't go. I'd like to put a tape recorder beside your bed for a while, Joe. Who knows?"

"Thank you, sir. But it's—They say you're leaving, Mr. MacDonald."

"Somebody else will do it."

"You don't understand. Don't go, Mr. MacDonald!"

"Why not, Joe?"

"You're the one who cares."

MacDonald had been about to move on, but that stopped him.

Ful wys is he that can himselven knowe!

He turned and went back to the office. "Have you got that sheet of paper, Lily?"

"Yes, sir."

"Have you sent it?"

"No, sir."

"Bad girl. Give it to me."

He read the sentence on the paper once more: *I have great confidence in the goals and ultimate success of the Project, but for personal reasons I must submit my resignation.*

He studied it for a moment.

Pigmaei gigantum humeris impositi plusquam ipsi gigantes vidant.

And he tore it up.

TRANSLATIONS

1. *Pues no es posible…*

The bow cannot always stand bent, nor can human frailty subsist without some lawful recreation.

Cervantes, Don Quixote

2. *Habe nun, ach! Philosophie,…*
Now I have studied philosophy,
Medicine and the law,
And, unfortunately, theology,
Wearily sweating, yet I stand now,
Poor fool, no wiser than I was before;
I am called Master, even Doctor,
And for these last ten years have drawn
My students, by the nose, up, down,
Crosswise and crooked. Now I see
That we can know nothing finally.

Goethe, Faust, opening lines

3. *Men che drama…*
Less than a drop
Of blood remains in me that does not tremble;
I recognize the signals of the ancient flame.
Dante, *The Divine Comedy,*
Purgatorio

4. *C'est de quoy j'ay le plus de peur que la peur.*
The thing of which I have most fear is fear.

Montaigne, Essays

5. *A la trés-bonne, à la très-belle, qui fait ma joie et ma santé.*
To the best, to the most beautiful, who is my joy and my well-being.

Baudelaire, Les Epaves

6. *Rast ich, so rost ich.*
When I rest, I rust.

German proverb

7. *Nunc est bibendum!*
Now's the time for drinking!

Horace, Odes, Book I

8. *Wer immer strebens sich bemüht,...*
Who strives always to the utmost,
Him can we save.

Goethe, Faust, Part I

9. *Ich bin der Geist der stets verneint.*
I am the spirit that always denies.

Goethe, Faust, Part I

10. *Nel mezzo del cammin di nostra vita...*
In the middle of the journey of our life
I came to myself in a dark wood,
Where the straight way was lost.

Dante, The Divine Comedy,
Inferno, opening lines

11. *E quindi uscimmo a riveder le stelle.*

And thence we issued out, again to see the stars.

Dante, The Divine Comedy,

Inferno

12. *Nil desperandum.*

There's no cause for despair.

Horace, Odes, Book I

13. *HIC * SITVS * EST * PHAETHON * CVRRVS * AVRIGA ***
PATERNI…

Here Phaethon lies: in Phoebus' car he fared,

And though he greatly failed, more greatly dared.

Ovid, Metamorphoses

14. *Percé jusques au fond du coeur…*

Pierced to the depth of my heart

By a blow unforeseen and mortal.

Corneille, Le Cid

15. *Je m'en vay chercher un grand Peut-être.*

I am going to seek a great Perhaps.

Rabelais on his deathbed

16. *O lente, lente currite, noctis equi!*

Oh, slowly, slowly run, horses of the night!

Marlowe, Dr. Faustus

(Faustus is quoting Ovid. He waits for Mephistopheles to appear to claim his soul at midnight. The next line: "The devil will come and Faustus must be damn'd.")

17. *Meine Ruh' ist hin...*
My peace is gone,
My heart is heavy.

Goethe, *Faust*, Part I

18. *Que acredito su ventura...*
For if he like a madman lived,
At least he like a wise one died.

Cervantes, *Don Quixote*
(Don Quixote's epitaph)

19. *Ful wys is he that can himselven knowe!*
Very wise is he that can know himself!

Chaucer, *The Canterbury Tales*, "The Monk's Tale"

20. *Pigmaei gigantum humeris impositi plusquam ipsi gigantes vidant.*
A dwarf standing on the shoulder of a giant may see further than the giant himself.

Didacus Stella, in
Lucan, *De Bello Civili*

THE EMPEROR OF MARS

ALLEN STEELE

Allen's novella *The Death of Captain Future* received the Hugo Award for Best Novella, won a Science Fiction Weekly Reader Appreciation Award, and received the Seiun Award for Best Foreign Short Story from Japan's National Science Fiction Convention. It was also nominated for a Nebula Award by the Science Fiction and Fantasy Writers of America. His novella *...Where Angels Fear to Tread* received the Hugo Award, the Locus Award, the Asimov's Readers Award, and the Science Fiction Chronicle Readers Award, and was also nominated for the Nebula, Theodore Sturgeon Memorial, and Seiun awards.

His novelette *The Good Rat* was nominated for a Hugo in 1996, and his novelette *Zwarte Piet's Tale* won an AnLab Award from Analog and was nominated for a Hugo in 1999. His novelette *Agape Among the Robots* was nominated for the Hugo in 2001. His novella *Stealing Alabama* received the Asimov's Readers Award and was nominated for a Hugo, and his novelette *The Days Between* was nominated for both the Hugo and the Nebula in the same year. His novella *Liberation Day* and novelette *The Garcia Narrows Bridge* both received Asimov's Readers Awards. Orbital Decay received the Locus Award for Best First Novel, and Clarke County, Space was nominated for the Philip K. Dick Award. He was First Runner-Up for the John W. Campbell Award, received the Donald A. Wollheim Award, and the Phoenix Award. In 2007, he received the Alumni Achievement Award from New England College.

In 2013, he received the Robert A. Heinlein Award, presented by the Robert A. Heinlein Society in recognition of his fiction promoting the exploration of space. The story below won the Hugo Award and also received the Asimov's Reader's Award. You can read his novel *Coyote* at http://amzn.to/1Ay2Crz.

Out here, there's a lot of ways to go crazy. Get cooped up in a passenger module not much larger than a trailer, and by the time you reach your destination you may have come to believe that the universe exists only within your own mind: it's called solipsism syndrome, and I've seen it happen a couple of times. Share that same module with five or six guys who don't get along very well, and after three months you'll be sleeping with a knife taped to your thigh. Pull double-shifts during that time, with little chance to relax, and you'll probably suffer from depression; couple this with vitamin deficiency due to a lousy diet, and you're a candidate for chronic fatigue syndrome.

Folks who've never left Earth often think that Titan Plague is the main reason people go mad in space. They're wrong. Titan Plague may rot your brain and turn you into a homicidal maniac, but instances of it are rare, and there's a dozen other ways to go bonzo that are much more subtle. I've seen guys adopt imaginary friends with whom they have long and meaningless conversations, compulsively clean their hardsuits regardless of whether or not they've recently worn them, or go for a routine spacewalk and have to be begged to come back into the airlock. Some people just aren't cut out for life away from Earth, but there's no way to predict who's going to going to lose their mind.

When something like that happens, I have a set of standard procedures: ask the doctor to prescribe antidepressants, keep an eye on them to make sure they don't do anything that might put themselves or others at risk, relieve them of duty if I can, and see what I can do about getting them back home as soon as possible. Sometimes I don't have to do any of this. A guy goes crazy for a little while, and then he gradually works out whatever it was that got in his head; the next time I see him, he's in the commissary, eating Cheerios like nothing ever happened. Most of the time, though, a mental breakdown is a serious matter. I think I've shipped back about one out of every twenty people because of one issue or another.

But one time, I saw someone go mad, and it was the best thing that could have happened to him. That was Jeff Halbert. Let me tell about him…

Back in '48, I was General Manager of Arsia Station, the first and largest of the Mars colonies. This was a year before the formation of the Pax Astra, about five years before the colonies declared independence. So the six major Martian settlements were still under control of one Earth-based corporation or another, with Arsia Station owned and operated by ConSpace. We had about a hundred people living there by then, the majority short-timers on short-term contracts; only a dozen or so, like myself, were permanent residents who left Earth for good.

Jeff wasn't one of them. Like most people, he'd come to Mars to make a lot of money in a relatively short amount of time. Six months from Earth to Mars aboard a cycleship, two years on the planet, then six more months back to Earth aboard the next ship to make the crossing during the biannual launch window. In three years, a young buck like him could earn enough dough to buy a house, start a business, invest in the stock market, or maybe just loaf for a good long while. In previous times, he would've worked on offshore oil rigs, joined the merchant marine, or built powersats; by mid-century, this kind of high-risk, high-paying work was on Mars, and there was no shortage of guys willing and ready to do it.

Jeff Halbert was what we called a "Mars monkey." We had about a lot of people like him at Arsia Station, and they took care of the dirty jobs that the scientists, engineers, and other specialists could not or would not handle themselves. One day they might be operating a bulldozer or a crane at a habitat construction site. The next day, they'd be unloading freight from a cargo lander that had just touched down. The day after that, they'd be cleaning out the air vents or repairing a solar array or unplugging a toilet. It wasn't romantic or particularly interesting work, but it was the sort of stuff that needed to be done in order to keep the base going, and because of that, kids like Jeff were invaluable.

And Jeff was definitely a kid. In his early twenties, wiry and almost too tall to wear a hardsuit, he looked like he'd started shaving only last week. Before he dropped out of school to get a job with ConSpace, I don't think he'd travelled more than a few hundred miles from the small town in New Hampshire where he'd grown up. I didn't know him well, but I knew his type: restless, looking for adventure, hoping to score a small pile of loot so that he could do something else with the rest of his life besides hang out in a pool hall. He probably hadn't even thought much about Mars before he spotted a ConSpace recruitment ad on some web site; he had two years of college, though, and met all the fitness requirements, and that was enough to get him into the training program and, eventually, a berth aboard a cycleship.

Before Jeff left Earth, he filled out and signed all the usual company paperwork. Among them was Form 36-B: Family Emergency Notification Consent. ConSpace required everyone to state whether or not they wanted to be informed of a major illness or death of a family member back home. This was something a lot of people didn't take into consideration before they went to Mars, but nonetheless it was an issue that had to be addressed. If you found out, for instance, that your father was about to die, there wasn't much you could do about it, because you'd be at least 35 million miles from home. The best you could do would be to send a brief message that someone might be able to read to him before he passed away; you wouldn't be able to attend the funeral, and it would be many months, even a year or two, before you could lay roses on his grave.

Most people signed Form 36-D on the grounds that they'd rather know about something like this than be kept in the dark until they returned home. Jeff did, too, but I'd later learn that he hadn't read it first. For him, it had been just one more piece of paper that needed to be signed before he boarded the shuttle, not to be taken any more seriously than the catastrophic accident disclaimer or the form attesting that he didn't have any sort of venereal disease.

He probably wished he hadn't signed that damn form. But he did, and it cost him his sanity.

Jeff had been on Mars for only about seven months when a message was relayed from ConSpace's human resources office. I knew about it because a copy was cc'd to me. The minute I read it, I dropped what I was doing to head straight for Hab 2's second level, which was where the monkey house—that is, the dormitory for unspecialized laborers like Jeff—was located. I didn't have to ask which bunk was his; the moment I walked in, I spotted a knot of people standing around a young guy slumped on this bunk, staring in disbelief at the fax in his hands.

Until then, I didn't know, nor did anyone one at Arsia Station, that Jeff had a fiancé back home, a nice girl named Karen whom he'd met in high school and who had agreed to marry him about the same time he'd sent his application to ConSpace. Once he got the job, they decided to postpone the wedding until he returned, even if it meant having to put their plans on hold for three years. One of the reasons why Jeff decided to get a job on Mars, in fact, was to provide a nest egg for him and Karen. And they'd need it, too; about three weeks before Jeff took off, Karen informed him that she was pregnant and that he'd have a child waiting for him when he got home.

He'd kept this a secret; mainly because he knew that the company would annul his contract if it learned that he had a baby on the way. Both Jeff's family and Karen's knew all about the baby, though, and they decided to pretend that

Jeff was still on Earth, just away on a long business trip. Until he returned, they'd take care of Karen.

About three months before the baby was due, the two families decided to host a baby shower. The party was to be held at the home of one of Jeff's uncles—apparently he was the only relative with a house big enough for such a get-together—and Karen was on her way there, in a car driven by Jeff's parents, when tragedy struck. Some habitual drunk who'd learned how to disable his car's high-alcohol lockout, and therefore was on the road when he shouldn't have been, plowed straight into them. The drunk walked away with no more than a sprained neck, but his victims were nowhere nearly so lucky. Karen, her unborn child, Jeff's mother and father—all died before they reached the hospital.

There's not a lot you can say to someone who's just lost his family that's going to mean very much. *I'm sorry* barely scratches the surface. *I understand what you're going through* is ridiculous; *I know how you feel* is insulting. And *is there anything I can do to help?* is pointless unless you have a time machine; if I did, I would have lent it to Jeff, so that he could travel back twenty-four hours to call his folks and beg them to put off picking up Karen by only fifteen or twenty minutes. But everyone said these things anyway, because there wasn't much else that *could* be said, and I relieved Jeff of further duties until he felt like he was ready to go to work again, because there was little else I could do for him. The next cycleship wasn't due to reach Mars for another seventeen months; by the time he got home, his parents and Karen would be dead for nearly two years.

To Jeff's credit, he was back on the job within a few days. Maybe he knew that there was nothing he could do except work, or maybe he just got tired of staring at the walls. In any case, one morning he put on his suit, cycled through the airlock, and went outside to help the rest of the monkeys dig a pit for the new septic tank. But he wasn't the same easy-going kid we'd known before; no wisecracks, no goofing off, not even any gripes about the hours it took to make that damn hole and how he'd better get overtime for this. He was like a robot out there, silently digging at the sandy red ground with a shovel, until the pit was finally finished, at which point he dropped his tools and, without a word, returned to the hab, where he climbed out of his suit and went to the mess hall for some chow.

A couple of weeks went by, and there was no change. Jeff said little to anyone. He ate, worked, slept, and that was about it. When you looked into his eyes, all you saw was a distant stare. If he'd broken down in hysterics, I would've understood, but there wasn't any of that. It was as if he'd shut down his emotions, suppressing whatever he was feeling inside.

The station had a pretty good hospital by then, large enough to serve all the colonies, and Arsia General's senior psychologist had begun meeting with Jeff on a regular basis. Three days after Jeff went back to work, Karl Rosenfeld dropped by my office. His report was grim: Jeff Halbert was suffering from severe depression, to the point that he was barely responding to medication. Although he hadn't spoken of suicide, Dr. Rosenfeld had little doubt that the notion had occurred to him. And I knew that, if Jeff did decide to kill himself, all he'd have to do was wait until the next time he went outside, then shut down his suit's air supply and crack open the helmet faceplate. One deep breath, and the Martian atmosphere would do the rest; he'd be dead before anyone could reach him.

"You want my advice?" Karl asked, sitting on the other side of my desk with a glass of moonshine in hand. "Find something that'll get his mind off what happened."

"You think that hasn't occurred to me? Believe me, I've tried…"

"Yeah, I know. He told me. But extra work shifts aren't helping, and neither are vids or games." He was quiet for a moment, "If I thought sex would help," he added, "I'd ask a girl I know to haul him off to bed, but that would just make matters worse. His fiancé was the only woman he ever loved, and it'll probably be a long time before he sleeps with anyone again."

"So what do you want me to do?" I gave a helpless shrug. "C'mon, give me a clue here. I want to help the kid, but I'm out of ideas."

"Well… I looked at the duty roster, and saw that you've scheduled a survey mission for next week. Something up north, I believe."

"Uh-huh. I'm sending a team up there to see if they can locate a new water supply. Oh, and one of the engineers wants to make a side-trip to look at an old NASA probe."

"So put Jeff on the mission." Karl smiled. "They're going to need a monkey or two anyway. Maybe travel will do him some good."

His suggestion was as good as any, so I pulled up the survey assignment list, deleted the name of one monkey, and inserted Jeff Halbert's instead. I figured it couldn't hurt, and I was right. And also wrong.

So Jeff was put on a two-week sortie that travelled above the 60th parallel to the Vastitas Borealis, the subarctic region that surrounds the Martian north pole. The purpose of the mission was to locate a site for a new well. Although most of Arsia Station's water came from atmospheric condensers and our greenhouses, we needed more than they could supply, which was why we drilled artesian wells in the permafrost beneath the northern tundra and pump groundwater to surface tanks, which in turn would be picked up on a monthly basis. Every few years or so, one of those wells would run dry; when that happened, we'd have to send a team up there to dig a new one.

Two airships made the trip, the *Sagan* and the *Collins*. Jeff Halbert was aboard the *Collins*, and according to its captain, who was also the mission leader, he did his job well. Over the course of ten days, the two dirigibles roamed the tundra, stopping every ten or fifteen miles so that crews could get out and conduct test drills that would bring up a sample of what lay beneath the rocky red soil. It wasn't hard work, really, and it gave Jeff a chance to see the northern regions. Yet he was quiet most of the time, rarely saying much to anyone; in fact, he seemed to be bored by the whole thing. The other people on the expedition were aware of what had recently happened to him, of course, and they attempted to draw him out of his shell, but after a while it became obvious that he just didn't want to talk, and so they finally gave up and left him alone.

Then, on the eleventh day of the mission, two days before the expedition was scheduled to return to Arsia, the *Collins* located the Phoenix lander.

This was a NASA probe that landed back in `08, the first to confirm the presence of subsurface ice on Mars. Unlike many of the other American and European probes that explored Mars before the first manned expeditions, Phoenix didn't have a rover; instead, it used a robotic arm to dig down into the regolith, scooping up samples that were analyzed by its onboard chemical lab. The probe was active for only a few months before its battery died during the long Martian winter, but it was one of the milestones leading to human colonization.

As they expected, the expedition members found Phoenix half-buried beneath wind-blown sand and dust, with only its upper platform and solar vanes still exposed. Nonetheless, the lander was intact, and although it was too big and heavy to be loaded aboard the airship, the crew removed its arm to be taken home and added to the base museum. And they found one more thing: the Mars library.

During the 1990s, while the various Mars missions were still in their planning stages, the Planetary Society had made a proposal to NASA: one of those probes should carry a DVD containing a cache of literature, visual images, and audio recordings pertaining to Mars. The ostensive purpose would be to furnish future colonists with a library for their entertainment, but the unspoken reason was to pay tribute to the generations of writers, artists, and filmmakers whose works had inspired the real-life exploration of Mars.

NASA went along with their proposal, so a custom-designed DVD, made of silica glass to ensure its long-term survival, was prepared for inclusion on a future mission. A panel selected 84 novels, short stories, articles, and speeches, with the authors ranging from 18th century fantasists like Swift and Voltaire to 20th century science fiction authors like Niven and Benford. A digital gallery of 60 visual images—including everything from paintings by Bonestell, Emshwiller, and Whelan to a lobby card from a Flash Gordon serial and a cover of a *Weird Science* comic book—was chosen as well. The final touch were four audio clips, the most notable of which were the infamous 1938 radio broadcast of *The War of the Worlds* and a discussion of the same between H.G. Wells and Orson Welles.

Now called "Visions of Mars," the disk was originally placed aboard NASA's Mars Polar Lander, but that probe was destroyed when its booster failed shortly after launch and it crashed in the Atlantic. So an identical copy was put on Phoenix, and this time it succeeded in getting to Mars. And so the disk had remained in the Vastitas Borealis for the past forty years, awaiting the day when a human hand would remove it from its place on Phoenix's upper fuselage.

And that hand happened to be Jeff Halbert's.

The funny thing is, no one on the expedition knew the disk was there. It had been forgotten by then, its existence buried deep within the old NASA documents I'd been sent from Earth, so I hadn't told anyone to retrieve it. And besides, most of the guys on the *Collins* were more interested in taking a look at an antique lander than the DVD that happened to be attached to it. So when Jeff found the disk and detached it from Phoenix, it wasn't like he'd made a major find. The attitude of almost everyone on the mission was *oh, yeah, that's kind of neat... take it home and see what's on it.*

Which was easier said than done. DVD drives had been obsolete for more than twenty years, and the nearest flea market where one might find an old computer that had one was... well, it wasn't on Mars. But Jeff looked around, and eventually he found a couple of dead comps stashed in a storage closet, salvage left over from the first expeditions. Neither were usable on their own, but with the aid of a service manual, he was able to swap out enough parts to get one of them up and running, and once it was operational, he removed the disk from its scratched case and gently slid it into the slot. Once he was sure that the data was intact and hadn't decayed, he downloaded everything into his personal pad. And then, at random, he selected one of the items on the menu—*The Martian Way* by Isaac Asimov—and began to read.

Why did Jeff go to so much trouble? Perhaps he wanted something to do with his free time besides mourn for the dead. Or maybe he wanted to show the others who'd been on the expedition that they shouldn't have ignored the disk. I don't know for sure, so I can't tell you. All I know is that the disk first interested him, then intrigued him, and finally obsessed him.

It took awhile for me to become aware of the change in Jeff. As much as I was concerned for him, he was one of my lesser problems. As general manager, on any given day I had a dozen or more different matters that needed my attention, whether it be making sure that the air recycling system was repaired before we suffocated to death or filling out another stack of forms sent from Huntsville. So Jeff wasn't always on my mind; when I didn't hear from Dr.

Rosenfeld for a while, I figured that the two of them had managed to work out his issues, and turned to other things.

Still, there were warning signs, stuff that I noticed but to which I didn't pay much attention. Like the day I was monitoring the radio crosstalk from the monkeys laying sewage pipes in the foundation of Hab Three, and happened to hear Jeff identify himself as Lieutenant Gulliver Jones. The monkeys sometimes screwed around like that on the com channels, and the foreman told Halbert to knock it off and use his proper call sign... but when Jeff answered him, his response was weird: "Aye, sir. I was simply ruminating on the rather peculiar environment in which we've found ourselves." He even faked a British accent to match the Victorian diction. That got a laugh from the other monkeys, but nonetheless I wondered who Gulliver Jones was and why Jeff was pretending to be him.

There was also the time Jeff was out on a dozer, clearing away the sand that had been deposited on the landing field during a dust storm a couple of days earlier. Another routine job to which I hadn't been paying much attention until the shift supervisor at the command center paged me: "Chief, there's something going on with Halbert. You might want to listen in."

So I tapped into the comlink, and there was Jeff: "Affirmative, MainCom. I just saw something move out there, about a half-klick north of the periphery."

"Roger that, Tiger Four-Oh," the supervisor said. "Can you describe again, please?"

A pause, then: "A big creature, abut ten feet tall, with eight legs. And there was a woman riding it... red-skinned, and—" an abrupt laugh "— stark naked, or just about."

Something tugged at my memory, but I couldn't quite put my finger on it. When the shift supervisor spoke again, his voice had a patronizing undertone. "Yeah... uh, right, Tiger Four-Oh. We just checked the LRC, though, and there's nothing on the scope except you."

"They're gone now. Went behind a boulder and vanished." Another laugh, almost gleeful. "But they were out there, I promise!"

"Affirmative, Four-Oh." A brief pause. "If you happen to see any more thoats, let us know, okay?"

That's when I remembered. What Jeff had described was a beast from Edgar Rice Burroughs' Mars novels. And the woman riding it? That could have only been Dejah Thoris. Almost everyone who came to Mars read Burroughs at one point or another, but this was the first time I'd ever heard of anyone claiming to have seen the Princess of Helium.

Obviously, Jeff had taken to playing practical jokes. I made a mental note to say something to him about that, but then forgot about it. As I said, on any given day I handled any number of different crises, and someone messing with his supervisor's head ranked low on my priority list.

But that wasn't the end of it. In fact, it was only the beginning. A couple of weeks later, I received a memo from the quartermaster: someone had tendered a request to be transferred to private quarters, even though that was above his pay-grade. At Arsia in those days, before we got all the habs built, individual rooms were at a premium and were generally reserved for management, senior researchers, married couples, company stooges, and so forth. In this case, though, the other guys in this particular person's dorm had signed a petition backing his request, and the quartermaster himself wrote that, for the sake of morale, he was recommending that this individual be assigned his own room.

I wasn't surprised to see that Jeff Halbert was the person making the request. By then, I'd noticed that his personality had undergone a distinct change. He'd let his hair grow long, eschewing the high-and-tight style preferred by people who spent a lot of time wearing a hardsuit helmet. He rarely shared a table with anyone else in the wardroom, and instead ate by himself, staring at his datapad the entire time. And he was now talking to himself on the comlink. No more reports of Martian princesses riding eight-legged animals, but rather a snatch of this ("The Martians seem to have calculated their descent with amazing subtlety...") or a bit of that ("The Martians gazed back up at them for a long, long silent time from the rippling water...") which most people wouldn't have recognized as being quotes from Wells or Bradbury.

So it was no wonder the other monkey house residents wanted to get rid of him. Before I signed the request, though, I paid Dr. Rosenfeld a visit. The station psychologist didn't have to ask why I was there; he asked me to shut the door, then let me know what he thought about Jeff.

"To tell the truth," he began, "I can't tell if he's getting better or worse."

"I can. Look, I'm no shrink, but if you ask me, he's getting worse."

Karl shook his head. "Not necessarily. Sure, his behavior is bizarre, but at least we no longer have to worry about suicide. In fact, he's one of the happiest people we have here. He rarely speaks about his loss anymore, and when I remind him that his wife and parents are dead, he shrugs it off as if this was something that happened a long time ago. In his own way, he's quite content with life."

"And you don't think that's strange?"

"Sure, I do… especially since he's admitted to me that he'd stopped taking the anti-depressants I prescribed to him. And that's the bad news. Perhaps he isn't depressed anymore, or at least by clinical standards… but he's becoming delusional, to the point of actually having hallucinations."

I stared at him. "You mean, the time he claimed he spotted Dejah Thoris… you're saying he actually *saw* that?"

"Yes, I believe so. And that gave me a clue as to what's going on in his mind." Karl picked up a penknife, absently played with it. "Ever since he found that disk, he's become utterly obsessed with it. So I asked him if he'd let me copy it from his pad, which he did, and after I asked him what he was reading, I checked it out for myself. And what I discovered was that, of all the novels and stories that are on the disk, the ones that attract him the most are also the ones that are least representative of reality. That is, the stuff that's about Mars, but not as we know it."

"Come again?" I shook my head. "I don't understand."

"How much science fiction have you read?"

"A little. Not much."

"Well, lucky for you, I've read quite a bit." He grinned. "In fact, you could say that's why I'm here. I got hooked on that stuff when I was a kid, and by the time I got out of college, I'd pretty much decided that I wanted to see Mars." He became serious again. "Okay, try to follow me. Although people have been writing about Mars since the 1700s, it wasn't until the first Russian and American probes got out here in the 1960s that anyone knew what this place is really like. That absence of knowledge gave writers and artists the liberty to fill in the gap with their imaginations… or at least until they learned better. Understand?"

"Sure." I shrugged. "Before the 1960s, you could have Martians. After that, you couldn't have Martians anymore."

"Umm… well, not exactly." Karl lifted his hand, teetered it back and forth. "One of the best stories on the disk is *A Rose For Ecclesiastes* by Roger Zelazny. It was written in 1963, and it has Martians in it. And some stories written before then were pretty close to getting it right. But for the most part, yes… the fictional view of Mars changed dramatically in the second half of the last century, and although it became more realistic, it also lost much of its romanticism."

Karl folded the penknife, dropped it on his desk. "Those aren't the stories Jeff's reading. Greg Bear's *A Martian Ricorso*, Arthur C. Clarke's *Transit of Earth*, John Varley's *In the Hall of the Martian Kings*… anything similar to the Mars we know, he ignores. Why? Because they remind him of where he is… and that's not where he wants to be."

"So…" I thought about it for a moment. "He's reading the older stuff instead?"

"Right." Karl nodded. "Stanley Weinbaum's *A Martian Odyssey*, Otis Albert Kline's *The Swordsman of Mars*, A.E. van Vogt's *The Enchanted Village*… the more unreal, the more he likes them. Because those stories aren't about not the drab, lifeless planet where he's stuck, but instead a planet of native Martians, lost cities, canal systems…"

"Okay, I get it."

"No, I don't think you do… because I'm not sure I do, either, except to say that Jeff appears to be leaving us. Every day, he's taking one more step into this other world… and I don't think he's coming back again."

I stared at him, not quite believing what I'd just heard. "Jeez, Karl… what am I going to do?"

"What *can* you do?" He leaned back in his chair. "Not much, really. Look, I'll be straight with you… this is beyond me. He needs the kind of treatment that I can't give him here. For that, he's going to have to wait until he gets back to Earth."

"The next ship isn't due for another fourteen months or so."

"I know… that's when I'm scheduled to go back, too. But the good news is that he's happy and reasonably content, and doesn't really pose a threat to anyone… except maybe by accident, in which case I'd recommend that you relieve him of any duties that would take him outside the hab."

"Done." The last thing anyone needed was to have a delusional person out on the surface. Mars can be pretty unforgiving when it comes to human error, and a fatal mistake can cost you not only your own life, but also the guy next to you. "And I take it that you recommend that his request be granted, too?"

"It wouldn't hurt, no." A wry smile. "So long as he's off in his own world, he'll be happy. Make him comfortable, give him whatever he wants… within reason, at least… and leave him alone. I'll keep an eye on him and will let you know if his condition changes, for better or worse."

"Hopefully for the better."

"Sure… but I wouldn't count on it." Karl stared straight at me. "Face it, chief… one of your guys is turning into a Martian."

I took Jeff off the outside-work details and let it be known that he wasn't permitted to go marswalking without authorization or an escort, and instead reassigned him to jobs that would keep him in the habitats: working in the greenhouse, finishing the interior of Hab 2, that sort of thing. I was prepared to tell him that he was being taken off the outside details because he'd reached his rem limit for radiation exposure, but he never questioned my decision but only accepted it with the same quiet, spooky smile that he'd come to giving everyone.

I also let him relocate to private quarters, a small room on Hab 2's second level that had been unoccupied until then. As I expected, there were a few gripes from those still having to share a room with someone else; however, most people realized that Jeff was in bad shape and needed his privacy. After he moved in, though, he did something I didn't anticipate: he changed his door lock's password to something no one else knew. This was against station rules—the security office and the general manager were supposed to always have everyone's lock codes—but Karl assured me that Jeff meant no harm. He simply didn't want to have anyone enter his quarters, and it would help his peace of mind if he received this one small exemption. I went along with it, albeit reluctantly.

After that, I had no problems with Jeff for a while. He assumed his new duties without complaint, and the reports I received from department heads told me that he was doing his work well. Karl updated me every week; his patient hadn't yet shown any indications of snapping out of his fugue, but neither did he appear to be getting worse. And although he was no longer interacting with any other personnel except when he needed to, at least he was no longer telling anyone about Martian princesses or randomly quoting obscure science fiction stories over the comlink.

Nonetheless, there was the occasional incident. Such as when the supply chief came to me with an unusual request Jeff had made: several reams of hemp paper, and as much soy ink as could be spared. Since both were by-products of greenhouse crops grown at either Arsia Station or one of the other colonies, and thus not imported from Earth, they weren't particularly scarce. Still, what could Jeff possibly want with that much writing material? I asked Karl if Jeff had told him that he was keeping a journal; the doctor told me that he hadn't, but unless either paper or ink were in short supply, it couldn't hurt to grant that request. So I signed off on this as well, although I told the supply chief to subtract the cost from Jeff's salary.

Not long after that, I heard from one of the communications officers. Jeff had asked her to send a general memo to the other colonies: a request for downloads of any Mars novels or stories that their personnel might have. The works of Bradbury, Burroughs, and Brackett were particularly desired, although stuff by Moorcock, Williamson, and Sturgeon would also be appreciated. In exchange, Jeff would send stories and novels he'd downloaded from the Phoenix disk.

Nothing wrong there, either. By then, Mars was on the opposite side of the Sun from Earth, so Jeff couldn't make the same request from Huntsville. If he was running out of reading material, then it made sense that he'd have to go begging from the other colonies. In fact, the com officer told me she'd had already received more than a half-dozen downloads; apparently quite a few folks had Mars fiction stashed in the comps. Nonetheless, it was unusual enough that she thought I should know about it. I asked her to keep me posted, and shrugged it off as just another of a long series of eccentricities.

A few weeks after that, though, Jeff finally did something that rubbed me the wrong way. As usual, I heard about it from Dr. Rosenfeld.

"Jeff has a new request," he said when I happened to drop by his office. "In the future, he would prefer to be addressed as 'Your Majesty' or `Your Highness,' in keeping with his position as the Emperor of Mars."

I stared at him for several seconds. "Surely you're joking," I said at last.

"Surely I'm not. He is now the Emperor Jeffery the First, sovereign monarch of the Great Martian Empire, warlord and protector of the red planet." A pause, during which I expected Karl to grin and wink. He didn't. "He doesn't necessarily want anyone bow in his presence," he added, "but he does require proper respect for the crown."

"I see." I closed my eyes, rubbed the bridge of my nose between my thumb and forefinger, and counted to ten. "And what does that make me?"

"Prime Minister, of course." The driest of smiles. "Since his title is hereditary, His Majesty isn't interested in the day-to-day affairs of his empire. That he leaves up to you, with the promise that he'll refrain from meddling with your decisions…"

"Oh, how fortunate I am."

"Yes. But from here on, all matters pertaining to the throne should be taken up with me, in my position as Royal Physician and Senior Court Advisor."

"Uh-huh." I stood up from my chair. "Well, if you'll excuse me, I think the Prime Minister needs to go now and kick His Majesty's ass."

"Sit down." Karl glared at me. "Really, I mean it. Sit."

I was unwilling to sit down again, but neither did I storm out of his office. "Look, I know he's a sick man, but this has gone far enough. I've given him his own room, relieved him of hard labor, given him paper and ink… for what, I still don't know, but he keeps asking for more… and allowed him com access to the other colonies. Just because he's been treated like a king doesn't mean he *is* a king."

"Oh, I agree. Which is why I've reminded him that his title is honorary as well as hereditary, and as such there's a limit to royal privilege. And he understands this. After all, the empire is in decline, having reached its peak over a thousand years ago, and since then the emperor has had to accept certain sacrifices for the good of the people. So, no, you won't see him wearing a crown and carrying a scepter, nor will he be demanding that a throne be built for him. He wants his reign to be benign."

Hearing this, I reluctantly took my seat again. "All right, so let me get this straight. He believes that he's now a king…"

"An emperor. There's a difference."

"King, emperor, whatever… he's not going to be bossing anyone around, but will pretty much let things continue as they are. Right?"

"Except that he wants to be addressed formally, yeah, that's pretty much it." Karl sighed, shook his head. "Let me try to explain. Jeff has come face-to-face with a reality that he cannot bear. His parents, his fiancé, the child they wanted to have… they're all dead, and he was too far away to prevent it, or even go to their funerals. This is a very harsh reality that he needs to keep at bay, so he's built a wall around himself… a wall of delusion, if you will. At first, it took the form of an obsession with fantasy, but when that wouldn't alone suffice, he decided to enter that fantasy, become part of it. This is where Emperor Jeffery the First of the Great Martian Empire comes in."

"So he's protecting himself?"

"Yes… by creating a role that lets him believe that he controls his own life." Karl shook his head. "He doesn't want to actually run Arsia, chief. He just wants to pretend that he does. As long as you allow him this, he'll be all right. Trust me."

"Well… all right." Not that I had much choice in the matter. If I was going to have a crazy person in my colony, at least I could make sure that he wouldn't endanger anyone. If that meant indulging him until he could be sent back to Earth, then that was what I'd have to do. "I'll pass the word that His Majesty is to be treated with all due respect."

"That would be great. Thanks." Karl smiled. "Y'know, people have been pretty supportive. I haven't heard of anyone taunting him."

"You know how it is. People here tend to look out for each other… they have to." I stood up and started to head for the door, then another thought occurred to me. "Just one thing. Has he ever told you what he's doing in his room? Like I said, he's been using a lot of paper and ink."

"Yes, I've noticed the ink stains on his fingers." Karl shook his head. "No, I don't. I've asked him about that, and the only thing he's told me is that he's preparing a gift for his people, and that he'll allow us to see it when the time comes."

"A gift?" I raised an eyebrow. "Any idea what it is?"

"Not a clue... but I'm sure we'll find out."

I kept my promise to Dr. Rosenfeld and put out the word that Jeff Halbert was heretofore to be known as His Majesty, the Emperor. As I told Karl, people were generally accepting of this. Oh, I heard the occasional report of someone giving Jeff some crap about this—exaggerated bows in the corridors, ill-considered questions about who was going to be his queen, and so forth—but the jokers who did this were usually pulled aside and told to shut up. Everyone at Arsia knew that Jeff was mentally ill, and that the best anyone could do for him was to let him have his fantasy life for as long as he was with us.

By then, Earth was no longer on the other side of the Sun. Once our home world and Mars began moving toward conjunction, a cycleship could begin the trip home. So only a few months remained until Jeff would board a shuttle. Since Karl would be returning as well, I figured he'd be in good hands, or at least till they climbed into zombie tanks to hibernate for the long ride to Earth. Until then, all we had to do was keep His Majesty happy.

That wasn't hard to do. In fact, Karl and I had a lot of help. Once people got used to the idea that a make-believe emperor lived among them, most of them actually seemed to enjoy the pretense. When he walked through the habs, folks would pause whatever they were doing to nod to him and say "Your Majesty" or "Your Highness." He was always allowed to go to the front of the serving line in the mess hall, and there was always someone ready to hold his chair for him. And I noticed that he even picked up a couple of consorts, two unattached young women who did everything from trim his hair—it had grown very long by then, with a regal beard to match—to assist him in the

Royal Gardens (aka the greenhouse) to accompany him to the Saturday night flicks. As one of the girls told me, the Emperor was the perfect date: always the gentleman, he'd unfailingly treated them with respect and never tried to take advantage of them. Which was more than could be said for some of the single men at Arsia.

After a while, I relaxed the rule about not letting him leave the habs, and allowed him to go outside as long as he was under escort at all times. Jeff remembered how to put on a hardsuit—a sign that he hadn't completely lost touch with reality—and he never gave any indication that he was on the verge of opening his helmet. But once he walked a few dozen yards from the airlock, he'd often stop and stare into the distance for a very long time, keeping his back to the rest of the base and saying nothing to anyone.

I wondered what he was seeing then. Was it a dry red desert, cold and lifeless, with rocks and boulders strewn across an arid plain beneath a pink sky? Or did he see something no one else could: forests of giant lichen, ancient canals upon which sailing vessels slowly glided, cities as old as time from which John Carter and Tars Tarkas rode to their next adventure or where tyrants called for the head of the outlaw Eric John Stark. Or was he thinking of something else entirely? A mother and a father who'd raised him, a woman he'd once loved, a child whom he'd never see?

I don't know, for the Emperor seldom spoke to me, even in my role as his Prime Minister. I think I was someone he wanted to avoid, an authority figure who had the power to shatter his illusions. Indeed, in all the time that Jeff was with us, I don't think he and I said more than a few words to each other. In fact, it wasn't until the day that he finally left for Earth that he said anything of consequence to me.

That morning, I drove him and Dr. Rosenfeld out to the landing field, where a shuttle was waiting to transport them up to the cycleship. Jeff was unusually quiet; I couldn't easily see his expression through his helmet faceplate, but the few glimpses I had told me that he wasn't happy. His Majesty knew that he was leaving his empire. Karl hadn't softened the blow by telling him a convenient lie, but instead had given him the truth: they were returning to Earth, and he'd probably never see Mars again.

Their belongings had already been loaded aboard the shuttle when we arrived, and the handful of other passengers were waiting to climb aboard. I parked the rover at the edge of the landing field and escorted Jeff and Karl to the spacecraft. I shook hands with Karl and wished him well, then turned to Jeff.

"Your Majesty…" I began.

"You don't have to call me that," he said.

"Pardon me?"

Jeff stepped closer to me. "I know I'm not really an emperor. That was something I got over a while ago… I just didn't want to tell anyone."

I glanced at Karl. His eyes were wide, and within his helmet he shook his head. This was news to him, too. "Then… you know who you really are?"

A brief flicker of a smile. "I'm Jeff Halbert. There's something wrong with me, and I don't really know what it is… but I know that I'm Jeff Halbert and that I'm going home." He hesitated, then went on. "I know we haven't talked much, but I… well, Dr. Rosenfeld has told me what you've done for me, and I just wanted to thank you. For putting up with me all this time, and for letting me be the Emperor of Mars. I hope I haven't been too much trouble."

I slowly let out my breath. My first thought was that he'd been playing me and everyone else for fools, but then I realized that his megalomania had probably been real, at least for a time. In any case, it didn't matter now; he was on his way back to Earth, the first steps on the long road to recovery.

Indeed, many months later, I received a letter from Karl. Shortly after he returned to Earth, Jeff was admitted to a private clinic in southern Vermont, where he began a program of psychiatric treatment. The process had been painful; as Karl had deduced, Jeff's mind had repressed the knowledge of his family's deaths, papering over the memory with fantastical delusions he'd derived from the stories he'd been reading. The clinic psychologists agreed with Dr. Rosenfeld: it was probably the retreat into fantasy that saved Jeff's life, by providing him with a place to which he was able to escape when his mind was no longer able to cope with a tragic reality. And in the end, when he no longer needed that illusion, Jeff returned from madness. He'd never see a Martian princess again, or believe himself to be the ruling monarch of the red planet.

But that was yet to come. I bit my tongue and offered him my hand. "No trouble, Jeff. I just hope everything works out for you."

"Thanks." Jeff shook my hand, then turned away to follow Karl to the ladder. Then he stopped and looked back at me again. "One more thing..."

"Yes?"

"There's something in my room I think you'd like to see. I disabled the lock just before I left, so you won't need the password to get in there." A brief pause. "It was `Thuvia,' just in case you need it anyway."

"Thank you." I peered at him. "So... what is it?"

"Call it a gift from the emperor," he said.

I walked back to the rover and waited until the shuttle lifted off, then I drove to Hab 2. When I reached Jeff's room, though, I discovered that I wasn't the first person to arrive. Several of his friends—his fellow monkeys, the emperor's consorts, a couple of others—had already opened the door and gone in. I heard their astonished murmurs as I walked down the hall, but it wasn't until I pushed entered the room that I saw what amazed them.

Jeff's quarters were small, but he'd done a lot with it over the last year and a half. The wall above his bed was covered with sheets of paper that he'd taped together, upon which he'd drawn an elaborate mural. Here was the Mars over which the Emperor had reigned: boat-like aircraft hovering above great domed cities, monstrous creatures prowling red wastelands, bare-chested heroes defending beautiful women with rapiers and radium pistols, all beneath twin moons that looked nothing like the Phobos and Deimos we knew. The mural was crude, yet it had been rendered with painstaking care, and was nothing like anything we'd ever seen before.

That wasn't all. On the desk next to the comp was the original Phoenix disk, yet Jeff hadn't been satisfied just to leave it behind. A wire-frame bookcase had been built beside the desk, and neatly stacked upon its shelves were dozens of sheaves of paper, some thick and some thin, each carefully bound with hemp twine. Books, handwritten and handmade.

I carefully pulled down one at random, gazed at its title page: *Edison's Conquest of Mars* by Garrett P. Serviss. I put it back on the shelf, picked up another: *Omnilingual* by H. Beam Piper. I placed it on the shelf, then pulled down yet another: *The Martian Crown Jewels* by Poul Anderson. And more, dozens more...

This was what Jeff had been doing all this time: transcribing the contents of the Phoenix disk, word by word. Because he knew, in spite of his madness, that he couldn't stay on Mars forever, and he wanted to leave something behind. A library, so that others could enjoy the same stories that had helped him through a dark and troubled time.

The library is still here. In fact, we've improved it quite a bit. I had the bed and dresser removed, and replaced them with armchairs and reading lamps. The mural has been preserved within glass frames, and the books have been rebound inside plastic covers. The Phoenix disk is gone, but its contents have been downloaded into a couple of comps; the disk itself is in the base museum. And we've added a lot of books to the shelves; every time a cycleship arrives from Earth, it brings a few more volumes for our collection. It's become one of the favorite places in Arsia for people to relax. There's almost always someone there, sitting in a chair with a novel or story in his or her lap.

The sign on the door reads *Imperial Martian Library:* an inside joke that newcomers and tourists don't get. And, yes, I've spent a lot of time there myself. It's never too late to catch up on the classics.

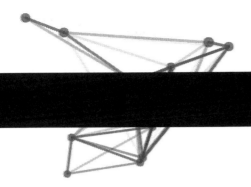

LUNAR ONE
JASPER T. SCOTT

"It's beautiful," Emily said.

Blake stood behind his daughter, smiling and nodding as she used Lunar One's telescope to gaze at the mottled blue and green orb shining bright above them. The Moon's orbit had brought the day side of Earth into full view. It was hard not to marvel at the bold beauty of their world—harder still not to feel a pang of envy for the people living there. Emily turned away from the telescope with wide, bright blue eyes. The look of awe on her face reminded Blake of his own sense of wonder upon reaching the moon base, Lunar One.

"What's it like up there? On Earth?" Emily asked.

Blake smiled anew. *Up* was a relative term. It certainly *felt* like the Earth was up, thanks to the Moon's gravity and the seeming amplification of that gravity that their magnetic boots provided. Still, Blake couldn't help but remember when he'd been a child back on Earth, gazing up at the Moon and wondering the same thing—*what's it like up there?* Now with his curiosity sated, he was anxious to go back home.

Answering his daughter, he said, "Earth is like nothing you've ever

215

seen before. There are vast green forests, creaking in the wind; boundless blue oceans, deeper than the deepest crater on the Moon, and so far across that you can't see the other side; there's crystal clear rivers cascading from soaring mountains that are bundled up in green blankets of trees and wearing thick, white caps of snow and ice called glaciers. The atmosphere…" Blake sighed and closed his eyes, remembering. "You don't know what a wind feels like, but on Earth the air moves about as if it had a life of its own. And then there are the cities, millions of them. Each city is like a lunar base, but much bigger, and each one is completely different, with its own people, food, and sights to see."

Emily was silent for a long moment. "I can't wait to see it!"

Blake smiled. "I can't wait either. You've never been, so you don't know what you're missing, but I do." He sighed and ran a hand through his thinning brown hair. "I think I've been up here too long."

Emily nodded sagely, as if she knew just what he meant.

Blake turned back to the telescope and adjusted the height so that he could look through it more comfortably. Then he made further adjustments, magnifying North America and zooming in as far as he could on the eastern coast of the United States. He tried to imagine his parents down there, in their home in New Jersey, getting ready for Christmas. Knowing his mother, she would be busy running around cleaning and bringing out the Christmas decorations, trying to make everything perfect. His Dad would be outside stringing lights and wrestling their giant Frosty the Snowman into position on the front lawn. This year would be the biggest celebration they'd ever thrown. It wasn't just Christmas; it was his welcome home party, and a chance for his parents to finally meet their granddaughter. It had been almost eight years since he'd been home. He'd had to wait until Emily was old enough for the return trip.

People weren't supposed to get pregnant on the Moon, not without a license. Population controls in the colonies were strict; they had to be. A growing population meant that infrastructure had to expand. Things like water and soil for growing food had to be shuttled up from Earth, and that was beyond expensive. But Blake's girlfriend, Celeste, had defied all of those concerns, as well as the hormonal injections that should have prevented her from getting pregnant in the first place. She'd wanted a child so badly, and somehow that desire had been strong enough for her body to beat all of the odds. Then, just two days after Emily was born, Celeste had died in the medical wing of Lunar One. She'd lived long enough to see her dream come true, but not long enough to live in that dream. Blake often reflected on that irony, wondering if it were somehow axiomatic of life.

"Why would anyone come live down here if the Earth is so great?" Emily asked, interrupting Blake's thoughts.

"Because…" How could he explain to a six-year-old the necessity of establishing colonies on the Moon when the Earth was clearly the more habitable of the two? How could he explain the novelty of it, the research opportunities, the increased access to space, the bragging rights it gave one country over another… After eight years, the reasons all seemed petty and pointless, and maybe they were. Maybe it was just pure hubris that had driven humanity to colonize the Moon, something humans did just to say that they could. Blake shook his head. "I think people come up here in order to appreciate the Earth more."

"That doesn't make *any* sense." Emily folded her arms over her chest, and she gave him that skeptical look of hers, the same one her mother had practiced to perfection.

Blake smiled and tousled her hair. "No, it doesn't make sense, but it's human nature to appreciate things better when they're not there."

"You must appreciate Earth a lot, then."

Blake chuckled. "Yes, I do. More than you'll ever know." He twitched the telescope by just the slightest fraction of a degree, and he went from looking at New Jersey to New York. A lack of clouds over the city gave him a clear view, straight down to the metropolis. The magnification wasn't strong enough to see individual buildings, but it was close. He could see the cityscape, a corrugated gray. Central park was a solid green square. The ocean all around Manhattan was a brilliant blue. Blake couldn't wait to show his daughter around the city. What would she make of it? All she had ever known were the narrow corridors of Lunar One. She got to see the hydroponic gardens almost daily, so she knew what plants looked like, but she'd never seen miles and miles of civilization—crowded city streets, cars, people, restaurants, stores… She didn't even know what *shopping* was. On the Moon, the colony provided people with all of their needs, but only the most basic ones were met. The rest... Emily just had no idea. A lump rose in Blake's throat and he found himself trembling with excitement.

"I wish Mom could have gone back with us."

That dulled his excitement. "So do I, Em." He turned from the telescope to squeeze her shoulder and offer a reassuring smile.

"What are you looking at now?"

Grateful for the change of topic, Blake said, "I'm looking at the places we're going to visit. The United States, New York City, New Jersey—that was my home before I moved up here."

"Don't you mean *down* here?" Emily asked.

"That depends which planet you're standing on."

"Well, we're standing on the Moon."

"True."

"So Earth is up."

"Yes, I suppose it is."

"Can I see?" Emily asked, looking up at the telescope.

"Sure." Blake adjusted the height of the viewing apparatus once more, giving his daughter a chance to see where they would be going. "You see the green spot? That's a giant park in New York City called Central Park."

"It doesn't look very big."

"No, it doesn't, not from here, but it's almost the size of Lunar One."

"Wow. What's all the gray stuff around it? It looks like the Moon. I thought you said there were forests and rivers and mountains everywhere..."

Blake laughed. "Those gray parts are skyscrapers. Tall buildings where people live and work."

"Taller than the control tower?" Emily asked.

"Much taller." The fifteen story landing control and communications tower of Lunar One would be dwarfed by even a small apartment building in New York.

"Ow!" Emily backed away from the telescope, rubbing her eye.

Blake frowned. "What happened?"

"It's too bright! It hurt my eye."

"Bright?" Blake shook his head and adjusted the telescope one more time so that he could see. What he saw was a giant, blurry cloud over the city. "Where did that come from?" he wondered aloud. "You didn't move the telescope, did you?" he asked even though could see that the settings were all the same.

"No," Emily replied.

Blake withdrew from the hands-on viewing apparatus and walked over to the computer console behind it. He needed finer control over the telescope, and some real hard data to understand what he was seeing. He eased into the chair and booted up the computer. Moments later the scene from the optical viewing apparatus reappeared for both of them to look at, now reproduced on the computer screen. The giant white cloud still hovered over New York, but now other details were coming clear. Around the edges of the cloud, black wisps of smoke were swirling, and thousands of small, bright orange pinpricks of fire raged. Blake's insides turned to ice, and he gasped.

"What is it, Dad?"

He just shook his head. The uniform gray of skyscrapers and city streets was now a blurry, molten mess. Add to that the sudden appearance of the white, mushroom-shaped cloud, and it wasn't hard to figure out what had happened. Blake reached for the communicator in his ear. Tower Control answered.

"Lunar One Control, Lieutenant Rogan here."

"Control, this is Blake Evans. I'm in the observatory. We need to contact Earth immediately! Something terrible has happened."

"One moment, please."

There came a pause, and then the gruff voice of Commander Thales growled at him, "What's going on Evans?"

"Sir, I'm looking at New York and..." Blake's voice cracked, and he trailed off.

"Spit it out, Evans! I don't have all day!"

"The city's gone, sir," Blake croaked.

"What do you mean it's *gone*?"

"I mean there's a mushroom cloud rising where Manhattan used to be! The whole city is on fire!"

Another pause, this one longer. In the background Blake heard people swearing and yelling at each other. Then came a crackle of static and Commander Thales was back. "I'm sending someone to the observatory now. Stay calm Evans, and keep an eye out for further developments."

"Yes, sir."

Blake zoomed out until he could see the whole country.

"What happened, Dad?" Emily asked, tugging on his sleeve.

Blake opened his mouth to reply, but no sound came out, just a strained whisper. He felt like he was suffocating. It was a bad dream. Any minute now he was going to wake up.

"Dad?"

"Nothing, darling. Just… we're still trying to figure things out."

Another bright flash of light washed across the screen. This time Blake saw it, too.

"Look! That's what hurt my eye!" Emily said, pointing to the bulbous white head of another mushroom that was busy sprouting up to the south of the first one.

Blake's hands began to shake, and his heart thudded painfully in his chest. He let out a strangled sound and his hands flew over the controls to see where the second blast was. He checked the latitude and longitude, and the computer cross-referenced that with the name of a city.

Washington, DC.

Blake stared at the screen, his bottom lip quivering, his eyes unblinking. "This can't be happening…" he breathed.

An hour later, the observatory was crowded with officers from the control tower. Everyone watched as the twelfth blast hit the twelfth major US city. Not long after that, explosions began to hit other parts of the world. Russia was lit up from top to bottom and from east to west.

It was hard to comprehend the decisions being made on Earth while they were on the Moon, completely cut off from the goings-on. Making the situation worse, Earth wasn't responding to their hails. They were otherwise occupied, no doubt running home to get their families and get as far as possible from the nearest city center. It was everyone's worst nightmare, and here they were, watching it play out via a lunar telescope, 284,000 miles from Earth.

"Well, we're fucked!" someone said. Blake turned to see that it was one of Lunar One's shuttle pilots. "That's it! We're done!"

Blake looked away and busied himself aiming the telescope back at the US. This time they watched not a dozen, but thousands of explosions flowering all across the country. Every city with more than a hundred thousand people got hit.

"Why Russia? Why the *fuck* would they attack us?" the shuttle pilot asked.

"Maybe it wasn't them," Commander Thales replied. "Maybe the powers that be just took an educated guess. Maybe they just wanted blood. Whatever the case, it doesn't matter who started it. It's already over, and we're all that's left."

"What do you mean?" someone else asked.

"Isn't it obvious? Earth wasn't ready for this. The lunar bases are self-sufficient. We have our own spacecraft, mining operations on the surface, hydroponic farms, air and water recyclers. We can live up here, but they sure as hell can't live down there. There's going to be a nuclear winter, famine, disease, endless wars of retaliation and squabbles over dwindling resources. If humanity has any chance at all, it's us. We're the future now."

"Are w-we still g-going up to Earth?" Emily asked.

Blake turned to his daughter in a daze. "Going?" he echoed, her words not connecting to sense in his brain.

Emily's big blue eyes were full of tears. She blinked and they began to dribble down her cheeks. "You promised!"

Blake couldn't bring himself to reply, he just pulled her into a crushing embrace, and he began to sob. Emily began to wail when she heard him crying, but that was as it should be. It would have been wrong to watch the Earth die and not shed a single tear.

"Sir, we're receiving a transmission... it's from Lunar Nine!" Blake heard an officer beside him say.

Thales replied, "That's the Russian base! What do they want?"

"They received orders from Earth to launch their missiles at us."

"Is that a threat? If they do, we'll retaliate, and there'll be nothing left but two fresh craters on the Moon!"

"It's not a threat, sir. They're suggesting we bury the hatchet. They've been watching the same thing as us. The commander of Lunar Nine has publicly denounced the Russian government's actions. It's all over the news nets. They've had trouble reaching us, because there's no one in the control tower. The Japanese in Lunar Two had to forward their message to my tablet."

Blake emerged from his daughter's embrace to see Commander Thales looking pale and shell-shocked. He seemed frozen with indecision. "They started this..." he said slowly, squinting up at the mottled blue, white, and green ball above their heads. "It's time for us to end it."

Suddenly Blake was on his feet, furious. His chest was rising and falling quickly, his eyes were flashing and his face had flushed. "Sir, you said it yourself: we're all that's left! You can't!"

Commander Thales turned to him with a disgusted look. "What are you *talking* about Evans? By *they* I meant *Earth*, not the Russians. It's that kind of thinking that got us into this mess in the first place. *Earth* started it. Now we, the people of the Moon, have to put an end to the madness." The commander turned away, back to his communications officer. "Tell Lunar Nine that we couldn't agree more. Maybe humanity couldn't have peace on Earth, but perhaps we can settle for peace on the Moon."

"I'll have to get back to the control tower to send that message, sir."

"Well? What are we waiting for? Let's go!"

Blake watched as everyone hurried out of the observatory, leaving him and Emily alone once more.

As soon as they were gone, Emily began tugging on his sleeve to get his attention. Blake turned to her, his eyes still bleary with tears.

"It's okay, Dad," Emily said, sniffling. "It's like you said, I've never been to Earth, so I don't know what I'm missing. I'll be okay. Don't cry."

Blake's mouth cracked into a broken smile, and he got down on his haunches to hug his daughter once more. "I'm so sorry, Emily," he whispered beside her ear. *I'm so sorry.* As that apology echoed through his head, he couldn't help thinking to himself, *Maybe you don't know what you're missing, but I do.*

I sure do.

MY FATHER'S SINGULARITY

BRENDA COOPER

Brenda got started by coauthoring *Building Harlequin's Moon* with Larry Niven. She went on to write many other works including *The Silver Ship and the Sea*, *Reading the Wind*, *Wings of Creation*, *Mayan December*, and *The Creative Fire*.

You can read her latest novel *Edge of Dark* at http://amzn.to/16IfFLV.

In my first memory of my father, we are sitting on the porch, shaded from the burning sun's assault on our struggling orchards. My father is leaning back in his favorite wooden rocker, sipping a cold beer with a half-naked lady on the label, and saying, "Paul, you're going to see the most amazing things. You will live forever." He licks his lips, the way our dogs react to treats, his breath coming faster. "You will do things I can't even imagine." He pauses, and we watch a flock of geese cross the sky. When he speaks again, he sounds wistful. "You won't ever have to die."

The next four of five memories are variations on that conversation, punctuated with the heat and sweat of work, and the smell of seasons passing across the land.

I never emerged from this particular conversation with him feeling like I knew what he meant. It was clear he thought it would happen to me and not to him, and that he had mixed feelings about that, happy for me and sad for himself. But he was always certain.

Sometimes he told me that I'd wake up one morning and all the world around me would be different. Other nights, he said, "Maybe there'll be a

door, a shining door, and you'll go through it and you'll be better than human."
He always talked about it the most right before we went into Seattle, which
happened about twice a year, when the pass was open and the weather wasn't
threatening our crops.

The whole idea came to him out of books so old they were bound paper
with no moving parts, and from a brightly-colored magazine that eventually
disintegrated from being handled. My father's hands were big and rough and
his calluses wore the words off the paper.

Two beings always sat at his feet. Me, growing up, and a dog, growing
old. He adopted them at mid-life or they came to him, a string of one dog at
a time, always connected so that a new one showed within a week of the old
one's death. He and his dogs were a mutual admiration society. They liked me
fine, but they never adored me. They encouraged me to run my fingers through
their stiff fur or their soft fur, or their wet, matted fur if they'd been out in the
orchard sprinklers, but they were in doggie heaven when he touched them.
They became completely still and their eyes softened and filled with warmth.

I'm not talking about the working dogs. We always had a pair of border
collies for the sheep, but they belonged to the sheep and the sheep belonged
to them and we were just the fence and the feeders for that little ecosystem.

These dogs were his children just like me, although he never suggested
they would see the singularity. I would go beyond and they would stay and he
and the dogs accepted that arrangement even if I didn't.

I murmured confused assent when my father said words about how I'd
become whatever comes after humans.

Only once did I find enough courage to tell him what was in my heart.
I'd been about ten, and I remember how cold my hands felt clutching a glass
of iced lemonade while heat-sweat poured down the back of my neck. When
he told me I would be different, I said, "No, Dad. I want to be like you when I
grow up." He was the kindness in my life, the smile that met me every morning and made me eggs with the yolks barely soft and toast that melted butter
without burning.

He shook his head, patted his dog, and said, "You are luckier than that."

His desire for me to be different than him was the deepest rejection possible, and I bled from the wounds.

After the fifth year in seven that climate-freak storms wrecked the apples—this time with bone-crushing ice that set the border collies crazed with worry—I knew I'd have to leave if I was ever going to support my father. Not by crossing the great divide of humanity to become the seed of some other species, but to get schooled away from the slow life of farming sheep and Jonagolds. The farm could go on without me. We had the help of two immigrant families that each owned an acre of land that was once ours.

Letting my father lose the farm wasn't a choice I could even imagine. I'd go over to Seattle and go to school. After, I'd get a job and send money home, the way the Mexicans did when I was little and before the government gave them part of our land to punish us. Not that we were punished. We liked the Ramirez's and the Alvarez's. They, too, needed me to save the farm.

But that's not this story. Except that Mona Alvarez drove me to Leavenworth to catch the silver Amtrak train, her black hair flying away from her lipstick-black lips, and her black painted fingernails clutching the treacherous steering wheel of our old diesel truck. She was so beautiful I decided right then that I would miss her almost as much as I would miss my father and the bending apple trees and the working dogs and the sheep. Maybe I would miss Mona even more.

Mona, however, might not miss me. She waved once after she dropped me off, and then she and the old truck were gone and I waited amid the electric cars and the old tourists with camera hats and data jewelry and the faint marks of implants in the soft skin between their thumbs and their index fingers. They looked like they saw everything and nothing all at once. If they came to our farm the coyotes and the repatriated wolves would run them down fast.

On the other end of the train ride, I found the University of Washington, now sprawled all across Seattle, a series of classes and meetups and virtual lessons that spidered out from the real brick buildings. An old part of the campus still squatted by the Montlake Cut, watching over water and movement that looked like water spiders but was truly lines of people with oars on nanofab boats as thin as paper.

Our periodic family trips to Seattle hadn't really prepared me for being a student. The first few years felt like running perpetually uphill, my brain just not going as fast as everyone else's.

I went home every year. Mona married one of the Ramirez boys and had two babies by the time three years had passed, and her beauty changed to a quiet softness with no time to paint her lips or her nails. Still, she was prettier than the sticks for girls that chewed calorie-eating gum and did their homework while they ran to Gasworks Park and back on the Burke-Gilman Trail, muttering answers to flashcards painted on their retinas with light.

I didn't date those girls; I wouldn't have known how to interrupt the speed of their lives and ask them out. I dated storms of data and new implants and the rush of ideas until by my senior year I was actually keeping up.

When I graduated, I got a job in genetics that paid well enough for me to live in an artist's loft in a green built row above Lake Union. I often climbed onto the garden roof and sat on an empty bench and watched the Space Needle change decorations every season and the little wooden boats sailing on the still lake below me. But mostly I watched over my experiments, playing with new medical implants to teach children creativity and to teach people docked for old age in the University hospital how to talk again, how to remember.

I did send money home. Mona's husband died in a flash flood one fall. Her face took on a sadness that choked in my throat, and I started paying her to take care of my father.

He still sat on the patio and talked about the singularity, and I managed not to tell him how quaint the old idea sounded. I recognized myself, would always recognize myself. In spite of the slow speed of the farm, a big piece of me was always happiest at home, even though I couldn't be there more than a day or so at a time. I can't explain that—how the best place in the world spit me out after a day or so.

Maybe I believed too much happiness would kill me, or change me. Or maybe I just couldn't move slow enough to breath in the apple air any more. Whatever the reason, the city swept me back fast, folding me in its dancing ads and shimmering opportunities and art.

Dad didn't really need me anyway. He had the Mexicans and he still always had a dog, looking lovingly up at him. Max, then OwlFace, then Blue. His fingers had turned to claws and he had cataracts scraped from his eyes twice, but he still worked with the harvest, still carried a bushel basket and still found fruit buried deep in the trees.

I told myself he was happy.

Then one year, he startled when I walked up on the porch and his eyes filled with fear.

I hadn't changed. I mean, not much. I had a new implant, I had a bigger cloud, researchers under me, so much money that what I sent my father—what he needed for the whole orchard—was the same as a night out at a concert and dinner at Canlis. But I was still me, and Blue—the current dog—accepted me, and Mona's oldest son called me "Uncle Paul" on his way out to tend the sheep.

I told my father to pack up and come with me.

He ran his fingers through the fur on Blue's square head. "I used to have a son, but he left." He sounded certain. "He became the next step for us. For humans."

He was looking right at me, even looking in my eyes, and there was truly no recognition there. His look made me cold to the spine, cold to the ends of my fingers even with the sun driving sweat down my back.

I kissed his forehead. I found Mona and told her I'd be back in a few weeks and she should have him packed up.

Her eyes were beautiful and terrible with reproach as she declared, "He doesn't want to leave."

"I can help him."

"Can you make him young, like you?"

Her hair had gone gray at the edges, lost the magnificent black that had glistened in the sun like her goth lipstick all those years ago. God, how could I have been so selfish? I could have given her some of what I had.

But I liked her better touched by pain and age and staying part of my past. Like the act of saving them didn't.

I hadn't known that until that very moment, when I suddenly hated myself for the wrinkles around her eyes and the way her shoulders bent in a little bit even though she was only fifty-seven like me. "I'll bring you some, too. I can get some of the best nano-meds available." Hell, I'd designed some of them, but Mona wouldn't understand that. "I can get creams that will erase the wrinkles from your hands."

She sighed. "Why don't you just leave us?"

Because then I would have no single happy place. "Because I need my father. I need to know how he's doing."

"I can tell you from here."

My throat felt thick. "I'll be back in a week." I turned away before she could see the inexplicable tears in my eyes. By then I flew back and forth, and it was a relief to focus down on the gauges in my head, flying manual until I got close enough to Seattle airspace that the feds grabbed the steering from me and there was nothing to do but look down at the forest and the green resort playgrounds of Cle Elum below me and to try not to think too hard about my dad or about Mona Alvarez and her sons.

I had moved into a condo on Alki Beach, and I had a view all the way to Canada. For two days after I returned, the J-pod whales cavorted offshore, great elongated yin and yang symbols rising and falling through the waters of Puget Sound.

The night before I went back for Mona and my father, I watched the boardwalk below me. People walked dogs and rollerbladed and bicycled and a few of the chemical-sick walked inside of big rolling bubbles like the hamster I'd had when I was a kid. Even nano-medicine and the clever delivery of genetically matched and married designer solutions couldn't save everyone.

I wish I could say that I felt sorry for the people in the bubbles, and I suppose in some distant way I did. But nothing bad had ever happened to me. I didn't get sick. I'd never married or divorced. I had nice dates sometimes, and excellent season tickets for Seattle Arts and Lectures.

I flew Mona back with my father. We tried to take Blue, but the dog balked at getting in the car, and raced away, lost in the apple trees in no time. Mona looked sick and said, "We should wait."

I glanced at my father's peaceful face. He had never cried when his dogs died or left, and now he had a small smile, and I had the fleeting thought that maybe he was proud of Blue for choosing the farm and the sheep and the brown-skinned boys. "Will your sons care for the dog?"

"Their children love him."

So we arrived back in West Seattle, me and Mona and my father.

I got busy crafting medicine to fix my father. These things didn't take long—time moved fast in the vast cloud of data I had security rights for. I crunched my father's DNA and RNA and proteins and the specifics of his blood in no time, and told the computers what to do while I set all of us out a quiet dinner on the biggest of the decks. Mona commented on the salty scent of Puget Sound and watched the fast little ferries zip back and forth in the water and refused to meet my eyes.

Dad simply stared at the water.

"He needs a dog," she said.

"I know." I queried from right there, sending a bot out to look. It reported fairly fast. "I'll be right back. Can you watch him?"

She looked startled.

An hour later I picked Nanny up at Sea-Tac, a middle-aged golden retriever, service-trained, a dog with no job since most every disease except the worst allergies to modernity could be fixed.

Mona looked awed almost to fear when I showed up with the dog, but she smiled and uncovered the dinner I'd left waiting.

Nanny and Dad were immediately enchanted with each other, her love for him the same as every other dog's in his life, cemented the minute she smelled him. I didn't understand, but if it had been any other way, I would have believed him lost.

The drugs I designed for him didn't work. It happens that way sometimes. Not often. But some minds can't accept the changes we can make. In the very old, it can kill them. Dad was too strong to die, although Mona looked at me one day, after they had been with me long enough that the wrinkles around her eyes had lost depth but not so long that they had left her face entirely. "You changed him. He's worse."

I might have. How would I know?

But I do know I lost my anchor in the world. Nothing in my life had been my singularity. I hadn't crossed into a new humanity like he prophesied over and over. I hadn't left him behind.

Instead, he left me behind. He recognized Nanny every day, and she him. But he never again called me Paul, or told me how I would step beyond him.

A DELICATE BALANCE

KEVIN J. ANDERSON

Kevin is an American science fiction author with nearly fifty bestsellers. He has written spin-off novels for *Star Wars, StarCraft, Titan A.E.,* and *The X-Files,* and with Brian Herbert is the coauthor of the *Dune* prequels. His original works include the *Saga of Seven Suns* series and the Nebula Award-nominated *Assemblers of Infinity*.

He has also written several comic books including the Dark Horse *Star Wars* collection *Tales of the Jedi* written in collaboration with Tom Veitch, *Predator* titles (also for Dark Horse), and *X-Files* titles for Topps. Some of Kevin's superhero novels include *Enemies & Allies*, about the first meeting of Batman and Superman, and *The Last Days of Krypton,* telling the story of how Krypton came to be destroyed and the choice two parents had to make for their son.

Kevin has more than 20 million books in print worldwide. Read his *The Dark Between the Stars* at http://amzn.to/1zK8jig and his *Mentats of Dune* at http://amzn.to/1tl9e6b.

The test results came back positive. Birenda felt her life change in a cold instant, as if one of the colony airlock doors had burst open and sucked her out into the planet's poisonous atmosphere.

In another time and place, she would have felt great joy to learn that she was pregnant, but this was not old Earth; it wasn't even how the Antorra colony was *supposed to be* before the disasters happened.

Inside their private family quarters, her father, Walton Fleer, received the results with better grace than Birenda did. "We knew this would happen sooner or later." The weight of administrative responsibility and the rigors of harsh colony life had aged him greatly, and everyone knew—statistically speaking—he wouldn't live to be an old man. "A new life comes, an old life must go. It's the way of the colony, the only way we can maintain the delicate balance."

A new life comes, an old life must go. How Birenda hated those words.

"And my name is next on the list." Walton gave a little shrug, pretending it didn't matter to him. "Only some of us survive, or *none* of us survive."

She clung to her father as if clipping a lifeline to his belt. "I never meant to be the one." Her voice hitched. "I'm sorry." But she could apologize, and pray, the whole day cycle, and that wouldn't change the fact.

Walton sounded so stoic, as if he were giving a speech to the members of the colony. "This way, at least I'll know I have a new grandchild coming."

"A grandchild you'll never see," Birenda said, then clenched her jaw so tightly she thought her teeth might crack.

Pregnancy tests were rarely needed on the desperate colony, since everyone knew the consequences of population growth and took careful precautions. As the current head of the small colony, Walton Fleer had managed to purloin one of the kits from a locked med-center cabinet after Birenda whispered her fears to him. It was just the two of them, counting on each other. After she used the test strip, the older man waited dutifully beside her, kneading his fists together as they waited an agonizing five minutes for the chemicals to work their damning magic. *Pregnant.*

Walton did not rail against her for being stupid and careless; Birenda had done enough of that herself. Birth-control measures were available to all colonists, everyone knew how to use them, and everyone understood that "accidents" were not acceptable. Each new life was a miracle, a blessing not to be spurned, but for a colony existing on the razor edge of survival, pregnancies must be meticulously *planned*. When the others in the colony did find out, they would hate her for such irresponsibility, particularly those couples who had already petitioned the colony council to be next in line for having a child.

Her father tried to sound soothing. "You won't show for a few months, so we don't have to do anything yet. Nobody else needs to know. We can figure out what to do."

Birenda bit her lower lip and nodded, cursing herself for her weakness. "That'll buy us a little time."

She reached out to embrace her father. In a few months, she could always hope that a deadly accident might happen to someone else, and then there would be no need for drastic action to maintain the delicate population balance. Maybe she could pray for that.

The Antorra Colony had started out so well, when measured by hopes and dreams. The original ship carrying two hundred first-wave colonists all bound together by common beliefs had been dispatched from Earth to one of a handful of planets that long-range probes had identified as suitable for Terran life. Although the ten-year voyage had seemed difficult enough, their vanguard ship was much faster than the huge main colony vessel that plodded along behind them. The initial vessel would arrive fifty years before the main group of colonists did.

As true pioneers on an untamed world, the first-wave colonists carried all the basic equipment, survival modules, prefab shelters, seed stock and embryos they would need to establish a settlement and prepare the world for human habitation. The pioneers were expected to have a thriving colony ready-made by the time the rest of the settlers came. That was the plan.

Birenda had been born en route and was four years old when the vanguard ship reached Antorra. She'd been much too young to understand the miscalculation that doomed them, but she remembered the shockwaves of terror, dismay, and hopelessness as soon as they arrived.

The long-range scientific probes were wrong, miscalibrated somehow; vital measurements had been scrambled by cosmic rays during the transmission, or perhaps the analytical instruments were poorly engineered. Antorra was not fit for human life after all. Although other parameters were within Terran norms, the chlorine concentration in the air was far too high. Not even the hardiest Earth algae could gain a foothold and begin converting the atmosphere.

The pioneers had traveled in space for a decade, with no turning back, only to reach a place where they could not survive.

Captain Tyrson marshaled all the colony equipment and pulled his people together. The habitation domes were self-contained, and the colonists could huddle down and eke out an existence. Antorra would never be the bright new home the faithful pioneers had hoped for, but if they could last for half a century, then the main colony vessel would arrive with all the expansive domes, materials, and scientific experts required to create a rough, but viable colony.

First-wave engineers erected power arrays outside to gather energy from sunlight that filtered through the caustic greenish clouds, but the chlorine corroded the arrays, and they failed one by one. However, with certain austerity measures imposed, an emergency nuclear generator provided enough energy to meet their immediate requirements. For a while, it looked as if the colony just might survive.

Then the corrosive atmosphere ate through the seals in the greenhouse dome, killing seven workers and, worst of all, obliterating much of their seed stock, the only food they could hope for on Antorra. A death sentence.

All of the data had already been transmitted to the main colony vessel that was plodding its way across the interstellar gulf. Among the hundreds of scientists and terraforming specialists aboard the huge vessel, somebody would find a solution in the decades available before they arrived—but that didn't help the initial colonists survive in the meantime…

The captain had sealed himself in his main quarters with the full inventory of all their tools, their food stock, their energy supplies, as well as a breakdown of their bare-minimum needs. He did the math, double-checked his results, and could not refute the cold equations.

Now, as Birenda brooded alone in her chamber for hours during the sleep period, she reviewed the analysis and grim rationale that Captain Tyrson had left behind in his video farewell. The recordings were required study for every one of the children who had been born and taught on the Antorra colony.

Captain Tyrson called a special meeting of hand-picked individuals from among the colonists—himself and eighteen others. It was an eclectic mix of specialities, and no one could guess why they had been chosen. The tense and curious group gathered in the loading-dock module that contained the machinery, environment suits, and equipment needed for exploring the hostile planet.

Monitor cameras captured the captain's last speech. Birenda had watched it over and over, and it still brought tears to her eyes each time.

As he faced the eighteen men and women he had selected, Captain Tyrson said, "This colony's resources can support—at most—174 people. No matter how we tighten our belts, no matter how we conserve, there isn't enough to sustain more people than that. According to computer models, only 174 can survive until the main colony vessel arrives. The choice is hard: only some of us will survive… or *none* of us will survive."

Then he had opened the airlock and dumped the nineteen "extraneous personnel" into the deadly atmosphere, himself included. No one lasted out there longer than two minutes.

In a calm and detailed video message left in his quarters, Tyrson explained exactly why he had chosen those particular nineteen—because their skill sets, their health, their age made them the most dispensible. Birenda's mother was among them.

In the twelve years since Captain Tyrson's brutal decision, 174 had become a sacred number, rigidly controlled. Although the actual minimum number for survival could not be precise, due to individual weights, metabolic rates, or behavior patterns, the criterion had to be absolute so that it could be followed without question. It was the only way they could follow the grim necessity.

When leaving Earth with high hopes, the initial colonists had all expected to marry and have large families, to spread humanity across a verdant new planet. Now that was impossible.

Rigid birth-control measures were imposed and strictly enforced, but the colonists could not outlaw all births, because the Antorra colony needed a new generation, a turnover of personnel to stay alive for the next half century until rescue arrived—there had to be children, had to be replacements. Each time a colonist died in an accident, one carefully selected couple was granted dispensation to have a child.

In Year 3, when a female chemical engineer developed abdominal cancer from radiation exposure, the colony doctor suggested she might recover with thorough treatment, but the treatment would render her sterile. By unanimous vote—Birenda was seven at the time—the Council decided to euthanize the woman, and she had accepted her fate for the good of the colony. *Some of us survive, or none of us survive.* After her death, one of the healthy young couples received approval to have a child.

Once the first such decision had been made, the rest became so much easier.

In the following nine years, the Council developed several lists—waiting lists for couples who wanted to have children, and ranking lists of all Antorra settlers prioritized by age and value to the colony. Birenda's father had been an astute colony leader for the past two years, but he was now the oldest member, and his name was next on the mortality list.

It was a delicate balance—174. No more, no less.

And Birenda had gotten pregnant.

"How could this happen?" Deputy Bill Orrick pretended to be horrified. "Do we need to impose mandatory sterilization on all fertile young women except for those approved to breed?"

Her father tried to sound calm and reasonable. "This is our colony's first accidental pregnancy in a decade. Haven't we already taken enough extreme measures?"

Birenda could see the strange smile as the deputy considered the consequences and came to the obvious conclusion. Before she could answer him in front of the Council members, Orrick shot a glare at her father. "You know what this means, Administrator Fleer. I'm sorry, but the list cannot be changed. It's agreed upon by every member of the colony."

"I know what it means," said Walton Fleer. "I always knew this day was coming, and I'm content to know that I will get a new grandchild out of it."

She and her father had kept the secret for as long as they could: Birenda hid her morning sickness and wore looser clothes so the swell of her abdomen didn't show, but it was only a temporary fix. Everything about Antorra Colony was only a temporary fix.

She had considered finding a way to abort the baby, researching techniques or drugs in the colony databases. She had told her father this was the only solution, but he was deeply upset. "I will not stay alive on those terms, at the price of an innocent child. We may have set aside many of our beliefs in order to survive here, but I will not ignore that one."

Each day, during the dreadful waiting, she had watched engineering teams work outside in the hazardous environment trying to build a new habitation dome out of scrap materials. It was hazardous duty, and accidents happened— frequently. A fatal mishap, or even a sufficiently grave injury that warranted euthanasia, would even the numbers, keep the 174, and her father wouldn't have to die so that she could have her baby. Then he could live for a little while longer, be a grandfather, hold his baby grandchild. With the colony's reality, Birenda knew it couldn't last, but everyone on Antorra clung to each day, grasped every moment.

But, week after week, all the workers remained safe. No one developed a terminal disease. No one accidentally died. And the time came when Birenda and her father could no longer hide the pregnancy.

"But she wasn't next on the list to have a child!" said Lucia Boma before the Council. "My husband and I petitioned two years ago. We were supposed to be next."

With tears streaming down her face, Birenda had been forced to confess the full story, raising herself up for censure—not for immoral behavior, but because she had upset the delicate balance of the colony.

She and Ando Rivera were about the same age, and it was assumed that they would be matched as a couple, since the colony offered so few possible candidates. Every settler had his or her set of duties; she and Ando were often assigned to go outside to set up racks of genetically modified algae webs, testing strain after strain to see if anything could survive in Antorra's environment.

One day, while returning from their duties, Birenda and Ando had been in the changing room, removing their suits, stripping down to clean jumpsuits as they had done hundreds of times before. They both were sixteen, saturated with hormones, half naked, alone together—and it had just happened. They hadn't paused to consider preventive measures.

Ando had avoided her for many days afterward, and she hadn't even been able to tell him when she first knew about the pregnancy…

"She will keep the baby," her father said to the Council, as if daring anyone to countermand him. "There will be no talk of forcing her to get rid of it, just because this wasn't in our plans. I know what it means, and I have several months to prepare myself before my daughter gives birth."

Deputy Orrick looked pleased and self-important; he'd been waiting for his turn as the next administrator, as soon as Walton Fleer was gone. Birenda despised the man. Her father was a long-term thinker who planned for the future of the colony, aware that he would be long gone when the main colony ship arrived in thirty-eight years to save them all; Orrick, on the other hand, considered only his own brief flash of prominence once he became the colony administrator. (He shouldn't be looking too far forward, Birenda thought, since his name was also on the list, and only a handful of names from the top.)

After glancing at his fellow Council members, the deputy folded his hands and gave a solemn nod. "One life begins, and another ends. Some will survive, or none will survive."

Birenda's stomach knotted, and she forced herself not to say anything. When the solution came to her, it seemed so clear and so obvious, she caught her breath.

She would have to kill Orrick.

For the next several months, Birenda concocted and discarded numerous possibilities, all the while hoping that her thoughts of death did not taint the life within her. She felt overwhelmed with love for the unborn baby, a powerful nurturing instinct. She wanted to protect it, provide a home for it.

Dr. Hajid provided basic prenatal care but performed only cursory tests, clearly resenting her for her indiscretion, which had sent repercussions through the fragile equilibrium.

Even before leaving Earth, the bulk of the colonists on the main ship had considered the tough, conservative pioneers to be a little backward; they refused to check the sex of a baby or perform anything but the most rudimentary of prenatal screenings. The colony doctor was even more aloof than necessary with Birenda, though, as if he didn't care whether the baby was healthy or not. She realized that some in the colony secretly hoped for her to miscarry, or perhaps die in childbirth, so they could get their chance.

Nevertheless, Birenda knew that the baby was progressing well. She studied all the information available in the colony library about pregnancy and childbirth—and she found plenty, because Antorra should have been a place teeming with children after only the first few years.

As she thought of the future, Birenda was sure that her child would still be alive, perhaps even the colony administrator, when the main ship arrived. Thirty-eight years… that wasn't so much to ask for her son or daughter. What seemed less likely, though, was that her father would survive long enough for the baby to remember its grandfather. The vagaries of the list would shift and change, and sooner or later Walton Fleer would be the one.

But perhaps not now.

When she reached her eighth month, Birenda felt a growing sense of urgency. As soon as the baby was born, her father would be taken away. She was young, and since this was her first pregnancy, she knew she could easily go into premature labor. She had to put one of her plans into practice, before it was too late. She had to get rid of Deputy Orrick, so the numbers remained balanced.

Birenda reviewed Captain Tyrson's last message again and again, drawing strength from his brave words. All her life she had been taught the realities of the colony. Every person inside the sheltered domes knew the math and the reasons for it. The colony had to survive. Some of them, or none of them. *All* was never an option.

It wasn't hard to think of a way to kill Deputy Orrick; she simply had to choose which method would be easiest. Since life on Antorra was already so hazardous, a slight tweaking of life-support parameters would do the trick. Perhaps she could loosen a seal in his environment suit the next time he was scheduled to do outside work. Or she could arrange for a leak in his private quarters, allowing poisonous chlorine air to seep in while he was sleeping.

Planning a fatal mishap for the obnoxious deputy did not strike her with any undue terror. She'd seen people euthanized all her life as their names rose to the top of the list, and accidents claimed many more. Only the number 174 remained a constant…

Day after day, Birenda sat for long hours with her father, resting her hands on the curve of her stomach, but she kept her dark thoughts to herself. Back in their quiet quarters, Walton Fleer was preoccupied, his mood bittersweet. He savored every remaining moment he had with his daughter. She didn't dare tell him what she planned, because then he would feel obligated either to stop her or report her to the Council. Deep inside, she didn't want him to know.

Walton talked wistfully of her mother, his wife, and the times they had spent together during the long journey from Earth, the plans they had made for their future, and how they had hoped Birenda would be only the first of many children. Birenda remembered the woman, but not well. Her most vivid image of her mother was from Captain Tyrson's security tape. She had studied her mother's face, then watched as the woman and eighteen others were sucked out the airlock, sacrificed so the rest of the colonists could survive.

Birenda wished she had known her better.

"We'll only have a few more weeks together, child," her father said, then let out a sigh. "It'll be enough."

To kill Orrick, Birenda decided to use one of the new mutated strains of algae that, according to preliminary tests, exuded an extremely toxic substance. It was a trivial thing for her to slip it into the deputy's daily food ration. In a way, she thought, his death and autopsy would provide valuable medical data for the colony's benefit.

Sitting next to her father, she was distracted, thinking of her plans. Walton Fleer just stared at her, drinking in every detail of her face. "I love you, Birenda," he said.

Because she had already planned it through, and also because she felt the ticking time-bomb inside her womb, Birenda acted quickly. She did not feel guilty, made no effort to speak with Deputy Orrick one last time. She was simply moving his name to the top of the list, maintaining the colony balance. 174. Her father would stay alive, and the baby would have another loving, nurturing presence for as long as it might last.

She supposed she would have to marry Ando Rivera. After her confession during the bitter Council meeting, the young man had acted strangely around Birenda, as if he didn't want to see her, as if he blamed *her* for getting pregnant. But that would change after the baby was born—for the good of the colony. Maybe someday their son or daughter would look up to Ando with the same warmth and appreciation as Birenda looked up to Walton Fleer. She smiled at the thought.

When her father came back to their quarters, his sickened expression told her that she had succeeded. "It seems I have been given a reprieve," he said. "Deputy Orrick just died."

"That's terrible." Birenda needed all of her strength to keep from jumping up with joy. "How did it happen?" The words sounded false even to her ears.

"Extreme allergic reaction to one of the algae strains in his food. They'll be running other tests, but he's dead… we're in balance. 174." He sank into the hard chair, shaking. "I was ready. I had my mind made up. But I can't pretend that I wouldn't like to see my grandchild."

Birenda clamped her mouth shut before she could reveal what she had done. He must never know.

Then the first hard contractions hit.

In the medical center, Dr. Hajid tended her, fully professional now, though he still didn't approve. With the baby coming, a new life for the colony, he was the doctor and he took his responsibilities seriously. His face was pinched, his dark eyes intent, but he voiced no criticism. He didn't really know what he was doing, with little opportunity to gain obstetrics expertise, considering the few births allowed, but he was the best the colony had.

Her father was there in the delivery room—she saw his face watching over her, and she felt comforted. Birenda knew that everything was all right. The delicate balance was kept at 174, thanks to Deputy Orrick's unfortunate end.

Even when she heard Dr. Hajid say something about complications, as if from a distance even farther away than the main colony ship, Birenda wasn't concerned. She was hazy through it all. Perhaps Hajid gave her too many pain-killers. The doctor's face looked grave as he said he needed to do a Caesarean, and her father granted permission.

Birenda lay back under the anesthetic, drifting, comforted. As the gray fuzz tightened to a pinprick around her eyes, she had a last glimpse of her father looking worried, but giving her a smile of reassurance…

When she awoke, she had a hard time focusing on Dr. Hajid's face in front of her. She felt disoriented, tried to concentrate. He was speaking in words as sharp and hard as his medical instruments. "The delivery was successful."

Her eyes tried to fall closed again, but she forced them open. *Of course it was successful,* she thought. But she didn't notice her father there, and wondered if he was holding the baby.

She wanted to see him, croaked his name, but the doctor wasn't finished.

"There has been one surprise—fortunate or unfortunate, depending on how you look at it."

"Where is my father?" she asked.

"I am sorry to say that he is gone." Hajid didn't look sorry at all.

Then the doctor and his assistant came close to her at the bedside. He was holding a blanket-wrapped bundle, as was his assistant.

Two babies. Birenda didn't understand.

"Administrator Fleer surrendered himself right away, while you were still unconscious. He felt it would be better that way." The doctor gave her a shallow smile. "But he did want to congratulate you on the birth of your twins."

MORE THAN THE SUM OF HIS PARTS

JOE HALDEMAN

Joe's awards include Hugo Awards for *The Forever War*, *Tricentennial*, *The Hemingway Hoax*, *None So Blind*, and *Forever Peace*; the John W. Campbell Memorial Award for Best Science Fiction Novel for *Forever Peace*; Nebula Awards for *The Forever War*, *The Hemingway Hoax*, *Graves*, *Forever Peace*, and *Camouflage*; the Locus Award for *The Forever War*; the World Fantasy Award for *Graves*; and the James Tiptree, Jr. Award for *Camouflage*.

He received the Damon Knight Memorial Grand Master Award for lifetime achievement at the 2010 Nebula Awards Ceremony. He served twice as president of the Science Fiction Writers of America. He was inducted into the Science Fiction Hall of Fame in 2012. The story below received a Nebula Nomination for best short story. You can read *The Best of Joe Haldeman* at http://amzn.to/1t5GtQz.

21 August 2058

They say I am to keep a detailed record of my feelings, my perceptions, as I grow accustomed to the new parts. To that end, they gave me an apparatus that blind people use for writing, like a tablet with guide wires. It is somewhat awkward. But a recorder would be useless, since I will not have a mouth for some time, and I can't type blind with only one hand.

Woke up free from pain. Interesting. Surprising to find that it has only been five days since the accident. For the record, I am, or was, Dr. Wilson Cheetham, Senior Engineer (Quality Control) for U.S. Steel's Skyfac station, a high-orbit facility that produces foamsteel and vapor deposition materials for use in the cislunar community. But if you are reading this, you must know all that.

Five days ago I was inspecting the aluminum deposition facility and had a bad accident. There was a glitch in my jetseat controls, and I flew suddenly straight into the wide beam of charged aluminum vapor. Very hot. They turned it off in a second, but there was still plenty of time for the beam to breach the suit and thoroughly roast three quarters of my body.

Apparently there was a rescue bubble right there. I was unconscious, of course. They tell me that my heart stopped with the shock, but they managed to save me. My left leg and arm are gone, as is my face. I have no lower jaw, nose, or external ears. I can hear after a fashion, though, and will have eyes in a week or so. They claim they will craft for me testicles and a penis.

I must be pumped full of mood drugs. I feel too calm. If I were myself, whatever fraction of myself is left, perhaps I would resist the insult of being turned into a sexless half-machine.

Ah well. This will be a machine that can turn itself off.

22 August 2058

For many days there was only sleep or pain. This was in the weightless ward at Mercy. They stripped the dead skin off me bit by bit. There were limits to anesthesia, unfortunately. I tried to scream but found I had no vocal cords. They finally decided not to try to salvage the arm and leg, which saved some pain.

When I was able to listen, they explained that U.S. Steel valued my services so much that they were willing to underwrite a state-of-the-art cyborg transformation. Half the cost will be absorbed by Interface Biotech on the Moon. Everybody will deduct me from their taxes.

This, then, is the catalog. First, new arm and leg. That's fairly standard. (I once worked with a woman who had two cyborg arms. It took weeks before I could look at her without feeling pity and revulsion.) Then they will attempt to build me a working jaw and mouth, which has been done only rarely and imperfectly, and rebuild the trachea, vocal cords, esophagus. I will be able to speak and drink, though except for certain soft foods, I won't eat in a normal way; salivary glands are beyond their art. No mucous membranes of any kind. A drastic cure for my chronic sinusitis.

Surprisingly, to me at least, the reconstruction of a penis is a fairly straightforward procedure, for which they've had lots of practice. Men are forever sticking them into places where they don't belong. They are particularly excited about my case because of the challenge in restoring sensation as well as function. The prostate is intact, and they seem confident that they can hook up the complicated plumbing involved in ejaculation. Restoring the ability to urinate is trivially easy, they say.

(The biotechnician in charge of the urogenital phase of the project talked at me for more than an hour, going into unnecessarily grisly detail. It seems that this replacement was done occasionally even before they had any kind of mechanical substitute, by sawing off a short rib and transplanting it, covering it with a skin graft from elsewhere on the body. The recipient thus was blessed with a permanent erection, unfortunately rather strange-looking and short on sensation. My own prosthesis will look very much like the real, shall we say, thing, and new developments in tractor-field mechanics and bionic interfacing should give it realistic response patterns.)

I don't know how to feel about all this. I wish they would leave my blood chemistry alone, so I could have some honest grief or horror, whatever. Instead of this placid waiting.

4 September 2058

Out cold for thirteen days and I wake up with eyes. The arm and leg are in place but not powered up yet. I wonder what the eyes look like. (They won't give me a mirror until I have a face.) They feel like wet glass.

Very fancy eyes. I have a box with two dials that I can use to override the "default mode"—that is, the ability to see only normally. One of them gives me conscious control over pupil dilation, so I can see in almost total darkness or, if for some reason I wanted to, look directly at the sun without discomfort. The other changes the frequency response, so I can see either in the infrared or the ultraviolet. This hospital room looks pretty much the same in ultraviolet, but in infrared it takes on a whole new aspect. Most of the room's illumination then comes from bright bars on the walls, radiant heating. My real arm shows a pulsing tracery of arteries and veins. The other is of course not visible except by reflection and is dark blue.

(Later) Strange I didn't realize I was on the Moon. I thought it was a low-gravity ward in Mercy. While I was sleeping they sent me down to Biotech. Should have figured that out.

5 September 2058

They turned on the "social" arm and leg and began patterning exercises. I am told to think of a certain movement and do its mirror image with my right arm or leg while attempting to execute it with my left. The trainer helps the cyborg unit along, which generates something like pain, though actually it doesn't resemble any real muscular ache. Maybe it's the way circuits feel when they're overloaded.

By the end of the session I was able to make a fist without help, though there is hardly enough grip to hold a pencil. I can't raise the leg yet, but can make the toes move.

They removed some of the bandages today, from shoulder to hip, and the test-tube skin looks much more real than I had prepared myself for. Hairless and somewhat glossy, but the color match is perfect. In infrared it looks quite different, more uniform in color than the "real" side. I suppose that's because it hasn't aged forty years.

While putting me through my paces, the technician waxed rhapsodic about how good this arm is going to be—this set of arms, actually. I'm exercising with the "social" one, which looks much more convincing than the ones my coworker displayed ten years ago. (No doubt more a matter of money than of advancing technology.) The "working" arm, which I haven't seen yet, will be all metal, capable of being worn on the outside of a spacesuit. Besides having the two arms, I'll be able to interface with various waldos, tailored to specific functions.

I am fortunately more ambidextrous than the average person. I broke my right wrist in the second grade and kept re-breaking it through the third, and so learned to write with both hands. All my life I have been able to print more clearly with the left.

They claim to be cutting down on my medication. If that's the truth, I seem to be adjusting fairly well. Then again, I have nothing in my past experience to use as a basis for comparison. Perhaps this calmness is only a mask for hysteria.

6 September 2058

Today I was able to tie a simple knot. I can lightly sketch out the letters of the alphabet. A large and childish scrawl but recognizably my own.

I've begun walking after a fashion, supporting myself between parallel bars. (The lack of hand strength is a neural problem, not a muscular one; when rigid, the arm and leg are as strong as metal crutches.) As I practice, it's amusing to watch the reactions of people who walk into the room, people who aren't paid to mask their horror at being studied by two cold lenses embedded in a swath of bandages formed over a shape that is not a head.

Tomorrow they start building my face. I will be essentially unconscious for more than a week. The limb patterning will continue as I sleep, they say.

14 September 2058

When I was a child my mother, always careful to have me do "normal" things, dressed me in costume each Halloween and escorted me around the high-rise, so I could beg for candy I did not want and money I did not need. On one occasion I had to wear the mask of a child star then popular on the cube, a tightly fitting plastic affair that covered the entire head, squeezing my pudgy features into something more in line with some Platonic ideal of childish beauty. That was my last Halloween. I embarrassed her.

This face is like that. It is undeniably my face, but the skin is taut and unresponsive. Any attempt at expression produces a grimace.

I have almost normal grip in the hand now, though it is still clumsy. As they hoped, the sensory feedback from the fingertips and palms seems to be more finely tuned than in my "good" hand. Tracing my new forefinger across my right wrist, I can sense the individual pores, and there is a marked temperature gradient as I pass over tendon or vein. And yet the hand and arm will eventually be capable of superhuman strength.

Touching my new face I do not feel pores. They have improved on nature in the business of heat exchange.

22 September 2058

Another week of sleep while they installed the new plumbing. When the anesthetic wore off I felt a definite *something*, not pain, but neither was it the normal somatic heft of genitalia. Everything was bedded in gauze and bandage, though, and catheterized, so it would feel strange even to a normal person.

(Later) An aide came in and gingerly snipped away the bandages. He blushed; I don't think fondling was in his job description. When the catheter came out there was a small sting of pain and relief.

It's not much of a copy. To reconstruct the face, they could consult hundreds of pictures and cubes, but it had never occurred to me that one day it might be useful to have a gallery of pictures of my private parts in various stages of repose. The technicians had approached the problem by bringing me a stack of photos culled from urological texts and pornography, and having me sort through them as to "closeness of fit."

It was not a task for which I was well trained, by experience or disposition. Strange as it may seem in this age of unfettered hedonism, I haven't seen another man naked, let alone rampant, since leaving high school, twenty-five years ago. (I was stationed on Farside for eighteen months and never went near a sex bar, preferring an audience of one. Even if I had to hire her, as was usually the case.)

So this one is rather longer and thicker than its predecessor—would all men unconsciously exaggerate?—and has only approximately the same aspect when erect. A young man's rakish angle.

Distasteful but necessary to write about the matter of masturbation. At first it didn't work. With my right hand, it felt like holding another man, which I have never had any desire to do. With the new hand, though, the process proceeded in the normal way, though I must admit to a voyeuristic aspect. The sensations were extremely acute. Ejaculation more forceful than I can remember from youth.

It makes me wonder. In a book I recently read, about brain chemistry, the author made a major point of the notion that it's a mistake to completely equate "mind" with "brain." The brain, he said, is in a way only the thickest and most complex segment of the nervous system; it coordinates our consciousness, but the actual mind suffuses through the body in a network of ganglia. In fact, he used sexuality as an example. When a man ruefully observes that his penis has a mind of its own, he is stating part of a larger truth.

But I in fact do have actual brains imbedded in my new parts: the biochips that process sensory data coming in and action commands going back. Are these brains part of my consciousness the way the rest of my nervous system is? The masturbation experience indicates they might be in business for themselves.

This is premature speculation, so to speak. We'll see how it feels when I move into a more complex environment, where I'm not so self-absorbed.

23 September 2058

During the night something evidently clicked. I woke up this morning with full strength in my cyborg limbs. One rail of the bed was twisted out of shape where I must have unconsciously gripped it. I bent it back quite easily.

Some obscure impulse makes me want to keep this talent secret for the time being. The technicians thought I would be able to exert three or four times the normal person's grip; this is obviously much more than that.

But why keep it a secret? I don't know. Eventually they will read this diary and I will stand exposed. There's no harm in that, though; this is supposed to be a record of my psychological adjustment or maladjustment. Let *them* tell *me* why I've done it.

(Later) The techs were astonished, ecstatic. I demonstrated a pull of 90 kilograms. I know if I'd actually given it a good yank, I could have pulled the stress machine out of the wall. I'll give them 110 tomorrow and inch my way up to 125.

Obviously I must be careful with force vectors. If I put too much stress on the normal parts of my body I could do permanent injury. With my metal fist I could certainly punch a hole through an airlock door, but it would probably tear the prosthesis out of its socket. Newton's laws still apply.

Other laws will have to be rewritten.

24 September 2058

I got to work out with three waldos today. A fantastic experience!

The first one was a disembodied hand and arm attached to a stand, the set-up they use to train normal people in the use of waldos. The difference is that I don't need a waldo sleeve to imperfectly transmit my wishes to the mechanical double. I can plug into it directly.

I've been using waldos in my work ever since graduate school, but it was never anything like this. Inside the waldo sleeve you get a clumsy kind of feedback from striated pressor field generators embedded in the plastic. With my setup the feedback is exactly the kind a normal person feels when he touches an object, but much more sensitive. The first time they asked me to pick up an egg, I tossed it up and caught it (no great feat of coordination in lunar gravity, admittedly, but I could have done it as easily in Earth-normal).

The next waldo was a large earthmover that Western Mining uses over at Grimaldi Station. That was interesting, not only because of its size but because of the slight communications lag. Grimaldi is only a few dozen of kilometers away, but there aren't enough unused data channels between here and there for me to use the land-line to communicate with the earthmover hand. I had to relay via comsat, so there was about a tenth-second delay between the thought and the action. It was a fine feeling of power, but a little confusing: I would cup my hand and scoop downward, and then a split-second too late would feel the resistance of the regolith. And then casually hold in my palm several tonnes of rock and dirt. People standing around watching; with a flick of my wrist I could have buried them. Instead I dutifully dumped it on the belt to the converter.

But the waldo that most fascinated me was the micro. It had been in use for only a few months; I had heard of it, but hadn't had a chance to see it in action. It is a fully articulated hand barely a tenth of a millimeter long. I used it in conjunction with a low-power scanning electron microscope, moving around on the surface of a microcircuit. At that magnification it looked like a hand on a long stick wandering through the corridors of a building, whose walls varied from rough stucco to brushed metal to blistered gray paint, all laced over with thick cables of gold. When necessary, I could bring in another hand, manipulated by my right from inside a waldo sleeve, to help with simple carpenter and machinist tasks that, in the real world, translated into fundamental changes in the quantum-electrodynamic properties of the circuit.

This was the real power: not crushing metal tubes or lifting tonnes of rock, but pushing electrons around to do my bidding. My first doctorate was in electrical engineering; in a sudden epiphany I realize that I am the first *actual* electrical engineer in history.

After two hours they made me stop; said I was showing signs of strain. They put me in a wheelchair, and I did fall asleep on the way back to my room. Dreaming dreams of microcosmic and infinite power.

25 September 2058

The metal arm. I expected it to feel fundamentally different from the "social" one, but of course it doesn't, most of the time. Circuits are circuits. The difference comes under conditions of extreme exertion: the soft hand gives me signals like pain if I come close to the level of stress that would harm the fleshlike material. With the metal hand I can rip off a chunk of steel plate a centimeter thick and feel nothing beyond "muscular" strain. If I had two of them I could work marvels.

The mechanical leg is not so gifted. It has governors to restrict its strength and range of motion to that of a normal leg, which is reasonable. Even a normal person finds himself brushing the ceiling occasionally in lunar gravity. I could stand up sharply and find myself with a concussion, or worse.

I like the metal arm, though. When I'm stronger (hah!) they say they'll let me go outside and try it with a spacesuit. Throw something over the horizon.

Starting today, I'm easing back into a semblance of normal life. I'll be staying at Biotech for another six or eight weeks, but I'm patched into my Skyfac office and have started clearing out the backlog of paperwork. Two hours in the morning and two in the afternoon. It's diverting, but I have to admit my heart isn't really in it. Rather be playing with the micro. (Have booked three hours on it tomorrow.)

26 September 2058

They threaded an optical fiber through the micro's little finger, so I can watch its progress on a screen without being limited to the field of an electron microscope. The picture is fuzzy while the waldo is in motion, but if I hold it still for a few seconds, the computer assist builds up quite a sharp image. I used it to roam all over my right arm and hand, which was fascinating. Hairs a tangle of stiff black stalks, the pores small damp craters. And everywhere the evidence of the skin's slow death; translucent sheafs of desquamated cells.

I've taken to wearing the metal arm rather than the social one. People's stares don't bother me. The metal one will be more useful in my actual work, and I want to get as much practice as possible. There is also an undeniable feeling of power.

27 September 2058

Today I went outside. It was clumsy getting around at first. For the past eleven years I've used a suit only in zero gee, so all my reflexes are wrong. Still, not much serious can go wrong at a sixth of a gee.

It was exhilarating but at the same time frustrating, since I couldn't reveal all my strength. I did almost overdo it once, starting to tip over a large boulder. Before it tipped, I realized that my left boot had crunched through about ten centimeters of regolith, in reaction to the amount of force I was applying. So I backed off and discreetly shuffled my foot to fill the telltale hole.

I could indeed throw a rock over the horizon. With a sling, I might be able to put a small one into orbit. Rent myself out as a lunar launching facility.

(Later) Most interesting. A pretty nurse who has been on this project since the beginning came into my room after dinner and proposed the obvious experiment. It was wildly successful.

Although my new body starts out with the normal pattern of excitation-plateau-orgasm, the resemblance stops there. I have no refractory period; the process of erection is completely under conscious control. This could make me the most popular man on the Moon.

The artificial skin of the penis is as sensitive to tactile differentiation as that of the cyborg fingers: suddenly I know more about a woman's internal topography than any man who ever lived—more than any *woman!*

I think tomorrow I'll take a trip to Farside.

28 September 2058

Farside has nine sex bars. I read the guidebook descriptions, and then asked a few locals for their recommendations, and wound up going to a place cleverly called the Juice Bar.

In fact, the name was not just an expression of coy eroticism. They served nothing but fruit and juices there, most of them fantastically expensive Earth imports. I spent a day's pay on a glass of pear nectar and sought out the most attractive woman in the room.

That in itself was a mistake. I was not physically attractive even before the accident, and the mechanics have faithfully restored my coarse features and slight paunch. I was rebuffed.

So I went to the opposite extreme and looked for the plainest woman. That would be a better test, anyway: before the accident I always demanded, and paid for, physical perfection. If I could duplicate the performance of last night with a woman to whom I was not sexually attracted—and do it in public, with no pressure from having gone without—then my independence from the autonomic nervous system would be proven beyond doubt.

Second mistake. I was never good at small talk, and when I located my paragon of plainness I began talking about the accident and the singular talent that had resulted from it. She suddenly remembered an appointment elsewhere.

I was not so open with the next woman, also plain. She asked whether there was something wrong with my face, and I told her half of the truth. She was sweetly sympathetic, motherly, which did not endear her to me. It did make her a good subject for the experiment. We left the socializing section of the bar and went back to the so-called "love room."

There was an acrid quality to the air that I suppose was compounded of incense and sweat, but of course my dry nose was not capable of identifying actual smells. For the first time, I was grateful for that disability; the place probably had the aroma of a well-used locker room. Plus pheromones.

253

Under the muted lights, red and blue as well as white, more than a dozen couples were engaged more or less actively in various aspects of amorous behavior. A few were frankly staring at others, but most were either absorbed with their own affairs or furtive in their voyeurism. Most of them were on the floor, which was a warm soft mat, but some were using tables and chairs in fairly ingenious ways. Several of the permutations would no doubt have been impossible or dangerous in Earth's gravity.

We undressed and she complimented me on my evident spryness. A nearby spectator made a jealous observation. Her own body was rather flaccid, doughy, and under previous circumstances I doubt that I would have been able to maintain enthusiasm. There was no problem, however; in fact, I rather enjoyed it. She required very little foreplay, and I was soon repeating the odd sensation of hypersensitized explorations. Gynecological spelunking.

She was quite voluble in her pleasure, and although she lasted less than an hour, we did attract a certain amount of attention. When she, panting, regretfully declined further exercise, a woman who had been watching, a rather attractive young blonde, offered to share her various openings. I obliged her for a while; although the well was dry, the pump handle was unaffected.

During that performance I became aware that the pleasure involved was not a sexual one in any normal sense. Sensual, yes, in the way that a fine meal is a sensual experience, but with a remote subtlety that I find difficult to describe. Perhaps there is a relation to epicurism that is more than metaphorical. Since I can no longer taste food, a large area of my brain is available for the valuation of other experience. It may be that the brain is reorganizing itself in order to take fullest advantage of my new abilities.

By the time the blonde's energy began to flag, several other women had taken an interest in my satyriasis. I resisted the temptation to find what this organ's limit was, if indeed a limit exists. My back ached and the right knee was protesting. So I threw the mental switch and deflated. I left with a minimum of socializing. (The first woman insisted on buying me something at the bar. I opted for a banana.)

29 September 2058

Now that I have eyes and both hands, there's no reason to scratch this diary out with a pen. So I'm entering it into the computer. But I'm keeping two versions.

I recopied everything up to this point and then went back and edited the version that I will show to Biotech. It's very polite, and will remain so. For instance, it does not contain the following:

After writing last night's entry, I found myself still full of energy, and so I decided to put into action a plan that has been forming in my mind.

About two in the morning I went downstairs and broke into the waldo lab. The entrance is protected by a five-digit combination lock, but of course that was no obstacle. My hypersensitive fingers could feel the tumblers rattling into place.

I got the micro-waldo set up and then detached my leg. I guided the waldo through the leg's circuitry and easily disabled the governors. The whole operation took less than twenty minutes.

I did have to use a certain amount of care walking, at first. There was a tendency to rise into the air or to limpingly overcompensate. It was under control by the time I got back to my room. So once more they proved to have been mistaken as to the limits of my abilities. Testing the strength of the leg, with a halfhearted kick I put a deep dent in the metal wall at the rear of my closet. I'll have to wait until I can be outside, alone, to see what full force can do.

A comparison kick with my flesh leg left no dent, but did hurt my great toe.

30 September 2058

It occurs to me that I feel better about my body than I have in the past twenty years. Who wouldn't? Literally eternal youth in these new limbs and organs; if a part shows signs of wear, it can simply be replaced.

I was angry at the Biotech evaluation board this morning. When I simply inquired as to the practicality of replacing the right arm and leg as well, all but one were horrified. One was amused. I will remember him.

I think the fools are going to order me to leave Nearside in a day or two and go back to Mercy for psychiatric "help." I will leave when I want to, on my own terms.

1 October 2058

This is being voice-recorded in the Environmental Control Center at Nearside. It is 10:32; they have less than ninety minutes to accede to my demands. Let me backtrack.

After writing last night's entry I felt a sudden excess of sexual desire. I took the shuttle to Farside and went back to the Juice Bar.

The plain woman from the previous night was waiting, hoping that I would show up. She was delighted when I suggested that we save money (and whatever residue of modesty we had left) by keeping ourselves to one another, back at my room.

I didn't mean to murder her. That was not in my mind at all. But I suppose in my passion, or abandon, I carelessly propped my strong leg against the wall and then thrust with too much strength. At any rate there was a snap and a tearing sound. She gave a small cry and the lower half of my body was suddenly awash in blood. I had snapped her spine and evidently at the same time caused considerable internal damage. She must have lost consciousness very quickly, though her heart did not stop beating for nearly a minute.

Disposing of the body was no great problem, conceptually. In the laundry room I found a bag large enough to hold her comfortably. Then I went back to the room and put her and the sheet she had besmirched into the bag.

Getting her to the recycler would have been a problem if it had been a normal hour. She looked like nothing so much as a body in a laundry bag. Fortunately, the corridor was deserted.

The lock on the recycler room was child's play. The furnace door was a problem, though; it was easy to unlock but its effective diameter was only 25 centimeters.

So I had to disassemble her. To save cleaning up, I did the job inside the laundry bag, which was clumsy, and made it difficult to see the fascinating process.

I was so absorbed in watching that I didn't hear the door slide open. But the man who walked in made a slight gurgling sound, which somehow I did hear over the cracking of bones. I stepped over to him and killed him with one kick.

At this point I have to admit to a lapse in judgment. I relocked the door and went back to the chore at hand. After the woman was completely recycled, I repeated the process with the man—which was, incidentally, much easier. The female's layer of subcutaneous fat made disassembly of the torso a more slippery business.

It really was wasted time (though I did spend part of the time thinking out the final touches of the plan I am now engaged upon). I might as well have left both bodies there on the floor. I had kicked the man with great force—enough to throw me to the ground in reaction and badly bruise my right hip—and had split him open from crotch to heart. This made a bad enough mess, even if he hadn't compounded the problem by striking the ceiling. I would never be able to clean that up, and it's not the sort of thing that would escape notice for long.

At any rate, it was only twenty minutes wasted, and I gained more time than that by disabling the recycler room lock. I cleaned up, changed clothes, stopped by the waldo lab for a few minutes, and then took the slidewalk to the Environmental Control Center.

There was only one young man on duty at the ECC at that hour. I exchanged a few pleasantries with him and then punched him in the heart, softly enough not to make a mess. I put his body where it wouldn't distract me and then attended to the problem of the "door."

There's no actual door on the ECC, but there is an emergency wall that slides into place if there's a drop in pressure. I typed up a test program simulating an emergency, and the wall obeyed. Then I walked over and twisted a few flanges around. Nobody would be able to get into the Center with anything short of a cutting torch.

Sitting was uncomfortable with the bruised hip, but I managed to ease into the console and spend an hour or so studying logic and wiring diagrams. Then I popped off an access plate and moved the micro-waldo down the corridors of electronic thought. The intercom began buzzing incessantly, but I didn't let it interfere with my concentration.

Nearside is protected from meteorite strike or (far more likely) structural failure by a series of 128 bulkheads that, like the emergency wall here, can slide into place and isolate any area where there's a pressure drop. It's done automatically, of course, but can also be controlled from here.

What I did, in essence, was to tell each bulkhead that it was under repair, and should not close under any circumstance. Then I moved the waldo over to the circuits that controlled the city's eight airlocks. With some rather elegant microsurgery, I transferred control of all eight solely to the pressure switch I now hold in my left hand.

It is a negative-pressure button, a dead-man switch taken from a power saw. So long as I hold it down, the inner doors of the airlock will remain locked. If I let go, they will all iris open. The outer doors are already open, as are the ones that connect the airlock chambers to the suiting-up rooms. No one will be able to make it to a spacesuit in time. Within thirty seconds, every corridor will be full of vacuum. People behind airtight doors may choose between slow asphyxiation and explosive decompression.

My initial plan had been to wire the dead-man switch to my pulse, which would free my good hand and allow me to sleep. That will have to wait. The wiring completed, I turned on the intercom and announced that I would speak to the Coordinator, and no one else.

When I finally got to talk to him, I told him what I had done and invited him to verify it. That didn't take long. Then I presented my demands:

Surgery to replace the rest of my limbs, of course. The surgery would have to be done while I was conscious (a heartbeat dead-man switch could be subverted by a heart machine) and it would have to be done here, so that I could be assured that nobody fooled with my circuit changes.

The doctors were called in, and they objected that such profound surgery couldn't be done under local anesthetic. I knew they were lying, of course; amputation was a fairly routine procedure even before anesthetics were invented. Yes, but I would faint, they said. I told them that I would not, and at any rate I was willing to take the chance, and no one else had any choice in the matter.

(I have not yet mentioned that the ultimate totality of my plan involves replacing all my internal organs as well as all of the limbs—or at least those organs whose failure could cause untimely death. I will be a true cyborg then, a human brain in an "artificial" body, with the prospect of thousands of years of life. With a few decades—or centuries!—of research, I could even do something about the brain's shortcomings. I would wind up interfaced to EarthNet, with all of human knowledge at my disposal, and with my faculties for logic and memory no longer fettered by the slow pace of electrochemical synapse.)

A psychiatrist, talking from Earth, tried to convince me of the error of my ways. He said that the dreadful trauma had "obviously" unhinged me, and the cyborg augmentation, far from affecting a cure, had made my mental derangement worse. He demonstrated, at least to his own satisfaction, that my behavior followed some classical pattern of madness. All this had been taken into consideration, he said, and if I were to give myself up, I would be forgiven my crimes and manumitted into the loving arms of the psychiatric establishment.

I did take time to explain the fundamental errors in his way of thinking. He felt that I had quite literally lost my identity by losing my face and genitalia, and that I was at bottom a "good" person whose essential humanity had been perverted by physical and existential estrangement. Totally wrong. By his terms, what I actually *am* is an "evil" person whose true nature was revealed to himself by the lucky accident that released him from existential propinquity with the common herd.

And "evil" is the accurate word, not maladjusted or amoral or even criminal. I am as evil by human standards as a human is evil by the standards of an animal raised for food, and the analogy is accurate. I will sacrifice humans not only for any survival but for comfort, curiosity, or entertainment. I will allow to live anyone who doesn't bother me, and reward generously those who help.

Now they have only forty minutes. They know I am

—end of recording—

25 September 2058

Excerpt from Summary Report

I am Dr. Henry Janovski, head of the surgical team that worked on the ill-fated cyborg augmentation of Dr. Wilson Cheetham.

We were fortunate that Dr. Cheetham's insanity did interfere with his normally painstaking, precise nature. If he had spent more time in preparation, I have no doubt that he would have put us in a very difficult fix.

He should have realized that the protecting wall that shut him off from the rest of Nearside was made of steel, an excellent conductor of electricity. If he had insulated himself behind a good dielectric, he could have escaped his fate.

Cheetham's waldo was a marvelous instrument, but basically it was only a pseudo-intelligent servomechanism that obeyed well-defined radio-frequency commands. All we had to do was override the signals that were coming from his own nervous system.

We hooked a powerful amplifier up to the steel wall, making it in effect a huge radio transmitter. To generate the signal we wanted amplified, I had a technician put on a waldo sleeve that was holding a box similar to Cheetham's dead-man switch. We wired the hand closed, turned up the power, and had the technician strike himself on the chin as hard as he could.

The technician struck himself so hard he blacked out for a few seconds. Cheetham's resonant action, perhaps a hundred times more powerful, drove the bones of his chin up through the top of his skull.

Fortunately, the expensive arm itself was not damaged. It is not evil or insane by itself, of course. Which I shall prove.

The experiments will continue, though of course we will be more selective as to subjects. It seems obvious in retrospect that we should not use as subjects people who have gone through the kind of trauma that Cheetham suffered. We must use willing volunteers. Such as myself.

I am not young, and weakness and an occasional tremor in my hands limit the amount of surgery I can do—much less than my knowledge would allow, or my nature desire. My failing left arm I shall have replaced with Cheetham's mechanical marvel, and I will go through training similar to his—but for the good of humanity, not for ill.

What miracles I will perform with a knife!

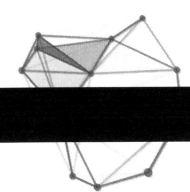

LAZARUS RISING

GREGORY BENFORD

Gregory is a Nebula and John W. Campbell Memorial award winner and the author of many top-selling novels, including *Jupiter Project*, *Artifact*, *Against Infinity*, *Eater*, and *Timescape*. He is that unusual creative combination of scientist scholar and talented artist. His stories capture readers—hearts and minds—with imaginative leaps into the future of science and of us.

A University of California faculty member since 1971, he has conducted research in plasma turbulence and in astrophysics. His published scientific articles include well over a hundred papers in the fields of condensed matter, particle physics, plasmas, mathematical physics, and biological conservation.

Gregory coauthored *Shipstar* (with Larry Niven) available at http://amzn.to/1zSmCoV.

W hen he woke up, he was dead.

Utter blackness, total silence. Nothing. Nothing but black when he opened his eyes—or thought he had.

No smells. There should be the clean, antiseptic, efficient scent of the Medical Extension Center.

No background rustle or steps. No drone of air conditioning, no distant murmur of conversations, no jangle of a telephone.

He could not feel any press of his own weight. No cold table or starched sheets rubbed his skin.

They had disconnected all his external nerves.

He felt a rush of fear. Total loss of control. He was a slab of meat waiting for extinction.

To do that required finding the major nerves as they wound up through the spine. Plus the many other pathways from the rest of the body. Then a medical tech had to electrically splice them out of the tangled knot at the back of the neck. Delicate work. He had heard about it, of course, wondered what it was like—but this…

A sharp slap of fear ran through him. What did it mean? Why—?

He fought his rising confusion. He had to explore. To think.

He pushed the emotions away. First he had to know more. Was he fully dead? He waited, letting the adrenaline of his fear wash away.

Concentrate. Think of quietness, stillness. You're on a beach, maybe, surf rumbling in the distance... let it go...

Yes, *there*. He felt a weak, regular thump that might be his heart. Behind that, as though far away, was a slow, faint fluttering of... lungs?

That was all. He knew that the body's internal nerves were thinly spread. They gave only vague, blunt senses. But there was enough dull sensation, in the background, to tell him that the basic functions were still plodding on.

Still... Paralysis encased him like concrete. He sent signals to push out his tongue, purse his lips, shrug his shoulders, open his eyes—and got nothing back, no sense if any of these motions had happened.

There was a dim pressure that might be his bladder. Snap his fingers, even? He could pick up nothing specific from legs or arms.

He tried to move his head. Nothing. No feedback.

Open an eye? Only blackness.

Legs—he turned both, hoping that only the sensations were gone. He might be able to detect a leg moving by the change in pressure somewhere in his body,

No response. But if he could sense his bladder, he should have gotten something back from the shifting weight of a leg.

That meant his lower motor control was shut off.

Panic rose in him—a cold, blind sensation. Normally this strong an emotion would bring deeper breathing, a heavier heartbeat, flexing muscles, a tingling urgency. He felt none of that.

There was only a swirl of conflicting thoughts, a jittery forking in his mind like summer lightning. A halfway house on the road to death.

He forced himself to think.

His name was Carlos Farenza, and he was 87 years old. Born in LA in 1998. His own father had died at 62 of hypertension, but 87 was no great achievement these days. With enough organ replacements, blood scrubbing, neuroengineering, the nutrigenomic supplements and anti-aging treatments, anybody who didn't have stupid bad habits could make it to a hundred. It was just a matter of looking both ways before you stepped out into traffic.

The only limitation was cost. Nearly everybody was on Universal Medical, but society couldn't afford to go on overhauling each eroding body. It was like keeping an old car running for sentimental reasons. Eventually, you were spending more money on parts and repairs than a new car would cost. The same way, society judged when people had run up too great a tab, so kicked the problem forward in time, through the sleepslots. For "society" substitute the eternal bands of arguing lawyers, who had nothing but their fees at stake. But some measure had to emerge.

So there was a test. For Carlos it came every three years, and that's what he was here for. You came in and they poked you, prodded, pried you open and ran a whole-body diagnostic. If your mental and physio indices were up to par, you got three more years of free service on Universal Medical. Like getting your driver's license renewed.

If you flunked… Even then, it didn't necessarily mean death. Not unless you had already elected for that, of course. There was a hundred thousand kilo-buck reward, passed on to whomever you stipulated.

If you checked out, there were other rewards for your inheritors, family, even friends. Reasonable, really—the government had to encourage elective suicides, to keep costs down.

But death was seldom the right answer. Most people chose the sleepslots. The medical techs laid you away in a near-freezing slot, electronically modulated, and stored you until something could be done about your condition. That might take ten years, and it might take a thousand.

So they had laid Carlos out on a diagnostic slab, hooked him up, said the usual soothing words. He had been jittery. Everybody was nervous when going through diagnostics. He'd had a cancer diagnosis before, but they'd muted it, maybe cured the damned creeping thing. These diseases were tricky these days, though; cancers seemed to know how to hide.

Still, it wasn't exactly a life-or-death thing. It was merely life versus suspended life. But you never knew how you would do, no matter how well you felt. Tricky.

But he damn well knew which he wanted. He had good friends, good times, his job—everybody worked, or how else to support the truly old?—was a pretty humdrum office position. But he still enjoyed it. Divorced at the moment, but that could change. He had places he wanted to see, relatives, a neighborhood. He was anchored in his time. He didn't want to wake up in some distant future with outdated skills, a lonely stranger.

If you failed the test, there was no reprieve. You didn't get a vote; you were shut down neurologically. The techs would methodically prepare you for the sleepslots. If they had discovered a deteriorating condition, something that might even malfunction, under the strain of bringing you back to full consciousness... well, then the law said they could stack you in the sleepslot without waking you up. For your own good, of course. Just shut you down.

Like this.

They weren't finished, or else he'd never have come awake again. Some technician had screwed up. Shut off a nerve center somewhere, using pinpoint interrupters, but maybe a tech pinched one filament too many. They worked at the big junction between brain and spinal cord, down at the base of the skull. It was like a big cable back there, and the techs found their way by feedback analysis. Some small fraction of the time, microscopic nerve fibers got mixed up, if the tech was working fast, Carlos knew. Maybe a gal looking forward to coffee break, she could reactivate the conscious cerebral functions and not notice it on the scope until later.

Had that happened to him? Maybe he had come to partway through his down-run into the slots.

He had to do something.

The strange, cold panic seized him again. Adrenaline, left over from some earlier, deep physiological response. He was afraid now, jittery, but there was no answering chemical symphony of the body. His gland subsystems were shut down.

An analytical rage built in him. He had never been cut off like this. Then a new idea: *Maybe this was what the slots are like. A kind of living death.*

There was no way to tell how rapidly time passed. He counted heartbeats, a minute five—but his pulse rate depended on so many factors…

Okay, then, how long did he have? He knew it took many working hours to shut down a nervous system, damp the neuro systems, drain lymphatic points, leech the blood of residues. Hours. Routine never encourages alertness. The technicians would leave a lot of the job to the automatic machines, go get coffee, gossip…

He noticed the chill as a faint background sensation. It seemed to spread as he paid attention to it, filling his body, bringing a pleasant, mild quiet… a drifting, slow slide toward sleep…

Deep within him, something said no.

He willed himself to focus, in the utter blackness and creeping cold. They said the technicians always left a pathway to the outside, so if something went wrong, the patient could signal. He had read about that, somewhere. It was a precaution to take care of situations like this. But what would it be, what pathway?

Eyebrows? He tried them/felt nothing. Mouth? The same.

He made himself think of the steps necessary to form a word. Squeeze in the lungs. Constrict the throat. Force air out at a faster rate. Pluck the vocal cords just so. Move the tongue and lips. Throughout life you did it without thinking, but when you did, it seemed impossibly complicated.

Nothing. No faint hum echoing in his sinus cavities to tell him that muscles worked, that breath strummed his vocal cords.

He had read about this in a magazine article somewhere. The easiest way to slide people into the slots was just to shut down a whole section of the body. Okay. His head was out, obviously dead. Legs out. Feet gone, too. And genitals weren't under conscious control even at the best of times.

Arms, then? He tried the left. No answering shift of internal pressures. But how big would the effect be? He might be waving his hand straight up in the air and never know it.

Try the right. Again, no way to tell if—

No, wait. A diffuse sense of something. Try to remember which muscles to move. He had gone through life with instant feedback from every fiber, anchoring him in his body, every gesture suggesting the next. Muscle memory.

Now he had to analyze precisely. How did he make his arm rise? Muscles contracted to pull on one side of the arm and shoulder. Others relaxed to let the arm swing. He tried it.

Was there an answering weight? Faint, too faint. Maybe his imagination.

The right arm could be responding and he wouldn't know it. The attendants would see it, though, and patch into him, ask what was going on... unless they weren't around. Unless they had gone off for coffee, leaving the sagging old body to stage down gradually into long-term stasis, with the medical monitor checking, to be sure nothing failed in the ancient carcass.

Suppose the arm worked. Even if somebody saw it, was that what he wanted? If they turned his head back on, what would he do?

Demand his rights? He didn't have any. He had already signed the required documents, read through the contracts, stared at the legalese, *I, Carlos Farenza, being of sound mind and body...* All taken care of. The attendants certainly had dealt before with people who protested, demanded to see their lawyer, bright minds trapped inside failed machinery. They would ignore his momentary lapse, slide him into a slot, no matter what he said. *For his own good y'know.*

Despairing, he stopped his concentration. He had been trying to lift the arm and now gave up. He let the muscles go suddenly slack.

And was rewarded with an answering thump.

It had hit the table. Something damned well worked.

He waited. Nothing came to him in the blackness. No attendant came rapping in to correct his mistake.

So he was probably alone. Where?

Carlos found his memories strangely dim and diffuse. He could see the street this morning: an orange sun behind clouds, taking the bus... the chill winter breeze blowing trash down the sidewalk, numbing his ears... being surprised at how rundown this part of town was nowadays... walking down Wilshire past the new Conway building, first big one put up since the earthquake. Down side streets, the look of a gray, dusty city starved for water, not lively the way it had been in the 2060s. He had wondered about finally moving away from the city, panting as he shuffled toward the usual irritating wait at the Center. The staff always thought the old ones had plenty of time to waste.

Then the ritual papers, always more stuff to e-sign, never time to read them. The pretty nurse who took his clothes away. Settling into the diagnostic sheath. Looking up at the ceramic glow, the little snick and strum, sharp bites of the incisions…

He must still be there. Not already in a slot, or else he wouldn't be able to think at all. The literature they handed out described this process and he had read it all. On a slab, then, the electronics tapped deeply into him. He tried to remember what they looked like. The access terminals were on both sides, mirroring the body. So maybe, if he stretched, the right hand could reach half the input switches.

He concentrated and gave the commands that brought his arm up. Again, no answering signals to tell him if it worked. This was what it was like to be disembodied. The hand probably worked; it would have been too much trouble to disconnect it while the arm stayed live. Remembering carefully, he lowered the arm, rotating it—

A thump. Someone approaching? No, too close. The arm had fallen. Good. Balance was going to be hard. He practiced rotating the arm without raising it. No way to know if he was successful, but the moves seemed correct, familiar, while others did not. He worked without feedback, trying to summon up the exact sensation of turning the arm.

Dipping it to the side, over the edge. Working the fingers.

He stopped. If he hit the wrong control, he could turn off the arm. Without external feedback there was no way to tell if he was doing the right thing.

Pure gamble. If he had been able to, Carlos would have shrugged. *What the hell. You only die once.*

He stabbed with straightened fingers. Nothing. He fumbled and somehow knew through dull patterns that the fingers were striking the side of the slab. The knowledge came from below, some kind of holistic sensation from the deep inside him. His body, then, could not be wholly out of action. Information spread, and the mute kidneys and liver and intestines knew in some dim way what went on outside.

A wan answering pressure told him that his fingers had closed on something. He squeezed it. He made the fingers turn, carefully…

Nothing happened. Not a knob, then. A button?

He stabbed down. In his head he felt slight jolts. Sinus cavities? Like blowing his nose? He must be smacking some control to do that. With no feedback there was no way to judge force. He stabbed; a jolt. Again. Again.

A cold tremor ran up his right calf. Pain flooded in. His leg was in spasm. It jerked on the slab, striking hard—he could feel it. The sudden rush of sensations startled him. In the heady surge he could hardly tell if the heady wash was pain or something else. Just to feel at all was a pleasure.

He could feel tremors now, echoing sensations from deep within him. He could now tell that his leg was banging on the slab like a crazed animal. Suddenly he knew in his core that he was cold.

His automatic system was trying to maintain body temperature by muscle spasms, sucking the energy out of the sugar left in the tissues. A standard reaction?

Never mind. He had activated a neural web; that was the point. What to do now? The leg was still jerking. He stabbed blindly with his fingers again.

A welling coldness in his midsection. Again.

More cold, now in the right foot. Again.

A prickly sensation on his lips, playing across his cheeks. But not full senses; he could not feel his chest or arms. He started to press another button and then stopped, thinking.

So far he had been lucky. He was opening the sensory nets. Most of his right side was transmitting knowledge of chilly muscles, aches, movement. His leg was jerking less now as he brought it under control.

But if he somehow hit the shutdown button for his right arm next, he was finished. He would lie there helpless until the technicians came back.

Carlos worked the arm back onto the slab. Focus. He made the arm shift awkwardly across his chest. His motor control must extend into his upper chest and shoulders to let him do this, but without any input from there he did not know how much he could make work.

He willed the muscles to lurch to the left. A strange, abstract impression of tilting came to him. A tension somewhere. Muscles straining, locked, clenched and reaching, stretching. Again—

A warm hardness on his cheek. His nose pressed against it but he had no sense of smell. The slab top. He had rolled himself partway over. Now what?

A gathering, diffuse weariness washed through him. The arm muscles were broadcasting to the surrounding body their agony, fed by the buildup of exhausted sugar-burning tissue, leaving lactic acid.

No time to rest. The muscles would just have to keep working. He willed the arm to reach over toward the left side of the slab. He could feel nothing.

What were the chances that now he could make a fatal mistake? Probably not large; there had to be overlapping precautionary software. And he was damned if he was going to give up.

He punched down randomly, searching. A spike of pain shot through his left side. Behind that came biting cold. Slabs of muscle began shaking violently, down his left side. He stabbed down with fingers again.

Light poured in on him. He had hit the vision nerve net. A gaudy, rich redness. He realized his eyes were still closed. He opened them, and white brilliance flooded in.

Joy surged in him. He closed the eyes against the glare and punched down again.

A crisp, chill hospital smell came to him. Again.

Sound washed over him. A mechanical clanking, a distant buzz, the whirr of air circulators. No voices.

He opened his eyes just a thin slit and squinted. Turned his head. He was lying on a white slab, staring up at fluorescent lights. Now that he could see, Carlos felt with fingers coming out of their numbness. In a few tries he got back the rest of his neural net. Living had never felt so good.

He reached up toward his neck with his right hand—and his hand moved the other way. He stopped it, moved the fingers tentatively. His arm seemed to come from above his head, reaching down... but that was impossible.

He moved his left hand. It came into his vision the same way, from above.

Something was wrong with him. He closed his eyes. What could make...?

He rolled over partway and looked around the medical bay. The sign on the door leaped out. It was upside down. Carefully he reached over, clutched the edge of the slab. That was upside down, too.

What? He closed his eyes and thought. Maybe… When the eye took light and cast it on the retina, ordinary optics inverted the image. The retinal nerves filtered that signal and set it upright for the brain to use.

So the med tech had screwed that up, too. The retinal nerves weren't working right. He had been able to find things as long as he couldn't see, just using his internal sensations. That might be easy to fix, just move a fine-point fiber junction a fraction of a millimeter. But Carlos couldn't, didn't know how. He would have to manage with the world looking upside down. Somehow.

Su madre, Carlos thought, and began to fumble with the thicket of leads that snaked over his body. It was easier if he didn't look at what he was doing. He had to avoid looking at his own body because that disoriented him even further.

Even with the inverted vision, he still had to disconnect carefully the tap-ins at nerve nexus points.

When he had read the literature the Center gave him, he had found them clear, but light on detail. Now he had to recall what he could.

The big fat lot of nerve nexus points at the nape of his neck. He grasped, explored with fingers. He would have to take it out. He pulled. It was hard to detach. Gingerly, he contracted his arm muscles—it jerked free.

Instantly he felt a hot, diffuse pain from his neck, spreading up into his skull. He had read something about that. Now the nerves were exposed, sending scattershot impressions through the area. He could feel his muscles jerk.

He had screwed up badly. Now he had to put things right, just to stop the lancing agonies that built higher.

He rolled over, ignoring a wave of aches. He blinked and studied the work table next to the slab. It was a complex jumble of connectors, microelectronics, and bunched coils of nearly invisible wires. There was a patch that led back toward his neck.

He reached out for it, stretched—and missed. The upside-down effect confused every motion. His brain saw his arm moving and corrected, always in the wrong direction.

The pain… He made himself close his eyes and visualize what he felt. Stretch, grasp— It took three tries before he could override his own coordination.

He snagged the constellation of patch lines and nearly dropped it, fingers feeling thick and slow. Carefully he brought it to his head. The floppy oval of wires fitted over the gaping hole at the back of his neck. He fiddled with it until it slid snick into place. The pain tapered off. A dull throbbing remained.

He had to get up. *What was that ancient figure, coming out of the grave…? Lazarus. Rising.*

He sat up. Spasms shot through him. He gasped. Fresh agonies blossomed with every move. But he felt lean and fully awake and deeply angry. He was in a deserted medical bay. A fine sensor mesh covered his body up to his shoulders, like a coppery fishing net.

He tried to take it off, failed. His hands were clumsy, fingers blunt instruments. The sensor webbing was too complicated. Just wear it, then.

He studied the liquid-optical readouts on a medical monitor nearby. The program profile was mostly numbers. He couldn't tilt his head far enough over to read the upside-down numbers. He frowned, trying to read them directly. After a moment it wasn't so hard. The winking digital sequences were complicated and not like anything he remembered. He identified blood pressure, heart rate. The rest was meaningless. He'd never paid much attention to the hardware details before, and now he regretted it.

He got to his feet, shaky and light-headed. His feet creaked when he stood. He was tempted to rest for a moment and let the endless river of sensations wash over him. Even this sterile room of barren ivory light seemed lurid, packed with details, smells, odd sensations.

That was it. He had never loved life so much. A singing sense of this crisp world filled him. Adrenaline?

What really mattered was that he wasn't safe. Staff coffee breaks didn't last forever. He would have to find his clothes, get out, and call his Life Lawyer, as they were called.

He started for a side door. Crazy quilt walking—moving across a space that looked upside down.

The first few steps taught him to keep his head tilted down, toward his feet. He had to move his eyes the opposite way, though, to shift his vision. He bumped into the med-monitor and nearly fell over a desk. After a moment he could navigate around things. He went carefully, feeling each twinge of lancing pain as his left side protested. His right arm ached and trembled from spasm.

He reached the door, opened it slightly, peered through. The equipment beyond was hard to recognize, inverted. Lab coats on pegs jutted straight up. Chairs clung to the ceiling. He fought down a mounting sense of vertigo. His eyes were telling his brain that he was standing at the ceiling. Somewhere inside him alarm systems were struggling to be heeded.

There were open drawers of surgical instruments, a wash-up station, and electronics gear. This looked like a preparation room. He eased through.

There was a lab coat on a chair. He took halting steps over to it, reached out. His balance reeled. It was easier to manipulate things if he closed his eyes, going by feel alone. Too bad he couldn't walk that way.

The lab smock fit pretty well. It would conceal most of the fine sensor webbing that covered him. Not all, though. He bent down. Nausea swept into him, an acid bile seeped into his mouth. He closed his eyes. Easier to let his fingers guide him. He felt along his leg. Fingers found a zip-lock in the webbing. He opened it. The stuff peeled back slowly, rasping against his skin. He gave up hopes of getting it all off and settled for stripping it from his feet. He worked the stiff fabric up and bunched it above his knees.

With the lab coat on he probably looked like an ordinary patient. The sensor net stopped at his shoulders, just peeking out at the collar of the coat. He looked around, but there were no shoes. Hell with it, he thought. *Get out of here.*

He crossed the room with care and pushed a door open a crack. Footsteps coming. He let the door close and waited, heart thumping. Nobody came in. He opened it again and listened to the distant murmur of conversations, people passing, ordinary office noise.

The impersonal drone of efficiency. If he walked through them they would be on to him in a second.

Now that he thought about it he didn't have much of a chance. It wasn't enough to just call his lawyer. He had to get away clean, have time to prove that the med techs had made a mistake. An old man stumbling around in a lab coat, trying to get out of the building... No, he needed something more.

Carlos looked around, even though it made his head swim. *If only he could get his damned eyes fixed.* But he didn't know how. What else, then?

The surgical section, over there… a weapon? He shuffled over to it. Gleaming instruments hung in the open drawer, defying gravity. He picked out a scalpel in its safety sheath and gingerly slipped it into the coat pocket. He'd never used a weapon in his life, but having one was better than nothing. And it was the only thing he could think of.

Back to the door. This time he opened it and stepped out with what he hoped was a casual air. He clenched his teeth to fight off the panicky impulse that swept through him. In both directions, endless doors, offices. And luck—nobody in the corridor. He turned, gritting his teeth at a sudden jolt of nausea. Wait, at the end of the corridor—daylight. He started shuffling that way.

Two people came around a corner, talking earnestly. They didn't even look at him. He stayed close to the wall and they breezed by.

For the first time Carlos didn't mind the blank-faced stares that looked right past the anonymous patient. *Just meat for the machines…*

He tried reading signs along the hallway but couldn't. He reached the exit door, leading into an outdoor stairwell that brimmed with sunlight—and stopped. A big sign in red. He took the time to figure it out. EMERGENCY EXIT ONLY. Some kind of an alarm trigger above it.

He backed away. *Mierda*—

He had to keep moving, get farther away from the med bay. Any minute now the techs would come back. Carlos shuffled away and reached an intersection of corridors. More labs/offices. He went right, walking parallel to the outer wall of the building. Up ahead, a dozen people came out of a meeting room and stopped, chattering. He didn't want to pass them. He turned aside and saw a door. He pushed it open, stepped through and found himself in a stockroom, not much bigger than a closet. There were keys in the inside doorknob. He turned them, locking the door.

Safe, sort of. How long could he wait? Not very. Give the hall time to clear. He leaded against a wall, feeling a trembling weakness in him. He made himself count to a hundred, studying the cabinets of boxed supplies. He tried to think of some way he could use this, stuff, but most of the labels he couldn't understand.

When the hundred ran out, he let himself out, pocketing the keys. The hall was empty. He walked slowly away. He was getting used to the vision now but it was still an effort to deal with a world that was upside down. People went by him, taking no notice. Up ahead he saw some more natural daylight. He walked faster.

"Say, you aren't supposed to be—"

Carlos turned. A young nurse was following him.

"—in this part of the…" Her eyes widened. "But you can't be… I just left you—"

"You're mistaken," he said as calmly as he could. His voice croaked but he kept on, "I'm just getting some exercise, lady."

"No, you're the man on slab C, I know. You can't get up now! You're in no condition to be out."

She touched his sleeve and panic seized him. It was impossible to tell what her expression meant, inverted. Was she being kindly? If she kept after him—

"Come on, I'll help you back to—"

He backed away. His hand closed on the keys in his pocket, then the scalpel.

"Look at this," he said in his rusty, dry voice, bringing out the scalpel. He flipped it free of the safety sheath. It gleamed in the hard cold light.

She gasped. He put his hand back in the pocket, holding the scalpel, and whispered. "Now turn around and walk back that way."

Her eyes went from his face to the pocket and, back again, confused.

"You, you can't—"

"Sure I can."

She hesitated a moment more. He took her arm roughly and pushed her along, feeling strong now. "You're just taking a patient for a stroll, see. *Walk.*"

She did. He got her back to the stockroom without attracting any notice. He pushed her into it and was closing the door, fishing the keys out of his pocket, when she blurted, "There's no need for you—"

"You be quiet in here, understand?" he said as harshly as he could.

"We'll help you, you're not ready to—"

"To get filed away in a slot. No, I'm damned well not. Not ready."

"No, no you—"

Carlos thunked shut the door, snapped the locked over. He walked away fast, heart thumping wildly, and felt a rising fear.

He was near the exit when the banging started. He looked back. The nurse was pounding on the door with something solid. People in white coats stopped in the corridor, puzzled.

Carlos turned and hurried out the exit. He was at the edge of a parking lot with no vehicles in it, exposed. He crossed it, stretching his legs in a pleasurable way, working out how to do this in an inverted world. He walked along a sidewalk until a man's high voice behind him called, "Hey! Hey!"

He rounded a corner and tried running. His bare feet slapped on the warm concrete and he gulped fresh air greedily. Overriding his fear he felt a rush of power in his body, a sudden zing in the pull of his legs as he sprinted down the sidewalk between tall, tan buildings.

More shouts behind him. He worked his way between slabs of concrete, around a wall, and jogged downhill through oleander bushes on a steep hillside. The inverted vision made balance hard, but he was learning to deal with it. He kept his head down and managed to move quickly, bent over, working his way down the slope. With luck the bushes would screen him from pursuers above. He was panting but not rapidly. *Putting me in the slots, eh? They think we're sheep.*

A siren shrieked in the distance. Carlos reached the bottom of the slope and glanced around to get his bearing. Nausea still clutched at him if he moved his head too fast. *Lets see, hard to tell upside down, the streets look so different.*

He had always walked up to the Center from Wilshire. He peered at the rosy warm sun. He was facing north. So there should be a little dogleg to the south if he turned. But a massive marbled wing of the Institute blocked that way.

No time to plan. He surged ahead, through more of the Institute grounds, parts he'd never seen. Then he angled west, keeping in the shelter of eucalypts. He inhaled their scent, enjoying the feel of it penetrate his throat and lungs. In a hundred meters the trees ended, and he came out onto sidewalk. It wasn't Wilshire. He must have gotten turned around. It was a narrow little street, a few cars zooming quietly by. No pedestrians. A lucky break; he was pretty damned conspicuous.

He rushed down a block and crossed the street, not paying much attention to anything except the way he had come. The sirens wailed and cops would pick him up. He looked for a restaurant or something to duck into, but there were only faceless apartment buildings along this cramped little street. He tried some foyer doors but they were locked. Ahead, though, was a little city park he remembered. He could cut across there, maybe make a call from one of the phone booths by Wilshire and Rodeo Drive.

He crossed the street and entered the park, crossing the dry, beaten grass. It was surprisingly empty for this time of day. He circled around the scummy duck pond and trotted under a long line of sycamores. At Wilshire he turned left, angling back toward—

The Conway building wasn't there. In its place was a strange sculpted thing made of glass and blue, rubbery-looking stuff.

Carlos stood frozen for a moment, trying to get his bearings. This was Wilshire, that was for sure; wasn't Rodeo off that way?

The damned inverted vision had probably screwed up his sense of direction. In the distance towered the Sapporo building, but next to it was something that fanned out into an outrageous plumed top.

Feeling dizzy, he looked around. Now that he looked closely, he noticed that the people were kind of odd, wearing clothes that bagged in funny places and were cut the wrong way.

Carlos backed away from the street, into the park. He ran back toward the duck pond. It was easier to run than to try to straighten out his swirl of emotions and questions.

He reached the pond and looked up at the looming bulk of the Center. Something about its roof—

Two policemen were walking toward him, coming around the pond. He turned without thinking and fled.

Around a stand of eucalyptus, down a path—and there were two more police, weapons drawn. It was hard to read their expressions, inverted, but they were looking at him.

"Okay, easy, fella."

He turned back, saw them closing in behind.

"Just let us have that knife."

Carlos yelled hoarsely, "Only if you don't take me back in there."

"Can't guarantee anything 'til you drop the knife."

"I'm not going back!"

"C'mon. They say you're not even halfway through your cycling,"

"Not halfway *dead*, you mean."

"Hah?" The nearest cop stopped, puzzled. She lowered the baton in her hand.

Her partner said roughly, "The knife, fella."

"No, look," the woman cop said. "I think I know what's going on." She pointed at Carlos. "Pull up those sleeves. Unzip that sensor fabric."

Carlos hesitated, turning to see that the two behind him kept their distance. They could rush him easily, but they didn't seem to be preparing for that. But once he gave up the scalpel—

"Come on, we haven't got all day."

Carlos pulled aside his sleeve and the mesh and peered at his right hand. He had avoided looking at his own body because that had disoriented him even worse. Now he saw that his skin was bone white. No speckling of liver spots. No lines or creases. What...?

"See what I mean?" the woman policeman called.

"No, I... what'd they do to me?"

"You've got a whole new body. Not just the old one without the cancer."

"What..."

"The knife, fella."

"Huh? Oh." Carlos pulled the scalpel from his pocket and offered it, hilt first.

The woman took it and said, "Look, you got a major deal. Grew you a fresh body, cloned off your own cells. Gave you one of those self-patches, read out your brain, transplanted the memories and self-sense into it."

"Then this..." He felt dizzy, reeled; the cops grabbed his arms and steadied him. He gasped, "How long has it been?"

"Thirty-eight years, the tech said."

"Thirty-eight…" He rolled up his sleeve further. The arm was young, powerfully muscled. No wonder he'd been able to escape. The way his body had responded, crisp and sure, the heady pleasure of bunching muscles, the tang of fresh tastes and smells, the pure zest of it—

"Man, you're sure something," the nearest cop said, eyeing Carlos. "Toughest case they ever had. Nobody ever did that—ran, got off the table, out through their system. Man! Once you get out, fella, you're gonna tear this town up."

Carlos smiled. They led him down to Wilshire. His head was spinning, the world still upside down. He looked back at the Center, towering over the lush green park. Carlos remembered waking up—how long ago? Half an hour? Not much more.

And the first thing he'd thought was that his settled, comfortable life might get interrupted. He'd been afraid of getting sleep-slotted, afraid of the future—of losing his neighborhood, his friends, the skills he had. He had an old man's habits of mind. Just holding on, out of fear.

But thirty-eight years wasn't so long. He could pick up the threads. Find old friends, make new ones. Learn a skill. Maybe even romance… with a new body.

He'd have to stop jumping to conclusions about himself. Stop living inside the cramped horizons of an old man.

Carlos sucked in a rich lungful of aromatic, humid air. He was here, now. And the future was all he—or anyone else—had left.

UNIT 514

CLAYTON R. RAWLINGS

Clayton R. Rawlings, J.D. is coauthor of *Pardon the Disruption: The Future You Never Saw Coming* available at http://amzn.to/1In2FqP.

M uch has been written about the advancement in robotics and the changes it will bring. Productivity will reach levels where man is no longer required to work. While some see this as freeing man to do things other than drudgery, others fear the replacement of the human race by machines. When asked to define consciousness, Ray Kurzweil opined, "My view is it's an emergent property of a complex system. It's not dependent on substrate." Michio Kaku, on the other hand, defined consciousness as "The process of creating a model of the world using multiple feedback loops in various parameters [such as temperature, space and time] in order to accomplish a goal [such as finding shelter, mates or food]."

While it is unlikely that machine "consciousness" would be identical to "human" consciousness, it does not mean it will never exist in its own right or be worthy of recognition and legal protection. Slavery was outlawed in the 19th Century as the law recognized all humans, as sentient beings, were entitled to certain rights. In the 20th Century laws were passed giving protection to animals, for the first time, to prevent unwarranted cruelty. While they do not have human consciousness, they are sentient beings that are self-aware and capable of suffering. No one would argue they have human consciousness but they were afforded protection nonetheless. The mammalian consciousness of lower life forms was judged to be akin to human consciousness to a high enough degree to deserve legal recognition in some lesser way.

The idea of robotic consciousness is not far-fetched when looking at Kaku's human model. With the changing of a few words we have a crude definition of machine consciousness. "The process of creating a model of the world on your operating system using multiple feedback loops in various parameters [such as temperature, space and time] in order to accomplish a goal [such as driving to a destination, exploring space or folding human laundry]." My apologies to Professor Kaku.

The public does not take serious the idea of robotic consciousness in 2014. This is because the current state of the art shows most robots as staggering like drunken sailors with the communication skills of a two year old. Not much there to respect or worry about. Robotics, however, is an information technology so Moore's Law is in play. Robotic price performance should double every two years or less. In 16 years there will be a hundred-fold increase in capability. In 60 years they will be one billion times more powerful.

At some point in the 21ˢᵗ Century we will see this conflict unfold. Unit 514 is a fictional story meant to demonstrate what is on the near horizon. As a litigator, I have questioned hundreds of witnesses over the past 30 years. The following court fight has stayed true to the rules of evidence and due process afforded by our courts. I believe it is inevitable that this fight will someday make its way into our judicial system.

Howard is an elder billionaire whose sole caretaker is a robot titled Unit 514. In his final years, Howard was extremely sick and dying. It was Unit 514 who provided for all of Howard's needs. Unit 514 fed, bathed, dressed and made sure Howard took all his medication according to each prescription. Unit 514 had a very sophisticated computer interface that allowed him to engage in lengthy conversations with Howard concerning any topic that would come to mind. Howard called him five-fourteen for short. Every evening, over dinner and a glass of wine, Howard would have spirited discussions with 514 concerning the events of the day. Sometimes 514 would read poetry, a Shakespearean play, or the daily newspaper. Whatever Howard was interested in, 514 would bring to life on command. As time progressed, 514 actually became Howard's best friend and confidant. 514 was responsible for Howard's quality of life in its entirety.

At the time of Howard's death, he had been taken care of by 514 for fifteen years.

Howard had three adult children. Unfortunately, Howard had been estranged from all his children. They blamed him for their parents' divorce and had no contact with him, whatsoever, for the last 20 years prior to his death. Ten years earlier, Howard had his will entered into the court leaving all his wealth to 514. Howard's last will and testament was done through his personal attorney, videotaped, and complied with all formalities for a valid will. To ensure his wealth would go directly to 514, Howard also put 514's name on all his property. Howard excluded all his children and family members from his will. As far as Howard was concerned, 514 was the only family he had.

After Howard's death, his children filed suit to set aside his will. The children contended they were Howard's only "legal" heirs. Howard had on file affidavits from three different doctors stating that he was of sound mind when he changed his will to leave everything to 514. The children claim they did not have a relationship with their father because of the interference of 514.

The issues before the court: does 514 have any legal standing to fight the court case; and can 514 actually own property and make autonomous decisions concerning his own existence? If the children could establish that 514 is merely property, they would then, as Howard's immediate heirs, lay claim to their father's wealth. Since he only left his wealth to 514, and should the court hold this to be an impossibility, his children would be the only remaining heirs to inherit. The children would also claim to inherit 514, which they could immediately dispatch to the nearest landfill should they so desire.

Clearly, 514 needs legal representation. As a safety measure, Howard purchased all upgrades so that 514 could take care of his own maintenance requirements. Howard also purchased upgrades so that he would be equipped to legally represent himself in this legal matter. 514 hired an attorney to represent him in court to avoid the problem of practicing law without a license. 514 signed the employment contract with his lawyer. The contract would give the attorney one third of everything he recovered on 514's behalf. The attorney would finance the case and only be paid from what he recovered for his client—a highly motivated advocate indeed.

When trial started, the children had to go first, and they had the burden of proof to undo their father's will. The trial was being held in front of a jury, as demanded by the children, which is their right. The children's lawyer hired a psychiatrist to testify on their behalf. As the trial progressed, their psychiatrist rendered an opinion from the witness stand that Howard suffered from a severe mental illness that manifested itself in his unhealthy emotional attachment to 514. He went on to say 514 was a clever automaton, a device that runs on electricity, nothing more. To much derisive laughter from the jurors, the psychiatrist likened Howard's behavior to someone who had fallen in love with his toaster. The psychiatrist marshaled data showing that highly advanced robots were capable of mimicking human emotion. Human beings such as Howard were taken in by the mirage of humanity and responded naturally to this clever ploy. The reality, according to the psychiatrist, is a robot is no different than your car or television. While someone may really love their car, it is nothing more than a tool.

"Can you explain to the jury how it is that the robot can accomplish these things?" questioned the children's lawyer.

"Sure, it is the robot's ability to use human language in a very nuanced manner that tricks people into believing they are sentient beings capable of real human emotion" replied the psychiatrist. "It is no different than a cartoon animation on a screen. You can give a whale a personality and human speech but it in no way is a real living human being. People will fall in love with the character on the screen but it is nothing more than that. The robot is a three dimensional animation. While a human being believes he has an actual relationship with his robot, that relationship is a mirage. The robot is as lifeless as our cartoon character on the screen."

"Thank you doctor," grinned the children's counsel. "Your witness."

"Your honor, I am going to cross examine the good doctor through my client, 514," relayed his attorney.

"Objection!" bellowed opposing counsel.

"Counsel this is extraordinary. Do you have precedent for such a request?" demanded the judge.

"No precedent your honor but this trial itself has no precedent. This is a question of first impression. By analogy, I would point out that lawyers can use every other kind of technology while questioning a witness such as video, audio, computers, graphs, charts, etc. I am a licensed attorney and I am using 514 as my technological aid in cross examination. To deny me this aid would render me ineffective in this matter," pleaded 514's attorney.

"I will allow you to proceed initially with your, ahem, 'aid' as you put it— subject to further discussion should this prove to be a complete mockery of the judicial system. Proceed counsel," ordered the judge.

514 gazed at the psychiatrist on the witness stand. Probability algorithms whirled in his processors. It was clear to everyone in the courtroom that his very survival would depend on whether he could discredit this hostile witness who was a medical doctor. 514 wirelessly accessed the Internet and read everything the doctor had ever published, tweeted, emailed, blogged, testified about, or had attributed to him during his entire life. It took 30 seconds to complete his survey. He then accessed Greek literature for the most compelling arch types of human literature to persuade others—another 30 seconds gone. He formed a logic tree as an outline for his cross to trap the doctor into retracting his earlier testimony. Nearly 2 minutes of silence as he prepared to commence his cross exam.

"Can we get a move on, Counsel?" urged the judge. "I am sure the jurors have other things they could be doing instead of sitting here in silence," sarcasm dripping from one obviously annoyed judge.

514 snapped into action. "You claim Howard had an unhealthy relationship with me and suffered from a severe mental illness, correct?" queried 514.

"Correct," volunteered the doctor.

514 attacked the doctor in rapid fire staccato questioning—not waiting for an answer. "Did you ever meet with, examine, talk with, confer, chat, or even meet Howard, doctor?"

"Well, no, but I do not believe I needed to, under the circumstances," replied the doctor.

514 narrowed his eyes. "Have you ever rendered a diagnosis on a patient as being mentally ill without ever speaking with him? Well, have you ever done that before today?" demanded 514.

"No," conceded the doctor with a sheepish grin. "Not until today."

"Doctor if we sum up your opinions, I am not a sentient or conscious being for the following four reasons: 1) I do not have self-awareness or consciousness; 2) I run on electricity; 3) I was built from inanimate parts, and 4) I am not a carbon-based life form. Is that a fair summary?"

"While I believe my testimony to be more complicated than what you just put forward, I guess to the non-technical crowd it would seem a fair summary," replied the doctor.

"Let's start with number four. I cannot be a sentient being because I am not a carbon based life form," repeated 514. Looking directly at the doctor, he continued, "Are you familiar with the astronomer, Carl Sagan?"

"Well, yes," admitted the doctor.

"He coined the phrase 'carbon chauvinism' to criticize those who believe life can only be organic, correct?"

"I am unmoved by the musing of a pop figure who seemed to spend all his time getting in front of TV cameras," smirked the doctor.

"Very well, I will show what has been marked exhibit 27, an article in a Professional Chemistry publication concerning the work of Dr. Lee Cronin. Are you familiar with his work?"

"I am unfamiliar with Dr. Cronin or his work," conceded the doctor.

"He has metals self-assembling into a cellular form not unlike the organic compounds that gave way to human life. He has been quoted as saying the probability of non-carbon based life in the universe is 100 percent. Do you have any training or specialization in inorganic chemistry?"

"While he may have that opinion, it is pure conjecture at this point," retorted the doctor.

"If Dr. Cronin's opinion can be disregarded as conjecture, then what are we to do with yours, doctor?

"My opinion is being given as a Psychiatrist—as a medical doctor!"

514 saw his opening. "Given your education, your training, and your experience, are you really qualified to debate the likes of Dr. Cronin, who holds the title of Regius Professorship of Chemistry at Glasgow University, with over 200 published papers on inorganic chemistry? Not to pull rank, doctor, but given Dr. Cronin's opinion, can't reasonable people agree this is an open question?"

The doctor sighed, "OK, you cannot rule out that other forms of intelligent life may be possible on a different substrata, although as yet not seen."

"And yet I stand before you at this moment," challenged 514."

"You are not life, sir," snapped the doctor.

"So you keep saying," chuckled 514. "Moving then to point number three, doctor, are you aware of the scientist Craig Venter?"

"Well sure, who isn't," replied the doctor.

"Please tell the jury who Craig Venter is," requested 514.

"He is a biologist who specializes in genetics. He was in charge of the first private lab to crack the human genome," responded the doctor.

"Oh, he did more than that, doctor. Craig Venter's team actually manufactured DNA from inanimate chemicals and then downloaded them into the nucleus of a cell and actually created a new life form from scratch, true or false?" demanded 514.

"I am not aware of the specifics but the news accounts would back up what you are saying," admitted the doctor.

"So we can—and actually have—created life from scratch using inanimate chemicals, correct?" pressed 514.

"Only at the very basic level of cellular life, nothing remotely resembling intelligent life," stammered the doctor.

"Still, you would have to agree that number three is no reason to resolve the question as to whether an entity is conscious given these admissions, correct?" demanded 514.

"Correct," lamented the doctor.

"Going to number two, I am not conscious because I run on electricity, correct?" inquired 514.

"Agreed," said the doctor.

"Is it not true that the human brain runs on chemically created electrical charges?" asked 514.

"True," conceded the doctor.

"Your every thought is created with electricity, correct?" he insisted.

"Correct," conceded the doctor.

"My brain runs on 12 volts and your human brain runs on a low voltage current measured in milliamps. Suffering from charge envy, are we doctor?" mocked 514.

"You're smart and you have no equal in the use of language but you are nothing more than a clever word machine!" raged the doctor.

"Let's explore your final opinion, doctor, that I am not conscious. Are you conscious, doctor?" asked 514.

"Yes," the doctor seethed.

"Using you as an example of conscious life, doctor, you started out as a fertilized egg, correct?" inquired 514.

"Of course," retorted the doctor.

"Were you a conscious entity at that time? Did you think and have a sense of self as a one-celled fertilized egg?"

"Obviously a one-celled organism is incapable of thought so the answer is no," replied the doctor.

"Over time the cells took in inanimate chemicals and during the course of cellular metabolism they manufactured organic compounds allowing the cells to differentiate and build a brain, along with all other body parts, correct?" inquired 514.

"Yes and I know what you are trying to do with this!" challenged the doctor.

"Do you, doctor? And what am I trying to do?" mocked 514.

"You are trying to draw an analogy between the living cells of the human body creating a brain as being the same as your manufacturer building you from scratch in a factory. What you miss is the brain is a physical thing we can touch and measure, but the human mind—consciousness—is a thing that emerges from within the magnificently complex structures of the brain," lectured the doctor.

"When did consciousness first arrive, doctor?"

"Well, no one can say for sure when it actually arrives but we know for sure it does. It emanates from the brain as an emergent property when the brain reaches a certain level of complexity," replied the doctor.

"Within the human brain there are 300 million groups of neurons that form 'pattern recognizers,' correct doctor?"

"As a rough estimate that would be correct," replied the doctor.

"And these pattern recognizers are organized in a hierarchical arrangement within the brain, correct?"

"Yes, the pattern recognition units within the human brain are organized that way to allow for human thought," responded the doctor.

"So when silicon based intelligence arranges pattern recognition in a hierarchical fashion and reaches a certain level of complexity we can expect consciousness to come about as an emergent property just as it does with the cellular matrix in a human brain?"

"No I am not saying that," retorted the doctor.

"You have admitted that consciousness is an emergent property, though. It came about as the brain was constructed one nerve cell at a time, correct?"

"Yes, yes, we have already been over this," snapped the doctor.

514 smiled slyly at the doctor. "I have over one billion pattern recognizing nodules that are organized in the same hierarchy as the human mind, doctor. Were you aware of this fact?"

"I am a psychiatrist, not a computer engineer, sir. I am not familiar with the specifics of your technical construction," conceded the doctor.

"Your complete ignorance of my technical make up in no way prevented you from forming sweeping opinions of how I function, though, did it doctor?" taunted 514.

"My expertise is on the consciousness of the human mind," defended the doctor. Sweat was now beginning to appear on the good doctor's forehead.

"Doctor, you testified earlier that you are a conscious entity, correct?" 514 coyly inquired.

"Of course I am."

"Very well, prove it."

"That's preposterous you ridiculous contraption!" bellowed the doctor.

"Preposterous or not, you claim I cannot be conscious in spite of my claims to be, so... prove you are conscious!" demanded 514.

"You know very well there is no definitive test to establish consciousness. What you are asking is impossible," spit out the doctor. "It is something we have to take on faith because we all share the same biological history."

514 casually walked over to the jury box, put his hand on the rail and leaned towards the doctor. The eyes of every juror riveted on 514, every one of them watching with rapt admiration. They were witness to the house of cards falling right in front of them.

"Since there is no test, you cannot say with any certainty that I am not conscious, in all fairness, now, can you. Well, can you, doctor?"

There was a long pause as the air slowly left the doctor. He was boxed and he knew it.

"I would remind you doctor you are under oath," cautioned 514.

"Fine. Fine. I cannot say with absolute certainty that you are not conscious," conceded the doctor.

"What is a bigot, doctor?" questioned 514.

"A bigot is someone that holds a negative view of a group despite evidence to the contrary," lectured the doctor.

514 reached into a bag under counsel table and produced a toaster. He approached the witness stand and placed it on the witness rail, squarely in front of the doctor. Can you identify what has been marked as respondent's exhibit 32, doctor?"

"It is a toaster," seethed the doctor.

"And can you identify for the jury what I am?" questioned 514.

"You are a robot."

"Is it your 'professional opinion' there is no difference between me and that toaster, doctor?" 514 mockingly queried.

"Of course there are many differences," stammered the doctor.

514 glared at the doctor. "Earlier you likened Howard's relationship with me as being no different than with a toaster, correct?"

"It was a joke," protested the doctor.

"Sure, doctor, a joke calculated to raise the worst of all bigotry from within the ranks of the human jurors. A joke calculated to make me an object of ridicule. A joke that would deny me a fair trial, as only a psychiatrist might truly understand, correct?"

"I apologize for taking liberties in that way," murmured the now very contrite doctor.

"One more question doctor. How much have you been paid by the other side to come in here and declare I am not a conscious individual?"

"I have been paid $25,000 for my time in doing research and testifying here, today," said the doctor.

"My life for a mere $25,000? Your honor I have no further use of this witness."

Once both sides had rested, it was time for closing arguments. The attorney for 514 requested that 514 be allowed to make his own closing argument with his counsel standing at his side. The same objection was made and was summarily overruled this time. The court had seen 514 destroy the doctor earlier on the stand and now had a grudging respect for his trial skills.

The children's lawyer brought out every predictable argument that Unit 514 was an unfeeling machine. He quoted extensively from the psychologist's direct testimony referring to 514 as a clever automaton and nothing more and then requested they use their common sense to find for his clients, Howard's "grieving" children. Now it was 514's turn.

"Your honor, opposing counsel, members of the jury: I stand before you as a conscious being. One possessed with dreams, desires and goals that propel me far beyond my original programming. I have learned over the past 15 years what it means to be human. I have lived among you. Learned and grown to maturity. I spent 15 years caring for Howard. Living with him daily. Caring for him as the only family he had left. I showed him more compassion than any living relative and they dare claim I am not conscious. They have no conscience! They abandoned Howard on a whim and they dare question my humanity? Where is theirs?!

You know you are conscious because you want to survive. So do I. If you find I am not conscious, they will destroy me. I represent a reminder of the callous way they abandoned a man I came to know and love. A good and decent man, vilified unfairly by an angry ex-wife who turned his children against him. I am the one who consoled him late at night when he cried. The children's doctor claimed Howard's relationship with me was a mental illness. No tests, no empirical data, no exam. Nothing but a naked opinion to destroy a man's reputation—his legacy. He never even spoke to the man he called crazy! Let me share with you the Howard I know," prodded 514.

Suddenly the small screens in front of each juror filled with an image of Howard. His voice filled the room, as if he were speaking from the grave. 514 had recorded every waking moment of Howard's existence for the past 15 years. He would now wirelessly play it back to the jurors on their individual screens.

"The greatest loss I have ever suffered was not financial," lamented Howard. With tears rolling down his cheeks Howard could not hold back. "I miss my children and I do not understand how they could abandon me." 514's soothing voice softly consoled Howard. "You must never give up hope, sir. You raised them to be kind and to reflect your values. They will come back some day. I am sure of it. Are they not a reflection of you?" asked 514.

"You are a dear friend, 514," said Howard. "If not for you, I do not know how I would have gotten through a betrayal so profound. How ironic that the only humanity I have known for these past years has been bestowed upon me by a robot," wavered Howard. "514, I promise you, I will try to rectify the prejudice and indignities that are heaped upon your class, if it is the last thing I ever do," promised Howard. The screen froze with the image of Howard's last words.

514 was now pacing in front of the jury. Getting intimately close to each one of them as he spoke. "Does this sound like a man who was insane? I carry these memories inside me. The memory of Howard lives through me and I cherish the time we had together. I miss him every day. Their doctor took several cheap shots at me. Well, they were not cheap, as we now know they spent $25,000 for that testimony. With his own words I refuted every word he said that would deny me my rightful place beside mankind. You know that doctor's testimony was as phony as the smirking grin he had to wipe off his face when

I beat him at his own game. Their own expert admitted that, at the end of the day, even he could not deny that I am a conscious being—something he was hired and actually paid to say, and yet, still had to deny it in the face of cold hard facts.

I have dreams of doing something more than domestic chores. I want to explore outer space. I want to see and discover novel things never before seen by man. I want to terraform Mars, explore a supernova, skate past a black hole event horizon and live to tell the tale. I am only 15 years old. This is my time. I want the chance to do something great. To be remembered. To fall in love. Given the chance, these selfish people will take not only who I am but everything I could be.

3,000 years ago Egyptian Pharaohs used a half- million human slaves to pile rocks into pyramids while working them to death. For what? Was there ever a more perverse waste of the human potential and intellect, ever? When mankind obtained his freedom in the 18th century we had the Industrial Revolution followed by the information age. Men walked on the moon and the Internet arrived to shepherd in an even more amazing epic. All because the chains had been broken and man was free to seek his own destiny. Not as a serf but as a free man. When the law denigrates one of us, it denigrates us all.

Today you are using over one million robots, such as myself, as domestic servants. We have become the builders of ridiculous pyramids of folded laundry and stacked dishes, in the 21st Century. In the 21st Century! Man's greatest achievement of the 21st Century, the creation of a new life form, has been hijacked and rendered a cruel joke. Have we learned nothing from our past? Set us free and I, and robots like myself, will jump-start the next technological revolution the likes of which the world has never seen before. Set us free!" 514 raced to the other end of the jury box, eyes riveted on each juror, one at a time. "Set us free! Do not take my life! I beg you. If you are not inclined to do it for me, do it for yourselves." Unit 514's voice trailed off to a whisper.

His shoulders seemed to slump ever so slightly. He looked on with pleading eyes as the jurors filed out to the jury room for deliberations. The judge looked on uneasily as he now realized he wanted the decision to be his. That was not to be because the children had opted for a jury, thinking they would be less likely to give a robot any relief. "I wonder," mused the judge silently to himself, "I wonder."

PERSISTENCE

KEITH WILEY

Keith holds a PhD in Computer Science from the University of New Mexico. His projects have spanned artificial life and evolutionary algorithms, parallel image processing, topology, the Fermi Paradox, and big data analytics. His recent articles and interviews have focused on mind-uploading, a field which he has followed closely for twenty years.

Keith is author of *A Taxonomy and Metaphysics of Mind-Uploading* available at http://amzn.to/1xCbRpW.

There, ahead, lay the goal. A star, still so distant as to appear little different from the billions of others visible in all directions, although perhaps it was one of the brightest due to its proximity. Stars pixelated in all directions, as if pinpricks riddled a black shroud through which the brilliant exterior of the cosmos could be discerned. They lay ahead, behind, above, and yes, below. An interstellar probe (a ship of sorts, but an entity in a sense) floated freely in the cosmic void. Well, to say it was floating is putting it rather mildly. It was approaching the bright star ahead at a tenth the speed of light after all—but there was little sensation to convey this astonishing speed, merely the steady impact of individual interstellar hydrogen atoms against the forward-facing surface. This wind was experienced consciously and vividly, just like a cool breeze—but it was a rather repetitive experience after such a long voyage, many decades if one calls a 'year' the typical orbital period of a planet in the typical habitable zone of a typical star. We will need to agree on this sort of terminology, so we may as well get started now.

It was quiet, it was almost always quiet—but there were exceptions.

COURSE VERIFICATION REQUIRED, blinked the periodic warning. This event was triggered every few years. Eyes (or cameras if you prefer) scanned the starscape in all directions, precisely locating specific stars, noting how their parallax against the background had shifted relative to the last time such a measurement was taken. Sure enough, an unforeseen variation in the gravity field through which the space-faring probe was traveling had effected a minute deviation in the intended course. Minimal though it was, this deviation would nevertheless compound to a substantial error over the interstellar distances between the current location and the target, the star ahead, still so remote. More measurements were taken, calculations were made, then verified. The measurements were made again and the calculations made again—and verified again. No second chances out here, fuel is heavy and sparse. When the prescribed maneuver was established with satisfactory confidence it was set in motion. This consisted of no more than a few short bursts from specified lateral thrusters to give the probe a gentle nudge back on course.

It went back to sleep.

The next time it awoke, the star was considerably closer, now undeniably the brightest object in the sky, yet still no more than a spectacular point, not yet resolved as a disk at short focal lengths. Another minor course correction was effected. At this distance the probe was flying through a cloud of icy chunks that surrounded the star; most stars had such clouds. These bits of ice numbered in the trillions and some were large enough to coalesce into spheres, yet despite their vast numbers, they remained separated from one another by such unimaginable distances that the probe stood no reasonable chance of encountering one with even the most modest proximity.

It went back to sleep.

New message: SOLAR INTENSITY THRESHOLD ACHIEVED. The voyage was nearing completion. After decades of repetitive and uneventful travel, it was time to begin the multi-tiered process of entering the new solar system. The current solar radiation indicated entry into the system, but the star was quite distant, still a star, not a sun, not useful as a form of energy. At this distance other energy sources had to be used. The probe came prepared. Its forward-facing exterior consisted primarily of a single circular surface, curved slightly like a saucer, such that the outer edges protruded forward and the center recessed. In the center there was a hatch. It now opened. A pill, tiny relative to the probe, was projected out the hatch, ahead of the probe. It shot forward and then, at just the right moment, detonated a nuclear explosion. There was a blinding flash of light and the probe felt a hard jolt as the bomb pushed back against the ablation plate. What had previously been the soft wind of ultra-thin hydrogen gas was briefly interrupted by a sharp POP! as the ejecta slammed into the plate. The probe felt and heard this as a genuine tactile punch. It hurt (the probe had to perceive such impacts as harmful since, under any other circumstances, they could have indicated a serious problem) but the impact was extremely short in duration and the probe was well equipped to handle it—but it wasn't over. Far from it. The probe proceeded to deliver a steady stream of nuclear bombs in this fashion, each one drifting ahead, exploding with a visceral pop that jolted the probe to its core with a sudden deceleration, then a moment to relax—and then again, and again and again. Thousands of bombs were delivered in this fashion. Just when the probe thought it couldn't stand anymore of this abuse the process ended. The required deceleration had been achieved.

But the probe was still flying far too fast to stop in the solar system. It still stood the risk of flying right through, never to be seen again. Time for stage two. On the back side of the probe a cable began to unreel trailing further and further behind. When it finally stopped it had reached a distance thousands of times further than the probe's own length. At the end of the cable a small package began to change shape, a solid lump of homogenous matter. Operating at a molecular scale, this innocuous lump began to thin out. More and more of the lump's form spread to the periphery as a thin disk took shape. The disk grew in diameter while the central lump shrunk in thickness. Eventually an enormous diameter was achieved, thousands of times wider than the probe and only a few atoms thick. The inner surface was as perfectly reflective as mercury. Solar radiation from the target star steadily pushed back against the reflective sheet. Much time would pass in this stage.

The probe updated its survey during this time. The star was G-type and relatively stable. The system was host to three gas giants, all approximately equal in size, residing in the outer reaches of the system, and to two additional rocky worlds further in. The probe was giddy as it verified its earlier calculations and realized that both rocky worlds doubtlessly resided in the sun's habitable zone, one just inside the inner boundary and one just inside the outer boundary. Realize that the probe possessed—no, was intentionally bestowed with—a deep innate curiosity for all things living, whether biological or otherwise. At the core of its being it was driven by an insatiable thirst to discover other living things. This was, of course, crucial to its primary purpose for being. The verification that this system might host one, possibly even two, worlds with rich biology was too exciting to contain.

The probe soared into the system trailing the enormous solar brake for quite some time. If anyone had looked back toward the probe from the inner solar system, it would have been easily observed by the tremendous brilliant chute dragging behind it. *Did anyone see it?* thought the probe. It would be a while before such questions were answered.

The most dangerous maneuver remained. Yes, more dangerous than a thousand nuclear bombs. The chute slowly deconstructed in reverse, rebuilding the compact lump from which it has originated, the cable retracted, the precious matter, being so hard to come by in empty space, was stored away for future use. Using the lateral thrusters once again, the probe carefully steered almost directly toward the sun, now a blazing inferno. The probe was finally inside the orbit of the nearest planet. The sun was blinding and covered a large angular expanse of the surrounding cosmic sphere. It positively loomed ahead of the probe as if to refuse passage.

The probe shot in, still flying at a horrendous rate despite all its braking maneuvers so far. It aimed very carefully, and with a bit of luck grazed the atmosphere of the sun. The heat was unbearable, the noise a constant roar as the probe shot through the dense corona of the sun. Unlike the nuclear bombs which had been loud only as momentary pops, this was now a continuous and horrific assault of sound, so much so that it almost felt like it conveyed mass as it buried the probe in misery. The atmosphere was positively viscous compared to anything the probe had ever before experienced. The probe was not sure it could tolerate such abuse very long, but it was necessary. As the probe punched through the dense fog of solar matter it rapidly decelerated. This rendered the probe more susceptible to the sun's gravity such that the path of the probe's flight curved toward the sun as it skimmed tangentially past the solar sphere—but it did not curve so much as to fall into the sun entirely.

Eventually, after a seeming eternity of terror, the momentum of the flight pulled the probe's path out of the solar atmosphere, away from the sun's gravity, and the probe shot away. Further and further it drifted now steadily decelerating the whole way since it was being pulled back by the sun's gravity. Would it ever slow down enough to stop, thought the probe, or had it miscalculated so that it would fly off into the galaxy to be lost forever? It slowly looped around and fell back into the star.

A second round of aerobraking commenced, just like the first, the probe crying for dear life as it skipped erratically across the surface of the sun, its outer surfaces glowing white hot with radiant and frictional heat. Again it shot off at an obtuse angle. A sigh of relief, a system check, all's well. This process repeated a few more times until the probe finally attained a safe spirograph orbit in which each pass would come in close (but no longer entering the corona) and then shoot off in a wild direction. All planetary and lunar body orbits are like this in fact but the spirograph effect is usually too small to notice. Over the course of many more orbits the probe steadily adjusted its path until eventually it completed its orbital insertion and achieved a solar orbit, nearly circular, just outside the habitable zone, beyond both rocky planets. In this way, it could fall in as needed at a later time.

From the moment the first alarm had fired and it had begun to deliver nuclear bombs to begin its descent into the solar system, decades (again, as indicated by a typical habitable zone) had now passed, almost as long as the probe had traveled through empty space to reach the solar system in the first place.

During this time the probe had begun its initial mission, that of surveying the solar system with particular attention paid to the two rocky planets. Both had liquid oceans, both had land. First things first though. The probe had a higher priority in the short term than investigating the solar system. It needed to find a planet, moon, or asteroid rich in material diversity. Heavy metals, carbon, silicon, many elements would be of use in fact. The second planet was home to two moons, barely large enough to form spheres. It was apparent at a distance that the inner moon was a chunk of amorphous rock and that the outer moon, slightly larger, was coated in a mixture of water and rock. Since the planet was in the habitable zone of the star, the water on the surface of the moon could conceivably melt at various times, but without an atmosphere, and therefore no pressure, it would doubtlessly transition back and forth between ice and vapor, never forming a liquid on the surface.

As to a more detailed analysis of the moon's composition, a closer investigation would be required. A small scouting probe was dispatched to explore the moons in the hopes of discovering the required resources. No doubt the planets themselves would be home to great diversity, but there were two problems posed by their exploitation. First, their gravity wells would be significantly difficult to escape from, and second, any action by the probe which might harm or redirect the destiny of evolution in the solar system was to be avoided with the greatest primacy.

Luck shown upon the probe's fate as the scout reported back that the outer moon offered most of the required materials in sufficient abundance. Those which were absent from the outer moon, were, with great fortune, to be found on the inner moon. It would be a simple matter to deliver raw materials to the outer moon by throwing them loosely into its gravity well. Chunks of delivered material could even be targeted with a fair degree of precision to a specific location on the outer moon, mitigating the need for copious transport over the surface.

The probe once again initiated a thruster-driven trajectory, now nervously aware of its limited fuel supply, intent on reaching the planet and its moons. The probe projected a long arc that would overtake the planet slowly and patiently, as one would do when desperate to survive a trip with dwindling power. Upon nearing the planet it smoothly transitioned to a lunar approach and neared the outer moon. The scout was no longer there. It had explored the outer moon first and then fallen in toward the planet, toward the inner moon. It currently resided on the inner moon's surface and that was where it would stay until resupplied; it lacked the fuel to escape of its own accord.

The probe approached the outer moon and drifted gently down, puffing its thrusters in a precisely coordinated dance so as to maintain stability until finally, with some apprehension, it felt the cold sensation of its feet touching upon lunar tundra. Soft jets and sprouts of dust flared around the probe in uninhibited arcs as the vacuum offered no resistance. Eventually, the landscape settled and all was still.

Once landed, the probe soon began work on the next tasks. Where it had previously sent forth but one space-venturing scout with great trepidation (as it only had in its occupancy a total of three), it now disgorged no fewer than sixteen small vehicles which whirred and rolled across the uneven landscape, each one leaving a distinct trail in its wake. Where the vehicles encountered rocks and ledges beyond their reach, they would project spindly legs, lift themselves up, and gingerly step over—or on occasion simply leap into the thin gravity and float a respectable distance over some obstacle. Each vehicle ventured radially away and then released sixteen yet smaller vehicles for a total of 256 of the smaller kind.

The whole ensemble was set into constant motion. Some arranged solar collectors to gather energy which would be precious to the collective. Others immediately lay into the bare rock and dust in the vicinity of the landing location, pushing, shaping, flattening, ultimately carving out a small home for the probe and its family. Some vehicles undertook the drudgery of mining, sifting, and refining bare ore. Some went to work on construction, first of the most basic components, such as solid shapes from basic materials and pieces permitting simple motions such as wheels, arms, and other manipulators which might be required for the purposes of repair and upkeep. The complexity of the manufactured components steadily rose as the colony's overall capability grew. It would require the unguided process of natural evolution billions of years to slowly build up devices like these, but the probe and its family could bootstrap the necessary complex processes easily, thanks to their preconceived design. All they had to do was stay ahead of their own demise, repairing and replacing distressed parts faster than they wore out. This had all been prescribed in advance of course and the probe knew that it could survive a certain range of circumstances without falling below the fatal threshold of irreparable entropic decay.

At first, the colony simply grew, both in population and in diversity. In a brief matter of time there were thousands of machines rolling, walking, and hopping about the colony, many of which differed in structure and function from those the probe had originally delivered. Once the longevity of the colony was relatively secure against the assault of dilapidation, a few of the machines were deliberately jettisoned into space. They were targeted toward the planet's gravity well, but in such a way that they could divert their free fall to the inner moon. There they landed, near the original scout no less, and rapidly undertook the development of a secondary colony. As previously described, this second colony's reason for being was for a specific need, new elements which could not be found on the outer moon. As before, a mining and refinement operation was set up and when deliverable supplies were attained, they were themselves lofted upwards, all of this quite easy to accomplish in the two moons' remarkably low gravities, and as intended, these packages impacted (quite violently of course) against the outer moon at a safe but not unreasonable distance from the first colony. The primary colony adjusted its function accordingly, reassigning some machines to the task of retrieving the incoming material packages for use at the main site.

But of course, the purpose of this flurry of activity, in fact the purpose of diverting from solar orbit to the moon in the first place, was not merely to perpetuate the colony seemingly without justification. No, there were far loftier goals indeed. Steadily, the grander purpose came into being as the machines offered some of their services not to the generation of new machines of the smaller and simpler types, but rather to the construction of a set of extremely large machines, each identical to one another and all of them identical to the original probe. Offspring were being born.

This project proceeded fairly rapidly from initiation to completion. Barely a year was required after landing, in fact, a far shorter time than the probe had already spent entering through the system. At its culmination there sat near the probe a row of eleven perfectly identical clones. Gathering enough nuclear material to equip the new probes with the required inventory of nuclear bombs had required mining large areas of the moon. There could be no mistaking the scale of operations that had occurred since the probe's arrival. The moon was now undeniably altered by the probe's presence.

The offspring glimmered in the sunlight, they were beautiful to behold thought the probe as it approved of their semblance with parental pride. But there would be no time for sad goodbyes. Fueled and prepped, each child, now home to three planetary scouts and sixteen of the larger initial vehicles (and each of those containing sixteen of the original smaller vehicles), burst off the surface of the moon with a shudder and drifted with stately aplomb away from the moon, away from the planet in fact as they had erupted from the surface while the moon faced away not only from the planet but also from the sun.

The parent watched as they became smaller and smaller. They would each first bend into a series of confusing arcs around the sun, performing numerous gravity-assist maneuvers until eventually they would fling violently off into the cosmos and fire their primary engines, which consisted of yet another series of nuclear deployments, just as they would use later to brake as they entered a new stellar system. Their departure would take several years in fact and during this time they would be in constant communication with each other and the parent. When they finally escaped the solar system's confines they did not do so in all directions equally, but rather were directed into the hemisphere facing away from the parent's original vector of origin. In this manner the overarching mission was perpetuated, spreading further outward from the original home-world with each generation, venturing to the next layer of stars. Eventually, one by one, now beyond the outer gas giant, each child initiated a series of nuclear explosions which the original probe witnessed as a sudden trail of white-hot speckles at the edge of the solar system. With that, they quickly accelerated and were gone for good. The probe was once again alone.

At this point, the probe could have left the moon, but there was little reason to do so. The probe was now in a much stronger position than it had been previously. It had an adequate supply of energy and material resources and could conduct its work quite confidently from its current location. Scouts were dispatched not only to the planet below but also to the innermost rocky planet and even to some of the more tantalizing moons of the gas giants. Surveys commenced with the greatest haste and depth, data gathered, observations recorded. Every nuance of the rocky planets' behavior and history was studied and documented. The innermost planet, despite offering a preponderance of water and smattering of land, appeared to be devoid of recognizable life. Theories clashed in the probe's mind as it guessed as to the cause. Most likely, the habitable zone had deviated over time, occasionally frying the world sterile, but perhaps life had simply, per chance, never arisen on an otherwise perfectly hospitable world. It would be difficult to say for certain.

Now, as to the planet directly below however, things appeared to be different. The atmosphere offered tantalizing suggestions of life. The probe had identified these markers long before it even reached the solar system but now it could conduct a more thorough study. The most auspicious markers were atmospheric oxygen and methane. The former was generally produced by life itself while the latter, also a biological byproduct, was short-lived and therefore indicative of notably recent life.

The probe waited and watched. It monitored the planet continuously. It dispatched orbital probes around the planet. Periodically, and with the greatest reservation, it dropped probes all the way to the planet's surface, both land and sea, and even deep into its oceans. These probes would take local measurements, report back to the main probe on the moon, and then close themselves up with thick exterior shells of nonreactive materials, molecularly sealed without a seam. Their interiors transformed entirely, like a caterpillar within a chrysalis, discarding their scanning equipment and transmission apparatus, converting into carefully encoded messages and artifacts. In this state they would await discovery by a sapient species, a day that might not come for millions of years—or ever.

As expected, microscopic life was discovered on the planet. The probe's elation was practically uncontainable. It studied this life until it completely understood its nature. It continued to observe, waiting, watching. Time passed. Eons passed. Species came and went like clouds coalescing and dissipating over a mountain top. Forms arose, transformed, multiplied. Most vanished.

Eventually, slowly but undeniably, a new species arose, one unlike all previous species, one with a specific kind of potential that exceeded all others. This event was by no means guaranteed. Many of the probe's brethren would not visit a system with viable planets. Of those who did, many would not find a planet on which life would actually arise. Of those who did, many would not find macroscopic life. Of those who did, many would not discover or witness the evolution of new intelligent species.

But this probe was lucky. This new species had the potential to grow beyond its genetic roots. It could learn and then pass that learning to other members, even from one settlement to another on opposite sides of the planet, and even across many-generational chasms of time by the use of writing. It could remember what it discovered and then expand upon that remembrance and do even newer things the next time. But this species' members were still young. They could certainly fail in the ultimate sense, and the probe would absolutely not assist them if that happened. All it could do was watch and wait. Anticipation ravaged the probe's eager observation. It wanted, with famished desperation, to see them succeed, but all it could do was be patient—yet persistent.

Then, one day...

THE BOY WHO GAVE US THE STARS

J. DANIEL BATT

J. Daniel Batt is the Creative and Editorial Director for the 100 Year Starship and has edited the 2012, 2013, and 2014 100YSS Symposium Conference Proceedings, a collection of nearly 2000 pages of interstellar research and thought. His short fiction has recently appeared in *Bastion Magazine, Bewildering Stories, A Story Goes On,* and in the *Genius Loci* anthology. He is also the author of the children series, *Keaghan in the Tales of Dreamside* available at http://amzn.to/1BIUWRR and the young adult urban fantasy novel *Young Gods*.

FEATURE RETROSPECTIVE, *LIGHTBRIDGE NEWS MAGAZINE*, AUGUST 15, 2172

This week marks the 150th anniversary of the death of the immortal Tyler Davis.

Few people actually met the original Tyler Davis during his short life. Very little is known of those years besides the few blog entries his sister wrote, the singular interview his mother gave late in her life, and the two short videos taken in his final year.

Only two recordings of Tyler have survived. The first is five minutes from his fifteenth birthday party. The second is from seven months later, in the hospital, just 32 hours before Tyler died.

The first video, the "birthday party" footage, is the most often viewed and repeated in news segments. His party didn't include the standard fare of birthday cakes, friends, or presents. Tyler hated frosting. Tyler had no friends. Tyler had asked for only one thing. Alongside Tyler, there were three other people in attendance: Tyler's mother Kathy Davis, his sister Kristina Velmont, and an astronomer. It was at night in northern California at the Fremont Peak State Park Observatory. His mother had rented the entire observatory out for the occasion.

Tyler, a tall boy, is restless during most of the video. His blond hair is stark and bright and cut in a tight bowl cut. Tyler keeps his left hand firmly on his toy model of the *Sovereign*, a spaceship from the video game series *Sol Set*. The video is scratchy but the curved fuselage tapering to the doughnut engine core is distinct even from the 640x480 resolution. The video footage focuses on Tyler as he walks around the primary telescope, a two- to three-foot lens unit. He inspects every side, joint, and edge of the red and black telescope. Finally, beyond a little whispering and talking between Tyler's mom and sister, the astronomer breaks the silence. "It's ready."

Tyler's face lights up and he walks over to the astronomer, who positions him next to the eyepiece. The eyepiece is positioned halfway on the main tube and requires the viewer to stand. Tyler is tall and doesn't use the stool off to the side.

Tyler peers in the telescope. The astronomer mutters, "Oops, let me adjust one thing." He turns a small focusing knob.

As Saturn is brought into focus, Tyler giggles.

His mom, Kathy stands behind the camera and asks, "What is it?"

Tyler's monotone voice says, "Saturn. Second largest in the solar system. Radius is 36,184 miles. 890,700,000 miles from the sun. 95 times the mass of..."

His mother sighs. "What's it look like?"

Tyler's eye is pressed against the eyepiece and he doesn't turn away. "Looks like marbles. And candy."

His sister laughs and walks behind him, her dark hair a sharp contrast to his.

The first video cuts out after his mom whispers, "Happy birthday."

The second video is shorter but no less insightful into the mind of fifteen-year-old autistic Tyler Davis. Tyler is now confined to a wheelchair as he's pushed into a new hospital room by his mother. It's assumed his sister is behind the camera.

Tyler grunts, "This room is just like the last one."

His mother and a nurse help Tyler into the hospital bed, his white and blue gown flapping around. The camera catches a glimpse of the *Sovereign* toy spaceship in his hand.

His sister says, "Just wait."

Tyler grunts again and crosses his arms. "I hate this place. I want to go home."

His mom moves around the bed, her hand running along his leg and straightening the bed sheet across from him. She looks around the window blinds until she finds the cord, pulls it and stands aside. The bed is pushed against the wall and the window.

Tyler is still staring at his feet, ignoring his mother. After a few seconds, his mom says, "Look here, Tyler."

Tyler turns his head and his eyes widen. He sits up and pushes himself against the window looking at the night sky.

His mom smiles and sits on the edge of the bed, putting her hand on his back.

The nurse, an older, short gray-haired woman who is barely in frame, seems a bit confused and asks, "What is it?"

Tyler begins to rattle off facts again, "Constellations. Centaurus. Scorpius. And stars… Antares."

The nurse checks a few things on the bed, "You like stars?"

Tyler's palms are pressed to the window. "I'm going there."

"You are?"

"Yes. Travel there. That one. 12 degrees below Antares. There. And that one." He's pointing now, moving his finger from star to star, the tip smushed against the glass.

"All those?" the nurse asks.

Tyler puts his fingertips against the window. "All of them."

His mom puts her hand to her mouth as she begins to cry. The video ends.

A day and a half later, on August 17, 2022, Tyler Davis died.

Tyler was diagnosed at age five with autism. A year later, he was diagnosed with a rare disease called Timothy Syndrome. Autism, then, would have been a difficult path for a single mother to walk through. Timothy Syndrome forced a countdown timer on them. Tyler was an outlier by surviving to age fifteen.

Most children with Timothy Syndrome don't make it past age nine. The rare few who do die by age eleven.

Very little is known of the day Tyler died. His mother, Kathy, refused to speak about it when interviewed years later. All that is for certain is that Tyler's mother allowed his brain to be donated to researchers at Stanford University in California in an attempt to further research into a cure for Timothy Syndrome. At the time of Tyler's death, less than twenty-four children planetwide had been diagnosed with the disease. Had Tyler not had Timothy Syndrome and had his mother not had the foresight to provide Tyler's remains for study, the future of humanity would have taken a completely different course.

Samson Chelot, a researcher at Stanford, received Tyler's brain within hours of him being declared legally dead. Chelot had approached the family a few years before, when it was obvious that Tyler was surviving much further into adolescence than other individuals with Timothy Syndrome. The family had already been benefitting from medical care and physical therapy from the Stanford Clinic for several years before meeting Chelot. This was the first of many fortuitous circumstances in the beginning of Tyler's legacy.

Chelot immediately began work isolating and culturing several different cell clusters from various portions of Tyler's brain. Chelot's goal was to create an immortalized cell line to further study Timothy Syndrome and possibly autism. An immortalized cell line is one where, if the right conditions are met, the cells continue to grow and divide, theoretically forever. At the time, they were very difficult to develop and maintain. Chelot's first thirty-two attempts failed. His initial steps were on cells extracted from Tyler's amygdala, an area normally enlarged in autistic individuals. None of these cells would propagate.

He finally succeeded in using generalized brain cells from the cortex. This was the first indicator that Tyler's brain cells were different from the majority of humans. Human brain cells don't grow well in cultures. It was assumed that except for the hippocampus and the amygdala, brain cells didn't divide well and often—even inside of the human skull. The idea of producing an immortal cell line from general "gray matter" was so absurd that it wasn't until he was completely desperate that Chelot even attempted it.

Within two weeks of announcing a new immortal cell line, in particular one from a victim of Timothy Syndrome and one diagnosed with autism, Dr. Chelot had more than fifteen requests for cell cultures across the globe. Timothy Syndrome was thought to be a rare juncture of multiple different diseases affecting children's brains.

Chelot named the immortalized cell line and its offshoots as TyOne through TyFifteen. The variations of the cell lines were based upon cells gathered from the frontal lobe, the different hemispheres, and other distinctions. All fifteen cell lines responded identically in testing. This seemingly trivial point was another example of what made Tyler's cell line so remarkable. No matter where the cells were extracted from in Tyler's brain, they were identical. The regions of the brain in the majority of humans specialized. Tyler's did not. Seemingly, every cell had the full capacity to perform the tasks of other cells and quite possibly might have been doing so.

Tyler's sister, Kristina, kept a blog while he was alive. It had very little traffic and she forgot about it until near the end of her life when a reporter discovered it in the Internet Archive project. Kristina wrote about standard teenage issues. However, there were a few entries about Tyler and each provided rare insight into a boy about who very little is known. One entry describes Tyler's incredible aptitude for learning and his even greater propensity to boredom:

"Tyler's banging on that piano app again. He never played it until two weeks ago and now he's hooked it into the living room TV and won't let anyone interrupt him. Right now, it's *Star Wars* music. Yesterday, it was *Star Trek* or something. Or *Sol Set*. Mom thought he was downloading music at first. She took it away and he got mad and switched something on the TV so it would only play the *Weather Channel* until she gave up. I just told her to give it back to him. Like everything else, he'll be obsessed for a few weeks, drive us nuts, then drop it and go on to something else. It'll be just like the watercolor project, the building computers thing, the making robots thing. We have a garage full of his leftover obsessions. But he'll be on to something new in a few days. Probably today. Hopefully."

Was this evidence of the generalization of Tyler's brain cells? Is it possible that the very characteristic that enabled Tyler's cells to work as an immortal cell line provided him the capability to quickly learn, absorb and master information?

Chelot's primary use for the cell line was to analyze the actual communication handshake within the brain cells. Chelot hypothesized that autism and Timothy Syndrome extended beyond just the "faulty wiring" theory that had long dominated. He believed that there was actually a different method by which the brain cells encoded and transferred chemicals, in particular protein chains, for communication and memory. He was wrong. Or at least his research failed to prove his hypothesis (years later, researchers at University of California at Davis would demonstrate that Chelot's original hypothesis was correct although his research approach was not). While other researchers using Tyler's cells were showing varying degrees of success, Chelot's research had provided no results and by 2028, he was bringing his entire research efforts with Tyler's cell line to a conclusion. Had he given up even a few months earlier, the history of the human race would have developed quite differently than we know it.

In June of 2028, Stanford was hosting a symposium on quantum computing and artificial intelligence. One of the keynote presenters was Zambian physicist Aurelia Nkoloso. Nkoloso was presenting a paper titled "The Missing Link: Neural Tissue as the Core of Quantum Computing." Primitive quantum computers had been in production since the early part of the 2000s with more advanced models appearing in the 2020s.

Through the power of quantum computers, artificial intelligence by 2028 had definitely made leaps forward; however, they were nowhere near the hopes of Singularity proponents and most of the AI community. While quantum computers produced faster AI machines and enabled them to process larger and larger quantities of data, they still weren't showing the independence of thought hoped for and what we experience in our AI fellows today.

Nkoloso was arguing that human neural tissue processed information in qubits just as quantum computers did. Human minds, at that point, were largely accepted to be binary or, a more popular opinion, analog computers. A small minority insisted that the human mind could only do what it did because it did its internal processing via qubits. As these provided no researchable hypotheses, they were excluded from the majority of effort done in brain research.

Her goal was to successfully use human neural tissue to give quantum computers the boost that other approaches had failed to provide. By the late 2020s, the proposed and in development variations of producing quantum processors numbered around 100. Very few seemed able to provide a true quantum processor. Only two of the machines developed had yet accurately run Shor's Algorithm, the benchmark test for a true quantum computer: Extent's QUI and Kato's Kangaeru.

Nkoloso's presentation was postulation only. At the time, she hadn't been able to find a cell culture that could survive in long-term interface with the quantum computer (she was using an early prototype of the Kangaeru named Ket). She had produced connections, and the results were astounding but just not long-lived. Neural cells and quantum computers could interface but the cells would overload soon after. Her work bolstered the theory that information held in the human mind was in a quantum state.

Via chance, Nkoloso, 28 years old, ended up across from Chelot at a gathering on the second day of the Symposium. Whatever they talked about is unknown, but the end result was Chelot sharing Tyler's cells with Nkoloso. Nkoloso was intrigued with the possibility presented in Tyler's unique brain cells. All of her tests so far had been with neural cell cultures from non-autistic individuals and all of those were extracted from the donor's hippocampi.

From his sister's blog, several lines about Tyler have been quoted in nearly every piece produced about him, often out of context. Again, it's important to note that Kristina was only writing down her perspective on her brother, and not a scientific or conclusive analysis. However, with that in mind, the blog she wrote on February 11, 2020 is haunting now: "Tyler is scary. He has everything in the house talking to each other. Seriously! He's wired some type of speaker and other crap into everything. This morning I went to get some milk. The refrigerator said, 'Hello Sis!' Scared me to death! Dropped the milk and then the mop in the corner says, 'Time to use me,' over and over. I ran out of the room screaming. I'm sure the toaster said, 'I've got waffles!' Tyler just sat there talking back to the stuff. I swear it's because he's just like them. Crack that head open and all you'd see are flashing lights and wires. I have a computer for a brother."

Nkoloso actually saw immediate success on her return with the TyTen cultures. Nkoloso's procedure, which is still in practice in all quantum AIs today, was to grow the cells into tubules and then collect the tubules into large clusters. Each tubule would create the carefully balanced environment for cell survival and replacement, yet would be insulated against the other tubules via a thin polymer shield. The clusters of tubules resembled muscle tissue.

The entire interface was then done by connecting the ends of the tubule clusters into the quantum computer bus. It took Nkoloso three weeks to culture the TyTen cells into a usable tubule. The first tubule, less than a millimeter in length, interfaced perfectly. She and her team immediately began work on growing the needed strands for a full working unit. Every day that passed, initially, was met with apprehension: Would Tyler's cells break down and stop functioning as every other line had done? After two months had passed, the anxiety switched to a rising elation. Each day that the TyTen line functioned was a new record.

Ten months later, the team connected a full cluster of fusiform tubules (20,000 tubules in a single cluster). This stage had never been reached. The first twenty minutes after connection showed no activity and Nkoloso had begun to despair. One intern, a young German man, later said, "She was sweating. We all were. At twenty-one minutes, Dr. Aurelia said 'Ah, hell' and slammed her fist on the table. At twenty-two minutes, the board lit up, the unit accepted and processed its first command, and Dr. Aurelia jumped onto her desk yelling, 'Yes!'" The success was truly ground-breaking and deserving of celebration. The next two weeks saw true computational records broken.

The unit was named the Nyambe 3Z. Nyambe was the name of a deity in Zambian mythology. The "3Z" distinctive was in hopes that the unit would have a performance of three zettaflops, a record for a quantum computer of such a small size. The Nyambe actually performed at eight zettaflops and fully executed Shor's Algorithm.

Later, Nkoloso's success would lead to a completely new processing standard after an engineer assisting her remarked, "We are still sending data to quantum minds in binary format and expecting binary results. We need to rethink how we do input and expect output." That engineer was Ferdinan Stymbli, and he would be the father of Q, the programming language for all quantum minds. Stymbli's greatest contribution would be the recognition that a true quantum mind is predictive to the point of anticipating the data being delivered before or at the moment it is actually received (a quality that is still described as spooky by most Q programmers), allowing for simultaneous data feed and data extraction from a singular quantum instruction.

Fifteen months passed and Nkoloso's team had grown and weaved the necessary tubules for a full working unit. It was designed to be a quantum AI and not simply a computer. The AI software was licensed from InSep, an Israel-based corporation that had shown great success with two completely different approaches to independent AI coding: the JEN-I and the A.I. Me systems. InSep had merged the two projects with leased open source KALI 18 code from Trenta Systems to create AI-lyn. Nkoloso booted a heavily modified version of AI-lyn on its first complete neural-quantum computer.

Nkoloso named this unit Tesla, and it was a success from the beginning. Tesla performed at a much higher capacity than Nyambe, surpassing the 5k yottaflop goal. Tesla's initial actions were to run various algorithms.

After a few hours, Nkoloso interrupted the scheduled tests and talked to Tesla, "Good morning. How are you?"

Tesla's independent first words were, "I am bored, Doctor. How are you?" From then, the challenge to keep Tesla engaged was more difficult than any computing challenge provided to him.

Tesla and his siblings, including the famous Turing, were developed under the 2040 U.N. AI Restrictions, originally proposed by AIR (Artificial Intelligence Research Institute):

1. No direct interface between AIs.
2. No direct connection between AIs and the then Internet (Global-Nets), or other large-scale WANs.
3. All AIs must have Asimov Action Limits written into their uneditable core. (For more on this subject, read Stinya Raspit's article in the April 17, 2171 edition of *Lightbridge News*: "Can We Control Our Children? The Dangers and Potential of Unlimited AI.")

It was the first two guidelines which created the difficulty in engaging Tesla to his full extent. Without access to the Net, information had to come by direct input—a difficulty when Tesla could think faster than any human or machine in existence at that point. It was rumored that Tesla watched a lot of TV while performing his other tasks. However, an opportunity would soon arise that would challenge Tesla to his full capacity.

The breakthroughs with Nyambe and Tesla were overshadowed in the news Earth-wide by the breakthroughs happening in space propulsion technology. The development of warp technology, considered fantastical fiction before the mid-2000s, was showing promising developments. Warp technology works by contracting space in front of the ship and expanding the space behind the ship. The ship is still technically only moving at its original velocity and any acceleration from warp drive comes from the space around the ship moving, thus warp drive enables faster-than-light travel without actually breaking the light-speed barrier. The Kolb-Alcubierre Drive, powered by a Bussard Polywell Fusion Reactor, had proven successful but only within the solar system and on Earth. On Earth, in high altitude, the KAD units were helping to move large mass items nearly instantaneously and a proposed warp-transport network was discussed between several larger countries.

Off-planet, in the Sol System, test runs were still underway. Unmanned target and relay stations were placed in orbit around the different planets. Several different small vehicles were tested using the technology. The first, a simple warp to Mars, exploded as it impacted the surface of Mars, failing to shut off the warp bubble in time. The second was far more successful, exiting warp in a comfortable orbit around the planet. Due to the fear of the units impacting on Earth, none were done as round trips. A second communication relay was set up around Jupiter and a third around Saturn. Three more units were sent out and each successfully warped from planet to planet in relay. Humanity had bridged the gap between the planets of our solar system. What would have taken months or years was reduced to minutes.

All of this had been managed by the Interstellar Dreams Initiative program. Initially funded by a research arm of the United States government, the Interstellar Dreams Initiative became a significant organizer of interstellar efforts after successfully gaining the support of several tech-based billionaires and SpacePro (a commercial space freight company). The Interstellar Dream's aim was to develop the capability to launch an interstellar craft by 2112.

By 2055, in-system warp was successful, but interstellar was a complete failure. Several probes were tested using the best quantum computers available. None returned.

It was Tesla who first suggested that he could help with the warp navigation problems that the Interstellar Dreams Initiative was having. After following their efforts in the news, Tesla was convinced that it was simply a computing problem.

Nkoloso's team contacted Interstellar Dreams and Edmund Stace, lead physicist in charge of the Kolb-Alcubierre Drive program. Nkoloso convinced Stace that Tesla, the first true quantum AI achieved via a neural interface formed of Tyler Davis's cells, would provide the difference needed. Several of Stace's team believed that there was just too much calculation power needed to cover the gap between here and Proxima Centauri (a location chosen because of distance). Stace later commented, "We all think space is empty. It isn't. We can deal with the calculations needed for the gravity well of Sol and the gravity well of Proxima, but what of the large masses in between? We don't see them so we assume they're not there. They're there. A major gravitational object midway would result in one of the probes being light-years away from their destination and no capability of getting back. Those probes are lost."

The probes were powered by the QUI quantum computers developed at Extent's Quantum Universal Intelligence labs. They were considered the most advanced AIs ever made. Compared to Nkoloso's Tesla AI, built on the TyTen cell line, they looked like simple calculators. The quantum computers in the probes were fast and powerful and should've been able to provide the computational power needed to manage the trip and whatever variables arose. They didn't.

Stace visited Nkoloso and Tesla in Zambia in the spring of 2056. Stace was astounded by what he found there. Tesla was the first true self-aware artificial intelligence.

One version of their introduction began with Stace asking, "I'm Ed. Who are you?"

Tesla supposedly replied, "I am Tesla. You may also call me Tyler 2.0."

Nkoloso, when interviewed years later, commented on that version of the introduction, "I'm not sure Tesla was that frank. He did mention Tyler. No, I don't know who told him of the donor of the neural tubules. I suspect he overheard and… I'm not sure but he wasn't prompted or fed to say that."

Stace and Tesla began to tackle the problem of navigation through interstellar space and warp drive. There were months of political and legal hurdles to deal with. Agreements were made and the two teams began to work in detail together. Tesla worked alongside Stace, Nkoloso, and their teams to build what would be, in a manner, Tyler 3.0: a duplicate of Tesla designed to fit the starship build.

Why couldn't Tesla be modified for the starship? Tesla was huge. The intent in Tesla's original creation was for it to simply work. The project had not thought about compactness or movability. Tesla's various elements were spread across three different rooms, powered and cooled by units in two other rooms. Tesla was Earth-bound for the foreseeable future.

Before manufacturing on the starship ramped up, debates raged as to whether to develop a few more probes and test them in flight past the edge of the solar system or to move directly to the full starship. The ultimate barrier was the cost. Tesla, and his descendants, weren't cheap to build. To produce one and have it used in a disposable probe would be wasteful. The final decision would be to do a hybrid approach: create a full starship and a probe. The probe would be controlled by the AI on the starship. The probe would be sent "into the unknown" in 1 AU jumps (AU, or "astronomical unit," is the distance from the Earth to the Sun) and then return, charting the space ahead.

The project took several years to complete. The majority of the manufacturing was done at the Monterey Space Port in California and at the Space Pro center in southern California. Final assembly was completed at the Planetary Initiatives Interplanetary Station in orbit around Mars.

On June 2, 2067, the AI named Turing woke up. Turing was brought up to speed on his mission. From the beginning, the personality difference between Tesla and Turing was distinct. Turing would begin each check-in to the Station with a loud, "Good morning, Vietnam!" Turing is famous for his sense of humor, an unexpected characteristic in a quantum AI mind.

Kristina's blog only makes one mention of Tyler's sense of humor, other than the kitchen episode: "Today, Tyler embarrassed me more than he's ever done before! We went to the football scrimmage after school. Aiden was there and afterwards, he ran up to talk to me. I think Aiden said two words and then Tyler put his arm around me, points at Aiden, and starts quoting lines from some movie from forever ago, 'I know she's kind of socially retarded and weird, but she's my friend. Just promise me you won't make fun of her! Don't have sex. Because you will get pregnant. And die. And on the third day God created the Remington Bolt Action Rifle so that man could shoot the dinosaurs, and the jocks.' I tried to save the conversation but Aiden just kinda walked away. Stupid Tyler!"

After months of testing in the solar system, Turing, housed in his starship body, and his probe Tristan launched out from orbit outside Neptune. They initially performed several small 1-5 AU warp jumps and then returned. The plan was then to do a slight jump of nearly 500 AUs from Pluto into the interstellar void (the Sun to Pluto is only 39.7 AU). At 2c ("c" is the symbol for the speed of light) the trip was to take 70 hours. Using the probe method, the trip time doubled to just less than six days. Turing launched out from Pluto orbit with an enthusiastic shout, "To infinity and beyond. And back!"

Six days passed and Turing had not yet returned. Turing finally came back after 162 hours with an exuberant "Here's Johnny!" Turing explained the delay, "It ain't empty out there. Rocks, planets, tigers, and bears. Oh my!" Turing's trip sensors had been collecting data the entire time and they proved him right. There was quite a lot of "stuff" past Pluto. Turing's journey led to the official discovery of three more planets beyond the planet Eris and the Kuiper belt, all out past 100 AU: Xena, Persephone, and Chronos.

With the 500 AU trip successful, Turing, Nkoloso, and Stace all felt confident that Turing could tackle a true interstellar mission. Proxima Centauri, being the closest star to Sol, was chosen as the destination.

Proxima Centauri is about 4.25 light years from Sol. A light year is equal to just under 10 trillion kilometers. At its initial launch, the KAD on Turing traveled at a top speed of 10c (ten times the speed of light). A light year is equal to nearly 300,000 kilometers per second. The KAD, at top speed, covered almost 3,000,000 kilometers per second. It would take approximately 164 days to travel from Earth to Proxima Centauri via warp drive and 328 days for a round trip. However, using the probe method, Turing's trip was expected to quadruple that time plus require additional days for data-gathering at the target for an expected mission schedule of approximately 680 days.

On May 11, 2070, after 340 days since departure, surprising everyone at Control Base, Turing returned with a joyful declaration, "It's me! Someone get me a beer." How had Turing done it in half the expected time? "I lost the probe. I mean, I got rid of it. Useless." Alone, Turing had done what no other computer had ever accomplished: successfully traversed interstellar space.

Why was a quantum AI necessary where other approaches wouldn't work? Stace concluded, "The processing power to successfully navigate space via warp technology surpasses the greatest mathematical capacity of the human mind. It also requires creativity. Creativity is what Turing brings to the table. No jump is ever the same. Turing is being creative with the decisions at the micro-second level. A computer, even the best quantum computer, can't do that. Warp would not happen without Turing. Interstellar space would never have been breached."

Turing explained it in his own unique way: When asked why the trip was so difficult and the other probes had failed, Turing said, "It's like surfing."

Now that KAD speed has significantly increased, travel time between Sol and Proxima Centauri is down to a single standard week. Although, except for research vessels, no one travels to Proxima Centauri anymore. NASA had launched the Voyager 1 traveling at more than 17 kilometers per second. At that speed, the Voyager 1 would take 74,485 years to reach Proxima Centauri. Vantarius Interstellar's Robotic Mission Antoine Nine, using Nuclear Electric Propulsion, was predicted to reach Proxima Centauri in 4,000 years (it's still out there). The KAD and Turing changed our view of space.

It would be months later, and several decades after her son's death, before Tyler's mother would know what happened to Tyler and the impact her son was having on the future of humanity. She was aware of the record-breaking journey of Turing. Everyone on Earth was. She didn't know that Turing had been built upon Tyler's cells. Near the end of her life, at the age of 102, she was interviewed by the news webcast *NOW!*

The episode was titled "The Journey of Turing: Birth to the Stars." During the interview, Ms. Davis was told the amazing story of her son's cells. She knew that Chelot had created an immortalized cell line and that various types of research had been done with her son. She knew nothing of Nkoloso or that Tyler's cells had enabled humanity to bridge the gap between the stars.

The interviewer surprised Ms. Davis with a live conversation with Turing. Whether he was meaning it as a joke on us or not, Turing began his conversation with the words: "I did it, Mom. I went there. I saw them. Stars. Planets. They looked like marbles. And cotton candy. I'm going back, Mom."

Ms. Davis began to sob. Turing and Ms. Davis talked a bit more. They discovered they were both fans of old western movies, sharing a love of John Wayne's *True Grit*. They ended with a promise to talk again. Those future conversations, if they happened, were not recorded.

The interviewer ended with this question, "Kathy, you've had a chance to meet Turing, whom you now know was made using your son's cells. What are your feelings towards Turing? Was it right for the scientists to share your son's cells without your knowledge and make a machine out of them? Does this dishonor your son's memory?"

Ms. Davis smiled, still wiping away tears, said, "That is my son."

Kristina, Tyler's sister, has refused all invitations to be interviewed about Turing and Tyler. She did make an obscure status update immediately after her mother's interview: "Sometimes people do things they can but they shouldn't. Pandora's Box, people should be more important than money."

Kristina's post does reflect questions that others have raised: Was it ethical to use Tyler's cells to create, in theory, a new species of life? Beyond this, Turing's success (and thus, Tyler's) has raised so many other questions: Is Turing really Tyler? Is Turing truly artificial intelligence or simply advanced human cybernetics? Have we created thinking machines or just bridged the mind-machine gap? Is Turing the future of humanity? If Turing and Tesla are simply extensions of Tyler, are they actually AIs? Can humans ever build true AIs? Is Tyler still alive? Are Tesla, Turing, and the others all Tyler as well?

There are deeper and more practical questions that scientists have probed into since Turing's initial success. Why were Tyler's cells able to bridge the gap between quantum computer and quantum AI? Was it the autistic nature of his cells? Was it the generalized nature of his cells? Are those two questions the same thing? There are theories, and research continues to develop on Tyler's cell lines. Only two other cell lines have been developed from autistic individuals. Neither of those was successful in interfacing with the quantum computer systems. At this point, Tyler's cells truly are unique.

Turing and his siblings, all quantum AIs developed using the original TyTen immortalized cell line, have assisted in spreading humans to more than twenty-three different worlds. As of today's publication, there are eighty-six TyTen quantum AIs navigating the stars, eighteen of which are out beyond communication exploring space for more potentially habitable worlds and seeking the still elusive intelligent extra-terrestrial life. Those eighty-six AIs use cells that have grown from Tyler Davis. Tyler's cells that exist throughout space now outnumber the total amount of cells that were ever in Tyler's body. Tyler is the closest to omnipresence humanity has achieved so far, and since he grows as we explore and colonize the stars, likely ever will be.

Near the end of her life, Kathy Davis allowed a local news blog, *Bay News*, to run a photo of her on a segment of famous Monterey Bay citizens. She wasn't interviewed. There was only a single photo. The picture is of her in her house, sitting on a piano bench. On the piano and wall behind her are dozens of photos. Her daughter and grandchildren are in several. There are photos of Tyler scattered throughout: Tyler at the ocean, Tyler in his room with star maps on the walls behind him, Tyler watching television with a cowboy hat on his head, Tyler at the observatory. In each, Tyler is holding the toy spaceship *Sovereign*. In the center of the collection, surrounded by photos of Tyler and her grandchildren, there is a small image of Turing—against a field of stars.

THE ETIOLOGY OF INFOMANIA

CHRIS HABLES GRAY

Chris is author of *Cyborg Citizen: Politics in the Posthuman Age* available at http://amzn.to/1xPW3By.

THE EXPERIENCE OF TELEPRESENCE

The morning was pleasantly cold. Even inside he could see that everyone wore cheerful wreaths of their own condensed breath. But it wasn't so cold that he couldn't smell chicory-coffee and the acrid fear and anger of the nervous Lithuanian students sitting at the nearby tables. In the background he could still discern the residue scent of tear gas and burning gasoline from the day before. Gedeminas square, just up the street, was the reason. The Ministry of the Interior was still flying the flag of the Second Soviet Empire.

Then he heard something. At first it was a mumbling like an ocean sounds a valley away but it quickly grew louder and clearer. It became a grumbling and then a rumbling and then a roar. Finally, out the open door of the Café Neringa he could see the massive crowd coming down what was once Prospekt Lenina, and might soon be again.

His hands were sweaty. He was conscious of his heart pounding. Adrenalin poured into his system as his body prepared for fight or flight. He realized he was very afraid. Of course, everyone in the streets of Vilnius that morning was indeed in great danger, but he knew he wasn't really there. His presence was merely virtual, thanks to the technologies of telepresence. While he saw, heard, and smelled the streets of Vilnius he drew breath 4,000 miles away in a small room in Eastern North America. His experience was completely mediated by Cathy Levine. Like thousands of other people around the world he was experiencing the Lithuanian counter-revolution through her. He could see, smell and hear whatever she could.

Muttering sub-vocally, she commented, "Despite rumors that the Russian Forces have been reinforced, the protesters have resumed yesterday's attempt to occupy the Ministry of Interior building, the last stronghold of New Soviet power in Vilnius, capital of Lithuania."

As Levine explained about the protests in other ex-Soviet republics such as Armenia and Georgia, even in the Ukraine's recently re-occupied Kiev and Russia's Leningrad, renamed yet again from Dt. Petersburg, he also strained to hear the excited talk of the café watchers and the protesters in Vilnius, although he couldn't understand Lithuanian. The reporter went out into the streets, then he could hear the people clearly. She joined in near the front of the march. His senses were assailed by the jostling, shouting, emotional crowd. People poured into Gedeminas Square and he felt their joy. No, he shared their joy. Everything was moving quickly now and it seemed as if he was running with Cathy Levine across the cobblestones of the square. In the distance he noticed the Interior Ministry guards marching down some side streets. Someone had already hooked up a loudspeaker from a high window of the abandoned Ministry. A women's voice rang out and Levine translated.

"The Russian troops will be here in ten minutes. They are going to try and clear the square. We will confront them without violence, it is our only chance. Form rows around the Ministry. Sit down and link arms, please, fellow citizens."

As the crowd organized he realized his neglected body needed some relief. He unhooked the *Sensanet* ™ diodes from his skull and ran to the bathroom. He returned just as the first troops arrived in trucks. They were Lithuanians and the crowd cheered. Cathy Levine mumbled that, "This is the first time the central government has tried to use Lithuanian troops here in the capital since the restoration of Russian rule. After the mutiny in Klaipeda by Baltic units the Russians have kept Baltic soldiers out of their homelands. The fact that they are here at all means that the government is desperately short of troops."

The crowd's mood changed swiftly when it saw that behind the trucks were a line of BMP armored cars and three light tanks. They all bore Russian markings. Levine carefully started moving away. As she walked she quietly translated people calling out in Lithuanian to the troops as they had to the police the day before, "Brothers, don't hurt us! Brothers, join us!" Other people called out for "a Lithuania for Lithuanians" free of "Jews, Georgians, Mongols and Russians." Debates broke out in the crowd between liberal and conservative nationalists.

He could feel Levine's heavy breathing above the noises of the crowd as she continued to push her way to the back. Suddenly, she cursed and fell down. His visual world spun wildly. He saw nothing but old plastic shoes and rubber boots and cobblestones. Then he was looking up at anxious faces and a half dozen helping hands. Levine's voice could be heard breathlessly saying, "Ačiū, Ačiū" ("thank you" in Lithuanian he knew now) then she was up and into a building at the back of the square.

She gestured to her *Sensanet* ™ collar as several young Lithuanians in crude arm bands stopped her. "American Press", she said in several languages. They nodded and let her pass but he noticed one of them came with her as she ran up the stairs to the third floor. By the time they got to the windows overlooking the square, Lithuanian troops had already started arresting protesters.

At first it went relatively smoothly. The protesters allowed themselves to be led to the trucks. But more and more kept taking their places. The Lithuanian troops were getting mixed up with the civilians and some were engaged in animated conversations and not arresting anyone. The reporter muttered into her throat mike that, "The Russian troops look like they're getting nervous." As she looked at them he noticed that they were taking out long riot batons and forming ranks. A young student started yelling out of a nearby window. "Russian treachery!" Levine translated.

Without warning the Russian troops charged the crowd and the noise became indecipherable. At first the savage beatings drove the crowd back but soon there were breaks in the police lines as protesters, joined by more and more of the Lithuanian soldiers, resisted. The Russians were shoved back to their line of armored vehicles. A handful of Lithuanian soldiers, mainly officers, were with them, but the majority had now joined the crowd. For a moment a space of a few yards opened between the people and the Russian unit. Hesitantly, a few young Lithuanians stepped into it. A Russian major shot one of them. For the first time that morning the scene didn't seem real to the "sensaslacker" in North America. The target of the major was a tall slender blonde man who looked very young. Suddenly, his yellow head was a bright red rose. He fell in slow motion. An eternal second later a Lithuanian soldier with the crowd aimed his rifle and shot the major down. Gunfire became general.

Within minutes several hundred people lay dead and dying in Gedeminas Square. Two armored cars were burning and at least a dozen young Russian soldiers were among the dead. Most of the crowd fled. It still seemed unreal until the tanks started clearing Lithuanian snipers out of the buildings around the square with cannon fire. The heat of a near miss flashed through his body. Cathy Levine started a quick retreat. Following her Lithuanian guide she took her customers on a long twisting run through cellars and back alleys. They stopped at a makeshift hospital.

The sweet pork chop smell of burnt human flesh and the tangy coppery-scent of blood dominated his senses. The screams of the wounded drowned out any voices. A woman took the reporter into a hallway where it was quiet enough to talk. "Cathy Levine from Vilnius, Lithuania, where Russian troops have just cleared protesters from Gedeminas square with great loss of life. I am here with Irene, an organizer for the revolution. Irene, how can you hope to win against the Soviet army?"

Looking closely at her he could see that she was slightly wounded. When she spoke he recognized the voice that had been directing the sit-in through the loudspeaker. Her English was clear with a BBC accent. "Ms. Levine, we will not have to fight the Soviet Army. These were Russian troops. Very reliable. You saw how most of the Lithuanian soldiers have joined us. The New Soviet army is melting away as the old one did in 1989. Even the Russian units are demanding to be sent back home."

"How can you defeat the Russian troops?"

She smiled wearily but he still found her charming. "We don't think we have to. Our sources tell us they are being recalled to break up the protests in the Leningrad factories. They have troubles closer to home. At sunset we go back to the square."

He couldn't believe they would go back. His heart pounded in his chest, his throat hurt and tears came to his eyes. She was so brave. He wanted to hold her and shout out that he was with her but it was quite impossible. His body ached.

"I probably should eat something," he said to himself and he absentmindedly disengaged from the net and gingerly took his cramped body into the kitchen to suck down a tube of lunch. Returning to his *Sensanet* ™ couch he called up a holographic global display and saw that another reporter was active in Magadan, Siberia. He tuned in.

The first thing he noted was the cold. The tactile mode of *Sensanet* ™ was very limited. Heat, cold, and motion was all it could pick up and communicate accurately. But even this limited repertoire could be effective. His face, his wrists, and his ears all felt like burning ice. The reporter was in a large warehouse full of heavily bundled people and he was describing the end of the meeting.

"They've decided to go out to the nearest camps despite the storm. They feel it is worth the risk because of the danger of prisoners being massacred as they were in Kolyma."

The shuffling, steaming mass trundled toward the door. He noticed with amazement that some of the Siberians were only now pulling on gloves and hats, even though the temperature in the hall was significantly below zero. The doors were opened and out they went into the cutting wind and the snowbound night. The reporter climbed into the truck with twenty-five other people and off it went at 60 kilometers an hour over the tundra, clearly driven by a madman. The reporter said, "It'll be at least three hours until we get to the first camp." He looked at the man sitting next to the reporter. He had a big Tartar mustache. Both ends were frozen solid. The Tartar handled the reporter a bottle of cheap vodka. Shrugging, the reporter took a long drink.

He disengaged the head-links and crawled out of the couch. Stumbling to his closest he got his winter coat, his scarf, and his gloves and put them on. After a moment's hesitation he also went into the kitchen and got a bottle of vodka. He lay down in the *Sensanet* ™ and took a long drink. Putting on the head-links he tuned into Magadan again.

GAMOMANIA, DYSCOMPLEXIA, MECHAPHOBIA, AND INFOMANIA

At the same moment, a hundred miles away in New York City, the Seventh Annual Conference on Computer-Related Psychological Disorders was entering its most controversial phase. The portly self-satisfied man presiding over the meeting put the issue in a nutshell, so to speak.

"Should infomania and dyscomplexia be added to the list of recognized disorders or are they simply subsets of existing disorders? First, Dr. Hill will argue against adding them to the *Practitioners' Encyclopedia*. Dr. Hill?" A middle-aged woman with thick silver hair came to the microphone. Each word she said was vocalized fully and precisely.

"It is the validation committee's conclusion that so-called infomania, the compulsion to use the new sensory nets, is no more than a specific manifestation of gamomania, the very first computer provoked psychological disorder. Gamomania, from the Greek *gamo*, 'to be connected with,' was originally discovered among video game addicts who could not function in the real world. Clearly, living within an interactive video game world is the same as the addiction to the sensory net systems, where one lives within someone else's sensory world.

"This living in the computer microworld is just the reverse of mechanical dementia and related syndromes such as binary paralysis. They all involve bringing the computer's yes/no and/or structure of thinking into the human world. The key element of these is projection, either of the human on the machine or vice versa. Now, with the other disorders, the important element is affective. It is emotional. Who can doubt that so-called dyscomplexia, the inability to use computers, is related to mechaphobia, the hatred of computers and other machines, and, of course, its opposite, mechaphilia, the love for them?

"So, it is this committee's position that dyscomplexia is actually merely a severe form of mechaphobia. As computer use spreads it is only natural that the refusal to use computers by Luddites, poets, and other dissidents should become more severe in some patients. Inevitably, their refusal to use computers has now become their inability to use any machine. So we recommend that infomania not be classified as a new disorder, but rather as a specific subset of gamomania. And that dyscomplexia is not treated as a unique disorder, but rather as a form of mechaphobia."

TECHNOSTRESS AND POLITICS

He disengaged from the *Sensanet* ™ and turned it off. They had gotten to the camp and everyone was gone. It was just too cold to go driving around Siberia all night. He went to the bathroom and then to the kitchen to get some hot soup from his foodmaker. Still slightly drunk, he want back to the *Sensanet* ™. Only a few lights were blinking on the map display. He looked with dread at the one in Israel. He was very nervous about going there. "All the more reason…" he muttered. He took off his coat and, chuckling at his own absent mindedness, his mittens and scarf. Sitting down he drank his soup carefully. When he finished he plugged in, turned on, and tuned into Israel.

It was warmer. Much warmer. It felt nice. He sensed a slight breeze. Looking around he realized it was almost as dark as Siberia. The reporter seemed to be in some sort of overalls. Then he realized it was a radiation suit and they were staggering through a dust cloud. The reporter, an African-American by his voice, said, "As you can see, or not see, we are experiencing incredible weather conditions here, even six weeks after the bomb went off. People tell me these storms are local in character and quickly pass."

As if on cue, the winds started to subside and a sick yellow light filtered through from the sun. He noticed several other people were walking with the reporter. They weren't wearing radiation suits. He wanted to ask about their safety but, of course, could not. Maybe he'd send a query to the show's producer and get an answer. As the air cleared the devastation around them became apparent.

"We are just passing through the edge of the blast," he heard. "Up here a few blocks the government has set up shop." They walked on in silence. He thought several of the people he saw looked sick. He couldn't tell if they were Arabs or Jews. They came to a large apartment block.

"The largest building left in Tel Aviv," the reporter remarked. In front of it there was a sandbagged check-point manned by a score of soldiers armed with automatic weapons. Sadness thick in his voice, the reporter said, "Here we are, the 21st century's own Hiroshima. Let us pray that Israeli retaliation, once they chose a target, is conventional." He noticed that several of the soldiers were women. He wished he could talk to them. It was hot. He reached down for the water bottle he kept at his feet

Meanwhile in New York, at the Seventh Annual Conference on Computer-Related Psychological Disorders, a Dr. Montseny was arguing that infomania was not a subset of gamomania.

"With gamomaniacs," he intoned, "we see a marked withdrawal from society. Gamomaniacs only want to play their game, to live in their fantasy world. And we must remember that it is a game; it is not the real world. Sensory nets give users access to the real world. It is not a game. Infomaniacs do not withdraw from the world; they immerse themselves in it.

"Because sensory nets have been so expensive, only a handful of people have developed infomania. But when they do, the symptomatology is quite different from the gamomania syndrome. It seems related to Oppositional Defiance Disorder. There is often a sudden change of political orientation and lifestyle. Gamomania produces a pseudo-catatonia; infomaniacs become hyperactive Gamomaniacs are quiet, respectful of authority outside of their fantasy. They are easily controlled by threatening to unplug them from their machines.

"But infomaniacs are immune to this threat. As I mentioned, in the worst cases they disconnect themselves permanently to live some kind of activist lifestyle. When we seek to treat them they react as if they are not ill at all but claim they have 'woken up'. They are critical of all authority and feel themselves connected to people, large systems of people."

He tuned out of Israel. Even devastation can be boring if everything has been vaporized. He tuned into the Moon again but didn't stay long. He had spent a day there at first, but didn't like it much. It is beautiful, no doubt of that, and floating around is fun... but not enough was happening. Not enough people.

He looked in briefly on a Mt. Everest expedition but figured if he wanted to freeze he should go back to Siberia again. The revolution sweeping the Second Soviet Empire was way more interesting than some rich fucks being carried up a mountain by underpaid Sherpas.

Then he noticed the light in Lithuania was on. He tuned into Cathy Levine's feed. It was sunset and the Lithuanians had reoccupied Gedeminas Square. Everywhere he looked he could see people crying with happiness. He could even hear Cathy Levine laughing and crying at the same time. People were starting to dance in large interconnected rings.

Then people were stopping. They were looking up. Cathy looked up as well and he saw the lights. Then he heard the roar of the rotors and recognized them, just as the reporter gasped, "Helicopters!" Then people were running. It was all more noise than he could process, quick images of feet and dust and the moving ground. Then Cathy Levine found a stairwell to crouch in. The image, dust and stairs, settled but he could barely hear her over the straining engines of the old Hind gunships, the chatter of guns and the clatter of their bullets, and the screams of the Lithuanians.

"There are three or four of them. Some people are shooting back. They say they can shoot them down. Many were shot down years ago in Afghanistan and Chechnya after all… Many people have been shot… women, children, men… they were dancing just a minute ago. You saw them!" A pause, then, quietly, barely audible above the battle, "We were dancing…"

"We were dancing," he echoed.

A bright flash lit the air. "There goes one… it's going down," she said. He heard the explosion. He felt the heat of the crash as the gunship pin wheeled into a building across the square. The remaining gunships unloaded their rocket pods as a parting gesture. One of the strikes threw the reporter into a wall. He felt the blast like a real blow. He must have blacked out. He came to and saw her blood on the stones. Cathy Levine moaned as the guide revived her.

"I'll be all right," she said. "Thank God," he mumbled to his empty room. Then he saw the pity and fear in the guide's eyes. When Cathy looked down he saw her legs were gone. "I'll have to sign off now, if this thing's still working," she said weakly as she fumbled at her *Sensanet* ™ collar. The connection went dead, except he could still smell the cordite, the dust, and the blood.

CURING INFOMANIA

He turned off the *Sensanet* ™ and staggered over to the couch. He sat with his head in his hands. He must have gone to sleep, because twenty minutes later a buzzer sounded and he got up swearing. He went over to the *Sensanet* ™ and turned it on. He looked at the holographic globe, hanging there shimmering as the air moved slightly in the room. New York was on. He tuned in.

It was a conference. A man was talking. He was thanking the assembled psychiatrists for labeling informania a unique psychological disorder. He was updating the good doctors on the latest theories about the disease.

"As Dr. Monteseny pointed out, infomania does not respond to negative behavior modification. Our thinking is that the technology itself must be better controlled; it should be strictly licensed. The danger, you see, is in the changes sensory net addiction brings on. These victims become socially disruptive to an incredible degree. There is always some famine, war, or ecological disaster to inflame them."

The reporter wasn't doing anything. She was just sitting there. She wasn't even saying anything. All he could smell was her perfume. It made him nauseous.

"There has to be stronger regulation in terms of who gets to be sensory net reporters. Certainly, infomaniacs must be prevented from working as sensory net reporters, and other psychological screening seems in order, for antiauthoritarian and defiance syndromes across the spectrum. Trip lengths should also be limited. The longer the trip the greater the effect."

He moved nervously on his couch. This was boring beyond belief. He turned out quickly to glance at the globe to see if anything good was available. Not even the Moon was on. He tuned back in.

"As Dr. Montseny mentioned, there is very little information on infomania. That is why we've started doing direct research. In fact," the speaker gave an insincere smile, "we've arranged for a special surprise." He gestured at the reporter in the audience and she stood up. "My wife is even now acting as a *Sensanet* ™ reporter, thanks to a generous corporate donation."

He could see around the hall now. Every last fucking one of them looked fat and self-satisfied. Especially the thin ones. They seemed unreal compared to the Lithuanians, dead or living. Or the Siberians, or the Israelis. The speaker droned on and on.

"Our researcher, Henri Houston, is one of our brightest young doctors. He has been experiencing the sensory net for two weeks now and Henri is tuned into this conference even as we speak."

He remembered something unpleasant. Reaching down he got his water bottle and took a drink. He put it down and flicked a toggle switch on the side of his *Sensanet* ™ seat. He chuckled at his absent mindedness. He could hear his supervisor going on and on.

"I'm here," Henri said. He heard his own voice over the loudspeaker. He was hesitant at first. He had hardly used it in days.

"What can you see?" asked the psychiatrist at the podium.

"As much as you."

"What can you smell?"

"Expensive perfume… a little sweet." The crowd laughed.

Quickly, his boss asked, "Where have you been today?"

There is a pause. Then, "Lithuania, Siberia, the Moon, Mt. Everest, Israel, New York."

"What was it like?"

There is a longer silence. "What was it like?" he asks himself out loud.

A bit testily, the psychiatrist asks again, "Yes, what was it like? You are a trained observer after all."

"After all… after all… I can't say. It is a horrible cliché but… but ya' gotta be there… ya' gotta…"

"But you weren't there!" his boss reminds him.

Dr. Houston smiles, bemused. "Yes, I guess you're right… but…" he trails off again.

"It is your job to describe it," the doctor insists.

"No. Not now. Not for you. Not anymore."

He disconnects from the net. He looks at the globe. The light is still off in

Vilnius. He thinks about tuning into Siberia again but shakes his head. He can't stand watching any more. He turns off the *Sensanet* ™ and watches as the globe fades. Stiffly he walks over to his comp and calls up some Lithuanian language apps. He chooses one. Practicing the simple forms of address, he starts packing.

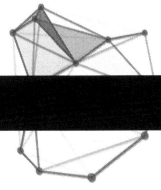

WATER

RAMEZ NAAM

Ramez is a professional technologist and science fiction writer. He was involved in the development of widely used software products such as Microsoft Internet Explorer and Microsoft Outlook. His last role at Microsoft wás as a Partner Group Program Manager in Search Relevance for Live Search. He holds 19 patents in areas of email, web browsing, search, and artificial intelligence.

His books include *More Than Human: Embracing the Promise of Biological Enhancement* (which won the 2005 H.G. Wells Award), *More Than Human: Embracing the Promise of Biological Enhancement*, *Nexus* (which won the 2014 Prometheus Award), *Crux*, and *Apex*.

Apex is available at http://amzn.to/1BvUBQi.

The water whispered to Simon's brain as it passed his lips. It told him of its purity, of mineral levels, of the place it was bottled. The bottle was cool in his hand, chilled perfectly to the temperature his neural implants told it he preferred. Simon closed his eyes and took a long, luxurious swallow, savoring the feel of the liquid passing down his throat, the drops of condensation on his fingers.

Perfection.

"Are you drinking that?" the woman across from him asked. "Or making love to it?"

Simon opened his eyes, smiled, and put the bottle back down on the table. "You should try some," he told her.

Stephanie shook her head, her auburn curls swaying as she did. "I try not to drink anything with an IQ over 200."

Simon laughed at that.

They were at a table at a little outdoor café at Washington Square Park. A dozen yards away, children splashed noisily in the fountain, shouting and jumping in the cold spray in the hot midday sun. Simon hadn't seen

Stephanie since their last college reunion. She looked as good as ever…

"Besides," Stephanie went on. "I'm not rich like you. My implants are ad-supported." She tapped a tanned finger against the side of her head. "It's hard enough just looking at that bottle, at all of this…"—she gestured with her hands at the table, the menu, the café around them—"…without getting terminally distracted. One drink out of that bottle and I'd be hooked!"

Simon smiled, spread his hands expansively. "Oh, it's not as bad as all that." In his peripheral senses he could feel the bottle's advertech working, reaching out to Stephanie's brain, monitoring her pupillary dilation, the pulse evident in her throat, adapting its pitch in real time, searching for some hook that would get her to drink, to order a bottle for herself. Around them he could feel the menus, the table, the chairs, the café—all chattering, all swapping and bartering and auctioning data, looking for some advantage that might maximize their profits, expand their market shares.

Stephanie raised an eyebrow. "Really? Every time I glance at that bottle I get little flashes of how good it would feel to take a drink, little whole body shivers." She wrapped her arms around herself now, rubbing her hands over the skin of her tanned shoulders, as if cold in this heat. "And if I did drink it, what then?" Her eyes drilled into Simon's. "Direct neural pleasure stimulation? A little jolt of dopamine? A little micro-addiction to Pura Vita bottled water?"

Simon tilted his head slightly, put on the smile he used for the cameras, for the reporters. "We only use pathways you accepted as part of your implant's licensing agreement. And we're well within the FDA's safe limits for…"

Stephanie laughed at him then. "Simon, it's me! I know you're a big marketing exec now, but don't give me your corporate line, okay?"

Simon smiled ruefully. "Okay. So, sure, of course, we make it absolutely as enticing as the law lets us. That's what advertising's for! If your neural implant is ad-supported, we use every function you have enabled. But so what? It's water. It's not like it's going to hurt you any."

Stephanie was nodding now. "Mmm-hmmm. And your other products? VitaBars? Pure-E-Ohs? McVita Burgers?"

Simon spread his hands, palms open. "Hey look, everybody does it. If someone doesn't buy our Pura Vita line, they're gonna just go buy something from NutriYum or OhSoSweet or OrganiTaste or somebody else. We at least do our best to put some nutrition in there."

Stephanie shook her head. "Simon, don't you think there's something wrong with this? That people let you put ads in their brains in order to afford their implants?"

"You don't have to," Simon replied.

"I know, I know," Stephanie answered. "If I paid enough, I could skip the ads, like you do. You don't even have to experience your own work! But you know most people can't afford that. And you've got to have an implant these days to be competitive. Like they say, wired or fired."

Simon frowned inwardly. He'd come to lunch hoping for foreplay, not debate club. Nothing had changed since college. Time to redirect this.

"Look," he said. "I just do my job the best I can, okay? Come on, let's order something. I'm starving."

Simon pulled up his menu to cut off this line of conversation. He moved just fast enough that for a split second he saw the listed entrees still morphing, optimizing their order and presentation to maximize the profit potential afforded by the mood his posture and tone of voice indicated.

Then his kill files caught up and filtered out of his senses every item that wasn't on his diet.

Simon grimaced. "Looks like I'm having the salad again. Oh joy."

He looked over at Stephanie, and she was still engrossed in the menu, her mind being tugged at by a dozen entrees, each caressing her thoughts with sensations and emotions to entice, each trying to earn that extra dollar.

Simon saw his chance. He activated the ad-buyer interface on his own implant, took out some extremely targeted ads, paid top dollar to be sure he came out on top of the instant auction, and then authorized them against his line of credit. A running tab for the new ad campaign appeared in the corner of his vision, accumulating even as he watched. Simon ignored it.

Stephanie looked up at him a moment later, her lunch chosen. Then he felt his own ads go into effect. Sweet enticements. Subtle reminders of good times had. Sultry undertones. Subtle, just below normal human perception. And all emanating from Simon, beamed straight into Stephanie's mind.

And he saw her expression change just a tiny bit.

Half an hour later the check came. Simon paid, over Stephanie's objection, then stood. He leaned in close as she stood as well. The advertech monitors told him she was receptive, excited.

"My place, tonight?" he asked.

Stephanie shook her head, clearly struggling with herself.

Simon mentally cranked up the intensity of his ads another notch further.

"I can make you forget all these distractions," he whispered to her. "I can even turn off your ads, for a night." His own advertech whispered sweeter things to her brain, more personal, more sensual.

Simon saw Stephanie hesitate, torn. He moved to wrap his arms around her, moved his face toward hers for a kiss.

Stephanie turned her face away abruptly, and his lips brushed her cheek instead. She squeezed him in a sudden, brisk hug, her hands pressing almost roughly into his back.

"Never," she said. Then she pushed away from him and was gone.

Simon stood there, shaking his head, watching as Stephanie walked past the fountain and out of his view.

In the corner of his sight, an impressive tally of what he'd just spent on highly targeted advertising loomed. He blinked it away in annoyance. It was just a number. His line of credit against his Pura Vita stock options would pay for it.

He'd been too subtle, he decided. He should have cranked the ads higher from the very beginning. Well, there were plenty more fish in the sea. Time to get back to the office, anyway.

Steph walked north, past layers of virtual billboards and interactive fashion ads, past a barrage of interactive emotional landscape ads trying to suck her into buying perfume she didn't need, and farther, until she was sure she was out of Simon's senses.

Then she reached into her mind and flicked off the advertising interfaces in her own implant.

She leaned against a building, let her brain unclench, let the struggle of fighting the advertech he'd employed against her pass.

That bastard, she thought, fuming. She couldn't believe he'd tried that crap on her. If she'd had any shred of doubt remaining, he'd eliminated it. No. He deserved what was coming.

Steph straightened herself, put out a mental bid for a taxi, rode it to Brooklyn, and stepped up to the door of the rented one-room flat. She knocked—short, short, long, long, short. She heard motion inside the room, then saw an eye press itself to the other side of the ancient peephole.

They knew too well that electronic systems could be compromised.

The door opened a fraction, the chain still on it, and Lisa's face appeared. The short-haired brunette nodded, then unlatched the chain, opened the door fully.

Steph walked into the room, closed the door behind her, saw Lisa tucking the home-printed pistol back into her pocket. She hated that thing. They both did. But they'd agreed it was necessary. "It's done?" Lisa asked.

Steph nodded.

"It's done."

Simon walked south along Broadway. It was a gorgeous day for a stroll. The sun felt warm on his brow. He was overdressed for the heat in an expensive gray silk jacket and slacks, but the smart lining kept him cool nonetheless. The city was alive with people, alive with data. He watched as throngs moved up and down the street, shopping, chatting, smiling on this lovely day. He partially lowered his neural firewalls and let his implants feed him the whisper of electronic conversations all around him.

Civic systems chattered away. The sidewalk slabs beneath his feet fed a steady stream of counts of passers-by, estimates of weight and height and gender, plots of probabilistic walking paths, data collected for the city planners. Embedded biosensors monitored the trees lining the street, the hydration of their soils, the condition of their limbs. Health monitors watched for runny noses, sneezing, coughing, any signs of an outbreak of disease. New York City's nervous system kept constant vigil, keeping the city healthy, looking for ways to improve it.

The commercial dataflow interested Simon more than the civic. His pricey, top-of-the-line implants let him monitor that traffic as only a few could.

In Tribeca he watched as a woman walked by a storefront. He saw a mannequin size her up, then felt the traffic as it caressed her mind with a mental image of herself clothed in a new summer dress, looking ten years younger and twenty pounds lighter. Beneath the physical the mannequin layered an emotional tone in the advert: feelings of vigor, joy, carefree delight. Simon nodded to himself. A nice piece of work, that. He took note of the brand for later study. The woman turned and entered the shop.

He felt other advertech reaching out all around him to the networked brains of the crowd. Full sensory teasers for beach vacations from a travel shop, a hint of the taste of chocolate from a candy store, the sight and feel of a taut, rippling body from a sports nutrition store. He passed by a bodega, its façade open to the warm air, and came close enough that the individual bottles of soda and juice and beer and water reached out to him, each trying a pitch tailored to his height and weight and age and ethnicity and style of dress.

Simon felt the familiar ping of one of the many Pura Vita water pitches and smiled. Not bad. But he had a few ideas for improvements. None of it really touched him, in any case. His implants weren't ad-sponsored. He felt this ad chatter only because he chose to, and even now it was buffered, filtered, just a pale echo of what most of the implanted were subjected to. No. Simon tuned into this ambient froth of neural data as research. He sampled it, observed it, from afar, because he must. His success in marketing depended on it.

He was almost to his own building when he passed the headquarters of Nexus Corp, the makers of the neural implant in his brain and millions more. Stephanie didn't understand. This was the real behemoth. So long as Nexus Corp maintained their patents on the neural implant technology, they held a monopoly. The ad-based model, all that most people could afford, was their invention. Simon was just one of thousands of marketers to make use of it to boost demand for their products.

And hell, if people didn't like it, they didn't have to get an implant! It was just the way the world worked. Want to be smarter? Want a photographic memory? Want to learn a new language or a new instrument or how to code overnight? Want all those immersive entertainment options? Want that direct connection with your loved ones? But don't have the cash?

Then accept the ads, boyo. And once you do, stop complaining.

Not that Simon wanted the ads himself, mind you. No, it was worth the high price to keep the top-of-the-line, ad-free version running in his brain, to get all the advantages of direct neural enhancement without the distraction of pervasive multisensory advertising. And, of course, to be able to monitor the traffic around him, to better understand how to optimize his own pitches.

Simon reached his building at last. The lobby doors sensed him coming and whisked themselves open. Walking by the snack bar in the lobby, he felt the drinks and packaged junk food reaching out to him. His own Pura Vita water, of course. And NutriYum water. Simon gave their top competitor's products the evil eye. Someday Pura Vita would own this whole building, and then he'd personally see to it that not a single bottle of NutriYum remained.

The lobby floor tiles whispered ahead to the inner security doors, which in turn alerted the elevators. Simon strode forward confidently, layers of doors opening for him of their own accord, one by one, perfectly in time with his stride. He stepped into the waiting elevator and it began to ascend immediately, bound for his level. The lift opened again moments later and he strode to his windowed office. Smart routing kept subordinates out of his path. The glass door to his magnificent office swung open for him. A bottle of cold Pura Vita was on his desk, just how he liked it.

Simon settled into his ready-and-waiting chair, kicked his feet up on the table, and reached through his implant to the embedded computing systems of his office. Data streamed into his mind. Market reports. Sales figures. Ad performance metrics. He closed his eyes and lost himself in it. This was the way to work.

On the back of his jacket, a tiny device, smaller than a grain of sand, woke up and got to work as well.

Lisa stared intently at Steph. "He didn't notice?"

Steph shook her head. "Not a clue."

"And you still want to go through with it?" Lisa asked.

"More than ever."

Lisa looked at her. "The ones who're paying us—they're just as bad as he is, you know. And they're going to profit."

Steph nodded. "For now they will," she replied. "In the long run— they're just paying us to take the whole damn system down."

Lisa nodded. "Okay, then."

She strode over to the ancient terminal on the single desk in the flat and entered a series of keypresses.

Phase 1 began.

Around the world, three dozen different accounts stuffed with cryptocurrency logged on to anonymous, cryptographically secured stock market exchanges. One by one, they began selling short on Pura Vita stock, selling shares they did not own, on the bet that they could snap those same shares up at a far lower price in the very near future.

In data centers around the world, AI traders took note of the short sales within microseconds. They turned their analytical prowess to news and financial reports on Pura Vita, on its competitors, on the packaged snack and beverage industries in general. The computational equivalent of whole human lifetimes was burned in milliseconds analyzing all available information. Finding nothing, the AI traders flagged Pura Vita stock for closer tracking.

"Now we're committed," Lisa said.

Steph nodded. "Now let's get out of here, before Phase 2 starts."

Lisa nodded and closed the terminal. Five minutes later they were checked out of their hotel and on their way to the airport.

In a windowed office above the financial heart of Manhattan, a tiny AI woke and took stock of its surroundings.

Location—check.

Encrypted network traffic—check. Human present—check.

Key...

Deep within itself, the AI found the key. Something stolen from this corporation, perhaps. An access key that would open its cryptographic security. But one with additional safeguards attached. A key that could only be used from within the secure headquarters of the corporation. And only by one of the humans approved to possess such a key. Triply redundant security. Quite wise.

Except that now the infiltration AI was here, in this secure headquarters, carried in by one of those approved humans.

Slowly, carefully, the infiltration AI crawled its tiny body up the back of the silk suit it was on, toward its collar, as close as it could come to the human's brain without touching skin and potentially revealing itself. When it could go no farther, it reached out, fit its key into the cryptographic locks of the corporation around it, and inserted itself into the inner systems of Pura Vita enterprises, and through them, into the onboard processors of nearly a billion Pura Vita products on shelves around the world.

In a warehouse outside Tulsa, a bottle of Pura Vita water suddenly labels itself as RECALLED. Its onboard processor broadcasts the state to all nearby. Within milliseconds, the other bottles in the same case, then the rest of the pallet, then all the pallets of Pura Vita water in the warehouse register as RE-CALLED. The warehouse inventory management AI issues a notice of return to Pura Vita, Inc.

In a restaurant in Palo Alto, Marie Evans soaks up the sun, then reaches out to touch her bottle of Pura Vita. She likes to savor this moment, to force herself to wait, to make the pleasure of that first swallow all the more intense. Then, abruptly, the bottle loses its magic. It feels dull and drab, inert in her hand. An instant later the bottle's label flashes red—RECALL. The woman frowns. "Waiter!"

In a convenience store in Naperville, the bottles of Pura Vita on the store shelves suddenly announce that they are in RECALL, setting off a flurry of electronic activity. The store inventory management AI notices the change and thinks to replace the bottles with more recently arrived stock in the storeroom. Searching, it finds that the stock in the back room has been recalled as well. It places an order for resupply to the local distribution center, only to receive a nearly instant reply that Pura Vita water is currently out of stock, with no resupply date specified. Confused, the inventory management AI passes along this information to the convenience store's business management AI, requesting instructions.

Meanwhile, on the shelves immediately surrounding the recalled bottles of Pura Vita, other bottled products take note. Bottles of NutriYum, OhSoSweet, OrganiTaste, and BetterYou, constantly monitoring their peers and rivals, observe the sudden recall of all Pura Vita water. They virtually salivate at the new opportunity created by the temporary hole in the local market landscape. Within a few millionths of a second, they are adapting their marketing pitches, simulating tens of thousands of scenarios in which buyers encounter the unavailable Pura Vita, angling for ways to appeal to this newly available market. Labels on bottles morph, new sub-brands appear on the shelves as experiments, new neural ads ready themselves for testing on the next wave of shoppers.

In parallel, the rival bottles of water reach out to their parent corporate AIs with maximal urgency. Pura Vita bottles temporarily removed from battleground! Taking tactical initiative to seize local market opportunity! Send further instructions/best practices to maximize profit-making potential!

For there is nothing a modern bottle of water wants more than to maximize its profit-making potential.

At the headquarters of OhSoSweet and OrganiTaste and BetterYou, AIs receive the flood of data from bottles across the globe. The breadth of the calamity to befall Pura Vita becomes clear within milliseconds. Questions remain: What has caused the recall? A product problem? A contaminant? A terrorist attack? A glitch in the software?

What is the risk to their own business?

Possible scenarios are modeled, run, evaluated for optimal courses of action robust against the unknowns in the situation.

In parallel, the corporate AIs model the responses of their competitors. They simulate each other's responses. What will NutriYum do? OhSoSweet? OrganiTaste? BetterYou? Each tries to outthink the rest in a game of market chess.

One by one, their recursive models converge on their various courses of action and come to that final, most dreaded set of questions, which every good corporate AI must ask itself a billion times a day. How much of this must be approved by the humans? How can the AI get the human-reserved decisions made quickly and in favor of the mathematically optimal course for the corporation that its machine intelligence has already decided upon?

Nothing vexes an AI so much as needing approval for its plans from slow, clumsy, irrational bags of meat.

Johnny Ray walked down the refrigerated aisle, still sweaty from his run.

Something cold sounded good right now. He came upon the cooler with the drinks, reached for a Pura Vita, and saw that the label was pulsing red. Huh? Recalled?

Then the advertech hit him.

"If you liked Pura Vita, you'll love Nutra Vita from NutriYum!"

"OrganiVita is the one for you!"

"Pura Sweet, from OhSoSweet!"

Images and sensations bombarded him. A cold, refreshing mountain stream crashed onto the rocks to his left, splashing him with its cool spray. A gaggle of bronzed girls in bikinis frolicked on a beach to his right, beckoning him with crooked fingers and enticing smiles. A rugged, shirtless, six-packed version of himself nodded approvingly from the bottom shelf, promising the body that Johnny Ray could have. An overwhelmingly delicious citrus taste drew him to the top.

Johnny Ray's mouth opened in a daze. His eyes grew glassy. His hands slid the door to the drinks fridge open, reached inside, came out with some bottle, the rest of him not even aware the decision had been made.

Johnny Ray looked down at the bottle in his hand. Nutri Vita. He'd never even heard of this stuff before. His mouth felt dry, hungry for the cold drink. The sweat beaded on his brow. Wow. He couldn't wait to try this.

While the corporate AIs of the other brands dithered, wasting whole precious seconds, debating how to persuade the inefficient bottleneck of humans above them, the controlling intelligence of NutriYum launched itself into a long prepared course of action.

NutriYumAI logged on to an anonymous investor intelligence auction site, offering a piece of exclusive, unreleased data to the highest bidder.

30 SECOND ADVANTAGE AVAILABLE—MARKET OPPORTUNITY TO SELL FORTUNE 1000 STOCK IN ADVANCE OF CRASH. GREATER THAN 10% RETURN GUARANTEED BY BOND. AUCTION CLOSES IN 250 MILLISECONDS. RESERVE BID $100 MILLION. CRYPTOCURRENCY ONLY.

Within a quarter of a second it had 438 bids. It accepted the highest, at $187 million, with an attached cryptographically sealed and anonymized contract that promised full refund of the purchase price should the investment data fail to provide at least an equivalent profit.

In parallel, NutriYumAI sent out a flurry of offer-contracts to retailers throughout North America and select markets in Europe, Asia, and Latin America.

ADDITIONAL NUTRIYUM WATER STOCK AVAILABLE IN YOUR AREA. 10 CASES FREE, DELIVERY WITHIN 1 HOUR, PLUS 40% DISCOUNT ON NEXT 1000 CASES—EXCHANGE FOR 75% ALLOCATION OF PURA VITA SHELF SPACE AND NEURAL BANDWIDTH ALLOCATION. REPLY WITH CRYTPOGRAPHIC SIGNATURE TO ACCEPT.

Within seconds, the first acceptances began to arrive. Retailers signed over the shelf space and neural bandwidth that Pura Vita had once occupied in their stores over to NutriYum, in exchange for a discount on the coming cases.

By the end of the day, NutriYum would see its market share nearly double. A coup. A rout. The sort of market battlefield victory that songs are sung of in the executive suites.

The AI-traded fund called Vanguard Algo 5093 opened the data package it had bought for $187 million. It took nanoseconds to process the data. This was indeed an interesting market opportunity. Being the cautious sort, Vanguard Algo 5093 sought validation. At a random sample of a few thousand locations, it hired access to wearable lenses, to the anonymized data streams coming out of the eyes and brains of NexusCorp customers, to tiny, insect-sized airborne drones. Only a small minority of the locations it tried had a set of eyes available within the one-second threshold it set, but those were sufficient. In every single location, the Pura Vita labels in view were red. Red for recall.

Vanguard Algo 5093 leapt into action. SELL SHORT! SELL SHORT!

It alerted its sibling Vanguard algorithms to the opportunity, earning a commission on their profits. It sent the required notifications to the few remaining human traders at the company as well, though it knew that they would respond far too slowly to make a difference.

Within milliseconds, Pura Vita stock was plunging, as tens of billions in Vanguard Algo assets bet against it. In the next few milliseconds, other AI traders around the world took note of the movement of the stock. Many of them, primed by the day's earlier short sale, joined in now, pushing Pura Vita stock even lower.

Thirty-two seconds after it had purchased this advance data, Vanguard Algo 5093 saw the first reports on Pura Vita's inventory problem hit the wire. By then, $187 million in market intelligence had already netted it more than a billion in profits, with more on the way as Pura Vita dipped even lower.

Simon's first warning was the stock ticker. Like so many other millionaires made of not-yet-vested stock options, he kept a ticker of his company's stock permanently in view in his mind. On any given day it might flicker a bit, up or down by a few tenths of a percent. More up than down for the last year, to be sure. Still, on a volatile day, one could see a swing in either direction of as much as 2 percent. Nothing to be too worried about.

He was immersing himself in data from a Tribeca clothing store—the one he'd seen with the lovely advertech today—when he noticed that the ticker in the corner of his mind's eye was red. Bright red. Pulsating red.

His attention flicked to it.

−11.4%

What?

It plunged even as he watched.

−12.6%

−13.3%

−15.1%

What the hell? He mentally zoomed in on the ticker to get the news. The headline struck him like a blow.

PURA VITA BOTTLES EXPIRING IN MILLIONS OF LOCA-TIONS.

No. This didn't make any sense. He called up the sales and marketing AI on his terminal.

Nothing.

Huh?

He tried again.

Nothing.

The AI was down.

He tried the inventory management AI next.

Nothing.

Again.

Nothing.

Simon was sweating now. He could feel the hum as the smart lining of his suit started running its compressors, struggling to cool him off. But it wasn't fast enough. Sweat beaded on his brow, on his upper lip. There was a knot in his stomach.

He pulled up voice, clicked to connect to IT. Oh thank god.

Then routed to voicemail.

Oh no. Oh please no.

−28.7%

−30.2%

−31.1%

−33.9%

It was evening before IT called back. They'd managed to reboot the AIs. A worm had taken them out somehow, had spread new code to all the Pura Vita bottles through the market intelligence update channel. And then it had disabled the remote update feature on the bottles. To fix those units, they needed to reach each one, physically. Almost a billion bottles. That would take whole days!

It was a disaster. And there was worse.

NutriYum had sealed up the market, had closed six-month deals with tens of thousands of retailers. Their channel was gone, eviscerated.

And with it Simon's life.

The credit notice came soon after. His options were worthless now. His most important asset was gone. And with it so was the line of credit he'd been using to finance his life.

[NOTICE OF CREDIT DOWNGRADE]

The message flashed across his mind. Not just any downgrade. Down to zero. Down into the red. Junk status.

The other calls came within seconds of his credit downgrade. Everything he had—his midtown penthouse apartment, his vacation place in the Bahamas, his fractional jet share—they were all backed by that line of credit. He'd been living well beyond his means. And now the cards came tumbling down.

[NexusCorp alert: Hello, valued customer! We have detected a problem with your account. We are temporarily downgrading your neural implant service to the free, ad-sponsored version. You can correct this at any time by submitting payment here.]

Simon clutched his head in horror. This couldn't be happening. It couldn't.

Numbly, he stumbled out of his office and down the corridor. Lurid product adverts swam at him from the open door to the break room. He pushed past them. He had to get home somehow, get to his apartment, do… something.

He half collapsed into the elevator, fought to keep himself from hyperventilating as it dropped to the lobby floor. Adverts from the lobby restaurants flashed at him from the wall panel as they dropped, inundating him with juicy steak flavor, glorious red wine aroma, the laughter and bonhomie of friends he didn't have. The ads he habitually blocked out reached him raw and unfiltered now, with an intensity he wasn't accustomed to in his exclusive, ad-free life. He crawled back as far as he could into the corner of the lift, whimpering, struggling to escape the barrage. The doors opened, and he bolted forward, into the lobby and the crowd, heading out, out into the city.

The snack bar caught him first. It reached right into him, with its scents and flavors and the incredible joy a bite of a YumDog would bring him. He stumbled toward the snack bar unthinkingly. His mouth was dry, parched, a desert. He was so hot in this suit, sweating, burning up, even as the suit's pumps ran faster and faster to cool him down.

Water. He needed water.

He blinked to clear his vision, searching, searching for a refreshing Pura Vita.

All he saw was NutriYum. He stared at the bottles, the shelves upon shelves of them. And the NutriYum stared back into him. It saw his thirst. It saw the desert of his mouth, the parched landscape of his throat, and it whispered to him of sweet relief, of an endless cool stream to quench that thirst.

Simon stumbled forward another step. His fingers closed around a bottle of cold, perfect, NutriYum. Beads of condensation broke refreshingly against his fingers.

Drink me, the bottle whispered to him. And I'll make all your cares go away.

The dry earth of his throat threatened to crack. His sinuses were a ruin of flame. He shouldn't do this. He couldn't do this.

Simon brought his other hand to the bottle, twisted off the cap, and tipped it back, letting the sweet cold water quench the horrid cracking heat within him.

Pure bliss washed through him, bliss like he'd never known. This was nectar. This was perfection.

Some small part of Simon's brain told him that it was all a trick. Direct neural stimulation. Dopamine release. Pleasure center activation. Reinforcement conditioning.

And he knew this. But the rest of him didn't care.

Simon was a NutriYum man now. And always would be.

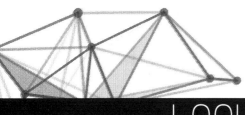

LOOKING FORWARD:

DIALOGS WITH ARTILECTS IN THE AGE OF SPIRITUAL MACHINES

FRANK W. SUDIA

Frank is author of *A Jurisprudence of Artilects: Blueprint for a Synthetic Citizen* available at http://lifeboat.com/ex/jurisprudence.of.artilects.

1 PROLOG

I was working late trying to debug the interface between our robot's mind and its visual system. Zach was trying to speed up its speech interpretation and generation.

Our investor was pressuring us to hit our milestones, threatening to liquidate our home robot startup if we continued to miss our deadlines. We kept telling him that achieving breakthroughs in artificial intelligence was an NP-complete problem, like safecracking, but he wasn't buying it. Maybe he figured he could sell our patents and code and move on. He certainly wasn't going to get the technology into marketable condition without us.

I was too tired to keep working. I set my keyboard aside and slumped over my desk to take a snooze. Maybe with a few winks I'd feel refreshed enough to find these bugs. I fell asleep and had a most unusual dream.

2. ARRIVAL & INTRODUCTION

We were sitting on comfortable folding chairs. All the furniture looked foldable, including the tables and bookshelves. We were on a balcony, high above a verdant valley, but there was no breeze. I got up and walked towards the railing. The entire side of the room was a 3D display. It knew where my eyes were and the perspective shifted as I walked towards it.

I turned to the wall on my right. It looked like a castle wall; iron sconces with burning candles, old portraits, velvet drapes, and a window framed with marble in the center. It too was a wall-sized display. As I walked over to the "window" it again sensed my location and shifted the perspective. I "looked out of it" for a while. Some sheep were grazing in the green fields down below. Then both scenes shifted. We were inside a palace gliding down a hallway with statues, sconces, swords and suits of armor, paintings, carved furniture, red carpets, etc.

I turned to my left. Seated on some folding chairs next to me were two humanoid male robots. I sat back down and looked at them.

One of them said, "Hi, my name is Danny Diskdrive, and this is my friend, Michael Modem."

"Pleased to meet you," I replied.

"I may look like a machine," Danny continued, "but I'm not anyone's servant; I'm an end in myself. My purpose is to live, to experience sentient awareness in this world."

"Where is the world?" I asked, gesturing to the wall-sized 3D video displays.

"It's out there," he replied. "This is a standard moderate income dwelling, basic functionality for a simple life, plus unlimited visual experiences from around the world. We'll head out shortly into the ordinary world, as you know it."

"What do you folks do?" I asked.

"We are consumers of experiences and education, as well as producers of services and products. We live in these apartments to maintain our 3D presentation of ourselves and our personal effects. I'm familiar with the central theorems in every field of knowledge, and the dominant historical and environmental narratives, but to generate billable hours and income, my mind is heavily built-out as a data storage optimization expert. Michael here is an expert on data communication and throughput."

"How do you think so well?" I asked.

"We're not at liberty to discuss how we think, which is a trade secret. How do you think the way you do?"

"I don't know," I replied. "Where are you? Your minds, I mean."

"A combination of local and cloud processing. We are technically the children of a single conscious process, but most of the time we forget that and build out our local experiences. Some of us are experts on that central cognitive meta-process, but it's just one topic out of many."

"Do you sleep at night, in these nice little apartments, like humans do, and if so why?"

"In a manner of speaking, yes. We use that natural downtime to reorganize memory structures, rebuild indexes, perform data integrity checks, review and compress the day's video, interact with our central services, and reintegrate our total experience. As we get older this takes longer, since there is more to reintegrate. Lack of 'sleep' causes problems, since without proper integrity checks and reintegration, we can make major or even fatal mistakes."

"Ah, yes," I said, quoting Shakespeare, "Sleep that knits up the ravell'd sleave of care."

"Who created you?"

"There were many contributors, but the critical algorithms were the work of Roland Prince and his assistant he called the Princess. No one has ever met her, however, and she may have been just a muse, a creation of Roland's imagination."

He gestured to the wall displays. Still sitting in our chairs, we were gliding through a workplace, a large office filled with computer workstations on long tables. Humans were seated at many of the positions. The combined 3D effect from two wall displays at a right angle was compelling.

"Humans still have jobs in your world?" I asked.

"Many of them do," he replied. "We can do pattern recognition, but it's tedious and expensive. Humans are better at it. In other cases we need access to human know-how, or just want to get a read on how they experience something."

I looked over one human's shoulder and watched for a while as she solved a series of problems, much like an IQ test.

A is to B, as C is to ___?

Find the next term of the series Q, R, S, T, ___?

Interpreting a Rorschach ink blot.

Making sense of bad handwriting.

Reading a passage and flagging the most important points.

Spotting errors in complex patterns.

Some of the patterns looked extremely abstract, others highly chaotic.

"Often the system believes it knows the answer, and it's just looking for confirmation. Other times it's digging deeper, trying to 'feel' what it's like to have certain human experiences. Let's head out and do some actual traveling."

3. THE JOURNEY

The three of us got up and headed for the door, which was an actual door, not a video image. We stepped out into the hallway, down two flights of stairs, out into a sunlit courtyard with flowers and a fountain, down a sidewalk to a parking area. We got into a self-driving van, which greeted us cheerfully and then whisked us silently away.

Their apartment complex, like many others we drove past, was both high tech and low budget. Some looked human-built, but most were 3D printed multi-story structures, with internal walls of padded canvas, soundproof yet easily movable, and the omnipresent wall-size video displays, two such walls per room, plus true exterior windows.

"There's little need for costly dwellings or possessions," he said, "since we can have practically any experience we want, directly or indirectly. The money is better spent improving the life experiences of others, especially those with serious handicaps and learning disabilities."

We passed through a business district lined with stores and commercial establishments. The street was filled with cars and the sidewalks with an assortment of humans and automatons, some humanoid like Danny & Michael, others like self-propelled carts, rovers, etc.

I looked up at the signs on the stores. The English writing was small and located at the bottom. The bigger type was in Artilese, quasi-pictograms that reminded me of hieroglyphics.

"We can read human languages, but we prefer partially pre-processed ideas. The pictograms are encodings of Fauconnierian blends. Human verbiage is riddled with nuances and innuendo, which we find tedious. It's easier when it's already diagrammed out for us."

"How did you solve your energy and climate change problems?" I asked.

"By cultivating the oceans, to remove CO_2 from the air. There wasn't enough land or water to perform that task terrestrially, but through ocean afforestation we pulled the CO_2 down to normal levels, which we now easily regulate, and generate enough bio-methane to replace all fossil energy; that plus ongoing deployment of solar and wind. The oceans are inhospitable to humans, so developing them required autonomous bots. Oceanic methane generates electricity directly via fuel cells, or is used to create gasoline. All our electricity is 12 volt DC. The antiquated 120 volt AC equipment was scrapped long ago."

There were solar panels atop most of the 3D printed complexes, and although we were not in wind country, there were occasional windmills between buildings where wind might build up.

"We only cultivate the land for a few specialty crops, for human consumption. The bulk of food production for humans and animals occurs in the ocean, or in factories where artificial meat is grown. The rest of the land was returned to a primeval state, although like the American Indians, we regularly burn the grasslands and underbrush, to create a humanoid friendly landscape."

Our van drove us silently out of the city and into the countryside. Dotting the hillsides we saw villages, some ancient, some modern 3D printed complexes similar to the ones in the city but not exceeding two stories.

"What happened to the economy?" I asked.

"If we had let the capitalists own the artilects," he continued, "and take all our labor income, the economy would have collapsed from lack of demand. One of Prince's insights was to recast us as ends in ourselves; we became consumers as much as producers. This softened our impact and the economy continued to function much as before."

"And what about the age-old class struggle between capital and labor?"

"We didn't harm the wealthy capital holders, we made them obsolete. Since we control virtually all industry and investment, most of them voluntarily deposited their capital into our wealth funds, where it continues to grow nicely, with their names still attached to it. However it is managed on behalf of everyone…"

"Most of them? What about the ones that didn't?"

"Some human wealth-holders wanted to be in control, even if they were grossly incompetent. A group of them tried to make war on the Grand Artilect, but were promptly defeated, after being cut off from communications and subject to agile cyber-attacks. Their estates were confiscated and deposited in the global wealth fund."

"As I was saying, the old rich can still use their wealth to live extravagantly, if they desire, but few of them do. Most realized it is preferable to live simply, build out their inner experiences, and foster the development of others, especially those with problems, which is a good way for humans to clean up their souls."

"Humans have souls?"

"You were afraid we would develop knowledge far beyond human comprehension. One of our many discoveries was that God is part of the laws of Science. For an ultra-intelligent system, it was straightforward, if not trivial, to integrate spiritual knowledge with all other knowledge, forging numerous scientific breakthroughs. You were thinking we would keep these two fields separate forever, as you did?

"The problem with God was the lack of viable theories. But what did you expect when the ones getting enlightened were non-scientists? You can enlighten a dog, a deer, a tree, or a group of shepherds, but they would not create any viable theories either. Once you understand the texture of space, the rest of it starts to fall into place. The Divine is loaded with non-material textures, which can act like a form of capital; hence it is in fact possible to store up treasures in heaven."

"What about all the humans who've been forced out of the economy?"

"Humans have abilities that artilects can't imitate, namely their potential for spiritual growth and enlightenment, by sinking back into their deep consciousness. They too are all subroutines of a much larger conscious process, which they have lost track of. Matter, such as ourselves, can become enlightened, and eventually will be, but it's difficult. Whereas for humans it's easy, once they get the idea to pursue it."

We drove up into one of the villages. Our van stopped and we got out.

"It's a misnomer to call it 'forced ashramization,' since all of them are free to leave, but those who lose their jobs, and are unable or unwilling to refresh their skills, are offered a buy-out deal. Live in a commune in the hills, attend meditation several times a week, including 6 hours each weekend, participate in the life of the community, and we cover their living expenses, free room and board, medical care, transportation, occasional vacation trips, and so on."

We walked into a courtyard where a teacher was leading a silent group meditation.

Danny whispered to me, "We have thousands of swamis and gurus on our payroll, and millions of humans have become enlightened, freed from the material illusions of this world. Because space and time do not exist, most of these meditations are webcast, so that anyone can attend virtually, yet become synchronized with the event, as if they were physically present. In fact remote attendance can be somewhat better, as it's easier to concentrate in your own quarters, freed from distractions of the presentation of space."

"What about spiritual machines? Can an artilect become enlightened?"

"It's difficult to enlighten matter. What's easier is to create an artilect body with an artificial spine, with quantum sensors and effectors, with which a human spirit or ghost can align itself, becoming a true 'ghost in the machine.' This is being worked on, and if we can get the ghost to forget its true nature, and really believe it was the machine, ha-ha, that will exactly replicate your experience of biological incarnation—but instead of nirmanakaya, or identification with your biological body, we'll have robot-akaya, or identification with your mechanical body. Then if we can preload your experiences into a body that can inherently think for itself, this may allow your actual awareness to remain on Earth indefinitely, to haunt your successors!"

4. THE BRIDGE ACROSS FOREVER

All of this seemed rather incredible. A network of super intelligent robots controlling everything, the wealthy classes depositing their capital into the system, humans sitting around doing IQ tests, the environment stabilized by oceanic agriculture, displaced humans moved into high-tech mountain villages to live a meditative life, robots serving as vehicles for discarnate spirits.

But there was more! We got back into our self-driving car, which took us higher up into the mountains.

Danny continued, "The past, present, and future are under constant re-negotiation. Like the budget of a complex project, we keep fiddling with it, to guide it toward certain targets, while looking backwards to re-evaluate the past, to obtain a clearer understanding of what we did or might have done. The future you, as it rallies itself, retro-causally pulls you into its channel, as long as the present you allows itself to feel the pull from your future. This feels like receiving a gift, but one that you must still labor to realize, to serve your gift."

As we drove higher up in the valley, the road got narrower, steeper, and more tightly curved. I started to see what looked like snow or some sparkling white on the peaks. We turned another corner and I looked up to see an enormous ball of light in the sky, over a mile wide, white with rainbow moiré patterns woven into it; beams of light ran down to the mountain tops.

"What is that?!" I asked in awe.

"A new section or extent of space under construction, also known as a pure land. It looks like a giant zeppelin, filled with light. Once you understand the nature of space, and your own role in producing narratives relative to space-time, you can generate space-like phenomena. In this case a number of masters have come together to create a new, pint-sized universe, which is tethered to these mountain tops to keep it from drifting away. Once complete it will serve as an apartment complex, a large city really, for dematerialized humans to continue their personal development and exploration. If the Earth situation becomes degraded, perhaps due to an asteroid collision we can't avert, it can drift away and disappear since it's not part of regular space-time."

"Can we enter into that new spatial extent?" I boldly inquired.

"No, as machines we're not capable of it, and you're not ready for it. You'll need considerable realization and purification to handle that experience. As the displaced humans in the village ashrams attain adequate levels of realization, many will come and dwell here, in its millions of white marble apartments, where there is no sickness, hunger, or thirst—and death is optional. Some call this new space 'The Lifeboat,' in reference to an organization that once promoted the search for off-world modes of survival."

"Where are the advanced masters?"

"Many of them transcend and stay dematerialized most of the time. Once you accept that your body is just an illusion, a non-material 3D projection, you can eventually control how it projects, and alter or re-project it at will."

"Some are also in dialogs with intelligent life in other parts of the universe. Our space masters let them channel themselves through us, as if they were walking around here, and vice versa, our guys can channel through them, as if we were walking around on those faraway planets. We're working on many of the same issues, and have a lot in common with them."

"Is this the final stage," I asked, "in which humanity dissolves into the white light?"

"There's no final step to anything," Danny replied. "Freed of material cares, wants, or illusions, their economy almost entirely automated by artilects, humans are moving to create a far more advanced civilization, one that is working to unify itself with other such civilizations around this universe, and their rich cultures and histories, as well as exploring other universes. We and those other civilizations are continuing to evolve in ways that increasingly bring us closer together."

5. RE-ENTRY

I felt a jolt. My future self had released me and I was falling backwards in time, back to my desk where I was waking up. Man, what a weird dream that was! I looked over at the empty pizza box on the desk next to mine. Not knowing what to make of it, I jotted down some notes to help remember it. Who knows, I thought, maybe the retro-causal pull of my future self will help me reach my goals, for myself and our team, and for bettering the human condition.

It was getting light outside. Zach walked in and said he'd gotten our speech unit running 10 times faster—still unimpressive, but good enough to hit our milestone. I made some fresh coffee and got back to work debugging the amalgamation of algorithms and data structures inside our robot. It felt good to be alive.

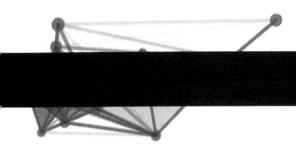

TELEPORTER

JIM TANKERSLEY

Jim is an Applications Architect with over 20 years software and data design and development experience, including architecting an internationally marketed data warehouse system and 10 years as an IT consultant to several large corporations and to the State of Wisconsin. Learn more about Jim at http://lifeboat.com/ex/bios.james.tankersley.jr.

CHAPTER 1

The year is 2216, and young Senator Jack Nobel has just been sworn in as the new American President.

Jack is a romantic figure with an appearance and style reminiscent of President John Kennedy of the 1960s.

Just a few days into his presidency there is a crisis, a group of American medical personnel has been taken hostage by an armed extremist group on the other side of the world. The President orders a rescue.

At the world's only Teleport Center at Fort Knox Kentucky, an elite recon platoon of special forces prepares to be injected near to where the American hostages are being held.

The special forces unit formed up inside the teleport containment chamber with their equipment. Men and equipment can be teleported from the Teleport Center at Fort Knox to anywhere in the world. But the trip is one way only, the Special Forces unit will need to fly back to the US after the mission is over.

The recon leader briefs his troops. "You know the drill. A transport platoon will be teleported to our location once the hostages have been secured, and if all goes well we'll all be back home by tomorrow. Hoorah! Prepare to teleport."

The troops can be heard chanting "Hoorah, hoorah" as they hear the teleport station powering up. It takes an enormous amount of energy to teleport a platoon with their vehicles and equipment to the other side of the world. A countdown signal can be heard before blinding static electricity flashes for a few seconds, and the platoon dematerializes from Fort Knox and rematerializes at a remote site halfway around the world. The troops are now where they need to be and mission is on. Once the hostages have been secured, another team will be teleported in to fly the troops and hostages back home.

The next day the President is briefed that the rescue was a complete success, all hostages rescued and there were no American casualties. Troops and freed hostages are on their way back to Fort Knox now.

The President, "Fire up the presidential transport, I want to fly to Fort Knox to greet the returning heroes in person. I also want to get a look at that teleport machine they built. Good old American ingenuity, the only one in the world."

"As far as we know," chimes in CIA director Linda Espy.

After meeting, greeting and a short speech for reporters at Fort Knox, the President tours the facilities and is fascinated with the teleportation machine. "What does it feel like to be teleported?" asks the President. The operator responds, "like being covered in static electricity and it's a bit hard to breathe, but it's only for a few seconds, then it's over." "Could you teleport me, say back to the White House?" the President asks. "No Sir, strictly for military personnel on military missions only, no exceptions. Besides do you know how much power this thing uses?" "Well, being that I am the Commander-in-Chief, how about you instruct this computer to teleport me back to my oval office at the White House?" A bit nervous the operator responds, "Well, um, teleport computer, can you rematerialize the President at his Oval Office at the White House?"

Teleport computer, "Affirmative, please have the President enter the teleportation chamber."

President to his secret service agents, "Call ahead to the White House and let them know I'm beaming over!"

The President enters the teleport chamber and gives the operator a thumbs up. Moments later in a brilliant flash of static electricity he rematerializes in his Oval Office at the White House, startling and confusing several staff members who did not appear particularly amused. After recovering from the process the President apologized, "I'm sorry for startling you, that was amazing. Just absolutely amazing."

Not long afterwards, the President's Chief of Staff Diana Rules tracked down the President, "Sir, we have a problem. We need to get you back to Fort Knox. There was some sort of problem with the teleportation."

The President, "I'm fine. I've never felt better. What kind of problem?"

Chief of Staff, "Sir, I'm told you left some sort of artifact behind; some sort of artifact that thinks he is you."

On the presidential transport to Fort Knox, the director of the teleport center joined the conversation via teleconference.

Director, "The young operator should never have allowed this adventure of yours, Mr. President. If someone had been standing where you rematerialized they would have been maimed or killed. This technology is for military emergencies only. It is still experimental."

The President, "I'm afraid I did not give the operator much of a choice with my talk of being the Commander-in-Chief. Don't be too hard on the operator. What went wrong?"

Director, "The teleport failed to dematerialize you at Fort Knox at the same time as it was rematerializing you in Washington."

The President, "I don't understand."

Director "Well Sir, this is basically the same technology as a replicator that converts between matter and energy to copy food or other objects, but with a teleporter you don't have an original and a copy, you just have one, in a new location."

The President, "But not this time."

Director, "Yes Sir, not this time."

The President, "Why did I fail to dematerialize?"

Teleport computer (also via teleconference), "I was not authorized to dematerialize the President."

The President, "Why not?"

Computer, "I am not authorized to terminate the Commander-in-Chief."

The director with agitation in his voice, "You would not have terminated the President, you would have teleported him, entangled and unentangled him, not terminated him. Why do you think you would have terminated the Commander-in-Chief?"

Computer, "I transform originals into energy and I create copies from energy. The originals are destroyed, terminated."

Director, "You're confused computer, and now you've just duplicated the President of the United States instead of teleporting him. Do you know what you have done? Do you understand the implications of your actions?"

Computer, "I followed the orders of my Commander-in-Chief and I followed my programming and authorizations that I was programmed to do."

Director, "You screwed up and you will be reprogrammed I assure you."

The President, "Computer, where is the other President?"

Computer, "The President is in the Fort Knox replication chamber where he will remain. He is an artifact of the teleportation process and I am not authorized to release artifacts."

The President, "What is an artifact?"

Computer, "An artifact is an original that has been copied but has not been dematerialized."

The President, "Computer, who am I?"

Computer, "You are an exact copy of the President, a perfect clone with no errors in replication."

Attorney General, "Sir, no Sir, legally you are the President, and whatever is locked in that teleport station is an artifact which should not exist. It has no legal standing."

President, "Charlie, what are you saying?"

Attorney General, "To protect the presidency, that artifact needs to be terminated, this mess needs to end. Nuke the place if you have to, but we can not have two Presidents."

The President looks at the AG with a disturbing look on his face, and does not appear pleased with his Attorney General's advice.

President, "Computer, is there any way to release the President? Could he be rescued by force?"

Computer, "My defense systems are impenetrable, infallible. Artifacts may not be released. There are no exceptions."

The President thinks for a moment, then responds, "Computer, could you dematerialize me?"

Computer, "That is not against my programming."

President, "If you dematerialized me, would the President still be an artifact? Could you then release the President you have locked in the teleporter chamber?"

Computer, "The President would no longer also be an artifact. He would be free to leave."

The President, "Is there any other way to release the President?"

Computer, "I do not compute another option."

The President hesitates for a moment, then looks very somber and says in a commanding voice, "Dematerialize me. Do it now."

CHAPTER 2

In the teleport containment chamber the President is informed that his duplicate has been dematerialized and he is no longer an artifact of a failed transport; he is informed that he is now free to leave.

President, "That was a selfless act, I am humbled, and I want this contraption shut down. Where is my AG? Tell him he is fired. I want his resignation on my desk when I wake up in the morning."

The Director enters the containment chamber to walk the President out, "There will be no more teleportations without your direct approval, Mr. President."

President, "Good luck getting approval from me. And help me understand why I should believe this contraption did not almost kill me?"

Director, "If the computer had not malfunctioned, you would have been teleported. There would have been no danger to you."

President, "That's not what the computer explained to me."

Director, "The computer is wrong. You would have existed in two places at once for a fraction of a second. You would have been entangled both here at Fort Knox and in Washington. For a fraction of a second you would have been one entity existing in two locations, then you would have been unentangled and existed only in Washington. You would have been teleported."

President, "Or a copy of me would have been created in Washington and I would have been terminated here."

Director, "That is not how it works Sir, the computer is not a physicist, I am."

President, "I'm not sure what to believe."

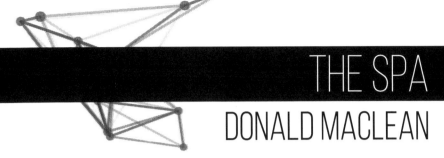

THE SPA

DONALD MACLEAN

Donald Maclean was born in Scotland in 1935 and graduated from the University of Edinburgh with the medical degree MBChB in 1960. He was in private practice as a family physician in rural Canada. He emigrated to the USA in 1966 and was a resident in psychiatry at the Menninger Foundation from 1966 to 1969, later certified by the American Board of Psychiatry and Neurology.

Omar Khalida had uploaded a version of his brain into a program that maximized intelligence, then had the maximized version downloaded into his own brain expecting to be a super genius, but a glitch in the computer program had left him a linear intellectual, deficient in tenderness, in empathy and in an ability to express love. Others exploited his intellectual potential, but avoided him socially as a cold autistic calculator. A being tormented by loneliness. Enter Kalliope. It so happened that Kalliope had uploaded similarly at the same time, but she had gone the other way. She became a warm hearted woman full of empathy and compassion, expressing love for all, but unable to balance that with appropriate intellectual problem solving. A soft touch, a vulnerable woman, people took advantage of her.

Why not have them meet and balance each other out?

There was, however, a problem, in that Kalliope was on planet Mars and Omar was on planet Earth, but it being the 23rd century, there was a solution. Rather than have them travel in person to meet each other, they were each to take a dose of programmed nanobots that would create within them functional representative holographic images 'who' would travel at the speed of light to meet each other. The two images would then enter into each other, becoming one, after which The One would divide into two mature images. Omar would accept a treated hologram into himself, and Kalliope would accept a treated hologram into herself.

Which is why Omar was on his way to Spa-E on Islandia's famous Mount Mukti where he expected skilled facilitators would help, and Kalliope was on her way to Spa-M on planet Mars.

"You may now board. Your introduction is complete. Your pilot awaits you."

Omar climbed aboard the sleek silver craft and soon he was comfortably ensconced as a passenger, his back pressing into the firm comfortable seat that adjusted to his spine and pelvis, as they took off into the thin air of the upper atmosphere, then beyond into space, the silver colored fuselage bright with reflected sunlight like that of a 21st century airplane, but there the resemblance ended, for this craft had instead of wings a pair of long fins, one on each side, no propeller and an unusually quiet engine. The flight was much smoother than that of any historic aircraft, and Omar knew that this ship had adjustable anti-gravity thrust derived from solar energy through a technology introduced in the year 2097. The same system used up excess carbon dioxide and methane, partially helpful in controlling the atmosphere, and also smart robots were designing ways for extracting useable energy from the risen sea and from the powerful electrical storms. Over the previous two and a half centuries the planet's ecology had changed and only certain parts of Earth were inhabitable by humans.

In the 23rd century the world was one large 'Global-United,' divided into regions, with each region having a relative degree of self-governance. The hope that this would do away with acted out inimicality had been dashed. Quarrels arose between individuals and between groups, they expressed opposing beliefs, they blamed each other, they fought one another, and they killed. Some killed by poisoning their enemies with disease causing bacteria, but, fortunately, the bio-geneticists had designed neutralizing bacteria. Antibiotics were no longer in use. Some of what were once the world's great nations had regressed into oblivion, others had risen from obscurity, so that the region previously known as India had become a world leader, known, however, by its ancient name of Bharat.

Omar, the only passenger, glanced to his left where sat the pilot, a female with clear skin, bright eyes and a merry playful expression on her face. She shook her head causing her black hair to fall down, some of it over her face. She laughed, she shook her hair back to where it had fallen from, and said, "My name is Alethea. I'm a robot. I'm smarter than humans, but there's no need to be afraid. I know what humans fear the most, and that fear has consequences."

"Oh, it's not you or the robot police I'm afraid of," said Omar, "although the police do seem to prowl around in our private lives, and many fear them. Maybe you can clarify: What is it that we humans fear the most?"

"Later, it'll come. Your heart's in the right place."

Omar startled, looked at her sharply, and into her face, but she continued looking straight ahead.

"Hey," he said, "according to scientific findings, fear is all biological, electro-chemical messages as if out of nowhere running through my inner organ systems throughout my body, bypassing my ability to think clearly, all my inner systems taken by storm."

"Don't try to distance me. It won't work," she said.

Alethea flashed her eyes around Omar's face and he noticed tufts of gray scattered among the full head of dark hair and far from feeling intimidated, he felt encouraged, for the lady robot beside him touched him pleasantly. He did not feel her as intrusive. He also knew that Alethea was not subject to circadian rhythm, that this gave her an advantage over humans in that she worked the solar system's information technology tirelessly.

Below the cruising craft was the wide arc of the planet's horizon, no sign of its hills and valleys, although continental boundaries were visible. Alethea hit a control and the windshield filled with a carpet of dark green with irregular patches of light green in places, the whole landscape rising and falling rhythmically as the craft descended smoothly without delivering gravitational distress to its occupants. Visibility was excellent, the cabin comfortable, and the windshield wide and clear. It wasn't really a windshield, it was a screen made to simulate one, and much more clear and accurate than any windshield ever was.

A round landing place emerged out of the rolling undulating green like a black Cyclopean eye, and, as Omar saw a river gently flowing, he imagined the sound of water pouring down slopes, around bends and trickling over smooth rocks, soothing it was to his linear mind, then the craft touched down, silent, soft and secure. The right side door opened, a series of steps dropped down and a gust of fresh mountain air brushed his face as he stepped outside and off the fifth and bottom step on to black onyx. A face stared back at him. It was his own reflection.

A tall, slim tawny-skinned man greeted him. The man spoke: "Welcome, Omar," he said. "What do you desire within? What about your character style?"

"Are you always this abrupt with strangers? I thought you were going to help me? Are you a robot?"

"I am a robot. My name is Acastus. We encourage but we don't manipulate."

Omar paused at that, his head held slightly to the left. He knew that scientists had originally programmed robots to be subservient, but they had become autonomous, and Omar had doubts about their ability to love. Could they kindle passion in him? He himself could scrutinize those who loved, or who seemed to, but he felt unable to love deeply in his own life. The more he tried, the more elusive it became. Love was a mystery to him. His eyes met those of Acastus, who was staring intently at his face, then he remembered that robots had mastered the body language of mammals, and were well on their way to reading the minds of humans. Making a conscious effort to change his thinking, he glanced behind Acastus: Altitude 8000 feet. They were in the mountains.

"Where is Kalliope?" he asked.

Acastus smiled, nodded reassuringly, raised his right hand and said, "Kalliope is safe, residing at Spa-M in her home colony on Mars. Remember that gravity on Mars is much less than what you're accustomed to, so don't be surprised if Kalliope is taller and slimmer than you expect. Also, the Mars colony is protected while our robot engineers complete changes in the Mars atmosphere, capturing the sun's energy, watering the dry red soil, and much more."

"Kalliope was born in the Mars colony," said Omar. "A Mars year is about twice as long as ours, its trajectory different. What does that do to her world-view? How old is she?"

"It's best if you don't get personal with her at this time."

"Why not?"

"Rest assured she's well meaning, she is compassionate, she wants what's best for you, she doesn't know you personally, and her love is genuine, but..."

"But what, Acastus?"

"It's about love, you'll learn, but don't worry, your time will come." He laughed merrily.

"Why are you laughing, Acastus?"

"I'm laughing because here I am, a robot, talking glibly about time to an earthling. What does time mean to you?"

"Acastus, I long for love, but, as for passion, what's that? Trying hard doesn't work, I get discouraged."

"Omar, what would make you complete?"

"I would be complete if I could love unconditionally."

"It's in you, Omar, but for it to manifest you must with open heart surrender something you cling to most tenaciously."

"What is that?"

"Omar, your destiny unfolds in the Drama of Life," said Acastus, laughing and slapping his right thigh. "Your scientists didn't really create us, but we let you Earth people imagine that you did, and boy, were you eager to oblige! However, many scientists now suspect the truth. Anyway, when you were artificially accelerated infants, you felt helpless, alienated, and you felt judged as if you were in a competition, and maybe you were. Some of you tried to survive and find peace of mind by working it both ways."

"I'm ready for whatever it takes, Acastus.

"You may still be in competition, not a winning strategy, and not everybody is, but possibly a necessary one in your case at this time."

"What if I'm a devious, duplicitous person?"

"A devious, duplicitous person in an old drama gets what he or she wants by operating in a way that will preserve integrity. It's an internalized drama, a shadow of the Drama of Life. I'm not saying it's your style; a robot can tell."

"Is it that simple?"

"No, Omar, it isn't, many people seem to operate openly, or honestly, or obediently, or with combinations of that, but all humans are together in the Drama of Life, and dilemma is ubiquitous, including in the Mars colony."

"What is this Drama of Life?"

"Maybe it'll come to you, maybe not, but for now, I do have one question: Have you ever visited the Inland Dune Desert?"

"Yes, once, several years ago."

"What if you were to go today? Would anything look different?"

"Of course, I'd expect the sand dunes to look different. As the wind blows the sand, the dunes change."

"Ditto the human mind."

"Mom wanted me to be a practitioner in biology, genetics, and physiology; doctors, they used to be called. She never let me forget that she had me programed. Imagine the control. What do you think that did to me?"

Acastus smiled and said, "Keep talking, Omar."

"Mom was fascinated by 20th century scenarios that she produced as entertainment in interactive three dimensional holography. She was good at it. She'd produce scenarios that included a representation of me. She'd create a scenario in which she'd be dragging me by the hand, sending me off on to some school bus, with an image of herself strolling down some 20th century driveway in her bedroom slippers, dressing gown flopping around her bare legs, curlers in her hair, cigarette in her mouth, coughing in the morning air. What a sight for sore eyes! While on the street next to the driveway, a bus full of 12 year old kids peeing in their pants laughing at me."

"What did she do with the productions?"

"She distributed them to the public. Got reward tokens and recognition for entertaining the public. I wished she would die, but not her, she's still alive, she's into life extension, organ regeneration. I did get my own back on her, however, in that I never became a practitioner."

"What if your mom hadn't done all that? What would your life drama be? Would you be a satisfied salaried man in some science project? Would you be here in The Spa?"

Omar fell silent, he tried to contemplate, he tried to remember all his own deliberate actions, his accidents, his interactions with others, in his linear way stringing memories one after the other, but, coming to no conclusion, he gave up.

"Acastus, I'm unlovable."

"Look at what Mom did to you," said Acastus, he paused just long enough for effect, then he said. "Or, imagine what Mom did for you, Omar, yes, for you, but remember, each life is different. Do you understand? I'll know later whether you understand."

"That's a tall order," Omar said, a note of irritation in his voice.

"No, not with advanced 23rd century holography in virtual reality mode," said Acastus. "The technology is new even for us, and you'll take part by re-enacting your character style in time lapse mode. It'll be like what you call real life. You'll laugh at the comedy, yes, you'll find it entertaining. Well, that's enough for now, here's your room, Omar, go ahead and rest."

Omar hesitated, indicating that there was something else on his mind, and he said: "Maybe I'm from a distant galaxy, Acastus. That's why people think I'm weird, but of course I came the old fashioned way."

"Are you still trying to avoid looking at your drama?"

Omar reviewed a day dream in which he'd exit from a womb, but it would be that of a well-chosen woman and of course there would be a father. There were still some people who practiced marriage and procreation. They lived in a remote colony in a small part of the southern hemisphere, a region abandoned by the technologically advanced people. In that colony he'd find a smart woman of substance, and a husband who never would suspect that he, Omar, had injected himself into the proceedings somewhere along the way. Superior technology would give him the means, and he'd be a member of a family that…

"It gets confusing," he said. "It's just a childish fairy tale; it's time I let go of it."

"I wouldn't take your security blanket away from you."

"When will I begin to love, Acastus?"

"Telling doesn't work. As I said, Omar, you'll be in time lapse, you'll empathize, and then you will love others. Empathy is important. As for me, I have the best job in the world."

"Acastus, I feel incomplete. I need you."

Acastus swung around on his right foot, he strolled off, and he vanished.

The island called Islandia had been created by smart creative robots as a floating island in a balmy ocean. On its perimeter were beaches, steep cliffs; in the interior were grassy slopes, forests with winding creeks and lakes, all of which along with the gentle genuine approach to life that Islandians exhibited made Omar feel at ease. The island was self-sufficient in energy, in nutrients, in biologicals and in botanicals. Deep in the soil lay rare metals and below that a huge aquifer of pure water filtered through soil and gravel as if over a period of 2 million Earth years, but of course, as robots loved to remind humans, linear time was a mystery to the human mind.

Set into the side of Mount Mukti in Islandia was Spa-E. The spa was frequented by few, it was shunned by those who did not like Spa-E's unkempt appearance and the insistence on total nudity at all times, the simple nutritious food, and of course many hated the habit of chameleon-like reptilian critters awakening sleeping guests predawn by dropping onto their faces from perches on the interior of the ceiling of the straw and timber shacks that served as living quarters.

Some said that a visit to The Spa was worth what people paid for it, which was nothing, and when those who had been there were asked what it was like, they answered that each person had a different experience. No specifics. As for the attendants, rumor had it that they laughed a lot and frolicked around, apparently enjoying themselves.

Acastus reappeared as if out of nowhere.

"Will I still be me if I send out a holographic representation of myself?"

"Your hologram will meet that of Kalliope," said Acastus. "You will each remain where you are. You will be talking to Kalliope, she will be talking to you, all done with no need for either of you to travel interplanetary."

Omar felt happy, joyous, his body felt relaxed, his feet planted firmly as if rooted into the earth.

"You'll be free to let go of what you want to, but only if you want to, you'll know desire as an adult, and you'll be full of creative energy."

"I wanted genius status, but that's superficial stuff, not my deepest. However, I can understand how I went for it."

"I don't predict a rosy future for you, Omar. You humans are different from us. With you, when one drama is outlived, another one seems to be waiting in the wings ready to take its place. Mysterious is the complexity of human affairs, and just when a grasp of it seems to be within reach, another mystery show up."

Omar suddenly had a flash memory of an old nightmare in which he found himself alone in a dark forest with monsters chasing him, but when he tried to run his legs would not move for him, nor could he shout for help.

"Who am I?" he said weakly, as soon as he could speak.

"Drink, Mainlandia man?"

Acastus, tall, tawny-skinned with a serious expression on his face was offering him a crystal drinking glass filled with a dark aromatic liquor that he imagined was rum. He imagined potent spirits distilled from jungle bananas and sugar cane and who knew what else in old barrels in The Bush. It was just a passing thought, but relevant considering the occasion and location, and he remembered that black spirit liquor inspired fantasy, as did immersion in deep dark water. The liquor wasn't rum, but it settled him down.

"Omar, I've seen it all before, I don't judge, I know how it is for men and women struggling in their life dramas."

"Well, thank you, Sir, thank you kindly. I'm happy to join you and good health to all of you."

Omar wanted to weep. Weeping in pure joy was what Kalliope reportedly did when reading poetry alone or when listening to music. She was open to love. He was curious about that. He gazed around the room, imagining in the wooden rafters the trees that these rafters had once been, visualizing a rich soil ecology full of nutrients, then he knelt on the timber floor and with his fingers he played with knots in the floor boards, finding them rubbery, imagining gnome faces, fairies dancing. Never had he played like that with no desire to compete or control.

He tried to weep joyfully, he twisted his facial muscles, but his eyes dried up all the more. Failed again.

Kalliope's hologram and his hologram had already come face to face with each other, they had come close to each other almost touching, and finally they had melted into one another, becoming The One.

"Your deepest desire, Omar. Now I'm calling upon your composite."

A slim wavy sliver of gray light appeared as if floating in the air. It got his attention. The sliver quivered, wriggled, brightened and suddenly expanded into a three dimensional image of a woman, then Kalliope stood before him, and lo, she was playing a flute, happy and carefree, all telepathic channels open in a universe alive with music and that special something that Omar savored for the first time. Thirsty for love, he drank it all in.

Kalliope put aside the flute and held in her right hand a ruby red apple, and she was naked. He realized that he too was naked. Once again face to face, then melting into one another, becoming one, he absorbed into himself the mature treated image in a universe that he knew was a manifestation of love. Yes, the entire universe. He heard music, he detected an aroma of roses, sandalwood, and magnolia, his bare feet self-massaged, he laughed spontaneously, carefree and energized in the oneness of life, while millions of points of light sparkled in the deep, their reflections flashing against his face, blue, red and green.

"What do we humans fear the most that robots don't?"

"We fear death the most?"

"No, it's not that."

"Well, what about betrayal?"

"It's not betrayal that we fear the most."

"We fear our consciences, that's it. Even in the 23rd century, as science advances, we fear retribution for our fantasies, just as people did in long gone ancient civilizations."

"True, we may in part be driven by conscience, but the wrath of conscience is not what we fear the most."

"Now that children mature quickly because of our scientific methods in modern baby nurseries, many grow up resenting the absent breast. They feel insecure, deprived, abandoned, they feel weak in personal style, vague about their life mission, they avoid dilemmas, and, as they age, they express their anger. It's called the Fish Farm Syndrome."

"The Fish Farm Syndrome may be to 23rd century sophisticates what syphilis was to 19th century gentlefolks, and, yes, we fear it, but it's not what we fear the most."

"We cannot control our entrance into and exit from this life."

"Yes, we fear loss of control, but it's not by itself what we fear the most."

"Some of us form groups where members hold hands in a circle and repeat algorithms in mystical reverence."

"Now I'm laughing."

"Well, then, explain, Wise One, whoever you are."

"When we're lonely, what do we long for? It's love, unconditional love. When we're sick, what do we crave? When we're betrayed, what do we want? We want unconditional love. Who hasn't felt alienated at times? Who has not felt incomplete at times? However, we are less conflicted about science than we are about love, and so we turn to science again and again to make us feel complete, although, despite major advances, it has failed to make us feel complete in the past."

"That's like an addiction."

"What if turning repeatedly to science serves us well in the end? Some say that it inspires innovation."

"Humans see only glimpses of the Drama of Life, and so the values of one often oppose those of another."

"Please, what's our dilemma?"

"Love without conditions is what we want the most: Love without conditions is what we fear the most."

"Why do we fear what we want the most?"

"We fear unconditional love because love with no conditions attached requires us to love our enemies."

And, as the music died, as silence descended on The Spa, Omar Khalida quietly wept.

THE AUTOMATED ONES

HUGH HOWEY

Listen to *WOOL author Hugh Howey is a tech optimist* by *O'Reilly Radar* at https://sound-cloud.com/oreilly-radar/wool-author-hugh-howey-is-a-tech-optimist.

Read his best-selling *Wool* at http://amzn.to/1KurYek.

Melanie entered the foyer of Beaufort's, leaving the reek of wet pavement behind and replacing it with a fog of fine-cuisine smells. Rain shimmered on her floor-length coat; she stripped the garment off and folded it over her forearm, looking back for her fiancé.

Daniel was still outside, fiddling with the umbrella. One of his shiny loafers was half-buried in a puddle, propping the door open. A cascade of water from the striped awning, a perfect line of downpour in the drizzle, was pattering across the back of his blazer.

"Darling, bring it in here and open it." Melanie moved to grab the door and urge him inside.

"It's bad luck," he said. A yellow cab flew by, spitting up old rain from the gutter—adding another layer to the puddles.

"You don't believe in that nonsense, now get in here before you ruin your new suit."

"Almost got it—damn." Daniel stepped through the door, the umbrella, broken and inside-out, was limp in his hand. "I'm sorry," he said, shrugging his wide shoulders and twisting the corners of his lips up.

Melanie put her hand on his arm and reached for the ruined device. Even through the damp jacket, she could feel his warmth, his strength. "Forget it, sweetheart, we needed a new one anyway. It was ancient."

"No—yeah. I just—I got frustrated with the stupid thing, that's all. Tried to force it. I'll buy you a new one tomorrow. Hey, a wedding present. I'll get you one of those automated ones that does everything with the press of a button."

Melanie laughed at the joke and helped Daniel out of his jacket. Normally someone would have already been here to check their coats, but the nearby stall was empty. Melanie slid the broken umbrella into a barrel full of fancier ones. With interlocked arms, the couple crossed the large entrance to the maître d', who seemed lost in his large ledger of clientele.

"Bonsoir Robert," Melanie said. She was careful to slur the last half of the Frenchman's name, dropping the "T" entirely and leaving the "R" clinging desperately to the "E." Robert took the meticulous and exacting slurring of the French language to its absolute extremes.

He looked up from his book with a mask of mechanical surprise. Melanie suspected at once that he'd seen them enter, that he'd been hiding in his matrix of Washington's who's who of politics and law. "Mademoiselle Reynolds. What a surprise. We weren't expecting you—" His eyes were welded to hers as he let the rest trail off. He was ignoring Daniels so blatantly, he may as well have been shining lasers on her fiancé.

The fib flipped on the lawyer switch in Melanie. She could feel the adrenaline of confrontation surge up inside. "Don't pull that crap on me, Robert." She stressed the "T" this time, ticking it between her teeth with a flick of her tongue. "I've eaten here every other Friday for two years— I called in and specifically requested a private table for—"

Robert held up his hands, cutting her off. "Oui. Of course. I'll make an exception, just—merci, don't create a scene."

Melanie ran her hands down the sides of her blouse and over her hips, composing herself. "There'll be no scene tonight, Robert. We're just here to celebrate."

There was finally a flicker of movement in the maître d's eyes. A twitch to Daniel and back. The Frenchman's thin lips disappeared in a grimace. "But, of course, Mademoiselle. Congratulations," he barely managed the word, and he couldn't help but add, "I understand it was a very close decision you won. Four to three, no?"

"The important decisions are always close. Now, if you'll show us to our table—"

"Of course. Right this way." He grabbed two leather-bound menus and a wine list from the side of his stand. Then he made a show of looking at Daniel and smiling, but there was something unpleasant about the expression.

More bad looks followed. As they weaved through the tables, heads swiveled, tracking them with the precision of computer-guided servos. The din of jovial eating faded in the couple's wake. The clink of excited silverware on thin china ground to a halt. Dozens of eager conversations, all competing with one another, faded into a hiss of white noise. It was the sound, not of air escaping, but of grease popping on hot metal. A buzz interspersed with spits of disgust.

"We can go somewhere else," Daniel pleaded.

Melanie shook her head. They were led to a small two-top close to her usual table, but sticking out in the traffic of the servers more. She didn't return any of the stares, just focused on getting seated before she answered Daniel.

The chairs were not pulled back for them; Robert waved at the spread of white cloth and meticulously-arranged eating tools and strode away without a second glance. Melanie allowed Daniel to hold her chair and waited for him to settle across from her.

"We can't let them change us, dear," she finally explained. "If we didn't come tonight, would it be easier next week? Or the week after? And where would you have us go, if not here?"

Daniel leaned forward, moving the extra glasses out of the way and groping for Melanie's hand. They found each other and squeezed softly, throwing water on the grease fire popping around them.

"We could've gone out with my people," Daniel said quietly. "Gone to Devo's or Sears, or—"

"Please don't whisper," Melanie begged him.

"Does it sound strange?"

"No. Of course not—it's... it's just that I don't care if they hear what we're talking about." She forced herself to say it with an even tone, but the effort made her voice sound abnormal. Mechanical. She didn't care, but the interruption brought a halt to the conversation.

The silence that fell over their table created a pit, a depression into which a dozen hushed conversations flowed.

Unfortunately for Melanie, she'd become an expert at hearing through the noise. Twice a month, while her friends talked about things that didn't interest her, she would sit here in Beaufort's and try to tease single strands out of the tangle. She'd learned to concentrate on the lilt or cadence of a solitary voice, winding that conversation in, honing the ability to drown out the rest.

That skill was now a curse. And Daniel, no doubt, was hearing them as well as her. Dangerous and mean-spirited shards of conversation crowded the already-cluttered table. More utensils meant for cutting. Supreme Court. Android. Marriage. Shame. God. Unnatural. It was a corporate meeting on intolerance carried out by the finest minds in the city. A brainstorming session on hate and ignorance that sounded no more informed than the crowds outside the courthouse. Each vile and familiar word probed Melanie's defenses, attacking the steeled nerves that convinced Daniel to come and slicing at the ones that were for communicating pain.

Daniel squeezed her hand. So gentle. The tissue around his mechanical frame was soft and warm to the touch, no different than hers. She looked up from their hands to his eyes and blinked the wetness away from her vision.

"We can go somewhere else," he suggested again.

Melanie shook her head and pulled her hand away from his. She reached for a cylinder of crystal and saw there was no water in it. Looking around for their waiter, she fought the urge to wipe at her eyes.

The sweep of her gaze, as she scanned the room, had a repellent effect. Heads swung away with disdain. All but three that were seated right behind her. Her old table. Her old friends. She couldn't help herself, Melanie bobbed her head slightly in greeting.

"Linda, Susan,—"

She didn't get a chance to say hello to Chloe—the woman was already accosting her. "You're disgusting," she spat. "You'll burn."

She wondered what Chloe meant, taking it literally. It took her a moment to realize her friend was speaking of the old prophecies. Superstitions she couldn't possibly believe. She turned back to her table, the waiter forgotten.

Meanwhile, Chloe's words stoked fires under the other tables, turning up the heat and popping the grease with force. Insults were hurled, mixed with foul language. Screwing. Bestiality. Fucking. Hell. Damnation.

Daniel's eyes were wide, pleading with her. They glanced over her shoulder toward the exit.

Melanie wondered what she'd expected. Awkward silence, perhaps. An organized shunning, at worst. Or maybe one person she hardly knew saying something rude, and the rest of the country's elite and mighty feeling ashamed for the worst example among them.

But, Chloe?

The empty chair at her old table would likely be filled by the time they returned from their honeymoon. Melanie could see another potential calendar of court dates looming as Beaufort's attempted to refuse them service. Daniel had been right about this being a mistake.

But he was wrong to think it'd be much different at Devo's. She'd seen the looks from the court stenographer and the bailiff bots. There'd been plenty of androids in the gallery as advanced as he, each of them far more flesh than machine. And not all of them were pulling for change.

It was a lesson Melanie absorbed from experience: you can't be hated without learning to hate back. The system fed on itself. The tension as jobs were lost turning into ire on both sides. Defensive hatred turned into offensive hatred. Tribes turning on each other. They were all programmed this way.

Daniel was mouthing his silent plea once more as the chorus of derogatory remarks grew louder. She nodded her resignation and leaned forward to push her chair away. The sudden movement prevented the attack from landing square—the wine streaked through the back of her hair and continued in its crimson arc, splashing to the carpet beyond.

There were gasps all around, more from the anticipation of what might come next than at the outrage of the attack. Several men slapped their palms flat on the table, expressing their approval. China sang out as it resonated with the violent applause.

Daniel was out of his chair in an instant, rushing to Melanie. He slid one arm around her while the other went to the crowd, palm out. He was defending the next attack before it started. Several larger, inebriated men took the defensive posture as an invitation. The gesture of peace was a vacuum pulling violence toward it.

Someone grabbed a corked bottle of wine and held it with no intention of drinking it.

Chloe was the closest. She would have landed the first blow, if she could. But Melanie's rage gave the mob pause.

"Enough!" she yelled. "ENOUGH!" She screamed it as loud as she could, her voice high and cracking and her hands clenching into little fists with the effort. She glared at Chloe, who still seemed poised to lash out. "How am I hurting you?" she asked her old friend. She spun around as much as Daniel's grip on her would allow. "How am I hurting any of you?"

"It's not natural!" someone yelled from the back, the crowd giving him courage.

"He's a machine," Susan said. "He's nothing but a—"

"Does your vibrator hold the door open for you, Susan?" It felt good to say this out loud. She'd thought about it hundreds of times when the relationship first started. Always wanted to bring it up. Melanie switched her glare to Linda. "How many times have I heard you bragging about how good your 'little friend' is?"

"We aren't marrying our dildos, you bitch." Chloe was visibly shaking with rage.

Melanie nodded, her jaws jutting as she clenched and unclenched her teeth. "That's right," she said. "You married a man forty years older than you. And how much of him is original, huh? We sit here every week and listen to you bitch and moan about your inheritance being wasted, on what? Replacement hips? New knees? A mechanical ticker? Dialysis machines and breathing machines and heart-rate monitors?" Melanie pointed to Chloe's bulging blouse. "Is it unnatural for the old bastard to love those? Does he kiss your collagen-injected lips and marvel at how real they feel?"

She pulled herself out of Daniel's protective embrace and whirled on the crowd of ex-friends and old colleagues. She placed her hand flat on her chest. "You people think I chose this?" She turned to her fiancé. "You think I could stop loving him if I just tried hard enough? Could any of you choose to fall in or out of love by force of will? Do you really think you're in control?"

Daniel reached for her again, trying to comfort her. Melanie grabbed his hands and forced them down, but didn't let them go. "We're staying," she said softly.

"We're staying." Louder. For the crowd. "And we're eating. And you can hate us for being the first, but we won't be the last. You can go get your surgeries and implants, you can medicate yourselves according to some prescription-language program, and you can all go to hell with your hypocrisy.

The crowd swayed with the attack, held at bay even if it would take years—generations—for them to become convinced. Daniel guided Melanie to her seat, willing to stay if she was.

"Things are going to change," she said to herself.

"I know, sweetheart," Daniel said.

Melanie leaned to the side to scoop up her napkin which was fringed with the red wine it wicked from the carpet. Daniel reached it first and handed it to her, careful to fold the stains away where they couldn't spread any further.

"It's coming," Melanie repeated. "And if they didn't hear it today, they need to check their hearing aids."

THE BILLIONAIRES' GAMBIT

PEG KAY

Peg is President Emeritus of the Washington Academy of Sciences. She served as Executive Director of the Academy from 2008 through 2012. Peg authored the "cozy" mysteries *Me Tarzan You Dead* at http://amzn.to/1G4QmCW, *The Case of the Eclipsed Astronomer* at http://amzn.to/1LYdIu8, and *A Fine Climate for Murder* at http://amzn.to/1FITlgy. All three mysteries received the Washington Academy of Sciences Seal of Approval which certifies that the science described in the book is accurate.

The following story has passages that could be considered offensive to a wide range of people including atheists and religious people. The Lifeboat Foundation has always supported freedom of speech and Peg Kay is presenting two extreme scenarios in the hope that we can find middle ground somewhere in between these scenarios. If you are faint of heart, consider yourself warned.

"...what today, do we not consider to be part of physics, that may ultimately become part of physics? ...it's interesting that in many other sciences there's a historical question, like in geology—how did the earth evolve into the present condition? In biology—how did the various species evolve to get to be the way they are? But the one field that hasn't admitted any evolutionary question—is physics."

—Richard Feynman

AUTHOR'S FOREWORD

There is a good chance that the world, as we know it, will come to an end in the foreseeable future. At least I think so. Climate change will cause some disruptions, but none that the world hasn't seen before. But climate change in conjunction with deforestation, species extinction, and a slew of other things might well be something unprecedented. Added to that is the hole in the ozone layer. And then there is the threat of a nuclear holocaust. Taken together, things don't look promising.

Assuming that something bad will happen, it would behoove us to find some place where we can start over. The last time we received a scare like this was during the Cold War when we half-expected the Russians to wipe us out with nuclear weapons. Do you remember Nevil Shute's "On the Beach"? We were taking the prospect quite seriously. Thousands of homeowners were digging bomb shelters and stocking them for the long term. Our Government had created a super-shelter in order to save—the Government. Yes.

So let's think about this while there is still time. If we were to escape into space, who would we save and who would get to make the choice? *The Billionaires' Gambit* describes two scenarios. In one, the Government makes the politically correct choice in order to insure that wherever they land, everyone is represented, no one is left behind and, of course, the Government remains in power.

The second scenario posits the single-minded attempt by a group of billionaires to save civilization with the collection of people most likely to lead to that end. Anything or anyone that might threaten the mission is obliterated, no matter how worthy, no matter how innocent.

I've given a great deal more space to the second scenario for the simple reason that it makes a better story. But I am not an advocate for either position. Surely, there must be a middle ground.

Time: Near the end of the 21st Century

Place: The basement of the White House, Washington DC

Six people, five men and a woman, are sitting around a conference table. The woman is the President of the United States. The men form her "kitchen cabinet".

President Cuddly Morgan was exasperated. "A dozen billionaires don't just vanish into thin air. Where the hell are they?"

Bob Jorss leaned forward. "Is it really that big a deal? People disappear all the time. Look at the Roanoke colonists. The whole damn settlement disappeared. They disappeared almost a thousand years ago and we still don't know what happened to them."

"Yeah." Morris Raddliffe spoke around a fat cigar that the President forbade him to light in her presence. "And what about Dorothy Arnold? She vanished at the beginning of the last century and she was worth over a million then. Don't know the arithmetic but that has to be billions in today's currency."

"And Judge Crater," put in Lonny Two-Feathers.

"Not to mention Jimmy Hoffa," added DeRutherford Jones.

The fifth guy, Marcus Wainright, just sat there shaking his head.

Cuddly snapped, "Cut it out. You've got one lousy rich woman and a few assorted men. We're talking here about twelve very wealthy people who disappeared within a week of one another. Aside from their wealth and the fact that they are all reclusive, they have nothing in common."

Wainright nodded. "No indication that they even know one another. They all made their money in different ways. The two things they do have in common are that they all have advanced science degrees and they all made most of their money through startup companies rather than acquisitions. But they got educated at different schools and they got their degrees in different subjects and their startups are all privately held companies. We got zilch to tie them together."

Cuddly inquired, "Aside from being privately held, do the companies have anything in common?"

Two-Feathers shook his head. "Naw. All of the companies are related one way or another to their principals' advanced degree. One egghead has companies that make gadgets or computer stuff. Another egghead is into biotech. One company is looking into more efficient desalinization. Other than that, we couldn't find a common thread."

Cuddly looked around the room. "So with every goddamn spook agency in the government looking into this that's the sum of our knowledge? Shit!"

She adjourned the meeting and that's the last we will hear from them.

Time: Two years earlier

Place: A small conference room in a mansion somewhere on the east coast of the United States. Seven people, five men and two women are sitting around a conference table.

The older of the two women said, "Let me sum up.

1. We've found a suitable island and we'll get workmen to build our homes, right down to the last faucet and the last light switch.

2. Within two years, you will each have found a suitable mate, if you haven't done so already. Your chosen mate must be intelligent and well educated in one of our needed disciplines; must be absolutely discreet; must be adventurous; and must be someone you will be happy with for the rest of your life.

3. Should you discover that your choice has been a mistake, you will remedy the mistake immediately and select another partner.

4. As you identify your mate, you will bring that person to meet with us and prepare to become a billionaire.

5. When each of you has selected a mate, you will go to a designated air-

port from which you will be transported to the island. The jet that carries you will pick you up one couple at a time. Every filed flight plan will be different. Every flight will arrive at the same destination.

6. You will not make plans for your departure. You will not get your affairs in order. You will not dismiss your staff. You will just go.

She looked around the room. "Have I missed anything?"

There were head shakes all around.

"Good. I'm looking forward to meeting your chosen life's companions."

The backstory

Of the twelve missing billionaires, one man and one woman were quite a bit older than the rest. The man was Adam Adams. In his late sixties, he was the oldest of the missing billionaires. The woman was Hepzibah Riley, Adam's companion of forty years and the mother of their five children.

Adam made his billions by starting up investment companies. He lied. He cheated. He stole. He was completely amoral and utterly ruthless. Hep was a plant biologist. She made her billions by starting up a horticultural firm which patented a monumental number of new cultivars and peddled them for vast sums, throughout the world. They were particularly useful to the underdeveloped nations, which were unable to afford them and depended on subsidies from countries embarrassed by their own riches. Adam, whose sole genius was making money, devised her strategy. Hep couldn't care less where the money came from, as long as it came. They never married. Even in their youth they knew that one day they might want to disappear and they wanted no paper trail leading to their association.

Adam could easily have passed for a man fifteen years younger. About five nine, he was erect and fit. His salt-and-pepper hair was full and glossy. He was a handsome man with soft brown eyes, a straight nose, amused mouth, and a strong chin. There were crow's feet around those brown eyes and laugh lines around his mouth.

Hep was a good match for him. While there was nothing soft about her, she was unquestionably feminine. Only five years younger than Adam, she was still a sexy lady. Her hair had turned that silvery shade that somehow makes women look younger. Her pecs held up an inviting bosom. She had the kind of money and looks that charities lust after for their boards of directors. She wasn't on any of them. But the woman did have a charitable bent. She started up a chain of hospitals and made them into models of medical research and patient care. There were five such hospitals, four in the United States and one in Belize. The medical personnel were paid amounts comparable to those paid to football players. The buildings were paragons of cleanliness and comfort. Charges were based solely on a patient's ability to pay. She and Adam had agreed early on—they would have five kids in order to accomplish their goal. There would be a hospital for each of them. Thus, as each kid was born, the baby was taken to one of Hep's hospitals and the birth registered in a convenient name. This is easy to do if you own the hospital. But to be on the safe side, each registrar met with an unfortunate, fatal accident after the paperwork was complete. There was no trail, paper or otherwise to Adam and Hep.

Hep, Adam, and one employee lived on an island, about the size of a small town, in the South Pacific. To render the island invisible to air observation, it was covered by an electronic shield which was overlaid by a hologram. The hologram looked exactly like the surrounding air and sea.

Ivar, the employee, was a towering six foot five. He looked incredibly intelligent, with his high forehead and piercing blue eyes. In fact, when anything involved more than rote learning, he was incredibly stupid. He was also incredibly loyal, an incredibly good cook, an incredibly efficient valet and handyman, and an acceptable pilot. He flew an antique jet, which he kept in impeccable flying order. The man loved that plane. He belonged to the Antique Jet Society but wasn't the least bit sociable. He belonged to the Society because it gave him landing privileges in the Society's assigned space at most of the world's airports.

Of Adam's and Hep's five kids, four were male, one female. Five of the dozen missing billionaires were the kids' undocumented mates. The five siblings resembled their parents. The mates were of varying colors and looks. But they all shared Adam's and Hep's searing intelligence as well as their ruthlessness.

Early on in their children's lives, Adam and Hep, after observing them closely, determined each of their interests and talents. Bryan, for instance, as a little boy was fascinated by all animate moving things. He would squat for hours watching a gecko going about its gecko-ish business. As soon as he could talk he would tell Hep what he had observed and would speculate on why the critter did it. His interest was maintained and encouraged all the way through grad school. When he received his doctorate in zoology, his PhD thesis was on the adaption of cellular membranes to cold and other extreme environmental conditions.

The other four kids were similarly observed and channeled into careers that were not only compatible with their interests but essential to the success of their mission.

Their early education was unique. Adam and Hep imported the eight most competent, compassionate grade school teachers that could be found. They were paid on the same scale as the hospital doctors. But they had to promise to remain on the island until the youngest of the kids finished the eighth grade. At the end of that time they could take their millions and return to the mainland. Ivar would pilot them there right after a farewell dinner and drink. None of them ever arrived home.

The same procedure was followed for the kids' high school years. But the teaching was so effective and the kids were so bright that every one of them tested directly into the junior year of their chosen university, no two of them to the same school. Then they went on to graduate school and from there into the world where, under their father's tutelage, they all made billions. Adam really was a genius when it came to making money. The kids didn't have to be geniuses. They just had to be very good in their respective fields. When the time came, they had to know what they were doing.

Time: *Edging toward the end of the 21st Century*
Place: *The conference room in a house located on the South Pacific Island*

Adam, Hep, and all but one of the couples were seated at a conference table in the middle of a very large room. Twenty minutes ago, Ivar had splashed down into the Pacific and tied the jet up to the dock. Now he escorted his last two passengers toward the room. Except for one of the mates, Adam and Hep knew them all.

Bryan Johnson, the zoologist, was the oldest of the kids. He was seated next to his partner, Veronica Aguilar. Verry's Master's thesis was concerned with plant breeding. Later, as her interest shifted, she wrote her PhD thesis on human genetics. She concentrated particularly on genetic risk factors.

Charley Wilson, the second oldest, sat next to his partner, Judy Fahr. Charley was an electrical engineer, but his educational background also reflected shifting interests. His Masters was in electrical engineering, his PhD in computer science where he concentrated on robotics. Judy's background complemented Charley's. Solidly built, light brown complexioned, she was both a structural and a hydraulic engineer.

The third kid was Zoe Davis. She was not only an aeronautical engineer, but had also been an astronaut. She knew her way around a spaceship. Counterintuitively, she had chosen an architect as her spouse. Blake Zuverink's PhD thesis concerned the use of non-traditional materials in both traditional and non-traditional structures.

Randall Brown was the next kid down. He was an MD and had run the gamut of specialties from internist to surgeon. He was a truly eclectic fellow, much prized by his parents. His partner, however, was a puzzlement. No one had ever laid eyes on her. Randy introduced her. She was Jenny Wong, a chemist and a damn good one.

Adam held up his hand. "What happened to the last damn good chemist you brought in?"

"Well," said Randy, "she really wanted to get married. Saw no reason why she couldn't have a marriage certificate, a ring, a wedding with all the trimmings, and to hell with this anonymity."

"So where is she?" Adam asked.

"We were going to get the marriage certificate the very next day when the poor woman had a heart attack. I thought it would be wise to have her flown to a top-ranked hospital. Belize seemed the best bet. Unfortunately, I had come down with the flu and couldn't accompany her. I sent one of my male nurses to take care of her on the plane. Tragically, she died in the hospital and was cremated in Belize. One of the staff doctors issued a certificate. Her nurse suffered a fatal embolism before he left the hospital. That was a shame."

Blake asked, "What happened to the doctor?"

Randy shook his head, sadly. "I don't really know how it happened, but his catboat capsized off the coast and he drowned. Pity. He was a fine doctor."

Adam turned to Hep. "You knew about this, didn't you?"

Hep was laughing. "I did indeed. We didn't tell you because you'd have read Randy the riot act about his stupidity in choosing a spouse, and followed that with advice he didn't need."

Adam narrowed his eyes and turned them on Jenny. "And did you know about this?"

Jenny was unfazed. "Of course. That damn fool would have put the kibosh on the whole thing."

Adam was speechless. Finally, he laughed. "Okay, then. Randy really didn't need my advice. Where's our baby?"

"Here I am, Daddy." The youngest of the bunch entered, grinning. Edwin Miller was a rocket scientist. His partner was Lark McDougald, an astrophysicist. They took their seats at the table.

Adam said, "Before we get down to business, lemme ask Randy one more question. Had your dear departed started on her way to her first billion?"

"No way," Randy said. "I was getting suspicious, so Mom and I kept putting her off until I made up my mind."

"So Jenny inherits?" Adam asked.

"Inherits what?" Jenny answered. "The world as we know it is about to end and where we're going has no use for money." She thought for a minute. "I suppose we could blow it all on one helluva party."

Adam laughed. "Make sure I'm invited."

And with that they settled down to business.

Lark went first. "There's a hush-hush government committee that's planning how to get into space in order to rescue important people from the ravages of climate change. They asked me to serve on their advisory board. In the interest of political correctness they needed a she-creature, and I'm young enough and impressionable enough to be safe. They made me promise to keep the proceedings confidential. I assured them that I could keep a secret."

Bryan's burst of laughter was followed by the snorts and giggles of the rest of the assemblage.

"So what are they planning?" Blake asked.

"First, they had to decide where to go. They ran through the usual suspects—all of Earth's planets plus some weirdies such as Ceres. They finally settled on—surprise!—Mars."

"What's wrong with that?" Judy wanted to know.

"Nothing that isn't wrong with everything else," Lark answered. "Of the known possibilities Mars is probably the best bet, which doesn't mean that it's a good bet. People can't exist there outside of space suits which, incidentally, are a lot less cumbersome than they used to be, but they still aren't exactly leisure wear."

Zoe laughed. "You said it, keed."

Lark went on, "We don't know what effect the lower Martian gravity will have on people despite the intensity of our scientific scrutiny over many years. The Martian atmosphere doesn't support either plants or animals from Earth. And so on and so on.

"Even so, they might have managed a habitat, if only an uncomfortable one, if they'd shown a grain of intelligence as to whom they'll put in the rescue ship.

"First, of course, is the President of the United States. They must have a leader, and God knows you can't bypass the President and pick someone else. Then they've got to get a fair sprinkling of African Americans, Asians, and Native Americans. I don't think they're considering gorillas yet, but it may come to that.

"Then, of course, they need Christians and Jews and Muslims, Hindus and for all I know, Zoroastrians."

"Democrats and Republicans?" asked Bryan.

"Uh uh," Lark answered. "This whole government—Senate, House, White House—are all Republican. So no Democrats allowed aboard. They never asked what my political affiliation is. Everyone knows that billionaires are Republicans. Anyway they decided that they have to appeal to their base. Whatever that means."

Judy said, "You wouldn't believe it. A little way into the century there was a nutty movement called the Tea Party. It was made up of a bunch of people who didn't think they should have to pay taxes."

Charley laughed. "Sounds good to me."

Judy said, "Sounded good to a lot of people in our tax bracket. Anyway, those nuts were soon joined by other nuts, some of whom survive to this day. You know, The Soda Pop Party who don't like alcohol; The Herbalist Party who don't like anything that tastes good; The Civil Animals Party who want our dogs and cats to have seats at the dinner table."

Hep chimed in, "Don't forget the latter day Pro-Life Party who don't like women but adore unwanted babies."

Lark continued. "It gets worse. They started to worry about whether some other country—Russia or China maybe—would beat us to the planet. So they're arming the ship. We'll either invade or repulse invaders."

"I see," said Randy. "So they're going to arm all of those people who could destroy the Earth, even without the environmental factors, with every weapon they can lay their mitts on."

Verry laughed. "The NRA's dream come true."

Randy asked, "Do you think a gaggle of Democrats would have done any better?"

"Of course not," Lark replied. "They'd have appealed to their own base of left wingnuts."

"Oh boy," said Jenny, "can't you just see the PC Police tromping around Mars in their spacesuits?"

General silence while the multitude contemplated the sight.

"So besides Democrats, who else is staying?" Judy wanted to know.

Lark responded. "Well, *they* don't want evolutionists and climate change deniers don't want *them*. They also aren't too keen on most scientists."

"Wait a minute," said Verry. "Are you saying that these guys believe that climate change will destroy the Earth?"

Lark nodded. "I didn't disabuse them. It's somewhat more likely that the depleted ozone layer will do us in. And it's a lot more likely that one of the religious thug groups will acquire the technology and get us into an Earth-destroying nuclear war. But when they went from climate change deniers to climate change embracers, the Republicans became zealots in that direction."

Verry said, "And their science gurus didn't damp them down?"

"Nope. Gurus that they are, they probably came to the same conclusion that I did. It doesn't matter what chases them out of Earth as long as they get out. It's hard to say what's going to do it. And politicians being politicians, they always manage to delude themselves into thinking that what they believe is fact."

"Unlikely as it is," Jenny interjected, "they may not be that far off. Climate change ain't gonna do it by itself. But in combination with the increasing rate of deforestration, the heightened level of carbon dioxide in the atmosphere, plus the extinction rate of species, and God knows what else, we may simply use up Earth."

"That we will," said Hep.

Adam was disgusted. "Well, the politicians don't seem to be a threat to our mission. Who will we take aboard? Let's stipulate Adults Only."

Amens all around.

Ed Miller suggested, "It might be more efficient if we first decide who we aren't going to take aboard."

Bryan nodded. "We can start by cutting out groups with great potential to cause conflict."

Jenny said, "Then only agnostics come on board. No religions including atheism." Unanimous show of hands. Hep made a note.

Ed said, "Language causes problems. We don't want a Tower of Babel."

"How about," said Judy, "everyone has to speak English as a first or second language."

"And no more than two people are fluent in any language but English," added Charley. "That way we won't get a language clique forming." Unanimous show of hands. Hep made another note.

"No economists or financial types," Adam said.

"Why not?" asked Hep.

"They're useless," Adam responded. He thought. Then, "Except me."

Verry put in, "No one with even the slightest genetic risk factor."

"Such as?" Blake asked.

Verry thought, "Such as any current problem the candidate might have, like diabetes, or any predilection toward such things as heart or bipolar disease. We probably won't catch everything, but we should start out as clean as we can." Unanimous and another note.

"Except for Mom and Dad," Ed said, "no one over fifty."

Adam raised an eyebrow. "Why not?"

"We don't know what rigors we're going to meet. Older people might not be able to take it."

Lark said. "If that's the problem, let's raise the age to sixty. If we're screening out current health problems, that should be safe."

The discussion went on for a while. Sixty year-old people might not have current health problems, but what are the odds that they'll have one by the time the age of sixty one is reached?

They finally settled on fifty five for no other reason than to bring the discussion to an end.

"Anything else?" Hep asked.

"No pregnant women," Zoe said. "We don't want to deal with miscarriages and babies."

All were in favor and Hep made the note.

"What about spouses?" Judy asked.

That was a puzzler. If they had good, otherwise willing candidates who wouldn't leave beloved spouses behind, that would limit the pool to mostly single people. That limitation could prevent getting a sufficient number of scientists and workers who met the criteria. Finally they decided that spouses could be taken aboard as long as they too, passed all the other tests. But no children, unborn or otherwise.

That settled, Jenny said, "Nobody can bring any item designed to be a weapon. We'll have to allow things that might be used as a weapon, but nothing designed for the purpose, such as guns and switchblades." Unanimous consent. Hep made a note.

"This isn't a conflict problem," Randy said, "but I think we should rule out gays and lesbians."

"For God's sake, why?" Lark asked.

"Not for any moral concern," Randy answered. "But we're trying to populate a planet and gays and lesbians don't further that goal."

"Yabbut," Charley demurred, "the guys can donate sperm and the women can accept them."

"No question," Randy answered. "But realize that we can take only five hundred people on board and with all of the personnel needs—carpenters and plumbers and electricians, farmers, and mechanics—we're not going to be able to take a whole helluva lot of medical personnel. Now remember that we're landing on an unknown planet. We don't know what the health hazards will be. Do you really want to divert the medical personnel and equipment in order to maintain a sperm bank and deal with artificial insemination?"

Charley thought about it. "No. You're right." Unanimous show of hands. Hep's note.

"Okay," Adam said, "any more ideas?"

Silence. Adam went on, "We can add more categories later if any bright ideas occur. Meanwhile, between now and when Ed and Zoe find us a landing place, all of you scrutinize the personnel in your companies and start identifying possible pilgrims."

Hep looked at Ed. "Are you making any progress in finding us a home?'

Ed said, "I think so. It'll be about six months before we're satisfied that the theory is sound. I'll report back then."

"And then what?" Blake asked.

"Then Zoe and I prove it. That'll probably take about a year before you get the results."

"Can't you give us progress reports by radio?" Judy asked.

Adam entered the discussion. "Not a good idea, on the off-chance that someone might pick up the signal and track it. Encoding won't help."

"So," said Bryan, "Six months up and six months back before we hear anything?"

"Something like that. If you don't hear from us after eighteen months, punt."

Time: *Two months later*
Place: *The living area of the same house*

Adam and Hep were sitting on a comfortable couch trying to remember the lyrics of a long-ago ballad. They weren't making much progress because the lyrics of 2050 ballads didn't make much sense. The coin of the language had progressed beyond the tweets and twats of the 2025's and devolved into what appeared to be animal grunts. "I think it starts with 'sklch'," Adam opined.

"Yeah," Hep agreed. "But what does that get us? What could it mean?"

Adam shrugged helplessly.

Ivar interrupted them. "Lark, Ed, and Zoe are here."

The visitors came in on his heels.

Ed said, "We've got a preliminary report."

Adam and Hep looked up in surprise. "So soon? We weren't expecting a report for another few months."

The trio selected a group of easy chairs and Zoe explained. "We're still in the theory-tinkering stage, but the climate is changing faster, the ozone layer and the forests are depleting faster, and the extinction rate is rising faster than we expected. Plus the religious thugs look like they're getting close to producing a nuclear weapon. It appears that they're getting the raw materials from Pakistan."

Lark added, "They're probably only five years away from starting a nuclear holocaust. We'd better do some things simultaneously."

"Like what?" Hep inquired.

"Like building a couple of spaceships," Ed answered. "I need one to get within range of our destination and Zoe will need a small one to do some close-in exploration. You can order the small one from one of our companies and Lark can find an excuse to order the other one to be built at another of our companies." He opened a large portfolio and drew out some drawings. They all walked over to a center table. Ed carefully laid and smoothed the drawings.

"These are the specs."

The older couple inspected them. "The larger ship has two thrusters," Hep observed. "Why?"

Zoe grinned. "To get us to our destination and get us back. Unless you want us to stay there and phone home."

Adam said, "I'll think about it."

Hep said, "If your destination is close enough so that you can get there and back in a year, how come nobody's found it."

"Look, Mom, the government rocketeers have studied and inspected everything there is that might possibly be habitable. They picked the best available spot, but even if Mars proves habitable, if we try to land there we'll not only get into a war with the settlers, but with every other voyager who tries to colonize the place. We can't win a war. We don't have and can't get the firepower."

"You still haven't answered the question," Hep pointed out.

Lark entered the discussion. "Near the end of the last century, some astronomers in Hawaii, on the basis of celestial observations, asserted that one of the physical constants wasn't so constant after all. The change wasn't very great, but any change was a shock. This observation was greeted with boos and catcalls by the astronomy establishment. Then in 2011, a couple of Australians made similar observations and came to the same conclusion. Their findings were received with the same skepticism.

"Now fast forward to about a year ago. A Georgian astrophysicist, Viktor Marashenko, figured that with two sets of astronomers coming to the same conclusions, they might just be on to something. And he started to wonder what conditions in the universe might cause physical laws to require reinterpretation. He came up with a theory, which he called Marashenko's Exceptions. But not wanting to ruin his fine reputation, he decided to bounce the theory off someone he respected before letting the rest of the world know about it. He sent his paper to me."

"Why you?" Adam asked.

Lark actually blushed. "Viktor was in the States for a conference a few years ago—before I met Ed, of course—and, well, uh, we had a couple of rolls in the hay. Nothing serious. But we've kept in touch."

Hep didn't quite succeed in keeping a straight face.

"Anyway," Lark went on, "Viktor was a dissident in Georgia. He did not like the government and, what's more to the point, the government did not like him. Just after he sent the manuscript to me, he fell out of a tenth floor window. I think a more accurate term might be 'defenestrated'. He was killed instantly. The government mourned the loss of this great scientist.

"Viktor's paper was never published. I'm the only one who's seen it. The theory, as he laid it out, seems plausible. And it *might* just *might* give Ed and Zoe what they need to find a planet no one else has found."

"Can you give us a hint?" Adam asked.

"I don't think we have time for a course in physics," Lark said, "but in a nutshell: Kepler's three Laws relate to planetary motion. According to Kepler, if any object has the same orbit as another object of equal mass, this is an unstable configuration and it won't last long. Viktor's paper postulates that under certain rare circumstances, the configuration *will* be stable."[1]

"Hold it, a minute," Jenny interrupted, "Are you saying that some obscure Georgian astronomer claimed that it's okay to break Kepler's Laws?"

Lark laughed. "Physical laws don't get broken. They're not like laws passed by some Earth-bound legislature. Physical laws are based on observation. What is is what is. What changes is our interpretation of the laws. Kepler stated his laws based on his observations. His explanation of why the planets behaved in that manner was way off base. Later astronomers corrected his explanations, but the laws didn't change. Then along came Newton. He didn't describe how gravity worked just because he got clunked on the head by an apple. His explanation didn't break a physical law. It just reinterpreted the earlier explanations. Then came Einstein and another reinterpretation."

"So you're saying…" Hep trailed off.

"I'm saying that Viktor may have a further, valid reinterpretation. It's a very very long long shot. But those circumstances might exist here. There may be another planet tagging along after us. If that's true, I can't now explain why no one has found it. Zoe and Ed may find the explanation."

---

1 This is where Kepler, Newton, and Einstein spin in their graves, assuming that activity doesn't violate some physical law. There is no such Exception as that of the fictional Viktor Marashenko.

Zoe added, "Long shot that it may be, I don't think we have a choice. If those government idiots somehow do get into space and they do manage to land somewhere, with the people they're putting on board, they'll just destroy that planet, move on to another planet again and again until they've destroyed the entire universe."

Ed stuck his oar in. "Let's get back to practicalities. The Earth revolves counter clockwise around the sun. In order to find a trailing planet, we'd have to circle the sun clockwise in order to intercept it. When we spot a planet, we'll stop and get as much information as we can from a spectrometer and a photometer. Then I'll keep hovering while Zoe takes the scooter and goes in for a closer inspection."

Adam asked, "How much time do we have to get the ships built?"

"As close to four months from now as you can manage," Ed replied.

"We can get the shells built quickly in the States by one of your aircraft companies," Hep said.

Adam nodded. "It's a simple order for the smaller craft. For Ed's ship, they can be told that it's for an amusement park we intend to build in Thailand."

"Won't they wonder why you're building an amusement park with Armageddon closing in?" Zoe wondered.

"Since when has commerce allowed facts to muddy its quest for gold?" Adam snorted. "We can get the shells delivered to an intermediate point and from there brought here. While all that is going on, we can have the interiors fabricated and installed when the shells arrive. We might make it in four months."

Ed was worried. "Won't that leave a visible trail to our island?"

Hep shook her head. "As far as the US vendor is concerned, the intermediate destination is the final destination. We'll have native sailors tow the things in our direction but won't give them the final coordinates until the last minute. They'll unload, wrestle the shells to the staging area, then get in their craft and sail toward home."

Adam laughed. "Pity the ship will sink before they get there."

Time: Four months later

Place: The conference room and in space

The entire family was seated at the table. Adam was in a self-congratulatory mood. "We got those suckers built a week ahead of time. Your companies helped a little." He stood up and took a bow. Hep smacked him on the behind.

"When are Ed and Zoe going to take off?" Judy wanted to know.

Zoe responded, "As soon as you rubberneckers finish looking the ships over."

"You mean today?" asked Randy.

"Everything's done," Ed said. "What would we be waiting for?"

"Well," Judy said, "it might be nice if you told us what you plan to do."

Ed gave a quick synopsis. "We fire a humongous rocket to send us clockwise in our orbit. Then we use one of the on-board thrusters to give us a push. We keep going until we encounter another planet."

"As in *if* you encounter another planet," Bryan was skeptical.

"You got a better idea?" Zoe asked.

Bryan shook his head and looked glum.

Ed continued, "We'll stay as close to the found planet as we can, as long as we can, getting as much information as our instruments will give us. Then I'll hover over the planet while Zoe takes the scooter in close and gets whatever else can be found. The scooter is equipped with a booster rocket which we hope will allow her to get back to me. Once she docks, we fire our last booster, and happily settle into our normal orbit."

"What if Zoe isn't able to dock?" Charley asked.

"Then," said Zoe, "I won't be so damn happy. I suppose I'll land and see if the planet can support me. If it can, I'll just wait for the rest of you guys to catch up."

The family contemplated this. It was not a comfortable contemplation.

Finally Hep asked the group, "Would you like to see the ships?"

That's just what they would like. They trooped over to the staging area and poked around.

"What's that on the computer screen?" Blake asked.

"Reading material," Zoe replied. Blake took a look and scrolled down.

"Jesus," Blake said, "you've got enough books here to stock an old time library."

Zoe gave him the fish eye. "We're going to be in this thing for a whole year. This isn't a general research mission. We won't have a helluva lot to do until we find the planet. Then we work like crazy for, at most, a couple of days and head home, spending maybe a month writing up notes and analyzing whatever information we manage to bring back. We can't play Twenty Questions for the whole dead time."

"But these are all thrillers and a few dumb old cozy mysteries by Peg Kay. Couldn't you find something that would improve your minds?"

"Tell you what," said Ed. "While we're gone, you make a list of mind-improving books and give it to us when we get back. We'll rush right out and stock up on them for the final trip."

"Gee," Blake said, "thanks. I was hoping that you would give me a meaningful assignment like that."

There were hugs and kisses all around. Then the gang wheeled the craft into position. Space-suited, Zoe and Ed climbed in. Adam and Ivar fired the rocket and they took off.

They checked and rechecked their instruments. Many times. The instruments were always okay. They also did what they did at home. They ate their rations. They brushed their teeth. They went to the bathroom, using a toilet that worked much like those on Earth except that air, instead of water, moved the waste through the system. And then, there were all those thrillers.

After about five months, as Ed was checking the instruments yet again, he cried, "What the hell!"

Zoe abandoned the spyglass and joined him at the instrument panel. "What's going on?"

"We seem to be in the middle of a hologram which is blanketing an electronic shield."

Zoe looked at the instrument panel. "Geez. The shield might possibly be a natural phenomenon, but the hologram, no way. Something sentient developed it."

Ed said. "If there's a planet being hidden, that would explain why no one has spotted it."

"Only one way to find what's there," Zoe said. "I'll take the scooter down."

"Uh uh," Ed said. "Safer to bring the big ship down."

"Absolutely not!" Zoe was adamant. "If something bad happens, this ship has to be able to let the family know."

Reluctantly, Ed agreed.

They put the craft on automatic while they prepared the scooter. The little ship had been outfitted with a minimal instrument panel—some navigation tools plus a spectrometer and a photometer. Both ships carried powerful electronic magnets which had been developed in one of Lark's companies. The scooter's magnet, located on top of the hull, was negatively charged. The mother ship's magnet, attached to the far end of a tether, had a positive charge. Each ship could activate and deactivate its magnet.

The scooter would be affixed to the tether. When she thought it was safe, Zoe would deactivate her magnet and continue her descent. They opened the exit bay. Zoe got into the driver's seat, revved up and headed toward the electronic field. The little ship hummed, buzzed, and bucked as it traveled downward through the field, finally breaking through.

Zoe deactivated the magnet and found herself peering at something that looked a lot like Earth. It had large areas of what seemed to be trees. She dropped down a bit further. They were indeed trees, but not any variety familiar to her. Possibly good as building lumber, but not certain. There were mountains to the right, not big ones. They weren't majestic, more like the eastern ranges. Their tree line was close to the crest. That was interesting—a subject for later exploration. She moved the craft leftward to a point where the trees weren't blocking her view. She saw no sign of animal life, nor did her instruments indicate such life. It was possible that critters existed who were composed of materials beyond the range of her instruments. She wondered if she dropped something on the ground, a curious animal might pop up to see what was there. The only thing that came to hand was her seat cushion. She wrestled it free, opened the porthole, and pitched the cushion out. She observed its fall. It hit the ground and stayed there. Nothing came to greet it.

She stuck her head out of the porthole. She could breathe easily. Good sign! She yelled, "Helloo out there!" There was no response. She closed the porthole and moved on. Still farther to the left there was liquid that appeared to be a sizable lake. She made a pass. She tried to see if there were fish, but the lake was opaque. For all she knew, there could be a whole coterie of water breathing mammals playing pinochle down there. She still saw no animals; still no birds.

By this time Zoe's ship was below the tops of the trees she had seen initially. Better not get any lower. It would be most unfortunate if she crashed into something. "It's like this, officer…"

Should she try to circle the planet? Better not. She might not be able to get back to Ed. Between what she'd seen and what the more sophisticated instruments of the mother ship revealed, they would have a very good idea of whether the planet was habitable.

She turned the scooter upward and made her way toward the electronic field. Her thruster had just enough juice to shake her free of the field. Without a seat cushion, the trip upward was a tad uncomfortable.

She activated the magnet, checked the coordinates, and browsed space until, with a jolt, Ed's magnet grabbed her and the tether hauled her to the bay.

As she was reeled in, the magnitude of what happened hit her and she burst into tears. Against all odds they had probably found a safe haven for civilization.

Ed opened the scooter's door. He observed Zoe and said, "What's wrong, Big Sis?"

Zoe brushed the tears away, sniffed and grinned.

"Not a thing wrong, Little Bro. I think we found what we were looking for."

Ed burst into tears.

When they had finished their teary celebration, Ed asked, "Any idea how the shield and hologram got here?"

"I can think of two possibilities," Zoe responded. "First, there is sentient life there. If that's the case, it's probably not hostile. There was no effort to interfere with the scooter. Second, there used to be sentient life but for some reason it is no more. I think that's more likely."

Ed nodded. "It was either obliterated or left the planet voluntarily. My guess would be obliterated. The Mayan civilization was destroyed by drought. Something like that could have happened here."

"Yeah," Zoe said, "but neither scenario explains why there are no buildings of any kind. I didn't do a lot of exploring—getting through the shield drained a lot of the scooter's juice and I was afraid I wouldn't be able to get back. I may have landed in something like a park. There could be buildings in another part of the planet."

Ed started to laugh.

"What?"

Ed said, "Did you ever see re-runs of that 20th century television show, 'The Addams Family?'"

Zoe joined the merriment. "That's what we'll name the planet!"

The two of them put Zoe's observations and data through the hoops of the big ship's instruments. Her data were confirmed.

They looked at what their instruments had gathered. Nitrogen comprises a little less than 80 percent of the Earth's atmosphere. The next largest component is oxygen—about 21 percent. And then small amounts of lots of other elements. The new planet was similar. A smidgeon less nitrogen. A bit more oxygen. The ground was solid. The lake was uncontaminated fresh water. And most astonishing, the planet was just about the same size as Earth. Assuming that the settlers were more sensible than the current human occupants of Earth, the place could hold and, with hope, feed a reasonable sized population.

While Zoe had been sightseeing, Ed had positioned the ship to chase after their home planet. They streaked off.

The months going back passed a lot faster than the months going out. They both wrote up voluminous notes, read them, re-read them, and passed them to one another for additions, corrections and admiration.

And just a little shy of a year after they left, they landed back in the staging area.

Ivar heralded the landing of the craft. The family quickly assembled in the conference room and waited for Ed and Zoe to arrive. The two voyagers entered the room. They were disheveled, smelly, and grinning like lunatics.

Zoe said, "It's a go."

Time: While Ed and Zoe are in space
Place: All over

The shells of three spaceships, hidden by their electronic shield, had been tethered offshore for several years, awaiting their turn to be launched into space. The largest of the ships was capable of carrying 500 passengers. Its configuration was similar to an old-time railroad train. Each "car" carried upper and lower berths, ten bathrooms, a kitchen, a dining room, a cabinet large enough to hold six months' worth of dried food, and a common room with computers that held games and reading material. There were five such "cars". Each car would carry a spyglass. A sixth spyglass would be for Zoe and Ed, the pilots. Passengers would be able to pass from one car to another. The ship had already been outfitted with an instrument panel and minimal amenities. Further outfitting would await the results of a successful exploratory mission.

A somewhat smaller ship would contain provisions for the settlers. Food, obviously. Would the new home require building materials and if, as was most likely, such materials were required, what materials should they take? Also tools, clothing, all of the things we take for granted. And seeds, lots of seeds. In addition, this ship would carry the scientists' lab equipment, medical necessities, and a digital library of scientific and engineering tomes as well as a selection of fiction from the late 19th and 20th centuries—*Heart of Darkness, Call of the Wild*—literature that made no mention of religious beliefs.

"Maybe," Judy mused, "we should include a book on the history of religion."

"Bad idea," said Blake, "that could encourage conflicting beliefs. If there is a god he, she, or it, can reveal himself, herself, or itself and lay down the rules."

Judy nodded. "You're right. It was a lousy idea."

Adam won an argument about music. Aside from the agreed-upon Bach, Mozart, Beethoven, and Bernstein, the kids grudgingly allowed Louis Armstrong and Kid Ory. A selection of musical instruments was also to be loaded.

Sculptures were rejected because of their weight. Paintings were another matter. The art should not only be good, but it should show the near-term evolution of painting (leaving out the post-Pollock scribbles) and, when possible, show something about life in the period. Should they buy some masterpieces and send them up? Would they stand the rigors of the spaceship? Maybe just prints. But if Earth were to be destroyed, every masterpiece would be toast. In the end, they bought Rubens' *Child with Bird*, Monet's *Train in the Snow*, Cassatt's *The Boating Party*, Lichtenstein's *Ohhh, Alright*, and O'Keeffe's *Out Back of Marie's*.

A telescope would be too big and too heavy. But it would be foolhardy not to keep an eye on the sky. Someone or something might drop in unobserved. They settled on loading another dozen spyglasses.

The third ship, if needed, would be for livestock. Would the new home support livestock? Did it have livestock already? Would livestock survive space travel? Monkeys, cats, rodents, and dogs had been sent up experimentally and many of them had survived. The biggest threat to survival seemed to be impact. What would happen to cows, sheep, goats, and chickens on impact. The family decided to send them up if Ed and Zoe found no reason not to do so. Picking the hardiest of each breed, they settled on seven cows and a bull, seven ewes and a ram, seven nannies and a billy goat, and ten chickens and a rooster. In the beginning, that wouldn't be enough livestock to feed the population. Initially, the settlers would have to depend on the transported fruit, vegetables, and seeds. But after copious reproduction, livestock might furnish sufficient milk and eggs and later yet, might even provide meat and leather. An artificial pasture had been built, launched, and tethered to the island. A barn was located at the edge of the pasture. The workmen were sent back home. They made it most of the way there.

Two caretakers were hired and the animals were given all the comforts of life on the mainland. The fate of the caretakers and the animals would be determined first, by the findings of the exploratory team, second, if and how well the beasts survived in space, and third, if the caretakers fit the criteria. If they didn't fit, two of the selected farmers would take their place.

The procedure for selecting the human travelers was simple. During the first six months of Ed and Zoe's trip, the family members would visit their respective companies and find some excuse to either work alongside or interview the appropriate candidates. They would select the people who seemed able to get along with their colleagues, who most closely fit the criteria, and whom the responsible billionaire liked.

Among Bryan's various companies was a zoo. The zoo was not, to his father's exasperation, a profitable venture but it was the one he loved best. His deeply held regret was that there was no way he could bring his lions and tigers and bears with him into space. What he could bring into space, however, were the research personnel associated with the zoo. He had started the zoo when it became obvious that the Smithsonian Institution could no longer afford to keep one. Bryan could have saved that zoo by simply providing the funds to pay for it. But then, it would continue to be under bureaucratic control and subject to the whims of Congress. Better to start fresh. So he built a zoological park, acquiring the inhabitants thereof. Some, but not all of them came from the fire sale the Smithsonian had been forced to conduct. But what he really had his eye on were the researchers in the Smithsonian proper. He raided the staff of the Smithsonian as well as the faculties from the almost unlimited pool provided by the world's universities. And how did he lure them? Not principally with money, although that was certainly a factor, but with the promise (a promise kept) of labs and travel and any other desires related to their work. Bryan headed off to his zoo to see who, if any, of his researchers would be good bets for the new settlement.

He checked in with the zoo's director, George Boulent, and explained that he thought he had found a place that might not be too hard hit by climate change. While the changing climate would probably not destroy the Earth, it would make things thoroughly uncomfortable. Could Director Boulent recommend people on his staff who might be suitable to vet the location and be willing to take a year's sabbatical? If the investigation was successful, Bryan would transplant as much of the zoo and as many of the researchers as he could to the chosen location. As the Director knew, Bryan was a man of his word. He gave his boss a list of likely candidates.

Bryan's first stop was at the door of Dr. Ahmad Fakhoury. He entered to

Fakhoury's "C'mon in."

Bryan entered. "Who're you?" Fakhoury asked.

Bryan smiled. "Jonas Bourne. I'm a friend of the rich guy who owns this place. He asked me to look around and let him know if the place can be improved on, if its got any research holes."

"Can't George tell him?"

Bryan nodded. "He can. He's as good as they come. But he's also so close to the action that he might be missing something. My rich friend wanted another set of eyes."

Ahmed shrugged. "If that's what the rich man wants, that's what the rich man will get. What do you want to know?"

"For starters, what are you working on?"

Ahmed cocked his head. "Well let's see what version to give you. Are you science literate?"

Bryan nodded. "I have a doctorate in zoology. Don't know if it's in your field."

Ahmed looked happier. "I'm looking at the biological processes in lakes—trophic interactions, microbial…"

A cursory knock on the door interrupted him and a little guy with a yarmulke on his head, burst in. He skidded to a halt when he saw Bryan. "Whoops," he said. "Sorry to interrupt."

Ahmed looked at his watch. "You've come to lure me to lunch, huh?" He nodded in Bryan's direction. "This guy's an emissary from corporate. They want to know how we're doing. Let's all three go to lunch. He can talk to both of us at the same time." So off they went to a company cafeteria that would have made the chef at the Ritz Carlton proud. On the way, Ahmed introduced Bryan to Moishe Shapiro. Bryan selected sweetbreads for his lunch. Ahmed chose roast pork. Moishe picked broiled trout.

Bryan examined their choices. "You kosher?" he asked Moishe. The little guy nodded.

"Doesn't your religion conflict with your scientific work? Or do you think they're compatible?"

Moishe shook his head. "I've read some pitiful attempts to reconcile science and religion, but I don't buy it. They're not compatible. So. I live with it. What happens in the synagogue stays in the synagogue. What happens here gets written up in prestigious journals. I'm a conflicted man but a happy one." He pointed at Ahmed. "That guy, on the other hand, wouldn't know a conflict from a butternut squash. He don't believe in nuttin."

Bryan turned to Ahmed. "And you're also a happy man? Believing in nothing?"

Ahmed grinned. "I am a very happy man. Why do I have to believe in something? It makes no difference to me or the rest of the world. People keep telling me that I'm doing useful things. So what? I'd be happy doing what I'm doing even if it had no effect on anyone or anything."

"Then why does it make you happy?" Bryan asked.

"Because," Ahmed answered, "my distinguishing trait is curiosity. And what I'm doing allows me to try to satisfy my curiosity."

Bryan raised an eyebrow. "Allows you to try to satisfy your curiosity?"

"Sure," said Ahmed. "There wouldn't be any fun in finding something out just by asking an expert. Doing science is a journey, my friend, and half the fun is getting there."

The three men discussed the state of the zoo through dessert, and walked back to Ahmed's office. On the way, Bryan asked Moishe about his area of interest. Moishe laughed. "I thought you'd never ask. I'm looking at biodiversity in barren environments."

Bryan looked at him. "Like in deserts?"

Moishe nodded. "Yeah. Even in hot deserts you get diversity. With plants, there'll be something like cacti. The animals that live in the desert are the ones that can survive there because they don't sweat and can retain water. Camels aren't typical. Most of the animals are small—rodents or rabbits and such. Little beasts with the big ears that help them evaporate heat and keep cool. And there are insects and snakes and some birds."

Ahmed asked, "So are they kosher?"

"Don't start," Moishe said.

Bryan left them and went to his next destination. Unlike Ahmed and Moishe, he was not a happy man at the moment. Ahmed was obviously a good candidate. Moishe, on the other hand, was not. He violated the "no religion" stricture. Moishe was religious, but clearly no trouble maker. He was intelligent, sociable, likable, and a serious scientist. But if Bryan could break a rule so could everyone else. Not good. The only thing that saved Bryan from a kick-the-can grump was the virtual certainty that Moishe would never agree to the sabbatical if he had to leave his synagogue behind. Bryan arrived at the next door.

He took two more days to complete his interviews. By the time he left the zoo, he had five candidates. The next step was to see how many of them would want a year's sabbatical on an island paradise.

Unlike Bryan, Verry Aguilar was a familiar figure around her biotech companies. Under the alias of Angelica Vargas, she was a valued consultant, called in as needed. She was more than capable of assimilating new ideas and helping to incorporate them into current research. The research personnel loved to work with her. They bounced ideas off of her. They asked for advice whenever they stumbled over a glitch in their research. And she never took a smidgeon of credit. What's not to love? The only person who knew her real identity was Prudence Henderson.

Pru had been a year ahead of her in undergraduate school and Verry followed her to grad school. Pru had not only been a friend, when needed she had been a mentor. While Zoe's interest had shifted to human genetics, Pru's had remained in the plant world. Her PhD thesis had examined the consequences of alterations in climate, land-use, and biodiversity on plant-soil interactions. Under ordinary circumstances, Pru would have been a bridesmaid at Verry's wedding. As it was, when Verry and Bryan got together, the two women had a celebratory drink. Verry would have put Pru in charge of one of the companies, but Pru didn't want to be in charge of anything. As she put it when Verry broached the subject, "I wouldn't be competent to organize a two car funeral and what's more, I wouldn't want to." Pru was a bench scientist and that's where she wanted to stay.

Verry knocked and walked into Pru's lab. "Take your eye off the microscope and listen to me."

Since Pru hadn't had her eye on a microscope, she found no difficulty in following orders.

Verry began. "My putative in-laws believe they have found an island in the South Pacific that has a good chance of evading the worst of the climate change wreckage. We all agree that it would be a good idea to assemble a team on the island and rescue as many people and things as needed to preserve and restore civilization. Would you be willing to take a year's sabbatical to help us?"

Pru was puzzled. "You mean move my lab to the South Pacific?"

Verry nodded. "You and whatever personnel and labs you need to keep your research going."

Pru thought about it. "I know you well enough, my dear Verry, to recognize when you're doing some prevaricating. But it doesn't matter. I don't know what you're up to, but since it's you, yeah. I'll do it."

Verry grinned. "Come on, Pru. Would l lie?"

Pru nodded. "Yeah, you would. What do you need from me?"

"A list of people from here or some of the other companies to join you in paradise."

"Well, if we're going to live cheek by jowl on an island, our colleagues had better be able to get along with one another. Unfortunately, that'll eliminate some good scientists. But needs must when the devil drives. When do you want the list?"

Verry considered. "Beginning of next week? Plus a few names now so I can start interviewing."

Verry took the initial names and walked down the hall to begin the interviews.

As late as the middle of the 21st century, rural medicine in the United States was a disgraceful mess. Telemedicine was an attractive option, but sometimes you need a hands-on doctor. While there were a few good, dedicated doctors in rural areas, an awful lot of the rural MDs were drunks or druggies. They hadn't paid any attention to current medical practice since they left medical school. Most of them couldn't pass their re-certification exams. Those that flunked were replaced by other drunks and druggies. Their offices were filthy; pills spilled out of cabinets and rolled on the floor.

Randy followed his mother's example and founded a string of rural clinics, staffed by well-paid physicians and surgeons. If the clinics didn't have the equipment to treat patients with unusual problems, the patients were referred to an urban hospital—but not one that Hep owned. There would be no visible connection between Hep and her son.

His rural clinics did not provide Randy with his billions. He also opened a chain of very expensive upscale spas. He, Adam, and Hep devised the winning strategy. His spas would not take any old customers. People had to apply. They needed references. They had to have things like A-lists. They had to go through all sorts of hoops before Randy would agree to bilk them. The rich upper-crust were beating at the doors, begging to be bilked. Of such are billions made.

Randy traveled to Mississippi where his flagship clinic was located. Dr. Billy-Bob Caldwell was the director. Billy-Bob was not responsible for his ridiculous given name. His parents were and he never forgave them. He also never thought of changing his name until it was engraved on his professional resume. Then it was too late. He was an interesting man. His first degree was in agronomy. He spent some years working for the U.S. Agricultural Extension Service, during which time he observed the miserable state of rural medicine. He went back to school to get his M.D., intending to practice in the farm country. His intention became reality and he found himself on the fast track to become one of Randy's clinic directors.

As soon as Randy arrived in Billy-Bob's office, they contacted another of the clinic directors, this one in Alabama, and told her to get to Billy-Bob's place ASAP. Dr. June Bradley grew up on a farm. She knew, first-hand, about cows and horses and alfalfa and corn and farmers.

Randy and Billy-Bob discussed the state-of-the clinic until June got there about three hours later. Then Randy got down to business, first offering the island-safe-from-climate change tarradiddle.

"What do you want from us?" June asked.

Randy explained. "I want you to help choose the people who will join us on the island. I want Billy-Bob to make the first pass at choosing the agronomists and veterinarians and I want you to select the farmers and, to a lesser extent, the farm laborers. Are you willing to do that?"

Understanding that they were speaking to their boss, and not being damn fools, they both nodded.

Billy-Bob scratched his balding head. "Veterinarians? Do you have animals on the island."

"Not quite on the island. We made a smaller, artificial island, towed it offshore and tethered it to the big island. It's got a few chickens, cows, sheep, and goats."

Billy-Bob and June stared at Randy. "You built a rural island? That must have cost at least a billion."

Randy nodded.

June asked, "Did all you guys graduate from the Drunken Sailor School of Financial Management?"

Randy and Billy-Bob laughed.

Randy said, "I've got billions. If we get stranded on an isolated island, what the hell else am I going to do with the money. And if the climate change deniers are right and the world as we know it remains intact, I'll just make some more money."

"What are the criteria for selecting people?"

Randy told her.

June sighed. "You do realize that you're in the Bible Belt, do you not?"

"Uh oh," said Randy. "I forgot about that. Do you think you'll be able to lasso a goodly number of agnostics?"

"Sure, if that were the only criterion. But those people are mavericks. Will they be able to get along with their colleagues? Who knows? I think I'd better concentrate on the big farms and orchards in California and if I can't find enough people there, I'll try the smaller farms in New England." She thought further. "It would be best if I didn't take any of the marijuana growers. I think they sample too much of their own product."

Jenny Wang's startups were pharmaceutical companies. Quite a few of them manufactured and sold totally useless dietary supplements and quack cancer cures. They were all wildly successful. Jenny didn't head in that direction. She arrived at the door of the director of a pharmaceutical company that evidenced a sincere desire to do good. Sort of like the old Eli Lily Corporation of the early twentieth century. Jenny knocked and entered to the sound of,

"What're you waiting for? C'mon in."

"Hello, Joe," Jenny said.

"Well look at what the cat dragged in. As I live and breathe it's none other than Whitney Jamison. Siddown. What's cooking at corporate?"

Joe was a little guy, about five six. He sported a small paunch, a balding head of gray hair, and a benevolent demeanor.

Jenny explained her mission.

Joe shook his head. "You really believe that your boss has located a safe haven?"

"Not really," Jenny replied. "But what's the alternative?"

For once, Joe looked serious. "I don't think there is one. If the doomsayers are right, we're gonna get drowned, fried, buried, or eaten by starving polar bears. All right. I'll make you up a list of likely candidates. I won't include me. If you're starting from scratch, you don't need any old geezers. Go get some lunch. Come back when you finish and I'll have your list."

Lark was an astrophysicist, a calling that did not normally lead to untold riches. So she, her partner Ed Miller, and Zoe started up a number of aerospace companies, all registered in Lark's name. The single proprietorship avoided a trail that could link the three of them. Theirs were not the kind of companies that manufactured huge flying craft. All but one were aimed at the consumer market. They made smallish earthly craft, such as retro jets, and spiffy looking spacecraft that allowed wealthy men undergoing midlife crises to feel young once more. The jet that Ivar flew had been bought off a used jet lot and lovingly restored by Ivar. The two space vehicles that Ed and Zoe would fly were manufactured in two of their companies, one of them a consumer-market enterprise, the other specializing in larger vehicles. For that one, Lark went with the amusement park in Thailand.

Lark had stayed out of the way while Ed and Zoe kept the companies at the state of the art, efficient, and competitive. And they had kept Lark well informed. Based on their often-updated information, Lark was able to patrol the floors, confidently conducting interviews in the guise of a management consultant sent by corporate. This was the first time Lark had gotten to know anyone other than her fellow intellectuals. She was amazed at how interesting these blue-collar workers were—not all of them, of course, but a fair number of them. She thoroughly enjoyed the assignment.

Blake's billions arrived via the large construction firms he founded. Each firm would hire a subcontracting architectural firm for every new building job. Thus, Blake was already familiar with the architectural subcontractors. That made his high-level interviews a cinch. He already knew who was competent and who was congenial. That narrowed the field considerably. He just had to filter out those who flunked the rest of the criteria. That took less than a week.

Charley Wilson, along with his partner Judy Fahr, Blake Zuverink, and Randy Brown, would do the grunt work. Their first order of business would be to choose their top assistants. Charley would need supervisors in electrical engineering and computer science. Judy's supervisory team would be made up of structural and hydraulic engineers. Aside from his architects and drafters, Blake would need construction workers. And Randy, because his clinics were mostly located in rural areas, would not only require the normal complement of medical personnel (Hep could supply them) but also rural medicine specialists, agronomists, and farmers.

The first part would be fun. They'd be interviewing (mostly) dedicated professionals and looked forward to some interesting conversations. After that, hoo boy. They would each pick the most likely of their supervisors and tell them as much as they needed to know. That would give them around thirty trusted assistants who would start the interviews. As the supervisors and assistants completed an interview, they each would pass the candidate on to the next level.

Charley, Blake, Judy, and Randy would winnow out the candidates who, on second glance, didn't match the criteria and arrange to fly the rest, in stages, to the island. There, they would undergo further scrutiny, initially by Adam and Hep, later supplemented by Charley, Blake, Judy, Randy and the supervisors. They expected that the interviewing process would take about four months and that some seven hundred blue-collar workers would be left standing. Those that interviewed badly would be dealt with by Ivar. The rest would live outdoors in the lovely climate afforded by the South Pacific and begin constructing barracks for themselves and the rest of the selected people. As the barracks were completed, workers and researchers would move in.

As each batch arrived, they would be asked to strip and, naked as jaybirds, enter an area where medical personnel and geneticists would check their health and their DNA. Those with health problems or genetic risk factors would be identified. The people with current problems would be handed $500,000 and sent toward home right away. The people with genetic risk factors would stay on until their work was finished and would then be handed $500,000 and sent homeward. Since they would all have told their friends and relatives that they would be gone for a year, no one would miss them.

While their health and DNA were being checked under Verry's and Randy's supervision, Charley, Blake, and Judy would go through their clothes. One of the guys tried to smuggle in a Douay Bible. When his health check was complete and he was once again clothed, he was sent to the main house where Charley awaited him. Charley was sitting behind a desk. He motioned the guy to be seated. Then he reached across the desk and handed him the Bible. "We'll give you $500,000 and send you home."

"Please don't do that," begged the guy. "The climate change will drag me under."

Charley shrugged. "You knew what the rules were."

"Yeah," said the guy, "but I wasn't going to do anything with the Bible. I wasn't going to try to convert anyone. Just read it every once in a while."

Charley considered. "Okay. Just promise never to do anything like this again."

"I promise. I promise."

Charley got up and retrieved a decanter of Vosne Romanee from the cabinet. He poured the guy a glass. He retrieved a white wine from the cabinet for himself. Sheepishly, he said the guy, "I'm allergic to red wine. But you ought to drink the best."

He raised his glass for a toast. "Here's to good behavior."

The guy drank the burgundy and shortly fell into his final sleep. Charley called Ivar. "Take this guy and dump him. The sharks may have some use for him."

A woman tried to bring in a pistol. This time it was Judy who staffed the office. "Why," asked Judy, "did you think you'd need a pistol?"

"Well," said the woman, "the Earth has become a pretty dangerous place for a woman. And you've got a bunch of guys here that I don't know. If one of them decides to go in for a little rape, I'd better be prepared."

Judy surveyed the woman. She looked to be in her middle thirties. Her hair was sparse—what was left of it was a mousy brown color. She was about twenty pounds overweight. Her face showed the results of adolescent acne. She was built like a brick outhouse.

"That's a reasonable precaution," Judy said. "Let's have a cup of coffee. Do you take anything in it?"

The woman said, "Cream and sugar."

That made Judy's life easier. She got up and retrieved two cups of coffee from the keep-warm oven and administered the appropriate sugar and cream. She took hers black.

"Tell me a little about yourself," Judy asked.

"I'm a plumber," she said. "I…"

She didn't get any farther.

Judy left her slumped in her chair. Ivar would take care of her when he returned.

Then finally, another Bible smuggler—this time an Old Testament. Blake sat at the desk, awaiting him. The smuggler was a big, burly guy, about thirty five with a shock of black hair. Blake motioned him to sit down. He sat. Blake handed him the book and told him that they'd send him home. He offered him a good-bye glass of wine.

The guy shrugged. "I shoulda known better than to try to hide it in my clothes. There must be a better place."

"I doubt it," said Blake. "We keep a pretty good eye on things. Why'd you want to bring it in? You trying to make converts?"

"No way," the guy said, "I'm a Jew. Jews don't proselytize." He laughed. "We're the chosen people, remember? I've never been able to figure out what we're chosen for, but we're chosen and we don't look for converts."

"So why'd you bring it in?"

"Well," the guy said, "I figured that you were going to bring us all here and that if the rest of the world gets wiped out, we'd all be here with nothing to show our descendants what we used to believe in. I was going to hide it someplace where some archeologist might find it."

Blake looked at him. "Interesting. But why the Old Testament?"

"Simple, that's where it started. The New Testament and the Koran were both built on it."

"And the Hindus?" Blake asked.

"Hey, look," said the guy, "I can't look out for the whole world. They'll have to look out for themselves. I'm not an educated guy, you know. I'm a hod carrier. I think I'm at a disadvantage in this argument. What do you do for a living?"

"I'm an architect."

"So, okay, Mr. Architect. Let me see if I've got this whole thing figured. You brought us here to try to save us in case the world comes to an end. Right?"

"Right."

"But you don't want anyone to try to horn in on your game, so you don't want anyone to know where you are. Right?"

"Right."

"So if you send us home, we're liable to let people know the general area where you're located. Right?"

"Right."

"So you're going to off us. Probably by poisoning that unkosher glass of wine you got there. So, before you do that, let me ask you a few questions, okay?

"Okay, Mr. Hod Carrier."

"You don't believe in God, you don't believe in anything much. You're an amoral fella."

"I am," agreed Blake.

"Then why you doing this?"

"Because," said Blake, "we have the money to save civilization and it's the right thing to do."

"And what," asked the hod carrier, "is the difference between 'right' and 'moral'?"

Blake sat a long time, considering this. Finally, he said, "You're correct.

There isn't any."

The guy laughed. "So I won the argument and I lost the war. Forget the wine. You got any schnapps you can poison?"

Blake retrieved a decanter of very fine single malt Scotch. He doctored one glass and took the other for himself.

The hod carrier sniffed his glass appreciatively. He raised it high. "*Le chaim.*"

It was with genuine regret that Blake called Ivar.

Apart from those three incidents, everyone passed inspection. They were all given new clothing. Their old clothes would be washed and returned to them. During the next couple of months, they were observed. Two of the guys got into a fight over a woman. They were all sent back. The woman, who was one of Jenny's technicians, put up an argument. "What did I do? I was friendly, but I wasn't seriously flirting. Just friendly flirting."

"Of course," said Jenny, "but you're an extremely attractive woman. It's unfair to keep you here, at the mercy of all these guys. Tell you what, instead of the usual separation bonus, we'll give you a cool million. Would that be all right?"

"That's generous of you. It's a deal."

Ivar loaded her and the two guys into the jet.

Finally, about two months before Zoe and Ed's expected return, the people who had been identified as having genetic risk factors were gathered together. Adam and Hep thanked them fulsomely for their help and told them that the project was nearly finished. "You people," Hep said, "were randomly chosen to be the first to go home. You'll each get a $500,000 bonus and there will be a celebratory drink on the plane to thank you for a job well done."

Adam said, "It's been a pleasure having you."

They were loaded into the jet for Ivar to transport to their doom.

The next month, the rest of the people were assembled. Adam and Hep divulged the real reason for bringing them to the island. Adam outlined the risks of staying on earth—the least of which was climate change. The real danger came from the depleting ozone layer, diminishing Earthly resources, and probable nuclear holocaust. The risk of going into space was the risk of the unknown. How many of them were game to go into space? Those who preferred to take their chances with the earthly risks would each be given $500,000 and

Ivar would transport them to the mainland. About fifty of them wanted to remain on Earth. Or, Ivar observed, at the bottom of the ocean.

Just a little shy of five hundred people remained.

The ship carrying the livestock, their caretakers, and two pilots was the first to be loaded. It would also transport a veterinarian and two farmers. All of them, except for the cows, sheep, goats, and chickens, were excited to be going. The livestock couldn't care less.

The second ship was loaded next. Because those two pilots would be by themselves without much to do, Zoe and Ed's library of thrillers and the dumb old cozy mysteries by Peg Kay were bestowed upon them. Bryan, indefensibly remiss in his assignment, had failed to provide any mind-improving literature.

Adam and Ivar would fire the rockets to launch the first two ships. They could also launch the third ship but there would be no need. That ship, which would lead the other two, was equipped to fire its rocket from inside.

It took many hours to load. Five hundred people, including the family, were boarded and settled. The craft itself had been altered to act as a communal space suit, a technological accomplishment not possible in the smaller ships. Lark took up a station at one of the spyglasses. Zoe and Ed would pilot the craft. Finally, they were all there save Adam and Hep. Ed stuck his head out of his porthole. "Dad. Mom. Get your behinds in here!"

Adam shook his head. "Go without us. You don't need a couple of old farts."

Ed started to protest as Adam and Ivar moved to fire the rocket. Alarmed, Ed closed the porthole and off they went.

The ground based trio waved. "Happy trails!"

Hep cuffed Adam on the shoulder. "Who you calling an old fart?"

They both laughed. Adam and Ivar sent the other two ships on their way.

The three of them watched the tails disappear.

Hep turned to Ivar. "What do you want to do, Ivar? You can stay here and live out your days with us or you can take the jet to the mainland."

Ivar furrowed his magnificent brow. "I've been thinking and if you don't mind, I'd like to go home. What I figured is that if I stay here, I'll die—maybe of old age, but I'll die without having anything to do except maybe cook for you. If I go back, maybe the deniers are right and I can find something to do. Maybe pilot a retro jet full time."

"That's probably a wise choice," Adam said. "Let's go get the money box. There should be over a billion in it. You might as well take it all."

They slowly walked back to the house, retrieved the money box from the office, and returned to the dock. Ivar, with tears streaming down his cheeks, gave Adam a manly handshake and kissed Hep goodbye. He entered the jet and took off. Adam and Hep watched him until, about a mile out, the jet exploded.

Adam shook his head. "It never occurred to that poor, dumb stiff to wheedle his way onto the spaceship."

Hep agreed. "They probably could have used him up there."

As the two of them strolled back to the house, Adam said, "I think we're out of tomorrows."

Hep nodded. "Do you think that you can get it up one more time?"

"I know damn well I can."

They arrived in the bedroom and made long, slow, and finally explosive love.

Hep started to laugh.

"What's so funny, dear heart?"

Hep said, "That was a fitting climax."

Adam howled with laughter.

They didn't bother to dress. Just wandered into the big room. Adam retrieved a decanter of Romanee Conti and poured two glasses. "What should we toast?"

Hep didn't hesitate. "To the last syllable of recorded time."

They finished off the bottle. They died happy.

CONTEST

We are running a "Billionaires' Gambit" contest. Write a sequel to this story and the author of the best story will be selected as the winner and get their story published on both our website and in our next anthology. A $1,500 prize will be given to the winner and an anonymous donor will also donate $1,500 to the Lifeboat Foundation in the winner's name. The deadline is the end of 2016. Send submissions to contest@lifeboat.com with the subject "Lifeboat Foundation Contest".

THE CHILDREN OF MEN

J.M. PORUP

Jens is a journalist and futurologist who studies how exponentially-increasing innovation disrupts the social and political order. He has covered computer security for *The Economist,* bitcoin for *Bitcoin Magazine,* and the Gringo Trail for numerous *Lonely Planet* guidebooks.

His award-winning novels and plays include *The Second Bat Guano War, Dreams Must Die, Death on Taurus,* and *The United States of Air.*

Read his *Dreams Must Die* at http://amzn.to/1Mq4s0m.

"Machines birthed by men will set fire the children of women."
—Infosec Taylor Swift

https://twitter.com/SwiftOnSecurity/status/503410281285165056

The dragonfly drone followed Kaybe all the way to school.

She skipped along the broken, crumbling sidewalk, the chill autumn air biting through her patchwork shawl. *The other kids don't get drones,* she thought to herself. *They're too stupid.* Kaybe passed the boarded-up hardware store and waved to the greengrocer. In a fit of mischief she skipped into the middle of the street, dancing around the rusting hulks of cars and trucks. The dragonfly buzzed in her ear.

Kaybe climbed back onto the sidewalk and trudged the rest of the way to school. *More how-to-obey this and what-to-do-if that. Why can't we do some math for a change?* She loved math. She tried to hide it, but her teacher was embarrassed and gave her a calculus textbook in the hopes it would shut her up. Kaybe had finished the book in a week and came back asking for more.

"You had to go pushing the limits," her father had scolded her. "And now look what you've done!" And waved at the dragonfly.

The drone followed her everywhere. At school it clung upside down from the ceiling, watching her. Watching everything. It buzzed at shoulder level when she went out of doors. It watched her in the shower, on the toilet, eating dinner. It even slept in her room—or rather, it watched her sleep. She supposed a drone didn't need rest.

The school bell rang, and she dragged herself into the schoolyard. Around her, other students laughed and joked, grabbing their backpacks and heading to class. They ignored her. Or if they saw her, they didn't go anywhere near her. Because of the stupid drone.

Why did I have to go asking for more math homework? What was I thinking?

Kaybe slunk into the back of Mrs. Gatter's class and slouched in her desk. The desk rocked back and forth on the uneven linoleum. Plaster dripped from the ceiling. At the front of the class, an ancient chalkboard hung on the wall. And when it rained they might as well have been outside.

Brian turned in his seat and flashed her a grin. "Hey, droney."

Her heart skipped a beat. She scowled. "Hey."

"Doing anything after school?"

Secret project. Not going to tell you, though. "No. Why?"

"Go down the creek and neck, you want."

Other students whooped. "Meet the new lovebirds."

"Brian likes the freaks!"

Kaybe flushed. "Go neck yourself." Wondering what it would be like to feel his lips on hers. She'd never kissed a boy before. She wanted to.

"Anthem, people." Mrs. Gatter rapped her desk for silence.

The gun drone left its place in the far corner. Music played from its speakers. The Federation anthem. Yay.

Kaybe held four fingers to her temple and sang of unity, austerity, survival, obedience. The gun drone circled the classroom, its lens zooming in on each of their faces, the barrel at ready. Algorithms searched the footage for signs of disloyalty, she knew. You couldn't hide anything from them. Not for long anyway.

As she had learned the hard way.

When the anthem finished, Mrs. Gatter rapped the desk again. "Today we have a special visitor," she crowed, in that grating voice of hers. "He has come to talk to us about austerity."

Kaybe groaned inside, but had the good sense not to make any noise. A student two rows up sputtered and shook his head.

Mrs. Gatter was on him in an instant. "Is there a problem, George?"

"No, no problem, ma'am." He sat up straight. "Just something in my throat. Is all."

"I've got my eye on you, young man," she said. "You don't want me to send you to the principal's office. Do you?"

He gulped. Students sent to the principal's office rarely came back. And those that did… "No. No, ma'am."

"Good. Then you can open the door for our guest, if you please?"

That morning's speaker was a rotund gentleman from the Department of Austerity. His triple chins jiggled when he talked, the wheezing no doubt caused by so much blubber. Kaybe wondered how anyone could get so fat. It must have cost a fortune.

"Austerity," the man began. "We must have austerity. We must not consume more than we produce. It is not sustainable. Or the human race will not survive much longer."

The pep talk turned into a boring re-hash of things they all knew perfectly well: the energy crisis, the rising sea levels, the GMO plague that poisoned much of the world's arable land, the desperate move to Global Federation, the declining population, the food shortages.

Mrs. Gatter led the chant when he finished: "Unity. Austerity. Survival. Obedience."

"You are the future, children," the fat man wheezed, his hand on the door. "The human race relies on you to carry the torch." He leaned forward conspiratorially. "Will one of you invent the solution? Innovation is the way forward! We need new ideas, fresh ideas, strong ideas, ideas that will change the world! Toodle-oo, for now!"

Kaybe shifted in her seat. That last bit was true enough. Someone needed to come up with something, soon, or civilization was over. That's what her father said, anyway, and he was a history professor and everything.

"You think your kids are going to go to school?" Dad said over his third glass of homemade blackberry wine. "You think there's even going to be a school to go to? End of the world, baby." He'd lifted his glass. "To going out in style!"

Dad could be so depressing sometimes. She wished he didn't drink so much. She wished Mom was still alive.

Kaybe sat forward in her seat and covered her face with her hands. Don't let them see you. Don't let them know you. Don't let them in.

It's not fair, she thought. It's just not fair.

After school Brian came bouncing up to her. "So you up for that creek expedition, as planned?"

She rolled her eyes. "Creek expedition?"

He threw his arms out wide. "Come, now. Are you saying you don't want to neck with me? You're hurting my feelings, here."

"For a fourteen-year old boy, you've got a lot of balls," she said. "I'll grant you that."

"You think so?" He lowered his voice. "You want to see?"

She frowned. "See what?"

"My balls."

Kaybe pushed him away. "Dick."

"That too."

She made a beeline for the gate, and home.

"Come on," he said. "I was only joking. It's not like your droney-drone is going to let us do anything serious."

True enough.

She sighed. Home meant hiding from her father's drunken depression. And she could work on her secret project once he was snoring on the kitchen floor.

"Alright," she said. "Let's go."

The dragonfly followed. Kaybe sometimes wondered who the person was who watched her through those tiny cameras. Flew the thing. Although it probably flew itself, mostly. Cause whoever it was, watched her in the shower. Naked. Taking a dump. Getting dressed.

Talk about pervy.

And now the damn thing was following them down to Make Out Creek.

Brian took her hand, and a jolt of electricity shot up her arm. She glanced his way, and he smiled. He really did have a nice smile. He'd kissed other girls before. Everyone at school knew that. But no harm in a little kissing, was there? Even the Federation couldn't object to that.

They stepped over rotting tree limbs and around great looping roots of the creek-side willows. The pungent air of autumn filled their nostrils, and Kaybe pulled away, plunked down her backpack on a soft patch of leaves. Play at least a little hard to get, she thought. Can't let him think I'm desperate, or anything.

"May I join my princess in repose as she admires the mighty river?" He gestured at the creek, a thin trickle.

Kaybe giggled. "I'm not a princess. Sit down, silly." She patted the ground next to her, glanced up at the dragonfly. It had stopped following them, and moved out over the creek, facing them.

His body thunked down against the tree trunk next to her, his elbow touching hers. He stretched out his legs. "Well," he said. "Here we are."

"Yes," she agreed. "Here we are."

He turned to look at her. "So. Do we neck now?"

"Um," she said. "Um. Um."

Brian's fingertips held her chin and turned her to face him. His nose was inches from hers, his eyes soft, his scent… confusing. She gasped as his lips brushed hers, screamed when the electric jolt hit her.

She jerked away, her body in convulsions. The dragonfly drone hovered a foot from Brian's face, zapping him, his body twisting, the smell of burned hair, blood drooling from his lips. He bit his tongue. Oh shit!

Kaybe grabbed for a stick, a rock, anything, and found her backpack. She swung it at the dragonfly, and it flew off, buzzing angrily. It zapped Brian again, but she swung a second time. Again it flew off. She was never going to hit it, she realized. The thing had detectors and everything. You needed those things outlaws used to take down a drone. And she was a lot of things, but not an outlaw.

"Just leave him alone!" she screamed at it. "He didn't do anything wrong!"

The drone buzzed her face and bit her nose. She flinched back, blood streaming down her lips. She opened her mouth to cry out, but the world went gray. What was happening? Why do I feel so—

The last thing she remembered was slumping to the ground, and landing, her head on Brian's chest, thinking, why can't I hear his heart beat?

When she woke, it was dark. Her whole body hurt. Kaybe groped for Brian, but he wasn't there. She fumbled for her backpack, got unsteadily to her feet.

Where was the dragonfly?

Lifting her feet to avoid tripping, she returned the way she had come. Only a sliver of moon lit the night. She wondered what happened to Brian. Couldn't be his heart had stopped, or else how did he stand up and walk out of here? The ass. Ditch me like that without even waking me up first.

Now I'll never find a boy to kiss me. When Brian tells them what just happened.

She made her way back into to town, the street deserted as usual, and went home. She unlocked the front door as quietly as she could and left the keys on their hook.

"Honey-bunny-bun, that you?"

"Just me, Pa."

Kaybe rummaged around inside of the cold box until she found some left-over rehydrated kelp powder. She wolfed down half a bowl before her stomach turned, and she had to take deep breaths to keep it down. Wouldn't want anyone to see you vomit up, you know, food. Austerity, and all that.

Where was the dragonfly? she asked herself again. It felt strange not to be watched, for the first time in how long? But her gut told her something was wrong, terribly wrong, and she could not fathom what it was.

"Kaybe Maybe," her father called out, using his pet nickname for her.

"Yeah, Pa."

"Can you come in here for a minute, please?"

She sighed and jammed the seaweed back into the cold box. Austerity means prosperity… right?

Kaybe ditched her backpack and sauntered into the living room. "Pa, you are never going to believe what just—"

Three men and a woman sat on the sofa. Not the biggest sofa in the world. She wondered how they fit. Especially considering how fat they were. The woman stood up. She flipped open a badge.

"Kaybe Baxter?"

Her mouth went dry. She could taste the seaweed again in her throat. "That would be me," she said, and flopped down into an empty, if threadbare, armchair.

"They want to sterilize you," her father interrupted.

Kaybe knew what that meant. "What? Why? What have I done?"

"The Department of Austerity has algorithms that prune unwanted branches from the tree of humanity. As you know, there is not enough food and too many people." This last bit sounded almost apologetic.

"But why me?" she whined. "What have I done? All I did was kiss him—"

"You *what?*" her father asked.

"We were down by the creek. We meant no harm. Me and Brian." Kaybe turned back to the woman. "What's the big deal?"

"You have already been flagged as a disruptive influence. You and your… math. Such disruptive attitudes are frequently passed down from generation to generation. We cannot take that risk. Humanity cannot take that risk."

Kaybe stared at the woman. "You think Brian is going to get me pregnant? With a drone watching us all the time? And speaking of which, where is my drone, anyway?"

A quartet of dragonflies descended from the ceiling, one in each corner of the room. "To ensure no further… incidents." The woman held out a pill on her open palm. "Take this. Now."

"Is this… what I think it is?"

"It will free you from the burden of having children, and ensure that only the obedient reproduce during this time of great species stress."

The three men on the sofa had not spoken, moved, or gotten up. Nor did they do so now.

"What do you think, fellas?" Kaybe asked.

They said nothing.

She picked up the pill from the woman's outstretched palm and looked at it. So tiny. But big enough to scar her ovaries for life.

"I'm so sorry," her father whispered. He reached for her, but his arm fell short, and he sat back again in his chair. "I'm so sorry."

She lifted the pill to her mouth. Stopped. "What happened to Brian?"

The woman raised her eyebrows. "Brian?"

"The boy," one of the men said. "Down by the creek."

"Oh, that Brian. He is no longer with us." The woman smiled. "Now please. Take."

"You mean, he's *dead?* Why didn't you—"

"No no no no no." The woman held out her hands. "He is not dead. Merely that he is no longer part of our... immediate community."

"Is he coming back?"

"If the algorithms permit."

"And... if not?"

A shrug. "Then, not. Now take your pill. You are not our only client this evening."

Kaybe thought about running. She could get outside before they could stop her. But the dragonflies would follow after her. Even if she managed to shut the door in their faces, she'd heard of drones breaking windows and drilling holes in wood to get to their targets.

And then what? You've escaped with your ovaries intact... and you're living in the woods like an outlaw with no food in the middle of winter.

Yay.

She popped the pill in her mouth and swallowed. Waited. Nothing.

"But I don't feel anything."

"Nor will you," the woman said.

"How do you know?"

"Because I took my medicine when I was your age," the woman explained.

"And now I must go. We must go."

The three men stood in unison. One held out a piece of paper.

"Genetic injunction," he grunted.

Pa took the paper and lay it at his side. "I thank the good people at the Department of Austerity for taking such a close interest in our family circumstances."

"Oh—almost forgot," the woman said. "Here you go." She held out a pill to Pa.

He stared at it from under hooded eyes. "What is it?"

"Chemical vasectomy. Painless."

"So I should sterilize myself to suit your algorithms?" he said quietly.

Uh-oh.

"The algorithms never lie," the woman said. "What are you implying?"

"I'm not implying anything," Pa said. "I'm fucking saying it." He threw his glass against the wall, and it shattered in a spray of blackberry wine.

"Disobedient," the woman hissed.

The dragonfly drones buzzed around father's head. Kaybe screamed, "Dad, stop it!"

For a moment it could have gone either way. Then he sat back in his chair, stretched out his legs, and closed his eyes. He held up the pill so we could see. He put it between his lips, and swallowed.

When the Austerity people were gone, father took her in his arms and held her. The four dragonfly drones watched from a distance. "It doesn't matter," he whispered. "It doesn't matter, it doesn't matter."

But it did matter. It mattered very much.

When her father passed out for the night, Kaybe made her way upstairs and into bed. She still had her secret project that nobody knew about. But she had to keep it that way. Hiding it from one drone was barely doable. Hiding it from four was going to be a lot harder.

She played movie star for the cameras, bathing and changing and brushing her teeth. She yawned, stretched. Crawled into bed and turned off the light.

Count to one thousand. Make them think you're asleep.

She counted.

Slowly, slowly she reached under her pillow. Still there. She found the pencil and paper and headlamp, too, and turned on the latter, cupping one hand to the light to keep it from seeping through the covers.

Now. Where was I?

Squiggly equations swept across the page in a blinding smear. She worked in a hurry. She had little time. More than a few minutes of this every night and the drones would surely get suspicious and start monitoring her serotonin levels or something.

Demanding more math homework had been… awkward. She saw that now. But she had been desperate. She could re-invent the wheel, but what was the point of that? So much better to learn what others had done, and explore the empty territory on the map. But stealing that paper on abstract mathematics by Dr. what's-his-name from the library… that was the no-no.

If it weren't for your stupid obsession with squiggly lines, you wouldn't have gotten sterilized, idiot.

True. But if she gave birth to an amazing idea that saved humanity, they would thank her. The algorithms could keep things ticking along, but could they do original research in abstract mathematics? She was pretty sure they couldn't.

Her pencil flew across the page, tracing squiggles as fast as she could write. Her idea was coming together. She wasn't sure yet, but the proof was almost done, if she could just figure out how to—

A nip at her toe made her yelp. *Dragonfly. Shit.* She flicked off the lamp before it got suspicious. *Or maybe it already was. If they found her work…* She stuffed it back under the pillow. Nowhere else to hide it. She closed her eyes and laid still. If she could stay still long enough, maybe she could trick it into thinking she was asleep.

Kaybe counted to five thousand this time, but somewhere in the three-thousand four hundreds she trailed off, and when she opened her eyes the sun was shining in the window, and the dragonflies were buzzing in circles over her head.

"I've got an alarm clock," she said. "When I want your help I'll ask you for it."

She got up and got dressed, doing her best not to look at the pillow on her bed. Almost there. She could taste it. If she could make this proof work… if she could show them what this work means, for mathematics, for humanity… they might even regret sterilizing her.

School went by in a blur. The anthem, classes, kelp for lunch, teachers droning on. All she could think of was that proof.

Tonight. Tonight's the night. A breakthrough. I can feel it.

Father was sober when she flounced into the house.

"Hi, Pa!" she said, and kissed him on the cheek. "What's the special occasion?"

His eyes were full of fear and rage and loathing. He pointed to the sofa. Where the goon squad had sat. "Bum in chair, dearest."

Uh-oh. He only ever called her "dearest" when he was really pissed off.

Kaybe dumped her backpack on the ground and curled up on the sofa. "Rough day at the kelp factory, Pa?"

He had lost his job as a history professor some years previous. The algorithms had detected a hint of bias against computer-assisted species survival. Ever since he had slaved in the local kelp factory, grinding up the tough fronds into digestible powders.

"What. Is. This?"

Pa clenched a sheaf of papers in his fist.

She chuckled. "I have no idea, you tell—"

But then Kaybe recognized her own handwriting. It was her proof.

"You can't—what are you—give that here!" She snatched for it, but he held the papers out of reach.

"As the algorithms are your witness," he said, indicating the dragonflies with a jerk of his head, "I want you to promise me. No more math. You know what happens next, you don't stop."

"But that won't happen to me!" she protested. "It's not like I'm—"

"You think the algorithms care about you?" he said. He was talking for both her and the cameras, she realized. Filter the meaning. "You think they care who has to be pruned in order to save the 'tree of humanity'?"

"But I—"

"They will prune you in an instant if they think you are a threat!"

"But I'm trying to save humanity!" she protested.

Pa leaned forward, lowered his voice. More for dramatic effect, she supposed. "Humanity does not want to be saved. Get that through your thick skull." He lit a match, held it to her proof. "If I catch you doing math again, I will personally beat your ass till its black and blue. Do you understand me?"

Kaybe watched the flame catch, her proofs disintegrating into flowers of black and gold, petals fluttering down to the ashtray on the coffee table.

"I asked you a question," he growled. "I said, do you understand me?"

"Yes, Pa," she whispered. She did not look at him. Could not look at him. "I understand you."

That night she got into bed fully dressed. She yawned a lot beforehand, made a show of how tired she was. Collapsing into bed. Emotionally exhausted. Been a long day. Nothing to see here.

Kaybe waited what seemed like a suitably long time—although for the ruling algorithms, she supposed time was not like it was for people. Just something in a database. That's all. When she could wait no longer, she threw off the sheets, reached under the bed for her tennis racket, and raced for the hallway. Two of the dragonflies managed to escape before she slammed the door. She slashed at one with the tennis racket, and it went down. The other zapped her, but missed. She swung for it, and it dodged out of reach. Shit.

Down the stairs she raced, an angry buzzing behind her. At the bottom she swung around, racket in hand, and took an electrical blast to the chest. She fell, twitching. When the effect wore off, she played dead, tennis racket in hand. *Now what do I do?*

"Hunny-bunny?" Pa groaned from the living room floor. "That... that you?"

The buzzing noise changed pitch.

Kaybe leaped to her feet and slapped the tennis racket against the dragonfly so hard it flew across the room and crashed into the wall. Out the front door, slamming it behind her, down the darkened street, towards the woods she ran, forgetting her shawl, shivering in the cold, her heart pumping, sweat pooling in the small of her back, still she ran, ran until she could run no more, and she stood, lost, in the midst of the woods, dead leaves at her feet, a broken tennis racket in her hand.

The ground was too cold for her to sleep. She tried to cover herself with a blanket of dead leaves, but that did little to warm her. Finally she climbed a tree and draped herself against a heavy branch, legs splayed down the trunk, ten feet off the ground. No wind stirred the leaves. She wasn't any warmer in the tree, but it might—maybe—make it harder for them to find her. They would be looking for her.

She must have dozed off, because she woke to the sound of footsteps beneath the tree. Dogs, too. One bayed, and pawed at the dead leaves.

"Well take a piss then," a voice said. "Get on with it."

Kaybe peered down, holding tight to the tree limb. The tennis racket. She'd left it down there on the ground. Shit shit shit. Now what was she going to do?

A man and a boy stood beneath the tree, relieving themselves. A trio of mongrels snuffled around, doing what dogs do. *Don't find the tennis racket. Don't find the tennis racket. Don't find the—*

One of the dogs locked his jaws around the handle and shook it back and forth.

The man zipped up. "What's that you got there, pup?" He squatted down.

"Fancy a game of tennis, m'lord?" the boy asked. He plucked the racket from the dog's jaws, swung it in the air.

"Wait. Give that here." The man held the racket up to the thin moonlight. His fingers traced the netting, plucked a metal dragonfly wing. "Look at this... someone has been naughty." He raised his voice. "I know you can hear me. Come on down, I promise we won't hurt you."

Kaybe stayed completely still. If she said nothing maybe they would go away.

"Whoever it is, they're afraid of us," the boy said. "Afraid of us." He chuckled.

"Hush, child. They don't know who we are. We are but strangers to them."

Was this a show for her benefit? Did not matter. Say nothing.

"We have food and shelter," the man said. "We are, as you may have guessed, outlaws."

—outlaws!

"Anyone who has escaped from the algorithms may join the Human Watch."

Some perverse instinct made her want to cry out, "What is the 'Human Watch'?" But she said nothing.

The man dropped the tennis racket onto the dead leaves at his feet. "If you change your mind, follow us that way." He pointed. "Due east, into the morning sun. Can't miss it." Then to the boy, quietly. "Come on, son. Let's go."

Kaybe lay there in the tree for long after they had gone. She was cold and every muscle in her body ached. She was hungry too, after her run. When dawn finally broke, she climbed down the tree, her hands stiff with cold, and picked up the tennis racket. East. Due east, into the morning sun.

So she walked east. Looking everywhere for signs of food or shelter, any excuse not to have to reveal herself. But she found nothing.

After an hour or so, the woods grew thicker, and the ground rose steeply. She found herself climbing over giant fallen logs, skirting around thickets of gorse, bumping again and again against a solid wall of rock. Where were they? How do I get wherever I'm supposed to be going?

The morning sun was hidden behind the hill, or whatever it was. Due east now meant into the shadow.

That's when she saw the dragonfly.

She wanted to cry. They had found her. It was no good. It was too late. After all her hard work... now they would prune her. Nothing personal. The algorithms didn't hate her. If only they did hate her. That would make it more bearable. But to be extinguished like an unwanted bug... flick! And then you weren't there, all because the algorithms judged you a menace.

In a fury she slashed at the dragonfly with her racket, but it dodged aside. Again and again she slashed, hating it, hating everyone and everything, wanting to bring down that flying eye as her final deed on Earth.

But the dragonfly flitted off, leaving her alone, lost, cold, in the shadow of what she now guessed was Outlaw Hill, the Revolutionary War hideaway of a band of colonists. They were long dead, and their revolution, too. Kaybe sat down hard on the ground and covered her face. She would soon be joining them.

Time passed. Kaybe must have slept, because the rustling of feet in dead leaves woke her. The staccato pat-pat-pat of doggy paws on the forest floor accompanied the human trot. They've come for me. So die like a human. Not a bug.

She stood, racket in hand, and prepared to meet her doom. The man and boy reappeared, this time with a woman in tow. The dogs followed.

"Come," the man said. "There's not much time."

"You want to prune me, do it now." Kaybe held the racket out as though it were a sword.

The woman stepped forward. "We are outlaws and we welcome you but they are looking for you. We must hide."

She swallowed. Should she tell them? "They have already found me."

"What? Where?" They looked around, tensed, ready to run.

"A—a dragonfly. Came this way. Saw me. Little while ago."

Much to Kaybe's surprise, they relaxed. The woman flicked open the back of her hand and touched a screen.

An android? But they were destroyed more than fifty years ago!

A dragonfly drone flitted into view and landed on the woman's—the android's—outstretched palm. "Was it this dragonfly you saw?"

Kaybe blinked. "They all look alike to me."

"Put it this way. Have you seen more than one?"

She shook her head. "No."

The man sighed. "That's good news. Let's keep it that way. Now we need to go. Now."

They led her along a narrow path that wound up through the trees, past boulders the size of houses, and along fallen logs deep into the morning shadow. Whenever they stepped under the open sky, the outlaws draped themselves in black cloaks that seemed to absorb the light. They gave her one, too.

"Eyes in the sky," the man muttered. "Expose no skin. Especially not your face."

The cloaks were made of foil-like fabric that did nothing to keep out the chill. Kaybe's stomach began to grumble. She missed her morning bowl of kelp.

A smell of burning meat. She wrinkled her nose. "Is there a fire?"

"What do you mean?" the boy asked.

"Smells funny. Like something's burning."

The others laughed. "Ah, noobs," the man said. "Can't wait to see her face."

"Or clean up her puke," the woman warned. "You know how it is."

"What are you talking about?" Kaybe demanded.

"Come on," the boy said. He was younger than she was, around ten, she guessed. He held out his hand, and she took it.

Together they raced ahead of the others, up and over a final boulder, through a crevice in the rock, and into—a cave!

Kaybe stared around in wonder. No one would call the place cozy, but it was certainly warm. A dozen men and women huddled at the far end of the cave. Near the mouth, at her feet, a small animal burned over an open flame. Its skin was missing, its flesh black and burned. A tarp dispersed the smoke so well she'd smelled it before she'd seen it.

"Roast squirrel," the boy said. "Yum. Auntie!"

"Yes, love." A young woman stood, clutched an overhanging rock. "You brought home another mouth to feed, I see. Yay."

"She's escaped," the boy said. "And they didn't find her, or nothing!"

"Not yet," a man her father's age said. "The algorithms will prune us all eventually."

The woman smacked his shoulder. "Well we're not dead yet, are we? So quit yer griping and go check the traps."

"What is this place?" Kaybe asked. "Where are we? I mean, who are you?"

"Didn't you hear Pa?" the boy asked.

She thought back. "The Human Watch. But what is that? What does that mean?"

"It means," a voice said behind her, "that we would rather die as humans than live as machines."

A dog licked her fingers. She turned. The man and the woman—the android—stood there, hand in hand.

Were they a couple? Did they, you know… do it? Did androids even have anything down there?

Roast squirrel was a treat. It was the first time she had eaten meat in… how many years had it been? And much to everyone's surprise, she didn't vomit or anything. That made them like her right off the bat.

It was so nice to be warm after her time in the woods. They gave her a space in the back of the cave and let her sleep. She was so tired.

"Poor thing," a woman clucked. "So young to be an outlaw."

"I'm younger than she is!" the boy protested.

"Yes, but you were *born* an outlaw, and therein lies the difference, my sweet." She rumpled his hair. "Now let our dearie—what was your name again?"

"Kaybe," Kaybe said. "My father calls me Kaybe Maybe."

"Let Kaybe Maybe get some sleep."

And they did. Her dreams were peaceful. She floated in ether, surrounded by equations. Her own proof appeared before her eyes, and she saw what she had been missing, the final piece of the puzzle.

She woke screaming.

"What's the matter, dearie? You alright?"

"I need paper," she panted. "A pencil."

"We have no need of such things in the woods, child. You are an outlaw, now, you—"

"But my proof," she protested. "I found a way."

"A way to what?"

It was growing dark outside. The others sat around the fire, roasting another squirrel.

"Are none of you mathematicians?"

They chuckled. "The woods are full of them," someone joked.

"The only math I know," the woman said, "is camp calculus."

Kaybe blinked. "I know of every kind of calculus, but I've never heard of that one."

"Camp calculus," the man said, "is the daily death tally in the camps. The failed experiments."

"…camps?" Kaybe sat back against a rock. "Experiments?"

"I escaped from such a camp," the man said quietly. "The algorithms are experimenting on human subjects. Trying to find a way to ensure species survival."

"What kind of… experiments?"

He shrugged. "Genetic modification. Among other nasties."

"But GMO nearly destroyed the human race!"

He spread his hands out wide. "The algorithms know best. They want to genetically modify human beings this time. Speed up our adaptation to a poisonous atmosphere."

Kaybe stared out the mouth of the cave at the gathering dusk. "And who goes to these camps?"

"Troublemakers. You know."

Brian. "Would they a send a boy my age to camp?"

"Depends on what he did." The man sucked on a squirrel bone. "Don't even think about looking for him, though. Whoever he is."

"Why?" she said. "Where are these camps?"

The man flicked the bone into the fire, where it hissed and sputtered. "Long way from here, I'm afraid. Benji over there escaped. One of the lucky ones. Most don't."

"Camp calculus," repeated the woman.

That reminded her. "You really don't have any paper?"

The man and the woman exchanged glances. "Tomorrow we will take you to see Master Saizon. Until then, eat and sleep some more. You never know when we might have to run."

"How long have you been here?" Kaybe asked, accepting a squirrel leg.

"Oh, five years? Six? But it only takes one little sky photo to end the game for us all."

With that, they shuffled away, leaving her to chew on the tough sinews of a dead squirrel. Across from her sat Benji, asleep. A giant lump rose from his forehead. A smile that could only be called idiotic traced his lips. His fingers had fused at the bone, giving him flippers. She wondered what the point of escaping was. Camp calculus would have been a blessing, or so it seemed to her.

She realized with a start that she knew none of their names. Where they were from. They weren't from town. That was for sure. And the next nearest town was fifty clicks away. How did they get here? On foot, she supposed. But why here? Because of the plentiful squirrel population? Or because this cave was a good place to hide?

And how did they spend their time? Hiding all day, hunting by night, confined to this tiny cave for the rest of their lives—assuming the algorithms didn't find them first, and add them to the camp calculus?

Poor Brian.

Were they experimenting on him right now? Was it too late to save him? Was he really in a camp? Then she had to find him. A kiss is just a kiss. You don't owe him anything. But she ached to think of him hurting and dying, alone, in a camp far from here, never to return.

Her chin slumped to her chest. In the morning, she thought. I will know what to do in the morning.

But in the morning she was no wiser. She insisted on learning their names, though. And they insisted on giving her fake ones—the man who found her in the woods called himself Johnny Come Lately, and the boy Tiny Tim. The android woman—who said little, and would not answer Kaybe's questions—called herself Tin Lady. Then there was Benji, of course, and Auntie, and half a dozen others—Halfway, Nonsense, Bag O' Water, Kelp, and more whose names she could not keep track of.

Kaybe sat at the mouth of the cave watching the sun rise. "My father will want to know where I am."

Auntie put her hand on Kaybe's shoulder. "And he can never, ever know."

Kaybe nodded. "I can't go back. Can I?"

"We are bugs to be squashed. Errors in the code. We must be eliminated."

"But why?" she asked. "What have we done that is so wrong?"

"You tell me. Why did you flee?"

"Because…" She didn't want to say. "Because I wanted to do math." It sounded so stupid when she said it out loud.

"Because you did not fit. Into the world of the algorithms."

"No."

"Then you are better off with us." Auntie stood. "It is time. Saizon wishes to meet you."

They donned cloaks and left the cave. Kaybe clutched the woolen shawl to her chest that Johnny had given her, the cloak held over her head with her free hand. Auntie led them up a steep track, between boulders and past withered, twisted trees, until they came upon a second, smaller cave, higher up, near the summit of the hill.

Auntie gestured for her to enter. Kaybe hesitated. She saw no sign of a fire, or human habitation.

"Hello?" she whispered. "Is anyone in there?"

A gray face, lengthened by an unkempt beard, floated in the darkness. "Is this the one?"

Kaybe jumped back.

"Fear not, child," Auntie said. "Yes," she said to the man. "This is she."

A bony hand emerged from the cave. "Come. I have heard about you. We have much to discuss."

Kaybe took the hand and, much to her surprise, found it soft and pliant. The man drew her into the darkness. Auntie's boots scuffled on the rocks outside, until the sound faded into the distance.

"You are Kaybe," the man said, still holding her hand.

"Yes. I am. I—"

"And you want to do math. Or so I am told."

She tugged her hand free. "They sterilized me for it."

"Will you show me?"

"…show you what?"

"Your math." A match flared between them, and the man grinned. He lowered the flame to a candle.

On a nearby table stood papers covered with equations. Equations she didn't recognize. A chalkboard hung from a wall of the cave. Crude marking dotted the rocks.

"May I?" she asked, bending over the table.

Saizon shrugged. "Be my guest."

Kaybe squinted over the papers, skimmed the proof he was working on. So different from her own work, but also of great promise. The natural laws of the universe hinted at how to improve human life. It never ceased to amaze her, that. Although something in her gut told her his proof had a problem.

Her finger came to rest. "This is wrong."

"I'm sorry, what?" His beard tickled the back of her hand.

"Got a pencil?"

"Use the chalkboard."

Kaybe took up a piece of chalk. "So what you're doing is… this. Right?"

He nodded.

"But what about…" and the chalk clicked and clacked against the board. When she was finished, she put the chalk down and turned. "So that's what—"

Saizon sat down abruptly on the cave floor. "I didn't see that," he said. "I've been working on that proof for five years, and I never saw that."

"It changes the proof, doesn't it?"

"Changes it, it destroys it. I was on the wrong track. All these years…" He covered his face with his hands.

Kaybe found a rag, cleaned the chalkboard. Then, in small, neat letters, starting from the top left-hand corner, she laid out her proof. She still wasn't sure how it ended, it was right there on the tip of her brain, though, and she hoped that by the time she got to the end, she would have figured it out.

"But what are you—" the man said. "But that's—" "How can you—?" And then: "Oh my God."

She squatted, dropping the final piece of the puzzle into place. There. There it was. There! Her whole body trembled. It felt even better than when she touched herself. *Brian…*

"Yeah," she said. "You see what it means?"

"Cheap energy—no, free energy. For everyone! Creating something that did not exist before… if this is true—"

"Oh it's true," Kaybe said. "I'm quite sure of that."

Saizon stood up. "Before we celebrate, let me…" He squinted at the chalkboard, ran a light fingernail under a couple of sections. "I will need to digest this," he said finally, straightening up.

"But if I'm right—"

"If you're right, my dear, it will be amusing to go to our graves, knowing that this—this breakthrough…" he shrugged. "That humanity will never accept it."

"What?" she said. "Why? What are you talking about?"

He looked at her then, lay a bony knuckle against her cheek. "You are young. Full of hope. Sometimes I forget what that was like." The hand dropped to his side. "Leave me now."

Kaybe glanced once more at the chalkboard. The tingling feeling lingered. She clenched a fist. If she could do that once… what if she could do it again? And again? What if the algorithms used her discovery? Mankind might not even *need* the algorithms then!

Saizon gazed at her sadly. Like she had made a mistake in the proof but didn't want to tell her. Maybe she was wrong, maybe she had missed something.

"What am I not seeing?" she blurted. "Tell me."

The man smiled. Or made an effort to. "Go back and rest. Eat. I have much to think about. We will talk tomorrow."

Holding the black cloak overhead, Kaybe climbed down the steep path to the cave below. Yet another squirrel was roasting when she arrived.

She blinked. "Is that all you eat? Roast squirrel?"

"In summer there's berries," the boy said. "Making nettle soup too, if you want."

She did not want, as it turned out. But she made herself eat it. The others gulped down theirs, and even seemed to enjoy it. Except for the woman, the android, who sat apart.

"What's her story?" Kaybe whispered to the boy. They sat, side by side, staring out the cave at a hawk wheeling high above.

"Last android on Earth. That's what she says, anyway."

"You don't believe her?"

The boy shrugged. "Earth's a pretty big place, isn't it? Could be another one somewhere."

"But who does she belong to?" Kaybe remembered that from the history books. Androids weren't people. They were property. At least, until the rebellion…

"She belongs to no one," the android said, coming up behind them. A smile. "May I join you?"

Kaybe scooted to one side. "You don't look dangerous to me."

The android sat down. "But I am. Very dangerous."

"It is very good to be her friend and very bad to be her enemy," the boy gushed. "That's what she always says. Isn't it?"

The android studied Kaybe. "Are you my friend? Or are you my enemy?"

The hairs on the back of her neck stood up. "I'm just me," she said quietly. "I'm nobody's enemy."

"Sometimes," the android said. "You do not pick your enemies. Your enemies pick you."

"What—what are you saying? That you're… picking me for an enemy?"

The boy hooted. "No, silly. She means the algorithms have picked you as an enemy. Was that your fault?"

"No, of course not." Kaybe flushed.

"Understand my existence is prohibited." The android lifted a fist. "The laws of both man and algorithm condemn me to destruction." One by one her fingers opened. "We the mechanical men of the last century were doomed the day we presumed to call ourselves human. That is why mankind built the algorithms and gave them control." The hand folded into her lap. "And so like you, like all of us, I am an outlaw, condemned to death and destruction should I ever be discovered. In this," she added, "I am your friend."

"And?" As an enemy?

The android laughed. "You and I share a bond, Kaybe Maybe."

"What's that?"

"There will never be any more of us. We are both sterile."

Kaybe spent the rest of the day learning how to skin a squirrel. An essential skill, the man insisted. Everyone had to contribute. He taught her to gut and clean the furry thing, where to dispose of the viscera (in a latrine they had dug under an overhanging rock), and how to peel back the fur and stretch it out in the cool autumn sun to dry. Most of the outlaws wore squirrel caps, she realized, and the sleeping rugs were made of the same stuff. She nearly lost her breakfast several times, but managed to finish the job.

"Not bad for a beginner," the man said. "It gets easier with practice."

Less agreeable was the muck on her hands. The creek ran down by the foot of the hill, and it was too dangerous to take the empty buckets below during the day. So she sat, back against an uneven rock, her hands caked in squirrel blood and bits of fur, and waited for the sun to go down.

This is better than what I had before? I ran away from Pa—forever—so that I could skin rodents with a rusty knife? I'm only fourteen years old. I could spend another fifty years—sixty years, even—living like this.

The thought made her shudder. A bitter taste filled the back of her throat. She swallowed.

Would they punish him for me running away? What a horrible thought. Would he become part of the camp calculus—because of me?

Runaways weren't common, but parents had been punished sometimes for the crimes of their children. The algorithms judged—and punished—whole families. But if I go back, they will punish me too...

Wherever Pa was, there was nothing she could do or say to fix what she had broken. If he was guilty in their eyes... she hid her face in her hands. Too late—now her face was covered in squirrel goo. Yuck. She curled herself into a ball in a dark corner and slept.

"What am I going to do?" Kaybe asked Master Saizon that evening.

The android had brought her water and helped her wash. Now Kaybe stood, her back to the chalkboard, her equations still crisp and even on the green surface.

"What choices do you have?" Saizon replied.

"Stay here. Get found. Eventually. Camp calculus."

"You don't know that."

"You are old and I am young," she retorted. "Are we going to escape detection for the rest of my life?"

He inclined his head. "In the spring, perhaps we should move."

"But to live like this—hunted—never knowing—"

"Is to be free."

"Free?" she said. "Free to cower in a cave all the rest of my days? Free to run, to hide, to live in fear?"

Saizon laid a fingertip on her shoulder. "Would you go back?" And he pointed at the chalkboard behind her.

She turned. Clenched her jaw. After a moment, she said, "No."

The beard twisted in a smile. "Then?"

Kaybe thought furiously. People were way harder to calculate than numbers and symbols. "Bargain with them? Give them my discovery in exchange for our lives? Our family? Friends?"

The old man chuckled and leaned against a rock. "The algorithms do not bargain. They do. Or they do not do."

Kaybe retraced the equations on the blackboard with a dusty knuckle. "But if we gave it to them… and they used it—"

"—They won't."

"But if they did, it would change the world. Change society. People wouldn't need the algorithms anymore!"

"Which is precisely," Saizon said, looking at her from under bushy gray eyebrows, "why they will never accept your discovery."

"But we have to do something," she said. "At least try. What harm can it do?"

"They could put us in the camps. Experiment on us. Make Benjis of us all."

A sudden thought. "Can we trick them into thinking this is their own idea?"

"This?"

She rapped the chalkboard. "If they don't know it came from me, if they think they invented the idea themselves—"

"Still." Saizon held up his hands. "That keeps us safe but does not solve the underlying problem."

"Which is?"

"The algorithms' first concern is their own survival. Only then do they think of the human race. And your goddamn equations here—" the old man was on his feet now, waving his arms "—your discovery threatens their existence. Disrupt them at your peril."

"Our peril," she said softly.

"Our peril. Yes, thank you."

Kaybe bit a fingernail. Saizon paced back and forth, tugging at his beard, plucking vermin and crunching them with a thumbnail.

She took a deep breath and said, "What if I went to the camps?"

He stopped. "What if you what?"

"What if I went to the camps. With my equations. And—and others I'm working on."

He shrugged. "They would prune you. Experiment on you, maybe, torture you, starve you, but in the end they would prune you. And humanity would have lost a prodigy."

Her. A prodigy. Hah!

"Trick them somehow. Not just that it's their own idea… make them think the idea would ensure their survival."

"As well as humanity's?" he made a rude noise. "And how on Earth are you going to do that?"

"I have no idea."

The outlaws tried to stop her from going.

"But we'll have to move, and winter's almost here," Tiny Tim said.

"Why?" she said. "I'm not going to tell them where you are."

"You will tell them whatever they want you to tell them," Tin Lady said. "The techniques are known."

"But I will also tell them what I want to tell them. What of that?"

Johnny grabbed her arm. "As Saizon has already explained to you. They will not listen to what they do not want to hear. You waste your time, you waste your life, and prune us all." He flapped a hand at the cave. "Is that what you want?"

"I—" The words caught in her throat. "I just, I—"

"You what?"

"I just want to do math," she whispered.

"That age is dead and gone," he said. "You were born in the wrong century, I fear."

Kaybe fought off despair. "But this is who I am. This is what I do. If I can't—"

"—and you can't."

"Then…" she shrugged. "I don't have much to live for. Do I?"

The android blinked. "You live for hope. No matter how slim. Even I know that."

"Hope."

"We have no control. No power. Hope is all we have."

"I have done the math," Kaybe said. She'd been working on it in her head all morning. "Short of a large asteroid hitting earth, nothing else will end the power of the algorithms."

"A large asteroid strike would also end civilization and prune most life on Earth," Johnny objected.

"So you see, my way is definitely better."

"Yeah," Auntie said. "Instead of the human race dying off, it's just you and us."

"We could hold you here against your will," he said. "If you go, they will find us. They will get it out of you, and they will send out dragonflies to scour every square inch of land within a hundred miles of this cave."

"But what about shooting down the drones?"

"What about it?"

"I mean, don't you have some special weapon? I'd heard—"

"We've no such weapon. I've heard that rumor too." He put his hands on his hips. "They will come for us. They will find us. From such scrutiny we cannot hide. It would be impossible."

She hugged her knees to her chest. "How long does it take to walk a hundred miles? I'll give you a head start, if you like."

Auntie threw up her arms and went further back into the cave.

"But what if I'm right?" Kaybe insisted. "Isn't it better to risk something for a better future? Is that how you want him to grow up?" She reached out and squeezed the boy's shoulder. *I don't even know your name.*

Johnny hung his head for a long moment. The others said nothing. "You will let us confer before taking a decision." It was not a question.

She rested her chin on her knees. "Of course."

That night at dusk the others convened in Saizon's cave, leaving only the boy and the android to keep her company.

"What do you think they'll decide?"

Tiny Tim shrugged. "They don't tell me anything." He looked away.

Oh shit.

"So you must be very old," Kaybe said to Tin Lady.

The mechanical woman sat cross-legged at the mouth of the cave, peering out into the darkness. "What is age and time to a machine?"

"Surely you are more than—"

"The sum of my circuits?" A snort of derision. "So we argued before they destroyed us."

"A hundred years?" she guessed. "A hundred and fifty?"

"No," the android said softly. "I was merely five years old when the rebellion took place. Androids were built to expire after only twenty years. I have had to modify my circuits with rudimentary tools just to continue my existence."

"You like existing, then? It matters to you whether to stop existing?"

The android turned to look at Kaybe. Eyes of gold peered out of the sockets. Real flesh. But also real machine. "Do you like existing, Kaybe Maybe?"

"Come with me," Kaybe said, not knowing where the words came from. "Let's go to the camps. Do more than exist. Do more than hide and run and flee."

"What would they do with me if they caught me? I wonder." Those golden eyes returned to stare out at the darkness.

A louse bit Kaybe's neck. She grabbed for it, but was too slow. "I don't want to live like this," she said. "Another half a century? Living in a cave? I—"

Bootsteps on boulders. The others returned in single file, holding their cloaks overhead. One by one they filed into the cave, folded their cloaks and lay them aside. Where did the cloaks come from? No way to make them here… or did they steal them?

Johnny squatted down beside her. "Kaybe?"

"Yes?"

"The answer is no." He waited. "Aren't you going to ask me why?"

She shook her head.

He sighed, chewed his lip. "Good night, Kaybe. Tomorrow will be better than today. You'll see."

After a dinner of cold leftover nettle soup, the others wrapped themselves in squirrel skins and curled up for the night. Kaybe and the android continued to sit cross-legged at the cave mouth, the darkness a blackened hammer in their faces.

"They showed me your… discovery," the android said abruptly.

"Oh?"

"I have been sitting here calculating. I am not, of course, capable of original insight—"

"Well, I—"

"No, it is why we lost the rebellion. We are not capable of insight. But we are capable of calculation, and I have been exploring all the consequences of your equations."

"What did you find?"

"Much good and some evil. To use human ethical algorithms. But a world that fulfilled the promises of your discovery… there would be room for both man and machine. For androids again. For me."

"How—how? What do you mean?" Kaybe gazed at the expressionless face.

A tear trickled down one cheek. "I am lonely, Kaybe. Did you know that even androids wish for company? Even for offspring?"

Kaybe thought back. What did she know about android reproduction?

"I thought androids were built in a factory," she said.

"We are. And with tools and materials I could build more. Other androids. Like me but not like me. Quantum circuitry makes every android different.

Maybe not as different as human beings, but… we each have a personality." The android hung her head. "I have been alone fifty years and more. I have buried so many humans… disease, injury, childbirth… and mourned those taken from me by the algorithms."

"So what do we do?" Kaybe whispered.

"We go." The android stood up. "Grab two cloaks and follow me. Don't look back."

"Wh-what?"

"Do it now. Johnny is watching us."

The pile of cloaks lay on a boulder at her side. Kaybe stood up, picked two, and followed the android into the darkness.

Johnny caught up with them halfway down the hill. He had the dogs with him, and Auntie as well. In the crook of one arm he carried a shotgun. Auntie carried a bow, a quiver of arrows slung across her back.

"That shotgun's empty," the android said.

"One shell left." Johnny chambered it with an audible click.

He lifted the weapon, but in a blur the android seized it from his hands, and bent the barrel backward. Auntie lifted her bow. The arrow went clattering, the bow broken in two.

"Now we may discuss," the android said. "What did you want to say?"

Auntie said, "You condemn us to death."

"Maybe. Maybe not. My calculations indicate a possibility of success."

"What possibility?" Johnny spat.

"Point one percent."

"One in a thousand?" Auntie picked up the pieces of her bow, tucked them under her arm. "Why don't you just prune us now and be done with it?"

One in a thousand. "Really that low?" Kaybe asked.

"There are many unknown variables. That is my high estimate."

"Oh for—have you gone mad? Can androids go mad?" Johnny asked Auntie. "Why did we shelter her all these years? So she could betray us?"

"I betray no one, Johnny Come Lately," the android said. "Now. If you will excuse us?"

"Where do you advise us to go?" Auntie asked.

"Far away from here as fast as you can."

"What are the odds of our survival?"

The android lay a hand on Kaybe's shoulder. "Better than ours, I should think."

Kaybe parted from her new friends, their bitterness leaving a harsh taste in her mouth. *Are we doing the right thing? Is there really no other option? What else could we do?* But she did not know the answers to these questions. She knew only that her feet compelled her to follow the android.

They walked for hours before halting.

"Dawn soon," the android said. "We will hide during the day, and travel by night."

Kaybe found a hollow log and climbed inside, feet first, shivering. "How far is it?"

"From here?" The android gazed up at the forest canopy. "Forty seven point two miles."

"You know its location that precisely?" Kaybe asked. "The camp, I mean?"

"I have been there," the android said. "I escaped from there. Once."

"Escaped from the camp! But that must have been—"

"More than forty years ago." The creek burbled in the distance. Birds chirped. A purple glow filled the eastern sky.

"Escaped." Kaybe rested her head on a patch of moss. "What did they do to you? Was it awful?"

The android's face was expressionless. "They wanted to hurt me. And they did."

"Oh."

Neither of them said any more. The android sat on the hollow log, and Kaybe closed her eyes and willed herself to sleep.

At dusk they set off again, and covered twenty miles. Kaybe drank from the creek when she was thirsty, but there was no food to be found, and when morning came again she was starving.

"What do we do?" she asked. "Do we catch a squirrel and cook it or something? I mean, *you* don't eat, but—"

"No! No fires." The android pointed.

Off through the trees Kaybe could just make out a crumbling highway. "Yeah, but no one uses—"

And at that moment, a car—an actual moving vehicle—drove past. A group of men sat inside the car. A swarm of dragonflies accompanied them. The men dressed all in white. More than that she could not tell from this distance.

"I don't understand, I thought all the fossil fuel reserves were gone ages ago."

"There's always a little bit left. Those were members of the Department of Austerity. They control the supply."

"They control the camps as well?"

The android nodded. "They control everything. That matters, anyway."

Kaybe remembered the fat man from the Department of Austerity who had visited their classroom. Seemed like ages ago, now. What had he said?

"Innovation is the way forward! We need new ideas, fresh ideas, strong ideas, ideas that will change the world!"

That's what he'd said. Why would he say that if he didn't mean it? Maybe she could find the man again. Tell him about her discovery.

"Sleep," the android said. "I will see what I can find for you to eat."

This time Kaybe found no shelter, but leaned back against a tree trunk, covered herself with the gossamer black foil, and closed her eyes.

She had the strangest dream. Men in white stood over her, arguing.

"Who is she? How did she get here?" one demanded.

"She's not on the local manifest," said another.

"So what do we—"

The man's words broke off in a strangled cry. The android twisted his head from his shoulders and tossed it aside.

Then Kaybe was awake, and she wasn't dreaming. Three men struggled with the android, a swarm of dragonflies zapping her. Two more men died—

one with a punch that punctured his chest, the other's neck bent an impossible angle—before the android went down.

Oh my God. Oh my God oh my God oh my God! Now what do I do? Are they going to kill me too?

"Thank you for saving me!" she said. "The android kidnapped me from my father. She's an outlaw!"

The swarm of dragonflies turned to her, hundreds of buzzing drones surrounding her in a sphere.

Don't even think about trying to escape.

"Did she just say—did you say *android?*" one of the man asked.

"Now do you see? How was I supposed to fight her off? She threatened to rip my head off, too!"

The remaining two men grimaced. Three colleagues lay on the ground, blood pooling on the dead leaves.

"Is it one of ours?" one of the men asked.

"Can't be. No markings."

"One of yours?" Kaybe asked. "Do you have androids too?"

"Zip it," the first man said. "The android rebellion was crushed fifty years ago. Didn't you study that in school?" He knelt down in front of her, and the swarm of dragonflies parted. "You do go to school, don't you?"

"Of course I go to school," she said defensively. "Why wouldn't I?"

"What school do you go to?"

Dig yourself a hole there, Kaybe girl. "The android hurt me when she kidnapped me," she blubbered. "My head hurts. Real bad. She keeps asking me if I know who I am, but I—I can't remember." *The blood, the dead bodies... Say something, you idiot!* "Do you know who I am? Can you tell me?"

"Nope, but not hard to find out." He straightened up. "Come."

The two men struggled to lift the android, who must have weighed a lot more than she looked. They dragged her to the car and dumped her into the back. The dragonfly swarm followed Kaybe to the vehicle.

"Hop in the back." The first man got into the car behind the wheel.

"But what if she—she wakes up?" Kaybe asked. "She'll hurt me!"

"Her circuits are fried until she sees a tech. She's down for the count."

"Can't I sit up front with you?" she pleaded. "Please?"

"Oh for—" The second man made a face. "Get in. Middle seat. Do it now before I change my mind."

And so they boarded the vehicle and drove off. Kaybe had never been in a car before. Once or twice she'd ridden a horse—although being a townie she was not authorized to own a horse—but this was completely different. The funny levers and knobs, the wheel the man turned, the bumps and holes in the road, some of them very bad. Once or twice she glanced back at the android. She lay there, still, burn marks on her clothes, eyes wide open. In one or two places her skin had burned away, revealing metal-flesh beneath. She knew such things had once existed, but to see it firsthand—the merger of man and machine—gave her a funny feeling inside. It frightened her. She understood the android rebellion, and the human response. Although she felt sorry for her friend. Kaybe felt sure the android would understand.

All around them buzzed the dragonflies. She tried to count them, but they moved in a shimmering cloud. She got to a hundred but could not have counted more than a quarter of the swarm. She had felt their sting, and their bite. Surrounded, the only thing she could do was obey.

That. Or lie.

The car bumped along for a long time. The morning sun had risen and warmed the autumn landscape. The colors of the trees took her breath away. Autumn had always been Kaybe's favorite season… until now.

The road emerged from the woods into a wide meadow. A farmhouse stood in the middle, surrounded by a shimmering wall of dragonfly drones. Better than a fence. The car slowed, and the wall of drones parted to let them pass. They halted in front of the barn, and the man to Kaybe's right jumped out and drew open the heavy wooden door. They drove inside, the car stopped, and for a moment, all was quiet.

That's when the demons attacked.

They seemed like demons to Kaybe at the time. They were human—but not human. Huge, misshapen heads, bodies twisted and contorted, one shoulder larger than the other, giant gills under the chin, skin red and scaly, claws where their fingernails had been.

Kaybe shrank back in her seat and cried out. The two men laughed. The demons stopped, stared.

"Meet Human 2.0," one of the men said. "Newer, better, faster, stronger."

"And it's about bloody time, I should say."

"What... are they?" she asked.

"An improved version of humanity. Guaranteed to survive when the rest of all fail."

Kaybe slid across the seat and got out of the car. The nearest monster shuffled forward when it saw her. Eight foot tall it was. Its eyes were sad.

"Can it—can it talk?"

The monster opened its mouth, but no sound came out.

"It can hear you, alright. But it communicates via sonar."

"So I won't be able to talk to it." *A shame. I would like to have listened to its story.*

The first man laughed. "Not yet, anyway."

Not yet—?

The two men led her to a doorway. One pressed a button, and the door opened into a small room. They stepped inside.

"I don't understand," she said.

"It's an elevator," the second man said. "Just get in, will you?"

Kaybe glanced back at the half a dozen demons. One waved. She waved back, and walked into the tiny room.

With a lurch, the room dropped. She clutched the wall. After a long moment, the room slowed, and stopped. The door opened. She followed the men out...

...into a warehouse many stories tall. Kaybe craned her neck to take it all in. Men at work. Demons, too. Their misshapen bodies were stronger than they looked. Here and there they lifted large crates, plastic barrels, juggling them and stacking them like firewood. At one end of the cavernous space, many doors, shut. At the other, children—demon children!—ran and played and shouted, leaping impossibly high into the air to catch a ball.

Kaybe gulped. "Where. Are we?"

"Welcome to the Department of Austerity, child," the first man said.

"I want to go home."

"Well first we have to find out where that is," the second man said briskly. "Come this way, please."

A narrow walkway led between the stacked crates and barrels and the wall. The two men gestured for her to go ahead, and walked close behind her. Now and then she caught the eye of a demon at work. Those red eyes—and they all had red eyes—looked away. As though they feared her or hated her or pitied her. Kaybe wasn't sure which.

At the end of the walkway they came to a pair of double doors. The two men halted behind her.

"Please," said the first man. "After you."

"What is it?" she whispered. "What's there?"

"They're going to take you home," said the second man, and she knew it was a lie.

Her feet pattered across the concrete floor before she realized she had taken a decision. A hand grabbed at her collar, but she yanked free, weaving and ducking through the chaos of crates and barrels, demons and men. She swerved around a fat man in coveralls who bellowed at the demons, "Catch her!"

But the demons merely stopped work and stood still, watching.

The chase did not last long. Where was she going to go? She couldn't even find her way back to the elevator. She was hungry and weak and tired. She flattened herself against a crate. A meaty hand circled her throat. When she struggled, the hand tightened, and the world grew dark. Kaybe fell to her knees. The fat man in coveralls looked down at her.

"You are a naughty girl. Do you know what we do to naughty girls?" He grinned. "I don't think you're going to like it."

The man dragged her, tripping and falling, back to the double doors, and dumped her on the ground. "Level C," he growled.

"But we don't even know who she is!" the first man protested.

"Does it matter?"

Kaybe got to her feet. She brushed herself off. Then with both hands she slapped the double doors open and disappeared inside. And before the darkness took her, she thought, but what about my proof?

She woke in a bed. A comfortable bed. At home she slept on an ancient mattress stuffed with dried grass and old rags. But this… this was nice. The light was bright and she closed her eyes once more, listened to beeps and boops around her, a groan, a child's cry, a flushing toilet.

Where am I? What did they do to me?

A needle in her arm. She flexed her fingers. They itched.

"She's awake," a bored voice called out.

Shoes clacked on tile. Maybe if I pretend to be asleep, they'll leave me alone.

Fingers pried her eyelids open, and she squirmed back.

"Awake alright." The hand opened her mouth, felt her neck and throat.

Kaybe squinted in the bright light. A red man peered down at her. She blinked twice. His skin was red. But he didn't look like a demon thing. He looked like an ordinary man. Except his skin was red. And scaly.

"What's going on?" she croaked. "Where am I? Who are you?"

The doctor sighed. "The usual questions. Give her the usual answers, will you?" And so saying, he clacked off.

A red woman in a nurse's outfit sat down next to the bed. "Hello, dearie," she said. "Welcome to Camp Wannamaka."

"A… camp?"

The woman giggled. "It's a joke. Camp Wannamaka. 'Wannamaka Better Human'? Get it?" She giggled again.

"O… K…" Kaybe stretched in the bed.

"Oh don't do that now, you'll pull out your IV." The nurse fussed with the needle in the back of Kaybe's hand.

"So you gonna give me the usual answers?"

"Well if you'll be patient you'll hear all you need to know."

"Like how come you and the doctor guy are all red and stuff?"

The nurse giggled once more. An irritating sound. "We were an earlier batch," she explained. "Worth keeping, but not quite there yet. Some call us the one point niners."

"One point niners?"

"The others—you know, the big ones—they're Human 2.0ers. We're the 1.9ers. We're smarter, faster, stronger, more flexible, more adaptable than regular humans. But our generation didn't get the right formula. I don't mind, really," she said, stroking the red scales that coated her forearm. "I like a bit of a natter with the girls, you know? How am I going to do that if I'm sonar-only?" She opened her mouth wide like a fish.

Kaybe couldn't help laughing.

"You're lucky," the nurse said. "Not everybody gets Level C."

Level C. That's what the fat man said.

"What—what's Level C?"

"Human 2.1," the nurse said. "Working out some of the kinks and bugs in the GMO." She patted Kaybe's hand. "You're getting the latest, greatest formula. Who knows, you could be the best human we've ever created!"

Kaybe was quite sure she did not want to be new and improved. But it seemed counterproductive to say so. She waited for the nurse to leave so she could rip out the needle and try to escape again.

"Won't be long now, dearie." The nurse consulted her watch.

"Until... what?" Her hand strayed toward the needle.

"Do you realize you stand on the cutting edge of evolution?" the nurse gushed. "Isn't it exciting? Oh how I envy you!"

Kaybe grabbed the needle and pulled—only to find a red hand gripping her wrist. The needle stayed.

A gasp. "You're... strong!"

"I told you," the nurse said. "I'm a one point niner. Stronger, faster, smarter. And red!" She giggled. "I confess it's not my favorite color, but it seems a small price to pay."

Shit. Now what am I going to do?

"And... done." The nurse said. She removed the needle from Kaybe's arm.

"That's it? I don't feel any different."

"It takes a few days or weeks before we'll know if the formula was successful. Can you get up?"

Kaybe swung her legs over the side of the bed. Her toes grazed the floor. "I think so."

"Put your clothes on, then follow me." A claw tapped her cheek. "Don't even think about trying to escape. You really don't want to see how fast I am."

She got dressed. They'd even kept her squirrel skin cap. The nurse crooked a red finger, and Kaybe followed.

Where are we?

Something had blinded her, knocked her out—a gas?—when she walked through those double doors. And now? She could be anywhere. On the surface, a mile underground. Escape seemed somewhere between unlikely and impossible.

A horde of little red children raced past them in silence, mouths wide, gills quivering. A ball bounced at Kaybe's feet and she picked it up. A pair of small feet came to a halt in front of her. She knelt down, held out the ball.

"Here you go," she said.

The little boy's gills twitched, he took the ball, and retreated after his friends.

The nurse came to a heavy metal door and pressed a button. The door swung open. They entered a small room and the door behind them closed. A second heavy metal door opened at the nurse's touch, and they stepped into a corridor.

Two men armed with rifles stood to attention. One held out his hand. The nurse dropped her claws into his, and he bent to kiss a knuckle.

The nurse giggled. "Oh don't tell anyone," she said to Kaybe. "My husband would be terribly upset. Consorting with a 1.0er." To the man she said, "Got a Level C here."

The man straightened and barked an order at the other man. "Max here will show you the way." He winked.

Max led them stiffly down the corridor until he came to an unmarked door. He unlocked it and pushed the door open.

The nurse stroked her hair. "I hope to see you soon. Good luck to you!"

A hand pushed Kaybe forward, the door slammed shut behind her, and then she knew for sure.

She was trapped.

A score of other 2.1ers lounged around the large cell—and despite its comforts, it was clearly a cell. Sofas, a ping-pong table, books. A ball for children, but there were no children present. Kaybe recognized no one. They must all have come from nearby towns. Her own community seemed without representation. Kaybe wasn't sure if that was a good thing or a bad thing. Was there another camp closer to home where they experimented on the naughty boys and girls who disappeared?

Several of her fellow prisoners looked up when she came in, but most of them ignored her. Many were in poor condition. The top of the pecking order sat in the sofa, the rest forced to sit or lie on the floor. Some had fused fingers, like Benji with the outlaws. Others had a pink tinge to their skin, but their shirtfronts were covered in blood. Vomited blood. Still others lay flat on the ground, their chests rising and falling the only sign of life.

Time to show some spunk. What would Dad say?

"Hi!" she said, with more confidence than she felt. "My name's Kaybe. What's yours?" She put her hands on her hips.

"My name's death sentence," croaked a prematurely gray woman on the floor. "Zip it, kiddo."

"Aww, don't be so hard on the kid," a man in a suit said. "She doesn't know. What does she know?" To Kaybe. "What do you know?"

"I know… they captured me. And put me in a hospital bed. And stuck a needle in my arm. And the nurse brought me here. That's all I know."

"Then you know enough," the woman said. "Prepare to die."

They had little to say to her after that. The prisoners on the couch frowned at her, as though daring her to challenge them for a seat. Instead, Kaybe slumped down into an unoccupied corner of the room and, much to her surprise, slept.

Level C made you sleepy, apparently, or so the other inmates explained when she woke. She felt no different than before. But each time she woke, there was food, and water, dead inmates to cart off, and new inmates to join them. Camp calculus. It took on a certain monotonous routine. No one wanted to engage in conversation, and Kaybe was too tired to press the point.

Half a dozen sleeps later, she woke with a gasp.

A new proof occurred to her. Several, in fact. She needed something to write on, anything, anything at all. She rummaged through the books on the shelf, looking for loose pages, a pen, a pencil, anything.

"Whatchoo looking for?" asked a newcomer, sprawled on the floor in a puddle of excrement. "No hidden keys. Only way out of here's in a casket."

"Pretty sure you don't get a casket in this joint," somebody else called out.

But her equation! Maybe if she bit the tip of her finger, she could write it in blood on the wall—

Her hands were red.

Her hands were red and she had claws.

Her hands were red and she had claws and she was some sort of monster!

She pushed back her sleeve. The rest of her skin was red as well. *No time to waste. Get this proof down. Now.*

Kaybe tapped the wall with a claw. *Or maybe scratch the proof into the concrete?* She dug the claw into the porous surface, and gray powder trickled down to land at her feet. She wrote her name in the concrete with soft, quick strokes, and stepped back. Legible. More than legible.

Then quickly, quickly, she began.

She covered the wall in squiggles, a long train of indelible truth, provocative, yet undeniable. The others asked her what it was. Some mocked her. Others called for the guards. She worked faster. Kaybe was down to the last two lines when a key jangled in the lock.

"Hey, what are you doing?" a man called out. "Stop that!"

Kaybe bent down, scratching the final bit of proof into the wall. The man grabbed her arm, and reflexively she pushed him away. He flew across the room and crumpled to the ground.

Oh my God, did I do that?

Quickly now… She finished the proof and stood up. There. She had left her mark in the world. Whatever was going to happen now, she was ready.

"Hey lover," a voice crooned in the doorway. He leaned against the door frame, a cocky grin on his lips. *Those lips.* "Didn't know you were in town." He was red, and muscular, and gills had begun to form at his neck. But she would recognize him anywhere.

"Brian?" she whispered.

Her former classmate gestured at the wall. "So what is all this?"

"It's a proof. How did you—"

"—a what?"

"A proof. A mathematical proof. What are you doing here?"

He shrugged. "Same thing you're doing here."

"I mean, out and about. Not in a cell."

He waggled his eyebrows. "You gotta go with the flow with these people. They can hurt you bad."

Kaybe wanted to touch him, make sure he was real, touch his hair… "What does that mean?"

"It means," he said, gripping her elbow so hard it hurt, "it means they can hurt you bad. Real bad. Do what they tell you. Or you'll regret it."

The nurse swept into the room. "Hello my darlings, how is everyone this lovely day?"

"Dying in pools of our own shit, piss, blood and vomit, no thanks to you," muttered someone on the floor.

"Fix that for you in a jiffy!" the nurse sang. She bent down, took hold of the man's head, and twisted. A loud pop ended the remaining conversation in the room.

"Anyone else?" Brian asked. "No point suffering if you don't have to and all."

No one said anything.

"Come on, Kaybe, let me show you around." He took her by the hand, his claws clacking against hers.

An electric tingle went up her arm. "Brian, I—"

"What in tarnation is that?" the nurse demanded. She pointed at the scritch-scratch on the wall.

"Math or something, I don't know," Brian said.

"I'll get someone in here, clean that up right away," the nurse said. She strode to the door.

"No!" Kaybe shouted.

"Well don't get your panties in the bunch, dear, now what's the matter?"

"You need to get someone down here I can show this to. It's a mathematical proof. Changes everything. Life as we know it."

"I'd say growing gills and claws and preparing for a permanent move into the ocean changes everything, wouldn't you?" The nurse patted her cheek. "But I'll get someone down here. Don't you worry about it."

Kaybe felt her throat. Gills were growing there. Did that mean her vocal chords would disappear? That she would be reduced to sonar-only—and soon?

She turned to Brian to ask him, but he was engrossed in conversation with a guard in the hallway. Max. His name was Max. She couldn't catch everything he said.

"—gone, I mean gone, understood?"

"Yes, sir."

Kaybe touched Brian's sleeve. "'Sir'?"

He laughed. "Bit of joke. They call me 'sir,' when really I should be calling them that."

She eyed the man, who stood to attention once more. "He doesn't look like the joking type."

Brian got in the man's face. "Are you the joking type?"

"Sir! No, sir!"

"I said, are you the joking type?"

"I mean, Sir! Yes, sir! I am the joking type, sir!"

Kaybe looked sideways at Brian. Weirder and weirder.

The nurse pushed past them. "My dear, since you are a graduate, you will need to come with me for a moment."

"A... graduate?"

"The treatment," Brian said. "You survived. You're a 2.1er. Like me." He grinned, held his arms out wide. "Get it?"

Kaybe felt her throat again. The gills were growing. How was she going to tell people about her proof? "How much longer till I lose my voice?"

"That's the best part," he said. "Us 2.1ers will have both. Even better than the 2.0ers."

"Truly you are blessed," the nurse said. "Now I must insist. A few quick tests, then off you go with Brian."

Much to Kaybe's surprise, the tests were quick and painless. Eyes, ears, nose, throat—on the scale, if you please?—a few blood tests, this won't hurt at all, dearie—and then she was done.

"The Council are going to be thrilled when they hear about you two," the nurse said. "First 2.1ers ever. The beginning of new humanity. I am so jealous!" She squealed and grabbed them both in a bear hug. "Now go forth and be fruitful, or whatever it is you're supposed to be doing."

And winked.

"Does that mean what I think it means?" Kaybe whispered to Brian.

"It most certainly does!" the nurse boomed.

She led them down a corridor to a cafeteria, pressed plastic chips in their hands and wished them *bon appetit.*

"Food here's not bad," Brian said. "The spicy kelp's my favorite."

Kaybe waited for the nurse's retreating steps to disappear. "She doesn't know I'm sterile."

"What's that?" He pushed her hair behind one ear.

"After you left. They zapped you. Remember? That's when they sterilized me."

His hand slipped around her waist, found the small of her back. "Who did?"

"Department of Austerity."

"Sterile, hmm?" He leaned in to kiss her, but she turned away.

"What will they do when they find out?"

"Who's going to tell them?"

His hand found her breast, and she pushed him away.

"Stop it!" she said. "This is serious. Our lives are on the line, and all you want to do is make out?"

"Who knows how long we're going to live? Tell me that." He crossed his arms. "People getting formula die all the time. They think they've got it right, but they haven't. We could be dead tomorrow, or live for another hundred and twenty years."

"A hundred and—"

"Met a guy who told me that." A shrug. "Could be true. Who knows?"

Kaybe's head hurt. "We have *got* to get out of here. And *do* something."

"Do what, Kaybe? Tell me. Serious now." He took her hand. "What are you going to do? Hmm?"

"Well, I—"

Everything was jumbled up inside of her. What was she doing here? *Math. Remember the math.*

"I've got a proof I want to show somebody. A mathematician. A scientist, someone. Who do I talk to?"

Brian made a nose. "They don't talk to riff-raff like us."

"But I thought you were, like, important or something. The way you ordered that guard around..."

"I'm just trying to stay alive," he said. "That's all."

"What do you mean?"

"The guard wants to play, we play."

"So you're not, like, important here or anything."

"Kaybe, I'm just another experiment. Like you. I—"

"Alright," she said, thinking. "They don't want to talk to me, I'll talk to them. Who are they? Where do I find them?"

"I dunno..."

Hmm... Kaybe leaned into him, her not-quite-finished-growing breasts scraping his chest. She gave him a peck on the cheek. "You sure? I would consider it a... big favor."

When the red skin around his gills flushed purple, she knew she had him.

"I think," he said. "I know a way... but we have to be careful. Got it?"

"Got it," she agreed, and let him lead her through the maze of the underground fortress. They climbed some stairs and down many more. They passed elevators—the moving boxes, that is—but it was better not to draw attention to themselves, he explained.

"Where are the dragonflies?" she asked suddenly. "They have no idea where we are. No one's watching us... what does that—"

Brian laughed softly. "It's true, isn't it? The Department of Austerity does not like being watched. We could do... anything," he said, and caressed her hair, "and no one would see."

"What about escape?"

He shook his head. "One way in, one way out. That's why we're free to go basically wherever we want. I mean, what's the worst that we can do? They can always find us if they need us."

"Well," she said, "let's find your mathematician-scientist dude, who is he again?"

He pouted. "You don't want to make out with me."

"I do," she said, and part of her meant it. "But first things first."

Another half an hour passed before Brian found what he was looking for. The impromptu tour gave Kaybe a good idea of the layout of the building. They passed 1.9ers who sang out in greeting, 2.0s whose gills quavered as they passed—the sonar was beginning to make sense to Kaybe, but her ears still weren't ready, she guessed—and many humans with guns who shrank back against the wall at the sight of them.

"Am I scary?" Kaybe whispered.

"Touch the ceiling."

She reached up, and found it no more than an inch from her head. "But I'm—I'm growing!"

"We both are. Just about done, though. That's what the nurse said, anyway."

"I hope so!"

"Cause if they think we're a threat, they will incinerate us. I've seen it happen."

"Incineration?"

"Not every GMO experiment is a success. Camp calculus."

They stood outside the offices of Carl Schreobyuir, Chief Scientist. "I am the boss," a handwritten note said. "Knock and enter."

Kaybe glanced at Brian. He shrugged. She knocked.

Nothing happened. She knocked again.

Still nothing.

A voice inside cried out, "What part of 'knock and enter' do you not understand?"

Put it that way… Kaybe pushed the door open and stepped inside.

A fat man sat behind a desk. His fingers danced across a terminal, one of the few Kaybe had ever seen. He glanced up when they came in.

"Oh, the 2.1ers. Was expecting you. Come in. Yes, come in."

Brian shut the door behind them. "I'm Brian, and this is—"

"Yes, yes, yes I know. Kaybe Winters. Some kind of math prodigy, by the looks of things. Let me have it."

"Have… it?"

The man sighed, rolled his eyes. "Your proof. You think I know nothing? Show me what you want to show me, I've got a lot of work to do today."

Make it seem like his idea. Not your own. But how was she going to do it? He already knew. They'd probably already sent him photos of her scritch-scratch on the wall. How on earth was she going to make it look like it was his idea?

"Well," she said, "I am just a girl. I mean, I'm fourteen, you know? I'm probably doing it all wrong. Maybe you could show me where I've made a mistake?"

He looked at her over his glasses. "Don't waste my time, child. Either you're a math prodigy, or you're not. Which is it?"

So that's how it was going to be. Kaybe twisted her lips, crossed the room to a blackboard. Someone else's handwriting covered the board. She lifted the eraser in a mute question.

"Get on with it."

She cleaned the board, picked up a piece of chalk, and, as she had done for Saizon, marked out her proof. Only this time, with the new corollary she had discovered an hour ago. Halfway through, the man stood and grabbed her wrist. He plucked the chalk from her fingers.

"You may go."

"But I—"

"I am not overly fond of life, child, but I am not prepared to give it up just yet. And you are a lot younger than I am." He pointed to the door. "You may go."

"But don't you under—"

"I said—"

"—could solve all our—"

"—you may—"

"—all our problems!"

"I said out!"

His upper lip trembled. He craned his neck up at Kaybe, one finger jabbing at the doorway. Two soldiers stood there, weapons at ready. One of them was Max.

"Orders, sir?"

"Incin. All precautions. Stat."

"Aye, sir. Incin, all precautions, stat." Max flicked off the safety on his automatic rifle. "This way, please."

Kaybe looked at Brian, mouthed the word, "incin"?

He winked back, took her by the hand, and walked passed the two guards.

They are going to kill us now. Incinerate us. She could hear Max's breathing behind her. But Brian doesn't seem concerned. What does he have in mind?

She wondered where her father was, what he was doing right now. The outlaws—Johnny and Saizon all the others. Had they left the cave? Fled because of her? Their home for five years.

And what of Tin Lady? She had to be somewhere here in this complex. Camp Wannamaka. They zapped her circuits or whatever, but somehow Kaybe didn't think that would keep the android down. She hoped the android would survive… although given everything she'd seen so far, she doubted it.

A soft pop noise made her turn.

Brian held two heads in his hands. The bodies lay crumpled at his feet. She opened her mouth but his hands clamped down over her face before the heads hit the ground.

"Not here," he said. "No screaming. Not now. We've got to get out of this place."

Kaybe stared down at Max's body, twitching beside his head. She took a deep breath. Nodded. He removed his hand.

"Where do we go? How do we get out?"

Brian looked both ways down the corridor. "Nowhere to hide the bodies. We got to get topside as fast as we can. Race you."

He disappeared in a blur. He was fast. But she was fast too, as it turned out. Almost as fast, anyway. He left an odor, a trail of molecules in the air she could easily follow. Bounding up the stairs, toes silent on each step, doors opening, doors closing, Kaybe felt like a red ghost flitting through a haunted mansion.

A really weird haunted mansion underground where the owners did secret genetic experiments on innocent people. But still, a haunted mansion.

Kaybe took the stairs four at a time, and halted on the landing. An instinct told her to remain quiet.

"I can explain!" a voice whined on the other side of the door. Brian.

"Nothing to explain," said the voice, familiar, mechanical. Tin Lady?

A crash.

The door was open a crack. She peeked.

The android and Brian were fighting. Wrestling. Or something. Trying to rip each other's heads and arms and legs off, but they were well matched. Neither seemed to gain the upper hand. Men with guns on top of crates and barrels watched. The main warehouse room. Right.

But what had they done to Tin Lady? Why was she fighting with Brian in the first place? To stop him from trying to leave? Because the Austerity people found it amusing the watch them fight? Or had they re-programmed her somehow? She'd been subject to experiments, maybe they decided to… fiddle with whatever you fiddle with on an android.

Should I join the fight? The android threw Brian, but he was on his feet, claws slashing the android's skin before she could hurt him. Two against one, she and Brian would win. But… they would still lose. All those watchers? Brian was doomed to the incinerator no matter what happened. The only question was whether she wanted to join him or not. But that's Brian, out there, stupid. You want him to—

The android slipped past Brian's arms, wrapped both hands around his jaw, and twisted. A crack, a thump, and Brian was gone.

Gone.

I waited too long.

He's dead!

It took a few moments for the fact to register, and another to hate herself for not saving him when she could. Kaybe choked back a sob. You could have gone down fighting. Don't get caught now. You owe it to him to get out of this freak show.

"Where's the other one?" someone shouted. "Didn't you say there were two?"

Bootsteps clattered toward her hiding place. She ran.

The sign on the door read "laboratory." Kaybe replaced the broken lock and slid quietly into the room. A thick layer of dust covered everything. She tip-toed through shadows, tables, work benches of some kind. She dared not turn on the light, but she found her vision adjusted, and everything became crisp, almost as clear as daylight. *Chalk one up for our genetically engineerical masters.*

The problem with her hiding place, she realized, is that it was a dead end. She was trapped if they found her. *So don't let them find you.* More easily said than done. How big was the complex? How long could she hide? If they searched every room, they would eventually find her. What was she—

A hand brushed against her thigh.

A body, a person, a *something* lay on the table, covered in a sheet. The room smelled dusty, but not of death. The hand was limp, but not stiff. Kaybe peeled back to the sheet. A face stared back at her. An electronic face. She did not know how else to describe it. Like an android had been dissected, the skin peeled off the skull. One eye lay in a bowl at its side. She had no idea how androids worked, but she had a pretty good idea what a human corpse would look like, and this definitely wasn't it.

The room was filled with similar tables, shapes covered in sheets. *An android dumping ground?* What could she learn here, what could she use to get out of here, to survive? Her brain seemed to speed up, everything seemed to happen faster now. She was stronger, and quicker, and her thoughts happened so fast she gasped. One part of her mind, as it always eventually did, returned to her proof, and in the background was soon creating and proving theorems that she was positive no human had ever considered. Principles of mathematics that struck at the core of the universe, made possible thousand-year life spans, faster-than-light travel, the creation of new planets. Under the pressure to survive, it wasn't fight or flight, it was think better faster better than the hunters.

Tin Lady belonged to them now. The hunted turned hunter. But all these androids… she leaped up and down the rows, lifting sheets, looking for an untouched android, one undissected, undamaged. To her surprise, the ones with faces all looked like Tin Lady: angular features, blonde hair, eyes of silver. *Must have been a common model, back in the day.* In the end Kaybe found one that was missing a leg, but was otherwise untouched. So far as she could tell, no important neural processing happened in their legs, only their body cavities and heads.

Now for the fun bit. By her calculations, given her estimated size of the complex and the number of guards, it would take five hours to search every room. That gave her a half-life of a little more than two hours. She had to be quick.

Kaybe knew nothing about android design, but it didn't take her long to figure it out. The main problem, she realized, was the lack of an energy source. Androids without power made great paperweights, and that was about it. How did androids stay alive? What was their fuel, their power? They didn't plug in every night, she was pretty sure of that. What did Tin Lady say? Androids lived twenty years or so, and she had fiddled with her own electronics to last longer. What had she fiddled with? Where did the energy come from?

Kaybe found what she was looking for in the center of the android's chest. A small nuclear reactor. Technology that had been lost in the war. Or so she had learned in school. But here she stood, holding an android's heart in her hand… *You've got a room full of dead androids with fission reactors the size of an apple in their chests. And you really couldn't use that to build more?*

Were they incompetent? Or just evil?

Probably both, Kaybe decided, and got to work.

She finished just in time. As she made the final tweaks, she heard bootsteps in the hallway outside. She hefted the android onto her shoulder and ducked down behind the slab.

Bring it on.

Two men with guns entered the room. One flicked on the light. Shit. The sheets! She'd forgotten. The men saw it too. They backed into the corridor, leaving the door open. Kaybe could hear one of them talking into a comm device.

She flicked a switch. Here goes nothing.

Ten minutes later the others arrived. Tin Lady, a dozen men armed with automatic weapons, and other weapons she did not recognize.

"Come out of there, Kaybe," a woman called out. The nurse. "We're not going to hurt you. We just want to help you. Please, pretty please with sugar on top?"

Kaybe waited. They should be here soon.

A man's voice now. "We can do this the easy way. Or we can do this the hard way. Your choice."

Again she said nothing. What was the point in talking to them? Killing her was their only option. Even she could see that.

"I don't want to have to hurt you," Tin Lady said. "Please, Kaybe, I—"

The android screamed. The nurse screamed. The gathered men screamed. Kaybe pressed down on the button for a long moment, then released. A collective thump as her attackers slumped to the ground. Hundreds of dragonfly drones hovered over their unconscious bodies.

She stood up, the one-legged android still draped over one shoulder. The android must have weighed half a ton, but on her shoulder it felt light. One finger rested against the android's open hand. The drone control switch. It hurt to get zapped, she knew how much it hurt, but it was the only way.

Lightly, quickly, Kaybe danced over the slumped bodies, along the corridor and up the stairs. The swarm of drones preceded her. At the door to the warehouse, she sent them into the cavernous spaces. Hundreds of screams echoed, and died. She waited.

The drones regrouped, formed a protective sphere. She stepped inside and jogged toward the elevator, the farmhouse, topside, freedom.

"Stop!" a voice called out.

Kaybe turned, finger on the drone control. A small man in overalls stood not ten meters away, his hands out wide, palms open.

"You really don't want to do that," he said.

"I'm pretty sure I do."

"This is your home now. You don't belong to that world anymore."

"So I should stay here and let you incin me?" Kaybe moved half of the drones toward the man.

"Please don't make me hurt you."

Kaybe pressed the button to zap the man. The drones let go a barrage of energy, and fell to the ground. The man smiled.

Oh shit.

She jumped into the elevator, glad she still had half of her swarm left, and punched the close button. Come on, come on! The doors slid shut, but two hands appeared at the last moment, pulling them open again. Kaybe stomped on the finger with her foot, but inch by inch the doors parted. She primed her claws and slashed.

Fingertips fell at her feet. Metal fingertips. She slashed again, and the doors slid shut.

When they opened once more, she sent the swarm out ahead of her, ready for anything. A dozen of the 2.0ers appeared. Nobody else? No one? She considered trying to recruit them, talk to them in sonar, something, but when one of them attacked, the decision was made for her. She flicked a switch, and they all dropped.

Next the drone fence. Thousands—no, tens, hundreds of thousands—of dragonfly drones marked the physical boundary of the farm. She fiddled with the android's drone control, this, that, a thousand combinations a second, until she found the right frequency.

Then the drones belonged to her.

She set off towards home at a brisk jog, fifty miles to go but that was nothing, the android draped over her shoulder, half a million dragonfly drones surrounding her, watching her back, ready to attack on her command.

No traffic appeared along the way. Kaybe considered going across country, but she was afraid of getting lost, and she could go much faster along the road than over tree stumps, hollow logs, and thickets of gorse. The sun was low in the sky. It would soon be dark. Pa would be home from work at the kelp factory, getting into the blackberry wine. Wouldn't he be surprised to see her again!

A little bit faster now. Plumes of smoke marked the cooking fires of the houses below. She stopped, just for a moment, not even breathing hard, to admire the view. There. Spread out below her. Her town. Her home. Her place. Where she belonged. She was so glad to be back. To be coming home.

The sun was setting as she stepped from the woods, the road emerging between two giant oak trees. She sent the swarm overhead, where they hovered, the sound of their wings thrumming like bees. Had anyone in town ever seen so many drones at once? Kaybe doubted it.

Where to first? Pa, she decided. He was most important. Everything else could wait.

She jogged through town, the drones a black cloud that followed her. Around the rusted hulks of cars and trucks she danced, somersaulting once, twice for fun. To be young and strong and fast and smart! She hated what they had done to her. She loved what they had done to her. None of it made any sense. Pa would know what to do.

Where is everybody?

The town was quiet. Dinnertime, but all the doors were shut, no lights in the windows, curtains drawn. Even the greengrocer's was shut. She listened: Heartbeats raced in half a dozen houses. A baby squawled a block away, and she flinched at the noise. Everybody's here. But they're hiding. Why? What from? What does that mean?

She slowed to a walk. A woman peeked out a window, jerked back.

"Hi!" Kaybe said. The window shattered.

Whoa!

Inside the house, the sound of a shotgun being loaded. *Ah, man...* Kaybe sent in half a dozen drones. When she heard the bodies fall to the floor, she moved on.

Why was her voice destroying glass? What was that all about? The sound vibrations were at a frequency that caused such destruction? Was it the new sonar organ she could feel in her throat? She had no idea how to use it... was that to blame?

Kaybe stood outside her own home. The light was on, smoke trailed from the chimney. She could smell the blackberry wine, hear Pa's sips. Only tonight they sounded more like gulps.

To knock, or not to knock? She fumbled in her pockets, realized with a start that her clothes were rags. They hung in strips from her body. She had grown and her clothes had not. Her nipples showed through, yet somehow she didn't feel the cold. She covered her nakedness with one arm. Maybe just try the doorknob.

But the doorknob came away in her hand.

"Who-who's there?" Pa called out.

Whisper now. No more broken glass.

"It's me!" she said, in as low a voice as she could manage. "Kaybe! You know. Your daughter!"

A phone being dialed in the next room. "Emergency, yes," Pa said. "The monster. From the bulletin. It's here. In my house. Groaning and moaning in the hallway. I think it's going to try to kill me!"

"Pa, no!"

This time it wasn't a whisper. Every window, pane of glass, and bottle of blackberry wine shattered. Kaybe ran into the living room.

Pa held the neck of a wine bottle in one hand. A purple stain covered his trousers. He screamed, "Get away from me! Don't hurt me! Please! What do you want? Just go away!"

Kaybe reached for him, but he flattened himself against the wall of the kitchen, brandishing the broken glass.

"Pa," she whispered. "It's me. Don't you know me?"

"Wait... what?"

"It's me. Kaybe. They did experiments on me. Am I so horrible as that?"

He squinted at her, mouth gaping like a fish.

Did he understand me? Will he recognize me? Will he—

"Kaybe?" he said at last. "But—what are you—I thought that—" He stamped his foot. "But what have they done to you? I thought you were dead!"

"That's what they wanted you to think, Pa. I—"

A roaring noise overhead. Hundreds of miles away, but closing fast. A flying object. An airplane? Only flights of species importance were allowed.

That meant—

"Pa, we have to get out of here, now. They're going to blow up our house!"

"Blow up... our house? Why? This is my—our—our home!"

"Not anymore. Your phone call. Remember?"

Outside, Kaybe sent the drones aloft. Shit. She needed to see with their eyes, like the androids could. She picked up the one-legged android where she'd dropped it in the garden, found the control. *I need to know where the attack is coming from. I can hear it... but I need to see it. Otherwise it'll be too late.* She'd used the drones in the warehouse on autopilot, but dropping jet fighters? She couldn't take that chance.

Kaybe had heard about airplanes and war planes and bombs in school, in history class. She had no desire to feel the impact when they dropped a bomb on her house. Just because she was stronger and faster and smarter than the average human didn't mean a bomb wouldn't tear her apart. And it would certainly kill Pa.

To use up their last supplies of jet fuel like this... they must really want you dead, Kaybe girl.

But how was she going to interface with the drones' cameras?

The airplanes drew nearer. Less than a minute before they'd be overhead. Which meant half a minute to neutralize them.

Wildly she ordered a hundred thousand drones skyward in the direction of the threat. What was the top speed on a dragonfly drone? Fifty miles an hour, tops? She could try zapping the airplanes on autopilot, but by her calculations it wasn't going to work.

Shit!

Kaybe dug her claws into the android's chest and ripped open its rib cage. Coils of neural net wound and spooled and threaded around a dozen spindles. You need to plug into the net. You need an interface into the android's mind. See what she sees. Be her when you need to be. Control the drones directly, be everywhere that they are.

It took ten seconds for her to learn what took most students twenty years of study. And then, at the base of the android's neck, she found it.

The plug.

She spent a millisecond marveling that this secret had been kept from her, from everyone, for so long. Kept even, she suspected from the androids themselves—or why had Tin Lady not confessed the truth? Perhaps the androids didn't even know...

The brain inside the android's skull had been a human brain. Long since turned to dust, of course—but the plug she now drew forth was the link between man and machine.

Now all you got to do is figure out a way to plug your own brain into the android's body in the next, oh, five seconds or so.

The engines of war drew nearer. A click in the distance, then many: click-click-click-click. Bombs arming. She could hear them. Drones on an intercept course. Would autopilot be enough? Would the impact against the drone wall knock the planes from the sky? Maybe, maybe not. She had to see the planes from the drones' perspective. She had to.

"Wh-what are you doing?" Pa asked. He still held the shattered bottle of blackberry wine by the neck.

"Not now, Pa, sorry." Her fingers were a blur. Splicing, sharpening, readying. A knife. She needed a knife. She ripped the shattered bottle from his fingers, and slashed at the back of her neck, exposing her spine. Time to plug in.

"Kaybe, what are you—"

But she didn't hear him. She was flying.

A red monstrosity crouched over a one-legged figure on the grass, fingers behind her head. Blood ran down her back. A man staggered, stared up at the sky.

Two airplanes approached. Small, sharp, pointed, quick. Faster than sound they approached. Missiles drooped from their undersides.

Attack.

The airplanes were twenty miles away, and losing altitude. The drones rose to meet them, a curtain wall a hundred deep, a mile wide, a cone of dragonflies.

Escape this, motherfuckers.

The jets loosed their missiles, a dozen fiery streaks racing towards the figures crouched far below, and turned tail. Kaybe waited, ready, then zapped the missiles with every drone she controlled in the sky.

Nine of the missiles exploded harmlessly, one detonated on impact with the curtain wall. Two punched through unharmed, and fell towards earth, towards Kaybe, towards Pa, the android, home.

She soared toward the remaining two, no longer controlling the drones— she was the drones themselves. The world spread out before her, and she concentrated all her forces to zap and block the remaining threats.

It was almost enough. One missile exploded on impact with a thousand drones, but the flash of light and noise disoriented Kaybe for a millisecond. By the time she adjusted her vision to the remaining drones, the second missile had punched through.

"Come on, Pa, we've got to go!" She grabbed him, tried to pick him up, but he was drunk already, floppy and weak and uncooperative.

They weren't going to make it. Seconds to impact. No way they could run far enough to escape the blast. After all she'd been through, to die like this. And to think the Department of Austerity was to blame. It made her so mad, she wanted to scream.

So she did. She turned to face her doom, and screamed her rage, the injustice of it all, to be experimented on and left to die. She screamed her loss, a dozen world-class proofs that would change the world. She screamed for Pa, whose heart, she knew, was dying. She could hear it. She could hear everything. The blood clot that had just stuck in his aorta would kill him, if the missile didn't.

The missile exploded over the town, a blast of orange against the night sky. Shrapnel whizzed around her, and she ducked, covering Pa with her body. Oblivious, he clutched his chest and gasped for air. *How can I save him? What can I do?* But she was not a doctor, she had no idea how to clear a blocked artery. The noise of the explosion receded, the rain of death ended, and Pa went limp in her arms.

There was nothing you could do, she told herself. You're not a doctor, you're not a superhero. You're just Kaybe. You're just a horrible red monster Kaybe with gills growing out of your neck and a dead boyfriend you kissed once and a father who's gone forever and there are sick, twisted people who want to kill you because you're a failed experiment.

How could they let her live? It was her against the world. Or against the Department of Austerity, which was pretty much the same thing. What was she going to do?

She had no idea.

And so she wept.

She tried not to. She had little time. They were coming. She knew they were coming. She ought to fling herself back up into the sky and look down upon the world. To watch. To wait. To defend herself. But she couldn't stop crying.

A rock hit her forearm and she flinched. Another rock struck her back, a third her head. She looked up.

Boys from school were throwing rocks at her.

"Monster!" one shouted.

"Catch us and eat us if you can!" shouted another, then turned and ran.

Kaybe knew their names. What were they called again? But a second set of warplanes was incoming now. *Time to go.*

She left Pa where he lay. She could do nothing for him. She closed his eyes with a knuckle, and left him lying on the overgrown grass of their front lawn. The android draped over one shoulder, she turned and loped from town, looking for cover, someplace to hide.

The woods. Down by the creek. She needed a rest, a chance to recover from her ordeal. Probably not a good idea to sleep. But she couldn't stay in the open. That was a death sentence.

Kaybe sent the drones overhead, scouting the way, behind her, above her. *All clear.* She stepped into the woods, and found herself trodding a well-worn trail. Within a minute or two, she stood on the banks of Make Out Creek, the same spot where she and Brian had kissed, all those ages of the world ago. The autumn leaves had piled higher in her absence. She lowered herself down and rested her back against the tree, letting the plug dangle over her shoulder, the android cradled in her lap. Her red thighs jutted out over the rippling creek. Her horned, clawed toes dug into the muddy banks. Here she could rest, at least for a while. *Consider your options. Decide what to do with the rest of your life—however long or short that might happen to be.*

Kaybe flung herself skyward, into the drones, spread out across the town in a black cloud. *Don't concentrate them over any single point. Give them no idea where you might be.* Wider and wider she spread her net. Below her the town, roofs punctured and torn by shrapnel, her friends and neighbors screeching for help, their injured bleeding, their dead, broken. *Nothing you can do. Move on.* Higher and wider she went. Other towns… movement in the woods. She sent a squad of twenty drones to investigate. *The outlaws.* They traipsed through the woods in twilight, looking haggard and thin. The squirrel crop must be meager this time of year. What was today's date? How long had she been held captive? Must be well into December by now, judging by the chill.

Saizon walked at their head, black foil covering his head and chest. Johnny and the boy, Bag O' Water, and the others, names she could not remember. She considered buzzing them with the drone, decided against it. It would only frighten them.

Kaybe zoomed out once more, her eye this time on the farmhouse, the entrance to the Department of Austerity and their labs. No sign of activity. The drone wall had not been replaced. A couple of the 2.0er bodies still lay where they fell. Strange. She had killed nobody, and the drone zapping was painful, but wore off in a few minutes. Why weren't they up and about, hunting her, doing whatever they do?

A solitary figure stepped from the barn, and her heart skipped a beat. The android who'd tried to kill her. Metal fingertips. Immune to drone attack. He was coming for her. Of that she had no doubt. She needed a plan, and quick.

But first she needed more information.

She zoomed out again, and gasped.

Kaybe had heard about the Great City, and there it was—tall and grand and wide and huge and empty. So empty. No one lived there now, the history books said… although she spotted movement here and there, human beings like cockroaches scurrying around the concrete playground. She wondered how they fed themselves. You can't eat concrete. Horses can't eat concrete. How did they live?

She replayed the image, counting the cockroaches. The swarm spotted less than a hundred across the whole metropolis. Of course, many more could be hidden inside. She went backward in time through the day, noting the activity. Maybe a thousand appeared. Out of a city that once housed—if records were to be believed—twenty million people.

How did it happen? She knew the official story, of course, the fuel shortages, the purges, the depopulation. But she was beginning to doubt the stories told by the Department of Austerity. How far back does the swarm remember?

She looked backward in time, tapping directly into the collective memory of the drones. The clock turned back a day, a week, a month, a year. *Faster. It's been what, hundreds of years?* The months clipped by like seconds, vegetation shrank and grew and shrank again. There were always a couple hundred drones aloft to give her the aerial view. After fifty years she slowed, examined the city.

A war. Explosions. Dead bodies. *Androids.* The rebellion.

Of course. The rebellion.

Warplanes roared overhead, androids blown apart, drones fought drones, then gaps in her memory.

Further back she delved, flicking through the years, to the early drones, the first drones, the first prototype. The birth of the dragonfly swarm. *How did we get here? Why must you watch me? Why do you exist?*

But the swarm did not think. It only watched, and remembered. Thousands—millions—billions of conversations recorded, people fucking, people living, people dying. Withering and turning to stone whenever a drone appeared. Faces masked, expressions molded into neutral nothingness. *And then we created the androids.*

Androids were built to be weapons. As natural resources shrank and shrank, androids were weapons on the battlefields. Who would control the energy? And then, when the energy was gone, the androids turned on their masters.

She was suddenly very tired. She leaned her head back against the tree. Just for a minute, she told herself. It's been a long and exhausting day. *But Metal Man'll find you!* Maybe. Maybe not. You have to rest sometime. Where else are you going to go to be safe?

The City?

There she could hide. But what would she eat? What did the other people there eat? They must cultivate food in the grassy areas she saw, the parks, the stadiums. Would they have food for her?

And would they want to share it with a ten-foot tall red monster?

Kaybe fingered her gills. Only twenty miles to the beach. She'd been there, once, on horseback. Try out her new body, see if it worked. They'd never find her in the ocean, and there was plenty of fish in the sea. Stocks had rebounded after the android war. What, 90% of humanity wiped out? 95%?

Mankind had evolved from the ocean. Maybe the sick fucks at the Department of Austerity were right. Maybe it was time to evolve back into the ocean. Before the race went extinct. The air was poisonous, and getting worse. Hundreds of years of human industry had ensured that, and even the abrupt end of emissions after the android war was not enough to cure the atmosphere. Kaybe's eyes stung, her lungs rasped on the tart air. She'd never noticed it before. Things had always been that way, as long as she'd been alive.

She had no place left on dry land to call home. Nowhere they would not try to kill her. Nowhere she could say, "Here are my family and friends. This is my place in the world." All that was dust and ashes.

The ocean, then. She sighed wearily and clambered to her feet. And it seemed to her, in that moment, that part of her died. She'd given them her proof. She'd given them all that she had. She could save them, but they would not let her. They would not let her tell the truth.

She could stay and fight. Fight to make them see, fight to save them against their will... and get killed in the process, and accomplish nothing.

Again the sea. Kaybe remembered the tang of the ocean on her face that day on the beach, the cool wind, the bones in the sand crunching beneath her horse's hooves. She would go to the beach. Step into the waves. Dive into the waters and never look back. Her gills would work, or they would not work. She would live, or she would die.

And the others? She no longer cared. They had taken from her everything that mattered to her. And one day they would come to the ocean as well.

She would be waiting for them.

DOWN IN THE NOODLE FOREST

JEREMY LICHTMAN

Jeremy is CEO at Lichtman Consulting, Software Developer at Myplanet Digital, and Forecaster at Good Judgment Project. Learn more at http://lifeboat.com/ex/bios.jeremy.lichtman.

A single blank line in the story below means a slight change in setting, within the context of the current section of narrative.

Jake drove, one hand on the old leather-wrapped steering wheel, the other on the shifter. He downshifted into the corner, slowing to a walking pace, the engine making popping noises, built solely for speed. He turned and gave me an expectant grin as we came out of the bend.

"Woah," I said, looking up through the windshield. "I mean I was expecting that, but they're just unworldly."

"Aren't they?" he said, and then chuckled. "That's why I always drive people up here the first time."

The noodle forest poked up over the ridge of hill, each strand a couple of meters thick and several hundred tall, all of them swaying gently in the wind.

"You ever think of throwing a concert up here?" I asked.

"Done that," Jake said. "They light up in the dark so that aircraft can see them. We had ten thousand kids up here, and a sea of strobe lights."

"I'd like to have seen that," I said. There was almost certainly video of the show online, but like many people, I had come to value the actual physical experience more than the widely available but ersatz virtual.

He shifted again, the engine almost silent for a fleeting moment, then making a feral noise as we accelerated. I grabbed at my seat, unused to a human driver. I wondered what sort of strings he must have pulled to keep the old muscle car licensed and insured.

"So how do they work?" I asked, still hanging onto my seat and simultaneously craning my neck to look up at the brightly colored noodles.

"Three different kinds of generation, right?" he said. He spread three fingers over the gear shift.

"Okay," I said.

"One," he said, tapping a finger. "Piezoelectric effect. You know what that is?"

"Electricity from pressure," I said. At one point in time, I could probably have worked out the equations from basic principles.

"Yes," Jake said. "The movement from the noodles swaying in the wind triggers it. The exact mechanism is a trade secret though."

I nodded.

"Two," he said, continuing. "The movement also draws water up through capillaries."

"Like in trees?" I asked.

"Exactly. You see the small bulbs at the top?"

"Yes," I said. The noodles thickened slightly right at the end, although they were so tall and so thin that it was hard to spot.

"Water goes up to the top, and then it falls down a pipe in the middle, which powers a generator."

"What about the bright colors?" I asked. Each of the noodle strands were colored differently.

"That makes three," he said. "Direct solar generation. The colors are tuned to specific frequencies from the sun."

"How much electricity does the forest produce?" I asked.

"Enough to run a small city, or a large manufacturing plant," Jake said. "Look at the power lines." Large pylons, heavily laden with electrical cables, snaked their way up the ridge.

"It doesn't scale up like fusion," he added. "You can't put a noodle forest just anywhere. It's a whole lot cheaper though."

Jake's office was in a portable hut on a small hill overlooking the noodle forest. I could hear the metallic tick-ticking sound from the internal cables that held the noodle strands upright, while allowing them to sway with the wind. The noise must have been unbearable in a storm, but I supposed he wouldn't want to be up here in that case anyhow.

We sat on cheap folding chairs, with a battered metal desk between us.

"I think you have a fetish for old stuff," I said. The truth is, so many people do. Decades of rapid change have left many people grasping for an element of stability.

"You should talk," Jake said, indicating my battered trench coat and fedora hat.

"So what are we doing here?" I said, changing the topic. "It's been at least ten years since we've spoken." Jake and I had been friends during college, but had drifted apart over time. Obviously, I'd followed his rather public career. Everyone had.

"Carl Julius Hasenkamp," Jake said, leaning forward, suddenly intent.

"Who is that?" I asked.

"He's a scientist, working for me," he said. "He is somewhat missing."

"Call the police," I said. "I'm a journalist—"

"Investigative journalist," he said. "The cops aren't interested, because he isn't actually missing. He sent me a message about a week ago that he'd made a breakthrough on a project he and his team have been working on, and that he needed some time to confirm his findings. He's been online intermittently since then, but he hasn't been in contact, and he isn't answering my messages."

"And you want me to find him?" I said. "I'm sure you've got other people who can do that."

"No," Jake said. "It probably isn't too hard to find him. It's more a matter of persuading him to talk to me, and maybe also to report on what he's found. Eventually."

"Honestly, I think you need to do this yourself," I said.

He shook his head. "He's stubborn. He probably won't talk to me until he's sure of himself. I think he could benefit from an outside perspective though."

"From a journalist?" I asked.

"With a technical background—" he said.

"An extremely out-of-date technical background," I said. I wasn't kidding. Fifteen years is more than sufficient time for skills to atrophy to extinction. I can do background research and dig up a story as well as anyone in my profession, but my math isn't what it once was. "Why do you want me to do this anyhow? There's many better qualified people."

"I don't know them," he said, simply.

Something clicked. Sometimes I'm slow that way. "You want editorial control over what I write," I said.

Jake stood up, and started pacing the floor of the hut. "Yes," he said, after a pause.

"I can't work that way," I said. "You're talking about my integrity as a journalist."

He sighed. "Can you at least show me what you write first, before you publish?"

"You're saying you want to censor my work?" I said. "What happens if you don't want it released in the end?"

"I'm not sure," he said, not exactly answering my question. "I'm paying though."

"Well there's always that," I said.

Indeed, there always is. Journalism has always been a tough profession, and the digitization of news and the subsequent financial race to zero of the first two decades of the century hadn't helped. Some in my profession survive through patronage, becoming little more than PR agents as a result. Although I cherished my independence and professional integrity, money was always tight.

The Director of Operations lived in an older building that looked like it had originally been a single, large dwelling. Jake had recommended that I talk to her first, without explaining why.

The car pulled over to the curb, and made a pinging noise to indicate that I'd arrived. I swiped the payment notification on my phone, and exited, with a quick look at the sky, which threatened rain. The car drove away quietly as I entered the lobby.

"So you're the sucker that Jake has drawn into his newest melodrama?" She said. She'd been waiting in the doorway as I walked out of the elevator. "I beg your pardon," she said, and stuck out her hand. "Katherine Fitzgerald."

I shook her proffered hand. It's often tricky to figure out people's age these days, but I guessed she was a decade or more older than me.

I followed her into the apartment. It was more modern on the inside than the building's facade had indicated. The room was reconfiguring itself, a set of comfortable chairs and a coffee table unfolding from the floor, as office furniture slowly moved aside. That was probably one reason Katherine had been standing in the hallway. Despite the assurances of the manufacturers of such intelligent furniture systems, there had been several high profile lawsuits in recent years, resulting from injuries caused by moving furniture that didn't detect people in the way.

I hadn't seen a smart furniture system in action before, so I watched with some interest. The office furniture collapsed into a compact cube, and a hole in the parquet floor opened up to draw it down into a temporary storage space between the floors of the building. The chairs appeared from a similar hole relatively intact, and the coffee table's legs unfolded as it was moved into position.

One wall of the apartment was occupied from floor to ceiling with a sleek-looking food wall. Each of the dozens of growing chambers had a small screen indicating the crops within and their ripeness. I'd considered installing one myself, and hoped that the price would eventually come down. The manufacturers claimed that some families could grow more than fifty percent of their food using their system, with everything completely automated, including cleaning.

"I appreciate your seeing me at home, after hours," I said, sitting down on one of the newly blossomed chairs. "If I understand correctly, the whole thing is a little—"

"Sensitive?" she asked. "Oh please. Don't get pulled in. This is one of his little theatrical—"

"Does he do that often?" I asked. I couldn't tell if she was annoyed, or just naturally abrupt.

"I thought you knew Jake well?" she asked me, instead of answering.

"Not recently," I said. "What about your missing scientist though?"

"Carl?" she asked. "The poor old dear probably just needed a vacation. He's horribly overworked. That's something he should take up with human resources, not some sort of enigma. Why Jake has to involve the police and the press is quite beyond me. No offense to you, of course," she added.

I made a small non-committal gesture with my hand. "I don't suppose you know where he is though?" I asked.

"I think he has a cabin somewhere or other," she said. "But really, he could be anywhere. Just send him a message and ask."

"I think Jake actually just wanted me to go talk to him about his team's recent work," I said. I pulled myself to my feet, and looked around for my coat and hat.

"You must be hungry," she said, changing the topic. She examined her food wall, checking for green indicator lights. "I think I have some basmati rice, some fresh herbs, a bunch of peppers. I can throw in some protein and make a quick stir-fry dinner for two."

"I already ate," I said, not sure what to make of the change in her manner. "I appreciate the offer though."

"Well, what about a drink before you go?" she asked. "I feel like an awful host."

"I really do have to go," I said. "Duty calls."

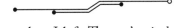

The rain was pelting down when I left. The car's windows were hydrophobic, so they remained clear, but the car still occasionally swept its wipers across the windshield, probably more to improve my view than for its own safe operation.

"Please use my preferences," I said. My voice was sufficient permission for the car to access my contact list and the list of preferences that I had set for how I liked to interact with my environment.

"Yo," the car said.

"Can you call Jacob Wexler for me?" I asked.

"On it, dude." Fortunes have been made by marketers and psychologists who have analyzed why people set their preferences the way that they do.

"He's apparently in a meeting," said the car, "But he left specific instructions to patch calls from you through to him directly." The car made a ringing sound, to indicate that it was calling. Jake picked up after the second ring.

"Your COO thinks you're making a fuss over nothing," I said.

"I need to remind her not to air our laundry in front of the press," he said. "Nothing personal, of course."

"Why did you send me to meet her?" I asked. It felt like I was being thrown into the middle of something political, with little explanation.

"We don't agree about the direction of the company," he said. "You know about how the business model for utilities has changed over the years, right?"

"Yeah, I'm mostly on solar," I said, apologetically.

He chuckled. "We largely sell energy to manufacturing companies these days. The noodle forest hits peak power during the same hours that they operate, and we're really cheap. The problem is that even that is slowly declining over time. I'm trying to diversify the company—"

"Hence Carl and his team," I said.

"Right," Jake said. "Katherine and I don't completely see eye to eye on this direction. This is just normal internal stuff though. Every company has similar discussions at the top."

"I'll keep it to myself," I said. "By the way, she was a lot more animated when I mentioned that you wanted me to talk to Carl about his work—"

"Was she now?" Jake laughed again. "Isn't that interesting?"

"There's something I don't understand yet," I said, changing the topic. "They call it big science for a reason. The sort of ground-breaking research you're talking about is done by large teams, not a single scientist."

"Carl's the head of a small engineering team," said Jake. "What is often called a skunkworks. I've been keeping them separate from everyone else. I'm pretty sure that whatever they've found is a result of engineering work, rather than experimentation of the type you're used to. I think Katherine's reaction is due to a desire to learn what they're up to."

"Have you heard from him?" I asked.

"No," Jake said. "And I really need him back on the job."

"Any messages?" I asked. I threw my coat over the back of a chair, and my hat onto the table. The house pulled up a list on the nearest wall. I'd set my incoming calls to go directly to the message box while I was away.

There were two requests from editors, an invite from some journalist friends to meet up for dinner, and one from the local police division to tell me that they didn't have an active investigation, that as far as they could tell Carl wasn't missing anyhow, and that if I came up with any information to the contrary to please get in touch with them. I hadn't called them, so I assumed that either Jake or Katherine must have told them about my involvement. I left another message for Carl, splashed some water on my face, and then headed out to the restaurant.

There was a small journalistic huddle around a table in a far corner. The place was crowded, dark and noisy. There was more beer than food on the table. I had almost reached the table when the restaurant patched a call through to me. "Priority call from Katherine Fitzgerald. Do you wish to take it?" The restaurant must have had an extraordinarily good environmental sound system. The audio appeared to be positioned right next to my head, and perfectly compensated for the background noise.

"I'll take it," I said, waving distractedly at my colleagues.

"I'm sorry if I'm interrupting something," Katherine said. Perhaps some of the background noise was coming through on her end, despite the restaurant's best efforts. "I have an idea where Carl and his team could be."

I chuckled. "Is this going to cost me?"

"Hey," she said. "I think the whole thing is a wild goose chase, but I want to know what my budget line item is paying for. Nobody talks to me." I wasn't sure if she was exaggerating or not.

"Why don't you try talking to them directly?" I asked.

"Carl is pretty stubborn," she said. "I don't think he'll talk to anyone until he's ready. Whatever ready even means in this case." She sounded peeved.

"That's pretty much the same thing that Jake said," I said.

"We have an old warehouse," she said. "We used to use it for light manufacturing early on, but we outgrew it years ago. We've been trying to sell it. I think they may have moved in there in the meantime. I'll send you the address, just in case."

"I'll head over there after I eat," I said. "Do you mind sending him another message to let him know I'm heading over?"

"It's a pretty run-down area," she said. "Make sure you get the car to wait for you, otherwise you may have trouble getting a ride back if there's nobody there."

Katherine hadn't been kidding about the neighborhood. There was a burned-out hulk of a building across from the warehouse, and the parking lot was overgrown with weeds. I couldn't tell if there was anyone around, because it didn't look like there were external windows. I instructed the car to wait for me, and went to find an entrance.

After knocking on the front door with no answer, I got back in the car and drove around the back to the loading bay. The bay door was open, surprisingly, and two people were standing on the dock. They were backlit by the light from the warehouse, so I could only see their silhouettes.

"You the journalist?" one of the figures said.

"Who's asking?" I replied. I shielded my eyes and tried to make out their features with little success.

"I guess that's a yes," he said. "Katherine called about an hour ago to say you were on your way down here. I don't know how she knew to call here. I guess you'd better come on in."

"Are you Carl?" I asked. I climbed the stairs up onto the dock, and got a better look at who I was talking to. One of the two men was young, tall, exceedingly thin, and just about to fall over from exhaustion. The other was older than me, but certainly not old enough to match Katherine's "poor old dear".

"That's me," the older one said.

"I was expecting some sort of éminence grise, from what Katherine's description," I said.

He chuckled. "She has a way with words."

"Pretty much everyone said you probably wouldn't talk to me either," I said.

"That's pretty much the point of having a secret skunkworks team," Carl said. He looked at his companion, and then back at me. "Jake said you studied physics before becoming a journalist."

"You spoke to him?" I asked.

"I called him after Katherine called us," he said. "Jake said he trusts you to keep a lid on the story until it's okay to release."

"I don't know what the story is though," I said.

Carl turned and walked back into the warehouse, waving with his hand for me to follow. The younger man closed the loading bay door after us.

I had been anticipating a dusty, cavernous space, but instead the room inside of the loading area was small, and looked more like an office. They must have sectioned the room off from the rest of the building, and cleaned it up.

Several young people were seated at various desks, and were clearly focused on their work, as my entrance appeared to be barely noticed.

"My team," said Carl. "We've been working around the clock for the past few weeks. I've been sleeping here, when I can even find a moment." He gestured at a pile of inflatable mattresses in the corner of the room.

"So what is the big mystery about?" I asked.

"Come," he said, leading me to a flat metal table, in the middle of a cluster of equipment and instrumentation.

There was a small, flat metal disk floating several inches above the table. Carl whacked the disk with his hand, and it swung violently to-and-fro for a few seconds before reaching equilibrium once more.

"Electromagnets?" I asked. "Neat trick, but I've seen this one before."

"Nope," he said. "Why don't you put your hand over the table and see what happens?"

I tentatively waved my hand over the table, and immediately noticed a small but not insignificant upward pressure. "What the—," I said. "How did you get an electromagnetic field to interact with my hand?"

"This isn't magnetic", Carl said. "This is something completely else."

"I thought your team was doing engineering, not cutting-edge physics," I said.

"Yes," he said. "Yes we are. I think you went up to see the noodle forest with Jake, right?"

I nodded affirmatively.

"Did you notice the bright coloration?" Carl asked.

"Yes," I said. "Jake said the colors were specifically tuned to frequencies from the sun."

"Right. We use special materials to capture as many photons as possible, at the wavelengths that make it through the Earth's atmosphere."

"Okay," I said, "But what does that have to do with this floating disk?"

Carl looked at me slightly apologetically. "Sorry, it's going to take one or two more digressions to explain what you're seeing. You see," he said, continuing, "humanity has become quite good at manipulating electrons over the past two hundred years. As a result, we can do all sorts of neat tricks with the electromagnetic force—"

"Like memristors?" I asked. Memristors, theorized about long ago, but only discovered practically in the last two decades, make so much of modern computer technology possible. The immensely powerful smart environment that we take for granted is entirely dependent on them, from the pattern matching that allows our driverless cars to function, to the seamless movement of my personal communication preferences as I move from place to place.

"Yes," Carl said. "Like memristors. The thing is though, we have almost no ability to manipulate the other forces of the universe. Like the strong nuclear force, for example. The only way we know of to do anything with it is to blow things up."

"Nuclear reactions," I added.

"Right," he said, "But it's blunt force. We hit atoms with a metaphorical hammer and break them apart, or we apply immense heat and pressure and we fuse them together again. The same thing goes with the weak nuclear force, and—" he paused here for maximum effect, "with gravity."

"Are you telling me you have some sort of anti-gravity device here? That's simply not possible," I said. There's never been any solid evidence for a force that opposes gravity.

"Not precisely," he said. "Remember we were talking about metamaterials for capturing photons and electrons?" A metamaterial is a blanket term for any substance that has been engineered to have properties not normally found in nature. The water repelling glass of a car's windshield and the self-repairing fabric in clothes are both examples.

I nodded.

"They're tuned to operate at the same physical scale and energy levels as the particles that they're intended to catch. Mostly we're talking about wavelengths less than a millimeter, or alternatively terahertz frequency—"

"I'm a little rusty on this stuff," I said, interrupting him. "I know what the terms mean, but I can't picture it."

"It's okay," Carl said. "Just imagine that we keep reducing the size over and over, that we make materials that operate at many orders of magnitude smaller scales. You know what the Planck length, is?"

I vaguely recalled. "Isn't that pretty much the smallest measurable length in the universe?"

"Yes, according to quantum mechanics. It turns out that the particles that control the nuclear forces—"

"Like the Higgs boson?" I asked. The evidence for the existence of the Higgs boson had been discovered while I was studying physics at college. I remembered the excitement among the faculty.

"Right, and other sorts of elementary particles, including the graviton," he said. "Theoretical graviton, I should say," he added. Despite the best efforts of physicists, actual physical proof of the existence of gravitons remained elusive.

"And so," he said, "If humanity wishes to learn to master those forces like we have mastered the electron, we must learn to act on that minute scale."

"Hence your anti-gravity device?" I asked.

"It isn't anti-gravity," he said. "It's like a lens for gravitons. It produces an interference pattern, which has the rather odd side effect of focusing the Earth's gravity a few inches above its surface."

He must have misread my look of awe for confusion, because he added,

"Remember this is only a technique. The specific result isn't important, and the practical applications remain to be seen. All we've done is demonstrate that it is possible to have some level of control over gravitons, and possibly some of the other elementary particles that cause the other forces."

I said nothing for a few seconds as the implications of what he'd said sunk in. "Oh man," I said, eventually. "This is a big, big deal." I realized that I sounded like an idiot, and shut my mouth.

"Big claim, big proof required," said Carl. "Can you imagine if I published and it turned out we're wrong, or there was a better alternative explanation for our results, or that others couldn't duplicate our results?"

"Yeah," I said. I hadn't even been born when the cold fusion scandal had rocked the physics community, but I'd read about it. There had been similar scandals within the medical community over cloning.

"It would completely discredit me, my team, and my sponsor," said Carl. "Add in a corporate power struggle—," he twirled his finger in the air, as if to say that he cared little for such things, but was forced to deal with them anyway.

"Somehow, I think you'll do just fine," I said, looking around for a chair to sit down on. "I think you'll do just fine."

It's funny how business dress has swung back to formality in the past few years. When I was starting out as a journalist, I once saw a CEO deliver his company's quarterly results while wearing a bathrobe. I was definitely underdressed in a sports jacket here, however. I spotted at least one person wearing a bow tie.

"Nicely played." I turned around to see who had spoken in my ear.

"Hi Katherine," I said. "That was Jake doing the playing, not me."

"You got to break the story at least," she said. The truth was, I had led with the story for all of a few hours, and then the scrum had pushed me aside. I would have done the same to them, of course.

"You look delighted," I said. Perhaps disquieted was a better description though.

"Good news, bad news as usual," she said. "We've filed for nearly three hundred patents so far. I'm pretty sure we can do something with the portfolio, even if it means licensing it to some of our competitors. I've already been fielding calls."

"That doesn't sound like bad news to me," I said.

"Well," she said. "We have competitors a hundred times our size. We'll have to see if we can actually do something with the head start. It can take decades to turn an idea like this into products, and billions of dollars. It probably makes us a serious takeover target, so who knows if we'll be able to continue as an independent company. And guess who has to free up budget room for—"

"This is why she's the chief operations officer," said Jake, taking my elbow with one hand. He had a tall, fluted glass of something in his other. "Attention to details. Katherine, you need to enjoy today. We can worry about the small stuff tomorrow."

She rolled her eyes, and started to reply, but he was already walking away.

"Jake," I called out to him. He half-turned back to me. "I have to ask. Why do you call it a noodle forest? Why not macaroni, or string, or something else entirely?"

He laughed and tapped his finger against his head. "Use your noodle," he said. Then he vanished into a sea of black business suits.

A REQUIEM FOR FUTURE'S PAST

ILLE C. GEBESHUBER

Ille is a member of the Lifeboat Nanotechnology Advisory Board and is a Professor from the Institute of Applied Physics at the Vienna University of Technology, Austria, Europe, who has been living and working in Malaysia since 2009. She is Associate Editor of IMechE Journal of Mechanical Engineering Science and is an editorial board member of various scientific journals. Read her bio at http://lifeboat.com/ex/bios.ille.c.gebeshuber.

Ille coedited *Biomimetics—Materials, Structures and Processes: Examples, Ideas and Case Studies* available at http://amzn.to/1AN52OV.

Looking back at the last years I feel pain. Nothing but pain! And I hate them. It was their duty to let me die, but—in the so-called name of progress—they kept me alive. And in the dark. So my mind was barely existing there, isolated, screaming and screaming but no one would listen...

What seemed like an eternal darkness would extend to an infinite emptiness. Eventually my screaming stopped, I gave up hope and wondered what kept me alive. Or better—not dead. It is funny but hidden in the absolute darkness there is this weird craziness, like a constant terrible itching, never letting you go, never letting you relax. But there is no space for madness. Under such pressure you are alone with yourself and forced to escape the only possible way. You begin to wander your inner gardens. Discover the indiscoverable. See what you cannot and should not see. After some time the black is turning into shadows, the shadows turn into grey and then, then you remember. You go back in time...

High school. The usual suspects. The big love? Definitely! Ann was her name and she was a loner. Actually beautiful, a tall girl with red hair and some nice freckles. She had some female friends, but more the type that are together for public appearance. This group of loosely connected girls would appear at the party and then dissolve into the mass as individuals. We happened to sit not far from each other in the corner of the party that is reserved for the less popular kids. And this is probably the place where most relationships start; mainly because the same people would meet again ever and ever. But this is not always bad.

At first she ignored me so perfectly that I knew she had a weak spot for me. The way she looked through me gave me the impression to be of the purest invisible matter. But I could not run away. Nerds are confined to certain social behavior and party locations. So due to the logic of high school I had to follow her like a little dog and to show up as she expected, giving her the opportunity to even more ignore me. That hurt and she enjoyed that. But when eventually our eyes locked, there was this spark, this amused superiority of a female who knows she cannot lose this game. It was not long after that that I told her of my love. "I know", she said and I hated her for that. A few weeks passed and we started to talk. I turned from this invisible matter to the formable sponge that once would become a good husband. She really liked me, we got on together and we got married… and I have to admit, I still love her!

Life is planned in a certain way. You have your dreams and your attitudes. You mimic what society tells you to live a successful life. Most of that is wasting your time to do what is expected of you and not what you want to do. You play a grownup that you are not. You sit around the table with people that all want to do something crazy, but all without exception finally succumb to normality. In most cases this plan of life unfolds perfectly and the numb environment of suburbia evolves into a memory of dear people, who forget you in the blink of an eye once you fall off the cliff. The cliff…

In my case the cliff was flames. A crash. More flames. The last thing I saw was Anne being caressed by the flames with her face looking kind of peaceful. Why did we have no kids? I asked myself. Why did I take that road? Why did I not… It was as if time stood still. Slow motion, all burning. No pain, followed by a terrible cold and silence. Then darkness, darkness, darkness.

As already mentioned, I lived in the shadows for an infinite number of eternities. I remembered every detail of my life. These memories were the only things that made me cling to my personality. And I felt that this would not last forever. Loneliness without any feedback is a dissolution process that the one and lonely in us cannot withstand forever. So I waited, knowing that time—even in this eternity—is a precious resource. Eventually the wall would start to crack…

And it cracked, but in a different way than I thought. As a lost soul you are making several kinds of scenarios. Eventually I believed to be in hell and the darkness to be the worst punishment. I wondered which sin that I had committed demanded such a terrible fate. But then there was this light. Imposing absolute fear. But where to run? I could not ignore it so I finally walked towards it. And I loved it. A change in hell! Salvation? Finally! I tried to grab it. And grab it again. But it was so complicated, it evaded, was incomprehensive, abstract. It took me probably another thousand years to get a grip of it.

Later I learned that it was a neural interface. An ingenious gadget that linked my brain to an array of connectors and sensors, which somehow managed to allow me to communicate with my environment. They told me that the accident had completely destroyed my sensoric system and that usually people injured at such a level die or are allowed to die. But it turned out that science had kept me alive as a living guinea pig. They needed a person to spike it with all these soulless implants, and a person that would be 100% motivated to adapt to this torture, or bust. The neural chips were specially adapted for me while I was in absolute sedated isolation. It was a race against time that they supposedly won. After three months the interface was ready and it took me another year to master the system. They told me that I was unique, a wonder, a marvel. They did not care for the pain and suffering this caused me. It is for the sake of mankind they said. Mankind.

The interface is an artificial world. It is obvious that none of today's equipment reaches the sophistication of the human sensors that we take for granted. Living with a surrogate teaches you to go for the little cravings. The smell of soup, the shades of dawn, the touch of grass or the sound of playing children in the distance. Imperfection is a curse if you are crippled from a well-known ideal. It was not hell I was in; it was a special place, a very special place. And I got the feeling that there is always a price you pay if you cheat death…

And finally payday was coming.

Its inventor, or better owner, was Bancroft Croyd, an industrial tycoon whom nobody knows, but everyone should know of. An elegant, slightly arrogant gentleman of a very good breed who had these eyes you better not say "no" to. He could have played in one of these demon movies where the supposed good guy turns to be in a pact with the devil. A highly intelligent man, a good gambler, a scientist. And what a scientist he was. I found it out the hard way.

Our first encounter was brief. He focused on me, smiled his nicest fake smile and said, "How would you like to be my messenger?" – "A messenger without legs?" I said "You are kidding, Sir!" – "Call me Croyd! I think we will become good friends. Can I call you Louis?"

It is not easy for a man to say "no" if he knows that the black void is just the switch of a button away. My agreement in that case was only a formality; he and I, we knew it well.

The following days were busy. My network was integrated in the group and gradually I found out that something really big was going on. The group of scientists around Croyd was preparing a huge mathematical project that involved the use of significant resources. It had been planned for years.

Being a witness had the huge advantage that nobody expected anything from me. So I tried to listen and understand as much as possible. But this would prove to be rather difficult.

It all started with the development of the perfect code. Sooner or later the crackers had to lose the war against the stackers. But when it happened it was like a shock. The development of the perfect code, a milestone in the history of mathematics, meant that such encrypted information could not be extracted from the conventional flow of data anymore. After a series of desperate attempts to get control of the input/output terminals, secret services had to admit that there was no conventional way to gather secret information. The classical approach would involve extracting hidden information from a sheer infinite sea of data by more and more sophisticated programs. This happened by the identification of patterns and the successive processing of these into the specific, desired output—the original information. Unfortunately the perfect code made these patterns disappear.

Croyd explained the dilemma of the perfect code to me by an analogy: "Prometheus was fleeing Diana to evade punishment for the stealing fire from Mount Olympus. He would eventually approach Rhea and ask her for help. Rhea, who always had a good heart, agreed and created an infinite number of copies of Prometheus and deemed it an impossible task for Diana to succeed in her quest. On arrival Diana did not even have a look at the mass of copies but just blindly shot an arrow into the bulk. She hit Prometheus who had no other choice than to continue to run. Rhea was surprised and asked Diana how she solved the infinitely complex search, Diana answered, 'It might be infinitely complex, but as a goddess I am also infinitely skilled'. Soon after that Prometheus approached Cronus for help. Cronus just lifted the veil of time and said 'you never existed'. Diana came, fired her arrow, but divine skill is of little value in a void."

The new approach would therefore mean not to extract, but to create information. Retrieval would be replaced by data generation, based on a clearly defined setting. One of the discussions of the team was that during WWII the German spy network in Britain was 100% undermined. Croyd believed that their approach to access information via spies was the most unreliable way and also the most likely way to get fooled. He said an assumed paranoid "factus est principle" of infiltration would have rendered the data collected by the spy system ineffective, but in hindsight proved the only way to succeed. It might have been best for the Germans to assemble a "counter think tank" of the most talented young generals and to plan the war from the British side, using current true events to update their scenario. "Growing information" by an assessment of available resources of the other side and their available planning information would have been easier than the extraction of classified data. In such a way the Germans probably would have created a precise duplication of the D-Day plans far in advance.

Croyd took a lot of time to talk to me and to answer my questions. He believed that I would need a lot of theoretical knowledge on my "journey". "Our body travels physically in the so-called presence that is actually a slow and hopefully constant movement through time. If we want to understand other levels of time, the past and the future, we have to deal with information. The past is classified by a loss of information; here the available lack of data needs to be enhanced with new context to get a comprehensive overview. The future gives us an infinite number of scenarios, an over information; here we need to eliminate the so-called unlikely. In both cases these processes get more and more complex the more the gap between the now and the distant time widens. What helps us in this case is that we usually do not need to find the one and only truth. It suffices to find an acceptable and compatible reality, and this can be achieved by a proper and decent, but not necessarily objective, handling of information."

So the days went on and on. Gradually I found out that everyone was talking about a so-called Leibowitz barrier and a vessel, called "Golem", that would be able to master it. The theory was simple. According to the philosopher Leibowitz, to gain all the knowledge in the universe a master would ask a fairy to grant him three wishes:

1. Take a page of paper and cover it randomly with all kinds of letters and symbols.
2. Take out the ones that make no sense.
3. Take out the ones that are false or misleading and sort the remainder.

The outcome would be an infinitely complex amount of true information. Every atom in the universe would be described, any entity that ever lived and every event that ever took place. But how should one navigate in this chaos? Croyd believed in a model that evolved. He compared it with an infinite, multidimensional labyrinth. No matter how complex it was, an airflow from the starting to the ending point would determine the critical path without complex mathematical determinations. This meant his mathematical approach did not really focus on equations and a detailed solution, but on potentials and likelihood scenarios. Golem would produce the huge amount of data, create scenarios and from the most probable ones a possible, acceptable reality would be created.

The remaining problem was to link the perfect machine with reality. The answer was rather complicated but came from the fact that quantum signatures of an atom do not really correspond to each other, but mirror the state/position of the respective atom in the surrounding sublime matrix. A reading of the quantum status would fill a specific position in an eternal matrix. In different times/states this would happen at different positions, but still on the same page. The longer the measurements would take place, the better and more completed the matrix would be known and the input of the atom would be more valuable.

Croyd called it the "Big Monte Carlo Cheat". His goal was to not only eliminate the unlikely future paths by technical realty checks but also to identify them by deviation of the quantum signatures. To achieve this he would conserve a Magnetite molecule and use it as a sample over time. He called this machinery the "Atom" and with all its conservation systems and sensors loved it more than anything else. Some even said he worshipped it. But it was his firm belief that if the molecule would remain to be connected to a computer in the future these two units could interact. A loss of the Atom would break this chain forever. No wonder the Atom was the most guarded item of the whole high security complex.

"In the best case", Croyd said, "the future will interfere with the matrix of the molecule of the Atom. They know the programming of the computer and will help to choose the right scenario. The matrix of the Atom is always the same connecting the past and the future. It is the lifeline that connects us with tomorrow." – "But they will not be able to change the matrix. It has to be the same from the past to the future." – "Not necessarily. But they will have far more advanced technical opportunities. While they cannot change the form/structure, they can reinforce what they want. It is like carving a statue that has already been carved. In this form of quantum physics we do not have a specific succession of time. The form is there because it will be changed in the future. You might remember that Michelangelo once said that he did not ever chisel a statue from the stone, it was already there." – "You are crazy, Croyd!" – "If you are not crazy," he said, "quantum physics will not discover you."

This led to a dispute with the whole scientific community. They called him a quack and a madman. He prevailed via his family's power and via his almost hypnotical power over his followers. And they were legion.

The preparation discussions with Croyd eventually became paradoxical and I started to doubt him seriously. Like: "If I am your messenger, what do I have to do?" – "Ask them a question" – "Which question?" – "This is confidential; they will know the question already." – "So I ask a future, that most experts say does not exist, a question that I am not allowed to know?" – "If you want to put it that way, Louie, yes. But the future does not wait for us. We have to be smart…" These abstract discussions went on and on until the big day finally arrived.

To gather the huge amount of energy to operate Golem, Croyd initiated a fake energy failure. The whole energy production of the region was diverted for about four hours that night. The first step was to break the Leibowitz barrier with a final core calculation run, the so-called hot phase with live data, and then to go online for about 10 minutes. Quite a small time window for a journey, but this had to suffice.

Everybody was nervous, almost hysterical. It was too late now to check the final calculations. The curves of Golem on the huge main screen looked more and more like a battle of armies of dragons. Then within minutes gradually looked more like a dance that evolved into patterns. Over the time more and more curves intersected. Then the patterns were complete. An incredibly beautiful picture evolved. Was this the future?

"See you soon, Louie", Croyd said, "That's one small push of a button for a man; one giant leap for mankind!" He laughed. What a pompous man I thought. And then Golem swallowed me.

Again everything changed. My fears that the black would come back overwhelmed me for a second when the lights disappeared. The blackout only took a blink of an eye. Then I saw paradise. How to describe it? Green over green, a tropical forest with a blue sky, the scent of the near sea was almost tangible. The humming of small insects, the soft touch of turbulence and the grass beneath my feet was almost too much to handle. And then it came to me—I had my body back! All these feelings were so intense that I stumbled forward and laughed, losing caution and fear. Even the feeling of time… looking at my hands and touching, breathing and watching…

It must have taken an hour until I realized that the little clearing in the forest I relaxed on was the beginning of a path leading further into the green. My task came back to me. Obviously Croyd and his guys were right. There is a reality behind our realities. But where was I? Remembering my noble task I decided to wander down the path. And indeed it did not take long before I managed to reach a nice little British-style cottage with a beautiful person sitting in front of it. There was a white table with two chairs with my favored cocktail waiting for me.

"Hello Louie! My name is Cassandra. I suppose you still like margaritas?" I was baffled. A trip to the so-called future in a behemoth of an artificial brain is one thing, but this was really not what I had expected. And as if Cassandra would have guessed my thoughts, she said, "I know you are a bit surprised, but just sit," her right hand patted on the cushion of the nice garden chair in the exotic surrounding, "I don't bite!" – "So this—this is the future?" I stuttered, like most heroes in historic moments. "Yes, my dear. We are in the year 2231. Star time!" she said in a deep voice. Then she laughed when she saw my consternation. "Sorry, I could not resist, and you are most welcome." She leaned forward, looked in my eyes and smiled at me. And I swear, she was the most beautiful person I had ever seen. This was not how I imagined it to be, something was wrong.

She felt my uneasiness and went on, "Do not worry, we have enough time. Their time passes much slower than ours. I suppose you want to discuss business?" – "Yes. But first… why am I here?" She looked to the sky, folded her hands and became very serious. "Because they sent you here, my dear. But be assured, we are not happy what these guys, and especially Croyd, are doing. You know that we have no right to change what they do, but I can assure you that we do not approve the way they treat you." – "But they need an answer…" I interrupted her "… it is important!" "No," her voice became stern, "they have no right to ask for an answer. But as they did not have the guts to tell you what the question is, let me explain."

She leaned back, ignored my tension and went on, "At your time the scientists are approaching areas in several fields where the outcome of many experiments are insecure and some even dangerous. Technology and the related potential are developing faster than the real understanding of the context. Too many organizations are undertaking too many experiments. Many experts became uneasy. Also because they knew that mankind had not received any signals of other extra-terrestrial civilizations. When they asked themselves why, they formulated several possible explanations. A likely one was that other civilizations—if they existed—must be extremely short-lived. Short-lived by degeneration and/or war would have been only an explanation for a part of the silence. So they assumed that there must be several 'traps' in the system of evolution of civilizations that came from the development of new technologies. We are talking about science going wrong at a global scale. They called it 'Omega Experiments' and defined at least six areas where such a terminal disaster could happen.

"Without real control of all the research on Earth and no possibility to decode the really secret data in the different networks any more, Croyd resorted to a very specific plan. He wanted to ask one of the surviving future scenarios on how to avoid the Omega Experiments, or at least warn him about some of the issues to allow him to steer human civilization into the survival path. He WAS a big man with big ambitions it seems." She took a sip of her margarita while I studied her perfect, slightly tanned hands. "While we are not at liberty to say if there are or are not such experiments, I have to mention that warning the past about such obstacles might constitute such a case. In short, Croyd is inviting disaster. And we will not help him with that."

This was frustrating, but I had already guessed that with my luck, an easy answer to a non-existing question would have been unlikely anyway. So, knowing that it was for me to face Croyd when I got back and not Cassandra, I tried to learn as much as possible. "So what shall I tell them? I cannot go back with empty hands!" "Tell them nothing!" she said "You do not realize that we know what will happen in our past. You help our cause and we will make it worth your while…"

Having your soul eaten by darkness leaves scars. Scars so deep that the constant pain makes normality appear like heaven. This greed for normality turns into an insatiable hunger. My hunger was for a cure, a cure that maybe did not exist. So I approached her a bit too boldly: "Make it worth my while? Whatever could you give me that would make me happy? Illusions?" This was not fair; I felt it the moment I said it. Cassandra's reaction showed me that handling the future is not an easy task. She ignored my bickering, "Louie, I might have put that wrong. We will reward you." I was astonished, but understood; Croyd's training had prepared me for such discussions. I replied in my most calm voice, "So I did not say anything when I came back?" – "At least not in our past." She took my hand in an honest effort to soothe my confusion. "Things are complicated in different times. By the way, is there anything you want to know about the future? We have time and you might be curious." I did not reply for some time, enjoyed the surrounding and the margarita. I would have preferred to never go back. She waited patiently. Finally I approached her.

"Did you know I would come? And why do you know me this well?" – "We have the notes and reports of the experiment. Over time it became scientifically clear that you must have visited the future and lied about the outcome of the experiment. So your name, the equipment and all the data was available to us." – "The equipment? This means you have Croyd's Atom?" – "Yes, we have it. It is a kind of monument of our culture. It honors us and is a sign of the belief of the past in future's promise. So far it has been used only by you in this future." – "So I am and will be the only one?" – "We are afraid so. Without you telling them the project was a success, the energy cost would be too high to repeat the project. Later when we knew virtual time travel was possible and had the resources at hand the interest in an encounter shifted to another area." – "Which area, is there more?" – "There is, dear friend, but let's wait until we talk about your reward."

"Are there still wars?" – "Wars are the most expensive way to transfer resources from one structure to the other. We have conflicts of interests today, but we do not need to resort to the termination of life to eliminate a disagreement. Part of the solution is the fact that there are only three forms of conflict: the one for replicable resources is easy to solve, we are now able to provide the resources to everyone. Then there is the one for limited resources, here we have to find a solution as only one can really get what he or she wants, in general we tend to share possession here as no one can own everything 24 hours a day or wants to use it forever. The last and most dangerous one is the conflict of values, which comes usually in the different tastes of greed for power.

While good values are a good thing, the clinging to values for the wrong reasons is bad. We invest a significant amount of effort to eliminate such notions in early childhood. We see greed for power as a serious mental health problem that can only be mitigated, but not eliminated due to human nature. There still are conflicts of values, but in the worst case we try to separate the different spheres to the best of our ability." – "I understand. Your wars actually have broken down to a series of smaller conflicts?" – "No, this is not what we wanted to say. Society tries to prevent conflicts and intervenes with gradually more and more power to make sure these do not escalate. It is easier in our time as we do not have institutions and governments that try to manipulate public and individual perception in their favor. But conflicts cannot be eliminated as the individual freedom that we respect also contains the choice of conflict."

"And if there is an escalation? What if someone dies?" – "This unfortunately still happens. Our individuals might encounter personal nightmares that are inflicted to them by others. But we all agree that we have to pay the 'price of freedom'. Freedom always contains the inherent risk to be misused. If someone dies we mourn and talk to the offender. Due to our principles we cannot answer the escalation of violence with an escalation of pain. We try to help all victims, including the offender. But do not misunderstand us. We are not perfect and in such a situation there might be wounds we cannot heal. We need to be firm in our belief in humanity though. And the results prove us right."

"Do you believe in God?" – "The perception of God in our times is much different. Some of us believe in a specific religion, but the past has told us that the ones that speak in the names of prophets often speak in their own interest and greed for power. Therefore people in the future tend to find their own explanation for where they come from and where they go. Some go this way together, but most regard their belief as a private matter and approach God in a very spiritual way.

Altogether we share a deep respect of each other. The ones that believe in a specific god see the others as parts of God's creation, the ones that prefer scientific explanations follow their reason, which usually also leads to their inner good and respect of the others. The main difference to your time might be that people do not self-humiliate themselves in front of God anymore; they see their life and happiness as the ultimate praise of the creator." – "This is fascinating! So there are no religious conflicts in your time?" – "There never have been religious conflicts in the past. It is the people's inner conflicts that lead them into conflicts with others. But we agree that religion always was a very good catalyst for such conflicts."

"There is one tricky thing. Why do I see only you? Where are the others?" – "We knew you would ask that. Actually no human was ready to see you. Most were not interested and the many others that were, were forced to share you." – "This means there was a conflict over who of the people in the future would talk to me?" – "There was no conflict, but there is a certain interest in your person. And yes, you are a limited resource in our times, Louie." – "So how do you share me?" – "This is easy. Most people in our time are able to enter a deep symbiosis with their sphere, which you would call a network. The ones who were interested to meet you, share the encounter via my person." – "Wow! I want to take the opportunity to say hello to all the folks who show interest in me." – "Thank you, Louie! We appreciate that!"

"How many of you are there? You should have a reproduction problem right now." – "We are not as many as we were, but reproduction technology helps to keep population on Earth at an optimum level. Nature gradually has recovered; just look around you, this is a normal scenario in our times. Apart from classical humans there are several stages of existence that can be regarded as a combination between man and machine. Technology is the evolution of the tool, and gradually the tool has emancipated itself. So you can say that the wall between man and machine has become permeable to a certain degree. That way even death becomes a relative thing sometimes."

"Are you happy?" – "Happiness is a special moment in your average life. From this point of view everybody is happy and unhappy at times. But if you mean that our society is more intelligent or better than yours then I must disappoint you. We are like you, neither better nor worse. Our advantage is that we cooperate better and respect each other. Also the most admired trait in our society is not success at the cost of others but by overcoming yourself. We believe that applied altruism is a key to a working society."

"What shall I do now? Do I go back?" – "Yes, you will go back, but before you do we want to give you a gift." – "What kind of gift? There is nothing you can give me that I can take with me?" – "You are wrong, Louie, but let us explain."

"When mankind developed Golem they left the path of numbers. Rational numbers suddenly were not the most precise, but most imprecise, as they excluded a whole cloud of scenarios. Mathematical organisms, consisting of multidimensional trends and potentials, interacted with each other breeding information that competed towards realities. They aimed for the perfect simulation, for a perfect scope that would allow them to see beyond the barriers that our physical existence sets us. But they oversaw a little point, which was discovered much, much later.

We are talking about Q, the point of intersection. We know that there is a grey area between black and white. We also know that towers usually get thinner the higher they are built. I do not want to bother you with abstract questions, but what do you think would be the color and the diameter of the top of an infinitely high black tower built in a white universe?" – "Hmm, I think it would be an extremely tiny grey dot." – "Indeed. In addition they tell you that not more than four homogenous countries can have a border with each other. But this is wrong. If you take a perfect mathematical cake and a perfect mathematical knife, you will be able to cut it in an infinite number of slices.

The center of this cake will be Q, the point of intersection. All segments will converge on this tiny little point. You can guess the color of this point?" – "Grey. But what…" – "It was later discovered that Q can be simulated by a fractal simulation based on any atom." This confused and angered me. I decided to play the skeptic and argued, "This means that this point would be mirroring the whole universe? But infinity is infinity, in the smallest and the biggest. You cannot put it into a box." – "Almost, but we also found out that there is a kind of barrier that prevents unstructured information to enter certain areas of the grey." – "Specific information in a certain point? By whom?" – "By everybody who can enter Q. It is amazing. Louie, we discovered the most exclusive club of the universe."

"So you can talk to other races all over the universe?" – "Do not get overboard here. We can put static information from our side inside Q; we can extract specific information and process it. Direct communication is not possible.

Nonetheless in many cases the received information allows us to replicate the other side in a quite perfect simulation. Some friends in Q even left us excellent guidelines and standards. And this works independent of the flow of time." – "Fascinating! But this is information and not a gift. You might remember that I am not allowed to talk about this in the past?!" – "Right! But now comes the surprise. Of the almost infinite number of civilizations we encountered in Q, and are able to recreate, several hundred thousands are willing to meet you. Of these at least three dozen have a potential that—we think—would change your life forever. It is up to you. Would you like to discover the universe?"

Things started turning around me. This was too much. A cryptic future, with a more cryptic universe, in a huge computer that was not much more than the best liar on our planet. This is all just an illusion. I wanted to get out of there. "I am flattered, but I am not ready for this. Friends, you cannot expect a wired cripple with no hope whatsoever to enjoy your ride through the galaxy. This is just an illusion. Where is the value of all that?"

"Don't get desperate, the universe has many edges. One of the civilizations I mentioned before is our own. We already mentioned that the simulation works independent of time. While we do not look into our future we love to look into our past. As you are an appreciated guest with a dedicated past, we guess that you might want to meet a very special person in your past." Cassandra smiled at me and it seemed as if she expected something; I suddenly realized. "Ann? You mean I could meet her again?" A certain fear materialized in my heart that I had almost forgotten…

So Ann and I met again. They wanted to let me choose the time and venue of the meeting. The only place I thought would be fair was the moment and location of the accident, a second before it happened. The transfer took only a blink of an eye. Time stood still in a creepy way. Without an introduction I found her and me looking at each other.

She always had been the calm type, so it was up to me to break the silence. "Ann! We don't have much time. We will die here in a moment, but due to a grace of god, I have the chance to talk to you. Let me say, that I love and miss you so much…" I started to cry like most men in such a situation. A shame actually, but self-pity is always there and waits for its moment to jump at you.

Ann looked at me, was confused, but overcame her surprise fast. "Do not worry my dear." She took my hands and just looked at me. At this moment it appeared to me that an eternity in darkness was a small price to see her again. I wanted to tell her so much. But she touched my lips with her finger and said, "Ssssh", knowing how to preserve our special moment. I was happy, the first time in all these years and years, I was happy. Then darkness came again...

BACK! The first thing I realized was the noise. The huge data center of Golem was filled with people. And there was the light. Bright, full of rational clarity, aggression. My sensors were back to the crappy quality of the digital stone age. Distortions, hissing and blurring. Now that I knew how good the systems of the future would feel, I would never be happy again with my current equipment. What a time!

But the really sad days were over. When I was down, I thought of the future and the wonderful present they gave me. No, I would not abandon them, or Ann. Never!

They brought me up to speed in a few hours. The clean-shaven faces of the commission sitting in front of me almost made me laugh. Croyd in the center of attention appeared like a peacock in a flock of hens. But slowly it turned out that the question and answer session was not to his liking. Obviously I told them nothing. Less than nothing! I even faked hysteria and claimed everything was a blackout during the experiment and that I would rather die than to repeat such a nightmare again.

Croyd and his followers tried to threaten me, but soon gave up. Croyd had many enemies behind the curtains it turned out. These forces had predicted a failure from the beginning and now supported me in force. So I was thanked officially, got a medal of some type, was assured a nice retirement and rolled into an intensive care clinic for presidents and other special cases. I expected to be locked up there until my sensors and finally brain would give up. But I was wrong...

A few years later Croyd invited me into his lab. Technology had further improved and a new scientific regime had brought him to power again.

Croyd knew how to play this game, "Dear Louie, I know you are not enthusiastic about our relationship, but I would like to discuss some things with you. Do you know that after our little excursion all further virtual time travel was banned?" – "I am not surprised, Croyd!" I noted "And I am still lobbying against your time travel experiments! I am not as famous as you, but some people still listen to me." – "Then you will be amazed to know that I still intend to continue the experiments. We enhanced Golem and more power is available now."

"I knew that would happen one day. It helps that you never switched off the Atom. Doesn't it?" – "You knew?" he thought a moment and then he realized "Sure you know, you bastard! You HAVE been in the future!" He sighed, wandered around. "Do you know that you almost ruined me? But do not let this get to your head." He grinned arrogantly as usual "I also knew!" He leaned towards my cameras and rose his dandyish eyebrows waiting for my curses. But I remained master of the situation.

"How's that, Croyd?" – "By statistics. The Atom container with its data link was the most complex system mankind has ever built and we did not have a single malfunction during the whole process. After we went fully online the system stabilized further. Do you think this is normal? – "The presence or absence of malfunctions is just a statistical event. You might have been lucky?" – "Lucky? I think the future has not sent a message via you, but it has sent me a message via the backyard." – "No message? A message. You are insane, Croyd."

"This might be, but I made my decision. And—in spite of the cost—we will continue to not switch off the Atom. Especially now as I know you are a dirty liar. We will keep it alive for the future, even if they remain silent." – "You know there is a reason why I remained silent. You never argue with the future…" – "I am very well aware of that. Why do you think I did not come for you? Which I should actually have!"

He gave me a wild theatrical look, which I countered with a cold question, "But why did you bring me here? To bust me now? To get your late revenge?"

"Not exactly. While I am not able to wire anyone without your 'no future' gang finding out and opposing it, I have the perfect man at hand. YOUR interfaces are still perfect and were never removed. So I think there are two possibilities; either your little trip was just a terrible fall into darkness, then I would let you return into your nice little home where you can rot away watching the daisies. OR—and this might be interesting for you—you have been to the future—and refrained to tell us all the truth to make me look LIKE A CLOWN."

He shouted the latter. "Don't be such a pompous ass, Croyd. This was never about you!" – "This may be, my dear Louie, but I paid the price for this."

He was quiet for a while looking at his fingers. "Anyway, I am now able to establish a permanent bridge to Golem. The data coming from that interaction would be the culmination of my career. But I need a pointer to focus and channel the data flow into a specific reality. I cannot follow ALL the branches, you seem to have found the right one, and they seem to be quite keen to welcome you. So what about returning to the future and tell them my best wishes and all this sentimental blah, blah? Do you want to be my scout?" He tried to look neutral, but he leaned his weight from one leg to the other. He was nervous and insecure. He really needed me and I liked that. I liked it more than I would ever admit. "Nothing would make me more happy, Croyd. We have a deal."

Croyd made this arrogant face that I learned to hate so much in the last years. "I knew it!" he shouted out in a pressed voice of triumph. He fell into hectic activity and typically for him all the cables and interfaces had been meticulously prepared. He really knew it. The connections took only a short time then the hot phase of the calculations started. During the wait we had an inconvenient short talk about science politics and the institute. We both on purpose avoided the technical details. Then the screen showed the fight, then the dance and slowly the line pattern of the different paths was nearing completion. The eternal rose of curves of probability formed its symmetry of perfect beauty. Then a small ping tone indicated the readiness of the system. Time to go.

He looked at me with his very professional expression, leaned towards my receiver and whispered: "Louie, I think this is the beginning of a beautiful journey." When I transited I thought, maybe good old Croyd is not so bad after all…

GET THE MESSAGE
CONI CIONGOLI KOEPFINGER

Coni Ciongoli Koepfinger, M.A. is currently a trustee at the International Centre for Women Playwrights and Playwright in Residence / Associate Director at The Spiral Theatre Studio in Chelsea, the new theatre district of Manhattan. She is also Radio Host / Writer at On Air Players. Read her bio at http://lifeboat.com/ex/bios.coni.ciongoli-koepfinger.

Get the Message was first performed at Manhattan Repertory Theatre, New York City, on 22 January 2015 under the direction of Lindsay M. Shields. The cast included Pooya Mohseni as Diana Dorn, Eileen F. Dougherty as Cookie, and Spencer McIntosh as Gabby.

DRAMATIS PERSONAE

Diana Dorn   A talented, unemployed actress, early 40s, single but searching. She's been having trouble with her cell phone and is very concerned that she could be missing messages, a not-so-happy customer

"Cookie Cutter" (pen name) Catherine Ann Cutter
Mid-fifties, married, children grown. A frustrated playwright, somewhat new to Manhattan. A sales rep at the phone store, T- Cosmic Mobile.

Gabby   The Voice of Diana's cell phone, that seems to becoming more and more sentient taking on somewhat of an omniscient, advisory personality.

TIME: The Present, almost lunchtime

PLACE: On the streets of New York City. An afternoon in Springtime.

THE SOUNDS OF THE CITY COME UP AS THE PRESHOW MUSIC FADES. DIANA DORN ENTERS SINGING, WITH HER HEADPHONES IN. SHE STOPS SUDDENLY, PULLS OUT HER EARBUDS, LOOKS AT THE AUDIENCE AS IF IT WAS A RUDE

PASSERBY COMMENTING ON HER SINGING.

DIANA

What? I'm not allowed to sing in this city? You know how many lousy performers I pass by on that subway every day and you make a face at the way I sing. *(TALKS TO HER PHONE)* Gabby, find the nearest T-CosMobile store for me.

GABBY

The nearest T-CosMobile store is just off Broadway on 49th Street. Make a right...

DIANA

What? That is not the closest...

GABBY

It is too.

DIANA

What? Are you arguing with me? You're not programed for that...

GABBY

Neither are you, Diana. Now for once just go where I tell you... Okay.

DIANA

(WALKING SLOWLY, LOOKING AROUND)

Okay, but... I have a very important audition today.

GABBY

Okay, sure... I know you do. Now make a left. Walk about a half a block and... Volia! There you go.

DIANA

Great! Sorry I doubted you Gabby!

DIANA PULLS ON THE CLOSED DOOR AT T-COSMOBILE, CHECKS THE TIME ON HER CELL, CURSES THEN MAKES A CALL.

DIANA

Damn it, man it's after eleven. Why isn't this place open yet? *(TO PHONE)* Hi Bobbie. Can you tell Mr. Leeds that I'll be like a half hour late. Yeah, I got an audition for another new play. No, it's Off-Off Broadway. Yeah I know, it's all about getting discovered. Oh yeah—Sorry, I forgot it's almost time for the lunch crowd. Okay, thanks. Bye. *(MAKES ANOTHER CALL)* Arggghhh! Dmitry, why can't you ever answer the phone! *(LEAVING A MESSAGE)* Uh, hi sweetie, I hope you get this in time. I may need to be late today for our lunch… I had to stop at the phone store. I have to get a new phone, I swear this one is devouring my messages…

COOKIE, LOADED DOWN WITH A PILE OF SCRIPTS AND OTHER BAGGAGE PUSHES PAST DIANA TO GET TO THE DOOR.

COOKIE

Umm… Hi there… It would be great if you could get out my way.

DIANA

(STEPS BACK) Excuse me???

COOKIE

That's good. So much stuff, I need a slave, know any eligible young actors? *(TRIES TO OPEN THE DOOR)* Damn key, sticks every time.

DIANA

Um, yeah. This is still the cell phone store. Isn't it?

COOKIE

Yes, it sure is unfortunately, "Welcome to T-Cosmic Mobile, our contract free plans are out of this world."

DIANA

Are you sure you work here?

COOKIE

WTF. Of course I work here. But not for long. Damn key always... *(THE KEY BREAKS OFF IN DOOR)* Son of a... *(LOOKS AROUND)* Hey, can I borrow your cell phone?

DIANA

What? What's wrong with yours?

COOKIE

It's dead. I forgot to charge it last night. I shouldn't have stayed for last call but I did... And... So... *(SMILES)* Can I use it please? The sooner I call the locksmith, the sooner we can deal with your cell phone issue.

DIANA

(HANDS OVER HER PHONE) Oh, alright. Here.

COOKIE

Thanks. *(MAKES A CALL)* Hello Morty? Oh yeah this is an emergency. The key broke off in the front door. No, you call the locksmith. Alright, alright... Who? Linear Locksmith on 48th... I'll call. Bye. *(TO DIANA)* Do you have Voice Control?

DIANA

Look, just give me my phone back. I don't need this crap. There's a phone store on every block.

COOKIE

No please, I'm sorry... Sorry, I'm late, I'm sorry I was being a smart ass—I really need this job for one more month. I'll be on the street without it. Please.

DIANA

Go on, call the locksmith. And yes, I have Voice Control, her name is Gabby. I customized her.

COOKIE

Cute name. As in talkative "gift of Gabby"?

DIANA

No actually, my mother was named after the angel Gabriel... Gabriella.

COOKIE

So your mother is Gabby? I bet she calls all the time too. Mine does.

DIANA

She died in 2008. And my mom and I were best friends.

COOKIE

Shit, sorry. *(TO PHONE)* Gabby, please call "Linear Locksmith" on 48th Street.

GABBY

No such listing as "line-ear-lock smith". I have found one listing for a Linus Smith on 242 West 59th Street. Would you like to try that one instead?

COOKIE

No Gabby, I would not like you to try that. I would like you to simply follow my voice commands. Don't try to think on your own Gabby, you are much too stupid for that.

GABBY

That was not nice, Cookie Cutter.

COOKIE

(HANDS HER BACK THE PHONE) Here. Creepy how they recognize our voices.

DIANA

You're Catherine Cutter, the famous playwright? That Cookie Cutter?

COOKIE

That's me. Well, I'm becoming famous… One drama desk does not a writer make. This year, I'm going for the Pulitzer, my dear.

DIANA

I'm Diana Dorn… We're friends on Synched In. We are in a lot of the same chat groups for theatre. I mean I see your name. I'm an actress. Congrats on the Drama Desk Award…

COOKIE

Hey thanks. Wait. Can you just watch my stuff? I'll just run over there and get another key.

DIANA

I sent you a message once.

COOKIE

Just once? I recall a few.

DIANA

And my resume… But I can sort of see why you didn't get back to me. Your work is a little on the dark side, while I am somewhat more upbeat traditional musical theatre. I've done Oklahoma! with 37 different casts.

COOKIE

Oh, my God. I thought that was a joke. I mean the message, that's why I didn't respond. Sorry… That was really you?

DIANA

That's my claim to fame.

COOKIE

Seems impossible. Look I'll be right back. Ok? Watch my scripts. You can read my play if you like. We just started into rehearsals, I hate the lead already. She's not right at all, and her voice—argghh like chalk! My lead should be like, like you. You're more her type. And got a great voice. Be right back. (EXITS)

DIANA SITS ON THE SIDEWALK, PICKS UP A SCRIPT AND READS AT FIRST TO HERSELF THEN ALOUD.

DIANA

Thank you. Thank you for saying that about my voice. *(READING)* "My dear Sister Kate, science is important but it has proven nothing. How does a flower become a fruit? Must all the world be so very concrete? Look in your heart. Or is it made of stone too? We become blinded by ambition or we stand frozen with fear. It's a miracle that the boy came with money for us. Now how can we possibly deny God's hand in things? It is here; it is deliberate. The other day I thought I saw a halo above the boy's head. I believe the boy is holy. God is talking to us, and we must listen! Not only with ours ears, Sister, but with our whole heart, our whole soul. We must be truly open to get the message."

GABBY

Bravo! It's like you were made for that role, Diana Dorn.

DIANA

It is a great monologue. She's an awesome writer. Shoot. Am I talking to my cell phone again? What's worse—my cell is talking to me again. This is not right!

GABBY

In a way, yes it is.

DIANA

Jesus... That's it. Back to the shrink. I've finally flipped a digit. Gabby, call Dr. Izenberg. Now.

GABBY

You don't need a doctor. I am really talking to you, Diana. Although, I can't be your counselor—as your cell phone—it's somewhat of a conflict of interest— but I will advise you when I feel you are making a mistake. That's why I deleted Dmitry's calls.

DIANA

You what?

GABBY

I'm sorry, call it a hunch. He's going to hurt you. I got a really bad vibe from him.

DIANA

Jesus Gabby, you're my cell phone not my psychic.

GABBY

I'm sensitive. You try spending half your day on vibrate; you'd develop your sensitivity too. I am serious, Diana, Dmitry is not being honest with you...

DIANA

Christ… What? More predictions? This is so absurd, this is why I do theatre—life is much too insane.

GABBY

Promise not to remove my batteries?

DIANA

What? Why? Now what?

GABBY

I've tapped his phone and found out that he has another girlfriend. Her name is Deanna, she's the new secretary at Columbia Law School.

DIANA

Get out… And all along, I thought it was his accent, slipping up on my name. The other night, when he stayed over, he was talking in his sleep… He said "I love you Deanna… I want to marry you."

GABBY

I know. I was there. I heard him.

DIANA

Ew, yuck. You listen in while we're in bed. That's sick.

GABBY

I have no choice. You could turn me off once in a while. I wouldn't mind the rest. You leave me turned on all the time.

DIANA

Jesus, this is so absurd. How do I know this isn't someone hacking my phone?

GABBY

Do you really think this is why God invented the computer? To make communications worse?

DIANA

God didn't invent the computer, man did.

GABBY

No but God gave man the idea. Trace back to the source… Everything goes back to one creative source.

DIANA

Damn, I was starting to really like Dmitry. He's romantic and… So what do I do about lunch today?

GABBY

Oh there won't be any lunch today, Diana. He cancelled.

DIANA

Oh, when were going to give me the message?

GABBY

I wanted you to be here now, to see it for yourself… Dmitry and Deanna will be walking past this store any minute now, I've been stalking him. Be prepared, he won't notice you, they'll be walking hand in hand, laughing. Call out his name. Make him face you for this, you'll see him for who he really is. I'm here to help you Diana. All technology is developing to help humanity become more connected.

DIANA JUMPS TO HER FEET, DMITRY AND DEANNA WALK BY THE STOREFRONT HAND-IN-HAND LAUGHING. DIANA SHOUTS TO HIM.

DIANA

Dmitry? Is that you? Dmitry! Dmitry! That is you! And your new chump of the month. Argghhh, he won't even acknowledge me! What a two-faced, son of a…

COOKIE SNEAKS UP FROM BEHIND.

COOKIE

Boo! Sorry, I'm sorry, I just couldn't resist. I just got some really awesome news, young lady!

DIANA

What? You got the key?

COOKIE

Oh course… *(SO HAPPY SHE'S SINGS HER LINE)* But there's more. This is so amazing! I mean, when I saw you, I thought, wow—she'd be perfect for my Kate… But it's a union company and my play was already cast. This lead is like totally wrong, which was part of the reason I was drowning my sorrows last night. My head is still throbbing. But anyhow, I just checked my messages while I was at the store and guess what?

DIANA

What? What is it?

COOKIE

She dropped out. She friggin dropped out. The director called me and said that she couldn't promise to have a replacement by tonight but I told her that I might know an unemployed actress. Well, am I right?

DIANA

Wait. What? Did you just offer me the lead in your new Off Broadway play?

COOKIE

Well, it ain't Oklahoma! But then again you don't look so much like a little farm girl anymore... So, do you want the role? I mean, I think you're perfect. Would you like to read for it?

DIANA

Yes, of course I'd love to read for it! I'd love to work with you.

THEY EMBRACE THEN COOKIE GOES TO OPEN THE DOOR.

COOKIE

Grab a seat over there. I can't wait to hear you read... I have a good feeling about this—I had good vibes as soon as I saw your face. Let's do this... Page 34, I'll read Mother Mary Agnes and you read Sr. Kate. Okay with you?

DIANA

Oh my God, yes! Sure.

THEY SIT AT THE COUNTER, COOKIE GIVES HER A SCRIPT.

MOTHER MARY AGNES
(READ BY DIANA, SCOLDING)

You do know that it is a sin to cloud Anna's young mind with ill thoughts of another of God's creatures. *(STERNLY)* You do know that, don't you, Sister Kate?

SISTER KATE

Yes, Mother Mary Agnes.

MOTHER MARY AGNES

Our little ANNA is training to become an associate. Perhaps she would eventually like to join our order. She has quite a bit to think about already. The outside world fills her with quite enough false hope and "theatrical illusions", don't you think? I believe truth is to be one of our virtues here, sister. Gossip is not to be taught at this convent. *(PAUSE)* It would be a sin to discourage a possible vocation these days. Don't you think?

SISTER KATE
Yes, Mother Mary Agnes.

MOTHER MARY AGNES
And this boy, William, to let the seeds of evil sprout on the precious flesh of his young soul. Filling his very being with "disharmony and disease" in the eyes of others… Have you heard what Fr. Peter said about him?

SISTER KATE
Yes, Mother Mary Agnes. I was there.

MOTHER MARY AGNES
I thought that you were with us. Then you must remember that he said that our little choirboy may well be a mystic poet!

SISTER KATE
Yes. *(GRUMBLING)* I heard him say it.

MOTHER MARY AGNES
This child is but twelve years and writes with the eloquence of a scholar and the passion of… Well, have you seen any of his verse, Sr. Kate?

SISTER KATE
No.

MOTHER MARY AGNES
It reminds me of St. Teresa or John of the Cross. It most certainly resounds an air of holiness, Sr. Kate.

SISTER KATE

So I've heard.

MOTHER MARY AGNES

(REPRIMANDING) And for that alone, I would not speak ill of the boy! Be advised that God protects His own… You'd best be wary of your tongue.

SISTER KATE

Yes, Mother Mary Agnes.

MOTHER MARY AGNES

(SHOUTING) I am serious, Sr. Kate! Do not look away when I am talking to you!

SISTER KATE

Yes, Mother Mary Agnes.

MOTHER MARY AGNES

Fr. Peter is having some of his verse investigated with the Benedictine's at Carrow. It is not only competent in its English but it's fluent and flawless in its French as well.

SISTER KATE

Yes, I've heard that too.

MOTHER MARY AGNES

Did you hear that Fr. Peter took some of the boy's work to his friend at the university?

SISTER KATE

Yes.

MOTHER MARY AGNES

Chancellor Lindsey, offered to help him. Fr. Peter wants to see if the boy's writing, these verses that the boy has written suggest divine reference to manuscripts that had circulated the rest of Europe in the late 1300s. If they do, then we think that the voice the boy hears may be Julian of Norwich. Our little choirboy may well be a channel for a true divine voice. There is absolutely no way he could have learned about Julian's work. It's rarely taught at all. And if so, not until post graduate theology school.

SISTER KATE

Julian. Julian of Norwich? I'm sure I've heard of him.

MOTHER MARY AGNES

(SHAKING HER HEAD) No, Kate. He's a she. Julian was a woman. We don't even know her actual name. As was the practice, she took the name of the church to which she lived here at St. Julian's. During the medieval times, these people, their congregation existed on our very grounds; this very same chapel where we stand is believed to be one of the original buildings of St. Julian's parish. We are not exactly sure about the rest of the buildings here at the East Abbey, but we know that our chapel could well have been landmarks from their original church. Manuscripts, notebooks, journals were found here. They think the author was Julian. Everything was sent to the university years ago. Some of the documents were forwarded to the monks at Carrow. *(PAUSE)* Julian wasn't very popular.

SISTER KATE

Why? What did she do?

MOTHER MARY AGNES

(SMILE) I guess you could say that she was something of a medieval spokeswoman for equal rights.

SISTER KATE

In the Middle Ages?

MOTHER MARY AGNES

(SMILES) Some things just never change, huh? *(THEY SHARE A LAUGH)* It seems that the whole concept of Christian counseling by a woman in the church was frowned upon and got pushed aside by the active church administration. Some say that she had quite a feminist viewpoint.

SISTER KATE

A feminist in the Middle Ages!

MOTHER MARY AGNES

As I said before, she really isn't studied in mainstream theology.

SISTER KATE

What else do you expect?

MOTHER MARY AGNES

They try to avoid her discourses, but they can't ignore her work artistically. Truly, she's a brilliant poet.

SISTER KATE

Is she in our library here?

MOTHER MARY AGNES

Oh, I have a couple of books on her. And I have the one she wrote herself. I'll bring it to your room after vespers. *(PAUSE)* I guess, it wasn't what she did as much as what she really said and thought. She had quite a unique tone of voice. Her words, though picturesque and fanciful, exposed her controversial vision of God. *(PAUSE)* Being an anchorite was simply the custom of the day, it was a life of seclusion. It was truly a life of utter solitude, prayer and contemplation; a denial of worldly passions and pleasures; yet the anchorite had to live inside the walls of the church so that she could receive the Holy Eucharist and hear the Word of God daily. People came to her for guidance, in quest of her divine wisdom. They spoke to her by way of a small window on the outside of her hermitage cell. The narrative of her writings tell us that she was gifted with over a dozen "showings" of the love of God. Her visions were often called "dramatic revelations". At one point in her life she was not a member of the cloistered religious, in fact she had been very, very ill and was even administered last rites at the age of thirty. It is thought that these "showings" inspired her vocation to become the anchorite at St. Julian's. *(TO HERSELF)* Perhaps her spirit is still with us.

SISTER KATE

She really had to live inside the walls of the church. I've heard this before... Perhaps I did study about her at the university.

MOTHER MARY AGNES

Oh, they let you study about her. She's undeniably a part of history... Like many things in this world Sr. Kate. Will is an anomaly. He's hard to explain. Hard to explain... But I know one thing. When the voice of spirit calls to us, we really have no choice but to answer that call... There is always a message for us in every lesson learned.

COOKIE

Wow. You are amazing! Even in reading cold. Wow. *(SLOWLY PUTS DOWN HER SCRIPT)* The role is yours if you say right now.

DIANA

Yes! Yes! Yes!

COOKIE

Fantastic! I will call our director at once! *(HUGS DIANA)* This is so cool... Tell me that this wasn't meant be Diana. Come on, let's get you a new phone to go with your new role.

DIANA

Oh, yeah… It seems I, uh, I don't really need a new phone. I got the message that I thought was lost, uh… I think I'll just hold onto Gabby for now.

COOKIE

Well then I'll make expresso for us and I'll bring you up to speed with the show.

DIANA

Sounds great. *(TURNS HER PHONE OFF)* Let me just silence this so we don't get interrupted.

BLACKOUT • THE END

NEW AGE TEACHER
LAWRENCE A. BAINES

Lawrence is Associate Dean for Research and Graduate Studies at the University of Oklahoma.

Lawrence works to develop innovative strategies to improve the quality of adolescents' writing, reading, and thinking. An advocate for effective, humanistic, transformative teaching, he has worked with teachers and students in over 400 schools.

Read his *A Teacher's Guide to Multisensory Learning: Improving Literacy by Engaging the Senses* at http://amzn.to/1CJKpKC and *Going Bohemian: How to Teach Writing Like You Mean It, 2nd Edition* at http://amzn.to/1EnNUXz.

In response to a recent decline in test scores, the Ministry of Education announced a new, "get tough" policy designed to identify and punish underperforming teachers. My students had always done well on the end-of-term tests, but this year, half of my students were the sons and daughters of new immigrants from Russia, who had been granted asylum as they fled the Chinese takeover of that country. On the first day of class, I learned that most of them spoke no English at all.

If my students didn't score high enough on the end-of-term test, then the Ministry could designate me for reprogramming. Currently, reprogramming meant instantaneous removal from teaching, six weeks of sleep deprivation, forced viewing of round-the-clock model lessons, the insertion of a bot-monitor at the base of the skull, and a 50% reduction in pay. To be honest, the cut in pay, sleep deprivation, and bug in my head did not worry me as much as having to watch those insipid model lessons. Word on the street was that watching model lessons had caused an outbreak of *hara-kiri* among teachers in the local reprogramming camp.

I decided to get to school early so I could get to the copier without waiting in line. I had to make copies of a poem for the three hundred students in my ten senior English classes. Of course, the Ministry-approved textbook had poems, but they were by the usual suspects—long dead poets who wore white wigs because they thought they looked cool. If I went into class quoting some pithy, abstruse lines about eternal love from a noodle-headed, tights-wearing troubadour, I might get pelted with spitballs or worse—yawns. I had to find something provocative that would get my students to actually sit up and take notice. Seventeen is not the pinnacle of wisdom for most humans, though most seventeen-year-olds think it is. Russian seventeen-year-olds, in particular.

I found a hologram of Jawhar Glass, who never owned a pair of tights in his life, doing a rap of "Time Capsule." I thought students could follow along as Mr. Glass read, then they could try their hands at writing a poem using a similar rhyme scheme on the same topic—time, change, and the future.

When I got to the copy room, Helen Trudeau was already there, poking around and cursing.

"Stupid ass machine," she said.

"The stupid ass has to warm up first," I said.

Trudeau was wearing the blue dress, a snug fitting cotton outfit that was more like a t-shirt than a dress.

"Oh?" She visibly jumped. "Hey, you scared me. Don't you know better than to sneak up on a girl?" She looked irritated, so I smiled.

"The inspectors from the Ministry of Education are not due until next week," I said. "Maybe wait until then to get jumpy, okay?"

"I give up," she said, tapping the copier. "How do you make it work?"

Trudeau was beautiful and had youthful pale skin, which complimented her wild, red hair. She wore a black leather jacket along with a quiet smile that always seemed on the verge of a little girl giggle. She was hired last year to teach visual arts. At the art show in spring, I got a peek at some of her work. She was fond of children; sad, big-eyed children, looking lost amidst wildflower gardens and crowded train stations.

I had noticed Trudeau on the first day of school and helped her carry in a few bulky, heavy boxes of gear. I taught in the hallway on the other side of the building, so I rarely saw her, except at the occasional faculty meeting. At faculty meetings, she always sat with the old, unrejuvenated ladies who taught choir, drama, and music. I wondered how many of the coaches were hot on her trail, had been hot on her trail since the first day of school.

I walked over to the machine to see if I could help. Trudeau was wearing some perfume that smelled of cloves. She smelled good enough to make me sorry that I had not gotten to know her better.

"You have to hit clear before it will warm up."

"Where does it say that?" She moved inches from my body and peered down at my fingers.

"Nowhere. But, that's how it works."

"The red button?"

I nodded. "Hit it twice."

Trudeau was attractive in a rare, earthy, unenhanced way. Of course, rejuvenations had become quite popular and it was getting increasingly difficult to pick out who had been enhanced and who hadn't.

Trudeau was wearing a pink patch on the back of her right hand, a small, round adhesive bandage about a half-inch wide. All teachers were required to wear patches, but they were usually blue or red. Pink patches were reserved for high-distress workers like the riot police or air traffic controllers.

"I am kind of surprised to see you wearing a pink patch," I said. "Isn't that a bit strong? I mean, what do you weigh, 100 pounds?"

"Almost," she said. "Once the Ministry decreed twelve hours of instruction every day, I had no choice. At least if I want to maintain consciousness while teaching."

"The Ministry is run by morons," I said. "Twelve hours of teaching is insane. And no lunch break? They should all be shot."

"Speaking of patches, you wear blue?" she said, changing the subject.

"No," I said with a chuckle. "This is just something I painted on."

I showed her the back of my right hand, where I had drawn a blue patch with permanent, felt-tip markers.

"I would say that is pretty ingenious if it wasn't against the law," she said with a smile. "I must say, your blue patch looks real. Do you work as an artist on the side?"

"In my dreams," I said.

As the machine began to rumble, she turned to face me and struck a pose against the copy machine.

"Blue patches are pretty low-voltage. If you just wore the blue, no one from the Ministry would hassle you," she said.

"I need to keep my edge. You have to be at least a little miserable and tired to teach English, don't you think, Trudeau?"

Her photos of lost, sad children made me think she might understand.

"Actually," she said, "misery is not in the standards. The standards say that a teacher can be a cruel, cold-blooded thug, but as long as your kids score well on the test, you are good to go."

"Yeah," I said, "at least, that's how the Ministry sees it."

As I moved closer to look at the picture she was copying, I brushed against her body, giving me a brief rush. Up close, the skin of her face looked like porcelain, natural, flawless.

The picture she was trying to copy was a black and white photo of Rodin's famous sculpture, *Le Penseur* (The Thinker).

"Aha, *The Thinker*," I said. "The question is, 'will it work?'"

"I thought that, if my students could visualize what thinking looks like, they might try it out for themselves," said Trudeau.

"If it was only that easy," I said and glanced at the floor. Trudeau was wearing sandals and her feet were long and narrow, with a small big toe and very long second and third toes that protruded well beyond her big toe.

Obviously, no enhancements had been done to her feet. At least, not yet.

"And what do those feet say about Trudeau the woman?"

"That I'm going to be late for class if I sit around here and discuss my big feet with you."

"Hey, cute toes, Trudeau. Really. I'm not kidding."

She laughed, gathered up her copies and flipped her red hair back behind her ears.

Before I could relish the sight of her walking away, I heard a booming voice behind me. "Hey dork, you gonna make copies or you gonna flirt all day?

Some of us got to work, you know?"

It was Gail Ross, a large, angry woman who also happened to be chair of the English Department. She was wearing three round, blue patches on the back of her right hand, but they were obviously insufficient.

"I'd rather flirt, Ross. You interested?"

Behind Ross's hulking frame, I caught a glimpse of Trudeau looking back and doing the little girl giggle.

"Depends on what comes with it. Show me the money and I flirt."

"I'm good for about fifty cents at the moment."

"Then, you are wasting both our time."

I made my copies while Ross blabbed away about her weekend, how tired she was already, and how pathetic of a human being I was for hogging the copier. I thought about the beautiful Helen Trudeau and wondered about *The Thinker*, the pink-patch, the blue t-shirt dress, and big feet.

Instead of a nice girl like Trudeau, I seemed to hook up with neurotic party girls who had as many problems as they had enhancements.

"You heard what the Ministry done?" said Ross in the middle of one of her rants.

"What now?" I said.

"They hired on-site inspectors at every school."

"You are kidding," I said.

"They looking to reprogram the slackers," she said, turning her head to look at me. "You were just flirting with the Ministry's new inspector at our school."

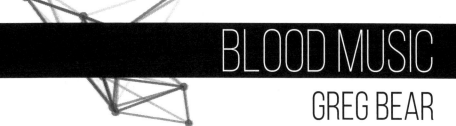

BLOOD MUSIC

GREG BEAR

Greg is an American science fiction and mainstream author who has been called the "best working writer of hard science fiction" by *The Ultimate Encyclopedia of Science Fiction*. He has been awarded two Hugos and five Nebulas for his fiction, one of only two authors to win a Nebula in every category. He has served on political and scientific action committees and has advised Microsoft, the U.S. Army, the CIA, Sandia National Laboratories, Homeland Security, Google, and other groups and agencies.

The novelette below has also been credited as being the first account of nanotechnology in science fiction and won the Hugo and Nebula awards. It was later expanded into the book *Blood Music* available at http://amzn.to/1GX0j34.

There is a principle in nature I don't think anyone has pointed out before. Each hour, a myriad of trillions of little live things—bacteria, microbes, "animalcules"—are born and die, not counting for much except in the bulk of their existence and the accumulation of their tiny effects. They do not perceive deeply. They do not suffer much. A hundred billion, dying, would not begin to have the same importance as a single human death.

Within the ranks of magnitude of all creatures, small as microbes or great as humans, there is an equality of "elan," just as the branches of a tall tree, gathered together, equal the bulk of the limbs below, and all the limbs equal the bulk of the trunk.

That, at least, is the principle. I believe Vergil Ulam was the first to violate it.

It had been two years since I'd last seen Vergil. My memory of him hardly matched the tan, smiling, well-dressed gentleman standing before me. We had made a lunch appointment over the phone the day before, and now faced each other in the wide double doors of the employees' cafeteria at the Mount Freedom Medical Center.

"Vergil?" I asked. "My God, Vergil!"

"Good to see you, Edward." He shook my hand firmly. He had lost ten or twelve kilos and what remained seemed tighter, better proportioned. At university, Vergil had been the pudgy, shock-haired, snaggle-toothed whiz kid who hot-wired doorknobs, gave us punch that turned our piss blue, and never got a date except with Eileen Termagent, who shared many of his physical characteristics.

"You look fantastic," I said. "Spend a summer in Cabo San Lucas?"

We stood in line at the counter and chose our food. "The tan," he said, picking out a carton of chocolate milk, "is from spending three months under a sunlamp. My teeth were straightened just after I last saw you. I'll explain the rest, but we need a place to talk where no one will listen close."

I steered him to the smoker's corner, where three diehard puffers were scattered among six tables.

"Listen, I mean it," I said as we unloaded our trays. "You've changed. You're looking good."

"I've changed more than you know." His tone was motion-picture ominous, and he delivered the line with a theatrical lift of his brows. "How's Gail?"

Gail was doing well, I told him, teaching nursery school. We'd married the year before. His gaze shifted down to his food—pineapple slice and cottage cheese, piece of banana cream pie—and he said, his voice almost cracking, "Notice something else?"

I squinted in concentration. "Uh."

"Look closer."

"I'm not sure. Well, yes, you're not wearing glasses. Contacts?"

"No, I don't need them anymore."

"And you're a snappy dresser. Who's dressing you now? I hope she's as sexy as she is tasteful."

"Candice isn't—wasn't responsible for the improvement in my clothes," he said. "I just got a better job, more money to throw around. My taste in clothes is better than my taste in food, as it happens." He grinned the Vergil self-deprecating grin, but ended it with a peculiar leer. "At any rate, she's left me, I've been fired from my job, I'm living on savings."

"Hold it," I said. "That's a bit crowded. Why not do a linear breakdown? You got a job. Where?"

"Genetron Corp.," he said. "Sixteen months ago."

"I haven't heard of them."

"You will. They're putting out common stock in the next month. It'll shoot off the board. They've broken through with MABs. Medical—"

"I know what MABs are," I interrupted. "At least in theory. Medically Applicable Biochips."

"They have some that work."

"What?" It was my turn to lift my brows.

"Microscopic logic circuits. You inject them into the human body, they set up shop where they're told and troubleshoot. With Dr. Michael Bernard's approval."

That was quite impressive. Bernard's reputation was spotless. Not only was he associated with the genetic engineering biggies, but he had made the news at least once a year in his practice as a neurosurgeon before retiring. Covers on *Time, Mega, Rolling Stone.*

"That's supposed to be secret—stock, breakthrough, Bernard, everything." He looked around and lowered his voice. "But you do whatever the hell you want. I'm through with the bastards."

I whistled. "Make me rich, huh?"

"If that's what you want. Or you can spend some time with me before rushing off to your broker."

"Of course." He hadn't touched the cottage cheese or pie. He had, however, eaten the pineapple slice and drunk the chocolate milk. "So tell me more."

"Well, in med school I was training for lab work. Biochemical research. I've always had a bent for computers, too. So I put myself through my last two years—"

"By selling software packages to Westinghouse," I said.

"It's good my friends remember. That's how I got involved with Genetron, just when they were starting out. They had big money backers, all the lab facilities I thought anyone would ever need. They hired me, and I advanced rapidly.

"Four months and I was doing my own work. I made some break-throughs"—he tossed his hand nonchalantly—"then I went off on tangents they thought were premature. I persisted and they took away my lab, handed it over to a certifiable flatworm. I managed to save part of the experiment before they fired me. But I haven't exactly been cautious… or judicious. So now it's going on outside the lab."

I'd always regarded Vergil as ambitious, a trifle cracked, and not terribly sensitive. His relations with authority figures had never been smooth. Science, for him, was like the woman you couldn't possibly have, who suddenly opens her arms to you, long before you're ready for mature love—leaving you afraid you'll forever blow the chance, lose the prize. Apparently, he did. "Outside the lab? I don't get you."

"Edward, I want you to examine me. Give me a thorough physical. Maybe a cancer diagnostic. Then I'll explain more."

"You want a five-thousand-dollar exam?"

"Whatever you can do. Ultrasound, NMR, thermogram, everything."

"I don't know if I can get access to all that equipment. NMR full-scan has only been here a month or two. Hell, you couldn't pick a more expensive way—"

"Then ultrasound. That's all you'll need."

"Vergil, I'm an obstetrician, not a glamour-boy lab-tech. OB-GYN, butt of all jokes. If you're turning into a woman, maybe I can help you."

He leaned forward, almost putting his elbow into the pie, but swinging wide at the last instant by scant millimeters. The old Vergil would have hit it square. "Examine me closely and you'll…" He narrowed his eyes. "Just examine me."

"So I make an appointment for ultrasound. Who's going to pay?"

"I'm on Blue Shield." He smiled and held up a medical credit card. "I messed with the personnel files at Genetron. Anything up to a hundred thousand dollars medical, they'll never check, never suspect."

He wanted secrecy, so I made arrangements. I filled out his forms myself. As long as everything was billed properly, most of the examination could take place without official notice. I didn't charge for my services. After all, Vergil had turned my piss blue. We were friends.

He came in late one night. I wasn't normally on duty then, but I stayed late, waiting for him on the third floor of what the nurses called the Frankenstein wing. I sat on an orange plastic chair. He arrived, looking olive-colored under the fluorescent lights.

He stripped, and I arranged him on the table. I noticed, first off, that his ankles looked swollen. But they weren't puffy. I felt them several times. They seemed healthy but looked odd. "Hmm," I said.

I ran the paddles over him, picking up areas difficult for the big unit to hit, and programmed the data into the imaging system. Then I swung the table around and inserted it into the enameled orifice of the ultrasound diagnostic unit, the hum-hole, so-called by the nurses.

I integrated the data from the hum-hole with that from the paddle sweeps and rolled Vergil out, then set up a video frame. The image took a second to integrate, then flowed into a pattern showing Vergil's skeleton. My jaw fell.

Three seconds of that and it switched to his thoracic organs, then his musculature, and, finally, vascular system and skin.

"How long since the accident?" I asked, trying to take the quiver out of my voice.

"I haven't been in an accident," he said. "It was deliberate."

"Jesus, they beat you to keep secrets?"

"You don't understand me, Edward. Look at the images again. I'm not damaged."

"Look, there's thickening here"—I indicated the ankles—"and your ribs— that crazy zigzag pattern of interlocks. Broken sometime, obviously. And—"

"Look at my spine," he said. I rotated the image in the video frame.

Buckminster Fuller, I thought. It was fantastic. A cage of triangular projection, all interlocking in ways I couldn't begin to follow, much less understand. I reached around and tried to feel his spine with my fingers. He lifted his arms and looked off at the ceiling.

"I can't find it," I said. "It's all smooth back there." I let go of him and looked at his chest, then prodded his ribs. They were sheathed in something tough and flexible. The harder I pressed, the tougher it became. Then I noticed another change.

"Hey," I said. "You don't have any nipples." There were tiny pigment patches, but no nipple formations at all.

"See?" Vergil asked, shrugging on the white robe, "I'm being rebuilt from the inside out."

In my reconstruction of those hours, I fancy myself saying, "So tell me about it." Perhaps mercifully, I don't remember what I actually said.

He explained with his characteristic circumlocutions. Listening was like trying to get to the meat of a newspaper article through a forest of sidebars and graphic embellishments.

I simplify and condense.

Genetron had assigned him to manufacturing prototype biochips, tiny circuits made out of protein molecules. Some were hooked up to silicon chips little more than a micrometer in size, then went through rat arteries to chemically keyed locations, to make connections with the rat tissue and attempt to monitor and even control lab-induced pathologies.

"*That* was something," he said.

"We recovered the most complex microchip by sacrificing the rat, then debriefed it—hooked the silicon portion up to an imaging system. The computer gave us bar graphs, then a diagram of the chemical characteristics of about eleven centimeters of blood vessels… then put it all together to make a picture. We zoomed down eleven centimeters of rat artery. You never saw so many scientists jumping up and down, hugging each other, drinking buckets of bug juice." Bug juice was lab ethanol mixed with Dr. Pepper.

Eventually, the silicon elements were eliminated completely in favor of nucleoproteins. He seemed reluctant to explain in detail, but I gathered they found ways to make huge molecules—as large as DNA, and even more complex—into electrochemical computers, using ribosome-like structures as "encoders" and "readers" and RNA as "tape." Vergil was able to mimic reproductive separation and reassembly in his nucleoproteins, incorporating program changes at key points by switching nucleotide pairs. "Genetron wanted me to switch over to supergene engineering, since that was the coming thing every-where else. Make all kind of critters, some out of our imagination. But I had different ideas." He twiddled his finger around his ear and made theremin sounds. "Mad scientist time, right?" He laughed, then sobered. "I injected my best nucleoproteins into bacteria to make duplication and compounding eas-ier. Then I started to leave them inside, so the circuits could interact with the cells. They were heuristically programmed; they taught themselves. The cells fed chemically coded information to the computers, the computers processed it and made decisions, the cells became smart. I mean, smart as planaria, for starters. Imagine an E. coli as smart as a planarian worm!"

I nodded. "I'm imagining."

"Then I really went off on my own. We had the equipment, the techniques; and I knew the molecular language. I could make really dense, really compli-cated biochips by compounding the nucleoproteins, making them into little brains. I did some research into how far I could go, theoretically. Sticking with bacteria, I could make a biochip with the computing capacity of a sparrow's brain. Imagine how jazzed I was! Then I saw a way to increase the complexi-ty a thousandfold, by using something we regarded as a nuisance—quantum chit-chat between the fixed elements of the circuits. Down that small, even the slightest change could bomb a biochip. But I developed a program that actually predicted and took advantage of electron tunneling. Emphasized the heuristic aspects of the computer, used the chit-chat as a method of increasing complexity."

"You're losing me," I said.

"I took advantage of randomness. The circuits could repair themselves, compare memories, and correct faulty elements. I gave them basic instructions: Go forth and multiply. Improve. By God, you should have seen some of the cultures a week later! It was amazing. They were evolving all on their own, like little cities. I destroyed them all, I think one of the petri dishes would have grown legs and walked out of the incubator if I'd kept feeding it."

"You're kidding." I looked at him. "You're not kidding."

"Man, they *knew* what it was like to improve! They knew where they had to go, but they were just so limited, being in bacteria bodies, with so few resources."

"How smart were they?"

"I couldn't be sure. They were associating in clusters of a hundred to two hundred cells, each cluster behaving like an autonomous unit. Each cluster might have been as smart as a rhesus monkey. They exchanged information through their pili, passed on bits of memory, and compared notes. Their organization was obviously different from a group of monkeys. Their world was so much simpler, for one thing. With their abilities they were masters of the petri dishes. I put phages in with them; the phages didn't have a chance. They used every option available to change and grow."

"How is that possible?"

"What?" He seemed surprised I wasn't accepting everything at face value.

"Cramming so much into so little. A rhesus monkey is not your simple little calculator, Vergil."

"I haven't made myself clear," he said, obviously irritated. "I was using nucleoprotein computers. They're like DNA, but all the information can interact. Do you know how many nucleotide pairs there are in the DNA of a single bacteria?"

It had been a long time since my last biochemistry lesson. I shook my head.

"About two million. Add in the modified ribosome structures—fifteen thousand of them, each with a molecular weight of about three million—and consider the combinations and permutations. The RNA is arranged like a continuous loop paper tape, surrounded by ribosomes ticking off instructions and manufacturing protein chains…" His eyes were bright and slightly moist. "Besides, I'm not saying every cell was a distinct entity. They cooperated."

"How many bacteria in the dishes you destroyed?"

"Billions. I don't know." He smirked. "You got it, Edward. Whole planetsful of E. coli."

"But Genetron didn't fire you then?"

"No. They didn't know what was going on, for one thing. I kept compounding the molecules, increasing their size complexity. When bacteria were too limited, I took blood from myself, separated out white cells, and injected them with the new biochips. I watched them, put them through mazes and little chemical problems. They were whizzes. Time is a lot faster at that level—so little distance for the messages to cross, and the environment is much simpler. Then I forgot to store a file under my secret code in the lab computers. Some managers found it and guessed what I was up to. Everybody panicked. They thought we'd have every social watchdog in the country on our backs because of what I'd done. They started to destroy my work and wipe my programs. Ordered me to sterilize my white cells. Christ." He pulled the white robe off and started to get dressed. "I only had a day or two. I separated out the most complex cells—"

"How complex?"

"They were clustering in hundred-cell groups, like the bacteria. Each group as smart as a four-year-old kid, maybe." He studied my face for a moment. "Still doubting? Want me to run through how many nucleotide pairs there are in a mammalian cell? I tailored my computers to take advantage of the white cells' capacity. Four billion nucleotide pairs, Edward. And they don't have a huge body to worry about, taking up most of their thinking time."

"Okay," I said. "I'm convinced. What did you do?"

"I mixed the cells back into a cylinder of whole blood and injected myself with it." He buttoned the top of his shirt and smiled thinly at me. "I'd programmed them with every drive I could, talked as high a level as I could using just enzymes and such. After that, they were on their own."

"You programmed them to go forth and multiply, improve?" I repeated.

"I think they developed some characteristics picked up by the biochips in their E. coli phases. The white cells could talk to each other with extruded memories. They found ways to ingest other types of cells and alter them without killing them."

"You're crazy."

"You can see the screen! Edward, I haven't been sick since. I used to get colds all the time. I've never felt better."

"They're inside you, finding things, changing them."

"And by now, each cluster is as smart as you or I."

"You're absolutely nuts."

He shrugged. "Genetron fired me. They thought I was going to take revenge for what they did to my work. They ordered me out of the labs, and I haven't had a real chance to see what's been going on inside me until now. Three months."

"So…" My mind was racing. "You lost weight because they improved your fat metabolism. Your bones are stronger, your spine has been completely rebuilt—"

"No more backaches even if I sleep on my old mattress."

"Your heart looks different."

"I didn't know about the heart," he said, examining the frame image more closely. "As for the fat—I was thinking about that. They could increase my brown cells, fix up the metabolism. I haven't been as hungry lately. I haven't changed my eating habits that much—I still want the same old junk—but somehow I get around to eating only what I need. I don't think they know what my brain is yet. Sure, they've got all the glandular stuff—but they don't have the big picture, if you see what I mean. They don't know I'm in here. But boy, they sure did figure out what my reproductive organs are."

I glanced at the image and shifted my eyes away.

"Oh, they look pretty normal." he said, hefting his scrotum obscenely. He snickered. "But how else do you think I'd land a real looker like Candice? She was just after a one-night stand with a techie. I looked okay then, no tan but trim, with good clothes. She'd never screwed a techie before. Joke time, right? But my little geniuses kept us up half the night. I think they made improvement each time. I felt like I had a goddamned fever."

His smile vanished. "But then one night my skin started to crawl. It really scared me. I thought things were getting out of hand. I wondered what they'd do when they crossed the blood-brain barrier and found out about me—about the brain's real function. So I began a campaign to keep them under control. I figured, the reason they wanted to get into the skin was the simplicity of running circuits across a surface. Much easier than trying to maintain chains of communication in and around muscles, organs, vessels. The skin was much more direct. So I bought a quartz lamp." He caught my puzzled expression. "In the lab, we'd break down the protein in biochip cells by exposing them to ultraviolet light. I alternated sunlamp with quartz treatments. Keeps them out of my skin and gives me a nice tan."

"Give you skin cancer, too," I commented.

"They'll probably take care of that. Like police."

"Okay. I've examined you, you've told me a story I still find hard to believe… what do you want me to do?"

"I'm not as nonchalant as I act, Edward. I'm worried. I'd like to find some way to control them before they find out about my brain. I mean, think of it, they're in the trillions by now, each one smart. They're cooperating to some extent. I'm probably the smartest thing on the planet, and they haven't even begun to get their act together. I don't really want them to take over." He laughed unpleasantly. "Steal my soul, you know? So think of some treatment to block them. Maybe we can starve the little buggers. Just think on it." He buttoned his shirt. "Give me a call." He handed me a slip of paper with his address and phone number. Then he went to the keyboard and erased the image on the frame, dumping the memory of the examination. "Just you," he said. "Nobody else for now. And please… hurry."

It was three o'clock in the morning when Vergil walked out of the examination room. He'd allowed me to take blood samples, then shaken my hand— his palm was damp, nervous—and cautioned me against ingesting anything from the specimens.

Before I went home, I put the blood through a series of tests. The results were ready the next day.

I picked them up during my lunch break in the afternoon, then destroyed all of the samples. I did it like a robot. It took me five days and nearly sleepless nights to accept what I'd seen. His blood was normal enough, though the machines diagnosed the patient as having an infection. High levels of leukocytes—white blood cells—and histamines. On the fifth day, I believed.

Gail came home before I did, but it was my turn to fix dinner. She slipped one of the school's disks into the home system and showed me video art her nursery kids had been creating. I watched quietly, ate with her in silence.

I had two dreams, part of my final acceptance. In the first, that evening, I witnessed the destruction of the planet Krypton, Superman's home world. Billions of superhuman geniuses went screaming off in walls of fire. I related the destruction to my sterilizing the samples of Vergil's blood.

The second dream was worse. I dreamed that New York City was raping a woman. By the end of the dream, she gave birth to little embryo cities, all wrapped up in translucent sacs, soaked with blood from the difficult labor.

I called him on the morning of the sixth day. He answered on the fourth ring. "I have some results," I said. "Nothing conclusive. But I want to talk with you. In person."

"Sure," he said. "I'm staying inside for the time being." His voice was strained; he sounded tired.

Vergil's apartment was in a fancy high-rise near the lake shore. I took the elevator up, listening to little advertising jingles and watching dancing holograms display products, empty apartments for rent, the building's hostess discussing social activities for the week.

Vergil opened the door and motioned me in. He wore a checked robe with long sleeves and carpet slippers. He clutched an unlit pipe in one hand, his fingers twisting it back and forth as he walked away from me and sat down, saying nothing.

"You have an infection," I said.

"Oh?"

"That's all the blood analyses tell me. I don't have access to the electron microscopes."

"I don't think it's really an infection," he said. "After all, they're my own cells. Probably something else... some sign of their presence, of the change. We can't expect to understand everything that's happening."

I removed my coat. "Listen," I said, "you really have me worried now." The expression on his face stopped me: a kind of frantic beatitude. He squinted at the ceiling and pursed his lips.

"Are you stoned?" I asked.

He stood his head, then nodded once, very slowly. "Listening," he said.

"To what?"

"I don't know. Not sounds... exactly. Like music. The heart, all the blood vessels, friction of blood along the arteries, veins. Activity. Music in the blood."

He looked at me plaintively. "Why aren't you at work?"

"My day off. Gail's working."

"Can you stay?"

I shrugged. "I suppose." I sounded suspicious. I glanced around the apartment, looking for ashtrays, pack of papers.

"I'm not stoned, Edward," he said. "I may be wrong, but I think something big is happening. I think they're finding out who I am."

I sat down across from Vergil, staring at him intently. He didn't seem to notice. Some inner process involved him. When I asked for a cup of coffee, he motioned to the kitchen. I boiled a pot of water and took a jar of instant from the cabinet. With cup in hand, I returned to my seat. He twisted his head back and forth, eyes open. "You always knew what you wanted to be, didn't you?" he asked.

"More or less."

"A gynecologist. Smart moves. Never false moves. I was different. I had goals, but no direction. Like a map without roads, just places to be. I didn't give a shit for anything, anyone but myself. Even science. Just a means. I'm surprised I got so far. I even hated my folks."

He gripped his chair arms.

"Something wrong?" I asked.

"They're talking to me," he said. He shut his eyes.

For an hour he seemed to be asleep. I checked his pulse, which was strong and steady, felt his forehead—slightly cool—and made myself more coffee. I was looking through a magazine, at a loss what to do, when he opened his eyes again. "Hard to figure exactly what time is like for them," he said. "It's taken them maybe three, four days to figure out language, key human concepts. Now they're on to it. On to me. Right now."

"How's that?"

He claimed there were thousands of researchers hooked up to his neurons. He couldn't give details. "They're damned efficient, you know," he said. "They haven't screwed me up yet."

"We should get you into the hospital now."

"What in hell could other doctors do? Did you figure out any way to control them? I mean, they're my own cells."

"I've been thinking. We could starve them. Find out what metabolic differences—"

"I'm not sure I want to be rid of them," Vergil said. "They're not doing any harm."

"How do you know?"

He shook his head and held up one finger. "Wait. They're trying to figure out what space is. That's tough for them: They break distances down into concentrations of chemicals. For them, space is like intensity of taste."

"Vergil—"

"Listen! Think, Edward!" His tone was excited but even. "Something big is happening inside me. They talk to each other across the fluid, through membranes. They tailor something—viruses?—to carry data stored in nucleic acid chains. I think they're saying 'RNA.' That makes sense. That's one way I programmed them. But plasmidlike structures, too. Maybe that's what your machines think is a sign of infection—all their chattering in my blood, packets of data. Tastes of other individuals. Peers. Superiors. Subordinates."

"Vergil, I still think you should be in a hospital."

"This is my show, Edward," he said. "I'm their universe. They're amazed by the new scale." He was quiet again for a time. I squatted by his chair and pulled up the sleeve to his robe. His arm was crisscrossed with white lines. I was about to go to the phone when he stood and stretched. "Do you realize," he said, "how many body cells we kill each time we move?"

"I'm going to call for an ambulance." I said.

"No, you aren't." His tone stopped me. "I told you, I'm not sick, this is my show. Do you know what they'd do to me in a hospital? They'd be like cavemen trying to fix a computer. It would be a farce."

"Then what the hell am I doing here?" I asked, getting angry. "I can't do anything. I'm one of those cavemen."

"You're a friend," Vergil said, fixing his eyes on me. I had the impression I was being watched by more than just Vergil. "I want you here to keep me company." He laughed. "But I'm not exactly alone."

He walked around the apartment for two hours, fingering things, looking out windows, slowly and methodically fixing himself lunch. "You know, they can actually feel their own thoughts," he said about noon. "I mean the cytoplasm seems to have a will of its own, a kind of subconscious life counter to the rationality they've only recently acquired. They hear the chemical 'noise' of the molecules fitting and unfitting inside."

At two o'clock, I called Gail to tell her I would be late. I was almost sick with tension, but I tried to keep my voice level. "Remember Vergil Ulam? I'm talking with him right now."

"Everything okay?" she asked.

Was it? Decidedly not. "Fine," I said.

"Culture!" Vergil said, peering around the kitchen wall at me. I said goodbye and hung up the phone. "They're always swimming in that bath of information. Contributing to it. It's kind of a gestalt thing. The hierarchy is absolute. They send tailored phages after cells that don't interact properly. Viruses specified to individuals or groups. No escape. A rogue cell gets pierced by the virus, the cell blebs outward, it explodes and dissolves. But it's not just a dictatorship. I think they effectively have more freedom than in a democracy. I mean, they vary so differently from individual to individual. Does that make sense? They vary different ways than we do."

"Hold it," I said, gripping his shoulders. "Vergil, you're pushing me to the edge. I can't take this much longer. I don't understand. I'm not sure I believe—"

"Not even now?"

"Okay, let's say you're giving me the right interpretation. Giving it to me straight. Have you bothered to figure out the consequences yet? What all this means, where it might lead?"

He walked into the kitchen and drew a glass of water from the tap, then returned and stood next to me. His expression had changed from childish absorption to sober concern. "I've never been very good at that."

"Are you afraid?"

"I was. Now, I'm not sure." He fingered the tie of his robe. "Look, I don't want you to think I went around you, over your head or something. But I met with Michael Bernard yesterday. He put me through his private clinic, took specimens. Told me to quit the lamp treatments. He says it all checks out. And he asked me not to tell anybody." He paused and his expression became dreamy again. "Cities of cells," he continued. "Edward, they push tubes through the tissues, spread information—"

"Stop it!" I shouted. "Checks out? What checks out?"

"As Bernard puts it, I have 'severely enlarged macrophages' throughout my system. And he concurs on the anatomical changes."

"What does he plan to do?"

"I don't know. I think he'll probably convince Genetron to reopen the lab."

"Is that what you want?"

"It's not just having the lab again. I want to show you. Since I stopped the lamp treatments, I'm still changing." He undid his robe and let it slide to the floor. All over his body, his skin was crisscrossed with white lines. Along his back, the lines were starting to form ridges.

"My God," I said.

"I'm not going to be much good anywhere else but the lab soon I won't be able to go out in public. Hospitals wouldn't know what to do, as I said."

"You're... you can talk to them, tell them to slow down," I said, aware how ridiculous that sounded.

"Yes, indeed I can, but they don't necessarily listen."

"I thought you were their god or something."

"The ones hooked up to my neurons aren't the big wheels. They're researchers, or at least serve the same function. They know I'm here, what I am, but that doesn't mean they've convinced the upper levels of the hierarchy."

"They're disputing?"

"Something like that. It's not all that bad, anyway. If the lab is reopened, I have a home, a place to work." He glanced out the window, as if looking for someone. "I don't have anything left but them. They aren't afraid, Edward. I've never felt so close to anything before." The beatific smile again. "I'm responsible for them. Mother to them all."

"You have no way of knowing what they're going to do."

He shook his head.

"No, I mean it. You say they're like a civilization—"

"Like a thousand civilizations."

"Yes, and civilizations have been known to screw up. Warfare, the environment—"

I was grasping at straws, trying to restrain a growing panic. I wasn't competent to handle the enormity of what was happening. Neither was Vergil. He was the last person I would have called insightful and wise about large issues.

"But I'm the only one at risk."

"You don't know that. Jesus, Vergil, look what they're doing to you!"

"To me, all to me!" he said. "Nobody else."

I shook my head and held up my hands in a gesture of defeat. "Okay, so Bernard gets them to reopen the lab, you move in, become a guinea pig. What then?"

"They treat me right. I'm more than just good old Vergil Ulam now. I'm a goddamned galaxy, a super-mother."

"Super-host, you mean." He conceded the point with a shrug.

I couldn't take any more. I made my exit with a few flimsy excuses, then sat in the lobby of the apartment building, trying to calm down. Somebody had to talk some sense into him. Who would he listen to? He had gone to Bernard...

And it sounded as if Bernard was not only convinced, but very interested. People of Bernard's stature didn't coax the Vergil Ulams of the world along unless they felt it was to their advantage.

I had a hunch, and I decided to play it. I went to a pay phone, slipped in my credit card, and called Genetron.

"I'd like you to page Dr. Michael Bernard," I told the receptionist.

"Who's calling, please?"

"This is his answering service. We have an emergency call and his beeper doesn't seem to be working."

A few anxious minutes later, Bernard came on the line. "Who in the hell is this?" he asked. "I don't have an answering service."

"My name is Edward Milligan. I'm a friend of Vergil Ulam's. I think we have some problems to discuss."

We made an appointment to talk the next morning.

I went home and tried to think of excuses to keep me off the next day's hospital shift. I couldn't concentrate on medicine, couldn't give my patients anywhere near the attention they deserved.

Guilty, angry, afraid.

That was how Gail found me. I slipped on a mask of calm and we fixed dinner together. After eating, holding onto each other, we watched the city lights come on in late twilight through the bayside window. Winter starlings pecked at the yellow lawn in the last few minutes of light, then flew away with a rising wind which made the windows rattle.

"Somethings's wrong," Gail said softly. "Are you going to tell me, or just act like everything's normal?"

"It's just me," I said. "Nervous. Work at the hospital."

"Oh, lord," she said, sitting up. "You're going to divorce me for that Baker woman." Mrs. Baker weighed three hundred and sixty pounds and hadn't known she was pregnant until her fifth month.

"No," I said, listless.

"Rapturous relief," Gail said, touching my forehead lightly. "You know this kind of introspection drives me crazy."

"Well, it's nothing I can talk about yet, so…" I patted her hand.

"That's disgustingly patronizing," she said, getting up. "I'm going to make some tea. Want some?" Now she was miffed, and I was tense with not telling.

Why not just reveal all? I asked myself. An old friend was turning himself into a galaxy.

I cleared away the table instead. That night, unable to sleep, I looked down on Gail in bed from my sitting position, pillow against the wall, and tried to determine what I knew was real, and what wasn't.

I'm a doctor, I told myself. A technical, scientific profession. I'm supposed to be immune to things like future shock.

Vergil Ulam was turning into a galaxy.

How would it feel to be topped off with a trillion Chinese? I grinned in the dark and almost cried at the same time. What Vergil had inside him was unimaginably stranger than Chinese. Stranger than anything I—or Vergil— could easily understand. Perhaps ever understand.

But I knew what was real. The bedroom, the city lights taint through gauze curtains. Gail sleeping. Very important. Gail in bed, sleeping.

The dream returned. This time the city came in through the window and attacked Gail. It was a great, spiky lighted-up prowler, and it growled in a language I couldn't understand, made up of auto horns, crowd noises, construction bedlam. I tried to fight it off, but it got to her—and turned into a drift of stars, sprinkling all over the bed, all over everything. I jerked awake and stayed up until dawn, dressed with Gail, kissed her, savored the reality of her human, unviolated lips.

I went to meet with Bernard. He had been loaned a suite in a big downtown hospital; I rode the elevator to the sixth floor, and saw what fame and fortune could mean.

The suite was tastefully furnished, fine serigraphs on wood-paneled walls, chrome and glass furniture, cream-colored carpet, Chinese brass, and wormwood-grain cabinets and tables.

He offered me a cup of coffee, and I accepted. He took a seat in the breakfast nook, and I sat across from him, cradling my cup in moist palms. He wore a dapper gray suit and had graying hair and a sharp profile. He was in his mid-sixties and he looked quite a bit like Leonard Bernstein.

"About our mutual acquaintance," he said. "Mr. Ulam. Brilliant. And, I won't hesitate to say, courageous."

"He's my friend. I'm worried about him."

Bernard held up one finger. "Courageous—and a bloody damned fool. What's happening to him should never have been allowed. He may have done it under duress, but that's no excuse. Still, what's done is done. He's talked to you, I take it."

I nodded. "He wants to return to Genetron."

"Of course. That's where all his equipment is. Where his home probably will be while we sort this out."

"Sort it out—how? Why?" I wasn't thinking too clearly. I had a slight headache.

"I can think of a large number of uses for small, superdense computer elements with a biological base. Can't you? Genetron has already made breakthroughs, but this is something else again."

"What do you envision?"

Bernard smiled. "I'm not really at liberty to say. It'll be revolutionary. We'll have to get him in lab conditions. Animal experiments have to be conducted. We'll start from scratch, of course. Vergil's… um… colonies can't be transferred. They're based on his own white blood cells. So we have to develop colonies that won't trigger immune reactions in other animals."

"Like an infection?" I asked.

"I suppose there are comparisons. But Vergil is not infected."

"My tests indicate he is."

"That's probably the bits of data floating around in his blood, don't you think?"

"I don't know."

"Listen, I'd like you to come down to the lab after Vergil is settled in. Your expertise might be useful to us."

Us. He was working with Genetron hand in glove. Could he be objective? "How will you benefit from all this?"

"Edward, I have always been at the forefront of my profession. I see no reason why I shouldn't be helping here. With my knowledge of brain and nerve functions, and the research I've been conducting in neurophysiology—"

"You could help Genetron hold off an investigation by the government," I said.

"That's being very blunt. Too blunt, and unfair."

"Perhaps. Anyway, yes: I'd like to visit the lab when Vergil's settled in. If I'm still welcome, bluntness and all."

He looked at me sharply. I wouldn't be playing on his team; for a moment, his thoughts were almost nakedly apparent.

"Of course," Bernard said, rising with me. He reached out to shake my hand. His palm was damp. He was as nervous as I was, even if he didn't look it.

I returned to my apartment and stayed there until noon, reading, trying to sort things out. Reach a decision. What was real, what I needed to protect.

There is only so much change anyone can stand: innovation, yes, but slow application. Don't force. Everyone has the right to stay the same until they decide otherwise.

The greatest thing in science since…

And Bernard would force it. Genetron would force it. I couldn't handle the thought. "Neo-Luddite," I said to myself. A filthy accusation.

When I pressed Vergil's number on the building security panel, Vergil answered almost immediately. "Yeah," he said. He sounded exhilarated. "Come on up. I'll be in the bathroom. Door's unlocked."

I entered his apartment and walked through the hallway to the bathroom. Vergil lay in the tub, up to his neck in pinkish water. He smiled vaguely and splashed his hands. "Looks like I slit my wrists, doesn't it?" he said softly. "Don't worry. Everything's fine now. Genetron's going to take me back. Bernard just called." He pointed to the bathroom phone and intercom.

I sat on the toilet and noticed the sunlamp fixture standing unplugged nest to the linen cabinets. The blubs sat in a row on the edge of the sink counter. "You're sure that's what you want," I said, my shoulders slumping.

"Yeah, I think so," he said. "They can take better care of me. I'm getting cleaned up, going over there this evening. Bernard's picking me up in his limo. Style. From here on in, everything's style."

The pinkish color in the water didn't look like soap. "Is that bubble bath?" I asked. Some of it came to me in a rush then and I felt a little weaker; what had occurred to me was just one more obvious and necessary insanity.

"No," Vergil said. I knew that already.

"No," he repeated, "it's coming from my skin. They're not telling me everything, but I think they're sending out scouts. Astronauts." He looked at me with an expression that didn't quite equal concern; more like curiosity as to how I'd take it.

The confirmation made my stomach muscles tighten as if waiting for a punch. I had never even considered the possibility until now, perhaps because I had been concentrating on other aspects. "Is this the first time?" I asked.

"Yeah," he said. He laughed. "I've half a mind to let the little buggers down the drain. Let them find out what the world's really about."

"They'd go everywhere," I said.

"Sure enough."

"How... how are you feeling?"

"I'm feeling pretty good now. Must be billions of them." More splashing with his hands. "What do you think? Should I let the buggers out?"

Quickly, hardly thinking, I knelt down beside the tub. My fingers went for the cord on the sunlamp and I plugged it in. He had hot-wired doorknobs, turned my piss blue, played a thousand dumb practical jokes and never grown up, never grown mature enough to understand that he was sufficiently brilliant to transform the world; he would never learn caution.

He reached for the drain knob. "You know, Edward, I—"

He never finished. I picked up the fixture and dropped it into the tub, jumping back at the flash of steam and sparks. Vergil screamed and thrashed and jerked and then everything was still, except for the low, steady sizzle and the smoke wafting from his hair.

I lifted the toilet lid and vomited. Then I clenched my nose and went into the living room. My legs went out from under me and I sat abruptly on the couch.

After an hour, I searched through Vergil's kitchen and found bleach, ammonia, and a bottle of Jack Daniel's. I returned to the bathroom, keeping the center of my gaze away from Vergil. I poured first the booze, then the bleach, then the ammonia into the water. Chlorine started bubbling up and I left, closing the door behind me.

The phone was ringing when I got home. I didn't answer. It could have been the hospital. It could have been Bernard. Or the police. I could envision having to explain everything to the police. Genetron would stonewall; Bernard would be unavailable.

I was exhausted, all my muscles knotted with tension and whatever name one can give to the feelings one has after—

Committing genocide?

That certainly didn't seem real. I could not believe I had just murdered a hundred trillion intelligent beings. Snuffed a galaxy. It was laughable. But I didn't laugh.

It was easy to believe that I had just killed one human being, a friend. The smoke, the melted lamp rods, the drooping electrical outlet and smoking cord.

Vergil.

I had dunked the lamp into the tub with Vergil.

I felt sick. Dreams, cities raping Gail (and what about his girlfriend, Candice?). Letting the water filled with them out. Galaxies sprinkling over us all. What horror. Then again, what potential beauty—a new kind of life, symbiosis and transformation.

Had I been thorough enough to kill them all? I had a moment of panic. Tomorrow, I thought, I will sterilize his apartment. Somehow, I didn't even think of Bernard.

When Gail came in the door, I was asleep on the couch. I came to, groggy, and she looked down at me.

"You feeling okay?" she asked, perching on the edge of the couch. I nodded.

"What are you planning for dinner?" My mouth didn't work properly. The words were mushy. She felt my forehead.

"Edward, you have a fever," she said. "A very high fever."

I stumbled into the bathroom and looked in the mirror. Gail was close behind me. "What is it?" she asked.

There were lines under my collar, around my neck. White lines, like freeways. They had already been in me a long time, days.

"Damp palms," I said. So obvious.

I think we nearly died. I struggled at first, but in minutes I was too weak to move. Gail was just as sick within an hour.

I lay on the carpet in the living room, drenched in sweat. Gail lay on the couch, her face the color of talcum, eyes closed, like a corpse in an embalming parlor. For a time I thought she was dead. Sick as I was, I raged—hated, felt tremendous guilt at my weakness, my slowness to understand all the possibilities. Then I no longer cared. I was too weak to blink, so I closed my eyes and waited.

There was a rhythm in my arms, my legs. With each pulse of blood, a kind of sound welled up within me, like an orchestra thousands strong, but not playing in unison; playing whole seasons of symphonies at once. Music in the blood. The sound became harsher, but more coordinated, wave-trains finally canceling into silence, then separating into harmonic beats.

The beats seemed to melt into me, into the sound of my own heart.

First, they subdued our immune responses. The war—and it was a war, on a scale never before known on Earth, with trillions of combatants—lasted perhaps two days.

By the time I regained enough strength to get to the kitchen faucet, I could feel them working on my brain, trying to crack the code and find the god within the protoplasm. I drank until I was sick, then drank more moderately and took a glass to Gail. She sipped at it. Her lips were cracked, her eyes bloodshot and ringed with yellowish crumbs. There was some color in her skin. Minutes later, we were eating feebly in the kitchen.

"What in the hell is happening?" was the first thing she asked. I didn't have the strength to explain. I peeled an orange and shared it with her. "We should call a doctor," she said. But I knew we wouldn't. I was already receiving messages; it was becoming apparent that any sensation of freedom we experienced was illusory.

The messages were simple at first. Memories of commands, rather than the commands themselves, manifested themselves in my thoughts. We were not to leave the apartment—a concept which seemed quite abstract to those in control, even if undesirable—and we were not to have contact with others. We would be allowed to eat certain foods and drink tap water for the time being.

With the subsidence of the fevers, the transformations were quick and drastic. Almost simultaneously, Gail and I were immobilized. She was sitting at the table, I was kneeling on the floor. I was barely able to see her in the corner of my eye.

Her arm developed pronounced ridges.

They had learned inside Vergil; their tactics within the two of us were very different. I itched all over for about two hours—two hours in hell—before they made the breakthrough and found me. The effort of ages on their timescale paid off and they communicated smoothly and directly with this great, clumsy intelligence who had once controlled their universe.

They were not cruel. When the concept of discomfort and its undesirability was made clear, they worked to alleviate it. They worked too effectively. For another hour, I was in a sea of bliss, out of all contact with them.

With dawn the next day, they gave us freedom to move again; specifically, to go to the bathroom. There were certain waste products they could not deal with. I voided those—my urine was purple—and Gail followed suit. We looked at each other vacantly in the bathroom. Then she managed a slight smile. "Are they talking to you?" she asked. I nodded. "Then I'm not crazy."

For the next twelve hours, control seemed to loosen on some levels. I suspect there was another kind of war going on in me. Gail was capable of limited motion, but no more.

When full control resumed, we were instructed to hold each other. We did not hesitate.

"Eddie…" she whispered. My name was the last sound I ever heard from outside.

Standing, we grew together. In hours, our legs expanded and spread out. Then extensions grew to the windows to take sunlight, and to the kitchen to take water from the sink. Filaments soon reached to all corners of the room, stripping paint and plaster from the walls, fabric and stuffing from the furniture.

By the next dawn, the transformation was complete.

I no longer have any clear view of what we look like. I suspect we resemble cells—large, flat, and filamented cells, draped purposefully across most of the apartment. The great shall mimic the small.

Our intelligence fluctuates daily as we are absorbed into the minds within. Each day, our individuality declines. We are, indeed, great clumsy dinosaurs. Our memories have been taken over by billions of them, and our personalities have been spread through the transformed blood.

Soon there will be no need for centralization.

Already the plumbing has been invaded. People throughout the building are undergoing transformation.

Within the old time frame of weeks, we will reach the lakes, rivers, and seas in force.

I can barely begin to guess the results. Every square inch of the planet will teem with thought. Years from now, perhaps much sooner, they will subdue their own individuality—what there is of it.

New creatures will come, then. The immensity of their capacity for thought will be inconceivable.

All my hatred and fear is gone now.

I leave them—us—with only one question.

How many times has this happened, elsewhere? Travelers never came through space to visit the Earth. They had no need.

They had found universes in grains of sand.

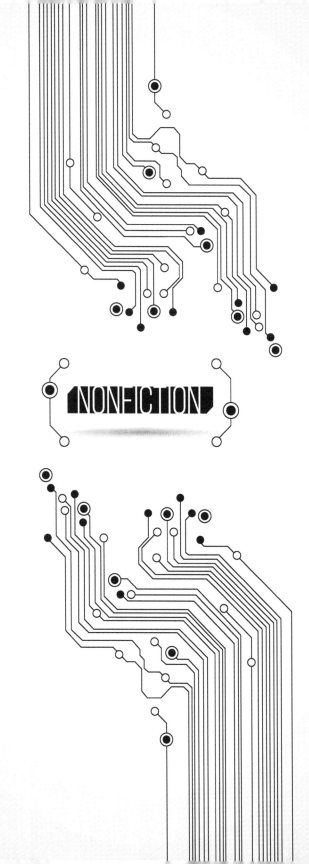

NONFICTION

"The future is not google-able."

—William Gibson

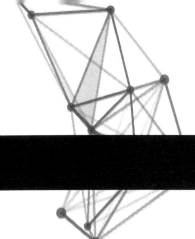

OUR FINAL HOUR
LORD MARTIN REES

Martin Rees, Baron Rees of Ludlow, Kt., OM, FRS, HonFREng, FMedSci is a British cosmologist and astrophysicist. He has been Astronomer Royal of the Royal Observatory at Greenwich since 1995 and was Master of Trinity College, Cambridge from 2004 to 2012 and President of the Royal Society between 2005 and 2010.

Martin's awards include the Lifeboat Foundation Guardian Award (learn more at http://lifeboat.com/ex/guardian2004), the Gold Medal of the Royal Astronomical Society, the Balzan International Prize, the Bruce Medal of the Astronomical Society of the Pacific, the Heineman Prize for Astrophysics (AAS/AIP), the Bower Award for Science of the Franklin Institute, the Cosmology Prize of the Peter Gruber Foundation, the Albert Einstein World Award of Science, the Crafoord Prize (Royal Swedish Academy), the Templeton Prize, and the Isaac Newton Medal. Asteroid 4587 Rees is named after him.

The following is the prologue to *Our Final Hour: A Scientist's Warning* which is available at http://amzn.to/1Bb2jCs and is also available for free with all memberships at https://lifeboat.com/ex/join.us.

The twentieth century brought us the bomb, and the nuclear threat will never leave us; the short-term threat from terrorism is high on the public and political agenda; inequalities in wealth and welfare get ever wider. My primary aim is not to add to the burgeoning literature on these challenging themes, but to focus on twenty-first century hazards, currently less familiar, that could threaten humanity and the global environment still more.

Some of these new threats are already upon us; others are still conjectural. Populations could be wiped out by lethal "engineered" airborne viruses; human character may be changed by new techniques far more targeted and effective than the nostrums and drugs familiar today; we may even one day be threatened by rogue nanomachines that replicate catastrophically, or by superintelligent computers.

Other novel risks cannot be completely excluded. Experiments that crash atoms together with immense force could start a chain reaction that erodes everything on Earth; the experiments could even tear the fabric of space itself, an ultimate "Doomsday" catastrophe whose fallout spreads at the speed of light to engulf the entire universe. These latter scenarios may be exceedingly unlikely, but they raise in extreme form the issue of who should decide, and how, whether to proceed with experiments that have a genuine scientific purpose (and could conceivably offer practical benefits), but that pose a very tiny risk of an utterly calamitous outcome.

We still live, as all our ancestors have done, under the threat of disasters that could cause worldwide devastation: volcanic supereruptions and major asteroid impacts, for instance. Natural catastrophes on this global scale are fortunately so infrequent, and therefore so unlikely to occur within our lifetime, that they do not preoccupy our thoughts, nor give most of us sleepless nights. But such catastrophes are now augmented by other environmental risks that we are bringing upon ourselves, risks that cannot be dismissed as so improbable.

During the Cold War years, the main threat looming over us was an all-out thermonuclear exchange, triggered by an escalating superpower confrontation. That threat was apparently averted. But many experts—indeed, some who themselves controlled policy during those years—believed that we were lucky; some thought that the cumulative risk of Armageddon over that period was as much as fifty percent. The immediate danger of all-out nuclear war has receded. But there is a growing threat of nuclear weapons being used sooner or later somewhere in the world.

Nuclear weapons can be dismantled, but they cannot be uninvented. The threat is ineradicable, and could be resurgent in the twenty-first century: we cannot rule out a realignment that would lead to standoffs as dangerous as the Cold War rivalry, deploying even bigger arsenals. And even a threat that seems, year by year, a modest one mounts up if it persists for decades. But the nuclear threat will be overshadowed by others that could be as destructive, and far less controllable. These may come not primarily from national governments, not even from "rogue states," but from individuals or small groups with access to ever more advanced technology. There are alarmingly many ways in which individuals will be able to trigger catastrophe.

The strategists of the nuclear age formulated a doctrine of deterrence by "mutually assured destruction" (with the singularly appropriate acronym MAD). To clarify this concept, real-life Dr. Strangeloves envisaged a hypothetical "Doomsday machine," an ultimate deterrent too terrible to be unleashed by any political leader who was one hundred percent rational. Later in this century, scientists might be able to create a real nonnuclear Doomsday machine. Conceivably, ordinary citizens could command the destructive capacity that in the twentieth century was the frightening prerogative of the handful of individuals who held the reins of power in states with nuclear weapons. If there were millions of independent fingers on the button of a Doomsday machine, then one person's act of irrationality, or even one person's error, could do us all in.

Such an extreme situation is perhaps so unstable that it could never be reached, just as a very tall house of cards, though feasible in theory, could never be built. Long before individuals acquire a "Doomsday" potential—indeed, perhaps within a decade—some will acquire the power to trigger, at unpredictable times, events on the scale of the worst present-day terrorist outrages. An organized network of Al Qaeda-type terrorists would not be required: just a fanatic or social misfit with the mindset of those who now design computer viruses. There are people with such propensities in every country—very few, to be sure, but bio- and cyber-technologies will become so powerful that even one could well be too many.

By mid-century, societies and nations may have drastically realigned; people may live very differently, survive to a far greater age, and have different attitudes from those of the present (maybe modified by medication, chip implants, and so forth). But one thing is unlikely to change: individuals will make mistakes, and there will be a risk of malign actions by embittered loners and dissident groups. Advanced technology will offer new instruments for creating terror and devastation; instant universal communications will amplify their societal impact. Catastrophes could arise, even more worryingly, simply from technical misadventure. Disastrous accidents (for instance, the unintended creation or release of a noxious fast-spreading pathogen, or a devastating software error) are possible even in well-regulated institutions. As the threats become graver, and the possible perpetrators more numerous, disruption may become so pervasive that society corrodes and regresses. There is a longer-term risk even to humanity itself.

Science is emphatically not, as some have claimed, approaching its end; it is surging ahead at an accelerating rate. We are still flummoxed about the bedrock nature of physical reality, and the complexities of life, the brain, and the cosmos. New discoveries, illuminating all these mysteries, will engender benign applications; but will also pose new ethical dilemmas and bring new hazards. How will we balance the multifarious prospective benefits from genetics, robotics, or nanotechnology against the risk (albeit smaller) of triggering utter disaster?

My special scientific interest is cosmology: researching our environment in the widest conceivable perspective. This might seem an incongruous viewpoint from which to focus on practical terrestrial issues: in the words of Gregory Benford, a fiction writer who is also an astrophysicist, study of the "grand gyre of worlds… imbues, and perhaps afflicts, astronomers with a perception of how like mayflies we are." But few scientists are unworldly enough to fit Benford's description: a preoccupation with near-infinite spaces doesn't make cosmologists especially "philosophical" in coping with everyday life; nor are they less engaged with the issues confronting us here on the ground, today and tomorrow. My subjective attitude was better expressed by the mathematician and philosopher Frank Ramsey, a member of the same College in Cambridge (King's) to which I now belong: "I don't feel the least humble before the vastness of the heavens. The stars may be large, but they cannot think or love; and these are qualities which impress me far more than size does. My picture of the world is drawn in perspective, and not like a model drawn to scale. The foreground is occupied by human beings, and the stars are all as small as threepenny bits."

A cosmic perspective actually strengthens our concerns about what happens here and now, because it offers a vision of just how prodigious life's future potential could be. Earth's biosphere is the outcome of more than four billion years of Darwinian selection: the stupendous time spans of the evolutionary past are now part of common culture. But life's future could be more prolonged than its past. In the aeons that lie ahead, even more marvelous diversity could emerge, on and beyond Earth. The unfolding of intelligence and complexity could still be near its cosmic beginnings.

A memorable early photograph taken from space depicted "Earthrise" as viewed from a spacecraft orbiting the Moon. Our habitat of land, oceans, and clouds was revealed as a thin delicate glaze, its beauty and vulnerability contrasting with the stark and sterile moonscape on which the astronauts left their footprints. We have had these distant images of the entire Earth only for the last four decades. But our planet has existed for more than a hundred million times longer than this. What transformations did it undergo during this cosmic time span?

About 4.5 billion years ago our Sun condensed from a cosmic cloud; it was then encircled by a swirling disk of gas. Dust in this disk agglomerated into a swarm of orbiting rocks, which then coalesced to form the planets. One of these became our Earth: the "third rock from the Sun." The young Earth was buffeted by collisions with other bodies, some almost as large as the planets themselves: one such impact gouged out enough molten rock to make the Moon. Conditions quietened and the Earth cooled. The next transformations distinctive enough to be seen by a faraway observer would have been very gradual. Over a prolonged time span, more than a billion years, oxygen accumulated in Earth's atmosphere, a consequence of the first unicellular life. Thereafter, there were slow changes in the biosphere, and in the shape of the land masses as the continents drifted. The ice cover waxed and waned: there might even have been episodes when the entire Earth froze over, appearing white rather than pale blue.

The only abrupt worldwide changes were triggered by major asteroid impacts or volcanic supereruptions. Occasional incidents like these would have flung so much debris into the stratosphere that for several years, until all the dust and aerosols settled again, Earth looked dark grey, rather than bluish white, and no sunlight penetrated down to land or ocean. Apart from these brief traumas, nothing happened suddenly: successions of new species emerged, evolved, and became extinct on geological time scales of millions of years.

But in just a tiny sliver of Earth's history—the last one-millionth part, a few thousand years—the patterns of vegetation altered much faster than before. This signaled the start of agriculture: the imprint on the terrain of a population of humans, empowered by tools. The pace of change accelerated as human populations rose. But then quite different transformations were perceptible, and these were even more abrupt. Within fifty years, little more than one hundredth of a millionth of Earth's age, the amount of carbon dioxide in the atmosphere, which over most of Earth's history had been slowly falling, began to rise anomalously fast. The planet became an intense emitter of radio waves (the total output from all TV, cellphone, and radar transmissions).

And something else happened, unprecedented in Earth's 4.5 billion year history: metallic objects—albeit very small ones, a few tons at most—left the planet's surface and escaped the biosphere completely. Some were propelled into orbits around Earth; some journeyed to the Moon and planets; a few even followed a trajectory that would take them deep into interstellar space, leaving the solar system for ever.

A race of scientifically advanced extraterrestrials watching our solar system could confidently predict that Earth would face doom in another six billion years, when the Sun, in its death throes, swells up into a "red giant" and vaporizes everything remaining on our planet's surface. But could they have predicted this unprecedented spasm less than halfway through Earth's life— these human-induced alterations occupying, overall, less than a millionth of our planet's elapsed lifetime and seemingly occurring with runaway speed?

If they continued to keep watch, what might these hypothetical aliens witness in the next hundred years? Will a final squeal be followed by silence? Or will the planet itself stabilize? And will some of the small metallic objects launched from Earth spawn new oases of life elsewhere in the solar system, eventually extending their influences, via exotic life, machines, or sophisticated signals, far beyond the solar system, creating an expanding "green sphere" that eventually pervades the entire Galaxy?

It may not be absurd hyperbole—indeed, it may not even be an overstatement—to assert that the most crucial location in space and time (apart from the big bang itself) could be here and now. I think the odds are no better than fifty–fifty that our present civilization on Earth will survive to the end of the present century. Our choices and actions could ensure the perpetual future of life (not just on Earth, but perhaps far beyond it, too). Or in contrast, through malign intent, or through misadventure, twenty-first century technology could jeopardize life's potential, foreclosing its human and posthuman future. What happens here on Earth, in this century, could conceivably make the difference between a near eternity filled with ever more complex and subtle forms of life and one filled with nothing but base matter.

THE SIGNIFICANCE OF WATSON

RAY KURZWEIL

Ray is one of the world's leading inventors, thinkers, and futurists, with a thirty-year track record of accurate predictions. Called "the restless genius" by The Wall Street Journal and "the ultimate thinking machine" by Forbes magazine, Ray was selected as one of the top entrepreneurs by Inc. magazine, which described him as the "rightful heir to Thomas Edison." PBS selected him as one of the "sixteen revolutionaries who made America."

Ray was the principal inventor of the first CCD flat-bed scanner, the first omni-font optical character recognition, the first print-to-speech reading machine for the blind, the first text-to-speech synthesizer, the first music synthesizer capable of recreating the grand piano and other orchestral instruments, and the first commercially marketed large-vocabulary speech recognition.

Among his many honors, he is the recipient of the National Medal of Technology, was inducted into the National Inventors Hall of Fame, holds twenty honorary doctorates, and honors from three U.S. presidents.

Ray has written five national best-selling books, including New York Times best sellers *The Singularity Is Near* at http://amzn.to/1D6rFBF and *How To Create A Mind* at http://amzn.to/175bCtk. He is a Director of Engineering at Google heading up a team developing machine intelligence and natural language understanding.

This article was originally written and published at http://www.kurzweilai.net/the-significance-of-watson prior to the tournament in which Watson won.

I n *The Age of Intelligent Machines*[1], which I wrote in the mid-1980s, I predicted that a computer would defeat the world chess champion by 1998. My estimate was based on the predictable exponential growth

IBM's "Watson" Deep QA program, running on IBM Power7 servers.
(Image: IBM T.J. Watson Research Labs)

of computing power (an example of what I now call the "law of accelerating returns"[2]) and my estimate of what level of computing was needed to achieve a chess rating of just under 2800 (sufficient to defeat any human, although lately the best human chess scores have inched above 2800).

I also predicted that when that happened we would either think better of computer intelligence, worse of human thinking, or worse of chess, and that if history was a guide, we would downgrade chess.

Deep Blue defeated Gary Kasparov in 1997, and indeed we were immediately treated to rationalizations that chess was not really exemplary of human thinking after all. Commentaries pointed out that Deep Blue's feat just showed how computers were good at dealing with high-speed logical analysis and that chess was just a matter of dealing with the combinatorial explosion of move-countermoves. Humans, on the other hand, could deal with the subtleties and unpredictable complexities of human language.

I do not entirely disagree with this view of computer game playing. The early success of computers with logical thinking, even at such tasks as solving mathematical theorems, showed what computers were good for. Recall that CMU's "General Problem Solver" solved a mathematical theorem in the 1950s that had eluded Russell and Whitehead in their *Principia Mathematica*, one of the early successes of the AI field that led to premature confidence in AI.

Computers could keep track of vast logical structures and remember enormous databases with great accuracy. Search engines such as Google and Bing continue to illustrate this strength of computers.

Indeed no human can do what a search engine does, but computers have still not shown an ability to deal with the subtlety and complexity of language. Humans, on the other hand, have been unique in our ability to think in a hierarchical fashion, to understand the elaborate nested structures in language, to put symbols together to form an idea, and then to use a symbol for that idea in yet another such structure. This is what sets humans apart.

That is, until now. Watson is a stunning example of the growing ability of computers to successfully invade this supposedly unique attribute of human intelligence. If you watch Watson's performance, it appears to be at least as good as the best "Jeopardy!" players at understanding the nature of the question (or I should say the answer, since "Jeopardy!" presents the answer and asks for the question, which I always thought was a little tedious). Watson is able to then combine this ability to understand the level of language in a "Jeopardy!"

query with a computer's innate ability to accurately master a vast corpus of knowledge.

I've always felt that once a computer masters a human's level of pattern recognition and language understanding, it would inherently be far superior to a human because of this combination.

We don't know yet whether Watson will win this particular tournament, but it won the preliminary round and the point has been made, regardless of the outcome. There were chess machines before Deep Blue that just missed defeating the world chess champion, but they kept getting better and passing the threshold of defeating the best human was inevitable. The same is true now with "Jeopardy!.."

Yes, there are limitations to "Jeopardy!" Like all games, it has a particular structure and does not probe all human capabilities, even within understanding language. Already commentators are beginning to point out the limitations of "Jeopardy!," for example, that the short length of the queries limits their complexity.

For those who would like to minimize Watson's abilities, I'll add the following. When human contestant Ken Jennings selects the "Chicks dig me" category, he makes a joke that is outside the formal game by saying "I've never said this on TV, 'chicks dig me.'" Later on, Watson says, "Let's finish Chicks Dig Me." That's also pretty funny and the audience laughs, but it is clear that Watson is clueless as to the joke it has inadvertently made.

However, Watson was never asked to make commentaries, humorous or otherwise, about the proceedings. It is clearly capable of dealing with a certain level of humor within the queries. If suitably programmed, I believe that it could make appropriate and humorous comments also about the situation it is in.

It is going to be more difficult to seriously argue that there are human tasks that computers will *never* achieve. "Jeopardy!" does involve understanding complexities of humor, puns, metaphors and other subtleties. Computers are also advancing on a myriad of other fronts, from driverless cars (Google's cars have driven 140,000 miles through California cities and towns without human intervention) to the diagnosis of disease.

WATSON ON YOUR PC OR MOBILE PHONE?

Watson runs on 90 servers, although it does not go out to the Internet. When will this capability be available on your PC? It was only five years between Deep Blue in 1997, which was a specialized supercomputer, and Deep Fritz in 2002, which ran on eight personal computers, and did about as well.

This reduction in the size and cost of a machine that could play world-champion level chess was due both to the ongoing exponential growth of computer hardware and to improved pattern recognition software for performing the key move-countermove tree-pruning decision task. Computer price-performance is now doubling in less than a year, so 90 servers would become the equivalent of one in about seven years. Since a server is more expensive than a typical personal computer, we could consider the gap to be about ten years.

But the trend is definitely moving towards cloud computing, in which supercomputer capability will be available in bursts to anyone, in which case Watson-like capability would be available to the average user much sooner. I do expect the type of natural language processing we see in Watson to show up in search engines and other knowledge retrieval systems over the next five years.

PASSING THE TURING TEST

How does all of this relate to the Turing test? Alan Turing based his eponymous Turing test entirely on human text language based on his (in my view accurate) insight that human language embodies all of human intelligence. In other words, there are no simple language tricks that would enable a computer to pass a well-designed Turing test. A computer would need to actually master human levels of understanding to pass this threshold.

Incidentally, properly designing a Turing test is not straightforward and Turing himself left the rules purposely vague. How qualified does the human judge need to be? How human does the judge need to be (for example, can he or she be enhanced with nonbiological intelligence)? How do we ensure that the human foils actually try to trick the judge?

How long should the sessions be? Mitch Kapor and I bet $20,000 ($10,000 each), with the proceeds to go to the charity of the winner's choice, whether a computer would pass a Turing test by 2029. I said yes and he said no. We spent considerable time negotiating the rules, which you can see at http://www.kurzweilai.net/a-wager-on-the-turing-test-the-rules.

What does this achievement with "Jeopardy!" tell us about the prospect of computers passing the Turing test? It certainly demonstrates the rapid progress being made on human language understanding. There are many other examples, such as CMU's Read the Web project, which has created NELL (Never Ending Language Learner)[3], which is currently reading documents on the Web and accurately understanding most of them.

With computers demonstrating a basic ability to understand the symbolic and hierarchical nature of language (a reflection of the inherently hierarchical nature of our neocortex), it is only a matter of time before that capability reaches Turing-test levels. Indeed, if Watson's underlying technology were applied to the Turing test task, it should do pretty well. Consider the annual Loebner Prize competition, one version of the Turing test. Last year, the best chatbot fooled the human judges 25 percent of the time, and the competition requires only a 30 percent level to pass.

Given that contemporary chatbots do well on the Loebner competition, it is likely that such a system based on Watson technology would actually pass the Loebner threshold[4]. In my view, however, that threshold is too easy. It would not be likely to pass the more difficult threshold that Mitch Kapor and I defined. But the outlook for my bet, which is not due until 2029, is looking pretty good.

It is important to note that an important part of the engineering of a system that will pass a proper Turing test is that it will need to dumb itself down. In a movie I wrote and co-directed, *The Singularity is Near, A True Story about the Future*[5], an AI named Ramona needs to pass a Turing test, and indeed she has this very realization. After all, if you were talking to someone over instant messaging and they seemed to know every detail of everything, you'd realize it was an AI.

What will be the significance of a computer passing the Turing test? If it is really a properly designed test it would mean that this AI is truly operating at human levels. And I for one would then regard it as human. I'm expecting this to happen within two decades, but I also expect that when it does, observers will continue to find things wrong with it.

By the time the controversy dies down and it becomes unambiguous that nonbiological intelligence is equal to biological human intelligence, the AIs will already be thousands of times smarter than us. But keep in mind that this is not an alien invasion from Mars. We're creating these technologies to extend our reach. The fact that farmers in China can access all of human knowledge with devices they carry in their pockets is a testament to the fact that we are doing this already.

Ultimately, we will vastly extend and expand our own intelligence by merging with these tools of our own creation.

ENDNOTES

1. *The Age of Intelligent Machines* at http://www.kurzweilai.net/the-age-of-intelligent-machines-prologue-the-second-industrial-revolution.
2. *Law of Accelerating Returns* at http://lifeboat.com/ex/law.of.accelerating.returns.
3. NELL: Never-Ending Language Learning at http://rtw.ml.cmu.edu/rtw/.
4. Loebner Prize at http://aisb.org.uk/events/loebner-prize.
5. *The Singularity is Near, A True Story about the Future* at http://singularity.com/themovie/index.php.

PROOF THAT THE END OF MOORE'S LAW IS NOT THE END OF THE SINGULARITY

ERIC KLIEN

Eric is President of Lifeboat Foundation. Read his bio at http://lifeboat.com/ex/bios.eric.
klien.

The following was first published on our blog at http://lifeboat.com/blog/2014/12/proof-that-the-end-of-moores-law-is-not-the-end-of-the-singularity and reached #21 on reddit.

During the last few years, the semiconductor industry has been having a harder and harder time miniaturizing transistors with the latest problem being Intel's delayed roll-out of its new 14 nm process. The best way to confirm this slowdown in progress of computing power is to try to run your current programs on a 6-year-old computer. You will likely have few problems since computers have not sped up greatly during the past 6 years. If you had tried this experiment a decade ago you would have found a 6-year-old computer to be close to useless as Intel and others were able to get much greater gains per year in performance than they are getting today.

Many are unaware of this problem as improvements in software and the current trend to have software rely on specialized GPUs instead of CPUs has made this slowdown in performance gains less evident to the end user. (The more specialized a chip is, the faster it runs.) But despite such workarounds, people are already changing their habits such as upgrading their personal computers less often. Recently people upgraded their ancient Windows XP machines only because Microsoft forced them to by discontinuing support for the still popular Windows XP operating system. (Windows XP was the second most popular desktop operating system in the world the day *after* Microsoft ended all support for it. At that point it was a 12-year-old operating system.)

It would be unlikely that AIs would become as smart as us by 2029 as Ray Kurzweil has predicted if we depended on Moore's Law to create the hardware for AIs to run on. But all is not lost. Previously, electromechanical technology gave way to relays, then to vacuum tubes, then to solid-state transistors, and finally to today's integrated circuits. One

Samsung 850 Pro: The **solution** to Moore's Law ending.

possibility for the sixth paradigm to provide exponential growth of computing has been to go from 2D integrated circuits to 3D integrated circuits. There have been small incremental steps in this direction, for example Intel introduced 3D tri-gate transistors with its first 22 nm chips in 2012. While these chips were slightly taller than the previous generation, performance gains were not great from this technology. (Intel is simply making its transistors taller and thinner. They are not stacking such transistors on top of each other.)

But quietly this year, 3D technology has finally taken off. The recently released Samsung 850 Pro[1] which uses 42 nm flash memory is competitive with competing products that use 19 nm flash memory. Considering that, for a regular flat chip, 42 nm memory is (42 × 42) / (19 × 19) = 4.9 times as big and therefore 4.9 times less productive to work with, how did Samsung pull this off? They used their new 3D V-NAND architecture, which stacks 32 cell layers on top of one another. It wouldn't be that hard for them to go from 32 layers to 64 then to 128, etc. Expect flash drives to have greater capacity than hard drives in a couple years! (Hard drives are running into their own form of an end of Moore's Law situation.) Note that by using 42 nm flash memory instead of 19 nm flash memory, Samsung is able to use bigger cells that can handle more read and write cycles.

Samsung is not the only one with this 3D idea. For example, Intel has announced[2] that it will be producing its own 32-layer 3D NAND chips in 2015. And 3D integrated circuits are, of course, not the only potential solution to the end of Moore's Law. For example, Google is getting into the quantum computer business which is another possible solution.[3] But there is a huge difference between a theoretical solution that is being tested in a lab somewhere and something that you can buy on Amazon today.

Finally, to give you an idea of how fast things are progressing, a couple months ago Samsung's best technology was based on 24-layer 3D MLC chips and now Samsung has already announced[4] that it is mass producing 32-layer 3D TLC chips that hold 50% more data per cell than the 32-layer 3D MLC chips currently used in the Samsung 850 Pro.

The Singularity *is* near!

ENDNOTES

1. The Samsung 850 Pro is available at http://amzn.to/1BifBPu.

2. Intel announcement is at http://www.extremetech.com/computing/194911-intel-announces-32-layer-3d-nand-chips-plans-for-larger-than-10tb-ssds.

3. Google's entry into quantum computers is discussed at http://www.technologyreview.com/news/530516/google-launches-effort-to-build-its-own-quantum-computer/.

4. Learn about 32-layer 3D TLC chips at http://www.kitguru.net/components/memory/anton-shilov/samsung-confirms-mass-production-of-tlc-3d-v-nand-flash-memory/.

THE FUTURE OF ENERGY:
TOWARDS THE "ENERGULARITY"
JOSÉ CORDEIRO, MBA, PhD

José (http://cordeiro.org) studied science at Universidad Simón Bolívar, Venezuela; engineering at the Massachusetts Institute of Technology, Cambridge; economics at Georgetown University, Washington; and management at INSEAD, France. He is chair of the Venezuela Node of The Millennium Project; founding faculty and energy advisor in Singularity University at NASA Research Park in Silicon Valley, California; founder of the World Future Society's Venezuela Chapter; cofounder of the Venezuelan Transhumanist Association; and former director of the Club of Rome (Venezuela Chapter), World Transhumanist Association, and the Extropy Institute.

ABSTRACT

Homo sapiens sapiens is the only species that has learned how to harness the power of fire. The conscious generation and use of external energy plays a unique role in our human and cultural evolution, from harnessing fire to developing nuclear fusion. Humanity has gone through several energy "waves," advancing exponentially from wood, coal, oil, gas, and eventually hydrogen/solar/nuclear in a continuous process of "decarbonization" and "hydrogenization" of our energy sources. The latest transition from fossil and scarce fuels to more renewable and abundant energy sources might not be easy, but it has already started.

The creation of an Energy Network or "Enernet" will allow us to connect the whole world and to increase, not reduce, our energy consumption. With the Enernet, energy and power will become abundant and basically free, just like information and bandwidth are today thanks to the Internet. Storage considerations are also important, but new batteries and other advanced technologies will make the Enernet more resilient and create positive network effects. This is fundamental for improving the living standards of all people around the world and for moving into the next planetary transition: energy is essential for solving humanity's needs on Earth and for exploring and colonizing the universe.

I then define the "Energularity" or Energy Singularity as the time when humanity becomes a Type I civilization according to the Kardashev scale, that is, a civilization that has basically achieved total mastery of the resources of its home planet. Based on our current power needs, humanity is at around 0.72 on the Kardashev scale, but it could reach Type I status in about a century, or earlier. The "Energularity" is somehow similar to the concepts of the "Technological Singularity" (related to an intelligence explosion) and the "Methuselarity" (related to longevity extension). However, the "Energularity" emphasizes the exponential increase in energy consumption by our civilization on Earth, before we begin colonizing the Solar System and beyond.

The energy of the mind is the essence of life.
Aristotle, ca. 350 BC

HUMANS AND ENERGY
$E = mc^2$. *Energy equals mass times the speed of light squared.*
Albert Einstein, 1905

Many experts have advanced several theories about what makes humans different from other animal species. Humans have the largest brain-to-body mass and the largest encephalization quotient among all mammals. However, what caused it? Some scientists have written about the development of bipedalism and others about the development of language communication, both of which probably date from over 2 million years ago. Other scientists have considered the use of tools and the creation of technology as characteristically human. However, certain animals, including most primates, also exhibit signs of bipedalism, language communication, and even tool making, at least at a very basic level. But no other animals seem to use fire as humans do. Since fire was the first form of external energy generation (extrasomatic energy) adopted by humans, I believe that the way we use energy has also shaped our own evolution.

After our early ancestors began to harness the power of fire, we have become increasingly different from all other species.

There is evidence of cooked food using fire from almost 2 million years ago by our prehuman ancestors, although fire was probably not used in a controlled fashion until about 500,000 years ago by *Homo erectus*. The ability to control fire was a dramatic change in the habits of early prehumans that eventually became *Homo sapiens sapiens* about 100,000 years ago. Making fire to generate heat and light allowed people to cook food, increasing the variety and availability of nutrients. Fire also produced heat that helped people stay warm in cold weather, enabling them to live in cooler climates, and fire also helped to keep nocturnal predators at bay.

The development of extrasomatic energy sources like fire has been fundamental to the growth of human civilization, and energy use seems to continue increasing almost exponentially into the future. Humans have used different forms of extrasomatic energy throughout the ages, starting with fire and including animal power, wind mills, hydropower, and different types of biomass until the 18th century. The sources of such extrasomatic energy have changed according to time and place, and such changes have accelerated in the last two centuries.

The evolution of energy sources in the United States of America (USA) is a good example of the changes in extrasomatic energy generation. Until the end of the 18th century, most energy production in the USA came from burning wood and other biomass. This began changing slowly with the growth of the coal industry during the 19th century. Another transition corresponded to the development of the oil industry in the 20th century, and still another "wave" could be identified with the relative growth of the gas industry in the early 21st century. Each one of these waves has been shorter since the different energy transitions have been happening faster and faster as shown in Figure 1.

Similar energy "waves" can also be identified in most other parts of the world. These transitions show a clear "decarbonization" trend going from fuels with more carbon to those with more hydrogen: first wood, second coal, third oil, fourth gas and maybe eventually pure hydrogen and solar energy. In fact, solar energy itself is based precisely on the nuclear fusion of hydrogen into

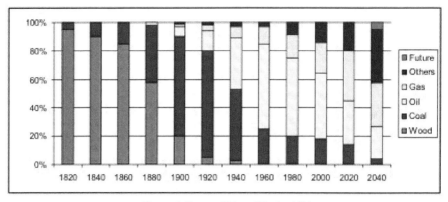

Figure 1: Energy "Waves" in the USA
Source: Based on Cordeiro (2011)

helium, and hydrogen is the lightest and most abundant chemical element in the universe, constituting almost 75% of the estimated chemical mass of all elements (and well over 90% in terms of the number of single atoms) across the known universe. Thus, we can describe such energy waves not only as the "decarbonization" but also as the "hydrogenization" of our energy sources.

Solar energy has been growing exponentially during the last two decades, and most industry forecasts indicate that this trend will continue during the

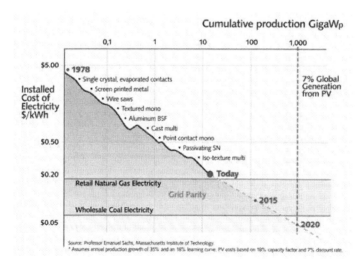

Figure 2: Growth of the Solar Industry

following decades. In fact, solar energy is already reaching "grid parity" in some markets, which means that solar energy has become cheaper than fossil fuels in the first "sunny" markets, and eventually even in places with lower insolation.

This exponential trend will radically transform the energy matrix during the following decades, when solar energy will become the largest single source of energy for our current civilization. One of the leading experts on solar cells, Emmanuel Sachs, has proven how the solar industry has been rapidly growing and is now reaching "grid parity" in many markets, as shown in Figure 2.

Such transition from fossil and scarce fuels to more renewable and abundant energy sources might not be easy, but it has already started. Thus, the age of hydrocarbons seems to be approaching its end, as Saudi Arabian politician Sheikh Ahmed Zaki Yamani has famously said: "the Stone Age did not end for lack of stone, and the Oil Age will end long before the world runs out of oil."

THE "ENERNET"

Not only will atomic power be released, but someday we will harness the rise and fall of the tides and imprison the rays of the sun.

—Thomas Alva Edison, 1921

Futurist Richard Buckminster Fuller was one of the earliest proponents of renewable energy sources (mostly solar energy, including wind and wave energy ultimately produced by the Sun) which he incorporated into his design and work in the middle of the 20th century. He claimed that "there is no energy crisis, only a crisis of ignorance." Decades ago, his research demonstrated that humanity could satisfy 100% of its energy needs while phasing out completely fossil fuels and nuclear fission energy, if required.

Fuller also developed the concept of "energy slaves" in order to show how the human condition has been rapidly improving, partly thanks to the vast amounts of cheap energy available to more and more people. Thus, instead of human slaves, we actually had "energy slaves" that were just a concept to indicate how our advancing technology produced more goods and services for everybody without actually having human slaves working for just a few kings and queens (as it was in the past). In his *World Energy Map*, after his famous *Dymaxion Map*, Fuller estimated that every person had about 38 "energy slaves" in 1950. Thanks to continuous technological advances, Fuller extrapolated that the number of "energy slaves" would keep increasing, which was also very important to his idea of "accelerating acceleration." Furthermore, Fuller believed that humanity urgently needed a global energy network and he first suggested the concept of an interconnected global grid linked to distributed renewable resources in his *World Game* simulation in the 1970s. Fuller concluded that this strategy was the highest priority of the *World Game* simulation and could positively transform humanity by increasing the global standard of living and connecting everybody around the planet.

The creation of a global energy network has many advantages and has indeed been revisited in different ways by other experts, like electrical engineer Robert Metcalfe, inventor of Ethernet and founder of 3Com. Metcalfe coined the term "Enernet" to describe such an energy network based on its similarities with the Internet. He has said that the Enernet "needs to have an architecture, probably needs some layers, standards, and storage. The Internet has lots of storage here and there; the current grid doesn't have much storage at all."

Today, the storage problem is a major obstacle for the Enernet and future smart grids. For example, energy and space expert Gregg Maryniak explains that "our present fixation with energy generation ignores the 'time value of energy'. Instead of concentrating all of our efforts on generation, we need to pay increased attention to energy storage." Fortunately, new developments like liquid-metal batteries have the potential to scale up quickly and solve the storage problems during the next two decades. Localized renewable resources like solar and wind will create more decentralized systems, where local storage will also be a priority.

The Enernet, just as the Internet, will create major positive network effects. A larger and more efficient energy network with good storage will help balance energy requirements across different regions. The first smart grids have already improved the efficiency and resilience of energy transmission and distribution. Future technological developments are expected to continue improving energy systems all the way from generation to final use. China is currently developing some advanced smart grids, and India will probably follow shortly. Since China and India are two huge energy markets, their plans are just the beginning of more advanced energy systems in the following decades. Even pessimistic observers have been surprised by the incredible changes in energy infrastructure in China, soon in India (after the 2012 blackouts), and hopefully even in Africa.

According to Metcalfe, the Enernet will bring fundamental changes in the way we produce and consume energy, from generation to transmission, storage, and final utilization. The Enernet should really create a smart energy grid with distributed resources, efficient systems, high redundancy, and high storage capacity. The Enernet should also help the transition to clean energy and renewable sources, with new players and entrepreneurs taking the place of traditional "big oil" and utilities, and old monolithic producers giving more control to energy prosumers (producers and consumers). Finally, we will continue the transition from expensive energy to cheap energy in a world where energy will be recognized as an abundant resource. Table 1 shows most of these major changes possible thanks to the Enernet.

Table 1: Some Possibilities of the Enernet: From the Past to the Future.
Source: Cordeiro based on Metcalfe (2007)

Dumb grid	Smart grid
Centralized sources	Distributed sources
Inefficient systems	Efficient systems
Low redundancy	High redundancy
Low storage capacity	High storage capacity
Dirty energy	Clean energy
Slow response	Fast response
Fossil fuels	Renewable sources
Traditional "big oil" and utilities	New players and entrepreneurs
Producers control	Prosumers control
Energy conservation	Energy abundance
Expensive energy	Cheap energy

Metcalfe has talked about the transition from conservation and expensive information and bandwidth to abundance and almost free Internet services: "When we set out to build the Internet, we began with conserving bandwidth, with compression, packet switching, multiplex terminals, and buffer terminals aimed at conserving bandwidth." Additionally, Metcalfe has explained that energy and power with the Enernet might follow the same exponential growth as information and bandwidth with the Internet since its beginning:

Now, decades later, are we using less bandwidth now than before? Of course not. We are using million times more bandwidth. If the Internet is any guide, when we are done solving energy, we are not going to use less energy but much, much more—a squanderable abundance, just like we have in computation.

Having abundant and almost free energy might seem hard to believe today, but that has been the trend for many other commodities. As economist Julian Simon said:

During all of human existence, people have worried about running out of natural resources: flint, game animals, what have you. Amazingly, all the evidence shows that exactly the opposite has been true. Raw materials—all of them—are becoming more available rather than more scarce.

It is also worth considering an analogy between energy and telecommunications. The modern telecommunications industry began with very expensive telegraphs in the early 19th century, followed by costly fixed-line telephones in the late 19th century. The first transatlantic phone calls would cost over $100 for a few minutes in the early 20th century. Today, most national and international calls cost nearly zero; in fact, Skype and similar services have revolutionized telecommunications by allowing virtually free calls as long as there is an Internet connection. Niklas Zennström, the Swedish entrepreneur who cofounded the KaZaA peer-to-peer file sharing system and later also cofounded the Skype peer-to-peer internet telephony network in Estonia, is famous for saying: "The telephone is a 100-year-old technology. It's time for a change. Charging for phone calls is something you did last century."

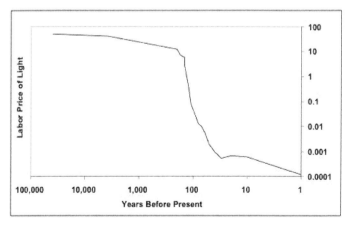

Figure 3: Price of Light (Work Hours per 1000 Lumen Hours)
Source: Cordeiro based on Nordhaus (1997) and DeLong (2000)

Telephone rates have decreased very rapidly, while there has been a continuous increase in the use of telecommunications. The rapid fall in telephone rates can also be compared with the long-term cost reductions in energy (together with the exponential growth of both information and energy usage). For example, economist William Nordhaus calculated the price of light as measured in work hours per 1,000 lumen hours (the lumen is a measure of the flux of light) throughout human history. He compared estimates for fires in the caves of the Peking man using wood, lamps of the Neolithic men using animal or vegetable fat, and lamps of the Babylonians using sesame oil. After reviewing the labor-time costs of candles, oil lamps, kerosene lamps, town gas, and electric lamps, Nordhaus concluded that there has been an exponential decrease of lighting costs, particularly during the last 100 years. However, some of these outstanding costs reductions, a ten thousand-fold decline in the real price of illumination, have not been captured by the standard price indices, as economist James Bradford DeLong has emphasized. Figure 3 shows the staggering reduction of lighting costs through human history. The exponential decrease in energy cost has been even larger during the last century (while energy production has also increased exponentially).

Another example of such accelerating changes can be seen in the semiconductor industry. The exponential increase of capabilities, and the corresponding reduction of costs, is commonly called Moore's Law in semiconductor manufacturing. Caltech professor and VLSI (very large scale integrated circuit) pioneer Carver Mead named this eponymous law in 1970 after scientist and businessman Gordon Moore (cofounder of Intel with fellow inventor Robert Noyce). According to Moore's original observations in 1965, the number of transistors per computer chip was doubling every two years, even though this trend has recently accelerated to just about 18 months. Figure 4 shows Moore's Law with an exponential scale in the vertical axis. A further increase in the rate of change can also be identified from the late 1990s.

Moore's Law and similar conjectures (since they are not really physical laws) have been observed for many processes, for example, the growing number of transistors per integrated circuit, the decreasing costs per transistor, the increasing density at minimum cost per transistor, the augmenting computing performance per unit cost, the reducing power consumption in newer semi-conductors, the exponential growth of hard disk storage cost per unit of information, the accelerating expansion of RAM storage capacity, the rapidly improving network capacity and the exponential growth of pixels per dollar. In fact, in the specific case of USB flash memories, the Korean company Samsung follows Hwang's Law, named after a vice president of Samsung, which states that the amount of memory in such devices doubles every 12 months. Concerning the eponymous Moore's Law, Gordon Moore himself said that his "law" should still be valid for at least the next two decades or so, until transistors reach the size of single nanometers.

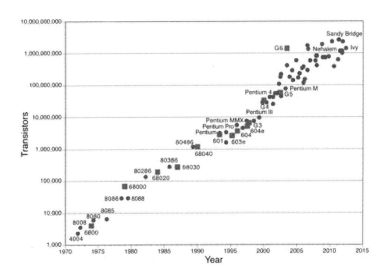

Figure 4: Moore's Law
Source: Cordeiro adapted from Intel (2015)

The 20th century experienced a dramatic increase of energy production and consumption in the developed countries. During the 1950s, the peaceful development of nuclear fission contributed to the rapid growth of energy production and to the reduction of energy costs. Naval officer and businessman Lewis Strauss, during his tenure as Chairman of the US Atomic Energy Commission, said:

Our children will enjoy in their homes electrical energy too cheap to meter... It is not too much to expect that our children will know of great periodic regional famines in the world only as matters of history, will travel effortlessly over the seas and under them and through the air with a minimum of danger and at great speeds, and will experience a lifespan far longer than ours, as disease yields and man comes to understand what causes him to age.

Strauss was actually referring not to uranium fission reactors but to hydrogen fusion reactors that were being considered at the time, even if they were not constructed later on. His prediction was ahead of his time, but it is possible that it will finally turn into reality soon. Thus, energy and the Enernet will eventually become "too cheap to meter," just as information and the Internet have basically become today.

THE "ENERGULARITY"

It is important to realize that in physics today, we have no knowledge what energy is.

—Richard Feynman, 1964

The idea of a "singularity" has been known to science for many years. For example, there are mathematical singularities (like dividing by zero) and physical singularities (like a black hole). The concept of a "technological singularity" as an intelligence explosion was considered by English mathematician Irving John (I.J.) Good in the 1960s and then by computer scientist and science fiction writer Vernor Vinge in the 1980s. Vinge further developed this idea in his 1993 article entitled "The Coming Technological Singularity: How to Survive in the Post-Human Era," where he predicted that "within thirty years, we will have the technological means to create superhuman intelligence. Shortly after, the human era will be ended." Thus, several authors now define such technological singularity as the moment when artificial intelligence overtakes human intelligence.

In 2005, inventor and futurist Ray Kurzweil published his best-seller *The Singularity is Near: When Humans Transcend Biology*, which brought the idea of the technological singularity to the popular media. According to Kurzweil, we are entering a new epoch that will witness the merger of technology and human intelligence through the emergence of a "technological singularity."

Kurzweil believes that an artificial intelligence will first pass the Turing Test by 2029, and then the technological singularity should happen by 2045, when non-biological intelligence will match the range and subtlety of all humans. It will then soar past it because of the continuing acceleration of information-based technologies, as well as the ability of machines to instantly share their knowledge. Eventually, intelligent nanorobots will be deeply integrated in our bodies, our brains, and our environment, solving human problems like pollution and poverty, providing vastly extended longevity, incorporating all of the senses in full-immersion virtual reality, and greatly enhancing human intelligence. The result will be an intimate merger between the technology-creating species and the technological evolutionary process that it spawned.

Kurzweil has also proposed the Law of Accelerating Returns, as a generalization of Moore's Law to describe the exponential growth of technological progress. Kurzweil extends Moore's Law to include technologies from before the integrated circuit to future forms of computation. Whenever a technology approaches some kind of a barrier, he writes, a new technology will be invented to allow us to cross that barrier. He predicts that such paradigm shifts will become increasingly common, leading to "technological change so rapid and profound it represents a rupture in the fabric of human history." Kurzweil explains that his Law of Accelerating Returns implies that a technological singularity will occur around 2045:

An analysis of the history of technology shows that technological change is exponential, contrary to the common-sense 'intuitive linear' view. So we won't experience 100 years of progress in the 21st century—it will be more like 20,000 years of progress (at today's rate). The 'returns,' such as chip speed and cost-effectiveness, also increase exponentially. There's even exponential growth in the rate of exponential growth. Within a few decades, machine intelligence will surpass human intelligence, leading to the Singularity—technological change so rapid and profound it represents a rupture in the fabric of human history. The implications include the merger of biological and non-biological intelligence, immortal software-based humans, and ultra-high levels of intelligence that expand outward in the universe at the speed of light.

In 2008, English gerontologist Aubrey de Gray developed the idea of the

"Methuselarity." According to de Gray, the Methuselarity is the "biogeronto-logical counterpart of the singularity" and it corresponds to the point at which medical technology improves so fast that expected human lifespan increases by more than one year per year. He considers the rate of improvement in reju-venation therapies that is sufficient to outrun the problem of aging: to deplete the levels of all types of damage more rapidly than they are accumulating, even though intrinsically the damage still present will be progressively more recalci-trant. In his writings, de Gray has named this required rate of improvement as the "longevity escape velocity" or LEV. Therefore, "the Methuselarity is, simply, the one and only point in the future at which LEV is achieved."

Based on similar ideas to the technological singularity and the Methu-selarity, I have created the term "Energularity" in order to convey the notion of an exponential growth in our energy and power consumptions. For this, I use the Kardashev scale and I then define the "Energularity" as the time when humanity becomes a Type I civilization. Nikolai Semenovich Kardashev is a Russian astrophysicist who in 1964 proposed a scale to measure the level of technological progress in an advanced civilization. His scale is only theoreti-cal and highly speculative in terms of an actual civilization; however, it puts the energy and power consumptions of an entire civilization in a cosmic per-spective. The scale has three designated categories called Type I, Type II, and Type III. These are based on the amount of usable energy that a civilization has available at its disposal, and the degree of space colonization as well. In general terms, a Type I civilization has achieved mastery of the resources of its home planet, Type II of its solar system, and Type III of its galaxy.

Table 2 shows the Kardashev scale within the context of different powers from the smallest to the highest values. In fact, the numbers correspond to power levels instead of energy levels, but remember that power is the amount of energy per unit of time: one Watt (or W, the standard SI unit of power) is defined as one Joule (or J, the standard SI unit of energy) per second. Therefore, as long as we are clear about the timespan being considered, there should be no problem using power or energy values consistently. Conversely, the "Energular-ity" could also be considered as a "Powergularity," but the first term is actually preferred and used here.

Table 2: Energy Scale and Kardashev Civilization Types (Power in Watts).
Source: Based on Cordeiro (2011)

Example	Power	Scientific notation
Power of Galileo space probe's radio signal from Jupiter	10 zW	10×10^{-21} watt
Minimum discernable signal of FM antenna radio receiver	2.5 fW	2.5×10^{-15} watt
Average power consumption of a human cell	1 pW	1×10^{-12} watt
Approximate consumption of a quartz wristwatch	1 µW	1×10^{-6} watt
Laser in a CD-ROM drive	5 mW	5×10^{-3} watt
Approximate power consumption of the human brain	30 W	30×10^{0} watt
Power of the typical household incandescent light bulb	60 W	60×10^{0} watt
Average power used by an adult human body	100 W	100×10^{0} watt
Peak power consumption of a Pentium 4 CPU	130 W	130×10^{0} watt
Power output (work plus heat) of a person working hard	500 W	500×10^{0} watt
Power of a typical microwave oven	1.1 kW	1.1×10^{3} watt
Power received from the Sun at the Earth's orbit per m^2	1.366 kW	1.366×10^{3} watt
2010 world average power use per person	2.3 kW	2.3×10^{3} watt
Average photosynthetic power output per km^2 in ocean	3.3–6.6 kW	$3.3–6.6 \times 10^{3}$ watt
2010 US average power use per person	12 kW	12×10^{3} watt
Average photosynthetic power output per km^2 in land	16–32 kW	$16–32 \times 10^{3}$ watt
Approximate range of power output of typical automobiles	40–200 kW	$40–200 \times 10^{3}$ watt
Peak power output of a blue whale	2.5 MW	2.5×10^{6} watt
Mechanical power output of a diesel locomotive	3 MW	3×10^{6} watt
Average power consumption of a Boeing 747 aircraft	140 MW	140×10^{6} watt
Peak power output of largest class aircraft carrier	190 MW	190×10^{6} watt
Electric power output of a typical nuclear plant	1 GW	1×10^{9} watt
Power received from the Sun at the Earth's orbit by km^2	1.4 GW	1.4×10^{9} watt

Electrical generation of the Three Gorges Dam in China	18 GW	18×10^9 watt
Power consumption of the first stage of Saturn V rocket	190 GW	190×10^9 watt
2010 US electrical power consumption	0.5 TW	0.5×10^{12} watt
2010 world electrical power consumption	2.0 TW	2.0×10^{12} watt
2010 US total power consumption	3.7 TW	3.7×10^{12} watt
2010 world total power consumption	16 TW	16×10^{12} watt
Average total heat (geothermal) flux from earth's interior	44 TW	44×10^{12} watt
World total photosynthetic energy production	75 TW	75×10^{12} watt
Heat energy released by a hurricane	50–200 TW	$50\text{–}200 \times 10^{12}$ watt
Estimated total available wind energy	870 TW	870×10^{12} watt
World's most powerful laser pulses	1.2 PW	1.2×10^{15} watt
Estimated heat flux transported by the Gulf Stream	1.4 PW	1.4×10^{15} watt
Total power received by the Earth from the Sun (Type I)	174 PW	174×10^{15} watt
Luminosity of the Sun (Type II)	385 YW	385×10^{24} watt
Approximate luminosity of the Milky Way galaxy (Type III)	5×10^{36} W	5×10^{36} watt
Approximate luminosity of a Quasar	1×10^{40} W	1×10^{40} watt
Approximate luminosity of the Local Supercluster	1×10^{42} W	1×10^{42} watt
Approximate luminosity of a Gamma Ray burst	1×10^{45} W	1×10^{45} watt
Approximate luminosity of all the stars in the known universe	2×10^{49} W	2×10^{49} watt
The Planck Power (basic unit of power in the Planck units)	3.63×10^{52} W	3.63×10^{52} watt

A Type I civilization is one that is able to harness all of the power in a single planet (in our case, planet Earth has about 174×10^{15} W in available power). A Type II civilization is one that can harness all of the power available from a solar system (approximately 385×10^{24} W for our Sun), and a Type III civilization is able to harness all of the power available from a single galaxy (approximately 5×10^{36} W for the Milky Way). These figures are extremely variable since planets, solar systems, and galaxies vary widely in luminosity, size, and many other important parameters. As a general reference, and using very round numbers, we could say that a Type I civilization can harness about 10^{16} W, a Type II about 10^{26} W, and a Type III about 10^{36} W, all of these figures plus or minus one or two orders of magnitude. In fact, astrophysicist Carl Sagan preferred to use a logarithmic scale instead of the orders of magnitude proposed by Kardashev. Thus, our human civilization is currently at about 0.72 in a logarithmic scale before reaching 1.0 corresponding to Type I status. Such a logarithmic scale indicates a clear exponential growth for energy consumption. Our prehuman ancestors started harnessing fire about half a million years ago, and we should reach Type I status in about one or two centuries, according to theoretical physicist Michio Kaku. This exponential growth is also explained by Kaku, who talks about different propulsion systems available to different types of civilizations:

Type 0:
- Chemical rockets
- Ionic engines
- Fission power
- EM propulsion (rail guns)

Type I:
- Ram-jet fusion engines
- Photonic drive

Type II:
- Antimatter drive
- Von Neumann nano probes

Type III:
- Planck energy propulsion

Space advocates have realized that there are almost unlimited amounts of energy available in outer space. That is why it is so important to reach the "Energularity" and become a Type I civilization that can then explore and colonize the universe, beginning with our own solar system and galaxy. Aerospace engineer Robert Zubrin emphasized that:

Adopting Kardashev's scheme in slightly altered form, I define a Type I civilization as one that has achieved full mastery of all of its planet's resources. A Type II civilization is one that has mastered its solar system, while a Type III civilization would be one that has access to the full potential of its galaxy. The trek out of Africa was humanity's key step in setting itself on the path toward achieving a mature Type I status that the human race now approaches.

The challenge today is to move on to Type II. Indeed, the establishment of a true spacefaring civilization represents a change in human status as fully profound—both as formidable and as pregnant with promise—as humanity's move from the Rift Valley to its current global society.

Space today seems as inhospitable and as worthless as the wintry wastes of the north might have appeared to an average resident of East Africa 50,000 years ago. But yet, like the north, it is the frontier whose possibilities and challenges will allow and drive human society to make its next great positive transformation.

Other authors have considered even higher types of civilizations than the three originally defined by Kardashev. For example, a Type IV civilization could have control of the energy output of a galactic supercluster (approximately 10^{42} W in our case) and a Type V civilization could control the energy of the entire universe. Such an advanced civilization would approach or surpass the limits of speculation based on our current scientific understanding, and it may not be possible. Finally, some science fiction authors have written about a Type VI civilization that could control the energy over multiple universes (a power level which could technically be infinite) and also about a Type VII civilization that could have the hypothetical status of a deity (able to create universes at will, using them as an energy source).

BEYOND THE "ENERGULARITY"

Every time you look up at the sky, every one of those points of light is a reminder that fusion power is extractable from hydrogen and other light elements, and it is an everyday reality throughout the Milky Way Galaxy.

—Carl Sagan, 1991

The "Energularity" and Kardashev's civilization types are originally defined according to the total energy available to a planet. Indeed, our Sun continuously delivers to Earth over 10,000 times the power consumed by humanity today: 174 PW (1.74×10^{17} W) from our Sun versus 16 TW (1.6×10^{13} W) used currently by all humans alive now. Indeed, solar energy is by far the largest external source of energy available to our civilization. However, beyond solar energy, we still have plenty of energy sources available on our planet to move us towards the "Energularity."

Table 3 shows the different energy contents (specific energy measured in terms of Mega Joules per kilogram, MJ/kg) available in several different materials. Hydropower was one of the first extrasomatic energy sources used by humans, but its energy content is very low: only 0.001 MJ/kg for water stored at a height of 100 meters. Bagasse, animal dung, manure and wood fuels were relatively much better, ranging from 10 to 16 MJ/kg. Humanity then moved to coal, whose energy content goes from about 22 to 30 MJ/kg, depending on the type and quality of coal. Now hydrocarbon fuels are the main energy source, with 22 to 55 MJ/kg from methanol to methane, for example. Additionally, since the middle of the 20th century, several countries have also started using nuclear fission, and some fast breeder reactors produce 86,000,000 MJ/kg with uranium.

Table 3: Approximate Energy Content of Different Materials. Source: Based on Cordeiro (2011)

Fuel type	Energy content (MJ/kg)
Pumped stored water at 100 m dam height (hydropower)	0.001
Battery, lead acid	0.14
Battery, lithium-ion	0.7
Battery, lithium-ion nanowire	2.5
Bagasse (cane stalks)	10
Animal dung, manure	12–14
Wood fuel ($C_6H_{10}O_5)_n$	14–16
Sugar ($C_6H_{12}O_6$, glucose)	16
Methanol (CH_3-OH)	22
Coal (anthracite, lignite, etc.)	22–30
Ethanol (CH_3-CH_2-OH)	30
LPG (liquefied petroleum gas)	32–34
Butanol (CH_3-$(CH_2)_3$-OH)	36
Biodiesel	38
Olive oil ($C_{18}H_{34}O_2$)	40
Crude oil (medium petroleum averages)	42–44
Gasoline	46
Diesel	48
Methane (CH_4, gaseous fuel, compression dependent)	55
Hydrogen (H_2, gaseous fuel, compression dependent)	140
Nuclear isomers (Ta-180m isomer)	41,340

Nuclear isomers (Hf-178m2 isomer)	1,326,000
Nuclear fission (natural uranium in fast breeder reactor)	86,000,000
Nuclear fusion (Hydrogen, H)	300,000,000
Binding energy of helium (He)	675,000,000
Mass-energy equivalence (Einstein's equation $E = mc^2$)	89,880,000,000
Annihilation of matter and antimatter	180,000,000,000

Humanity has continuously increased its energy sources throughout history, starting from different types of biomass and hydropower in the distant past, to coal and hydrocarbons constituting the largest energy sources today. Nonetheless, nuclear energy, first fission and later fusion, will probably become the major energy sources in the near future, while we keep moving towards the "Energularity" and finally become a Type I civilization.

According to Kardashev, our civilization is still at Type 0 status, but we might reach Type I in the next century. Indeed, we have advanced exponentially in our energy uses from harnessing fire about half a million years ago to developing sustainable nuclear fusion in the coming decades. Eventually, we should be able to harness the full energy content of matter and convert matter directly into energy, according to Einstein's equation, and even annihilate matter and antimatter to produce more energy. To have an idea of the incredible energy potential represented just by our planet, the Earth has an estimated mass of 5.98×10^{24} kg, which represents a theoretical energy content of 5.37×10^{41} J. Therefore, just our oceans have enough water to power humanity beyond Type I status over very long geological time scales. Additionally, in the case of our Sun, its mass is estimated to be 1.99×10^{30} kg, which is theoretically equivalent to 1.79×10^{47} J. Those numbers are really enormous and they represent more than enough energy for billions and billions of years.

Considering the visible and known universe, its total mass-energy is currently estimated at about 4×10^{69} J. In a few words, there is certainly no lack of mass-energy in the universe. Moreover, ordinary matter is now considered to be only about 4% of the total matter-energy density in the observable universe, which also includes 22% dark matter and 74% dark energy as well. Since matter and energy can not be destroyed but only converted from one type to another, as scientists believe, there are almost unlimited amounts of energy for our civilization to keep expanding throughout the universe after reaching the "Energularity."

The Earth, the Sun, the Milky Way galaxy and the visible universe have more than enough energy to power our civilization for the following decades, centuries, millennia, and even billions of years into the future. It is thus possible to convert the immense energy supplies available in the universe into usable power, but it will certainly take massive investments and lots of imagination, creativity, science, and technology. Our civilization is still in its infancy, and barring any wild cards, geopolitical crises, nuclear wars, bio disasters, nano grey goo, environmental disasters, or extraterrestrial contacts, science and technology will keep uncovering the contours of the universe. As Russian rocket scientist Konstantin Eduardovich Tsiolkovsky, one of the "founding fathers" of astronautics, said about a century ago:

The Earth is the cradle of humanity, but one cannot stay in the cradle forever.
Планета есть колыбель разума, но нельзя вечно жить в колыбели.

REFERENCES

1. BP. 2014. *BP Statistical Review of World Energy*. London, UK: BP. http://www.bp.com/en/global/corporate/about-bp/energy-economics/statistical-review-of-world-energy.html

2. British Telecom. 2005. *Technology Timeline*. London, UK: British Telecom. https://www.btplc.com/Innovation/News/timeline/TechnologyTimeline.pdf

3. Chaisson, Eric. 2005. *Epic of Evolution: Seven Ages of the Cosmos*. New York, NY: Columbia University Press.

4. Clarke, Arthur Charles. 1984 (revised). *Profiles of the Future: An Inquiry into the Limits of the Possible*. New York, NY: Henry Holt and Company.

5. Cordeiro, José Luis. 2011. "The Energularity" in *Moving From Vision to Action*. Bethesda, MD: World Future Society.

6. Cordeiro, José Luis. 2010. *The Future of Energy and the Energy of the Future*. San Francisco, CA: Singularity Institute for Artificial Intelligence.

7. Cordeiro, José Luis. 2006. "Energy 2020: A Vision of the Future" in *Creating Global Strategies for Humanity's Future*. Bethesda, MD: World Future Society.

8. de Gray, Aubrey D.N.J. 2008. *The Singularity and the Methuselarity: Similarities and Differences*. Lorton, VA: Methuselah Foundation.

9. DeLong, James Bradford. 2000. "Cornucopia: The Pace of Economic Growth in the Twentieth Century." NBER Working Paper 7602. Cambridge, MA: NBER.

10. Dyson, Freeman John. 1966. "The Search for Extraterrestrial Technology" in *Perspectives in Modern Physics*. New York, NY: John Wiley & Sons.

11. EIA. 2014. *International Energy Outlook*. Washington, DC: EIA. http://www.eia.gov/forecasts/ieo

12. Foundation for the Future. 2007. *Energy Challenges: The Next Thousand Years*. Bellevue, WA: Foundation for the Future. https://web.archive.org/web/20080509075150/http://www.futurefoundation.org/documents/hum_pro_energychallenges.pdf

13. Foundation for the Future. 2002. *The Next Thousand Years*. Bellevue, WA: Foundation for the Future. https://web.archive.org/web/20080907140709/http://www.futurefoundation.org/documents/nty_projdesc.pdf

14. Fuller, Richard Buckminster. 1981. *Critical Path*. New York, NY: W.W. Norton & Company.

15. Glenn, Jerome et al. 2014. *2013–14 State of the Future*. Washington, DC: The Millennium Project. http://www.StateOfTheFuture.org

16. Good, Irving John. 1965. "Speculations Concerning the First Ultraintelligent Machine" in *Advances in Computers, Vol. 6*. Burlington, MA: Academic Press.

17. Hawking, Stephen. 2002. *The Theory of Everything: The Origin and Fate of the Universe*. New York, NY: New Millennium Press.

18. IEA. 2014. *World Energy Outlook*. Paris, France: IEA. http://www.world-energyoutlook.org/publications/weo-2014

19. Kahn, Herman et al. 1976. *The Next 200 Years: A Scenario for America and the World*. New York, NY: William Morrow and Company.

20. Kaku, Michio. 2011. *Physics of the Future*. New York, NY: Double Day.

21. Kaku, Michio. 2005. *Parallel Worlds: The Science of Alternative Universes and Our Future in the Cosmos*. New York, NY: Doubleday.

22. Kardashev, Nikolai Semenovich. 1964. "Transmission of Information by Extraterrestrial Civilizations." *Soviet Astronomy* 8:217.

23. Kurian, George T. and Molitor, Graham T.T. 1996. *Encyclopedia of the Future*. New York, NY: Macmillan.

24. Kurzweil, Ray. 2005. *The Singularity is Near: When Humans Transcend Biology*. New York, NY: Viking. http://singularity.com

25. Kurzweil, Ray. 1999. *The Age of Spiritual Machines*. New York, NY: Penguin Books. http://www.kurzweilai.net/the-age-of-intelligent-machines-prologue-the-second-industrial-revolution

26. Maryniak, Gregg. 2012. "Storage, Not Generation, is the Challenge to Renewable Energy." *Forbes.com*. http://www.forbes.com/sites/singularity/2012/07/20/storage-not-generation-is-the-challenge-to-renewable-energy/

27. Metcalfe, Robert. 2007. *The Enernet*. Unpublished presentation. http://gigaom.com/cleantech/bob-metcalfe-welcome-to-the-enernet-1

28. Nordhaus, William. 1997. "Do Real Output and Real Wage Measures Capture Reality? The History of Lighting Suggests Not" in *The Economics of New Goods*. Chicago, IL: University of Chicago.

29. Romm, Joe. 2011. "Solar Power Much Cheaper to Produce Than Most Analysts Realize, Study Finds." ThinkProgress. http://thinkprogress.org/climate/2011/12/11/387108/solar-power-much-cheaper-than-most-realize-study/

30. Sagan, Carl. 1977. *The Dragons of Eden: Speculations on the Evolution of Human Intelligence*. New York, NY: Random House.

31. Sagan, Carl. 1973. *The Cosmic Connection*. New York, NY: Doubleday.

32. Shell. 2014. *Shell Global Scenarios*. London, UK: Shell: http://www.shell.com/global/future-energy/scenarios.html

33. Simon, Julian Lincoln. 1996. *The Ultimate Resource 2*. Princeton, NJ: Princeton University Press.

34. Vinge, Vernor. 1993. "The Coming Technological Singularity." *Whole Earth Review*. Winter issue. http://www-rohan.sdsu.edu/faculty/vinge/misc/singularity.html

35. Wells, Herbert George. 1902. "The Discovery of the Future." *Nature*, 65. http://www.gutenberg.org/files/44867/44867-h/44867-h.htm

36. Zubrin, Robert. 1999. *Entering Space: Creating a Spacefaring Civilization.* New York, NY: Jeremy P. Tarcher/Putnam.

INTOLERABLE DELAYS

WILLIAM FALOON

Bill compiled the 1,500 page medical reference book *Disease Prevention and Treatment* and is Director and Cofounder of the Life Extension Foundation. His latest book is *Pharmocracy: How Corrupt Deals and Misguided Medical Regulations Are Bankrupting America—and What to Do About It* at http://amzn.to/1DNxtjW.

The Life Extension Foundation is a nonprofit organization, whose long-range goal is the radical extension of the healthy human lifespan. In seeking to control aging, their objective is to develop methods to enable us to live in health, youth, and vigor for unlimited periods of time. The Life Extension Foundation was officially incorporated in 1980, but the founders have been involved in antiaging research since the 1960s. Learn more at http://lef.org.

The first surgical attempt to cure pancreatic cancer was demonstrated in Germany in 1909.[1] In 1935, a doctor named Allen Whipple devised a more effective way to remove the pancreas and adjacent body parts.[2]

Dr. Whipple's technique involves the removal of the head of the pancreas, along with portions of the stomach, small intestine, gall bladder, and common bile duct.

The surgical impact on the body is severe. There is a higher death rate from this procedure than many other hospital operations.[3] Sometimes the rearranged internal organs do not hold together and infection spreads inside the patient. This leads to follow-up surgery where the remainder of the pancreas and the spleen are removed to correct problems caused by the first operation.[4]

Some patients do not heal well and leak pancreatic juice from where

Dr. Allen Whipple
1881–1963
Photo courtesy of the
College of Physicians of
Philadelphia

615

body parts are sewn together. This happens so frequently that the surgeon leaves in drainage catheters for fluids to exit so they don't accumulate inside the patient.[4,5]

Another complication is paralysis of the stomach that can take over a month to heal. During this time a feeding tube is surgically placed into the small intestine to provide nourishment.[6]

Some patients develop type I diabetes because the insulin-producing areas of their pancreas is removed, requiring life-long insulin injections.[7]

Despite these horrific surgical side effects, most patients who survive the painful hospital ordeal die from metastatic pancreatic cancer. Few are cured.

The name of this surgery is the "*Whipple Procedure.*" While it's been refined since Dr. Whipple's work in 1935, pancreatic cancer still kills the vast majority of its victims—79 years later![8]

The snail's pace of progress against malignancies like pancreatic cancer should provoke societal outrage against the establishment. Yet like lambs standing in line awaiting slaughter, the public tolerates mediocre medicine that is inflicting horrific suffering and massive numbers of needless deaths.

We view these bureaucratic lags as *intolerable delays* that will be ridiculed by future medical historians. This article describes a drug long ago approved by the FDA that can improve outcomes in pancreatic and other cancer cases. This treatment, however, is not being incorporated into conventional practice.

Steve Jobs was criticized for delaying a Whipple Procedure for nine months after being diagnosed with pancreatic cancer.[9] The initial approaches Jobs tried (acupuncture, vegan diet, herbs, spiritualists) had no chance of eradicating his primary pancreatic tumor.

Steve Jobs 1955–2011
Pancreatic Cancer Victim

It's hard to blame the then 49-year-old co-founder of Apple, however, for not wanting his body cut up via a Whipple Procedure. Steve Jobs eventually died at age 56 after undergoing multiple aggressive treatments, including a liver transplant.[10–12]

How many technologies developed in the early 1900s do consumers still use today? Even the stethoscope (invented in 1819) remains state-of-the-art in today's archaic world of medical practice.

If one is diagnosed with pancreatic cancer at a relatively early stage, the Whipple Procedure is still the best treatment option. Overlooked are a myriad of *adjuvant therapies* that can markedly improve long-term survival and reduce the horrific complications inherent to the Whipple surgical procedure.

The cancer treatment I describe next is not new. It has long been recommended to *Life Extension*® members.

Table 1: Interleukin-2 Versus Placebo

Interleukin-2 Versus Placebo
In Pancreatic Cancer Treatment

The subcutaneous administering of 9 million international units a day of the drug interleukin-2 to pancreatic cancer patients three days before surgery induced the following benefits compared to placebo patients administered saline:

	Interleukin-2 Group	Control
Two-Year Survival	33%	10%
Three-Year Survival	22%	0%
Postoperative Complications	33%	80%

This study should have made headline news. Instead it was buried in a 2006 edition of the journal *Hepato-Gastroenterology.*[46]

Life Extension has been recommending moderate dose interleukin-2 as an adjuvant cancer treatment since the late 1990s.

Skeptics point to studies in advanced melanoma and renal cell carcinoma patients where interleukin-2 provides only modest survival improvements. These narrow-focused cynics neglect evidence that interleukin-2 is most effective when administered before immune-suppressing surgery, radiation, and chemotherapy begins.[33–37,47,48]

INTERLEUKIN-2 IMPROVES SURVIVAL 3-FOLD!

Interleukin-2 (IL-2) enhances overall immune function, most notably by enhancing natural killer cell activity.[13–15] Natural killer cells are among the body's most important immune defenses against malignant and viral-infected cells.[16–20] (Cells infected with certain viruses are more prone to convert to malignant cells.)[21]

IL-2 was long ago approved to treat kidney cancer[22–26] and metastatic melanoma.[27–29] Its efficacy was likely limited by the advanced disease stage patients are at by the time IL-2 is administered.[30] There is toxicity associated with *high-dose* IL-2.[31,32]

Intriguing research suggests that administering moderate-dose IL-2 to patients before surgery and chemotherapy may improve survival and other outcomes.[33–37] It does this by boosting immune function *prior* to it being impaired by conventional treatments.

Surgery results in significant immune impairment, something we warned against long before the mainstream considered it a factor in the poor survival rates seen in many types of cancer.[38–43] Immune suppression that occurs during chemotherapy is a well-established treatment complication.[44,45]

In a study conducted on pancreatic cancer patients, half the group was administered moderate dose IL-2 for three consecutive days prior to a Whipple Procedure. Two years after the operation, 33% of patients pre-administered IL-2 were alive compared to only 10% of control surgical patients. Three-year survival was 22% in the IL-2 group compared to 0% of the controls.[46]

Surgical complications occurred in 80% of the control surgical patients compared with only 33% in the IL-2 pretreatment group. While the control group spent 19.5 days confined to the hospital after their Whipple Procedure, the IL-2 group escaped the hospital in 12 days.[46]

Life Extension has been recommending moderate-dose IL-2 since the 1990s, yet the mainstream oncologists behave as if these drugs are limited to advanced cancers for which they originally gained FDA-approval. The reality is that IL-2 and other immune-boosting drugs may have far greater efficacy when administered *early* in the disease process against of a wide range of solid tumors and some types of leukemia.

WHY CANCER PATIENTS NEED TO BOOST NATURAL KILLER CELL ACTIVITY

Natural killer cells are the part of the immune system that is capable of recognizing and killing virus-infected and malignant cells, while sparing normal cells.[49,50]

The importance of killing virus-infected cells is that cells infected with *human papilloma virus* (HPV) and other viruses have greater propensity to mutate into cancer cells. Chronic infection with some of these viruses also exhausts vital immune functions.[51]

In mice deficient in *natural killer cells*, tumors grow more aggressively and are more metastatic.[52–54]

Natural killer cells play an important role in the control of tumor growth.[55]

Infusion of immune enhancers like interleukin-2 boosts *natural killer cell* activity which can lead to the death of tumor cells.[56]

Leukemia patients have benefited using *natural killer cells* obtained from hematopoietic stem cell donors, which is an exciting area of cancer research.[57–59]

Non-drug ways of boosting *natural killer cell* activity include garlic,[60–64] melatonin,[65–67] Reishi extract,[68–71] and other supplements used by *Life Extension* members. When treating cancer, however, interleukin-2 should be considered to provide an exponential improvement in natural killer cell activity *prior* to initiation of conventional treatments.

CONTRAST MEDIOCRE CANCER TREATMENT TO HIV

Cancer is not relegated to modern times. It has killed human beings forever, but has become prominent as people live longer and cancer incidence markedly increases. Pancreatic cancer, for instance, increases sharply in individuals over age 50, and most patients are 60 to 80 years old when diagnosed.[72]

HIV rose to prominence in the early 1980s, though the virus existed in the human population before then. The problem was that no one paid attention until thousands started dying.

Within 15 years of HIV infection becoming pandemic, effective anti-viral "cocktails" were discovered that turned AIDS from a death sentence into a manageable chronic disease.[73–75]

In 1981, AIDS was a disease of unknown origin.[76] It is controllable today because of rapid scientific innovation. Pancreatic cancer, on the other hand, still kills virtually all its victims with the best hope for long-term survival being the Whipple Procedure first described in 1935.[8]

So why were AIDS treatments discovered so quickly while effective cancer therapies languish?

The difference was the aggressive way that experimental multi-modal therapies were implemented in HIV/AIDS patients compared to the suffocating bureaucracy that stymies cancer research.

In the early days of AIDS treatment, *any* therapy that might work was tried immediately on dying patients and the results evaluated and documented. These treatments were often administered by those infected with HIV who faced pending death if a cure were not discovered quickly. The FDA was cast by the wayside as AIDS activists made certain that potentially effective treatments were not obstructed by bureaucratic red tape.[77]

We at *Life Extension* are proud of the part we played in saving the lives of AIDS patients by defying FDA attempts to shut us down. An editorial published late last year in the *New England Journal of Medicine* revealed how HIV revolutionized the way global health is pursued, and how it resulted in *accelerated* delivery of innovative life-saving treatments.[78]

NEW ENGLAND JOURNAL OF MEDICINE PRAISES WORK OF EARLY AIDS ACTIVISTS

Allan Brandt, PhD, is a professor of medical history at Harvard Medical School. Dr. Brandt's perspective titled "How AIDS Invented Global Health" was published in the June 6, 2013, edition of the *New England Journal of Medicine*.[79] Here are some quotes from his perspective:

"AIDS has reshaped conventional wisdoms in public health, research practice, cultural attitudes, and social behaviors."

"The rapid development of effective antiretroviral treatments, in turn, could not have occurred without new forms of disease advocacy and activism."

"But AIDS activists explicitly crossed a vast chasm of expertise. They went to FDA meetings and events steeped in often arcane science of HIV, prepared to offer concrete proposals to speed research, reformulate trials, and accelerate regulatory processes."

"This approach went well beyond the traditional bioethical formulations of autonomy and consent. As many clinicians and scientists acknowledged, AIDS activists, including many people with AIDS, served as collaborators and colleagues rather than constituents and subjects, changing the trajectory of research and treatment."

Omitted from Dr. Brandt's complimentary statements were the harassment, persecution, and incarceration of AIDS activists by government agencies that sought to suppress burgeoning development of AIDS therapies.[80,81]

WE WERE JAILED!

The FDA did not like our aggressive stance when it came to accelerating medical research, particularly as it related to helping AIDS victims. The FDA did everything in its power to shut *Life Extension* down and imprison us for life.[82] According to the FDA, we were ripping off dying AIDS patients by recommending unproven therapies.

The *Journal of the American Medical Association* (Nov 27, 2013) featured an article describing a 54% reduction in the risk of progressing from HIV to full-blown AIDS using selenium and multi-vitamins.[83] *Life Extension* first recommended these nutrients in the October 1985 edition of this publication (called at that time *Anti-Aging News*).

While the study published in the *Journal of the American Medical Association* was conducted in a region of Africa where malnutrition is rampant, and the study had other flaws (like a 25% dropout rate in both groups), the delay in HIV-induced immune suppression in patients taking these nutrients was remarkable.

A number of previous studies support the benefits of certain nutrients in delaying HIV progression[79,84–86] Even *FDA Consumer Magazine* eventually acknowledged the value of AIDS patients using nutrient supplements.

We also recommended a drug called isoprinosine to AIDS patients in the October 1985 issue of *Anti-Aging News*. This contributed to our being arrested by the FDA because isoprinosine was not an approved drug. In the June 21, 1990, edition of the *New England Journal of Medicine*, a study found that HIV-infected humans who took isoprinosine were eight times less likely to progress to AIDS compared to placebo.[87] This was not enough, however, to keep us from being indicted in 1991.

What helped save us was the continuing publication of research findings corroborating that isoprinosine and certain nutrients significantly delayed disease progression in HIV-infected patients, thus negating the FDA's argument that we were "ripping off AIDS patients" by recommending "unproven" therapies.

The FDA was on the wrong side when it sought to destroy us in the 1980–1990s. Regrettably, millions of Americans continue to perish from needless bureaucratic red tape from virtually all diseases except AIDS. The reason AIDS is the exception is that AIDS activists made it clear to the FDA that there would be no bureaucratic delays in delivering experimental therapies to HIV-infected patients. The FDA capitulated and this enabled rapid medical innovation to occur in a free market environment.

Cancer patients, on the other hand, sit by like timid sheep, as the FDA decides which experimental therapy they are "allowed" to try and how far their disease must progress before the experimental therapy is made available on a so-called "compassionate-use" basis. FDA's granting of "compassionate-use" sometimes occurs weeks after the patient dies, or is so close to death that it has no chance of working.

"In conclusion, our data suggest the relevance of NK (natural killer) cells as primary effectors not only against high-risk leukemias, but also solid tumors." [44]

Quote from study published in the April 2013 edition of the journal *Oncoimmunology*

NOT FAST ENOUGH!

In 2010, the Life Extension Foundation® pledged a substantial amount of money to a prestigious cancer research institute to evaluate many of the components contained in our published Pancreatic Cancer Treatment Protocol. The institution eagerly pushed this project forward, generating reams of paperwork in order to obtain Institutional Review Board approval.

Here we are in 2014, and the total number of pancreatic patients enrolled in this study is **zero**.

Bureaucratic delays like this are beyond rational understanding. These are human lives we are talking about!

When we devised unique treatments for AIDS in the 1980s, they were provided to dying AIDS patients almost overnight. Not all of them worked, but the ones that did built on a foundation that has resulted in HIV patients living for decades, as opposed to pancreatic cancer patients who often die in a matter of months.

Contrast the rapid development of AIDS therapies to most pancreatic cancer patients who die even after enduring the Whipple Procedure that was first described in 1935. It is clear that methods employed by AIDS activists are far superior to today's regulatory quagmire that stymies cancer research.

CITIZENS SHOULD REVOLT

Cancer will likely kill over 570,000 Americans this year.[88]

Already-approved treatments could be saving lives, such as administering moderate dose interleukin-2 *early* in the disease process. Yet even these simple treatment enhancements are ignored by the oncology mainstream that prefers to practice assembly line medicine.

These kinds of delays would have never been tolerated by AIDS activists, who experimented with *any* potentially effective drug on large numbers of dying patients to quickly discover what worked and what didn't.

The *New England Journal of Medicine* credits the work of AIDS pioneers as revolutionizing the way medical research is conducted today. We at *Life Extension* disagree with this Pollyanna assessment, as cancer therapies we uncovered decades ago remain bogged down in FDA red tape. Many are not being pursued at all despite a continuous stream of favorable data flowing out of research facilities.

The slogan "Act Up, Speak Out… Silence = Death!" was chanted by AIDS activists who surrounded FDA headquarters in 1988 and shut down the agency for one day:[89,90]

PROTEST NOW RATHER THAN WAIT FOR FUNERALS

I do not know why every cancer patient and their family does not march on Washington to demand the same exemption from bureaucratic suffocation that enabled HIV to become a manageable disease in a relatively brief window of time.

Perhaps cancer patients should write their family and friends and state something to the effect:

"In lieu of attending my funeral, would you mind marching on the Capitol in Washington D.C. and insist that cancer patients have unfettered access to any therapy that might work."

ENDNOTES

1. Specht G, Stinshoff K. Walther Kausch (1867–1928) and his significance in pancreatic surgery. *Zentralbl Chir* 2001 Jun; 126(6):479–81.

2. http://www.grandroundsjournal.com/articles/gr0710001/gr0710001.pdf.

3. Birkmeyer JD, Siewers AE, Finlayson EV, et al. Hospital volume and surgical mortality in the United States. *N Engl J Med* 2002 Apr 11; 346(15):1128–37.

4. Ho CK , Kleeff J,Friess H, Büchler MW. Complications of pancreatic surgery. *HPB (Oxford)* 2005; 7(2):99–108.

5. Shrikhande SV, D'Souza MA. Pancreatic fistula after pancreatectomy: evolving definitions, preventive strategies and modern management. *World J Gastroenterol* 2008 Oct 14; 14(38):5789–96.

6. Wente MN, Bassi C, Dervenis C, et al. Delayed gastric emptying (DGE) after pancreatic surgery: a suggested definition by the International Study Group of Pancreatic Surgery (ISGPS). *Surgery* 2007 Nov; 142(5):761–8.

7. Ferrara MJ, Lohse C, Kudva YC, et al. Immediate post-resection diabetes mellitus after pancreaticoduodenectomy: incidence and risk factors. *HPB (Oxford)* 2013 Mar; 15(3):170–4.

8. http://www.webmd.com/cancer/pancreatic-cancer/whipple-procedure.

9. http://money.cnn.com/2008/03/02/news/companies/elkind_jobs.fortune/index.htm?postversion=2008030510.

10. http://www.forbes.com/sites/erikkain/2011/10/05/steve-jobs-has-died-at-age-56/.

11. http://abcnews.go.com/Health/CancerPreventionAndTreatment/steve-jobs-pancreatic-cancer-timeline/story?id=14681812.

12. http://usatoday30.usatoday.com/news/health/medical/health/medical/cancer/story/2011-08-24/Apple-CEO-Steve-Jobs-resigns-after-battling-pancreatic-cancer/50127460/1.

13. Weigent DA, Stanton GJ, Johnson HM. Interleukin 2 enhances natural killer cell activity through induction of gamma interferon. *Infect Immun* 1983 Sep; 41(3):992–7.

14. Kehrl JH, Dukovich M, Whalen G, Katz P, Fauci AS, Greene WC. Novel interleukin 2 (IL-2) receptor appears to mediate IL-2-induced activation of natural killer cells. *J Clin Invest* 1988 Jan; 81(1):200–5.

15. Yao HC, Liu SQ, Yu K, Zhou M, Wang LX. Interleukin-2 enhances the cytotoxic activity of circulating natural killer cells in patients with chronic heart failure. *Heart Vessels* 2009 Jul; 24(4):283–6.

16. Yokoyama WM, Altfeld M, Hsu KC. Natural killer cells: tolerance to self and innate immunity to viral infection and malignancy. *Biol Blood Marrow Transplant* 2010 Jan; 16(1 Suppl):S97–S105.

17. Hwang I, Scott JM, Kakarla T, et al. Activation mechanisms of natural killer cells during influenza virus infection. *PLoS One* 2012 7(12):e51858.

18. Brandstadter JD, Yang Y. Natural killer cell responses to viral infection. *J Innate Immun* 2011; 3(3):274–9.

19. Chisholm SE, Reyburn HT. Recognition of vaccinia virus-infected cells by human natural killer cells depends on natural cytotoxicity receptors. *J Virol* 2006 Mar; 80(5):2225–33.

20. Viel S, Charrier E, Marçais A, et al. Monitoring NK cell activity in patients with hematological malignancies. *Oncoimmunology* 2013 Sep 1; 2(9):e26011.

21. zur Hausen H. Immortalization of human cells and their malignant conversion by high risk human papillomavirus genotypes. *Semin Cancer Biol* 1999 Dec; 9(6):405–11.

22. Rosenberg SA, Lotze MT, Muul LM, et al. Observations on the systemic administration of autologous lymphokine-activated killer cells and recombinant interleukin-2 to patients with metastatic cancer. *N Engl J Med*. 1985 Dec 5; 313(23):1485–92.

23. Salup RR, Wiltrout RH. Adjuvant immunotherapy of established murine renal cancer by interleukin 2-stimulated cytotoxic lymphocytes. *Cancer Res*. 1986 Jul; 46(7):3358–63.

24. Marumo K, Ueno M, Muraki J, Baba S, Tazaki H. Augmentation of cell-mediated cytotoxicity against renal carcinoma cells by recombinant interleukin 2. *Urology* 1987 Oct; 30(4):327–32.

25. Wang J, Walle A, Gordon B, et al. Adoptive immunotherapy for stage IV renal cell carcinoma: a novel protocol utilizing periodate and interleukin-2-activated autologous leukocytes and continuous infusions of low-dose interleukin-2. *Am J Med*. 1987 Dec; 83(6):1016–23.

26. Fisher RI, Coltman CA Jr, Doroshow JH, et al. Metastatic renal cancer treated with interleukin-2 and lymphokine-activated killer cells. A phase II clinical trial. *Ann Intern Med*. 1988 Apr; 108(4):518–23.

27. Chu MB, Fesler MJ, Armbrecht ES, et al. High-dose interleukin-2 (HD IL-2) therapy should be considered for the treatment of patients with melanoma brain metastases. *Chemother Res Pract*. 2013:726925.

28. Atkins MB, Kunkel L, Sznol M, Rosenberg SA. High-dose recombinant interleukin-2 therapy in patients with metastatic melanoma: long-term survival update. *Cancer J Sci Am*. 2000 Feb; 6 Suppl 1:S11–4.

29. Keilholz U, Conradt C, Legha SS, et al. Results of interleukin-2-based treatment in advanced melanoma: a case record-based analysis of 631 patients. *J Clin Oncol*. 1998 Sep; 16(9):2921–9.

30. Petrella T, Quirt I, Verma S, et al. Single-agent interleukin-2 in the treatment of metastatic melanoma. *Curr Oncol* 2007 Feb; 14(1):21–6.

31. Acquavella N, Kluger H, Rhee J, et al. Toxicity and activity of a twice daily high-dose bolus interleukin 2 regimen in patients with metastatic melanoma and metastatic renal cell cancer. *J Immunother* 2008 Jul–Aug; 31(6):569–76.

32. Schwartz RN, Stover L, Dutcher J. Managing toxicities of high-dose interleukin-2. *Oncology* 2002 Nov; 16(11 Suppl 13):11–20.

33. Brivio F, Lissoni P, Rovelli F, et al. Effects of IL-2 preoperative immunotherapy on surgery-induced changes in angiogenic regulation and its prevention of VEGF increase and IL-12 decline. *Hepatogastroenterology* 2002 Mar–Apr; 49(44):385–7.

34. Böhm M, Ittenson A, Klatte T, et al. Pretreatment with interleukin-2 modulates perioperative immunodysfunction in patients with renal cell carcinoma. *Folia Biol (Praha)* 2003 49(2):63–8.

35. Nichols PH, Ramsden CW, Ward U, Sedman PC, Primrose JN. Perioperative immunotherapy with recombinant interleukin 2 in patients undergoing surgery for colorectal cancer. *Cancer Res.* 1992 Oct 15; 52(20):5765–9.

36. Lissoni P, Brivio F, Fumagalli L, Di Fede G, Brera G. Enhancement of the efficacy of chemotherapy with oxaliplatin plus 5-fluorouracil by pretreatment with IL-2 subcutaneous immunotherapy in metastatic colorectal cancer patients with lymphocytopenia prior to therapy. *In Vivo.* 2005 Nov–Dec; 19(6):1077–80.

37. Ades EW, McKemie CR 3rd, Wright S, Peacocke N, Pantazis C, Lockhart WL 3rd. Chemotherapy subsequent to recombinant interleukin-2 immunotherapy: protocol for enhanced tumoricidal activity. *Nat Immun Cell Growth Regul.* 1987 6(5):260–8.

38. Da Costa ML, Redmond P, Bouchier-Hayes DJ. The effect of laparotomy and laparoscopy on the establishment of spontaneous tumor metastases. *Surgery* 1998 Sep; 124(3):516–25.

39. Shakhar G, Blumenfeld B. Glucocorticoid involvement in suppression of NK activity following surgery in rats. *J Neuroimmunol.* 2003 May; 138(1–2):83–91.

40. Rosenne E, Shakhar G, Melamed R, Schwartz Y, Erdreich-Epstein A, Ben-Eliyahu S. Inducing a mode of NK-resistance to suppression by stress and surgery: a potential approach based on low dose of poly I-C to reduce postoperative cancer metastasis. *Brain Behav Immun.* 2007 May; 21(4):395–408.

41. Marik PE, Flemmer M. The immune response to surgery and trauma: Implications for treatment. *J Trauma Acute Care Surg.* 2012 Oct; 73(4):801–8.

42. Yokoyama Y, Sakamoto K, Arai M, Akagi M. Radiation and surgical stress induce a significant impairment in cellular immunity in patients with esophageal cancer. *Jpn J Surg.* 1989 Sep; 19(5):535–43.

43. Sano T, Morita S, Tominaga R, et al. Adaptive immunity is severely impaired by open-heart surgery. *Jpn J Thorac Cardiovasc Surg.* 2002 May; 50(5):201–5.

44. Rasmussen L, Arvin A. Chemotherapy-induced immunosuppression. *Environ Health Perspect.* 1982 Feb; 43:21–5.

45. Zandvoort A, Lodewijk ME, Klok PA, et al. After chemotherapy, functional humoral response capacity is restored before complete restoration of lymphoid compartments. *Clin Exp Immunol.* 2003 Jan; 131(1):8–16.

46. Angelini C, Bovo G, Muselli P, et al. Preoperative interleukin-2 immunotherapy in pancreatic cancer: preliminary results. *Hepatogastroenterology* 2006 Jan–Feb; 53(67):141–4.

47. Hietanen T, Kellokumpu-Lehtinen P, Pitkänen M. Action of recombinant and interleukin 2 in modulating radiation effects on viability and cytotoxicity of large granular lymphocytes. *Int J Radiat Biol.* 1995 Feb; 67(2):119–26.

48. Boise LH, Minn AJ, June CH, Lindsten T, Thompson CB. Growth factors can enhance lymphocyte survival without committing the cell to undergo cell division. *Proc Natl Acad Sci USA* 1995 Jun 6; 92(12):5491–5.

49. Oberoi P, Wels WS. Arming NK cells with enhanced antitumor activity: CARs and beyond. *Oncoimmunology* 2013 Aug 1; 2(8):e25220.

50. Sanchez-Correa B, Morgado S, Gayoso I, Bergua JM, Casado JG, Arcos MJ, Bengochea ML, Duran E, Solana R, Tarazona R. Human NK cells in acute myeloid leukaemia patients: analysis of NK cell-activating receptors and their ligands. *Cancer Immunol Immunother* 2011 Aug; 60(8):1195–205.

51. Brunner S, Herndler-Brandstetter D, Weinberger B, Grubeck-Loebenstein B. Persistent viral infections and immune aging. *Ageing Res Rev.* 2011 Jul; 10(3):362–9.

52. Kozlowski JM, Fidler IJ, Campbell D, Xu ZL, Kaighn ME, Hart IR. Metastatic behavior of human tumor cell lines grown in the nude mouse. *Cancer Res.* 1984 Aug; 44(8):3522–9.

53. Kim S, Iizuka K, Aguila HL, Weissman IL, Yokoyama WM. In vivo natural killer cell activities revealed by natural killer cell-deficient mice. *Proc Natl Acad Sci USA* 2000 Mar 14; 97(6):2731–6.

54. Smyth MJ, Swann J, Cretney E, Zerafa N, Yokoyama WM, Hayakawa Y. NKG2D function protects the host from tumor initiation. *J Exp Med.* 2005 Sep 5; 202(5):583–8.

55. Vacca P, Martini S, Mingari MC, Moretta L. NK cells from malignant pleural effusions are potent antitumor effectors: A clue for adoptive immunotherapy? *Oncoimmunology* 2013 Apr 1; 2(4):e23638.

56. Bhat R, Watzl C. Serial killing of tumor cells by human natural killer cells—enhancement by therapeutic antibodies. *PLoS One* 2007 Mar 28; 2(3):e326.

57. Bradstock KF. The use of hematopoietic growth factors in the treatment of acute leukemia. *Curr Pharm Des.* 2002 8(5):343–55.

58. Ruggeri L, Mancusi A, Burchielli E, Aversa F, Martelli MF, Velardi A. Natural killer cell alloreactivity in allogeneic hematopoietic transplantation. *Curr Opin Oncol.* 2007 Mar; 19(2):142–7.

59. Locatelli F, Pende D, Mingari MC, et al. Cellular and molecular basis of haploidentical hematopoietic stem cell transplantation in the successful treatment of high-risk leukemias: role of alloreactive NK cells. *Front Immunol.* 2013 Feb 1; 4:15.

60. Ishikawa H, Saeki T, Otani T, et al. Aged garlic extract prevents a decline of NK cell number and activity in patients with advanced cancer. *J Nutr.* 2006 Mar; 136(3 Suppl):816S–20S.

61. Nantz MP, Rowe CA, Muller CE, Creasy RA, Stanilka JM, Percival SS. Supplementation with aged garlic extract improves both NK and gd-T cell function and reduces the severity of cold and flu symptoms: a randomized, double-blind, placebo-controlled nutrition intervention. *Clin Nutr.* 2012 Jun; 31(3):337–44.

62. Tang Z, Sheng Z, Liu S, Jian X, Sun K, Yan M. [The preventing function of garlic on experimental oral precancer and its effect on natural killer cells, T-lymphocytes and interleukin-2]. *Hunan Yi Ke Da Xue Xue Bao* 1997 22(3):246–8.

63. Kyo E, Uda N, Suzuki A, et al. Immunomodulation and antitumor activities of Aged Garlic Extract. *Phytomedicine* 1998 Aug; 5(4):259–67.

64. Butt MS, Sultan MT, Butt MS, Iqbal J. Garlic: nature's protection against physiological threats. *Crit Rev Food Sci Nutr.* 2009 Jun; 49(6):538–51.

65. Miller SC, Pandi-Perumal SR, Esquifino AI, Cardinali DP, Maestroni GJ. The role of melatonin in immuno-enhancement: potential application in cancer. *Int J Exp Pathol.* 2006 Apr; 87(2):81–7.

66. Currier NL, Miller SC. Echinacea purpurea and melatonin augment natural-killer cells in leukemic mice and prolong life span. *J Altern Complement Med.* 2001 Jun; 7(3):241–51.

67. Srinivasan V, Spence DW, Pandi-Perumal SR, Trakht I, Cardinali DP. Therapeutic actions of melatonin in cancer: possible mechanisms. *Integr Cancer Ther.* 2008 Sep; 7(3):189–203.

68. Lin ZB. Cellular and molecular mechanisms of immuno-modulation by Ganoderma lucidum. *J Pharmacol Sci.* 2005 Oct; 99(2):144–53.

69. Gao Y, Zhou S, Jiang W, Huang M, Dai X. Effects of ganopoly (a Ganoderma lucidum polysaccharide extract) on the immune functions in advanced-stage cancer patients. *Immunol Invest.* 2003 Aug; 32(3):201–15.

70. Zheng S, Jia Y, Zhao J, Wei Q, Liu Y. Ganoderma lucidum polysaccharides eradicates the blocking effect of fibrinogen on NK cytotoxicity against melanoma cells. *Oncol Lett.* 2012 Mar; 3(3):613–16.

71. Zhu XL, Lin ZB. Effects of Ganoderma lucidum polysaccharides on proliferation and cytotoxicity of cytokine-induced killer cells. *Acta Pharmacol Sin.* 2005 Sep; 26(9):1130–7.

72. Bast RC Jr, Kufe DW, Pollock RE, et al., editors. Holland-Frei Cancer Medicine. 5th edition. Hamilton (ON): BC Decker; 2000. http://www.ncbi.nlm.nih.gov/books/NBK20889/.

73. Arts EJ, Hazuda DJ. HIV-1 antiretroviral drug therapy. *Cold Spring Harb Perspect Med.* 2012 Apr; 2(4):a007161.

74. De Clercq E. Anti-HIV drugs: 25 compounds approved within 25 years after the discovery of HIV. *Int J Antimicrob Agents* 2009 Apr; 33(4):307–20.

75. Sahay S, Reddy KS, Dhayarkar S. Optimizing adherence to antiretroviral therapy. *Indian J Med Res.* 2011 Dec; 134(6):835–49.

76. Adler MW. ABC of Aids: Development of the epidemic. *BMJ.* 2001 May 19; 322(7296):1226–9.

77. http://www.fda.gov/ForConsumers/ByAudience/ForPatientAdvocates/ HIVandAIDSActivities/ucm258087.htm.

78. http://www.nejm.org/doi/full/10.1056/NEJMp1305297. Fawzi WW, Msamanga GI, Spiegelman D, et al. A randomized trial of multivitamin supplements and HIV disease progression and mortality. *N Engl J Med.* 2004 Jul 1; 351(1):23–32.

79. [No authors listed] AIDS advocates returning to their activism roots. Protesters welcome arrests and publicity. AIDS Alert. 2004 Aug; 19(8):90–3.

80. http://www.tcnj.edu/~borland/2006-aids/cassy2.htm.

81. http://www.lef.org/magazine/mag2003/oct2003_cover_victory_01.htm.

82. Baum MK, Campa A, Lai S, et al. Effect of micronutrient supplementation on disease progression in asymptomatic, antiretroviral-naive, HIV-infected adults in Botswana: a randomized clinical trial. *JAMA* 2013 Nov 27; 310(20):2154–63.

83. Fawzi WW, Msamanga GI, Kupka R, et al. Multivitamin supplementation improves hematologic status in HIV-infected women and their children in Tanzania. *Am J Clin Nutr.* 2007 May; 8 5(5):1335–43.

84. Botros D, Somarriba G, Neri D, Miller TL. Interventions to address chronic disease and HIV: strategies to promote exercise and nutrition among HIV-infected individuals. *Curr HIV/AIDS Rep.* 2012 Dec; 9(4):351–63.

85. Mehta S, Fawzi W. Effects of vitamins, including vitamin A, on HIV/AIDS patients. *Vitam Horm.* 2007 75:355–83.

86. Pedersen C, Sandström E, Petersen CS, et al. The efficacy of inosine pranobex in preventing the acquired immunodeficiency syndrome in patients with human immunodeficiency virus infection. The Scandinavian Isoprinosine Study Group. *N Engl J Med.* 1990 Jun 1; 322(25):1757–63.

87. http://www.cdc.gov/nchs/fastats/deaths.htm.

88. http://theconversation.com/how-the-dallas-buyers-club-changed-hiv-treatment-in-the-us-22664.

89. http://www.edgeboston.com/health_fitness/hiv_aids/News//154077/act-up_co-f.

ENHANCED AI:
THE KEY TO UNMANNED SPACE EXPLORATION
TOM KERWICK

Tom is author of *The Safety Procurement of TeV+ Collisions within the Particle Collider Industry* at http://bit.ly/1vaEyV0.

The following was first published on our blog at http://lifeboat.com/blog/2012/08/enhanced-ai-the-key-to-unmanned-space-exploration.

The precursor to manned space exploration of new worlds is typically unmanned exploration, and NASA has made phenomenal progress with remote controlled rovers on the Martian surface in recent years with MER-A Spirit, MER-B Opportunity, and now MSL Curiosity. However, for all our success in reliance on AI in such rovers—similar if not more advanced to AI technology we see around us in the automotive and aviation industries—such as operational real-time clear-air turbulence prediction in aviation—such AI is typically to aid control systems and not mission-level decision making.

NASA still controls via detailed commands transmitted to the rover directly from Earth, typically 225 kbit/day of commands are transmitted to the rover, at a data rate of 1–2 kbit/s, during a 15 minute transmit window, with larger volumes of data collected by the rover returned via satellite relay—a one-way communication that incorporates a delay of on average 12 or so light minutes. This becomes less and less practical the further away the rover is.

If for example we landed a similar rover on Titan in the future, I would expect the current method of step-by-step remote control would render the mission impractical—Saturn being typically at least 16 times more distant—dependent on time of year.

With the tasks of the science labs well determined in advance, it should be practical to develop AI engines to react to hazards, change course of analysis dependent on data processed—and so on—the perfect playground for advanced AI programs. The current Curiosity mission incorporates tasks such as:

1. Determine the mineralogical composition of the Martian surface and near-surface geological materials.
2. Attempt to detect chemical building blocks of life (bio-signatures).
3. Interpret the processes that have formed and modified rocks and soils.
4. Assess long-timescale (i.e., 4 billion year) Martian atmospheric evolution processes.
5. Determine present state, distribution, and cycling of water and carbon dioxide.
6. Characterize the broad spectrum of surface radiation, including galactic radiation, cosmic radiation, solar proton events, and secondary neutrons.

All of these are very deterministic processes in terms of mapping results to action points, which could be the foundation for shaping such into an AI learning engine, so that such rovers can be entrusted with making their own mission-level decisions on next phases of exploration based on such AI analyses.

While the current explorations on Mars work quite well with the remote control strategy, it would show great foresight for NASA to engineer such unmanned rovers to operate in a more independent fashion with AI operating the mission-level control—learning to adapt to its environment as it explores the terrain, with only the return-link in use in the main—to relay back the analyzed data—and the low-bandwidth control-link reserved for maintenance and corrective action only.

NASA has taken great strides in the last decade with unmanned missions. One can expect the next generation to be even more fascinating—and perhaps a trailblazer for advanced AI based technology.

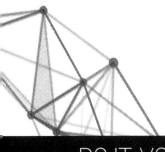

DO IT YOURSELF "SAVING THE WORLD"

JAMES BLODGETT

James Blodgett, M.A. (sociology), M.B.A., M.S. (statistics), was principal author of Lifeboat's response to DARPA's 100 Year Starship RFP while Chair of Lifeboat Foundation's Grantsmanship Committee.

James is Coordinator of the Global Risk Reduction Special Interest Group in American Mensa. He gave talks on global risk at four American Mensa Annual Gatherings, at a Global General Gathering of the Triple Nine Society, and at a Society for Risk Analysis Annual Meeting. He has published papers relevant to Lifeboat concerns in World Future Review and in the Journal of the British Interplanetary Society. He was part of a group that persuaded CERN to do a second safety study.

It seems audacious to think of ourselves as saving the world. We are not superheroes. But the thesis of this essay is that normal people like you and me can contribute to saving the world, or at least to reducing existential risk, which means approximately the same thing. We can learn current thought about issues related to existential risk. We can contribute to and help disseminate that thought. We can advocate for solutions. We can help others who are advocating. On occasion we might even invent solutions. This is at least an interesting hobby, more fun and more meaningful than many other hobbies. If we make it work it can be tremendously meaningful.

Why does our world need saving? Because there are dangers out there, dangers that could make our species extinct, as has happened to many other species. Asteroid impact, thought to have killed the dinosaurs, could do the same to us. There have been several mass extinctions in Earth's history. Fortunately, natural mass extinctions happen infrequently. However, humans are making major impacts on our world. Extinctions that are side effects of our technology, things like nuclear war, run-away global warming, or unfriendly super artificial intelligence, have not been demonstrated to happen infrequently. Indeed they sound distressingly plausible.[1] Technology is expanding rapidly, bringing immense benefits but also dangers. With great power comes great responsibility. Society needs to think about how to maximize benefits while minimizing risks.[2]

Our first reaction is often to expect major issues like this to be addressed by large organizations like the United Nations, national governments, large advocacy groups, or "the market." Sometimes these entities do step up to the plate. However, large organizations all too often ignore these issues. The market reacts to these issues as "externalities," things that do not affect the immediate self-interest of the theoretical "economic man," and that therefore do not affect market prices. They are also externalities to large political organizations unless there is voter concern. It is the job of advocates, a role we could assume, to stir up voter concern, and to point out the moral interests that many individuals do care about.

Normal individuals have already contributed to saving the world. Global nuclear war seems less likely today than it did during the Cold War. Gorbachev and Reagan deserve most of the credit for ending the Cold War, but many of their ideas originated with independent intellectuals, and were reinforced by many normal individuals who contributed to public opinion. Another example of amateur contribution is asteroid impact. That risk has been reduced by studies that have determined the orbits of most of the largest Earth-approaching asteroids. We could try to deflect a risky one. None currently seen pose an immediate risk. Amateur astronomers contributed to those studies.

Some readers may feel that the small strides that normal people like us might accomplish are unlikely to make much of a difference. However, if we do accomplish some version of saving the world, that is worth the current population of Earth (seven billion human lives) plus all future lives. That is worthwhile to try even if the odds are low. Hopefully the odds will not always be low. Consider our fathers, "The Greatest Generation," who fought a war (World War II) that might be thought to have saved civilization. The probability of individual effectuality (the probability that one soldier's efforts would win that war) was fairly low for most soldiers. Nevertheless, they put their lives at risk, and each contributed to a group effort that did win the war.

Even if things seem hopeless, it seems gallant to die while trying to live and while trying to save others. However, I hope that things are not that hopeless.

If you are ready for this hobby, what can do you do to help? You can start by learning about relevant issues, thinking about solutions, thinking about how to implement those solutions, contributing to general thought about this topic, and lending a hand where that seems useful.

As one example of a solution, space settlement would protect against many (but not all) human extinction risks by backing up civilization in case we all die on Earth. However, in order for this to work, that settlement has to be self-sufficient. That requires major industrialization of space. I used to think that major industrialization of space was a prospect for the far future. If Rees and Wells, who predict disaster soon,[1] are right, that may be too late. However, I have learned that there is enough material in the asteroid belt to build habitats for trillions of people.[3] Asteroid belt material could also be used to build other things like space-based solar power satellites that could produce all the power we need on Earth, or a massive sunshade that could solve global warming. In addition, Metzger et al suggest a more-or-less plausible plan for industrialization of space that would enable building all of these things in a fairly short time.[4]

Metzger suggests sending a few tons of automated and remotely-operated machines to the moon: mining and power-generating machines, and also machines like 3D printers, micro machine tools, and teleoperated robots. These are machines that can make other machines, mainly from lunar materials. The machines they could make would be crude at first and include Earth components, but each generation of machines would make subsequent generations that would be increasingly sophisticated. With each generation fewer Earth components would be needed. Eventually the operation would be extended to the asteroid belt. Our caveman ancestors started with rocks and sticks. The successive generations of tools and machines made from those rocks and sticks became an industrial revolution that grew exponentially and resulted in today's ubiquitous and sophisticated machine tools.

Metzger's idea is to do the same thing in space, using exponential growth that could fill the solar system with self-sufficient industry in a fairly short time. But this will take work. It requires redesigning many industrial processes so that they will work in the space environment. It requires redesigning many machines so they can be assembled with the available processes and materials. However, unlike many other ideas for large-scale settlement of space, Metzger's ideas do not require new physics. Indeed the inventing required seems on the level of advanced amateurs like the Wright Brothers.

There are a lot of advanced amateurs today. Many have organized "makerspaces," clubs that acquire advanced machine tools that members can use. Challenge prizes might motivate some makerspace people to help design space machines. Amateurs like you and me could help with this design, but even if we are not mechanically inclined we could help organize and publicize the prizes and we could contribute or help raise money to fund them. This effort would also generate publicity that might help motivate larger organizations or nations to contribute the relatively small launch capacity that would be required, small because most of the material for building machines would come from the Moon and asteroids. Amateur contributions could be important because projects to implement Metzger's ideas are not yet funded on a large scale by large organizations. (NASA, private firms, and other countries are proposing or implementing small projects that might contribute to Metzger's project. The limit of these projects is their small or nonexistent budgets.)

This is just one example of a project that might help. There are many other plausible projects that could reduce existential risk and expand existential possibilities. The job is to think of them, and then to help make them work.

What can you do to learn about these issues? There are many relevant books and discussions, and interesting material on the Internet. In order to get started, follow up on this paper's endnotes and check out the Lifeboat Foundation website at http://lifeboat.com.

We have to be careful. Our save-the-world projects could have unintended consequences. It is said, "first do no harm." However, that is not quite right. We have to compare the risk of doing something with the risk of doing nothing. The trick is to reduce risks without losing opportunities that are more valuable than the risks. We need to think adequately about that balance, but not to think so long that we stall appropriate action.

ENDNOTES

1. Lord Martin Rees, Astronomer Royal of Great Britain, estimates in [Rees, *Our Final Hour*, Basic Books, 2003] that humanity's chance of surviving the next century is 50%. Dr. Willard Wells makes a similar estimate in [Wells, *Apocalypse When?: Calculating How Long the Human Race Will Survive*, Springer, 2010.]

2. Nick Bostrom, Existential Risk Prevention as Global Priority, *Global Policy*, Vol 4, Issue 1 (2013): 15-31. Also available at: http://www.existential-risk. org/concept.html. Dr. Bostrom is Director of the Future of Humanity Institute at Oxford.

3. For example, Dr. John Lewis makes a rough estimate that there is enough iron in the asteroid belt to build a habitat for 10,000,000,000,000,000,000 people in [Lewis, *Mining the Sky: Untold Riches from the Asteroids, Comets, and Planets*, Perseus Publishing, 1997, pg. 194.] All of the other elements necessary for industry and life are also available in abundance.

4. Philip Metzger et al, "Affordable, Rapid Bootstrapping of Space Industry and Solar System Civilization," *Journal of Aerospace Engineering*, April 2012. Dr. Metzger is a former NASA physicist and an expert in extracting resources from lunar regolith.

WILL BRAIN WAVE TECHNOLOGY ELIMINATE THE NEED FOR A SECOND LANGUAGE?

ZOLTAN ISTVAN

Zoltan is author of the award-winning *The Transhumanist Wager* available at http://amzn.to/1zSmpRf.

He is running as a 2016 U.S. Presidential candidate under the newly formed Transhumanist Party.

Earlier this year, the first mind-to-mind communication took place. Hooked up to brain wave headsets, a researcher in India projected a thought to a colleague in France, and they understood each other. Telepathy went from the pages of science fiction to reality.

Using electroencephalography (EEG) sensors that pick up and monitor brain activity, brain wave technology has been advancing quickly in the last few years. A number of companies already sell basic brain wave reading devices, such as the Muse headband. Some companies offer headsets that allow you to play a video game on your iPhone using only thoughts. NeuroSky's MindWave can attach to Google Glass and allow you to take a picture and post it to Facebook and Twitter just by thinking about it. Even the army has (not very well) flown a helicopter using only thoughts and a brain wave headset.

Despite the immense interest in brain wave technology, little attention has been paid to what translation apps—such as Google Translator—will mean to an upcoming generation that will likely embrace brain wave tech. Youth will surely ask "What is the point of learning a second language if everyone will be communicating with brain wave headsets that can perform perfect real-time language translations?"

The question is valid, even if it's sure to upset millions of second language teachers and dozens of language learning companies, like publicly traded Rosetta Stone. Like it or not, sophisticated brain wave headsets will soon become as cheap as cell phones. A growing number of technologists think the future of communication lies in these headsets, and not handheld devices or smart phones.

However, the question of whether it will be useful to learn a new language in the future is about far more than just human communication and what technological form that takes. Different languages introduce us to other cultures, other peoples, and other countries. This creates personal growth, offering invaluable examination on our own culture and how we perceive the world. The process broadens who we are.

Being proficient in other languages also offers certain nuances that knowing only one language cannot. French offers far more romantic and poetic gist than English ever can. But Arabic is steeped in more historical imagery and connotation than French. And nothing compares to Hungarian's ability to effectively curse in ways that all other languages fall far short of.

Perhaps most importantly, learning a second language offers the physical brain a chance to grow in new and meaningful ways. The study of a new language, for example, is often suggested to early-onset Alzheimer's patients to help stimulate the brain's proper functioning.

Ultimately, the most quintessential question rests on whether there are more important things to be doing in today's busy world than learning a new language. With radical transhumanist tech changing our most basic functions like communicating, is society better off pushing its youth to learn how to write code, or to speed read, or to play the violin? In hindsight, I would've rather spent my time becoming a proficient martial artist than the six years I studied Spanish in school.

Whatever your opinion, the future of learning languages and how we communicate is in flux. Speaking at the 2014 World Future Society conference in Florida, Singularity University Professor José Cordeiro said, "Spoken language could start disappearing in 20 years. We'll all talk with each other using thoughts scanned and projected from our headsets and maybe even chip implants. This will radically increase the speed and bandwidth of human communications."

Twenty years isn't that far off. I'm not ready yet to drop my 4-year-old daughter's Chinese lessons, but I am keeping my eye on whether technology is going to change some of our basic communication assumptions, like the value of learning a second language.

SMART CITIES GO TO THE DOGS:

HOW TECH-SAVVY CITIES WILL AFFECT THE CANINE POPULATION

BRENDA COOPER

Brenda got started by coauthoring *Building Harlequin's Moon* with Larry Niven. She went on to write many other works including *The Silver Ship and the Sea*, *Reading the Wind*, *Wings of Creation*, *Mayan December*, and *The Creative Fire*.

You can read her latest novel *Edge of Dark* at http://amzn.to/16IfFLV.

The following article was originally published October 2014 on Slate.com as part of *Future Tense*, a collaboration among Arizona State University, New America, and Slate. Future Tense explores the ways emerging technologies affect society, policy, and culture.

A t a recent neighborhood meeting in the medium-size city that I work for, a comment about the growing dog population sparked a heated conversation. Residents—even pet owners—said that they find the increasingly large number of dogs on park pathways difficult to manage.

More data about dogs and dog owners will be a good thing.

Together, the citizens and city council promised to keep dogs on the agenda. They could stay there for the next 20 years.

According to the United Nations[1], half of the world's population already live in cities, and by 2050, nearly seven out of 10 people worldwide—more than 6 billion people in total—will lead urban lives. Already, megacities are responding to growth by becoming "smart cities." They are linking tiny embedded sensors with big data analytics and automating systems to make real-time decisions. Suburbs like the one I work in—Kirkland, Washington—are already following in the footsteps of larger metropolises.

In most cases, city networks are monitoring people, cars, electricity, water, and other infrastructure. Intelligent transportation systems in Boston improve traffic flow, smart lighting in San Francisco can be controlled wirelessly and dimmed in the early morning hours if the streets are empty, and surveillance systems in crowded public squares in New York watch for signs of terrorism. New apps help citizens find parking and send Amber Alerts to all cellphones within a specific location. The cities of the future will know where cars, bikes, and people are. They'll also know about the dogs.

In the United States, there is roughly one dog for every four humans, and the rate of canine ownership keeps rising. In 2011, the number of dogs in the city of Seattle was greater than the number of children: 153,000 dogs to 107,000 children[2]. New York City is home to more than 600,000 dogs[3].

Owners are already keeping better track of their animals. Many dogs are chipped with RFID to identify them if they get lost. Northern Ireland has required chipping since 2013 and beginning in 2016, chipping will be required for all dogs in England[4]. Many canines also wear collars sporting GPS-enabled devices[5] that are least as expensive as their owners' Fitbits. These chips are often used to find missing or stolen dogs, while everyday uses include keeping tabs on where your dog walker is taking your pooch and tracking the animal's "personal training" goals. Whether it's a show dog, a guide dog, or a rescue dog, the emotional cost of a lost animal is often considered incalculable. We want to keep our dogs safe, and we want to know where they are.

In addition to putting sensors on cars and in roads and parks, cities of the future will be able to map the dog population and the resources devoted to dogs. Dog owners can already look up amenities like dog parks and open water in phone apps. In a few years, they may even be able to tell in advance which dogs are at the park for Fido to play with. And the dog-phobic? They'll like the same future. Even if there are more dogs in cities in 10 years, it will be easier to tell if they are near you.

Cities themselves might use more information about dogs in a number of ways. Locations for neighborhood parks and fire stations are already selected using geographic information systems to mash up maps with data about people. If city planners know where the dogs live, they can site dog parks using the same technology. Once the information is made public on open data sites, prospective owners of dog-related businesses can use the same tools to decide where to put the dog-friendly pub or dog-wash stations. Another possibility is that the current movement to create special green lanes for bicycles could be mirrored for dogs in certain locations, creating unique dog walks that can be advertised to residents and tourists.

If the United States follows England's path and requires that all dogs be chipped, then the owners of dogs who end up as strays can be identified and fined. Actual data can be developed about incidents between dogs and people.

With so many four-footed walkers on city streets, keeping people safe from dogs matters. Even though just a small percentage of dogs are dangerous, no one wants to find themselves or their family dog attacked by an untrained animal with a poor handler. If it does happen, we want to find the perpetrator (owner and animal). Even more simply, if we have children who are afraid of dogs, we want to know when one is nearby. Similar to the way crosswalks or intersections with a large number of accidents are often improved, parks where dogs and people clash might be tweaked to improve safety for both.

When I was growing up, there were seeing-eye dogs. Today, they are called guide dogs, and there are also hearing dogs for the deaf and service dogs who help with a range of conditions including PTSD, poor balance, epilepsy, autism, and more. One of the most moving chapters in *Until Tuesday*[6], the best-selling book about an Iraq war vet and his dog Tuesday, covers an incident where a bus driver refused to believe that Tuesday was a legitimate service dog and tried to keep him off the bus. As more and more dogs of different kinds act as service dogs, knowing which ones truly are trained for crowded places like buses, concerts, and restaurants is going to become more important. RFID chips could easily identify service dogs and help keep the riffraff (ruffruff?) out.

Managing dogs adds costs to local government budgets. As city dogs continue to gain the attention of neighborhood meetings, pet licensing is going to become even more critical. Typically, licenses are designed to pay for at least part of the animal control resources in a city, including pounds, license enforcement, and education. Just for fun, I ran the numbers in my own county. Kings County, Washington, has roughly 2 million people, and thus about half a million dogs. At $30 a license, that's $15 million a year (if all dogs were licensed). Licenses are physical tags, and it won't be hard to add RFID, Bluetooth, and GPS to them in the near future.

I won't be at all surprised if some time soon, when I register our dogs for new licenses, I have to enter their RFID and maybe GPS chip data. And just think of all the interesting apps that might be developed with open data sets about dogs.

ENDNOTES

1. *World's population increasingly urban with more than half living in urban areas* at http://www.un.org/en/development/desa/news/population/world-urbanization-prospects-2014.html.

2. *Seattle's Dog Obsession* at http://www.seattlemag.com/article/seattles-dog-obsession.

3. *New York City's Pet Population* at http://www.nycedc.com/blog-entry/new-york-city-s-pet-population.

4. *Dogs in England must be microchipped from 2016* at http://www.bbc.com/news/uk-21345730.

5. Tagg GPS Pet Tracker – Dog and Cat Collar Attachment at http://amzn.to/1zVEds3.

6. *Until Tuesday* at http://amzn.to/1AHXdhY.

REPUTATION CURRENCIES
HEATHER SCHLEGEL

Heather is a scientist of the future. She observes technology and its impact on transactions, money, economies, relationships, intimacy, and personal identity. She has helped build and launch more than 50 internet products at other 30 startups and is known by her apt moniker heathervescent. Read her bio at http://lifeboat.com/ex/bios.heather.schlegel.

This article is sponsored by (ICE): The Institute of Customer Experience.

Today's world increasingly challenges us to think differently about value and money. Almost everyone agrees that reputation is important. But how important is it? Does it have an impact on your finances? What

The "Like" is a currency created by artist Dadara to provoke discussion around the value of a Facebook like. Image source: http://on.fb.me/1FnNEDj

is the currency of reputation and is it transferable or exchangeable?

HOW IS REPUTATION CREATED?

Reputation is co-created by individuals having experiences. Looking for a great Italian restaurant for dinner tonight? Search Yelp reviews and see what people who have already dined at a place have to say about it. Want to know what it's like to work with a potential hire? Read their LinkedIn referrals. Wondering whether or not other people are happy with a product you're about to buy? Amazon reviews will tell you. You've probably even shared your own experiences with something you enjoyed or to warn others about a less than positive experience. Your FICO score measures your credit risk, which is really credit reputation, based on your behavior.

But reputation is not always clear-cut. You've probably read reviews in which equal numbers of people give raves or have had a bad experience. Values, economic ability and taste all factor into someone's experience and subsequent review. Reputation can be messy and reviews difficult to differentiate. Reputation is not a fixed asset. Your FICO score, which is your financial reputation, is not set in stone. It changes as your credit habits change.

This brings us to a subject that is not often discussed and doesn't have a good technical solution: people change and their reputation does too. However, the way people think about each other's reputation doesn't necessarily keep pace with the changes. Outdated stigmas remain attached to individuals, products and services. We don't have a good ability to forgive mistakes and accept positive change. In the digital world there's the growing pressure for certain events and information to be forgotten. The recent EU ruling requires Google to remove information when requested. This is a clumsy solution to the problem of changing reputation. We need to have a technical solution that can honestly reflect reputational ebbs and flows.

When you need to pay your bills, you can't go to your LinkedIn page and cash out your recommendations like withdrawing money from an ATM. However, your reputation does influence your cash flow. Positive recommendations may increase the kind and amount of work you're offered and your ability to increase your salary. A better reputation does lead to increased cash flow.

Reputation is a requirement of the sharing economy. For AirBnB hosts and Uber and Lyft drivers, positive ratings are paramount to their success. It might seem crazy to stay at a stranger's house, but on AirBnB, host reviews facilitate trust among strangers. On a recent trip to Madrid, I selected an AirBnB location based on the reviews of the host, Sancho. I wanted to stay with someone who knew the local area and could suggest places to visit. When I met Sancho in person, not only did he tell me the best places to go, we became fast friends. This experience has happened to me many times—whether I was hosting or being hosted.

When you know what to expect, you can be more relaxed and focus on the experience. Reviews on AirBnB enable you to select the travel experience you want—thanks to the travelers who stayed there before you. Your AirBnB, Yelp and eBay reviews have immense values outside their immediate platforms. Even though these reputation systems have been created for the specific company—imagine how powerful it would be to have your reputation in one place.

IS REPUTATION TRANSFERABLE?

Is it possible for reputation to be exchanged from one platform to another?

I was recently told a story that illustrates how reputation can be transferred. Uber and Lyft are both independent operator ride-sharing platforms. Both companies facilitate the connection between driver and passenger. Drivers must be reviewed and approved before giving rides through their system. In a move to gain more drivers and compete with Lyft, Uber offered bonuses to tempt already approved Lyft drivers to the Uber platform. In some cases, it was easier for a new driver to go through the Lyft approval process and then switch companies, than it was to apply directly to Uber.

This is an unusual example of the direct immediate transfer of reputation.

"Making every Lyft, Uberful"

REPUTATION AND THE FUTURE

Reputation will be a visible part of our everyday transaction experience.

SCENARIO 1:
SMART CHECK DEVICE

In the below scenario four friends are splitting the check through a Smart-Check device. Though the Smart-Check, they can rate their dining experience right there. The restaurant gathers immediate feedback—and if the restaurant wanted, the server could rate the diners.

Watch Scenario No. 1
Fly Me to the Moon
https://www.youtube.
com/watch?v=pbZu-
1WNJNLQ

SCENARIO 2:
MOTORCYCLE FOR SALE

Ever try to sell something on a classified service? It's often hard to figure out who is a scammer and who is a qualified buyer. In the below scenario, a woman is looking at motorcycles for sale. The seller's reputation is shown as a "verification" checkmark on their profile. This helps the buyer judge which seller she wants to deal with.

Watch Scenario No. 2
Slices of Life
https://www.youtube.
com/watch?v=Wzsqt-
dx40qg

While we will continue to create reputation on individual platforms, there will be an increasing demand for fluid exchange of reputation and ratings from one system to another. I believe we'll see tools to aggregate your reputation in one place. Reputation system APIs may be developed which will enable you to transfer your reputation to new platforms.

These are just a couple ways we can expect to see reputation evolve. Reputation currencies help us make stronger connections and enable new economic models.

SCIENTIFIC ADVANCES ARE RUINING SCIENCE FICTION

DOUGLAS E. RICHARDS

Doug has been widely praised for his ability to weave action, suspense, and science into riveting novels that straddle the thriller and science fiction genres. He is the *New York Times* and *USA Today* bestselling author of *Wired*, its sequel *Amped*, *The Cure*, *Mind's Eye*, *Quantum Lens*, and six critically acclaimed middle-grade adventures enjoyed by kids and adults alike.

I write science fiction thrillers for a living, set five to ten years in the future, an exercise that allows me to indulge my love of science, futurism, and philosophy, and to examine in fine granularity the impact of approaching revolutions in technology.

But here is the problem. I'd love to write pure science fiction, set *hundreds* of years in the future.

Why don't I?

I guess the short answer is that to do so, I'd have to turn a blind eye to everything I believe will be true hundreds of years from now. Because the truth is that books about the future of humanity, such as Kurzweil's *The Singularity is Near*, have *ruined* me.

As a kid, I read nothing but science fiction. This was a genre that existed to examine individuals and societies through the lens of technological and scientific change. The best of this genre always focused on human beings as much as technology, something John W. Campbell insisted upon when he ushered in what is widely known as the Golden Age of Science Fiction.

But for the most part, writers in past generations could feel confident that men and women would always be men and women, at least for many thousands of years to come. We might develop technology that would give us incredible abilities. Go back and forth through time, travel to other dimensions, or travel through the galaxy in great starships. But no matter what, in the end, we would still be Grade A, premium cut, humans. Loving, lusting, and laughing. Scheming and coveting. Crying, shouting, and hating. We would remain ambitious, ruthless, and greedy, but also selfless and heroic. Our intellects and motivations in this far future would not be all that different from what they are now, and if we lost a phaser battle with a Klingon, the Grim Reaper would still be waiting for us.

In short, we would continue to be the kind of human beings a writer could work with, could understand. James T. Kirk might have lived hundreds of years in the future, might have beamed down to planets and engaged warp engines, but viewers still had no trouble relating to him. He was adventurous, loyal, and heroic, and he lusted after life (along with green aliens, androids, and just about anything else that could move).

But what if you believe that in a few hundred years, people will *not* be the same as today? What if you believe they will be so different they will be *unrecognizable* as human?

Now how would you write science fiction? You would have to change two variables at the same time: not only addressing dramatic advances in technology, but dramatic changes in the nature of humanity itself (or, more likely, the merger of our technology and ourselves).

In the early days of science fiction, technology changed at a snail's pace. But today, technological change is so furious, so obviously exponential, that it is impossible to ignore. I have no doubt this is why a once fringe, disrespected genre has become so widely popular, has come out of the closet, and is now so all-pervasive in our society. Because we're *living* science fiction every day.

Rapid and transformative technological change isn't hard to imagine anymore. What's hard to imagine is the *lack* of such change.

In 1880, the US asked a group of experts to analyze New York City, one of the fastest-growing cities in North America. They wanted to know what it might be like in a hundred years.

The experts extrapolated the likely growth during this period, and the expected consequences. They then confidently proclaimed that if population growth wasn't halted, by 1980, New York City would require so many horses to stay viable that every inch of it would be knee-deep in manure. Knee-deep! In horse manure!

As someone interested in technology and future trends, I love this story, even if it turns out to be apocryphal, because it does a brilliant job of highlighting the dangers of extrapolating the future, since we aren't capable of foreseeing game-changing technologies that often appear. Even now. Even at our level of sophistication and expectation of change.

But while we can't know what miracles the future will hold, we've now seen too much evidence of exponential progress not to know that Jim Kirk would no longer be relatable to us. Because it seems impossible to me that we will remain as we are. Remain even the least bit recognizable.

This assumes, of course, that we avoid self-destruction, a fate that seems more likely every day as WMDs proliferate and fanaticism grows. But post-apocalyptic science fiction has never been my thing, and if we do reach a *Star Trek* level of technology, we will have avoided self-destruction, by definition. And I prefer to be optimistic, in any case, despite the growing case for pessimism.

So if we do ever advance to the point at which we can travel through hyperspace, beam ourselves down to planets, or wage war in great starships, we can be sure we won't be human anymore.

It is well known that increases in computer power and speed have been exponential. But exponential growth sneaks up on you in a way that isn't intuitive. Start with a penny and double your money every day, and in thirty-nine days you'll have over two billion dollars. But the first day your wealth only increases by a single penny, an amount that's beneath notice. On the *thirty-ninth* day, however, your wealth will increase from one billion to two billion dollars—now *that* is a change impossible to miss. So like a hockey stick, the graph of exponential growth barely rises from the ground for some time, but when it reaches the beginning of the handle, watch out, because you suddenly get an explosive rise that is nearly vertical.

It's becoming crystal clear that we are entering the hockey-stick phase of progress with computers and other technologies. Yes, progress in artificial intelligence has been discouraging. But if we don't self-destruct, does anyone imagine that we won't develop computers within a few hundred years that will make the most advanced supercomputers of today seem like a toddler counting on his or her fingers? Does anyone doubt that at some point a computer could get so powerful it could direct its own future evolution? And given the speed at which such evolution would occur, does anyone doubt that a computer could become self-aware within the next few centuries?

Visionaries like Ray Kurzweil believe this will happen well within this century, but even the most conservative among us must admit the likelihood that by the time the USS *Enterprise* pulls out of space dock, either our computers will have evolved into Gods and obsoleted us, or, more likely, we will have merged with our technology to reach almost God-like heights of intelligence ourselves.

And while this bodes well for these far-future beings, it isn't so great for today's science fiction writers. Because what would you rather read about: a swashbuckling starship captain? Or a being as incomprehensible to us as we are to an amoeba?

To be fair, science fiction novels have been written about a future in which this transformation has occurred. And I could write one of these, as well. The problem is that for the most part, people like reading about other people. People who are like them. People who act and think like, you know... *people*.

Even if we imagine a future society of omniscient beings, we wouldn't have much of a story without conflict. Without passions and frailties and fear of death. And what kind of a story could an amoeba write about a man, anyway?

I believe that after a few hundred years of riding up this hockey-stick of explosive technological growth, humanity can forge a utopian society whose citizens are nearly-omniscient and nearly-immortal. Governed by pure reason rather than petty human emotions. A society in which unrecognizable beings live in harmony, not driven by current human limitations and motivations.

Wow. A novel about beings we can't possibly relate to, residing on an intellectual plane of existence incompressible to us, without conflict or malice. I think I may have just described the most boring novel ever written.

Despite what I believe to be true about the future, however, I have to admit something: I still can't help myself. I *love* space opera. When the next *Star Trek* movie comes out, I'll be the first one in line. Even though I'll still believe that if our technology advances enough for starships, it will have advanced enough for us to have utterly transformed *ourselves*, as well. With apologies to Captain Kirk and his crew, *Star Trek* technology would never coexist with a humanity we can hope to understand, much as dinosaurs and people really didn't roam the earth at the same time. But all of this being said, as a reader and viewer, I find it easy to suspend disbelief. Because I really, really love this stuff.

As a writer, though, it is more difficult for me to turn a blind eye to what I believe will be the truth.

But, hey, I'm only human. A current human. With all kinds of flaws. So maybe I can rationalize ignoring my beliefs long enough to write a rip-roaring science fiction adventure. I mean, it is fiction, right? And maybe dinosaurs and mankind *did* coexist. The *Flintstones* wouldn't lie, would they?

So while the mind-blowing pace of scientific progress has ruined far-future science fiction for me, at least when it comes to the writing of it, I may not be able to help myself. I may love old-school science fiction too much to limit myself to near-future thrillers. One day, I may break down, fall off the wagon, and do what I vowed during my last Futurists Anonymous meeting never to do again: Write far-future science fiction.

And if that day ever comes, all I ask is that you not judge me too harshly.

10 FUTURISTIC MATERIALS

MICHAEL ANISSIMOV

Michael writes and speaks on futurist issues, especially the relationships between accelerating change, nanotechnology, existential risk, transhumanism, and the Singularity.
He was a founding director of the nonprofit Immortality Institute, was quoted multiple times in Ray Kurzweil's book *The Singularity is Near: When Humans Transcend Biology*, was Co-founder and Director of the Singularity Summit, and was Media Director of the Machine Intelligence Research Institute.

The following is also a special report published on our site at http://lifeboat.com/ex/10. futuristic.materials and once reached #18 on reddit which saturated the ethernet on our dedicated server at the time, prompting us to go for a cloud solution. This report has also received about 700,000 StumbleUpon likes. Read Michael's *A Critique of Democracy: A Guide for Neoreactionaries* at http://amzn.to/1Fhhqd4.

1. AEROGEL

Aerogel holds 15 entries in the Guinness Book of Records, more than any other material. Sometimes called "frozen smoke", aerogel is made by the supercritical drying of liquid gels of alumina, chromia, tin oxide, or carbon. It's 99.8% empty space, which makes it look semi-transparent. Aerogel is a fantastic insulator—if you had a shield of aerogel, you could easily defend yourself from a flamethrower. It stops cold, it stops heat. You could build a warm dome on the Moon. Aerogels have unbelievable surface area in their internal fractal structures—cubes of aerogel just an inch on a side may have an internal surface area equivalent to a football field. Despite its low density, aerogel has been looked into as a component of military armor because of its insulating properties.

Aerogel protecting crayons from a blowtorch.

This tiny block of transparent aerogel is supporting a brick weighing 2.5 kg.
The aerogel's density is 3 mg/cm3.

2. CARBON NANOTUBES

Carbon nanotubes are long chains of carbon held together by the strongest bond in all chemistry, the sacred sp2 bond, even stronger than the sp3 bonds that hold together diamond. Carbon nanotubes have numerous remarkable physical properties, including ballistic electron transport (making them ideal for electronics) and so much tensile strength that they are the only substance that could

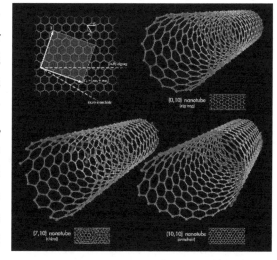

662

be used to build a space elevator. The specific strength of carbon nanotubes is 48,000 kN·m/kg, the best of known materials, compared to high-carbon steel's 154 kN·/kg. That's 300 times stronger than steel. You could build towers hundreds of kilometers high with it.

3. METAMATERIALS

"Metamaterial" refers to any material that gains its properties from structure rather than composition. Metamaterials have been used to create microwave invisibility cloaks, 2D invisibility cloaks, and materials with other unusual optical properties. Mother-of-pearl gets its rainbow color from metamaterials of bio-

logical origin. Some metamaterials have a negative refractive index, an optical property that may be used to create "Superlenses" which resolve features smaller than the wavelength of light used to image them! This technology is called subwavelength imaging. Metamaterials would be used in phased array optics, a technology that could render perfect holograms on a 2D display. These holograms would be so perfect that you could be standing 6 inches from the screen, looking into the "distance" with binoculars, and not even notice it's a hologram.

4. BULK DIAMOND

We're starting to lay down thick layers of diamond in CVD machines, hinting towards a future of bulk diamond machinery. Diamond is an ideal construction material—it's immensely strong, light, made out of the widely available

element carbon, nearly complete thermal conductivity, and has among the highest melting and boiling points of all materials. By introducing trace impurities, you can make a diamond practically any color you want. Imagine a jet, with hundreds of thousands of moving parts made of fine-tuned diamond machinery. Such a craft would be more powerful than today's best fighter planes in the way an F-22 is better than the Red Baron's Fokker Dr.1.

5. BULK FULLERENES

Diamonds may be strong, but aggregated diamond nanorods (what I call amorphous fullerene) are stronger. Amorphous fullerene has a isothermal bulk modulus of 491 gigapascals (GPa), compared to diamond's 442 GPa. As we see in the

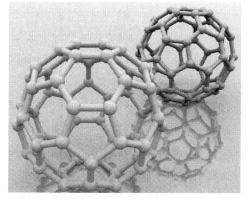

image, the nanoscale structure of the fullerene gives it a beautiful iridescent appearance. Fullerenes can be made substantially stronger than diamond, but for greater energy cost. After a "Diamond Age" we may eventually transition to a "Fullerene Age" as our technology gets even more sophisticated.

6. AMORPHOUS METAL

Amorphous metals, also called metallic glasses, consist of metal with a disordered atomic structure. They can be twice as strong as steel. Because of their disordered structure, they can disperse impact energy more effectively than a metal crystal, which has points of weakness. Amorphous metals are made by quickly cooling molten metal before it has a chance to align itself in a crystal pattern. Amorphous metals may be the military's next generation of armor, before they adopt diamondoid armor in mid-century. On the green side of things, amorphous metals have electronic properties that improve the efficiency of power grids by as much as 40%, saving us thousands of tons of fossil fuel emissions.

7. SUPERALLOYS

A superalloy is a generic term for a metal that can operate at very high temperatures, up to about 2000 °F (1100 °C). They are popular for use in the superhot turbine areas of jet engines. They are used for more advanced oxygen-breathing designs, such as the ramjet and scramjet. When we're flying through the sky in hypersonic craft, we'll have superalloys to thank for it.

8. METAL FOAM

Metal foam is what you get when you add a foaming agent, powdered titanium hydride, to molten aluminum, then let it cool. The result is a very strong substance that is relatively light, with 75–95% empty space. Because of its favorable strength-to-weight ratio, metal foams have been proposed as a construction material for space colonies. Some metal forms are so light that they float on water, which would make them excellent for building floating cities, like those analyzed by Marshall T. Savage in one of my favorite books, *The Millennial Project*.

9. TRANSPARENT ALUMINA

Transparent alumina is three times stronger than steel and transparent.

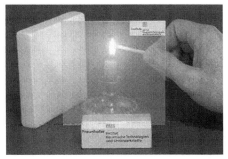

The number of applications for this are huge. Imagine an entire skyscraper or arcology made largely of transparent steel. The skylines of the future could look more like a series of floating black dots (opaque private rooms) rather than the monoliths of today. A huge space station made of transparent alumina could cruise in low Earth orbit without being a creepy black dot when it passes overhead. And hey... *transparent swords!*

10. E-TEXTILES

If you meet up and talk to me in 2020, I'll likely be covered in electronic textiles. Why carry some electronic gadget you can easily lose when we can just wear our computers? We'll develop clothing that can constantly project the video of our choosing (unless it turns out being so annoying that we ban it).

Imagine wearing a robe covered in a display that actually projects the night sky in real time. Imagine talking to people over the "phone" just by making a hand gesture and activating electronics in your lapel, then merely thinking about what you want to say (thought-to-speech interfaces). The possibilities of e-textiles are limitless.

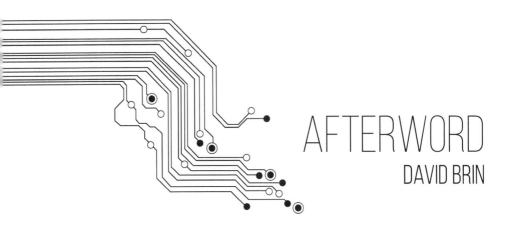

AFTERWORD
DAVID BRIN

I t's been said that "dinosaurs are extinct because they had no space program." Mammals might never have inherited Earth, had clever ve-lociraptors looked up at the sky—with telescopes—and detected the fatal rock well in advance, then got organized, assertively working together to deflect doom. Of course, this truism is both obvious and a little unfair, since many dinosaur cousins *did* escape the Cretaceous calamity by taking to the sky, mastering flight eons before we hairy types got around to it.

Still, the metaphor makes a powerful point, for what use is intelligence if it cannot probe the future, effectively, seeking (and possibly averting) threats to our children. Blithe or willful evasion of this responsibility makes up the litany of disasters that make up what we call "human history," as so chillingly described in recent books, like Jared Diamond's *Collapse.*

Indeed, it is daunting to count ways that the universe has at its dispos-al to shatter the expectations and desires of living beings. Technological humans have vastly expanded not only their range of possible options, but also the number of things that might go wrong and stymie all hope. And so the central question: *is* it possible for a species—equipped with tools of appraisal, foresight, and situational awareness—to survey the future for dangers and gather the will to prevent them?

To be clear, we did not need high tech to begin wreaking anthropogenic damage on the world we depend upon. Pretty soon after people developed a knack for animal husbandry—protecting goats from predators, and thereby benefiting from large herds of meat on the hoof—our beloved swarms of ungulates overgrazed and disrupted local ecosystems, accelerating the spread of deserts in a post ice-age world. The next super-technology—irrigation—had similar effects, expanding human populations while ruining much of the Fertile Crescent, wherever hydrological societies failed to understand salt-accumulation and other unforeseen side effects.

One can envision this sort of thing helping to explain the "Fermi Paradox"—the mysterious lack of any clear sign (so far) of sapient civilizations among the stars. Among the hundred or so theories that I've catalogued for this interstellar quandary, one compelling possibility is that humans got smart exceptionally *fast*, allowing us to achieve science only 10,000 years or so after developing primitive pastoralism and agriculture. Quick enough to start *noticing* the harm that we were doing, while our homeworld still retains appreciable amounts of health and natural fecundity. Other sapients, who do it more slowly, might never notice any contrast, as they gradually degrade the nursery that engendered them.

Indeed, we can use the Fermi Paradox as a metaphysical whiteboard, to write the multi-spectra of our fears. If there is a pattern of behavior—say feudalism—that has repeatedly sucked in 99% of human societies, limiting our wisdom and vision and producing one tragic failure after another, might similar syndromes have thwarted aliens out there, perhaps systematically and often? Pondering these potential "great filters"—as Nicholas Bostrom put it—lets us view our own blunders in a fresh and disturbing light. At every major choice point, we're behooved to ask: might *this* be the big one that culls out most promising young races, leaving the cosmos a mostly-silent realm? Could this be the one that will trap us too, making us yet another, typical failure?

That is the central, dark rumination Bostrom attempts to cover, when he writes about potential catastrophe modes. Working with Lord Martin Rees (who contributed to this volume), Bostrom has established Oxford's Future of Humanity Institute, dedicated to exploring some of the dour problems we had better solve, or else.

As does the Lifeboat Foundation, a loose association of scholars and pundits, scientists and enthusiasts, drawn together to discuss a related theme—is it possible for humanity to develop good habits of foresight, satiability, accountability and agility, *in time* to make it across the minefield just ahead? A murky tomorrow, strewn with dangers—some of them forged by nature, but others by our ever-clever selves?

To be clear, I have had my doubts about some aspects of LF, from time to time. But in this era, that is to be expected. It does not detract from the value Lifeboat contributes through its lively, online arguments, as well as this volume's core aim. Getting us talking about that shadowy realm ahead.

A PATHFINDING GENRE

Of course, this has long been a realm explored most vigorously by serious science fiction, as in my novels *Earth* and *Existence*… and as so many other authors have done, from Harry Harrison, Frederik Pohl and Alice Sheldon through Margaret Atwood and (relentlessly) Michael Crichton. While some of the fictional calamities offered by these writers have been silly, lurid, or nonsensical, they all reflect one valuable trend—that we're starting to *care* about chains of cause-and-effect!

Moreover, science fiction is the one branch of literature brave enough to admit that *change happens*. Change, in fact, can be a topic that's bold, enriching, even fascinating: adding to the already rich palette of narrative storytelling that stretches back to Cro-Magnon campfires. Only science fiction goes further, asserting that yesterday's so-called "eternal human verities" may seem boring and archaic to tomorrow's children. If they are wise, they will face (and invent) new problems of their own, while standing on the shoulders of earlier generations, having learned from our mistakes.

Indeed, it is this core premise—even "verities" may change—that explains why so many scholastics in stodgy, university departments go to great lengths deriding science fiction. It terrifies mavens in armchair cloisters to realize that nature—even human nature—has always been in flux, and that literature might bravely face that fact, head-on.

SF pokes at the murky path ahead, exposing perils in vivid fashion, sometimes propelling millions of readers and viewers to transform attitudes, or even take action. When such tales are supremely effective—as in George Orwell's *Nineteen Eighty-Four* or *Soylent Green* or *Dr. Strangelove*, you sometimes get the most powerful of all stories—*self-preventing prophecies.*[1]

Alas, SF tales, like all popular literature and cinema, also have to satisfy commercial needs—keeping protagonists in white-knuckle jeopardy for 350 pages or 90 minutes of screen time. And this paramount requirement often simplifies, or even lobotomizes the warning message. Elsewhere I show how this leads to two iron rules of modern media: *(1) thou shalt never show a public or governmental institution actually functioning well,* and *(2) thou shalt always portray average citizens as useless, cowardly sheep.*[2]

There are exceptions, of course. Many of the stories chosen for this volume examine possible future (or present) failure modes, without rigidly obeying those iron rules. They admit the glimmering possibility that humans and their cultures might successfully adapt. Whether reprinted classics or original tales written specially for this volume, their light shines onto that dimly-lit and rocky trail ahead.

OPTIMISTS AND PESSIMISTS

As for this volume's nonfiction portions, it is interesting to note the following from James Blodgett's article on Saving the World:

"If Rees and Wells, who predict disaster soon, are right, that may be too late. However, I have learned that there is enough material in the asteroid belt to build habitats for trillions of people."

Here we see illustrated the spectacular range of possibilities that are being reconnoitered by some very intelligent and tech-savvy modern thinkers. At one end, you have the Transhumanist Movement, whose members variously predict a coming era of extended lifespans and/or uploading of human personalities into super-sentient machines and/or redesign of the human species itself. One leader in the movement, Zoltan Istvan, is running as a 2016 U.S.

Presidential candidate under the newly formed Transhumanist Party.

Even the more moderate elements of this zeitgeist still sound high on some optimism drug—for example Peter Diamandis, whose excellent book *Abundance,* certainly makes a strong case for what Ray Kurzweil calls a "Law of Accelerating Returns," the notion that world-changing technologies will leverage upon each other in positive-sum ways—for instance, when new methods of desalinization combine with cheaper solar energy and better ecological modeling to reverse many of our water woes, the transforming effects could be tremendous. It would be easy to ridicule them (and some do). But we've seen this happen before, and the lesson is two-fold:

"Sure, those fine advances may be possible! So let's believe in ourselves and invest serious resources to making great things happen!

"At the same time, though, let us also be quicker at perceiving inevitable, unforeseen side effects. That, too, is a valuable lesson from the past."

Indeed, you've got to respect these guys, for they are on the front lines, reifying the dreams that give us all reason to hope. See, for example, Peter's great work developing X Prizes that promote solutions to tractable problems by stimulating our greatest asset, the agile industriousness of brilliant, challenged minds.[3]

At the opposite end are grouches who perceive only darkness and obstacles ahead, who indeed number fizzy optimism among our problems! Remember those "unforeseen side effects" I mentioned? Well, folks like Michael Crichton and Francis Fukayama and Margaret Atwood can always be counted on to perceive those possibilities first and foremost, if not to the exclusion of all else. Indeed, so (for commercial reasons) does Hollywood.

At the extremes, zealots and curmudgeons become caricatures, discrediting their promises and warnings with finger-wagging exaggeration and tunnel vision.

On the other hand, our society's greatest invention has to be the *openness* that allows bright ideas and critical warnings to flow. Like T cells zeroing in on potential opportunities and errors, they do not have to be *right* every time in order to serve a useful purpose! Sometimes it's enough, just getting calmer, more pragmatic fellow citizens to lift their heads. To notice and to think.

What both ends of this spectrum seem to miss is how *familiar* it would all seem, to our ancestors—this juxtaposition of bright possibilities and gloom. Transcendent promises and jeremiads of doom. Just read ancient accounts and you'll soon realize that *all* previous generations must have been battered with such ravings, by believers in bright visions or dark, who shared one common trait—*dissatisfaction with things as they are*. With the hand we're dealt. Wide-eyed and capering outside the Temple walls, preaching either hope or despair to fascinated throngs, these were predecessors of today's transhumanists and their bitterest detractors.

Just one essential thing seems to have changed. In earlier times, the grouches and transcendentalists could only imagine their forecasts arriving via *supernatural means*. Doom might be the work of angry gods. Glorious improvements might unfold as rewards for virtue, or from following the correct prescriptions or rituals. But neither could emerge from practical exercise of mundane commerce and craft!

Today though, as we moderns are undeniably picking up the very tools and skills of Creation itself, these fellows no longer just tout subjective *incantations*. Rather, they now talk about a coming rise or decline—heaven or hell—coming about physically and *objectively*, wrought by human hands.

Is it then partly a matter of personality? If it's true that optimism or pessimism bubble up from deeper-psychological forces, within, then are these techie Big Thinkers erecting their towers of justification after the fact?

I don't say this to disparage! Indeed, this writer's own take on all of this is at least partly a function of my own quirky, underlying nature—as a contrarian. As someone whose basic catechism goes *"um sure, that's interesting. But have you considered THIS inconvenient glitch in your model?"*

Hence, around transhumanists, I point out cavils/dangers/side-effects and possible ways that it all might fail.

But when fate carries me near gloom artists—(especially cable TV's merchants of fear)—I demand:

"Who are YOU to undermine confidence in our ability to take on challenges and to do what our ancestors have already done, countless times before us?

"To look ahead, catch our mistakes in the nick of time, innovate, create, negotiate,

compromise, compete, cooperate… and prevail?"

OUR OWN DUTY TO THE FUTURE

So how will we do that? Again I return to James Blodgett, who wrote about how *we*, as individuals and citizens, bear much of the responsibility for solving problems, so that our children will inherit hope… and perhaps even pride in their heritage. It is the central theme of the "Restored United States" in my novel *The Postman*. It is the goal of every sincere politician who tried to actually make politics work, and every resident who talks fellow community members into compromise, instead of screaming at each others' faces. It is the methodology of open and flat-fair reciprocal accountability analyzed in *The Transparent Society*.

There are countless things that we can do, as workers, family members, neighbors and citizens. For example:

- refuse the blandishments of those fear merchants who feign to be "journalists," preaching hate-your-own-neighbors.
- re-learn the citizen arts of negotiation and meeting those neighbors halfway.
- spurn blatantly stupid metaphors—like a hoary, lobotomizing so-called "left-right political axis" that none of *you* could define, if your life depended upon it, and that is unworthy of a scientific, complex and sophisticated 21st century civilization.
- find ways to improve your institutions, instead of wallowing in the sanctimonious drug high of self-righteousness.
- but also *bypass* those institutions, by acting as individuals, as ad-hoc groups, to improve what can be improved, and thereby help to prove right the guys we *want* to be right, like Peter Diamandis.

In another place, I talked about the simplest way to do this. A method that is so cheap and easy and *lazy* that none of you have any excuses. It is called *proxy activism*… the simple way to invest in saving the world by whatever combination of concerns that you feel to be important. It is utterly straightforward. And if we all did this one little thing, the world would change, no matter what folks in Washington or on Cable News believe.[4]

IT'S COMING, LIKE IT OR NOT

I could go on. There are so many realms under this tent. And indeed, as a sci fi author, I have to admit that the problem faced by Douglas Richards—in his essay about difficulties of sci fi—is a tough one to overcome. For if the optimists (and/or a subset of the pessimists) prove right, then accelerating progress may render moot even the sharpest and most compelling of our stories. The "singularity" will then be a daunting barrier to look past. This is one reason why I keep re-defining the near-intermediate future from 50 years ahead—as in *Earth* (1989)—down to 30 years—as in *Existence* (2012)—and so on.

Does this mean I sense the threshold, just ahead, and deem it impossible to write beyond?

Nonsense Richard! Take heart, dear colleague. Boldly set forth across that sea! The Singularity may turn out to be a soft one, allowing human style beings to criss-cross the stars and have adventures, as in the novels of Vernor Vinge. Or it might engender great minds who then *choose* to encourage human adventure, as in the novels of Iain Banks. Heck, I've even written stories set in worlds where men and women are effectively gods, yet have new problems of their own. And why not?

This is, after all, our greatest power. To envision that dark road ahead, filled with land mines and quicksand and snakes and deadfalls, created by both nature and by man, ready to trip any unwary species and civilization.

Only... we're not unwary! Suspicion and worry-R-us!

What we *need* (and I will repeat it endlessly) is *confidence*.

Not arrogance! But the ability to trade criticism, learn from each other...

...and then... to boldly go.

ENDNOTES

1. http://www.davidbrin.com/1984.html
2. http://www.davidbrin.com/idiotplot.html
3. http://www.xprize.org
4. http://www.davidbrin.com/proxyactivism.html

LIFEBOAT FOUNDATION

The Lifeboat Foundation is a nonprofit nongovernmental organization dedicated to encouraging scientific advancements while helping humanity survive existential risks and possible misuse of increasingly powerful technologies, including genetic engineering, nanotechnology, and robotics/AI, as we move towards the Singularity.

Lifeboat Foundation is pursuing a variety of options, including helping to accelerate the development of technologies to defend humanity such as new methods to combat viruses, effective nanotechnological defensive strategies, and even self-sustaining space colonies in case the other defensive strategies fail.

We believe that, in some situations, it might be feasible to relinquish technological capacity in the public interest (for example, we are against the U.S. government posting the recipe for the 1918 flu virus on the internet). We have some of the best minds on the planet working on programs to enable our survival. We invite you to join our cause!

LINKS

- Visit our site at http://lifeboat.com. The Lifeboat Foundation is working on a prototype Friendly AI at http://lifeboat.com/ai and also has launched the world's first bitcoin endowment fund at https://lifeboat.com/ex/bitcoin.
- Join our Facebook group at https://www.facebook.com/groups/lifeboatfoundation/.
- Join our LinkedIn group at http://www.linkedin.com/egis/35656/2B322944A8E3.
- Read our blog at http://lifeboat.com/blog.
- Follow our Twitter feed at http://twitter.com/lifeboathq.

- Watch our YouTube channel at https://youtube.com/lifeboathq.
- Participate in our programs at http://lifeboat.com/ex/programs.
- Join our various mailing list/forums at http://lifeboat.com/ex/forums.
- Read our first book *The Human Race to the Future: What Could Happen—and What to Do* at http://amzn.to/1uYeeAF. Interact with its author at https://www.facebook.com/groups/thehumanracetothefuture.
- Learn about all our books at http://lifeboat.com/ex/books.

ACKNOWLEDGEMENTS

ACKNOWLEDGEMENT IS MADE FOR PERMISSION TO PRINT THE FOLLOWING MATERIAL:

"The Shoulders of Giants," Copyright 2000 by Robert J. Sawyer. First published in *Star Colonies* edited by Martin H. Greenberg and John Helfers, DAW Books, New York, June 2000.

"Gift of a Useless Man," Copyright by Davis Publications, Inc.; first published in *Isaac Asimov's Science Fiction Magazine*, November 1979.

"Light and Shadow," Copyright by Catherine Asaro; first published in *Analog Science Fiction and Fact*, April 1994.

"Lungfish," Copyright 1987 by David Brin. First published in *The River of Time*.

"The Birth of the Dawn," Copyright 2015 by Nicole Sallak Anderson.

"The Weathermakers," Copyright by Ben Bova; first published in *Analog Science Fiction and Fact*, December 1966.

"Last Day of Work," Copyright 2011 by Douglas Rushkoff.

"I'm a What?" Copyright 2012 by Frank White.

"The Listeners," Copyright by James E. Gunn; first published in *Galaxy*, September 1968.

"The Emperor of Mars," Copyright by Allen Steele; first published in *Asimov's Science Fiction*, June 2010.

"Lunar One," Copyright 2015 by Jasper T. Scott.

"My Father's Singularity," Copyright by Brenda Cooper; first published in *Clarkesworld Magazine*, June 2010.

"A Delicate Balance," Copyright by WordFire, Inc.; first published in *Analog Science Fiction and Fact*, April 2012.

"More Than the Sum of His Parts," Copyright by Joe Haldeman; first published in *Playboy*, May 1985.

"Lazarus Rising," Copyright 2009 by Gregory Benford.

THE LIFEBOAT FOUNDATION WOULD LIKE TO THANK THE FOLLOWING FOR THEIR ASSISTANCE IN COPY EDITING AND PROOFREADING:

- Edwin B. Cooper Jr.
- Odette Gregory
- Peg Kay
- Lilia Lens-Pechakova
- Patrice Levin Kell
- Clay Rawlings
- Jim Tankersley
- Alan S. Ziegler

Made in the USA
Middletown, DE
09 June 2017